UNTIL
THE
END

ALSO BY
Christopher Pike

THE THIRST SERIES
REMEMBER ME
THE SECRET OF KA

UNTIL THE END

INCLUDES *THE PARTY*, *THE DANCE*, AND *THE GRADUATION*

Christopher Pike

Simon Pulse

New York London Toronto Sydney

"LET IT BE" by John Lennon and Paul McCartney © 1970 NORTHERN SONGS LTD. All Rights for the U.S., Canada and Mexico Controlled and Administered by SBK BLACKWOOD MUSIC INC. Under License from ATV MUSIC (MACLEN). All Rights Reserved. International Copyright Secured. Used by Permission.

〜〜〜

SIMON PULSE

An imprint of Simon & Schuster Children's Publishing Division
1230 Avenue of the Americas, New York, NY 10020
This Simon Pulse paperback edition August 2011
The Party copyright © 1988 by Christopher Pike
The Dance copyright © 1988 by Christopher Pike
The Graduation copyright © 1989 by Christopher Pike
All rights reserved, including the right of reproduction
in whole or in part in any form.
SIMON PULSE and colophon are registered trademarks
of Simon & Schuster, Inc.
For information about special discounts for bulk purchases, please
contact Simon & Schuster Special Sales at 1-866-506-1949
or business@simonandschuster.com.
The Simon & Schuster Speakers Bureau can bring authors to
your live event. For more information or to book an event contact
the Simon & Schuster Speakers Bureau at 1-866-248-3049
or visit our website at www.simonspeakers.com.
Designed by Mike Rosamilia
The text of this book was set in Adobe Garamond.
Manufactured in the United States of America
10 9 8 7 6 5 4 3 2 1
Library of Congress Control Number 2011927749
ISBN 978-1-4424-2252-0
These books were previously published individually.

Contents

THE PARTY

For Ashley

Chapter One

I *should never have gone on vacation in Europe,* Jessica Hart thought. *After climbing the Matterhorn, starting high school again feels ridiculous.*

The day was a Friday, the last day of the first week of school, but Jessica's first glimpse of Tabb High. Less than twenty hours earlier she had been enjoying the crisp, cool air of Switzerland's Alps. Now she had Southern California's worst to breathe; the morning was as smoggy as it was hot. Plus she had a terrible case of jet lag. She probably should have skipped what was left of the school week and rested up over Saturday and Sunday, but she had been anxious to see her friends and to check out the place where she was doomed to spend her one and only senior year. So far it had not impressed her.

"I want to have a party," Alice McCoy was saying to her as they wove through the crowds in the outdoor hallway toward

Jessica's locker room. "We could get, say, thirty kids from Mesa, with thirty kids from Tabb."

Mesa High had been their alma mater until midsummer, when those in power had decided that the district could not afford two partially full high schools. Tabb had absorbed perhaps three-quarters of Mesa's students. Although Tabb was older than Mesa, it was far bigger. The other twenty-five percent had ended up at Sanders High, five miles farther inland. Fortunately for Jessica, the majority of her friends had moved with her to Tabb, not the least of whom was Alice McCoy. Two years younger, she was—in Jessica's unbiased opinion—the sweetest girl in the whole world.

"You mean as a get-to-know-each-other sort of thing?" Jessica asked.

"Yeah. I think it would help break the ice between us."

"I wouldn't worry about any ice today," Jessica said, brushing her dark hair off her sweaty forehead. On hot days like this she wished she had Alice's bright blond curls; they seemed to reflect most of the sun's rays. "Does this joint have air-conditioning?" Jessica asked.

"In some of the rooms."

"Some?"

"The teachers' lounge is real cool. I was in there yesterday. They want me to paint a mural on the wall." Alice laughed. "They want a mountain glacier."

"It figures. I hope you're charging them?"

"I'm not."

"Fool. Back to this party business. How would you know which thirty Tabb kids to invite?"

Alice nodded. "That's a problem. But maybe in the next week we'll meet some neat people. Have you run into anyone that you like yet?"

Jessica shook her head. "No, and I've been here all of thirty minutes. But maybe by lunch I'll get some guy to fall in love with me."

The words came out easily, but were accompanied by a slight feeling of uneasiness. She had gone on few dates while at Mesa High. Guys just didn't ask her out much. Her best friend, Sara Cantrell, said it was because they were intimidated by her beauty.

"You're right, Sara, that must be it. All those guys watching me from across campus and thinking to themselves that there's a babe beyond their reach. Really, they have a lot of nerve even looking at me."

Actually, Jessica knew she was pretty. Enough people had told her so for enough years, and they couldn't all be wrong. Besides, she had only to look in the mirror. Her face was a perfect oval, with a firm chin and a wide, full mouth that she had trained to smile even when she didn't feel much like smiling. Her hair and eyes matched beautifully. The former was dark brown, long and wavy, with a sheen that had stayed with her from infancy; the latter, an even darker brown, large and round, giving her either a playful or nasty look, depending on her mood. And with a carefully controlled diet and daily jogs around the park, she kept her figure slim and supple. She'd even picked up a tan this summer.

I sound practically perfect!

But, no, she wasn't perfect. She believed, like most teenage girls who don't date much, that there was something wrong with her, something missing. Yet she didn't know what it could be. She didn't understand how Alice—a nice enough looking girl, but certainly no fairy princess—drew girls and guys alike to her in droves. Some people were charismatic, she supposed, and others weren't, and that was that.

Just then Jessica caught sight of a girl in a cheerleader's uniform standing beside a tree and chatting with a group of what appeared to be football players. A stab of envy touched her. The past spring she had successfully tried out for the cheerleading squad. And all summer she had been looking forward to entering the mainstream of her school's social life. But then *her* school had disappeared, and those who decided such things—who were those jerks, anyway?—had felt that Tabb High should be allowed to maintain its pep squads without integrating those from Mesa High.

God, now there's a girl that looks out of reach.

Jessica stopped Alice, gestured in the direction of the cheerleader. Her blond hair teased and highlighted, the girl appeared hip, arrogant in a flirty way. Even from a distance,

Jessica could see the eyes of the guys gathered around her flickering down her long tanned legs. "Who is that?" she said.

"Clair Hilrey," Alice replied. "Funny you should ask. She was one person I had already decided should come to my party."

"Why?"

"She knows everybody. She's probably the most popular girl on campus. She's gorgeous, isn't she?"

Jessica had already taken a dislike to her. It had been a dream of Jessica's, since her freshman year, that she might be nominated homecoming queen. Back at Mesa, she would have had an excellent chance. Here it already looked as if the odds were stacked against her. She shrugged, started up the hallway again. "She's all right."

Jessica had been at her locker half an hour earlier to deposit her notebook before checking in with her senior counselor. The man had seemed nice enough, but sort of slow and boring, and she couldn't remember his name any more than she could now remember her locker combination. Stopping in front of the locker, she searched her pockets for the slip of paper with the three magic numbers.

"Whoever you put on your list," she said, finding the paper and twisting the steel dial, "be sure to invite that new guy you're seeing. What's his name, Kent?"

Alice looked doubtful. "Clark. I don't know if he'd come. He doesn't like to be around a lot of people."

The dial felt as if it had gum stuck under it. This school was gross. "Where does he take you when you two go out, the desert?"

Alice smiled briefly. "We don't really go out. He just comes over." She added quickly, almost nervously, "He's an incredible artist. He's helped me so much with my painting."

Jessica paused, studying her. The topic of Clark disturbed Alice, and Jessica wondered why. More than that, she was concerned. She had always felt the urge to take care of Alice. Perhaps because Alice had lost both her parents when she was only ten.

"I'll have to meet him someday," she said finally, brushing a curl of hair from Alice's face. The younger girl nodded, kissed Jessica quickly on the cheek, and began to back away.

"I'm glad you had a happy vacation. I'm even more glad you're home! Catch you later, OK?"

"At lunch. Where should we meet?"

Alice had already begun to slip into the crowd. "I'll find you!" she called.

After waving a quick farewell, Jessica turned and opened her locker and discovered that the light blue cashmere sweater her mother had bought for her in Switzerland for two hundred francs was being spotted with *somebody's* grape juice. The juice was leaking from a soggy brown-paper lunch bag perched on top of a thick notebook that didn't belong to her and which she felt by all rights did not belong in her locker.

"Damn," she whispered, hastily pulling the bag and the

notebook out of the locker and dumping them on the ground. Her face fell as she unfolded her prize gift and held it up. She had known it was to be in the high nineties today; she'd only brought the sweater to show off to her friends. Now it had a big stain over the heart area. It was dark enough to be a bloodstain. Suddenly she wished she had never gotten on that plane in Zurich.

"Excuse me, I think these are mine," somebody said from below her. There was a guy crouched down at her feet, picking up the notebook and lunch bag. When he had his things in hand, he glanced up, clearing his throat. "Are we sharing the same locker?"

Jessica let her sweater down and sighed. "You mean you don't even get your own locker in this school? What kind of place is this? I had my own locker in kindergarten."

The guy stood, frowning as he noticed the juice dripping from his bag. "I guess it does take some getting used to. But I don't think I'll be getting in your way much. I only keep my books in my locker."

"And your lunch."

The fellow noticed her sweater and did a quick double take, from it to his bag. "Oh, no, did my grape juice leak on your sweater?"

"Somebody's grape juice did."

He grimaced. "I'm sorry, I really am. Do you think the stain will come out?"

"I'll probably have to cut it out."

"That's terrible." He reached a hand into the bag. "It's all my fault. Boy, can I make it up to you? Could I buy you a new one?"

"Not around here."

"Well, how much did it cost? I could pay you for it at least."

"Two hundred Swiss francs."

"How much is that?"

"I don't know." Jessica leaned an elbow on the wall of lockers, rested her head in her hand, blood pounding behind her temples. What a lousy way to start the day, the whole school year for that matter. "I can't remember."

The guy stood staring at her for a moment. "I really am sorry," he repeated.

Jessica closed her eyes briefly, taking a deep breath, getting ahold of herself. She was making a mountain out of a molehill. Fatigue often made her overreact. Chances were the dry cleaners could get the stain out. And if they didn't, they didn't. Her bedroom closet was overflowing with clothes. When she thought about it, she realized she had little right to blame this guy. After all, she was invading his territory. He had probably had this locker since he was a freshman.

She straightened up, letting the sweater dangle by her side, out of the way. "Don't worry about it," she said. "I have another one at home just like it." She offered him her hand, lightening her tone. "My name's Jessica Hart. I'm a Mesa High refugee."

The guy shook her hand. "I'm Michael Olson."

"Pleased to meet you, Michael." She wondered if this were their first meeting. She could have sworn she had seen him before. "Are you a senior?"

"Yeah."

"So am I."

"I thought so. Did you just get here? I didn't see you earlier this week."

"Yeah, my family's vacation ran a few days too long."

Michael nodded, looking her straight in the face, and as he did, Jessica realized that, besides seeming familiar, he was rather attractive. He had thick black hair and eyebrows, pleasant friendly features. Yet it was his eyes that sparked her interest. There was an extraordinary alertness and intelligence in them, a sharpness she had never seen before in anyone her age. But perhaps she was imagining it. For all she knew, he could be the local druggie, high on something.

But he seems nice enough.

"I bet you were in Switzerland," he said.

She laughed. "How did you guess?"

"Your accent." He glanced about. "I suppose this place looks old to you after Mesa."

She nodded. "And crowded. And hot. We had air-conditioning."

"Some of our rooms are cooled. The gym is. We take our basketball very seriously here at Tabb."

Jessica brightened. "Oh, now I know who you are! You're on the basketball team. I saw you playing last year. You killed us, didn't you?"

Michael shrugged. "It was close most of the way."

"Yeah, right, all through warm-up."

"Well, you guys were never very nice to our football team. What did we lose to you, the last nine in a row?"

"The last ten. And you know what's worse? Practically our whole varsity was transferred to Sanders High."

"I guess we couldn't expect to get beauty and brawn both."

Did he just compliment me? It sounded like a compliment.

Jessica didn't take compliments well. To simply accept them, she felt, was to acknowledge that her looks were important to her, and she always thought that was the same as saying to the world that she was superficial. On the other hand, she did love to be complimented. She was nuts, and she knew it.

She laughed again. "Before the football season's over, I know you're going to think Tabb got the raw end of the deal."

"I hope not," he muttered, lowering his head, pulling a handkerchief from his pocket, and wiping up the few remaining drops of juice from the locker. "I'm going to pay you for that sweater no matter what you say. What's a Swiss franc in U.S. money these days?"

"One and a half pennies. Forget about it, really. I have parents who can't spend enough on their darling daughter."

"It must be nice. Did you enjoy Switzerland?"

"Yeah. And the Greek islands. It was neat floating on a raft in the Mediterranean. The Vatican was far-out, too."

He nodded, repeated himself. "It must be nice." Then he began to back up. "Well, I have to go. I hope you like Tabb. I'm sure you will. If you need help finding your way around, just let me know."

"Thanks, Michael. See you later."

"Sure."

Michael was gone no more than ten seconds when Sara Cantrell appeared. It had been Sara who had been kind enough to pick Jessica and her parents up at the airport at three that morning. Sara had grumbled about it, naturally, but that was to be expected, and wasn't to be taken seriously. The two of them went back to the beginnings of time; they had taught each other to talk. Or rather, Jessica had learned to talk, and Sara had learned to make astute observations. Sara had a biting wit and was usually hungry for potential victims. Tabb High did not yet know what it had inherited. It would know soon, though.

"Hello, Jessie, can't believe you dragged yourself in today. God, you look wasted. You should go home and put your face back under a pillow."

Jessica yawned. "I didn't even go to bed. I was too busy unpacking. What are you doing here? When you dropped us off at home, you said you were taking the day off."

"I was until I remembered my mom wasn't working today.

She would just drive me nuts. Hey, do you know who that guy you were talking to is?"

"Michael Olson."

"Yeah. I hear he's the smartest guy in the school. Better get on good terms with him. You're taking chemistry, and I hear our young Olson wrote the lab manual they use here."

"Are you serious? I thought he looked clever." Then she winced. "Did you really sign me up for chemistry?"

"You told me to."

"My *dad* told you to. What do I need chemistry for?"

"So you can get into Stanford and find a smart young man to marry who'll give you smart little kids to play with in a big stupid house."

Jessica groaned. "I didn't know that's why I was taking chemistry."

Sara pointed to her sweater. "Did your ears explode while going up in the plane or what? That looks like a bloodstain."

"I didn't get it on the trip. It's something old. I got it at Penney's."

Sara grabbed the tag. "Is Penney's charging us in francs these days?"

Jessica pulled the sweater away and shut it in the locker. "Don't hassle me, all right? I'm still getting acclimated." She wiped at the grape juice on her hands. "Last night you said we share first period. What class is it? I lost my schedule already."

Sara wrinkled her nose. She could do a lot with her nose.

She had the same control over it that most people had over their mouths. This did not mean, however, that it was an unusually large nose. Sara was cute. By her own estimation—and Sara could be as ruthless on herself as she was on everybody else—she rated an eight on a scale of one to fourteen. In other words, she was slightly above average. She had rust-colored hair, cut straight above her shoulders, hazel eyes, and a slightly orange tan that somehow got deeper in the winter. Because she frequently wore orange tops and pants to complement her coloring, Jessica told her she looked like Halloween.

"Political science," Sara said. "And we've got this real liberal ex-vet for a teacher. He was in Vietnam and slaughtered little babies, and now he wants us selling the communists hydrogen bombs so he can have a clear conscience."

"He sounds interesting." Jessica didn't believe a word of it. "Come on, let's get there before the bell rings. I'm already four days late."

The teacher's name was Mr. Bark, and Sara hadn't been totally off base in her analysis. The first thing the man did when they were all seated was dim the lights and put on a videotape of a nuclear attack. The footage was from the big TV movie *The Day After.* They watched a solid ten minutes of bombs exploding, forests burning, and people vaporizing. When the lights were turned back on, Jessica discovered she had a headache. World War III always depressed her. Plus she wasn't wearing her glasses as she was supposed to; watching the show had strained her eyes. Sitting to her right, Sara had put her head down and nodded off. Jessica poked her lightly, without effect. Sara continued to snore softly.

"I hope my purpose in showing this movie is clear," Mr. Bark began, leaning his butt on the edge of his desk. "We can *talk* on and on about how incredibly destructive nuclear weapons are, but I think what we have just seen creates an image of horror that will stay with us a long time, and will remind us that above all else we can't allow the political tensions of the world to reach the point where pushing the button becomes a viable alternative."

If Sara hadn't been lying about his being a vet, then Mr. Bark hid it well. He didn't look like someone who had seen battle. In fact, he looked remarkably like a plump, balding middle-aged man who had taught high school political science all his life. He had frumpy gray slacks, black-rimmed glasses, and an itch on his inner left thigh that he obviously couldn't wait to scratch.

Jessica poked her friend again. Sara turned her head in the other direction and made a low snorting sound.

"One Trident submarine," Mr. Bark continued, raising one finger in the air for emphasis, striding down the center of the class, "has the capacity to destroy two hundred Soviet cities. Think about it. And think what would happen if the captain of a Trident sub should go off half-cocked and decide to make a place in history for himself, or to put an end to all history.

Now I know most of you believe that the fail-safe device the president has near him at all times controls—"

We should have had someone else pick us up at the airport.

Mr. Bark paused in midstride, suddenly realizing he didn't have Sara's full attention. Impatience creased his wide fleshy forehead. He moved to where he stood above her.

"She had a late night," Jessica said.

Mr. Bark frowned. "You're the new girl? Jessica Hart?"

"Yes, sir."

"And you're a friend of Sara's?"

"Yes, sir."

"Would you wake her, please?"

"I'll try." Jessica leaned close to Sara's head, hearing scattered giggles from the rest of the class. Putting her hand on the back of Sara's neck, she whispered in her ear, "You are making fools of both of us. If you don't wake up this second, I am going to pinch you."

Sara wasn't listening. Jessica pinched her. Sara sat up with a bolt. "Holy Moses," she gasped. Then she saw the stares, the smirks. Unfazed, she calmly leaned back in her chair and picked up her pen as if to take notes, saying, "Could you please repeat the question, Mr. Bark?"

"I didn't ask a question, Sara."

Sara stifled a yawn. "Good."

"But I'll ask one now. Were you awake through any of the movie?"

"I got the highlights."

"I'm glad. Tell me, what was your gut reaction while watching the bombs explode?"

Sara smiled slowly. "I thought it was neat."

Mr. Bark shook his head. "You might think you are being funny, but I can assure you that you are—"

"No, no," Sara interrupted. "I'm telling you exactly how I felt. The whole time I was watching it, before I nodded off, I was thinking, Wow."

Mr. Bark grinned in spite of himself. "Granted, Sara, the visual effects were outstanding. But didn't the wholesale destruction of our civilization upset you?"

"No."

"Come on, be serious. I had girls crying when I showed this movie in fifth period yesterday."

"Mr. Bark," Sara replied with a straight face, "when I was watching that part where the bomb exploded outside that university, I honestly thought to myself, 'Why, those lucky kids. They won't have to go to school anymore.'"

The class burst out laughing. Mr. Bark finally gave up. He tried to dig up more heartfelt testimonials from the less bizarre minded, and while he did so, Jessica noticed a handsome blond fellow sitting in the corner. She had to fight not to stare. What kind of place was this Tabb? First there was Clair Hilrey, who belonged in *Playboy*, and now there was this hunk. It was a wonder that they couldn't put together a halfway decent football team with all these great genes floating around. She poked Sara again.

"Who's that in the corner?" she whispered.

"The football quarterback," Sara whispered back.

"What's his name?"

"He hasn't got one. But his jersey number is sixteen."

"Tell me, dammit."

"William Skater, but I call him Bill. Pretty pretty, huh?"

"Amazing. Do you know if he has a girlfriend?"

"I've seen him hanging out with this cheerleader named Clair."

"God, I hate this school."

"Miss Hart?" Mr. Bark called.

"Yes, sir?"

He wanted to know about her feelings on radiation, and of course, she told him she thought it was just awful stuff. When the class was over, Jessica did her best to catch Bill's eye, but he wasn't looking.

I've been here less than two hours. I can't be getting a crush on someone already.

She ditched Sara and trailed Bill halfway across campus. He had a great ass.

The following period was the dread chemistry, and the teacher's lecture on molecular reactions proved far harder to absorb than Mr. Bark's on atomic explosions. This was definitely one class she wouldn't be able to BS her way through.

Toward the middle of the period, they started on the first lab of the year. Jessica ended up with a quiet Hispanic girl named Maria Gonzales for a partner. They hardly had a chance to talk, but she struck Jessica as the serious type. Jessica just hoped she was smart and took excellent notes. She wondered if Michael Olson really was a wizard at science. It would be asking too much, she supposed, to hope William Skater was.

Maybe Bill will be in another one of my classes.

Break came next. Before leaving for school that morning, Jessica had spoken to another friend of hers, Polly McCoy—Alice's older sister—filling her in on everything that had happened on her vacation. She had known Polly almost as long as she had Sara, although she was not nearly so close to Polly. A lot of their friendship was founded on simple geography; since they were kids they had lived only a few hundred yards apart; it was hard not to be friends with someone your own age who lived so close.

Polly had what at best could be described as a nervous disposition. It showed particularly when she was around Sara, who enjoyed picking on Polly. Keeping the two girls apart was difficult, however, because none of them really had any other close friends, and they usually ended up going to movies, the beach, or wherever together. Three bored girls each looking for one exciting guy.

When Polly and Alice's parents had died, they left the girls a large construction company. It was at present managed by a board of directors, but both girls were potential bosses and millionaires. They lived in a big house with a partially senile aunt who was their legal guardian. They lived as they wanted. Only the McCoy sisters could think of throwing a party to introduce two schools to each other.

But it turned out that Alice had not told Polly about the party.

"She's going to do what?" Polly asked as they waited in line at the soda machines. Polly had already gotten ahold of a candy bar. She ate a lot of sweets these days, and it showed, especially in her face. It was a pity. When thin, Polly was a doll.

"She's going to invite thirty of our own people and team them up with thirty of Tabb's people," Jessica said, casting an eye toward the front of the line. Apparently the machines here took kicks as well as quarters. The guy up front was busting a toe for a Coca-Cola Classic.

"She never told me."

"Maybe she just thought it up."

"I don't care. We're not having it. They'd rip up the house."

"No, they wouldn't." The guy kicked the machine one final time and then stalked off. He was from Mesa. "But let's not invite that guy. Hey, is there another place we can get something to drink?"

"There's the mall. It's less than five minutes away in the car. But I don't want to go there now. And I don't want a party at my house."

Jessica decided she'd let Sara and Alice argue with Polly. She had already made up her mind that they had to have the party if only to invite Mr. Football Quarterback. "All right, all right, we'll have it in my bedroom. What did you do while I was gone?"

"Nothing." Polly took a bite of her candy, her bright green eyes spanning the jammed courtyard. Then she grinned. "I take that back. I did do something funny. They were running a contest on the radio to see who could send in the best album cover for a new heavy-metal band. I can't even remember the group—it was Hell and Steel something. Anyway, I sent in one of Alice's paintings. She won!"

"What did she win?"

"A free trip to one of their New York shows and a backstage pass. The disc jockey said the group is seriously considering using her artwork."

"Is Alice going to go?"

"No. You know she hates loud music."

"Wait a second. One of Alice's paintings on the album cover of a heavy-metal band? Since when does she paint anything that doesn't have flowers and clouds in it?"

Polly shrugged. "It's none of my business."

"What's none of your business?"

"What Clark has her drawing."

"Her boyfriend has her drawing whips and demons? Boy, I hope he hasn't seduced her."

Polly did not appreciate the remark. She was fanatically protective of her younger sister. "He's not her boyfriend. He's just someone who comes over and eats our food."

"What's he look like?"

"Not bad, pretty good."

"You wouldn't want to give me too many details, would you?"

Polly smiled. Unlike her sister, her hair was dark, almost black, with red highlights. Indeed, in almost every respect, their looks differed. Alice was a waif. Polly was a peasant. She had big breasts and a bigger butt. "He's got great hands," she said.

"How do you know?"

"I'm not saying anything."

"For someone who doesn't like to pry into Alice's business, you've said a lot." The subject was beginning to bore Jessica. She noticed a booth near the center of campus, pointed it out. "What can we sign up for over there?"

Now Polly was bored. "Student office. They've lengthened lunch today so all those who want to play politics can tell us why we should vote for them. You're not thinking of running for anything, are you?"

Jessica had a brilliant idea. "No, but Sara is."

"Sara? She doesn't like to get involved in choosing what to wear in the morning."

"You say the candidates are supposed to speak at lunch today?"

"In the gym, yeah. It's the only cool building on campus."

"Let's sign her up."

"We can't. You have to sign up in person."

"Then you be Sara for a few minutes."

"We'll never get her out on the floor to speak."

"We'll worry about that later."

"She'll be furious." Polly paused, thought about that a moment. "All right, I'll be Sara. What should we have her run for?"

"What else? Student body president."

Chapter Two

Michael Olson had not heard Jessica Hart's comment to Alice McCoy about finding a guy to fall in love with by lunch, but had he been listening, he might have believed her to be a beautiful witch capable of casting potent spells. Michael had thought of Jessica, and nothing else, all morning. He had a terrible feeling he was going to spend a substantial portion of the remainder of the year thinking about her.

And I'm going to have to see her every day, several times a day, until June.

Whereas most guys would have been delighted with a setup that would bring them repeatedly in contact with a girl they found attractive, Michael didn't for the simple reason that he knew he'd never be able to get past the hello-how-are-you? stage. It was true that he had said much more to her than that during their first meeting, but that had been before he'd had a chance to fantasize about her. Now just the memory of her made him uneasy. He didn't know what it had been about her that had hit him so hard. He wondered if her effect on him hadn't been largely because of his own state of mind. His summer had been particularly lonely. He had worked and read a lot, and gone out seldom; and never with anyone of the opposite sex. Since school started he'd been looking over the new girls from Mesa. There was no doubt he was ripe for a crush.

Or a heartache.

"Remember that scene in *War Games* when Matthew Broderick changes the girl's grade with his home computer?" Bubba asked as he and Michael strolled across the deserted campus. Fourth period had just begun, but neither Bubba nor Michael was cutting. Because of extremely high scores on IQ tests taken when they were in junior high, both guys were in the MGM (Mentally Gifted Minors) Program. They had a free period each day to pursue individual projects that their superior intelligence qualified them to pursue. In actuality, they probably were cutting. So far this year, they had used fourth period primarily to get an early start on lunch.

"I remember the scene," Michael said. "You couldn't do that here, though, could you?"

Bubba was a wizard at computers, and at life itself. He was five feet four, and because he enjoyed food and denied himself nothing, he was also rather round. But stature and weight were no obstacle to Bubba. He went out with practically any girl he wanted and enjoyed the reputation as the coolest person in Tabb High.

"Not without the codes that give access to the school district's data files."

"I didn't think the scene was very realistic," Michael said. "Hey, why are we going to the administration building?"

"To get the codes."

"What?"

Bubba smiled faintly. He endeavored to maintain a serene countenance, like the holy Buddha, from whom his nickname had been derived. Michael couldn't remember who had thought up the nickname. Perhaps it had been Bubba himself. His real name was John Free.

"Mr. Bark wants me to write a program that will automatically read and count the votes on the cards that will be used in the voting for student body officers," Bubba explained.

"But you don't need the district data files to do that."

"Does Miss Fenway know that?"

Miss Fenway was a secretary in the administration building. "What does Miss Fenway have to do with any of this?"

"She has the codes written on a little piece of white paper taped to a board that slides out from her desk above her top left drawer. I saw them there yesterday."

"Did you memorize them?"

"No, I didn't have a chance. But I will today."

"But what does this have to do with the program you're writing for Mr. Bark?"

"Absolutely nothing."

Once inside the administration building, they went straight to Miss Fenway's office. She was busy sorting files at a corner cabinet when they entered. Michael had always liked Miss Fenway. She enjoyed playing mother to every kid in school, and she took special pride in him because he got straight A's. But she was no dummy, and he doubted Bubba would trick her into giving out confidential information. She had a computer terminal on her desk.

"May I help you boys?" she asked, putting down her papers and stepping toward them. A thin woman with a warm, wrinkled face, she had never married nor had any kids.

"Yes," Bubba said. "Mr. Bark has put me in charge of tabulating the votes for student body officers this afternoon. I need the codes that will allow me to connect the old card reader in this building with the new PC in the computer science class."

Miss Fenway was puzzled. "I hadn't been informed about this."

"Mr. Bark is free this period. You'll find him in the teachers' lounge, I believe. He'll explain what I mean." Bubba took a seat, making it clear he was going to wait in her office until she did what he wanted. Miss Fenway looked at Michael.

"Do you know what this is all about?"

"Not me."

The instant Miss Fenway left, Bubba sprang to his feet—he was remarkably agile given his physique—and closed the door. He had the desk board with the page of codes pulled out in two seconds. Swiftly, but carefully, he began to copy them down.

"I didn't see you do this," Michael said.

"See me do what?"

Miss Fenway returned a minute later with Mr. Bark. The latter explained to Bubba that all he had to do was write a program that broke the count down into freshmen, sophomores, etc. He would do the rest. Bubba nodded and apologized for not understanding the first time. As they were leaving, Mr. Bark told them about a video he wanted them to see.

"From the TV movie *The Day After*?" Bubba asked.

"Yes."

"I've seen it," Bubba said.

"What did you think?"

"It was neat."

Mr. Bark sighed. "I have this new student you should meet."

The computer room was empty fourth period. They had the place to themselves. Using the stolen codes, Bubba called up the files containing the transcripts of every kid in the school district. Michael wondered at his motivation. Although as intelligent as himself, Bubba never worried much about his grades. He had no intention of attending college. He wanted to go straight into business. In fact, he already invested in commodities and stock options. He also bet the horses through his uncle, who was a bookie with mob connections. Financially speaking, Bubba's family occupied the same position as Michael's, lower middle class. And yet Bubba drove an old but well-kept Jaguar and wore only the finest clothes. And he didn't even have a job. Since Michael had to slave six days a week at a local 7-Eleven to help his divorced mother make ends meet, he knew if he were to criticize Bubba's *businesses*, he would only be doing so out of jealousy.

"Here you are," Bubba said, pointing to the screen. Michael leaned closer. Semester after semester—rows of A's, except for one C his junior year. He'd gotten it last year in calculus. A pal of his had desperately whispered for help in the middle of a test. Being such a swell guy, Michael had slipped him a piece of paper with a few answers that, through bad timing and bad luck, had ended up in the hands of the teacher. Regrettably, the test had been the final exam and the teacher had given them both automatic F's. It had slashed his overall semester grade in half. His hopes of being valedictorian had gone out the window then and there.

"You can't change it," Michael said. "Everyone on the faculty knows I got that C."

Bubba's fingers danced over the keyboard. Then he frowned. "We can't change it, anyway. The file's protected. I should have known. Once transferred to the district offices, the grades are carved in stone." He thought for a moment, then jumped out of the file and into another that was the same except for the absence of recorded grades.

"What's that?" Michael asked.

"This semester's records." Bubba moved the cursor beside Michael Olson's MGM fourth period, put in an A. "This file hasn't been transferred yet. We can manipulate it up until the day it is." He erased the A. "You know, Mike, I think this is going to be a pretty laid-back year for the two of us. Would you like me to pull Dale Jensen's record?"

Dale Jensen had the only grade-point average higher than Michael's. It was a perfect 4.00. But Dale hadn't taken a difficult class in all the time he had gone to Tabb. He specialized in subjects where he could get up and indulge in long-winded monologues about how screwed up all the screw-ups in the world were. He was really a despicable character. If anyone stopped to tell him something, he always interrupted with the sarcastic line "I'm impressed."

"No, leave him alone."

"Are you sure? Who wants to listen to him graduation day?"

"We're not going to sneak a phony grade onto his transcript for this year without him knowing it."

"I suppose you're right," Bubba replied without much conviction, sitting back from the screen and stretching.

"I wanted to tell you about this girl I met," Michael began.

"Ask her out."

"No, let me tell you about her first."

"What for? I'm sure she's the greatest discovery since sliced bread. Just ask her out. What's her name?"

"You probably haven't seen her. She just got here this morning. Jessica Hart."

Bubba nodded approvingly. "I know her, a quality chick. A friend of hers is having a party for the whole school."

"Where did you hear that?"

Bubba shrugged. He seldom revealed the sources of his information. He was seldom wrong about anything. "I don't think you should wait until the party to go after her. She won't last, not around here. Someone will nab her. It may as well be you."

Michael chuckled at the crude manner in which Bubba referred to Jessica. He knew that Bubba had a strong admiration for the female species, or at least a powerful appreciation of them, which was almost the same thing. Girls who went out with Bubba once wanted to go out with Bubba twice. He knew how to satisfy them.

"Why don't you ask her on a date?" Michael asked.

"I can't. I've got to save myself for Clair Hilrey."

"I thought Clair was going with our esteemed quarterback, Bill Skater?"

"They've dated a few times. They went to the Baked Potato Restaurant last Saturday night. But it's nothing serious."

"Does Clair know this?"

"Give me a couple of weeks, and I'll make it clear to her."

Michael scratched his head. "Didn't Clair tell you last spring that she thought you were the most disgusting human being in the whole school?"

"It makes no difference. Over the summer your average teenage girl forgets nine-tenths of what happened the previous school year. I'll ask her out at tonight's game, during halftime. She'll say yes."

Michael shook his head in amazement. "I'm going to enjoy watching this."

Bubba sat up, speaking seriously. "I'll let you in on a profound secret. Only the very select of males in our society know this. And once you know it and ponder its significance for any length of time, your whole perspective will change."

"The earth is really flat?"

"No." Bubba leaned closer. "Girls want to have sex exactly as much as boys want to."

Michael laughed. "Bubba, I just met Jessie. I don't even know her. I don't want to sleep with her. I'm afraid to talk to her."

"It is much easier to have sex than to talk. When you talk, you have to think. You think too much, Mike. That's your problem. And you're lying to yourself. Of course you want to sleep with Jessie. You don't have to be ashamed. Chances are she probably wouldn't mind sleeping with you if she thought she could do it and not have to pay for it later in some way. That's why girls love me so much. I let them know that with me everything is OK."

"But you kiss and tell. With what you just said, that makes you a hypocrite. Take how you carried on about Cindy Fosmeyer."

"Who do I tell except you? And I know you would never damage a girl's reputation." He smiled. "And since we're talking about Cindy, did I ever tell you she has the hots for you?"

Cindy Fosmeyer had huge breasts. They were so huge they fairly blotted out any personality she might have had. "You never did because it's not true."

"Believe what you want, buddy." Bubba stood. "But I give you my word on this—if you don't ask Jessica out by Monday, I will."

Michael was not amused. He had known Bubba a long time. They'd had a lot of good times together. But there was a lot about him he didn't know, that he didn't want to know. "Is that a threat?"

"Think of it as an incentive."

"What about saving yourself for Clair?"

Bubba patted his bulging gut. "There's enough of me to go around." He turned toward the door. "I'll be back in a minute."

Bubba was gone much longer than a minute. While waiting, Michael entertained himself scanning Jessica Hart's transcript. He felt mild guilt at prying, but couldn't resist. He was mildly surprised to discover she was taking chemistry. She must have some smarts, but then, he had observed that talking to her. Perhaps she would need a tutor. He knew the subject so well that a rumor had gone around last year that he had written the lab manual. It was incredible the things people would believe.

When the door opened behind him, he assumed it was Bubba. The cool, soft hug from behind caught him by surprise.

"Hi, Mikey!"

"Alice, what are you doing here?"

Michael had met Alice McCoy the previous winter, a couple of weeks before Christmas. Wearing what he was later to discover to be her typical sunny expression, she had popped into his 7-Eleven and asked if she could paint Santa Claus and Frosty the Snowman on his windows. He had been immediately taken by her enthusiasm. She told him he could pay her what he thought it was worth, and if he didn't like it when she was done, he wouldn't have to pay her at all. It sounded like a good deal, but the owners of the store were Muslims from Lebanon, and he didn't know if they'd appreciate Christmas decorations all over their place of business. A quick call dispelled his fears; the two brothers were eager to have their store look as American as possible.

The next day was a Saturday. Alice showed up at nine o'clock in the morning. He expected her to chalk out a few reindeer and spray on a couple of featureless snowmen and call it done. Her supplies threw him for his first loop. She had a huge, flat black case of paints and brushes. She spent a half hour cleaning and polishing the windows before starting, and when she finally did begin, she worked steadily for seven hours, slowly, patiently, meticulously unfolding a rich colorful tapestry of sparkling elves, joyous children, and racing sleighs. When she finished, she sprayed on a sealer that she promised would protect the paintings. When he finally did wash away her work, near Easter, it had been with a heavy heart. But by then he'd had something greater than her pictures to enjoy. He had Alice herself, as both a regular visitor and a good friend. She was a true gift of holiday magic. She had charm and grace, kindness and wit.

She was everything he had imagined his little sister would have been.

Michael's mother was only seventeen and in high school when she had given birth to him. Old man Jerry Olson split for parts unknown five years after that—Michael still had a few clear memories of his dad—and since then his mother had dated a seemingly endless succession of men. Two years ago one of them had gotten her pregnant. The guy had had no wish to marry her—he, too, would eventually disappear—and his mother had vacillated about having an abortion. Finally, over Michael's bitter protests, she had decided on the operation— sort of late. He did not understand why the doctor had told his mom it had been a girl, or why she had told him.

By a strange quirk of fate, he'd always thought of his

unborn sister as *Alice*. After the incident, he often dreamed of what she would have been like. His little Alice. He still loved his mother more than anyone, but he doubted he'd ever totally forgive her for what she had done.

But now, with Alice McCoy here to see him, it was easy to pretend what had gone before had been only a bad dream.

"What am I doing? I'm cutting, just like you," she said, releasing him and walking around the room, lightly tapping the keyboards on Tabb's brand-new PCs, touching a printout page. Like a perpetually curious child, Alice was fascinated with everything around her.

"You have an art class now, right?"

"Yeah, I'm supposed to be at the park across the street studying tree branches. But they've just sprayed there with an awful-smelling insecticide." She giggled. "I did start on this one sketch of a giant mosquito sucking the sap out of a tree. It was really gross."

"Can I see it?"

"No."

"Did you throw it away?"

She shook her head. "But I'm going to, right after I show it to Clark. It really is weird. I can't believe I drew it."

"Clark's your new boyfriend, isn't he?"

"He's not that new. I see him a lot."

"I'd like to meet him. What's he like?"

Alice shrugged, tossing her bright head of hair. "I don't want to talk about him. I want to tell you about a friend of mine I want you to meet. She's from Mesa, like me. She's really wonderful."

"What's her name?"

"I'm not going to tell you. I want to be the one to introduce you so that when you both fall in love, and get married later on, you'll be able to look back and say it was *I* who made it all possible. Are you going to the game tonight?"

"I'm going to try. I have to work, but I should be able to catch the second half."

"Could you get there at halftime? I could introduce you to her then."

Michael chuckled. He wasn't really interested in Alice's friend, not after meeting Jessica Hart, but he saw no harm in saying hello to the girl. "What's wrong with today at lunch?"

"I won't be here. I have a doctor's appointment."

He paused. "What for? I mean, are you sick?"

Alice brushed aside the question. "It's nothing, I just have to stop in."

"How are you going to get there? I could give you a ride." For some reason, the thought of Alice going all alone to the doctor disturbed him. He knew she had no parents, and that her guardian aunt didn't get out often.

"I'm taking a taxi."

"They're expensive."

"I have money. Don't worry about it. Just be there tonight at halftime. I'll get her to come."

"I'll do my best," he promised.

She smiled. "Thanks, this means a lot to me. Oh, what's that you have on your screen? It looks like a report card."

Michael explained how through the use of special codes—he didn't say where they had obtained them—he and his friend were able to tap into the school's files. Alice was fascinated, but before she could ask any questions, Bubba returned. And when Bubba realized that Alice had been made privy to what he obviously considered inside information, he quickly tried to present a more innocent picture of their doings.

"What's on this screen is only a photocopy of existing records," he said. "It's not the records themselves. We're just looking at them, that's all. It's no big deal."

Alice grinned slyly. "Sure, you're getting ready to turn the school upside down, and it's nothing? I'm not that dumb. Come on, where did you steal these codes?"

"What codes?" Bubba asked, glancing at Michael. "These photocopies aren't confidential. You don't need codes to access them."

Alice laughed gaily, much to Bubba's displeasure. "I don't believe you!"

Bubba feigned nonchalance, quickly maneuvering out of the file, leaving the screen blank. "Suit yourself," he said.

"In fact, I think you could get into lots of trouble if certain people knew about this," Alice said playfully.

Bubba stopped, stared at her a moment. "No one's going

to get into trouble. No one's going to talk about this. OK?"

She didn't understand what he was really saying. "He's right," Michael said. "This isn't something that should get around. Do me a favor, Alice, and forget what I showed you here."

"All right," she said cheerfully. "But I know it was all your idea, Bubba. Michael wouldn't fool with people's grades."

"Nor would I," Bubba said curtly.

Alice laughed again, oblivious to the tension in the room. Giving Michael a quick kiss on the cheek, she reminded him to be sure to get to the stadium by halftime. The instant she was gone, Bubba turned off the screen and shook his head.

"Mike, you're not improving your chances of being valedictorian by trying to get us both expelled."

"Alice won't talk. She's my friend."

"Alice is a fifteen-year-old girl who is not my friend. I don't trust her."

"Don't worry about it. She was only kidding."

Bubba thought for a moment. "All right, Mike, whatever you say."

Michael and Bubba went to the mall for lunch shortly after that. It was crowded. Michael remembered when the mall had been nothing but a piddling collection of failing stores. Put a roof over something and people swarmed in.

Michael ordered a turkey sandwich from Ed's Sandwich

Selection. His mother was usually too tired after working all day as a secretary in a downtown high-rise to cook; he had grown up eating most of his food wedged between two slices of bread.

He was practically finished with his sandwich before Bubba had even decided what to order. Bubba finally opted for Indian food, which took time to prepare (to his specifications). By then many of Tabb's students had already come and gone so they could be back for the special assembly of candidate speeches. Michael also had a mild interest in hearing the talks. Plus he hoped to run into Jessica Hart again. He had begun to take Bubba's threat seriously. At Michael's prodding, Bubba got his dishes to go.

The assembly was well under way when they entered the gym. The bleachers were jammed. They stood near the ticket booth beside the entrance, Bubba holding his aromatic spiced dahl and rice in a white cardboard container, surveying the audience for a seat. In a high, cracking voice, a girl at the microphone was talking about school spirit and how far-out she was.

"Do you see her?" Bubba asked.

"I'm not looking for her."

"I believe you. I see her."

"Where? Don't point."

"Sixth row on the far right, two rows behind Fosmeyer's body."

Michael saw her. It was amazing how her beauty had magnified since morning. The shine of her long brown hair seemed to jump right out from the crowd. "All right, let's leave," Michael said.

"But you dragged me back here. No, we're going to sit behind her."

Michael didn't like that idea. "There's no room."

Bubba ignored him. "Come on."

They didn't actually get the seats directly behind Jessica, but a couple of rows back. Bubba obtained the space by gesturing to a couple of sophomores to move to the rear. Bubba did not have a reputation for being violent; nevertheless, the kids jumped when he pointed. Climbing the steps, Michael had kept his head turned away from Jessica. He didn't know if she'd noticed him.

Sitting in the row between Michael and Jessica were a couple of Tabb's football players. They cheered loudly as the next speaker was announced: Bill Skater. Bubba began to lay out his Indian delicacies, opening a bottle of Perrier and spreading a cloth napkin across his lap. Michael saw Jessica lean forward as Bill strode toward the microphone. She had a pudgy girl with dark hair on her left and an orange-haired girl on her right. These two girls turned and spoke to Jessica when Bill appeared. Michael leaned forward, trying to block out Bill's opening statements, straining to hear what the girls were saying.

"He walks like a stiff board," the one on the left said.

"I hear he's the worst quarterback in Tabb's long history of terrible quarterbacks," the one on the right said.

"Shut up, both of you," Jessica said.

"Oh, but I think he's cute," the one on the left said.

"He should take his shirt off and give his speech," the one on the right agreed.

"Shh. I want to hear what he has to say," Jessica said.

"What for, we've heard it all before," the one on the left said.

"Yeah, I wish I could get down there and tell them what this school really needs," the one with orange hair said.

This last comment caused Jessica and her pal on the left to break into laughter. Michael didn't know what was so funny. He wondered if Jessica was interested in Bill Skater.

Michael listened to Bill's speech with an open and unprejudiced mind, but never did figure out what he was running for, much less why anyone should vote for him. Bubba continued to savor his meal. When Clair Hilrey's name was announced next, however, Bubba looked up.

"Isn't she something?" he muttered as Clair swaggered to the microphone in her cute blue-and-gold cheerleader uniform.

"She's an empty phony devoid of an iota of intelligence."

Bubba nodded. "True. But if you look past those superficial qualities, you'll see her true value."

"Which is?"

"It's hard to express in words. Just imagine her naked."

Clair's speech had a content similar to Bill's, which is to say it had no content at all. But she giggled a lot, whereas Bill had been as stiff as the board Jessica's friend had compared him to, and she did have an alluring way of propping her hands on her hips at the top of her undeniably gorgeous legs. Clair made it clear she wanted to be school president.

The name Sara Cantrell was called next.

"What the hell?" the girl on Jessica's right said.

"Go ahead, tell them what this school really needs," Jessica said.

"No way. I'd have to start by telling them it doesn't need me."

"Coward," the girl to Jessica's left said.

"Don't call me a coward, you spineless fish."

"Sara Cantrell, please?" the announcer repeated.

"It took you three years to alienate everyone at Mesa," Jessica said. "Just think of the power you'll have behind that microphone. You can do it all in one afternoon here."

The logic appealed to the strange girl named Sara. Michael watched as she stood and made her way down the bleacher steps and onto the gymnasium floor.

"Hi, I'm Sara," she began, completely at ease. "I'm not really running for anything. My friends Jessica Hart and Polly McCoy signed me up because they thought it would be funny to get me down here." Sara pointed toward her friends. "They're sitting right over there. Let's give them a big laugh to show them that at least we think *they're* funny."

The audience cheered loudly. Jessica and Polly turned beet red and buried their faces in their knees. Michael burst out laughing.

"But since I am here," Sara continued, "I do have a few things I'd like to say. First, I don't think you should vote for anybody who's spoken this afternoon. They all struck me as a bunch of insecure idiots, looking to get their egos stroked. Second, I don't believe we need student officers at all. What do they do? I'll tell you. Nothing! And finally, I don't know who out there stole the chewing gum from my locker, but I hope you choke on it. Thank you."

Sara received a standing ovation and thunderous applause. She walked back to her place as though she were just another spectator taking her seat. But she grinned when she reached her friends.

"How did I do?" she asked.

"You'll probably be expelled," Polly said.

"Or elected," Jessica said.

"I think your girlfriend's right," Bubba whispered in Michael's ear.

Chapter Three

Nick Grutler did not go to the mall for lunch nor did he attend the afternoon assembly. He didn't own a car to drive anywhere, and no one had told him about the election. Indeed, although Nick had been in school every day since Monday, no one at Tabb had even spoken to him outside of class, and that included his teachers. Nick Grutler was six feet four, wiry as a hungry animal, and as black as midnight. No one had spoken to him for the simple reason that they were afraid of him.

Tabb High had several black students—four to be exact, two girls and two boys—but none of them was a recent transfer from East L.A. where youth gangs ruled. None of them had the pent-up emotion that came from having to master the use of a switchblade by age twelve just to survive. Nick had not killed anybody—no one he had been forced to stab, at least, had died in his presence—but he had seen more violence than most war vets. And he had always hated it, and worse—in his own mind, for someone of his size and strength—had been afraid of it. None of the teachers that had yet to speak to him had noticed that the new boy from the other side of the city who sat so still during class actually had tremors beneath his skin. Nick had a lot he wished he could forget.

But it was his intention to forget, or if that was not possible, at least to put the past behind him. He considered the new job his divorced father had landed in a nearby aerospace firm as a gift from above. Another summer in East L.A. like the past one, Nick knew, probably would have seen him killed. On the other hand, Tabb High was no paradise either, so far.

He was enrolled as a senior, but he had to admit to himself that he hardly qualified as a freshman in this part of town. He was going to have to read the textbooks they had given him. He was going to have to *learn* to read.

He had absolutely no one to talk to. The white kids at school were all caught up in things that he had always imagined were just for TV characters. They went to the beach and parties and worried about what they were going to wear to the next dance. In a way they were like children to him. They had never stared down the barrel of a sawed-off shotgun and been ordered to kiss cold metal. They had lived incredibly sheltered lives. And yet, they were light-years beyond him. They knew all kinds of stuff. They could get up in front of a whole class and speak what was on their minds. They had nice clothes, nice cars, and lots of money. They could laugh at the drop of a hat. He had spent Monday through Thursday feeling superior to them. But now that it was Friday, he realized he was jealous—and all alone.

His counselor had put him in sixth period P.E., where all the athletes were. The only connection Nick had had with any sport was basketball. He used to play in a lot of pick-up games in the inner city. Of course, basketball season was months away. The coach who oversaw the P.E. class hadn't known what to do with him. Finally he'd asked if Nick would like to lift weights. Sure, Nick had said.

Nick was working up a sweat with over two hundred pounds on the bench press that Friday afternoon when the big, fat-legged dude with the thin-lipped mouth began to hassle him.

"A little heavy for you?" the dude asked, taking up a position near Nick's knees. Lying on his back, Nick could see that the weight room was fairly crowded, about twenty guys pumping iron. He suspected they were all on the football team, and that not a single one of them would rally to his side if this guy started to get rough. He knew instantly the guy was looking for a fight. He had an instinct for such things.

"It's not bad," he muttered, letting go of the bars and sitting up. Perhaps if he went on to another machine, he thought, there was a chance the guy would leave him alone. Unfortunately, the guy was blocking his way.

"What did you say, boy?" the big white kid asked.

"Nothing."

"Yeah, you did. I heard you say something. What was it?"

Nick scooted back to where he was able to swing his leg around the bench press table without touching the guy. "I said, it was not bad. The weight wasn't."

The guy smiled. A couple of his buddies behind him stopped lifting to watch. "You must be pretty strong, boy. How many pounds were you lifting there?"

"I don't know."

"You don't know? How come you don't know?"

Nick stood up. "I wasn't keeping track."

The guy followed him to the next machine, which exercised the hamstrings. To use it, Nick would have to lie face down, which was not something he wanted to do at the moment. He stood undecided as all around him more guys stopped working out to stare.

"What are you waiting for?" the dude asked, moving closer. Nick estimated the guy had forty pounds on him, but knew that his gut was soft, a swift fist in the diaphragm and the white kid would go down. Nick also estimated that about twenty guys would jump him the moment the guy hit the floor.

"Nothing." Nick had never mastered the art of talking his way out of a fight.

"Aren't our machines good enough for you?"

Nick lowered his head. "They're all right."

"Just all right? You sure spend enough time on them, time that someone else on the team could be using. Are you getting my meaning, boy?"

Nick got it very well. But suddenly he didn't feel that he should. This is how it had always been with him. He would try to avoid a confrontation up to a point—and then he just wouldn't bend anymore. He would explode. He hated being called boy.

"No."

The guy lost his smile. "No what?"

Nick looked him straight in the eye. He hadn't really looked anyone in the eye all week. "I have as much right to use this equipment as you do. If you think I don't, that's your problem."

"Really? Well, I think it just became your problem." And with that, the guy shoved him hard in the chest.

Nick had been expecting the move, and it was still his intention to floor the guy without seriously injuring him. But what followed proved unexpected. Absorbing the blow without losing his balance, Nick moved slightly to the right and forward. He planned to grab the guy by the left arm, spin him around, and put him in a choke hold. He figured that would be the best way to keep his teammates at bay. He couldn't believe it when the overweight tub anticipated *his* move and caught his right hand, whipping him into the nearby wall with incredible force. On the wall hung a mirror the guys used to admire themselves.

It splintered on impact beneath Nick's skull, cutting into his scalp. Then he was on the floor, trying to stand. Blood trickled down the side of his face. The guy's feet were approaching.

"You goddamn piece of—" the dude swore as he let fly a kick toward Nick's forehead. Nick was through treating him carefully. He ducked the fat foot and crouched, coiling the power of his legs. The momentum of the misplaced kick left the white dude twisted at an awkward angle. Nick launched himself upward, grabbing the guy's hair with both hands and snapping his right knee into his groin. The bastard couldn't even scream out. Doubling up, making a strangled gasping sound, he fell to the floor, turning a sick pasty color.

"Who's next?" Nick barked, glaring at the remainder of the room. He doubted that he'd scare off the whole gang, and he was right. You couldn't bluff people out of a twenty-to-one advantage. A few of the stockier fellows began to close in. Instinctively, Nick knelt and grabbed ahold of a large jagged slice of mirror. The players paused warily, glancing at one another. It was then that the head of the football team, Coach Campbell, barged in.

Nick had seen the man before. Approximately forty years old, he had tan leathery skin and a wide blunt face Nick thought particularly ugly. Although below average in height, he was built like a tree trunk and had one of those thick raspy voices that was usually the result of years of shouting.

"What's going on here?" he demanded. He saw his player

rolled up on the floor and then saw Nick bleeding, with the glass knife in his hand. A look of pure disgust filled his already disgusting face. "Put that down!"

Nick set the piece of mirror on the floor. He had been gripping it so hard, it had cut into his fingers, and they were bleeding as well. Coach Campbell moved so close to Nick that Nick could feel his hot breath on his bare chest. "What did you do to Gordon?" he asked.

"He attacked m-me," Nick stuttered.

"He attacked *you*? Why would he attack someone carrying a knife?" The coach backed off a step, scowled down at Gordon. "Skater, Fields, help The Rock to the infirmary."

The Rock, Nick thought.

The players did as told and soon the guy had been cleared away. From the outside, Nick knew he was standing perfectly still, but inside he was shaking. He half expected the coach to belt him in the face. Worse, he had no doubt at all that he was to be expelled, and that his father would kick him out of the house when he heard.

"What's your name, son?" Coach Campbell asked.

"Nick Grutler."

"Where you from? What are you doing here?"

"This is where I go to school."

"Who gave you permission to use the facilities in this room?"

"The other coach."

"Who?"

"I don't remember his name."

Coach Campbell folded his arms across his chest, nodding to himself. "I know who you are. You're that transfer from Pontiac High downtown. I was warned about you. I see I should have listened."

Nick swallowed. "He started it."

Coach Campbell looked around the room. "Is this true?" He waited for an answer. No one spoke up. The coach sighed, shook his head. "Grutler, either you're a liar or else no one here gives a damn about your hide. I don't know which is worse. But I can tell you one thing, you're on your way out, out of this room and off this campus." He began to walk away. "See someone at the infirmary about your cuts. Then come to my office."

A heavy weight descended on Nick, and for the first time an outsider might have noticed a crack in his reserve. He was stooped over slightly; he couldn't quite catch his breath. He really had wanted to fit in.

Then the unexpected happened for the second time in a few minutes. One of the guys in the corner began to laugh. The sound caused Coach Campbell to stop in the doorway and glance over his shoulder. The guy in the corner kept right on laughing, louder and louder. The coach turned toward him, glaring.

"What are you giggling about, Desmond?" Coach Campbell demanded.

The guy got up slowly, shaking his head. "It's just that you remind me, Coach, of a sheriff in a movie I saw last night on TV. The sheriff tried to put a black fella behind bars just 'cause he didn't like his looks. Sitting here, I was thinking you talked just like him. You see that movie, Coach? You would have liked it. The sheriff ended up going to jail."

"What's your point?"

The guy yawned. "Seems to me if The Rock wants to pick on people that can kick his ass, I don't see why it's anybody's business except his and the guy he's hassling."

"Are you saying The Rock started this? Why didn't you speak up earlier?"

"Couldn't be bothered, I guess."

Coach Campbell glanced at Nick, then back at the guy. Nick could see Desmond was no slouch, either. About six feet with a head of thick brown hair, he had a powerfully developed physique. More important to Nick, though, when he had begun to laugh, the other guys in the room had backed off slightly, as though even his humor intimidated them. Coach Campbell seemed to take him seriously enough.

"What are you doing in here, anyway, Desmond?" the coach asked. "Don't you have a cross-country race to run this afternoon?"

"I do, yeah. So what?"

"You shouldn't be tiring yourself out beforehand lifting weights." Then his tone took on a bitter edge. "You shouldn't be running at all. Why don't you suit up for tonight's game? We need some help at fullback."

"I'll tell you why, Coach. 'Cause I don't feel like it."

"You're wasting God-given talents. You could go to college on a scholarship. You have the potential to go to Notre Dame!"

Desmond looked bored, sat down. "No way, I ain't even Catholic."

Coach Campbell let out an exasperated breath, turned to Nick. "All right, Grutler, we'll let it pass this time. But in the future, try to stay out of trouble."

Nick had not expected an apology. "Yeah, sure."

When the coach had left, everyone went back to pumping iron, except for Desmond, who pulled on a torn cross-country jersey and strolled outside. Nick caught up with him on the hot asphalt between the weight room and the gym.

"Hey, I just wanted to thank you," Nick said.

The guy didn't even slow down. "No problem. I got a real kick out of seeing you knee The Rock between the legs. I bet that pig can't stand up straight for a week."

"Well, I won't forget it. I owe you one."

"You don't owe me nothing. But if you want to buy me a case of beer someday, I'll drink it." And with that, Desmond walked away.

Nick did not go to the infirmary. He didn't know where it was, and he didn't want to run into The Rock and his pals if he *was* able to find it. He took a shower instead and afterward held a wad of toilet paper to the cut on his scalp. Eventually the bleeding began to subside. The resulting scar would be hidden under his hair, but because he had hit the mirror with the side of his head, and not the back, the flesh between his left temple and left eye had also begun to swell. He worried what his father would say when he saw it. His father had a violent temper.

Besides having given him walking orders to stay out of trouble, his father had also told him not to come home that afternoon without a job. Nick had figured his best bet would be the nearby mall. He knew roughly where it was and thought he might be able to walk there in less than an hour. He'd worked before, in his old neighborhood, loading freight at the docks. He wondered if the stores in the mall would want him to fill out all kinds of papers before letting him show what he could do. He hoped not.

Before he set out for the mall, he stopped at the soda machines in the courtyard. He was disappointed to discover he didn't have enough money to buy a Coke. He was standing there, fishing through his pockets for a possible hidden dime, when a small Hispanic girl came up at his side.

"May I?" she asked. He was blocking her way. He stepped aside hastily.

"I don't have the right change," he mumbled. He'd seen the girl before, at lunch, sitting by herself beneath a tree hugging her knees. She had long black hair tied back in a ponytail that reached to her waist.

"Oh." She put in her change, made her selection. A can of orange soda popped out below. "What do you need?"

"Nothing, I wasn't that thirsty." He was dying for a drink. "Thanks, anyway."

"No," she said, glancing up at him with big, lustrous eyes, a serious, perhaps sad, expression. "I have change."

Nick shrugged. "I need a quarter."

She reached in her tiny purse. "I have three dimes."

He took out his dime and three nickels. This was all the money he had in the world. He'd gone without lunch. This was another reason he needed a job in a hurry. He had to buy almost all his own food. He took her dimes and bought his Coke, giving her back the spare nickel. "Thanks," he said, opening the can, shifting nervously on his feet. She was staring at him.

"Do you know you're bleeding?" she asked finally.

He touched the side of his head. It had started again. "It's nothing. I cut it."

"Does it hurt?"

"No. A little. It will stop in a minute."

She went to touch the area. He recoiled automatically, and she quickly withdrew her hand. "I'm sorry," she said.

"It's really nothing," he said quickly.

"You were in a fight, weren't you?"

He began to shake his head, stopped. "Yes, I was."

Her next question caught him off guard. "Did you win?"

"I don't think he'll want to fight me again."

She offered her hand. "I'm Maria Gonzales. You're Nick, aren't you?"

He shook her hand briefly. Her skin was cool, very soft. "How did you know?"

"I've watched you this week. You walk from one place to another. You never talk to anyone. I did that when I first got here."

She had a strong Spanish accent. He wondered if she had only recently come into the United States. He'd had experience with a variety of ethnic groups in his old neighborhood. He suspected she wasn't from Mexico, but from farther south, from El Salvador or Nicaragua. "I don't know many people here," he said.

"Do you know anybody?"

"I know the name of the guy who threw me into the mirror."

She smiled faintly. She had deep red heart-shaped lips, smooth high cheeks untouched by makeup. Her pink dress hung loose and cool but he could tell she had a fine figure. She had a freshness about her he had seldom seen in his old neighborhood. She had probably led a clean life.

"And I bet he knows your name," she said.

Nick smiled, too, pleased with himself for having made a mildly funny remark, and happy to be talking to someone who was kind. Yet at the same time he felt the sudden urge to curtail the conversation. Perhaps he wanted to quit while he was ahead. Maybe he didn't think he was good enough to be talking to someone like Maria.

"Nice meeting you," he mumbled, backing up a step. "I better be going."

"Do you take the bus home?"

"No."

"Oh, you have a car?"

He stopped. The truth sounded so poor. "Not really."

"Where do you live?"

In a shack.

"Near Houston and Second."

"I live over that way. You don't walk home every day, do you?"

"Sometimes I hitch a ride." No one had picked him up so far.

"You should take the bus. There's one coming in about ten minutes. You shouldn't be walking home after getting hit like that on the head."

The urge to get away intensified. He felt exposed, as though any second this girl was going to see something repulsive in him. He took another step back. "I'll be all right. I've got to go. Thanks again for the Coke."

"Take care of yourself, Nick."

He hurried off the campus, walking in the direction of the mall. He didn't understand it. She had sounded concerned about him.

Chapter Four

Sara Cantrell approached the soda machines seconds after Maria Gonzales and Nick Grutler finished talking. Sara was feeling pretty good. She was glad she had spoken her mind about the candidates in the assembly that afternoon. The whole country was in love with phonies, she felt. The bimbos on sitcoms, the rock dopers on MTV, the rich liars in D.C. It made her sick just going into the supermarket and having to look at all those fakes on the covers of *People* magazine. One day she'd like to start a magazine of her own where she could interview people like herself, people who knew it was all a big joke.

Sara had a bad thirst. But when she put her quarters in the soda machine and punched the 7-Up button, nothing happened. She tried the other buttons, then the coin return, and still nothing happened. Her good mood went right out the window. Those were the only two quarters she had! What did this stupid machine expect her to do, drink water? She pounded it with her fists, kicked it with her feet. Her quarters must be stuck.

The administration's probably behind this. Trying to weasel extra money out of us kids to buy themselves magazines for their goddamn lounge.

She remembered a move a guy had done on one of the soda machines at lunch. He had grabbed ahold of it with both hands and tilted it slightly on edge, coughing up not only his money but a couple of free cans as well. Setting down her books, she stretched out her arms, trying to get a grip on it. She was not a big girl, nor was she particularly strong. Nevertheless, when she tilted the machine to the right, she was surprised to see it rock right out of her hands. It hit the asphalt with an incredible bang, causing her to jump. Taking a quick look around to make sure no one had seen her, she collected her books and hurried toward the front of the campus. At Mesa High she'd never once had a soda machine fall over on her. This was a stupid school.

Sara was supposed to meet Polly and Jessica in the parking lot directly across from campus. They had been forced to put their cars there; Tabb's lot was filled. Sara was temporarily without wheels. Her dad had taken them away when she had received her third ticket in a month for running a red light. It was a real drag—and totally unfair. She had only gone through the lights after stopping and looking both ways. Why, she thought, should she have to sit and wait on a mechanism that didn't care if she crossed the road or not?

Her dad didn't know she had picked up Jessica and her folks at three in the morning. She'd run half a dozen red lights driving to the airport.

A row of bushes separated the school from the sidewalk that ran along its west side. They were tall, thick shrubs, and putting one foot onto the sidewalk, Sara couldn't see more than a few yards in either direction. She didn't even hear Russ Desmond coming.

When he hit her, she hardly felt a thing. One second she was walking, the next, flying. She must have closed her eyes. When she opened them, she was sitting in the bushes with a branch running up her pant leg and a flower stuck in her ear.

"Oh, wow," she breathed. A guy with the greatest set of legs she had ever seen was standing over her breathing hard.

"You all right?" he asked.

"What happened?"

"You got in my way."

"Really?" Did this guy throw every chick that got in his way into the bushes? She sat up with effort, a muscle in her lower back protesting. The guy grabbed her arm and pulled her onto the sidewalk as if she were light as a feather. The second he let go of her, she reeled backward. The sidewalk wobbled under her feet. "Thanks a whole bunch," she muttered, blinking. "Who the hell are you?"

"Russ Desmond." He wiped his sweaty face on his arm,

still panting like a dog. "You've got leaves in your hair."

"I didn't grow them, believe me." She tried to brush them away and poked herself in the ear. Her hands were trembling. Maybe she had a concussion or something. The guy looked pretty far-out, like a biker in a track uniform. "I'm Sara Cantrell. You must have seen me at lunch."

"Huh?"

Just then a multicolored herd of various-shaped teenage boys came storming down the sidewalk. They had appeared from around a corner, and there was only a second to get out of their way. Russ Desmond watched them pass without a great deal of interest.

"Do the guys migrate at Tabb or what?" she asked, getting back down from the steps where she had run for safety.

"We're just having a little race is all. What did you mean, I must have seen you at lunch? What happened at lunch?"

It hit Sara then what was going. "Wait a sec, you're in the middle of a race?"

"That's what I just said."

"No, I mean, *you're* in the race?"

"Yeah."

"But you were winning!" She looked down the sidewalk in the direction of the rapidly vanishing group of cross-country runners. "Get going. Go after them. Hurry!"

"I will," he said, sounding vaguely annoyed. "In a minute. I just want to make sure you're all right."

"I'm all right. Get out of here."

"First tell me what happened at lunch?"

"I gave a speech. Didn't you hear my speech? It doesn't matter. I'm sure someone taped it. You can listen to it after your race. Now get out of here. Go. Scoot. Good-bye."

He nodded, gave a quick smile. "You've wrecked my time, Sara."

Watching him run off, pulling leaves from her hair, she muttered, "Well, you wrecked my makeup, Russ."

Russ Desmond.

Polly and Jessica showed up a few minutes later. They were talking about Alice's party, or rather, arguing about it. Sara loved arguments. She hated to simply discuss things.

"Food doesn't have to be a big deal," Jessica was saying. "We don't have to feed everyone dinner for god's sake. All we need are a few sweet and salty dishes, and plenty to drink. Isn't that right, Sara?"

"That is true."

"But people are going to be showing up with beer," Polly said. "You remember what happened at Alice's last party? Claudia Philips got drunk and threw up all over Kirk Holden."

"So we won't invite Claudia," Jessica said.

"Or Kirk," Sara added.

"And we can put on the invitations that no alcohol will be allowed," Jessica said.

66

Polly grimaced. "We have to print up invitations?"

"Of course," Sara said. "We have to show these barbarians we have class."

"Who's going to pay for all this?" Polly asked. "Me?"

"No, of course not," Sara said. "Alice will."

"Alice has the same account as I do," Polly complained. Then she paused, staring at Sara. "What happened to you? You have leaves in your hair, Sara."

"Well, you have a fat ass, Polly. And this evening I'll wash my hair and look just wonderful, and you'll still have a fat ass."

"You wouldn't look wonderful if a car full of plastic surgeons ran over you on the freeway," Polly retorted.

Sara wrinkled her nose. "Huh?"

"Stop it, you two," Jessica said. They had reached Jessica's and Polly's cars. Jessica had a Toyota; Polly, a Mercedes. Both cars were brand-new. Sara had had a nice car once, before she had run into a stupid telephone pole. Jessica continued, "We have to decide whether we want to make it a swimming party or not. What do you think, Sara?"

"Definitely. We can go skinny-dipping."

"We're not going skinny-dipping," Polly said. "It's against the law."

"Only when you've got a fat—" Sara stopped, looking around. "Where's Alice?"

Jessica and Polly glanced at each other. "She went home early," Jessica said.

"What's the matter?" Sara asked. "Does she have cramps?"

Polly hesitated. "Yeah."

"That's a shame," Sara said. She liked having Alice around. That girl could take an insult better than anybody; she always just laughed.

Jessica yawned. "Let's talk about this later, at the game. I've got to take a nap now or I'm going to turn into a pumpkin." She opened her car door. "You want Polly or me to take you home, Sara?"

"I'll go with you."

"I can drive us to the game," Polly said eagerly.

"Whatever," Jessica nodded, still yawning. "Get in, Sara."

When they were cruising down the road, the air conditioner on full and Polly following on their tail, Sara asked, "Why are you going to the game? You should stay home and rest."

Jessica rubbed her tired eyes beneath her glasses. She had only put on the glasses at Sara's insistence. Lately Jessica's sight had gotten so bad that Sara hated to get in the car when she was driving. That morning in political science, before she fell asleep, Sara had noticed Jessica straining to see the screen. The girl had a history of allergies; her eyes were too sensitive for contacts, even for soft lenses. Yet she resisted wearing her glasses, even when there was no one else around; simple vanity, there was no question about it.

"I would, but I told my journalism teacher I'd take some pictures for the paper," Jessica said.

"You volunteered?"

"Not exactly. The teacher saw the pictures I'd taken last year for Mesa's annual. She likes my work. I think she's been waiting for me and my camera to show up. I don't mind. I've got to do something now that I'm not a cheerleader anymore. And I promised Alice I'd come. She has this guy she wants me to meet."

"What's his name?"

"I don't know."

"Bill Skater?"

Jessica smiled. "I wish. It'll be fun watching him play tonight."

"It might be *funny.* I wasn't kidding in the assembly when I said I'd heard he was awful."

Jessica shrugged. "I could care less what he can do with a football."

Sara sneered. "What makes you think you're ever going to find out what he can do with you?"

Jessica grinned. "It's only September. I've got till June. I'm going to invite him to the party."

"I know."

Jessica lost her grin. "You don't think we're pressuring Polly into something she doesn't want to do, do you?"

"Polly's just being Polly. If we didn't give her a shove every now and then, she'd be mummified in her bedroom closet. Besides, the party was Alice's idea." Sara rubbed her aching arm. A purple bruise was beginning to appear below her elbow. "I have someone I'm going to invite, too."

"Who?"

"This guy I ran into."

Chapter Five

Michael Olson was doing inventory at the 7-Eleven when Nick Grutler walked in. Michael had seen Nick at school—it was hard not to see that tall, black body—and wondered if he played basketball. He had thought of asking him. It was not fear of Nick that had kept Michael quiet. Once Bubba had accused Michael of being especially kind to minorities because he felt guilty about not fully trusting them. It was Bubba's contention that everyone was prejudiced to a degree, and the best anyone could do was to try not to let it interfere with how he treated other races. But Michael was genuinely color blind. People were people to him.

Michael had not approached Nick because Nick did not look as if he wanted to be approached. It was as simple as that. The Rock probably wished he'd had as keen instincts. Michael had heard what had happened in the weight room. But unlike Russ Desmond, he did not take pleasure in The Rock's downfall. Michael disliked violence in any form.

But now that Nick had come into his store, Michael felt no qualms about introducing himself. He nodded as Nick approached the counter. "Hi, how are you doing? Don't we go to school together?"

A flicker of surprise crossed Nick's eyes. "I go to Tabb," he mumbled.

"So do I." Michael offered his hand. "I'm Michael Olson. Nick Grutler, right?"

Nick shook his hand. He had a mean grip. "How did you know?"

"You can expect most people at school to know your name after you floored The Rock."

A note of wariness entered his voice. "Was he a friend of yours?"

"The Rock doesn't have many friends." Michael had only brought up the weight room incident because he wanted to answer Nick's question honestly. He wanted to get off the subject. "You look like you've been out in the sun all afternoon. Can I get you something to drink? You know we sell soft drinks in glasses here as well as bottles and cans." Michael picked up the king-size cup behind him. "These are only fifty-five cents."

Nick looked vaguely uncomfortable. He pulled a couple of

silver dollars out of his pocket and laid them on the counter. "These are good, aren't they?"

Michael picked one up. "Yeah, sure. Though you don't see many of them around. Did you get them at the bank?"

"No. At the Italian market."

"In the mall? Man, I love the smell in that place."

"Their warehouse in the back don't smell so good."

"What were you doing back there?"

"They needed some boxes moved."

Michael knew the owner of the market. He had probably worked Nick to death for a couple of hours and then given him the two silver dollars, probably thinking Nick would imagine they were worth more or something.

Michael was looking for a new employee. The owners had told him to hire whomever he wanted. They trusted his judgment.

"Was it a temporary job?" he asked, knowing it was. Who would hire a guy with bloody hair?

"Yeah. I'll have one of those big Cokes for fifty-five cents."

"Sure." Michael reached over, scooped some ice into the paper cup. "Have you done enough work for one day?"

Nick seemed interested. "I could do more."

"I'm rearranging our storeroom. But because I have to keep coming back up front to handle the register, it's taking me forever. It's back-breaking work—all you're doing is lifting—but someone like you could probably finish most of it in a few hours. I could give you thirty bucks under the table, no tax taken out?"

Nick accepted his Coke, took a deep swallow. "Show me where to start."

Michael led Nick to the rear of the store and gave him an overview of how disorganized things were. Nick grasped immediately what had to be done. After a couple minutes of discussion, Michael left Nick alone. He needed help with the storeroom, true, but Michael was also using the chore as a test. If Nick did good work, he would offer him a permanent part-time job. It would be handy having someone around who could reach the top shelves without a ladder.

Two hours later, as it began to get dark outside and the faint sounds of Tabb High's band drifted through the open door from the direction of the school stadium, Nick reappeared and announced he had finished. One look in the back and Michael was astounded. Not only was everything neatly arranged, Nick had obviously used his own initiative—and used it wisely—in setting up certain sections. This meant a lot to Michael. He'd previously had a couple of employees who had been fine workers except that they had required constant supervision. Obviously Nick had common sense as well as powerful biceps.

Getting three tens out of the cash register, Michael made his offer. He could guarantee him at least twenty hours a week, although some weeks he'd need Nick close to thirty. He gave him a brief summary of what his responsibilities would be, and what he would start at. Nick listened patiently, and from his stoic expression, it was impossible to tell what was going on in his head. He asked only two questions.

"Will I be working with you all the time?"

"Most of the time," Michael said.

Nick thought for a moment. "Why are you doing this for me?"

"I'm offering you the job because you've proven to me you know how to work. I'm not *doing* anything for you."

Nick nodded. "I appreciate it, anyway. The only one who would even talk to me at the mall was that Italian guy, and I know he just ripped me off." He put his thirty dollars in his pocket. "Can I just keep working now?"

Michael smiled. "You'll take it then?"

Nick smiled, too, finally letting his pleasure show. "Yeah. But I'll have to call my dad to tell him I've got a job."

Michael pulled the phone from beneath the counter. "Sure, then take a break. There's a lot to do here, but you don't have to kill yourself."

A half hour later Michael wondered if he'd lied to Nick about not killing himself. They got held up by a guy with a gun.

Nick was in the cooler, putting the beverages in from behind, and Michael had returned to the inventory report and the register when the masked man entered. He wore a dark nylon stocking over his head on top of a blue knitted cap and a pair of silver sunglasses. He had his gun drawn as he entered.

"Get your hands up!" he snapped, waving his revolver nervously. Michael carefully set down his note board and pen. His first reaction was not one of fear, but of pure amazement. It was only eight-thirty. Who would be stupid enough to try to pull off a holdup now, when anybody could walk in at any second? The 7-Eleven was open twenty-four hours a day, for god's sake. But Michael didn't consider suggesting to the guy he come back later.

"What can I do for you?" he asked calmly, slowly raising his hands. There was a button located beneath the counter that would sound an alarm at the local police station. Unfortunately, it was so situated that Michael would have to ask permission of any thief to use it. The clink of bottles continued to sound from behind the cooler. Nick must not know they had uninvited company.

"What's that?" the fellow demanded. He wasn't very good at this. Outside of his obvious anxiety, he had a rather squeaky voice. Shifting the gun from one hand to the other, he scratched under his nylon stocking.

"What was what?" Michael asked.

"Do you have someone back there?" He peered toward the cooler. It must have been hard to see through the disguise. "Hey, you back there! Get out here before I blow your buddy away!"

"Yeah, come out here, Nick. We've got a guest."

Nick appeared a moment later, his arms hanging by his sides. "Mike?"

"It's nothing to worry about," Michael said, trying to relax everybody concerned. "We're all cool here, aren't we?"

"Yeah, it's cool," the guy spat out, cocking his revolver. "Give me your goddamn money. No funny business." He gestured toward Nick. "And you, get your hands up and come over here."

Michael did not want to give him the money. In no way did he plan on risking his or Nick's life to save it, but he did feel a responsibility to the owners of the store to get to the alarm button if at all possible. Opening the register, he rapidly began to toss all the change on the counter, like he was scared and didn't know what he was doing. The masked man shook his gun angrily.

"Just the bills, man! Just the bills!"

"Yes, sir, the bills," Michael answered breathlessly, pulling the drawer out still farther, past the point of no return. The drawer slipped from the register, the money pouring loudly onto the floor. Michael feigned shock. "Wow, I'm sorry." He bent over. "Here, I'll pick it up."

"Man, you're a peach." The masked man chuckled, falling for Michael's chicken act, leaning forward to watch him better. But it was already too late. Michael had hit the button the instant he had crouched down. At this very second, several patrol cars would be changing direction and moving toward them.

Michael didn't know when he had hired Nick that Nick had never depended on a cop for anything in his life. He didn't know about Nick's incredible reflexes.

As Michael began to collect the money behind the counter, Nick lashed out with his foot at the gun, sending it ricocheting off the ceiling and into the cereal row. Startled, the masked man twisted around to retrieve it. Before he could get halfway there, Nick grabbed ahold of his arm and whipped him into a stack of beer bottles. The guy slid toward the freezer on a wave of broken glass, foam, and noise.

"Oh, God," Michael whispered. Moving quickly, Nick collected the gun and turned on the fallen thief. Seeing him coming, the guy frantically began to rip at the nylon over his face.

"Mike, don't let him kill me!" he cried. "It's me! It's Kats!"

"Kats," Michael said, disgusted. "I should have known."

Carl Barber, better known as Kats, was a nineteen-year-old loser. He had gone to Tabb High for five years, taken advanced pottery and Shop I, II, and III, and still hadn't graduated. He'd had a life-long dream of joining the marines, but without the diploma, they wouldn't take him. He worked at the gas station up the street from Tabb High. He had oil under his fingernails a surgeon couldn't have removed. Whenever kids from the school drove into the station—dozens of students cruised by every morning and afternoon—Kats got into a fight with them. Admittedly, Kats usually didn't start the fights. He was one of those rare people that *no* one respected. Guys would pull into the full-service area and tell him to dust their tires. According to Bubba—who took Kats about as seriously as everyone else but who nevertheless spent a fair amount of time in his company— Kats had been genetically cloned from Rodney Dangerfield. Nothing ever went his way, that was for sure.

"Stop, Nick," Michael said. "I know this guy."

Nick looked bewildered. He shook the weapon in his hand. "This is real, Mike. He was pointing it right at us."

Michael came from behind the counter, furious. "So you hold us up with a real gun! What the hell do you think you're doing?"

Kats grinned, his ugly teeth protruding from beneath his thin black mustache. It was not true, like some said, that he greased his hair and mustache with oil from the gas station, at least not intentionally. But it was a fact he was always running his hands through his hair even when he was laboring beneath filthy dripping heaps.

"I was just trying to give you boys a little scare." Kats giggled. "I did, too. I saw the way you fumbled that cash register!"

Michael turned to Nick. "All right, go ahead and waste him."

"Mike!" Kats cried, squirming in a pond of Miller Lite.

Michael took a step closer. "I fumbled the drawer on purpose!

I hit a button to call the police. It also trips an alarm in the homes of the owners. They're all going to be here in minutes. What am I supposed to tell them?"

Kats tried to get up without cutting himself, brushing off scraps of glass knit together with torn beer labels. "Christ, Mike, what's the big deal? The gun wasn't loaded. It was just a prank." He grinned again. Michael really wished he would stop. "How'd you like my disguise? I knew you wouldn't recognize me with that voice I was using. Got it off an old gangster movie I watched last night. What do you think of my piece, huh? Picked it up at the swap meet last Saturday. It fires a twenty-two—"

"Shut up," Michael said wearily. "Just take your piece and get out of here before the police arrive. I don't know what I'm going to tell them." He tried to count the broken bottles. "But I do know one thing, you're paying for this mess."

Kats tried to snap the revolver from Nick's hands, failed. Nick did not appear to trust Kats any more now than when Kats had been holding them at gunpoint. Nick gave the weapon to Michael, instead, who accepted it reluctantly. Michael had never understood why anyone made handguns. They were no good for hunting. They were only good for killing people. Had Kats been stowing it in his refrigerator, he wondered. The steel felt unreasonably cold in his hand. He was anxious to be rid of it.

"Why should I?" Kats said angrily. "It was this big lug here who tripped me. I ain't paying for it, no way."

"If you don't," Michael said flatly, "I'll give the police your address."

Kats saw he was serious, nodded. "OK, lighten up. I'll pay for the beer. And I'll leave now." He started toward the door.

"Go out the back," Michael said. "I don't want some cop taking a shot at you." He held out the gun. "Take this with you."

Kats smiled as he accepted the revolver, slipping it into his belt beneath his shirt. He had a fetish for guns. It was probably part of the reason he wanted to join the marines. His crummy single-room apartment was packed with rifles, shotguns, all kinds of ammunition. "Good thinking. Hey, you're not really mad at me, are you, Mike? You know I would never try to rob you. You and me, we go way back. Coming to the game later?"

"Yeah, maybe." Michael chuckled in spite of himself. This was turning out to be a weird day. "Go ahead, get out of here. Go home and take a shower. You stink."

"Thanks, Mike. See you later."

When he was gone, Michael called the police. Turned out they had received no alarm. He called one of his bosses, told him he had accidentally bumped the button. The boss gave him the same story as the police; no alarm had gone off. Hanging up the phone, Michael pulled on the wiring attached to the button. It was burned out, shorted.

"At least now we've got your feet to protect us," he told Nick. "That is, if you haven't changed your mind and want to quit?"

"I'm not quitting, Mike. I'm just beginning to feel at home."

Between the two of them, they cleaned up the mess. The equivalent of three cases had been destroyed. Michael decided to juggle the numbers on the store inventory until Kats came up with the money, if he ever did. Michael figured he'd probably end up paying for the damage out of his own pocket.

Michael's replacement, the twenty-year-old son of one of the bosses, came in at nine o'clock. Amir went full-time to the local junior college and spent most nights at the store. As a result, he was chronically exhausted, and did little during the wee hours of the morning except run the cash register and study. He simply nodded when Michael introduced Nick as their new employee. Michael hoped Amir's father had the same reaction.

Michael and Nick were walking out the front doors of the 7-Eleven when the phone rang. An hour had passed since the phony holdup. It was Bubba. Michael took the call in the small office in the back.

"Did you invite Nick Grutler to come to the game with us?" Bubba asked.

"Yeah." The invitation had surprised Nick, but he had accepted without hesitation. He seemed to be looking forward to it. "Where are you? You said you'd pick me up at nine."

"Kats is here," Bubba said, lowering his voice. "He tells me Grutler tried to kill him."

"Did Kats also tell you that he pulled a gun on us?"

"Yeah, but that was a joke, Mike. What's wrong with this guy? I hear he practically cut The Rock's throat this afternoon."

"Get off it, Bubba. You know as well as I, The Rock started it. Nick's cool. Are you going to pick us up or not?"

"If it was just up to me, I'd be there already. But Kats wants to go to the game, and he says if Nick comes with us, things might get ugly. He's full of it, I know, but why don't you and Nick go on alone?"

"Since when does Kats tell you what to do?"

"It's no big deal. Let's not fight about it. I'll meet you there. Come on, it's getting late, and I want to talk to Clair before half time ends."

Michael was disappointed in his friend. "Whatever you say, Bubba."

Michael owned his own car, an off-white Toyota that had had over a hundred thousand miles on it when he bought it. The interior was clean, and although the engine drank a quart of oil every month, it ran smoothly. Yet as he opened the passenger door and adjusted the seat for Nick's long legs, Michael thought how plain it would look to a girl like Jessica Hart who had just returned from sunbathing in the Aegean Sea. He was hoping to see her at the game, maybe say hello.

The school lot was packed; they had to park a block away in a residential area. Walking toward the stadium, Michael caught a glimpse of the scoreboard: Tabb High 0; Visitors 6.

The marching bands and drill teams had taken the field. The snack bar was beset with thick lines. They had definitely made it for half-time.

"Have you ever played any sports?" Michael asked Nick as they hurried up the steps that led to the entrance.

"Nope."

"How about some pickup basketball games?"

"Oh, yeah, we used to play those." Nick chuckled. "But we never followed many rules. You had to knock a guy unconscious for a foul to be called."

"Have you ever thought of going out for the team here?"

Nick looked uncomfortable. "I don't think I'd fit in on a team." He reached for his back pocket. "How much is it to get in?"

"When you're this late, it's free."

Once inside the gate, they both caught a whiff of the hot dogs and decided they were starving. Nick insisted it would be his treat and went to wait in line while Michael made a quick stop at the rest room. He was heading back to the snack bar when he ran into Alice McCoy. She had a guy with her, a thin redhead who was literally dragging her toward the exit.

"Mikey!" she called, disengaging herself from her date and running to give him a quick hug. "Where have you been? I've been looking for you all night. Remember, I wanted you to meet my friend?"

"Well, I'm here now," he said cheerfully.

She glanced back over her shoulder. Her date had turned

away, staring into the brick wall behind the snack bar. Alice smiled quickly, nervously. "Did you have to work late?"

"No later than usual. Do you have to leave now?"

"Yeah. We—we have to go somewhere."

"That's too bad. I can always meet your friend another time."

"No, I want to be there when you meet her." Again, she glanced at her date, obviously trying to come to some sort of decision. Michael nodded toward the guy.

"Is that your new boyfriend?"

She didn't seem to hear him. "Could you stay here a sec?"

"Sure."

Alice walked back to the guy, spoke softly to him. First he shook his head. But as Alice persisted, he shrugged, pulling out a comb and running it through his long, thin red hair. Touching him gratefully on the arm, Alice returned to Michael.

"I'll go get her," she said. "Stay here, right here. OK?"

"All right." Watching her disappear into the crowd, Michael wondered why Alice had not introduced him to her date. Ordinarily she was extremely polite. Something about the way the guy stood, his hands plowed into his pockets, completely ignoring everyone around him, disturbed Michael. He decided he'd introduce himself.

"Hi, I'm Michael Olson," he said, walking up and offering his hand. "I'm a friend of Alice's. You're Clark, right?"

The guy had the brightest green eyes Michael had ever

seen. They practically glowed in the dark. His gaze lingered on Michael's outstretched hand for a moment before he lazily shook it.

"I suppose," he said. He had a deep southern accent, a disconcerting stare. His black leather biker jacket hung loose over his shoulders; Michael suspected there was nothing but skin and bone beneath it. The guy needed to see a doctor. His palm was warm and clammy.

"Alice tells me you're also an artist?"

Clark found the comparison amusing. "She loves pretty colors. I like sharp lines, black and white."

"Huh. What's that mean?"

"That I'm unique."

What does she see in him?

The question made Michael pause and consider how well he knew Alice. From day one, he'd neatly classified her as a carefree darling. He should know better by now that no one was that neat, or that unique.

"She told me you've had a big influence on her work?" he asked.

"She's talked about me?"

"On occasion."

"Alice doesn't work. Alice's got too much money to work. Alice's got too many dresses." He grinned suddenly. "Do you like the dress she's wearing tonight? I like when her sister wears it. It looks a lot different on Polly."

Michael had met Polly once. Alice had brought her by his store last spring. He assumed Clark was making a lewd reference to her large breasts. His dislike for the guy deepened. "Where are you from?" he asked.

Clark lost his grin. "Why?"

"I was just wondering, that's all. Do you go to school around here?"

"No."

"Where do you go?"

"The other side of town." Clark's gaze wandered toward the playing field. "Our team's as lousy as yours. But in our stadium, you can always lean your head back and look at the trees in the sky."

Michael frowned. "I don't mean to be rude, but are you stoned?" He was worried about Alice driving home in the car with him.

"I'm here man, right here." Clark yawned, turning again to face the wall behind the snack bar. "Alice had better get back soon. I've got to get out of here."

"Why?"

Bubba and Kats appeared. Since Clark had not bothered to answer his last question, Michael felt under no obligation to introduce him to them. Bubba had on a black suede jacket, a red handkerchief tucked in the pocket, a white silk shirt underneath. Kats was no longer dripping but still stunk of beer. Bubba had probably thrown Kats's clothes in the dryer without washing them. Clark continued to stare at the wall. It didn't even have graffiti on it. Michael allowed Bubba to pull him aside.

"Have you seen Clair?" he asked.

"No, I haven't been here long," Michael said. "But I think the cheerleaders are finished with their halftime routine."

"Good." Bubba gestured in the direction of Clark.

"Who's that?"

"A friend of Alice's."

"Wonderful. He looks dead." Bubba turned to Kats, pulling out his wallet. "Get me a large buttered popcorn and a medium-size Dr Pepper without ice." He handed Kats a ten. "Treat yourself to whatever you want. Bring it to the fifty-yard line. But if I'm talking to Clair, keep your distance."

Kats accepted the money. The side of his face had begun to color from his bout with Nick. "Going to bag her, Bubba?"

"I'm going to wrap her up in aluminum foil and toast her. Go get in line. Tell them to watch the salt on the popcorn." When Kats was gone, Bubba said, "Let's do it, Mike."

"I'm waiting for Alice and Nick. I should stay here."

Bubba waved his hand. "Don't worry, they'll find you. Come on."

Michael really did want to see Bubba in action, especially going after Clair. He figured he'd be able to catch Alice on her way back to Clark. And locating Nick would be no problem. He followed Bubba out onto the bleachers. The mood of the crowd appeared upbeat; Tabb High hadn't been down at halftime by only six points in years. The cheerleaders were gathered beneath the stands on the track, near center field. Standing nearest to the microphone, Clair was giving her voice a rest, sucking on a soft drink while waiting for the team to return to the field. With her shiny blond hair tied up in twin gold-ribboned pony tails, her legs deeply tanned beneath her short blue skirt, Michael had to admit she looked awfully sexy.

"Are you sure you want me with you?" Michael asked.

"I consider this a necessary part of your education. Just stay close, like we're hanging out together. But let me do all the talking."

A chest-high chain-link fence separated the audience from the track. Leaning casually into it, Bubba waved to Clair, calling, "Hey, come here. I want to talk to you."

Clair did not quite know what to make of the order. Holding on to her drink, she approached slowly. "Yeah, what?" she said, looking up at him.

Bubba smiled. "How are you doing, Clair? Good? You look good."

Clair took her straw out of her mouth. "I'm all right. What can I do for you, Bubba?"

Bubba rested an elbow on the top of the fence, dropped his smile for an unhappy expression. "I don't know, maybe you can do something. I'm having a bad day, a really bad time."

"What's wrong?" Clair asked.

"Well, like I was telling Mike here—you know Mike, sure you do—it's no wonder they speak of the stock market like it was a woman. You never know what she's going to do. The same day you think you've got her figured out, she turns around and stabs you in the back."

Clair showed interest. "Oh, yeah, someone told me you fooled around with stocks. What happened, did you lose some money?"

"It was all on paper, you understand. I was investing dollars I'd made on earlier trades. But it still pisses me off to be outguessed. I probably shouldn't talk about it. But the market, she's one nasty lady. How are things with you? I love your hair up like that. You should wear it like that all the time, even when you're taking a shower."

Clair played with one of her ponytails. "If I did that, I'd get my ribbons wet."

Michael recognized Bubba's strategy. It was Bubba's opinion that money and sex were inseparable in the female mind; thinking about credit cards and spending power, in his opinion, got them more excited than browsing through a *Playgirl* magazine.

"Then you could blow them dry," he said. "Hey, can I ask you something? This has really been a miserable day."

"What?"

"Let's go out together sometime. I'm always working, I've got to have more fun in life. Let's go out next weekend, next Saturday night."

Clair nodded. "Sure, we could—wait a second. I don't know. I don't think so. I'd like to, but I'm seeing Bill Skater. I don't think he'd like it if I went out with someone else."

Bubba waved his hand. Sometimes Michael thought Bubba could convince the pope to break his vows with a wave of that hand. "Bill won't, I know the guy. He doesn't want to totally monopolize your life. Don't worry about it, we'll have fun." He smiled. "I just got new leather upholstery in my Jaguar."

"That's right, you've got a Jag."

"I sure do. Hey, you like music, Clair? You like U2?"

Bubba must have researched Clair's taste in music. She lit up. "They're one of my favorite bands!"

"They're going to be in town next week. We'll go see them."

"But I heard they were sold out."

"I've already got tickets. Third row, dead center. We can eat first and then head on over to the Forum. Give me your phone number."

Clair glanced around uneasily. Bubba had come a long way in less than a minute, but Clair was obviously hesitant about handing out her number to a short, overweight guy in front of the entire community. "You really have third-row tickets?"

"They could be second row."

She paused, sizing him up. She wasn't a total airhead. "You're not just throwing me a line, are you? I've heard about you."

Bubba was sly. "What have you heard?"

Clair blushed. "Stories."

"Well, they're all true." Bubba leaned over the fence, spoke seriously. "If you don't want to go, Clair, just say so. A lot of guys don't mind wasting their time. But I do."

Michael had followed Bubba's moves perfectly up until this point. But when Clair suddenly blurted out her number, he realized he was completely lost.

"Five-five-five-four-three-two-six," she said. "I don't have anything to write on. Will you remember it?"

Bubba nodded, moved back from the fence, straightening his jacket. "I'll call you tomorrow."

Clair returned to the microphone, her fellow cheerleaders quickly gathering around. Bubba led Michael back in the direction of the snack bar. "No sweat," he said.

Michael nodded. "All right, you were smooth. But if you hadn't brought up the concert, she would never have given you her number. Do you really have tickets in the third row?"

"Nope, I don't have any tickets. And I'm not going to pay scalper prices to get them."

"You're kidding? She'll freak when you pick her up."

"No, she won't. Ten minutes alone with me and she won't even remember how to spell U2."

Michael laughed. "I'd like to see that."

"I'm hoping you will. You noticed I made the date for next Saturday, and not tomorrow? I wanted to give you time to talk to Jessica Hart. We can make it a double date."

"I don't think I can move that fast."

"Then stop where you are and let her come to you." Bubba stopped, gestured toward midaisle. "She's coming down the steps now. See her? She's got that Sara chick with her."

Michael would not have believed his heart could start pounding so hard so quickly. Jessica had changed into white pants, a bright green blouse. A 35mm camera with a telephoto lens hung around her neck. Her long brown hair bounced with each step she took down the bleachers. He turned away.

"Let's get out of here," he said.

"Leave if you want. I've been looking forward to a private conversation with Jessie about her tastes in music."

"I'll stay," Michael grumbled. He hoped—and feared— that Jessica and Sara would pass them by without noticing them. Perhaps they would have. But Bubba stepped right into their path.

"Ladies," he said. "My name is Bubba. You may have heard of me. This is my friend, Michael. You may have heard of him, too. We are both fairly popular." He extended his hand. "We would like to welcome you to Tabb High."

Giggling, Jessica shook his hand, introducing herself. Sara was more reserved. "I *have* heard about you," she said. "This girl in my P.E. said I should watch out for you."

"Did she tell you why?" Bubba asked innocently.

"No."

"Then she must have a guilty conscience, and you shouldn't

listen to her." Bubba pulled his gold pocket watch from his jacket. "I have a few minutes, Sara. Come with me. I want to discuss your political future."

"I'm not running for anything."

"But you like hot dogs, don't you?" Bubba asked.

Sara threw Jessica a quick glance. "I love hot dogs," she said slowly.

Bubba reached over and took Sara by the arm. "Then you should have one, with *everything* on it. Nice meeting you, Jessie. See you later, Mike."

When they were gone, Jessica continued to giggle. "Is he really your friend?" she asked.

"I think he considers me more of an apprentice." He cleared his throat. "I hope he doesn't overwhelm your friend."

"Sara can take care of herself."

"That's right, I almost forgot. I was there at lunch."

"I saw you when you sat down."

"Really?"

"Yeah."

The conversation ran into a hitch right there. Michael couldn't think of anything to say. Jessica started to fiddle with the focus on her camera. It was a Nikon 4004. The previous year, Michael had constructed an eight-inch reflector telescope. He had a dream of taking time-lapse photos of the sky through it from out in the desert. Jessica's camera would have been ideally suited for the job. Except it cost close to five hundred bucks.

"It's jammed again," she muttered, getting frustrated. A roar went up from the crowd. Wiping her hair out of her eyes, Jessica looked up. The team was coming back on the field. "Damn, the teacher wanted me to get a shot of the players running out of the tunnel."

"May I see it?" Michael asked.

"It does this all the time," she said, holding it out without removing the strap from her neck. He gently twisted the lens, trying not to brush up against her breasts; they weren't all that far away. She added, "I think I was sold an incompatible attachment."

It was indeed jammed. "Did you just take the telephoto lens out of its case and screw it in a moment ago?"

"Yeah, how did you know?"

"The camera's warm. You must have been holding it in your hands most of the night. But the lens is cool. Let them both sit out for a moment. When the temperatures average out, the jamming will stop."

She nodded. "That makes sense. You know a lot about cameras?"

He shrugged. "I've played around with a few."

"You should be the one taking these pictures, not me."

"Are you doing this for the paper or the yearbook?"

"Both, I guess." Jessica's attention wandered to the football players. She had a striking profile. He hadn't realized she had such thick lashes, such big eyes. He wondered what it would be like to touch her face.

"Who are you looking for?" he asked.

"A girlfriend."

"Is she on the football team?"

"She plays quarterback." Jessica turned his way again. "Hey, do you know a guy named Russ Desmond?"

Michael felt a pang of jealousy. "Yeah. But he's not on the football team this year."

"He runs cross-country, right?"

"Yeah."

"Do you know him well?"

"Not really."

Jessica smiled. "I suppose I can trust you. Sara's been searching for him all night."

Michael felt better. "She's searching in the wrong place. Russ would never come to a football game."

"Why not?"

"He hates the coach. And the coach hates him. It's a long story."

Jessica nodded, her lovely brown eyes drifting up into the stands this time. "Where is she?" she whispered.

"Sara?"

"No, the girlfriend I mentioned. You wouldn't know her. She's from Mesa. She's only a sophomore, an old friend." Jessica chuckled. "All day she's been telling me about this fantastic guy I've got to meet."

"What's her name?"

"Alice McCoy."

Michael leaned into the fence. He was lucky he didn't flip over and land on the track. "Oh, my," he said.

"Pardon?"

"Nothing."

Jessica suddenly turned her head toward the field. Tall, blond, and handsome number sixteen was walking toward the sidelines. Jessica quickly raised her camera, trying to focus her jammed telephoto lens. "Damn," she muttered.

Had Jessica not tried so eagerly to take Bill Skater's picture at that precise moment, Michael probably would have admitted he was the fantastic guy Alice wanted Jessica to meet. Later, he was to wonder if he *had* told Jessica, if the tragedy that was to follow Alice's party would have been avoided. It would be a possibility that would haunt him the entire year. It would be a possibility based solely upon a young girl's strange dream.

"You might want to give it a few more minutes," he said softly.

Jessica did not appear to hear him. She had lowered the camera, and her eyes. Bill had stopped at the microphone to talk to Clair.

"I better go," Michael said.

Jessica raised her head. "Huh? No, don't go, please. I'm sorry. What were you saying?"

"Nothing." He edged away. "I really have to go."

"That's too bad. Thanks!"

"For what?"

She forced a smile. "For everything, what else?"

Michael did not head in the direction of the snack bar, but away from it. Alice would have to forgive him for ditching her. He couldn't bear the thought of witnessing Jessica's probable—if she went for the likes of Bill Skater, it was virtually certain—disappointment when she learned Michael Olson was Mr. Fantastic.

He only remembered that Nick had gone for their dinner when Nick came up to him with a box full of goodies.

"I hope you like junk food," Nick said. "I live on it."

Michael accepted a hot dog, a tub of popcorn, and a large orange. Nick again refused Michael's offer to help pay for the stuff. They continued to walk in the direction of the scoreboard. "I bet you've had to search all over for me," Michael said. "Sorry I took off."

"I knew where you were," Nick said. "I was watching you talk to that girl."

"Jessica? You should have come over. I could have introduced you."

"No, I couldn't do that."

"Why not?"

"I don't know. I would have gotten in your way."

"Don't say that."

Nick glanced over at him. For an instant, something glimmered deep within Nick's black eyes. But all he said was "OK, Mike."

They sat at the end of the bleachers, away from the crowd. Nick began to dig into his food. Michael realized he'd lost his appetite. He sipped his drink, stared at the clock on the scoreboard. He didn't even know what he was doing at the game. She had smiled at him, thanked him, all the while thinking about the quarterback. Bubba would steal Clair away from Bill. Bill would find solace in Jessica's arms.

It's like the earth going around the sun—a vicious cycle.

"This is going to be a long second half," he muttered, referring to the rest of his life.

"Want to leave?"

"Do you?"

"Whatever you want, Mike."

"Whatever I want," he repeated quietly. He chuckled sadly, shook his head. "No, not today. Maybe tomorrow." He slapped Nick on the back. At least he'd made a new friend. "Tell me about yourself, Nick."

"What do you want to hear?"

"Everything." He thought of Jessica's line. "What else?"

It took them awhile until they returned to the topic of girls. Finally, however, Michael heard of Maria, and spoke of Jessica. They both agreed that something had to change.

Chapter Six

Polly McCoy noticed that her arm was bleeding. A drop of red trailed from beneath the bandage inside her left elbow all the way to her wrist. She had given blood that afternoon; it was a habit of hers to give blood every two months, as frequently as she could. Once Jessica had joked that she must have been a vampire in a past life, that she was working off karma. Polly didn't know about that. She had all this money and she had never done anything to earn it. She felt as if she had to help people, give something back. And she didn't believe in reincarnation, anyway, or even life after death. When you died, you were dead. It was pretty simple. On the other hand, she occasionally did wonder about vampires, about demons in general. So many terrible things happened to so many nice people. There had to be something evil behind it all.

Taking out a Kleenex and wiping away the blood, Polly saw Alice making her way up the stadium steps. Polly was sitting in the very top row. She liked the view. She could see what everyone was up to. Of course, when halftime finished, she would rejoin Sara and Jessica closer to the field. They had all come together. But for now she didn't mind being alone. Actually, she preferred it. She was not in the best of moods. She was mad at her sister. Sara and Jessica had been looking for him, but only she had seen Clark. She'd watched him and Alice carrying on the whole night.

And it was me who saw him first.

Polly had met Clark three months ago, during the last week of school at Mesa High. The day had been beautiful. She and Alice had decided to go for a hike in the woods. They had driven up into the nearby mountains and set out along a trail adjacent to a stream. They quickly ran into trouble.

Approximately two miles from the car, Polly stepped on a loose stone and twisted her ankle. The sprain was nasty. They both decided she should stay where she was while Alice went for help. While waiting for her sister's return, Clark appeared.

Polly's initial reaction to him had been one of fear. He talked weird. He looked weirder. But he had a certain *touch.* When he took her swollen ankle in his delicate hands—over her shy protests—and began to massage points on either side of the bone, the pain vanished. Polly had read about acupressure and stuff like that. What he did went beyond that. The swelling even stopped.

And the more she listened to his voice, the less strange it sounded. He had lots of interesting ideas. He told her how the mountain they were on had once been used by the Indians as a sacred spot for the channeling of the spirits of long-dead medicine men. What made his point of view so unique was that he neither believed nor disbelieved what he said. He was just being "open." He told her she had to open up. He had a pad and pencil with him. He wanted her to take off her top and let him sketch her. When she refused, he began to draw her as if she were completely nude. He finished the sketch minutes before Alice returned with the ranger. He gave it to her as a present. She didn't remember having given him her number. But he called her the next day.

Over the next two months, they never went out once. They spent most of their time together necking in her bedroom with the door locked. She finally did take her top off for him, and her pants, but they never had sex. He would push her right to the limit and then back off. She knew it was probably for the best—what with all the talk of herpes and AIDS going around—nevertheless, it still frustrated her. She wondered if he truly found her attractive. She wondered that a lot when he started chasing Alice.

It happened just like that. Overnight. Hello, how are you, Polly? Let me speak to Alice. And from then on Alice and

Clark were always together. The only thing that kept Polly from freaking out all together was that their relationship appeared to be a brother-sister sort of thing. Alice said it was, and of course being the considerate sister that she was, she had still asked Polly a thousand times if it was OK. Polly told her not to worry. She wanted what was best for Alice. And there was no denying Clark was "opening" her up to all kinds of artistic inspirations. Alice had paintings in progress in her studio that the special-effects people in Hollywood couldn't have dreamed of.

Yet Polly was finally beginning to wonder if she hadn't gotten a raw deal. Tonight, for the first time, she had seen Clark put his arm around Alice. If you would do that in public, there were a lot of other things you might do in private. Clark had such hypnotic green eyes, like a cat. And those long fingers. She couldn't stand the thought of them all over her baby sister.

"Hi. Have you see Jessie?" Alice asked, panting from her hop up the steps.

"Last time I saw her, she was down by the cheerleaders. But she's not there now."

Alice searched the stands, sighing. "I've got to find her right away. Clark wants to leave."

"I could give her a message for you."

"No, it's not that. I want her to meet somebody."

"Why are you leaving with Clark now?"

"I told you, he wants to leave."

"Why does he want to leave?"

"He didn't tell me." Alice stopped. "What's wrong?"

"With my arm? It's bleeding, can't you see? I gave blood today. You should, too, sometime. There're a lot of sick people out there who need it."

"No, I mean, you sound mad?"

"Why would I be mad?"

"I don't know."

"I'm not mad."

Alice smiled. Polly could remember the first time Alice had ever smiled. Polly had only been two years old at the time, and Alice two months, but Polly remembered everything. "Are you having fun?" Alice asked.

"Sure. How about you?"

Alice beamed at the whole stadium. "I'm having a great time. I love this school. I love the people here." Suddenly she leaned over and embraced her sister. "And I love you most of all!"

Polly returned the hug. "I know you do," she said softly, feeling the bones of Alice's rib cage under her fingers. When they had both been kids, Alice had tended toward chubbiness. Now, Polly could barely get her to eat one full meal a day. "Would you like a candy bar?" she asked, reaching for her purse.

Alice straightened herself. "No, chocolate gives me acne."

"It doesn't do that to me," Polly replied, getting the candy out for herself. The nurse at the hospital this afternoon had told her to go home and have a big meal. She had to make up for what she had lost. She didn't appreciate Alice suddenly staring at her as if she were a pig. "I gave blood today," she repeated.

"What about your diet?"

"Leave me alone, all right?"

Alice knelt back down beside her, holding her hands. "Are you upset 'cause Clark's here?"

Polly swallowed on the lump in her throat. "No. I see Clark all the time at the house. What difference should it make seeing him here? Anyway, why have you been hiding him away all night? Jessie and Sara want to meet him."

Alice leaned back on her heels. "I don't want them to see him."

"Then why did you bring him here tonight?"

A note of anger entered her voice. "I didn't. He insisted he come. Now he wants to leave early." She looked away, her expression strangely flat. "I've got to get away from him," she whispered.

Polly felt a thrill. She softened her voice. "Why?"

"He's not very nice."

"What?"

"He talks about mom and dad."

Polly closed her eyes, the thrill gone. "What does he say?"

"Nothing."

"Tell me!"

"No, it has nothing to do with you."

Polly opened her eyes, took a bite of her candy, smiled slowly. "All right, let's drop it. Let's talk about the party."

Alice brightened. "Can we have it?"

Polly nodded. The bad moment had come, and the bad moment had gone. All of a sudden she felt greatly relieved. "Yes, I think it would be all right. But we'll have to take Aunty over to Uncle Tom's for the night. The noise might upset her."

Alice nodded, leaned over, and kissed her cheek. "Thanks! I owe you a million."

Polly smiled at her. "You only owe me a penny. Don't invite Clark to the party."

Alice didn't hesitate. "I won't even tell him we're having one."

Alice left to search for Jessica. Polly remembered a textbook she had forgotten to take home that afternoon. She debated about waiting until after the game to get it from her locker. She finally decided that Sara would get mad if she did. Sara had been getting mad at her a lot lately; it was really beginning to bother her.

Polly accidentally ran into Sara at the bottom of the steps.

"Do you know where Jessie is?" Sara demanded.

"No. Alice doesn't either."

"What are you talking about? Where is Alice?"

"I don't know."

Sara rubbed her stomach, groaned. "I just ate three hot dogs."

"Why three?"

"My political adviser insisted. Where are you going?"

"To my locker."

"Is the locker hallway open now?"

"The door lock is busted. It's always open."

"What did you forget?"

"Nothing. Don't say anything mean."

Sara laughed loudly. "Don't get mugged. I could see the school from the snack bar. They don't waste electricity here. There isn't a light on."

No greater truth had ever passed Sara's lips. After leaving the stadium and heading around the silent gymnasium, Polly found herself in a disquieting land of darkness. Tabb High had a lot of trees. The branches blocked much of the sky, as did the overhanging roofs. She wished she had a flashlight. She had never cared much for the dark. It had been on a dark and lonely road her parents had died. She remembered it well. She remembered everything.

What did that bastard say about them?

Her steps echoed softly as she strode down the empty open hallway. She was uneasy, yes, but she also enjoyed the emptiness. Sometimes during the day she wished she could be this alone, strolling the campus free and easy, meeting only those people she chose to meet, hearing only those voices she wanted to hear, touching only those who wanted to touch her. . . .

What did Clark say about me?

Polly was crossing the courtyard, passing beneath what she had heard referred to as the varsity tree, when the can landed on top of her head. It startled her something awful; she practically had a heart attack right there on the spot. She jumped away from the tree and cried in a trembling voice, "Who's there!?"

A vague figure shifted above her in the branches. She leaned slightly forward—all the while telling herself to run the other way—straining to see better. "Hello?" she croaked.

The figure croaked back. No, it was more of a belch. She reached down, picked up the can that had struck her on the head, smelled the beer. Her fear disappeared as quickly as it had come. Somebody was just getting drunk in private. Laughing, she walked toward the tree trunk.

"Hey, if I was you, I wouldn't be drinking up there. You could slip and hurt—"

A flash of metal and wood whipped by, inches from her face. Polly leaped back a step. Embedded in the ground in the grass at her feet was a huge ax.

Polly screamed bloody murder.

The guy fell out of the tree. Polly kept screaming. He rolled over and looked up at her. "What time is it?" he mumbled.

Polly bit her lip. "Past nine-thirty."

The guy sat up, rubbed his head. "Where are the birds?"

"What birds?"

"I heard birds." He burped again, deep and loud, and reached for his ax.

"That was me. Excuse me, what are you doing with that?"

He was using it, Polly realized a moment later, to climb to his feet. She relaxed a notch. There were empty beer cans littering the ground. This guy wouldn't be chasing her anywhere.

"Do you need some help?" she asked tentatively. He briefly gained an upright position, clinging to the ax handle, before swaying forward and smacking his skull directly into the tree trunk. "Oh, no!" she cried, jumping to his side. "You'll kill yourself."

"What time is it?" he breathed in her face. With the lack of light, she couldn't see what he looked like. She could, however, smell him. He must have poured half the beer over his shirt.

"I told you, past nine-thirty. Why do you keep asking me that?"

He tried to get up again. "Got to chop this down before morning, before the birds get here."

"You can't do that." She tried to pull the ax from his hands. "No."

He wouldn't let go of the handle. "Why not?"

"Because it's a pretty tree. Leave it alone."

The guy turned, stared at the trunk, and then spat on it. "Those faggot foots—footballs. They all stand here." He leaned into the ax, pushed himself up. "It's got to go."

Polly moved back a step. He'd raised the ax over his head. It looked capable of flying in a dozen different directions. "Stop!" she pleaded.

He let go with a wild swing. The tip of the ax sliced into the bark. Leaning back, he tried to pull it free. His hands ended up slipping from the handle, and he was back on his ass. Before he could get up, Polly knelt by his side, putting both her palms on his chest. Even through his soggy shirt, she could feel the curves of his well-developed pectoral muscles. "Look, you've got to stop. If you kill this tree, you'll be killing all the birds who live in it."

"I can't hurt the birds," he said, trying repeatedly to get up, not realizing it was she that was holding him down.

"That's right. So why don't we take your nice ax and put it in my car and I'll drive you home." She wasn't exactly sure why she had made the offer. It could have been because of some distant streetlight. A sliver of white had fallen across his face, revealing a rugged—rough would probably have been closer to the truth—handsomeness. He belched again, his jaw dropping open.

"Is it you?" he asked, amazed.

"Who? What?"

"You! I stopped the race for you. The foots—Coach made them kick me off the team. All because of you."

"No, it wasn't me."

He wiped the back of his arm across his nose. "You're pretty, Sara."

"Thank you. Let me take you home."

"Your place or mine?" he slurred as she helped him up.

"Your place. What's your name?"

"Rusty—Russ."

"I'm Polly."

"Sara Polly?"

"I'm whoever you want me to be."

It took time getting the ax out of the tree. It took longer getting Russ and the ax into her car. Fortunately, he remembered where he lived. She assumed it was the right house. She deposited him in the front yard without knocking on the front door and then headed back for the stadium. She decided to keep the ax for now. In his intoxicated condition, there was no telling what he might do with it.

She liked him. And she didn't care that he was the guy Sara had been searching for all night. She'd seen Clark first and look where that had gotten her. Nowhere.

When it came to love, you were a fool to be nice.

Chapter Seven

Mr. Bark stopped Sara the following Monday morning as she was leaving his political science class. Jessica was with her.

"What is it?" Sara asked defensively. "I stayed awake the whole period."

"It's not that. I have some news for you." He paused, and there was no denying from his expression that he thought it was bad news. "You know I am the faculty adviser to the student government?"

"It doesn't surprise me," Sara said cautiously. "What's up?"

"You've been elected student body president."

Sara laughed. "What the hell? No, you're kidding. What are you talking about?"

"You were elected by a landslide."

Sara swallowed. "But I wasn't running. Jessie, tell him it was all a joke."

"You didn't want to be president?" Jessica asked in surprise.

"Your name was on the ballot," Mr. Bark said.

"Now hold on a second," Sara said. "I explained this to the whole school last Friday. Jessie put my name down."

Jessica smiled. This was great. "No, I didn't."

"Polly did then. It makes no difference. I can't be president. I hate politics. I hate politicians. No, absolutely not."

"I don't want you as president, either," Mr. Bark said. "I think you have a bad attitude. But the student body doesn't think so. Your nearest competitor didn't get a quarter of your votes. You have a responsibility to your peers. There's a lot of business that has to be taken care of immediately. We don't have time for another election."

"Who's the new vice-president?" Sara asked.

"Clair Hilrey."

"I thought she was running for president," Jessica said.

Mr. Bark frowned. "I thought she was, too. Maybe she put herself down for both offices. She shouldn't have done that."

"Make her president," Sara said quickly.

"I can't do that," Mr. Bark said.

"Then I'll do it," Sara said.

"No, you can't do that, either. It's against the rules."

"The President of the country never follows the rules, why

should I? No, wait. If you won't accept my resignation this instant, I'll intentionally break every rule in the book. Then you'll have to impeach me."

Mr. Bark was getting angry. "You don't impeach student body presidents."

"Why not? This is a free and vicious society."

"Why are you being so difficult? There are kids in this school who would give almost anything to have the honor that's been bestowed on you."

Sara started to speak, stopped, silently shook her head.

"It might be fun," Jessica said. "It might make you popular."

Sara glared at her. "No," she said firmly.

Mr. Bark had run out of patience. "I can't stand here all day arguing with you. We're having our first student council meeting tomorrow at lunch in Room H-Sixteen. If you should change your mind and want to accept the office, see me sometime this afternoon. There're notes on the student body's financial status you should go through before the meeting. If not, then I guess we'll have to carry on without you."

Jessica had chemistry next. She had to go. Once outside Mr. Bark's class, Sara refused to speak to her, anyway. She went off in a huff. Jessica couldn't help laughing.

The laughter did not stay with her. She'd had a miserable weekend. She was still sleepy and tired from her travels. She'd had to take long naps Saturday and Sunday afternoons just to be awake at dinnertime. Also, she'd been lamenting Bill Skater's obvious interest in Clair Hilrey. The disappointment was silly, she knew. She had only started at the school. She couldn't realistically expect the resident fox not to have some sort of girlfriend. Nevertheless, she had spent hours since the football game wondering how she could get his attention. In Mr. Bark's class just now, Bill hadn't looked at her once. And she'd worn her shortest skirt.

Her gloom deepened when her chemistry teacher announced a surprise quiz in the middle of lab. She practically fell off her stool. "He didn't say anything about a quiz on Friday," she complained to her lab partner, Maria.

"Last Monday he warned us to be ready for a quiz at any time," Maria said, pushing aside their rows of test tubes, getting out a fresh sheet of paper. "You weren't here. But I wouldn't worry, it shouldn't count for much."

Jessica worried anyway. To get accepted at Stanford, she had to keep her GPA close to a perfect four. She hadn't even glanced at the textbook over the weekend.

The teacher let them stay at their lab desks. He wrote several molecular formulas on the board and asked for their valence values. It appeared no big deal for the bulk of the class; they went right to it. Jessica sat staring at the board. She'd left her glasses at home again. She could hardly read the formulas.

What's a valence value?

When Jessica finally looked down, she saw that Maria had slipped her a piece of paper with two rows of positive and negative values. Sitting across the gray-topped table, Maria nodded.

"I can't," Jessica whispered.

"Just this once," Maria whispered back. The teacher wasn't watching. Jessica scribbled the numbers onto her paper.

The teacher collected them a few minutes later. Then he wrote the answers on the board. Maria knew her stuff; they each got a hundred. Jessica thanked her as they returned to the lab.

"I've never cheated before," she said, embarrassed.

"But you didn't know there could be a quiz," Maria said, adding softly, "Sometimes it's hard not to lie."

"Well, if I can ever make it up to you, let me know."

Maria nodded—she didn't talk a lot—and they continued with their acid-base reactions, which made no more sense than they had before the quiz. Jessica swore to herself that she would study chemistry for at least two hours every night until she caught up. She even entertained the idea of asking Michael Olson for a couple of tutorial lessons. She wasn't getting much out of the teacher; he talked too fast, and seemingly in a foreign language. Michael obviously had a sharp mind. She'd felt rather silly when she'd needed his help at the game with the camera. He had been right about the jamming disappearing when the temperatures evened out. Although she found his intelligence somewhat intimidating, he was easy to talk to. Yet she worried what he thought of her. He would start out friendly enough, and then after a couple of minutes talking to her, he'd be in a hurry to get away.

He probably thinks I'm an airhead.

Sara had cooled off by lunch. When Jessica met her near the snack bar, she even laughed about how her election had proved beyond doubt the substandard intelligence of the majority of Tabb's students. She had not changed her mind about the job.

Polly joined them midway through break. She had not heard of the election results, and neither Jessica nor Sara brought it up. She had, however, already printed up the party invitations—elegantly lettered orange cards in flowery orange envelopes. Jessica and Sara both agreed the printers had done a fine job. Polly gave them six each.

"But don't invite anyone weird," she warned.

"You'll have to give one to Russ," Jessica told Sara.

She fingered the envelopes uneasily. "I'll think about it."

"Are you talking about Russ Desmond?" Polly asked suddenly.

"Yes," Sara said warily.

Polly giggled. "You can't invite him. You're the one who got him kicked off the cross-country team. He hates you."

Sara didn't respond immediately, which surprised Jessica. "What are you talking about?" Jessica asked.

"Russ had to stop in the middle of his race last Friday to help Sara up. She had jumped right in his way, and he accidentally knocked her down. He ended up losing the race, and the football coach got furious and kicked him off the team."

"How does the football coach have the authority to kick someone off the cross-country team?" Jessica asked. Sara had told her about the race incident, but from a slightly different perspective.

"He's also the athletic director," Polly said.

An odd look had crossed Sara's face. She was angry, certainly, but also—was it possible?—upset. "You lie," she said.

"I'm not," Polly said indignantly. "The whole school knows about it."

"If that's true, then why did the whole school just nominate me president?"

Polly sneered. "Since when are you president?"

"I am president. Ain't I president, Jessie?"

"Unquestionably. But why does Russ hate Sara? He can't blame her for what happened."

Polly shrugged. "He does."

"How do *you* know?" Sara demanded.

"He told me so when I took him home Friday night."

Sara snorted. "You took him home? Where did you take him home from?"

"It's none of your business," Polly said.

Sara held up her finger. "Polly, if you're lying to me or even if you're telling me the truth, you're going to have a party at your house you're never going to forget 'cause I'm going to drown you in your goddamn swimming pool."

And with that, Sara whirled around and stalked off.

"What's gotten into her?" Polly asked.

"I don't know," Jessica said. "Maybe it's love."

Polly departed to eat large quantities of sugar. Jessica was left holding her six invitations and wondering who to give them to. It took her all of a fraction of a second to realize she had to get one to Bill Skater. It didn't take her much longer to spot him. He was alone, walking toward the parking lot. She had never seen him alone before; he usually had a bunch of guys around him. This could be a rare opportunity. Quickly she strode toward the other exit. She should be able to circle around a portion of the lot and run into him coming the other way.

Her plan worked better than she expected. She ended up coming up the aisle where he'd parked his car. He stopped when he saw her, nodded.

"Hi."

She looked up, smiled. "Hi! You look familiar. Do we share a class?"

He put the key to his red Corvette in the door, his eyes on her. They were as blue as the Bill in her fantasies. "I don't think so," he said. "What's your name?"

"Mr. Bark. I mean, we're in Mr. Bark's class together. My name's Jessie. What's yours, Bill? Is your name Bill?"

He nodded. He did not appear to notice she was suffering from momentary brain damage. She was so nervous. "I remember you," he said. "You sit next to the girl who snores."

What notoriety. "That's me," she gushed.

"Right." He opened his car door. "See you around, Joan."

"Jessie. Wait!"

He sat inside on the black leather upholstery. "Yes?"

"Ah—you were great last Friday, you know, in the game. I thought you were." Tabb had lost sixteen to three. Bill had thrown only one interception and an equal number of completions.

"Thanks. Bye."

"Bye. Would you like to go to a party?"

He shut his car door, rolled down his window. "What did you say?"

"My friend's having a party. She gave me all these to pass out." Jessica waved her half-dozen invitations as if they might multiply into hundreds any second. "Would you like come? It's not this Saturday, but next Saturday. In the evening."

He took one of the envelopes, opened it, nodding as he read the contents. "Are you going to be there?" he asked.

"Sure, yeah. The whole time."

He nodded again, tossing the card onto the passenger seat. "I'll see you then."

He drove away. Her approach had set women's lib back twenty years, she realized. But she didn't care! He had asked if she'd be there! He was only coming to see her!

Right, and your name's Joan.

Jessica decided to dwell on the positive. It didn't require much willpower. She floated back up the steps and into the courtyard. She bought a milk and sat by herself in the shade beneath a tree. Polly had specified on the cards that everyone was to bring a bathing suit. Jessica had a new bikini she could wear—blue with white polka dots. It left little to the imagination. Maybe he would bump up against her in the water . . .

If she went in the water. She'd almost drowned as a child in a backyard pool. She didn't know how to swim.

Jessica looked up. Michael Olson was coming over to say hi. How sweet.

They were in the computer room. Nick was listening. Bubba was talking. Michael wanted to get it over with. They had finally decided to do it, Nick and himself. They were going to ask the girls out.

"It's important you do everything in its proper order," Bubba was saying. "Get her alone. Start a conversation. Bring up a movie. A movie doesn't sound as heavy as dinner. Of course, once you're on the date, you can always go to dinner. But it's easy to work a movie into the conversation. Do each of you know what's playing?"

"Yes," Michael said.

"No," Nick said, hanging on to Bubba's every word. He had looked more relaxed during Kats's holdup. Then again, Michael wasn't exactly enjoying a period of low blood pressure. It struck him as ironic that the fear of one little word could have such an effect on two grown boys. Would you like to get together this weekend?

No.

A big little word.

"It doesn't matter," Bubba continued. "She'll know what's playing. Then ask if she's busy this weekend. This is a better question than asking outright if she'd like to go out. It eliminates a possible objection before she can raise it."

"But you asked Clair outright?" Michael said.

"Yes, but neither of you is Bubba. Now, after she has said no—"

"What if she is busy?" Nick interrupted.

"Then ask about another time. Don't be discouraged if this weekend is not good. Even teenage girls have other commitments. But if she puts you off twice, then back off. Keep your dignity."

"Go on," Nick said.

"Arrange the date. Set a definite time and get her phone number and address. Be sure to paint a picture that the whole thing is casual. That way she'll know how to dress without asking. Also, you don't want her to think she's overly important to you."

"Get off it," Michael said.

Bubba spoke seriously. "That may offend your romantic ideals, Mike, but it's a fact the human animal only desires what it can't have. True, you have to make her feel wanted, but never *loved*. If she knows you can't live without her, then she'll also know she can see you whenever she wants. You want to operate from a position of strength. Always keep her in the dark, unsure of where she stands."

"Go on," Nick said again.

"That's it, for now. When the date's set, come back here and I'll give you the next lesson: how to get her clothes off."

"We have a problem," Michael said. "Nick doesn't have a car."

"Let him borrow yours," Bubba said.

"Then what is Mike supposed to use?" Nick asked.

"He can borrow my car. And I'll get Clair to pick me up."

"You'll make her drive, and you don't even have the concert tickets?" Michael asked.

Bubba smiled. "Mike, you worry about the most unimportant things." He stood and slapped them both on the back. "Make me proud of you, boys."

Michael and Nick left Bubba to his computers. Lunch was more than half over. They had to locate the girls quickly. They hurried toward the courtyard.

"Why are we doing this?" Michael muttered.

"We don't have to," Nick said with more than a note of hope in his voice.

"Let's not start that again." They had talked about this moment all weekend at work. Without this mutual encouragement, Michael realized, neither of them would have gotten this far. Yet Michael had another reason for having decided to ask Jessica out. He'd had a dream.

It had been beautiful. He had been on a roped bridge stretching between two lands, one a desolate desert, the other a lush green forest. There had been a churning river running beneath his feet, and above—in contrast to the brightly lit lands—a black sky adorned with countless stars. He had been standing in the middle of the bridge facing the desert, hesitating, when a female voice had spoken at his back.

"I will follow you," she said. And when he started to turn around, she added quickly, "No, don't. You can't see me."

"Why not?"

"Because of the veil. I'm still wearing it. But you're young. Go forward, I will follow you."

The desert beyond looked most unappealing, particularly compared to the green woods that he could glimpse out the corner of his eye. "Who are you?" he asked.

"You have forgotten." There was no censure in her voice, only mild amusement and a rich, enduring love. Michael could almost, but not quite, figure out who it was. "It happens sometimes. It doesn't matter. Just remember that I am behind you. That you can't fall. No, don't look down, either. Go forward."

"Then can I see you?"

"Yes, but not today. Later, another time. I will see you first, and then we will meet again, like we always do. Go now, and don't be afraid. You are my love, Michael Olson. . . ."

And then he had woken up, and the stars outside were fading with the approaching dawn. He hadn't gone back to sleep.

He had just lain there feeling content. That had been Saturday morning.

The dream had left him with a measure of courage. Enough to risk the big No. Walking beside Nick, he continued to wonder who the girl had been.

They split up when they reached the center of campus. Nick had spotted Maria. She was by herself, next to the low adobe wall that surrounded Tabb. Michael wished him luck. He had to chuckle when Nick crossed himself.

Michael sighted Jessica minutes later. She was sitting alone beneath a tree, drinking a milk. And he had thought Nick superstitious; he would have recited a Hail Mary on the spot had he been able to remember the opening line. Jessica waved to him. He was trapped.

"How are you doing?" she asked as he approached. She looked positively radiant. Could she be this happy to see him?

"Fine. How about you?"

"Fantastic." She patted the grass beside her. "Have a seat. I was just thinking about you today, in chemistry class."

He sat down. The ground felt solid, better than his feet. "Really? I thought they only studied guys like me in psychology."

She laughed, and he secretly congratulated himself on his witty remark. "No, I was remembering how you wrote the lab manual they use."

Michael almost gagged. "Who told you that?"

She paused. "It's not true?"

"No. All I did last year was discover a couple of procedural errors in the manual. I didn't write it." He smiled. "I am still in high school, after all."

She laughed. "With your reputation, it's hard to remember that."

Michael had never thought of himself as having a reputation. "Are you having trouble in the class?" he asked.

She set down her milk, folded her hands between her bare legs. He couldn't help noticing how much of her legs there was to notice. Nice skirt. Nice legs. "Yes," she admitted quietly. "I think missing the first week has thrown me off. We had a quiz today, and I didn't even know what the questions meant."

"Did you flunk it?"

She giggled. "No, I got an A." She continued in a serious voice, "No, I really am confused. And I was wondering if maybe you could possibly tutor me a tiny bit? I could pay you for your time and all." She looked at him with her big brown eyes. "I really need the grade, Michael. My parents are on top of me all the time about my GPA."

He couldn't believe his luck. It almost seemed unnatural. A corner of his mind wondered if Bubba had not somehow set it up. "Sure, I could help you. But you wouldn't have to pay me. I think you'll catch on quickly, once you get used to the chemical language. Physics, calculus, chemistry—they all have a jargon that can be frightening at first. I sometimes think scientists keep it that way to make themselves look smart. Honestly, chemistry is as easy as basic math."

"I have a lot of trouble with that, too."

"When do you want to start?"

"I want to do something for you first." She brightened. "I know what! I'll take you to a movie. Yeah, that would be fair. I pay for the movie and you teach me about valence values. How does that sound?"

Michael had to take a breath. Very unnatural, this whole conversation. "I have some free time this Saturday. Can you get by in class until then?"

"Yeah, we won't have another quiz that soon." She pulled a pen from her purse, began to write on one of the funny orange envelopes by her side. "I'll give you my number and address, and you give me yours. If you want, I can drive."

"No, that's OK, I have a car." He would have a Jaguar Saturday night. He began to feel rather happy about the whole dating business. All these lonely years he had suffered in silence. There was nothing to it. All you had to do was decide to ask them out and then they asked you. Sure.

This won't happen again in another three hundred years.

They exchanged the vital information. He noticed she lived in Lemon Grove. Big bucks. Maybe he wouldn't tell her he had borrowed the Jag. He nodded to the orange envelope in his hand. "What is this?"

"Oh, an invitation to a party my friend's having. Alice McCoy—I told you about her at the game? You're welcome to come."

His heart skipped as it had last Friday when she had mentioned Alice's name. But this time the reasons were different. This time there was no reason at all, only the voice in the dream. *"I will follow you."* Why would Alice have been standing behind him, covered in a veil? Even his subconscious should have a purpose in putting her there.

"Thanks." He began to get up. He didn't think he would go to the party. He would have to be Mr. Fantastic again. For now, he was doing all right as Michael Olson. He hadn't seen Alice at school today. He hoped she wasn't sick. "I've got to go," he said.

Jessica looked up, surprised, got slowly to her feet, brushing off her bottom. "I didn't mean to keep you."

"You haven't. I'm not that busy. I'll give you a call."

She smiled. "Or leave me a note in our locker. I seem to keep missing you between classes."

He had missed her on purpose today. "We'll talk," he said, turning away. "Take it easy."

"Bye!"

He wanted to be happy. He had been looking forward to this moment—he had better be happy. He was going out with Jessica Hart, he told himself. She was sweet, beautiful, charming. He had her number. She needed him. Bubba would be proud of him. . . .

Do you want her to need you? Or to care about you?

He decided, as long as he got to see her, *he* didn't care.

He hoped Nick was all right.

"Hello, Nick," Maria said. "How's your head?"

"My head? It's OK."

She put down her sack. It appeared packed with oranges, nothing else. He felt as if he had an orange stuck between his ears. He couldn't remember what Bubba had told him to say first. "The swelling looks like it's gone down?"

"Yeah."

She nodded. "Would you like an orange?"

Nick accepted the fruit. "You have a lot of them."

"My dad brings them home."

Her dad probably worked the orchards. The possibility reinforced his suspicion she had not been in the country more than a year, two at the outside, that her father was working for slave wages picking the fruit. Bubba had told him to bring up the movies. "You can't get oranges like these at the movies."

Maria blinked. "They don't sell them there."

"Yeah, that's what I mean." He put his hand on the nearby wall for support. Unfortunately, he used the hand that held the orange, and crushed it. A squirt of juice hit Maria right in the eyes. "Damnit, I'm sorry!" he cried, dropping the offending fruit. She calmly reached for a handkerchief in her bag.

"You got a ripe one," she said.

"I'm really sorry."

"It's nothing."

"It must hurt."

She looked up at him, her face serious. "If I ever did get hurt, I don't think I could take it like you did last Friday."

"That was nothing."

"Someone told me this morning that you got thrown into a mirror."

Nick scratched his head. "Well, yeah, I didn't walk into it." She liked that. She smiled. She was the kind of girl who needed to smile more often. So solemn.

"Would you like another orange?" she asked.

He waved it away, feeling a sudden surge of confidence. She admired how he had fought! She wasn't afraid of him. "Would you like to go to the movies Saturday night?"

She nodded. "Could you pick me up at the library? I'll be there studying."

"I could, yeah." He would have to ask Michael where the library was. "What time would be good?"

"Six. That's when the library closes."

That Bubba was a genius. "I'll see you then."

Chapter Eight

Sara had decided to attend the student council meeting Tuesday at lunch after all. When she arrived with Mr. Bark's papers on the financial status of the council tucked under her arm, the other officers were already gathered around the large table in Room H-16. She recognized only three: Clair Hilrey, Bill Skater, and that football player everyone called The Rock. She knew of the latter because of the stories that had been circulating about his fight with the tall black guy. The Rock sat slightly hunched over in his chair. He had not played in Friday's game. Sara heard the black guy had almost killed him.

Two adults were also present: Mr. Bark and Tabb's principal, Mr. Smith, both sitting unobtrusively in one corner. They were there to oversee, she had heard, not to interfere. The promise of the principal's presence was one of the reasons she had decided to come. She hoped to speak to him about allowing Russ Desmond back on the cross-country team. That lying Polly had been feeding her a line—there was no doubt about that—but she did feel somewhat guilty about having stepped in his way. She certainly didn't want him hating her.

Another factor had brought her to the meeting. The biggest problem she had with school, and life in general, was that it bored her. After thinking about it awhile, she had come to the conclusion that being president couldn't make the situation any worse. Of course, if the job ever got to be more of a hassle than it was worth, she could always walk away from it—and to hell with any responsibility she owed to her peers.

"Have you been waiting for me?" Sara asked, sitting at the head of the table, all eyes on her.

"Yes," Mr. Bark said.

"That's a shame." She cleared her throat, glancing around. "What are we supposed to do first?"

"I'm the sergeant at arms," The Rock said. "I have to call the meeting to order."

"Do it," Sara said.

The Rock stood and smashed his gavel on a wooden block and mumbled a few lines about the date and the time. Sara thought it a pathetic comment on student councils across the land that the sergeant at arms was an elected position. The Rock sat back down.

"Can I begin?" Sara asked. No one moved to stop her. "All

right, I want this meeting to be short. I haven't eaten yet. I want all our meetings to be short, no longer than ten minutes."

"Sara," Mr. Bark said, interrupting. "That is ridiculous. A lot has to be accomplished during these meetings. Ten minutes is not enough time. But we don't want to keep you from eating. We offer a class here at Tabb called leadership. All the students in this room, except you, are in that class. Of course, we understand you did not expect to be nominated. For that reason, the faculty would be happy to rearrange your schedule so that you may join the class. That way we can take care of business during leadership and you can have the majority of your lunches free."

"Does leadership replace political science as a requirement?" Sara asked.

"No, it doesn't," Mr. Bark said.

"Then I don't want my schedule rearranged."

"Be serious—" Mr. Bark began.

"Rocky," Sara interrupted.

"I'm called The Rock."

"Whatever. Don't I have to recognize someone before they can speak?"

The Rock nodded. "It's in the bylaws."

"Mr. Bark," Sara said. "I don't recognize you. I'll tell you when I do." She glanced at her notes on the financial papers Mr. Bark had given her to review. "Let's get going. First, we're broke. We have a sum total of nineteen hundred and sixty-two dollars and thirteen cents in our activities account. With this we're supposed to put on both the Sadie Hawkins and the homecoming dances in the fall quarter. Now the senior class controls homecoming—and I'll get to that in a second—but the juniors are supposed to take care of Sadie Hawkins. Who's junior class president?"

A thin Japanese girl on her near right raised her hand. "I am."

"If I give you half of what we've got," Sara said. "Can you book a band, print up tickets, buy a truck-load full of hay, and do whatever else you need to get this thing going?"

The girl hesitated. "I don't know everything involved."

"It's a question of cash flow. Figure out approximately how many people will attend, how much you'll have to spend to keep them happy. Then decide on a ticket price. The grand or so I'll give you will be to get you started until you can start collecting money. Do you understand?"

"Yes."

"Can you do it? I don't want to have to think about it."

The girl nodded. "The junior officers will take care of it."

"Good. We're making progress. Let's discuss homecoming. I think we should cancel it this year."

Now they were really staring at her. Clair—sitting to her left and looking sickeningly gorgeous—protested. "Are you out of your mind? It's the biggest event of the year."

"I have to recognize you," The Rock said. "Can I?"

"Yeah, she's recognized," Sara said, leaning toward Clair. "What do you mean it's the biggest event of the year? For you maybe, and four other *princesses* in the school. But for the rest of us slobs it's just another occasion to have dirt rubbed in our faces. So we're not as pretty as you? Whoever said good looks make a good person? Look at history. It's full of ugly kings and queens. Look at all the suffering that's gone on— Wait a second. Never mind. If the kings and queens had all been good-looking, it probably would have been worse. Let's get back to the issue. How many dances do we really need? Last year at Mesa, I never went to a single one. We already have Sadie Hawkins. I say that's enough. The alumni won't be coming back, anyway. I went to the game last Friday. I felt like leaving after the first quarter. What a bunch of clods."

Bill Skater raised his hand. "Can I speak?"

Sara sat back. "Rocky, recognize our quarterback."

The Rock did so. Bill stood, and Sara had to admit he had an imposing physique. She could see Jessica's reasons for wanting to get him alone in a dark and secluded spot. She wondered if perhaps she should have skipped the clods part.

"I don't think you have any right to knock our football team," he said. "One game doesn't mean nothing. Last year, the Super Bowl champs lost their first four games. And they ended up with the gold ring."

"Yeah," The Rock said.

"But that's not what I want to talk about," Bill went on.

"I'm the treasurer. I've looked at our books, too, and I think we can afford homecoming. How much money do we need, anyway? It doesn't have to be that fancy. Homecoming is a tradition. Traditions are important. They're what makes this country great." He sat down.

"Yeah," Clair said. "Just because no one's going to vote you onto the homecoming court doesn't mean you've got to spoil it for the rest of us."

"What officer are you?" Sara asked.

"I'm vice-president," Clair said proudly.

"You were running for president. How did you get nominated for vice-president?"

Clair frowned. "I don't know."

Sara sighed. "I should have you all shot." The whole gang went to protest. Sara raised her hand. "All right, we'll keep homecoming. But we can't have it in the next few weeks, and I don't care what our treasurer says. We simply don't have the money. We're going to have to raise it somehow, and to do that, we need time. Let's have it during basketball season."

"That's absurd," Clair exploded. "Homecoming is always during football season. You can't change that."

"Why not?"

"Because you can't, that's why."

Sara strummed her fingers on top of the table. "I will give you another reason why it must be postponed. If the elections are held in the next couple of weeks, the girls from Mesa won't stand a chance of being nominated to the court. Transfers from Mesa like myself make up only a quarter of the student body. Hardly anyone who was originally from Tabb knows us. It wouldn't be fair."

Clair grinned. "Does Mesa have anyone we would vote for if we knew them ten years?"

The group giggled. Sara leaned toward Clair again. "Jessica Hart—remember that name. When the final count comes in, pimple brain, you won't be smiling."

Uncertain, Clair turned to Bill. "Who?" she whispered.

Bill nodded. "I've met her. She's pretty."

"How pretty?"

Bill shrugged.

"Rocky?" Sara said.

He pounded his gavel. "Order in the council."

Mr. Smith, the principal, raised his hand. "May I speak?"

"I recognize you myself," Sara said.

He stood. An older man close to retirement, he always wore—no matter what the weather—tailored three-piece suits. He had a faint English accent and was known for his exquisite manners.

"What you people decide is, of course, strictly up to you," he began. "But I would like to say that, in my opinion, Sara has made a persuasive argument for a postponement. This is, however, not the reason for my interruption. I was curious, Sara, how you plan on raising funds for homecoming outside of ticket sales and the like?"

"I don't know, maybe we can have a raffle."

Claire scowled. "This isn't a church. What are we going to raffle? A new TV set?"

Sara smiled faintly. "Maybe your body."

There followed cries of outrage and protest, plus plenty of good laughter. In the midst of it all—especially when Clair called for a presidential impeachment—Sara realized she was having fun. The remainder of the meeting—she let it run twenty minutes—passed quickly. It was decided homecoming could wait until winter. Naturally, she didn't recognize the vote of anyone who thought different.

Sara caught up with the principal in the hallway afterward. "Excuse me, Mr. Smith?"

He turned. "Ah, Sara, you're a strong-willed young lady. You've put a spark back into the council that's been missing for a number of years. But a word of advice from an old gentleman. In the future, please watch the personal attacks. I realize you say all those things in the spirit of jest, but as you must know, not everyone shares your sense of humor."

"I'll remember that, sir. Could I ask a favor of you?"

"Certainly."

She told him about Russ Desmond's expulsion from the cross-country team and the reason behind it. When she had finished, he said, "Russ is one of our finest athletes. It sounds like a misunderstanding that can easily be patched up. I'll have a word with Coach Campbell."

"Thanks a lot. I appreciate it."

"I do have a piece of bad news for you. It doesn't have to be taken care of immediately by the student council, but we have a soft drink machine that needs to be replaced. The accountants at the school district refuse to cover the cost. Apparently, one or more students had the bad sense to tip the machine over. It can't even be repaired."

Sara shook her head. "The barbarians."

Chapter Nine

Stepping onto the track near the runners, Jessica had to shield her eyes from the sun. Heat radiated in rippling waves off the ground over her bare legs. She couldn't imagine how anyone could run three miles on a day like this.

"They should postpone their race till evening," Alice said, wiping the sweat from her brow. "They'll get heat stroke in this."

"Maybe it'll rain," Sara said. There wasn't a cloud in the sky. She pointed toward the shadow cast by the scoreboard. "Let's go over there."

"Where's Polly?" Jessica asked.

"She said she was stopping for a drink," Alice said.

"Not a bad idea," Jessica said, turning to Sara. "See Russ?"

"No."

"You haven't even looked for him," Jessica said. "You've got to tell him you're here."

"I'm under no contractual obligation to do so," Sara said.

"Why wouldn't you?"

"He's here to run a race. Why should I bug him?"

"You're just afraid he won't remember you," Jessica said.

"You're right, I should have him knock me down again in case he's forgotten," Sara snapped. "Get off my case, Jessie. If he wants to talk to me, he can come over and talk to me."

"Sorry," Jessica muttered, surprised at her tone. Sara was usually about as sensitive to personal remarks as a brick wall.

They reached the shade and sat down. The grass tickled Jessica's legs. Alice continued to wipe at her head, the sweat literally pouring off her. "Are you all right?" Jessie asked.

Alice smiled quickly. "I'm fine, just glad I'm not running."

"But you were sick, weren't you? You didn't come in Monday or Tuesday."

Alice found a tiny yellow flower, plucked it. "I was painting."

"What?" Jessica said.

Alice threw her flower into the air, watched it fall directly to the ground. No breeze. "The blue wind."

"Really? Sounds interesting," Jessica said. "You'll have to show me. Hey, what are you doing this weekend? Want to go to the beach?"

"I'm painting."

"Couldn't you set it aside for a few hours?"

"I've got to finish it."

"That's too bad." Jessica paused. "I'm going to the movies

Saturday night. You won't believe it, I asked the guy. His name's Michael Olson."

Alice nodded slowly, leaning back, looking up into the clear sky. "Polly told me. That's neat that you found—someone you like."

"We're just friends. He's going to help me with chemistry. That reminds me, where's that fantastic guy you were going to introduce me to?"

Alice lay down, closed her eyes. "Ask me after your date." She yawned. "I could go to sleep here and never wake up."

Jessica patted her arm. "You go ahead and rest."

Polly reappeared a few minutes later. Seconds before she reached them, however, Sara nodded in the direction of the stadium ramp. "That's him over there with the shaggy brown hair, the muscles," she said.

Jessica cupped her hand over her eyes again. "He looks tough."

"You don't like him?"

"I didn't say that. He's very attractive." He belonged in a black leather jacket on the back of a motorcycle. "He's the one who stopped that black guy from killing that football player?"

"Yeah," Sara said. "So what do you think?"

"I just told you," Jessica said. "He's attractive."

"Attractive. Phonies on TV are attractive. Do you like him?"

"Yes, I *really* like him. He's totally bitchin'," Jessica said.

"Shut up. I was only asking."

Polly waved. "What are you guys doing over here? They start and finish by the bleachers. Come on, let's move. What's Alice doing?"

"Dreaming," Alice whispered, her eyes still closed.

"She's taking a nap," Jessica said. "Sara wants to stay here in the shade."

Polly plopped down beside them, her face flushed with blood. "You won't believe who I was just talking to. Russ Desmond. He—"

"Shut up," Sara said.

Polly looked to Jessica. "What did I say?"

"It's the heat," Jessica said.

They stood—except for Alice, who appeared to have caught an early train to sleepyland—for the start of the race. The bang of the gun echoed off the mostly deserted stands. In a colorful jumbled herd—Russ lost in the center—the runners circled the track and vanished out the gate. "That's exciting," Jessica remarked. "What happens now?"

"We wait till they come back," Polly said.

Jessica preferred races where she got to see the runners running. She contemplated joining Alice in sleep on the grass.

Fifteen minutes later Russ reappeared, coming up the ramp. He had company, a short Japanese fellow clad in green dogging his heels. A cheer went up from the people gathered near the finish. Jessica leaped to her feet, her interest level taking a sharp upward climb. It was going to be close.

"Come on, Russ!" she yelled.

Russ accelerated sharply as he hit the track, opening up a ten-yard lead. He added another five yards as he went into the curve of the track, momentarily heading away from the finish but quickly approaching their vantage spot. Jessica poked Sara in the ribs.

"Cheer."

"Shh," Sara said, intent upon the race.

"Shout his name," Jessica said.

"Shh."

"Go!" Jessica yelled with Polly.

"Damn," Sara muttered. With a surge of his own, the Japanese guy had cut his lead in half. "Russ!!" Sara cried.

At the sound of her voice, he twisted his head toward them. He even raised his hand, shielding his eyes to see better. Then his left foot stepped onto the slightly upraised narrow cement strip that circled the inside of the track. The rhythm of his stride faltered; he practically tripped. When he had recovered, the Japanese guy was ten yards in front. Russ went after him.

"Go!" they screamed.

He lost by inches. Maybe he would have lost, anyway, without the stumble. His competitor obviously had a powerful kick. Jessica told Sara as much. Sara would have none of it.

"I should have kept my mouth shut," she said. "Two races, two screw-ups."

"But it sure was exciting," Alice remarked, still on the ground, fresh from her snooze.

"What makes you think he was looking for you?" Polly asked Sara. "He could have been looking for me."

Jessica expected Sara to explode. Sara, however, ignored Polly completely. "Let's get out of here," she said.

"No, you should congratulate him on his effort," Jessica said. "I'll go with you."

Sara surprised her again. His loss seemed to have depressed her. "All right."

"I'm coming, too," Polly said.

"No," Jessica said. "Stay here. Stay with Alice."

"Why should I?"

"Because I'm asking you to. Please?"

Polly gave in reluctantly. Jessica and Sara approached the gang at the finish slowly, watching as the winner embraced Russ, hanging back for a few minutes while the coach and several of the other runners spoke to him about the race. Finally he separated himself from them and grabbed a can from the ice chest, heading for the shade behind the bleachers.

"You want to talk to him alone?" Jessica asked as they followed after him.

"No."

He must have been totally exhausted. Sitting with his back to a wooden plank, he didn't notice them coming. He had a beer in his hand, Jessica realized. Quite an ice chest they had here. Or else he filled it with his own private stock.

"Hi," Sara said.

He glanced up briefly. "Hi."

"This is my friend, Jessie."

Russ grunted. Sara looked at Jessica, uncertain. "That was a great race you ran," Jessica said quickly. His rough edges were more apparent up close, and yet, he also seemed somehow younger, more of a boy than she had thought from a distance.

"I've run better." He took a slug of beer, his eyes wandering to the baseball field.

"It's a shame you lost," Jessica said.

"You win some, you lose some."

"I didn't mean to distract you," Sara said.

Russ belched. "Hey, you got my ax?"

Sara paused. "What?"

"My ax. You took it the other night."

"No, I didn't."

"I need it back. It belongs to the store where I work."

"I don't have your ax."

"What did you do with it?"

"Nothing. I don't have it."

"What are you talking about?"

"What are *you* talking about?"

Russ looked vaguely annoyed. "You know, you're a weird girl."

Sara sucked in a sharp breath. "I'm weird? I'm weird? I'm not the one who's worried about some goddamn ax that he thinks he's lost."

He sharpened his tone. "I didn't lose it. You took it."

"Why would I take it?"

"You didn't want me to chop down the tree."

"What tree?"

Russ rubbed his head, growing tired of the whole discussion. "What are you doing here?" he muttered.

Sara chuckled. "I came over so *you* could thank *me* for getting you reinstated on the cross-country team."

"Huh?"

"In case you didn't know, I'm the school president. It was I who talked to the school principal. It was I who made it possible for you to run today."

She'd caught his attention. "No kidding?"

Sara nodded. "You better believe it."

He had a short attention span. He finished his can, crumpled it up in one hand, and threw it aside. "You shouldn't have bothered."

She stared at him for a long moment, and Jessica was just thankful Sara didn't have the missing ax in her hands. She probably wouldn't have killed him, but she might have taken a foot off. As it was, she turned and stalked off. Russ observed her departure with mild surprise. "Is it that time of month or what?" he asked.

"I think you might have hurt her feelings," Jessica said diplomatically.

"Oh, really?" he said innocently. "Well, I didn't mean to. Tell her I'm sorry."

Jessica knelt by his side. "This is probably none of my business, but do you like Sara?"

"Huh?"

"When she shouted for you in the race, I couldn't help noticing how you looked over. I was wondering if you liked her?"

"Yeah, she's all right. She's got a temper, though. God."

"Would you want to go out with her?"

"Where?"

"Anywhere, you know, like on a date?"

"I don't know. I guess."

She supposed that would have to do in place of yes. "Are you busy tomorrow night?"

"No."

Jessica took a pen and paper from her purse. It would be hopeless to give him Sara's number. He would only lose it. "I'll tell you what. Come over to my house tomorrow at six. Sara will be there. You can pick her up and the two of you can go out to dinner. How's that sound?"

"I don't know where you live."

"I'll draw you a map. Will you come?"

He shrugged. "All right. As long as she gives me back my ax."

Chapter Ten

Michael was no expert when it came to dressing for a date. Part of the reason, he supposed, was he had never gone on a date before. The other problem was his lack of nice clothes. He finally settled on a pair of gray slacks and a white shirt. He figured he was playing it safe. Bubba said he looked like an altar boy.

The three of them—Michael, Bubba, and Nick—were spending the last minutes before the *Big Night* in Michael's house. Bubba only lived around the block, and of course Nick had had to come over for the car. Michael's mom had already left for the weekend. Her current boyfriend, Daniel Stevens, owned a condo by the beach. Michael liked the man. Mr. Stevens taught music at UC-Irvine. He had an easygoing manner and treated his mother like gold. Michael suspected his mom liked him, too. Maybe this one would work out. She deserved someone nice.

"Did any of you go to the game last night?" Michael asked, sitting on his bed, sipping a lemonade. Nick—he couldn't seem to relax—had glued himself to the far wall. And Bubba was at the desk in front of the mirror, trying on a bag full of garish forties ties his gangster uncle had left him in a will.

"I didn't," Nick said.

"We got stomped: thirty-seven to fourteen," Bubba said. "There's a rumor circulating that Bill Skater's quarterback days are over."

"Did you start the rumor?" Michael asked.

"I did, but it's gathering momentum. I've also started a Draft Russ Desmond campaign, whether he wants to play or not." He turned away from the mirror. "What do you think of this one?"

Not only was it a depressing brandy-red color, it had a dime-size hole in the center. "It's awful," Michael said.

"That looks like a bullet hole," Nick said.

Bubba nodded. "My uncle was wearing it when he got wasted." He tightened the collar. "Clair will love it."

"What did Clair say when you told her she had to drive?" Michael asked.

"We'll see," Bubba said, reaching for the phone. He dialed the number from memory. She answered on the second ring. "Clair? This is Bubba. How are you doing? . . . Hey, that's great. I can hardly wait myself. But I've got a small problem. You know Michael Olson? . . . Yeah, he sure is smart. He's going out with Jessica Hart tonight. . . . What? No, she's cool. Never mind what you've heard. Anyway, he has to borrow my car. Could you pick me up? . . . What a sweetheart! Let me give you my address."

He chit-chatted a minute longer before signing off. "She loves me," he said as he put down the phone.

"Do you swear you don't have those tickets?" Michael asked.

"U2 played their final L.A. show last night. How could I have tickets?"

"What did she say about Jessie?"

"She called her a stuck-up bitch. Don't take it personally. It's only because Jessie's pretty. Pretty girls always hate other pretty girls. It's biological."

Nick ventured away from the wall. "I better get going." He had a long face.

"Hey, loosen up, Nick," Bubba said. "You're just going out with her. You don't have to kill her afterward."

Michael stood, setting down his lemonade. "Are you worried because she's having you pick her up at the library?"

Nick looked at the floor. "I don't know, when I think about it, maybe she's ashamed of me."

"She's probably just worried her dad will blow your head off when he sees how dark you are," Bubba said sympathetically.

Nick smiled faintly. "Yeah, that must be it."

Michael escorted Nick to the front door. "I filled the car with gas this afternoon," he said. "The air conditioner works, but the window's usually a better bet. And forget about the radio. It only gets AM."

"Thanks, Mike."

"The car's ten years old. It's no big favor."

Nick went to touch his shoulder, hesitated. "I mean, thanks for everything. You're a real friend. Where I come from, you learn to appreciate your friends. Anytime you need a favor, no matter what it is, I'll be there for you."

Michael was touched by the sentiment. "You just have yourself a good time."

Nick promised him he would. Michael watched him drive off, and was heading back to his room when Kats pulled up. Kats drove an old Mustang that never needed an oil change; it leaked a quart a week. "Don't park that thing in the driveway!" Michael called.

"You let that black dude take your car?" Kats asked a minute later, after having stowed his heap out of sight around the corner. He had obviously just come from work. He needed a bath. "You must be out of your mind, Mike."

Michael ignored the comment—people did that all the time with Kats—fetched him a glass of lemonade, and told him not to sit on anything. Bubba came out of the bedroom with a box of condoms in his hands.

"You sure you don't want at least one of these?" he asked.

"That's all right, you might need the whole box," Michael said.

Bubba nodded. "I did use a whole box once. Lost three pounds that night. Gained it right back, though. It was mostly water."

Michael groaned. "If you're going to talk like that, we better go in the bathroom."

"Don't be a prude. They advertise condoms on national television. Safe sex, all that stuff." Bubba pulled one from the box, offered it to him. "Come on, she'll thank you for it afterward."

"Give it to Kats."

Kats was excited. "How many of those have you got to wear?"

Bubba glanced at Kats's filthy fingernails. "You? Eleven."

Michael pointed to the orange envelope with Jessica's address on it. "Kats, hand me that paper on the oven, would you?"

Kats picked the invitation up, stopped to read it. He was nosy on top of everything else. His grin widened. "Polly and Alice McCoy! They come into the station all the time. Always pay with a gold credit card. You know them, Mike? Are they having a party? I'd like to go to that. Wooh, that Alice sure is a tasty number."

Michael took a step forward, snapped the invitation from Kats's hand. "Shut up. You have to be invited. You can't come."

"Hey, Mike," Bubba said. "Cool down."

Michael realized he was overreacting. "Sorry."

Kats stared at him a moment, his black eyes strangely flat. Then he grinned again. "I bet you were just afraid I'd break in carrying my gun, hey, Mike?"

Michael folded the invitation, put it in his back pocket, out of sight. He remembered that gun all too well. "Yeah, I guess, something like that."

He had asked Jessica yesterday if she'd like to get a bite to eat before the movie. She had said sure. He was supposed to pick her up at six-thirty. He would be early if he left now, but suddenly he wanted to get out of the house, get away from the others. He told them he had to hit the road. Bubba left with Kats in the dripping Mustang.

Michael was familiar with Jessica's neighborhood. And although he had never been to the McCoy residence, he knew Alice lived around the block from Jessica; he had both addresses on the invitation. Cruising down the road in Bubba's Jaguar, he decided to swing by and say hello to his favorite artist.

He had expected a huge house. He wasn't disappointed. You could use up a lot of gas, he thought, going up a driveway like this every day; it was as long as a football field. He parked beside a silver gray Mercedes, climbed out.

An elderly lady answered the door. He assumed she was the guardian aunt Alice talked about. Her posture was terrible; in better years, she must have been half a foot taller. She was one of those old ladies it was hard to imagine had ever been young. She had a sweet smile, however, which reminded him of Alice's. Parents and relatives always smiled when they saw him. As Bubba had observed, he had that altar boy aura.

"Is Alice here?"

"She's around back. Are you a friend from school?"

"Yeah, I'm Michael Olson." He offered his hand. She shook it feebly.

"Alice has told me about you. Please come in."

They had cream-colored carpet, deep and soft. The living room cathedral ceiling went way up; twin tinted skylights spread a faint rainbow of color over the elegant contemporary furniture and towering fireplace. The place was spotless. *They'd better lay down protective sheets for the party,* he thought. The aunt pointed toward a sliding glass door. "You'll find her near the rose bushes."

"Thank you. Is Polly here?"

"She's at a friend's."

The pool was large even for a house as big as this one. It was not, however, exotically shaped, simply rectangular. Mr. or Mrs. McCoy had probably enjoyed swimming laps.

Alice had set up her easel in the corner of the yard, between the wall of the house and the beginnings of an exotic garden of flowers, bushes, and trees that stretched perhaps fifty yards to a tall adobe brick wall. The McCoys could do all the shouting they liked and their neighbors wouldn't even know about it.

An overhang from the second-story roof cast a shadow over her spot. She had compensated by erecting a silver-dished lamp behind her right shoulder. He thought the arrangement unusual since she could have painted practically anywhere else in the yard and enjoyed direct sunlight. Perhaps the strange mixture of artificial and natural lighting was what suited her mood best. Although he could scarcely see the painting, her work in progress appeared—from the colors—to have a distinct surreal quality.

He thought how content she seemed with a brush in her left hand, a song on her lips. Maybe she was in the middle of a creative high. He decided not to interrupt her, after all. He circled around to the other side of the house and climbed back in the Jaguar. The aunt would probably wonder what had become of him.

It hit him then, hard as a rock, that he was going to pick up Jessica. *Jessie!* The nervousness came quick, but also, an exhilarating joy. This could be the start of something. She could fall in love with him. It was theoretically possible.

He drove around the block, parked in the street in front of her house. Ringing the doorbell and waiting for her to answer, he aged five years.

When the doorbell rang, Jessica was upstairs in her bedroom with Sara and Polly, trying on earrings. She sent Polly down to answer it. "If it's Michael, tell him I'll be down in a minute. Offer him a Coke."

"What if it's Russ?" Polly asked.

Jessica glanced at Sara. "Give him a beer," she said.

When Polly had left, Sara went to the bedroom door and peeked out. "It's Mike," she said a moment later, disappointed.

"He'll be here, Sara. He's only a few minutes late."

"Thirty-two minutes is not a few."

"Guys have a different sense of time than girls."

"Are you absolutely positively sure it was his idea to go out?"

"Yes."

"You're lying. You talked him into it."

"He likes you. He told me so."

"Did he say that? What were his exact words?"

"He said you were an all-right girl." She decided against any earrings at all. They were just going out for fun, after all. She turned to Sara. "Look, why don't you call him? He may have gotten lost."

"Right, it'll be a snap reaching him on his car phone."

"You've got a point there. Maybe you could talk to his mom. I'm sure their number is listed. She could tell you when he left."

Sara folded her arms across her chest. She'd broken from tradition and put on a beautiful white dress. "I'm not talking to his mom."

Jessica squeezed Sara's arm. "Be patient. He'll be here. Now, I've got to go. Wish me a good time."

"Have a good time," Sara grumbled.

"Don't you want to come down and say hi to Michael?"

Sara plopped on the bed. "No. I hate men. All of them."

Michael was sitting on the couch with Polly when Jessica entered the living room. He stood up quickly when he saw her and smiled. His gray slacks and white shirt looked a bit plain next to her bright yellow pants and silky green blouse, but who gave a damn? The degree of her pleasure at seeing him again surprised her. He had such lovely black eyes.

"You look nice," he said casually, stepping toward her. On impulse, she gave him a quick hug.

"Thanks, so do you." His arms felt strong beneath his shirt. She took a step back. "Did you have any trouble finding the place?"

"No."

"Where are my manners? Have you met Polly?"

"I met Mike last year," Polly said. "He's a good friend of Alice's."

Jessica stopped, frowned. "You are? Alice didn't tell me that."

Michael was watching her. "She's a nice girl."

"Alice? She's a doll." Jessica picked her purse off the TV. "I'd introduce you to my parents, but they went out for dinner. Which reminds me, where do you want to eat? Remember, I'm paying."

He mentioned a local restaurant—one of her favorites—but insisted it would be his treat. She told him they could argue about it when the bill came.

As she was leaving, she remembered that Maria would be coming over later to spend the night. All this last week, since Maria had helped her on the quiz, they had begun to talk more, outside of class as well as during chemistry lab. Maria was a different sort of friend for Jessica. She was serious, someone who weighed every word before speaking it. She appeared totally uninterested in local gossip, and yet she was fun to be around. She had a quiet dignity that Jessica found inspiring.

On Thursday Maria had admitted she had a problem. Nick Grutler, the tall black guy, had asked her out. She wanted to go; she had, in fact, told him she would. But her parents would kill her if they found out. They weren't prejudiced, she said, just *extremely* conservative. She had told Nick to pick her up at the library, but she knew that when he dropped her off at home, her parents would be awake and waiting. She didn't know what to do.

To Jessica, the solution was obvious. Spend the night at her house. The offer had delighted Maria. To further insure that Maria's parents did not learn of the date, Jessica had called Friday afternoon after the cross-country race and had casually spoken to Mrs. Gonzales about Maria's coming over. The lady had sounded pleased her daughter had made such an upstanding friend. You just had to know how to handle parents.

"Are you going to hang around for a while?" she asked Polly. "I forgot to tell my mom and dad about Maria spending the night."

"I might stay for a while."

"Until Russ shows up, right?" Polly started to get mad. "Don't say it. If you do leave before they get back, could you leave them a note for me?"

"Sure, Jessie. I hope you two have fun."

Michael probably was going to think she was a jerk. The second they left the house, she asked if they could stop at the nearest gas station. "I have to make a call," she explained.

"Your phone's not working?"

"Yeah."

They stopped at an Exxon not far away. Excusing herself, she shut herself in the booth and rang information. There were three Desmonds. The first one didn't have a Russ. The second—it sounded like his dad—said he'd go get him. Russ didn't seem all that wide-awake when he came on the line.

"Hello?"

"Hi, Russ, this is Jessica Hart. Remember me?"

"Yeah."

Jessica gestured to Michael that she would be off in a moment. "Russ, where are you? Don't you remember you were supposed to go out with Sara tonight?"

He yawned. "It was tonight?"

Jessica wondered if she should stop where she was. Chances were, Sara would eventually kill a guy like this. "Yeah, how could you forget?"

"I don't know. Can I come tomorrow? I'm watching *Star Trek*."

"No, you can't come tomorrow. Sara's waiting for you at my house this minute. She's all dressed up. You get over there right away."

"Right now? I'm hungry."

"You made a date, Russ. You should keep it. Do you still have that map I drew you?"

"I think so."

"Good. Now whatever you do, don't tell her I called. All right?"

"All right."

Nick's worst nightmare was coming true. They were in the car together, driving down the road, and they had absolutely nothing to say to each other. He didn't even know where he was taking her. He had assumed she would suggest a place she wanted to eat, the movie she wanted to see. Now he suspected she was waiting for him to make the decision. Unfortunately, he hardly knew the area. He didn't want to risk taking her to the local doghouse. The silence between them dragged on and on.

"How was the library?" he asked finally.

"Fine."

"Did you get a lot of homework done?"

"I should have done more. What did you do today?"

"I worked at the store in the morning. Then I just hung out."

"Oh."

They'd had a couple of other mini-conversations like this. They had also ended with "oh." The word could be used in practically any situation. Nick worried that they would keep coming back to it all night. He felt he had to say something different, something to break them out of their rut. Actually, he wanted to tell her how happy he was that she had agreed to go out with him, but since he was feeling rather miserable at the moment, he was afraid it would come out sounding insincere. He decided on a different tack.

"How do you feel?" he asked.

"Good."

"That's good."

"How do you feel?"

"Good. I mean, I'm OK."

"Is something wrong?" she asked.

"No. Why do you ask?"

"No reason. I was just asking."

"Oh."

See—now he had said it. He was seriously debating whether he should give up right then and there and take her home when he noticed her staring at him. "What is it?" he asked.

"You're mad at me, aren't you?"

"Why would I be mad? I'm not mad."

"I didn't invite you to my house."

"That's all right. You were working at the library."

"That didn't fool you, Nick."

Her saying his name—on top of her confession—seemed to loosen something in the air. At home, he seldom heard his name. He didn't think his dad had said it in the last five years. "Is it your parents?" he asked.

She nodded. "They don't know I'm out with you."

"They don't let you date?"

She hesitated. "Not exactly."

"Oh." The light turned red. Stopping, he rolled down the window. The outside air had cooled significantly. They must be getting close to the beach. Naturally, what she said did not surprise him. That was the thing about being one of the few blacks in the neighborhood—you got used to everything. "Do you feel guilty?"

"No. I'm not doing anything wrong."

"But I could be getting you into trouble?"

"You won't. I'm spending the night at a friend's."

It stung to hear how she'd had to set everything up beforehand. Maybe he was mad at her, a little. "Does this friend have parents?" he asked. "You know, they might see me accidentally."

She turned toward him. "I'm sorry."

The regret came swift. "No, Maria, I shouldn't have said that."

"My parents are good people. They just feel they have to be cautious. They haven't had easy lives."

He waited till the light turned green, then drove across the street and parked near the curve. Behind Maria, through a patch in the bushes along the sidewalk, he saw a blue slice of ocean, the warm brown of sand. He turned off the engine. "And you feel you have to be cautious, too, right?"

She nodded, watching him.

"Why?"

"I just have to be."

"Then what are you doing with me?"

She didn't answer, but continued to stare. She seemed scared, not of him, but of what he might say. He said it anyway. "You and your parents are illegal aliens, aren't you?"

She trembled, ever so slightly. "Yes," she whispered.

"There were lots in my old neighborhood."

She nodded. "I knew."

"What?"

"You would know. When I met you at the soda machines, you looked like someone—who knew who didn't belong."

He chuckled. "I suppose a bloody head might give someone that idea." Then he got serious. "What's the big crime? They've loosened the laws. Stay here a few years and they'll make you a citizen."

"That's not how it works. We got here after the amnesty deadline. In Washington there's talk about changing the requirements, but until then we could be sent home anytime."

"How did you get registered at school?"

"My dad paid this man some money. He made me a phony birth certificate."

"How long have you been in the country?"

"Almost two years. We're from El Salvador."

"How is it there?"

She tensed. "Not good. I like it better here." She gently touched his knee. He could not remember when he had last been touched by a female. Probably by his mom, before she had split eight years ago. "I'd rather not talk about it, if you don't mind? I worry too much about it as it is."

"What would you like to do?"

She brightened. "Eat. I'm starving. You don't know where you're going, do you?"

He smiled. "No."

She told him about a Mexican restaurant next to the pier. Nick restarted the car. She hadn't asked him to keep her secret. She'd automatically trusted him to do so. He was glad.

Russ had half a roast beef sandwich in his hand when Sara answered the door, the other half in his mouth. "Sorry I'm late," he mumbled, chewing.

He had on blue jeans, a torn red T-shirt, and sandals. Sara silently cursed Jessica for talking her into dressing up. He hadn't even combed his hair. "Did you have trouble finding the place?" she asked diplomatically.

"No."

Polly popped her head out the side of the door. "Hi, Russ! How are you doing?"

He grinned. "Hanging in there, babe. How are you?"

Sara pushed Polly out of the way. "We've got to go. Remember to feed the cat." She stepped outside, shutting the door in Polly's face. That girl only liked a guy when he belonged to someone else. "Where's your car?"

"I don't have a car. I've got a truck. It's right there."

Sara grimaced. It looked like he used it for hauling. She pointed to the mound of grass piled in the back. "Do you keep a cow, or what?"

He didn't think that was funny. "My old man's a gardener. What's yours do?"

"He shuffles papers." He was a bank president.

"Does he use a truck to deliver them?"

Jessica had warned her to watch her mouth. Jessica said guys didn't appreciate being made fools of. "Ah, yeah."

"What do you want to do?" he asked as they walked toward his truck.

"I'm hungry."

He took another bite of his sandwich. "You haven't had dinner?"

"No. I thought we were going to eat together?"

"That's cool. Let's go to the McDonald's in the mall."

"The McDonald's?"

He opened the passenger door, and as he did so, she caught a whiff of his breath. The empty beer cans littering his front seat only confirmed her fears. "You've been drinking," she said.

"Is there a law against it? If you want, we can go to the Burger King instead."

"How many beers have you had?" Judging by his empties, he'd put away several six-packs; but that seemed unlikely.

"Why? I can drive."

"How many?"

"I can't remember."

"I'm driving." She held out her hand. He stared at it a moment before giving her the keys.

"Do you know how to drive a stick?"

"I learned on a stick," she said, reaching into the passenger side and removing what was left of a six-pack. "I'm putting these in the back, under the grass. I don't want some cop stopping and arresting us." As it was, her license was still in suspension.

"They'll get warm," he protested. "One of them's half-full."

"I don't care."

The driver's seat was encrusted not only with dirt, sweat, and more dead grass, but also had a dozen or so of those little thorny balls that get stuck on clothes at picnics. She looked down at her white dress, running her fingers over the clean smooth fabric. She'd bought it in Hollywood at a designer shop for big bucks. Then she looked over at Russ: food in his mouth, hair in his face, not much going on behind his eyes.

What the hell am I doing with this guy?

But it was right then that he showed the first trace of

decency he had since their collision when he stopped during the race to see if she'd been hurt. Without her even asking, he pulled off his shirt and draped it over her seat. And sitting there naked from the waist up, his powerfully developed chest warm and brown in the evening sunlight, he seemed to her, if not perfect, at least worthy of consideration. She got in.

"You've got to watch the brakes," he said as she fiddled with the clutch. King Kong could hardly have pressed the thing in.

"What's wrong with them?"

"They don't always work."

She stopped. "You can't be serious?"

He shrugged. "If you don't like it, let's take your car. That'll give me a chance to look in your trunk."

She didn't have her car; Jessica had picked her up. "What's in my trunk?"

"I think that's where you put my ax."

Sara leaned her head on the steering, totally reversing her opinion of a moment ago. "Jesus," she whispered.

Dinner had been fabulous. Probably because the restaurant overlooked the ocean, they'd both been in the mood for seafood; she'd had a shrimp salad, and Michael, swordfish. Although she was already stuffed, the pastry tray the waitress had brought by a moment ago was too much of a temptation. Fortunately, Michael promised to eat half the chocolate cake she had ordered. She was going to have to jog a few miles this weekend to make up for tonight. She didn't care. She was having a great time.

Initially, while thinking about the date that afternoon, she had worried she would come off seeming stupid, shallow. She had always done well in school, but since third grade, she had felt she was faking it. She got good grades, she thought, because she studied twice as much as anybody else. She saw herself as an overachiever and feared that one day, someday, she would be found out. Everyone would know she didn't really belong in the accelerated math class, or chemistry for that matter.

Yet rather than trying to hide her insecurity from the smartest guy around, she found herself confiding in him about it. She wasn't even sure why, other than that Michael was an excellent listener.

"I keep reading about the average GPAs of the kids who get into Stanford," she said. "And their SAT scores. They're so high! I'm not taking the test until December, and I've already bought a couple of those study guide books. I took a trial test a couple of nights ago. I won't tell you what I scored. Let's just say if I do as well on the real test, I'm going to save my dad a lot of money on tuition fees. I swear to God, sometimes I think I'm going to end up at the local junior college."

"What do you want to major in at Stanford?" he asked. He had taken a fancy to the candle on their table and was playfully running his fingers above the flame. She didn't doubt she had his full attention, however; he wasn't staring, but his eyes seldom wandered far from her face. Once again, she wondered how he saw her.

"My parents eventually want me to get into broadcasting. They tell me I've got the voice, the personality. They think a major in journalism, with a minor in communications, would give me a solid background. I know some of those girls on the news make a lot of money. What do you think?"

"I think I asked the wrong question."

She smiled. "What do you mean?"

He momentarily took his hand away from the candle, caught her eye. "You keep telling me what your parents want."

She started to answer, stopped. He'd hit pretty close to home with that one. "They are paying the bills," she muttered.

He backed off. "I didn't mean they were giving you bad advice. They obviously care a great deal about you."

"No, you're right. I need to hear this. I should major in what *I* want. It is my life, after all. But that's the problem. I don't know what I want. Being an anchorperson on TV looks glamorous. Everyone knows who you are. You're where the action is. But that's looking at it from the outside in. For all I know, I might hate it."

He nodded. "That's true. But if you really are interested, you probably could get a summer job at a TV station. You might only change lights, but at least you'd get a feel for the environment."

"That's an idea." She made a mental note to check on that. "What about Stanford?"

"What about it? Don't you think it's a good school?"

"It's one of the best. Is that why you've chosen it?"

He'd caught her again. "My dad went to Stanford," she admitted. "I grew up browsing through his college yearbooks. I know all the sororities on campus, even the Stanford school song. I don't know, it's so hard to get into, I've always felt that if you graduated from Stanford, you would be one of the elite." She leaned forward. She really wanted his approval. "Does that sound like too snobbish a reason?"

He chuckled. "I'm the last person to ask."

"Why?"

"'Cause I'm jealous. *I* won't be going to Stanford."

"Why not? You've got the grades. You'll probably get super-high SAT scores."

He looked down. "I can't afford it."

She had to remember that not everybody's dad made six figures a year. He must have borrowed the Jaguar for their date. "Couldn't you get a scholarship?"

He shrugged. She may have been embarrassing him. "It's a possibility, but I'd hate to be that far away from my mom. She sort of likes having me around."

He'd said nothing about his family. "Is your mom divorced?"

"Yeah."

"You don't have any brothers or sisters, do you?"

"No."

"Neither do I. I wish I did. I sort of envy Polly sometimes. She's got Alice." He glanced up suddenly. "What is it?"

"Nothing," he said.

"It really surprised me that you knew her. She never told me. When did you meet?"

"Last Christmas?"

"Really? Where?"

"At the store where I work. The 7-Eleven on Western."

"I've been in there a couple of times. I never saw you. Is it a part-time job?"

"Fifty hours a week."

"Wow." He lived in a different world, she realized. He made money, carried his own weight. She charged everything, ran up the phone bill. And from what he said, he watched out for his mom, when all she did was fight with her parents about nothing. She lived such a superficial life.

But what can I do? I'm already spoiled.

She decided she couldn't possibly accept his help with chemistry. He undoubtedly had little time to himself.

She leaned over, blew out the candle beneath his hand. "Come on, Michael. We don't need the cake. I'm taking you to that movie I promised."

They called for the check. She put up a fight, but he insisted on paying. Out in the car, they checked a paper he'd brought. They couldn't make up their minds what to see and decided to head back to the mall near campus where they would have six shows to choose from.

Driving along Pacific Coast Highway, the salty air pouring in through the open windows, the sun setting over the water, they slipped into a quiet spell. Relaxing into the seat, she glanced over, studying his profile. For a moment she wished that it had been he who had asked her out, that this was a *real* date. He didn't have Bill Skater's startling blue eyes, his strong jaw. But his face was appealing, particularly now, with his dark eyes intent upon the road, his thoughts seemingly far away. And he had something else she liked. He was kind.

Twenty minutes later, while reviewing the movie posters outside the mall's theaters, they heard their names called.

"Maria!" she cried, turning.

"Hi, Nick," Michael said. "It's a small city."

They made an interesting couple. Maria couldn't have been five feet tall, and Nick had to be pushing six and a half. They were not holding hands, but Jessica noticed how close they stood, how their arms and sides brushed as they approached. She had been curious to meet Nick. She'd heard such contrasting stories: that he was a bloodthirsty maniac; that he had risked his life to protect Russ Desmond from a huge toppling mirror; that he had the strength of ten guys. Watching him now shaking Michael's hand, shyly saying hello to her, she marveled at his politeness.

They decided to team up. But if it was difficult for two to

choose a movie, it was impossible for four. Not that they were each insisting their own personal taste be the deciding factor. On the contrary, Michael, Nick, and Maria refused to volunteer any preference, and Jessica didn't know what she wanted to see. They had time. They decided to have ice cream first.

They ran into Bubba and Clair inside the 31 Flavors.

Meeting him at the game, Jessica had thought Bubba a wonderful character, not someone she would like to get too close to, but a guy it would be nice to run into from time to time when she needed a taste of the extraordinary. He obviously had Sara's highly developed sense of self-confidence, as well as her wit. Yet he seemed somehow both more fun loving and more devious. She had been surprised to learn he had been a friend of Michael's for many years.

Bubba took charge of the introductions. When it was time for Jessica to formally meet Clair, Jessica found herself becoming defensive. She'd heard what Clair had said in the student council meeting about how all the female transfers from Mesa were dogs.

"Clair, this is someone you have to know," Bubba said, excited. "Miss Jessica Hart. She used to be a cheerleader at Mesa. The best they had, I've been told. Jessie, meet my pal, Clair Hilrey." He chuckled. "Clair *is* the best."

Clair blushed at Bubba's remark, remaining seated beside a half-consumed banana split. She had an overall flushed look, as if she had just been out in the sun, or exercising. A thin gold necklace glittered at her throat. Crossing her exquisite long legs, she offered her hand. "I've heard about you," she said sweetly. "I've been wanting to meet you."

Jessica shook her hand. She wondered what Clair was doing with short, fat Bubba, whether this meant Bill and she weren't a couple, anymore. She forced a smile. "I've seen you at the games."

"Yeah?"

"Cheering, you know." Who did this girl's hair? Jessica wondered. That person should be doing her own.

Clair glanced at Bubba, giggled. "That's what we cheerleaders do here at Tabb."

"Yeah," Bubba said. "They're full of spirit. They never get tired. Hey, why don't you guys join us? We're going to go to the movies in a few minutes."

Michael and Nick didn't react to the suggestion one way or the other, although Maria did not seem particularly enthusiastic. The three of them appeared to be waiting for her decision. Clair smiled at her again, the fine lines of arrogance beautifully arranged around her wide, sensual mouth. Jessie almost felt as if Clair were challenging her to stay. *Come on, girl, see who all the boys start fawning over.* Jessica met her eyes. "That sounds like fun," she said.

They ate ice cream, lots of it, until they were all sick and groaning. Then they headed back to the theaters. They didn't have to worry about selecting a movie. Bubba did it for them.

He'd read the reviews and heard the inside Hollywood buzz, he said, and they would be crazy to see anything else. It was something about a female vampire from outer space who didn't wear any clothes.

Michael had been right. It *was* a small city. They bumped into Sara and Russ next, standing in line for the same movie. Russ must have picked it; Jessica knew how much Sara hated anything sci-fi. Indeed, Sara didn't appear to be having a thrilling night. She pulled Jessica aside the first chance she got.

"I'm going nuts," she hissed, while the others talked together in line. "Do you know where he took me for dinner?"

"Where?"

"I'll let you guess. The menu was fabulous. We had a choice of hamburgers: single patty, double patty, cheese on top, and cheese on the bottom. Then we had our choice of shakes: vanilla, strawberry, chocolate. Of course, if you ordered the full dinner, you got complimentary french fries."

"That sounds like McDonald's?"

"Very good. But dinner was the fun part. Before that, he let me take him for a scenic drive in his garbage truck. And guess what? Two local civil servants stopped us to point out the twenty bushels of dead grass we had flying out the back."

"You were driving? Did they ask for your license?"

"That they did. Fortunately, my less than sober male companion ingeniously told them I had accidentally left it in the back before we had piled in the grass. The cops didn't mind.

They told me to dig it out. They even helped me. And guess what they found?"

"More dead grass?"

"No. Beer. Alcohol. That stuff they sell to people after they are twenty-one years of age. They found three cans, and one of them was open. That's against the law, in case you didn't know."

"Did you get a ticket?" Sara's license was already in suspension; another ticket and they would probably tear it up.

"No, I got arrested!"

"No!"

"I had to take a sobriety test. I had to walk in a straight line and breathe in a bag. And get this, all the while Russ—drunk out of his gourd—got to sit there and watch!"

"Did you get a ticket?" she repeated. Sara had not been arrested.

"No, I got humiliated! Then I had to eat a greasy hamburger, which gave me indigestion. And now I've got to watch some goddamn flick about a blood-sucking pin-up." She glared in the direction of her date, fuming. "I wish the cops had given me a urine test. Then I could have thrown it in his face."

"But do you like him? Are you having fun?"

"Shut up. What are you guys going to see?"

"The same thing you are." Jessica noticed Clair fixing Michael's collar, her polished nails brushing the back of his neck. Bubba noticed, too, and didn't seem to care. Jessica couldn't say the same for herself.

Am I jealous? I can't be jealous. He's just a friend.

"Let's get back in line," she said.

Clair backed away from Michael the moment they returned. For the first time that night, Jessica took Michael's hand. Clair whispered something in Bubba's ear, causing him to laugh.

"What's up?" Michael asked innocently. Jessica pulled him close, squeezed the top of his arm, smiled.

"I am." Maybe, just maybe, he would be more than a friend.

The fireworks between Sara and Russ were not over. When Russ reached the ticket window, he discovered he didn't have enough money for two admissions. He asked Sara if she could spring for a few dollars. Sara stared at him for a long time before responding. Jessica silently hoped Sara was using the time to calm herself. She might just as well have been hoping for a gallon of gasoline to put out a fire.

"What?" Sara asked softly. "You want money from *me*? You want *me* to pay for *your* movie? Is that what *you* want?"

Poor Russ, he was looking right into the face of a volcano and he couldn't feel the heat. The girl behind the ticket window waited with an expression of infinite boredom. "Yeah," he said.

Sara took out her purse, opened it for all to see. She must

have had forty bucks, in tens and fives, and plenty of change. She smiled when she saw the money, and Jessica shivered. It was a crooked smile Sara saved for special occasions, immediately before she exploded into a frenzy.

"Hey, why don't we make this my treat," Jessica said quickly, stepping up to the window, pulling out a twenty. "Why don't I—"

"She's got plenty of dough," Russ interrupted. He stretched his hand over to pluck a bill from Sara's purse. Sara held it out of reach. He frowned. "Hey, come on, we're holding up the line."

"No," Sara said.

"What do you mean, no?" Russ demanded.

"You didn't say please."

"Please what? Please give me a couple of bucks? Man, you're— All right, all right, please give me a couple of bucks."

Sara stopped smiling. "No."

"What do ya want to see?" the chick in the window finally asked. The people behind them began to stir.

Michael took out his wallet. "Russ, I could lend you a ten if you need—"

"No," Sara interrupted, her eyes fixed on Russ. "No one's loaning this buffoon a red penny."

Russ shook his head, disgusted. "You know what your problem is, girl? You're spoiled. You get everything handed to you on a platter. You've got no class."

Sara started to laugh, loud and high, like a hyena. She did this for maybe three seconds, then suddenly cut it off and poked a sharp finger into Russ's chest. "I have no class!" she screamed. "You're an hour late! Your truck smells like a cow stall! You practically get me thrown in jail, and now you're pinching money out of my purse!"

"That's telling him," Bubba said, enjoying the exchange. The others held back. It was too late, Jessica knew, to go back.

"My truck doesn't stink," Russ said indignantly. "And I'm not pinching your money. I'm just short is all. I didn't know I was going to have to pay for all this tonight."

Sara went to snap at him, stopped. Jessica began to feel faint. "What do you mean?" Sara asked quietly.

"I didn't know we were going out until your friend called me. If I'd known, I would have went—"

"Stop," Sara said. She glanced at her, spoke to Russ. "Jessie called you? When did Jessie call you?"

Russ lowered his head, realizing his mistake. "I don't know."

Sara nodded. "Jessie set this all up, didn't she? Yeah, that makes sense. You're being a jerk 'cause you don't want to be here. Well, I can understand that." She took a breath. "I'm sorry."

"What do ya want to see?" the girl asked again. She had the line down pat. Sara reached into her purse, threw all her money under the window.

"The vamp flick," she told her, glancing at the rest of them. "It's on me."

Then she left, in a hurry, and Jessica was not able to catch up to her until they were halfway across the mall, near the central fountain. Fortunately, none of the others followed. Sara was crying. Jessica would not have thought it possible.

"I didn't know this would happen," Jessica said. "I didn't know."

Sara didn't tell her to go away, didn't blame her. Removing a handkerchief from her bag, she slowly wiped away her tears, blew her nose. Jessica watched with a mixture of guilt and amazement. Who was this fragile creature? It couldn't be her best friend. That girl *never* cried, not in the twelve years she had known her. Sara looked at her with red eyes.

"I would call a cab, but I spent all my money," she said.

"I'll go get Michael. We'll give you a ride home. You stay here until I get back." She put her arm around her. "I really am sorry."

Sara smiled faintly, embarrassed. "This is stupid."

Jessica hugged her. "No, this just means you like him."

Michael met her midway between the theaters and the fountain. She explained how Sara would rather not have to see the others any more tonight. He understood immediately; he went for the car.

They drove to Jessica's house; Sara had planned to spend the night, anyway, and Jessica wanted to talk to her. Sara didn't say a word, except to thank Michael when she got out of the car. Jessica watched her hurry to the front door, disappear inside. She turned to Michael.

"I guess I still owe you a movie," she said.

"That's OK."

"You know, you're being awfully cool about all this. I think I would feel better if you were a little put out or something."

He played with the keys in the ignition. Now he wouldn't look at her, and for a moment she wondered if he was nervous. But he hadn't asked her out. He couldn't be thinking of kissing her good night.

What if I kissed him?

"Sara seemed pretty upset," he said, rolling down his window and placing his left elbow halfway outside. In the confines of the front seat, he had placed himself as far away from her as possible. She decided to take the hint. He didn't want her kisses. He probably just wanted to get back to see the movie. She couldn't blame him.

"Yeah, she is. I better go see her."

"OK." He glanced up the street. "I have some free time tomorrow evening, if you still need help with chemistry?"

He probably had to work all day, and would be exhausted when he got home. She would be stealing his own study time. "Oh, that, never mind. I've been reading the textbook like mad the last few days. I think I've caught up on my own."

"Are you sure? It's no bother."

"I'm sure." She reached over, touched his arm. "Thanks."

Now he turned his keen dark eyes on her. "For everything?"

He remembered! She smiled. "What else?"

A sweet note to finish the evening. Nevertheless, walking toward her front door, alone, the sound of his car disappearing around the corner, she felt a little sad. She would have to remember to make sure Michael came to Alice's party next Saturday.

Chapter Eleven

A week later, riding to the party in the Jaguar with Bubba and Nick, Michael was still thinking of Jessica's good night, and feeling bad. A couple of hours alone with him and she decides she doesn't even want his help with her homework. Hell of an impression he must have made. Yet for a few happy minutes here and there, over dinner and standing in line for the tickets before the Sara-Russ blowup, he had actually believed she liked him. He'd caught her staring at him a couple of times, watching him, thinking, he had imagined, how far-out he just might be.

She had probably been wondering when the night would be over.

Since then he had spoken to Jessica only in passing. He had taken to timing his trips to their locker so he would avoid her. He did so not because he was angry with her, but because he didn't want to bother her. She was so sweet; she might feel obligated to be nice to him even if she didn't feel like it. And he had another reason. She'd been spending a lot of time with Bill Skater the past week, at lunch and during break. Beyond their mutual great looks, Michael couldn't imagine what those two had in common. Of course, from their point of view, that was probably more than enough.

"You're awfully quiet back there, Mike," Bubba said, driving. Nick sat to his right in the passenger seat. After dropping Sara and Jessica off the last Saturday, Michael had gone straight home. He had, however, seen Nick the next day at work and heard how well things had gone with Maria. But he had not spoken to Bubba about the *Big Night*, about Clair or Jessica. After all these years, Bubba usually knew when to leave him alone. Then again, it was Bubba who was dragging him to this party. If it hadn't been for him, and a fear of offending Alice, he would be at home now reading a book.

"That happens to me when I don't talk. You make a left here, in case you didn't know."

Bubba took one look down the road and drove past it without turning. Michael quickly saw his reason. The street was jammed, with cars everywhere. Though a quarter of a mile away from Polly and Alice's house, he could clearly hear the rhythm of the music, the sound of people laughing and carrying on.

"Your babe's going to be here, isn't she?" Bubba asked Nick.

"Yeah, Jessie invited her. And me, I guess."

"It doesn't look like they're turning away anyone," Michael said. Bubba couldn't find a spot anywhere.

"Is Clair coming?" Nick asked Bubba.

"Yeah. Wait till you see her in this new bikini I bought her. For all the material they used, it could have been cut from a red handkerchief."

"How did you keep her from exploding when she found out you weren't going to the concert?" Nick asked.

Bubba looked over at him. "Do you consider yourself a gentleman?"

"I suppose."

Bubba pointed to the glove compartment. "Open that, take the box out."

Nick did as he was told. Bubba was referring to the box of condoms he had been showing off last week. "There're only two left," Nick said, peering inside.

"That's why," Bubba said simply.

Michael snorted. "You didn't have sex with her eight times before ice cream and the movies."

"Four times before, three and a half times after," Bubba said.

"I don't believe it," Michael said. "I bet you didn't even kiss her good night."

"Maybe I didn't kiss her good night. I don't remember. She fell asleep in my arms."

"That's B.S.," Michael said. "How could you get her in bed?"

"For the faithful romantic, no explanation is necessary. For the unbeliever, no explanation is possible."

"You probably got her loaded."

"I confess to offering her a couple of drinks."

"I bet she was unconscious the whole time," Michael said. He didn't know whether to believe him or not. In either case, he realized he was jealous.

"What was the halftime like?" Nick asked, curious.

Bubba smiled. "And you said you were a gentleman."

They ended up parking two blocks away. Climbing out of the car, Bubba donned a pair of sunglasses and a hat, even though the sun had set two hours earlier. He already had on a flowery Hawaiian shirt and a pair of brilliant red baggy swimming trunks. Nick offered to carry the case of Heineken Bubba had purchased—with the help of a phony I.D. Michael tucked his trunks in his towel, lagging behind his friends as they walked toward the huge, brightly lit house.

A number of people were gathered on the long steep front lawn. Michael thought he saw Dale Jensen, his main competitor for valedictorian honors, sucking on a joint. Neither of them let on he had seen the other.

Loud and crowded, the beautiful living room had changed from the last time he'd been there. Furniture had been cleared away from the center of the floor, a thick clear plastic laid down. The dancers could have used a referee. You couldn't even hear yourself talking.

Nick deposited the beer in an ice chest in the kitchen, then he and Michael followed Bubba down the hall to a relatively quiet game room. The main attractions here were a pool table and three separate video games. Michael searched for Jessica, hoping to find her so he could avoid her.

Russ had planted himself in the corner in front of the full-color graphics Demon Death. He had a joy stick, a full pitcher of beer, and Polly to help him back to safety from the realm of the dead. She was all over him. Sara mustn't be around.

On the other side of the room, on a low couch behind a table covered with snack bowls, sat Bill Skater, Clair Hilrey, and The Rock. The latter glanced up the instant Nick entered, leaned over, and whispered something to his quarterback. The team had lost the previous night: 17 to 7. Bill had thrown two interceptions and had spent the entire second half on the bench, when Tabb had scored its only touchdown. The Rock had played the whole game and had sacked the opposing quarterback four times. He was a strong SOB.

"Maria might be outside," Michael said to Nick.

"She might be in this room," Nick said. He had gained a measure of self-confidence in the last two weeks.

"She's not in this room," Michael said. "And there's no sense looking for trouble."

"All right," Nick said, turning to leave. "But I can't keep avoiding him. You know that."

"We'll see."

Nick left. Apparently Bubba saw trouble, too. He didn't approach Clair right off the bat. He waited till Bill and The Rock were distracted, caught her eye, gesturing for her to meet him outside. Clair shook her head. She didn't mind hanging on to Bubba as long as no jocks were around. Yet Bubba persisted with his gestures, and finally she stood, excusing herself and silently passing within inches of Bubba as she left the room.

"There's a girl in love," Michael observed.

"Even the best of them suffer from guilt now and then," Bubba responded, not worried.

"Face it, she doesn't want to be seen with you when all her friends are around."

Bubba didn't appreciate the remark. "I didn't see Jessie running to welcome you with open arms at the door." He went after Clair.

"Sorry," Michael called after him. He was off to a great start. He noticed a Ping-Pong table set up in the garage off the game room. He often played against his mom at home; they were both good. He went and got in line for the next game.

He was a point away from being handed the paddle when he saw Jessica enter the game room and sit down beside Bill on the couch. They seemed happy to see each other. Bill handed her his drink. She offered him a pretzel. Michael accepted the paddle and crushed his opponent's initial serve into the table.

They needed to get a fresh ball. He handed the paddle to the guy behind him and got out of line.

I could walk home. It would only take a couple of hours.

He once had read a discussion about which was the worse pain: severe emotional or severe physical pain. The article had come to no conclusions. Now he could see why. One always brought the other. He actually felt as if he had been knifed through the heart. He felt the urge to shout, to run away, but he didn't have a shred of energy to move. Most of all, he felt angry at himself for caring. What did he have to care about? They hadn't gone together. He had nothing to feel sad about losing. What he had was exactly that—nothing. Looking at her didn't even bring him pleasure anymore.

He would have left if Alice hadn't suddenly appeared at his side. He felt her before he saw her. She was hugging him. "Mikey, you're very, very late," she scolded.

He hugged her back. Touching her seemed to lessen his disappointment. "How come I hardly ever see you at school?" he asked.

She stood back a step. She looked thinner than he would have liked, but color had returned to her cheeks. Her clothes surprised him: plain blue jeans, an oversize green sweatshirt—and she had a closet of dresses to choose from. She read his mind, as she often did.

"I wore this for you," she said. "Don't you remember?"

He smiled. "When you came into the store at Christmas? Yeah, but you were ready to paint then."

"I'm going to paint tonight," she said, suddenly serious. "When everyone's gone." Then she smiled. "I'm happy you're here. I have to talk to you."

Bubba chose that moment to reappear, hat and dark glasses still in place. "Hello, Crackers," he said to Alice.

"Hi, Johnny," she replied in the same flat tone. Michael understood Alice's choice of greeting—John was Bubba's real name after all—but he had never heard the Crackers nickname before.

"Clair's changing," Bubba told him. "So are Nick and Maria. It's time for a little dip."

Alice warmed at the suggestion. "Yeah, Mike, let's go in the pool. Polly's been on me all night about playing the hostess, and I'm getting sick of it. I'll dump a half gallon of bubble bath in the filter. It'll be great! You dive off the board, and you don't know what you're going to land on."

"Isn't that dangerous?" Michael asked. He supposed he couldn't leave now.

"No, that's a great idea," Bubba said. "With the bubbles, we can all go skinny dipping." He glanced at Alice. "As long as that doesn't offend the kids?"

Alice didn't answer immediately, sizing him up. "Sara's here. She's upstairs, in case you didn't know."

"So?" Bubba said.

Alice slowly stepped around him, forcing Bubba to turn to follow her. "She didn't expect to be elected president," she said.

"She was really surprised. Everyone was, except me. I know you used your computer to change the vote count."

It was Bubba's turn to size her up, his thoughts effectively hidden behind his dark glasses. Michael had of course suspected Bubba had altered the outcome of the election. After studying how the votes were collected, however, and the structure of the program used to count them, he had been unable to figure out how it could have been done. He had, therefore, not confronted Bubba with it. In reality, Michael couldn't have cared less who was school president.

"I didn't," Bubba said finally, his voice low and even. "And I don't care whether you believe that or not. But I do insist you stop accusing me of having access to confidential files, especially when other people are around. I told you on that first day—talk like that could get Mike and me expelled."

Alice laughed at his seriousness. "You're such a wonderful liar! I love it! Don't worry, Johnny, I'm not turning you in. Not tonight at least. Come on, let's go swimming. Let me go change."

As Alice left, Bubba looked at Michael and shook his head.

Polly was upset. She'd printed up sixty invitations and at least three times that number had barged through her front door. These people—they didn't care how much they ate, what they dropped on the floor. And they were so noisy! At Alice's insistence, she'd combined the speakers from their two bedroom stereos and arranged them in the corners of the living room. When the dial on the receiver was set at six, the house vibrated. Naturally, someone had jacked the setting up to ten! She already had a splitting headache. She almost hoped the police showed up when ten o'clock rolled around and neighborhood noise restrictions went into effect. It was going to take something drastic to get this herd out of here. She wished she had never allowed herself to be talked into this blasted party. That Alice—she got her way too much.

Polly had another reason to be angry at her sister. Despite her promise, Alice had invited Clark to the party.

"How do I kill these ugly critters here?" Russ asked, nodding at the TV screen, slurring his words. He'd asked for a little whiskey in his beer. She didn't mind obliging him, though ordinarily she hated the smell of alcohol. She considered Russ a very special guy. He seemed to like her.

"You have to identify who they are first, what their powers might be. Most witches you can just shoot at and kill. But a disembodied spirit, you need a magic potion to get rid of them."

"Huh," Russ grunted, rubbing his red eyes. The poor dear, it had been hot again yesterday afternoon when he'd run the cross-country race. She'd been one of the few present, shouting her support. She'd been glad when he won. Sara and Jessica hadn't bothered to stop by. "What are these?" he asked.

"Witches," she said. "Just blow them away and go on."

He fumbled with the button on the joy stick. "They won't

die," he complained. They wouldn't die because he kept missing them by several inches. Frustrated, he dropped the joy stick on the floor and took a gulp of his beer. She had never seen anybody, teenager or adult, who had his thirst. He belched loudly. "Where's Sara?"

She smiled pleasantly. "She not here. She's sick."

"Sick?"

"She gets sick a lot. I never get sick. I'm one of the healthiest people I know. At the hospital, they're always having me come back to donate blood."

Russ looked confused. "I've got to talk to Sara."

"Why? You can talk to me."

He tried to stand, without much success. "She's got my ax."

Polly put him back in his chair. She had just spotted Alice heading for the living room, possibly for upstairs. That girl had better not be planning to go in the pool. Someone had to keep up with all these guests. Polly felt she had already done more than her fair share.

"Stay here," she said, getting up. She still had the ax in the trunk of her Mercedes. "I'll try to find it for you."

Russ scratched his head. "Why did Sara give it to you?"

Leaving the game room, Polly noticed Jessica gossiping with Bill Skater. Clair Hilrey vanishes for a second and Jessica takes her place. The same thing had been going on all week at school. Polly thought Jessica a fool. She had a sharp guy like Michael Olson interested in her, and she pursued a lug like

Bill. If she had a guy, Polly swore, any guy, who really respected her, she would treat him right. Jessica had a lot to learn.

Alice did indeed head upstairs. Polly followed her carefully. They'd placed a sign on the front door stating the top floor was off limits. A few people had ignored it, to use the second-floor bathrooms, which Polly supposed was better than their using the bushes.

Two short flights of stairs led to the upper floor. Polly paused on the landing. Alice was talking to that greasy guy from the gas station near the turn in the hall. *Kats*—another example of someone they had not invited. With the loud music, Polly couldn't hear what he was saying. But she didn't like how he was grinning at her sister. She wouldn't be surprised if Alice was encouraging him.

She changed her mind a moment later. Kats wouldn't let Alice into her room. He'd stretched his hairy arm across her bedroom door. Alice looked around uneasily. Polly hurried up the remaining flight of stairs, strode down the hallway.

"Hi," she said to Kats. "How are you?"

He took his hand off the door frame, stepped back. "Great! Far-out party you're having."

She smiled. "I'm glad you're enjoying yourself." She took Alice by the arm. "Excuse me, I have to speak with my sister."

She led Alice around the corner and into the room at the end of the hall. It used to be their parents' bedroom years ago. Polly opened the door, turned on the light. A sudden flash dazzled her eyes. The light died. Old bulb, burned out. She stumbled forward, searching for the lamp on the nightstand in the corner. They were the only two pieces of furniture in the room. There wasn't even a rug.

"What was that all about?" she asked, turning on the lamp.

"Nothing," Alice said, closing the door behind her. "He wanted to talk, and I wanted to get into my room and change."

The floor had recently been polished. The glare of the light from the lamp's naked bulb reflecting on the hard wood irritated Polly's eyes.

"You're not going in the pool."

Alice put her hand on her hip, pouted. "Yes, I am."

"That isn't fair. I'm sick and tired of running all over the house making sure everybody's having a good time. I'd like a few minutes to relax."

"Fine, relax. The party will carry on just fine without either of us."

"Sure, just drop everything. In case you didn't know, we're out of paper cups downstairs."

Although the room appeared empty, its closets were jammed. They kept Christmas decorations, party stuff, etcetera in the space where their parents had hung their clothes. Earlier, while preparing for the party, they had gone through the closets. There was still an aluminum ladder parked against the wall. Taking hold of the middle rungs, Alice spread it out beside one closet.

"I'll get the cups," she said. "Then I'm going in the water. I don't care what you say."

"Who'll greet the guests? Not me."

"Most of the guests are here. A lot of them are already leaving."

Polly moved closer, stepping in front of the lamp, casting a shadow over her sister. "Somebody is not here yet."

Alice paused halfway up the ladder. "He's not coming," she said.

"He said he was when he called this afternoon. That's what he told me." She took another step closer, put her hand out to support the ladder. It was old, unsteady. "Why did you tell him about the party?"

"I didn't."

"Then how did he find out about it?"

"I don't know."

"I don't believe you."

Alice closed her eyes briefly, leaning her head back, taking a deep breath. Her doctor had taught her that, just breathe and blow your troubles away. A bunch of hogwash. "I told you, I'm not seeing him anymore. I didn't tell him about the party. He must have heard about it from someone else. Jessica, or Sara maybe."

"Neither of them has even met Clark."

"He could have called when they were helping us get ready this morning. One of them could have answered the phone."

"Did they say that?"

Alice shook her head, went up another step. "Leave me alone."

"You want me to let go of the ladder? If I do, you'll fall and break your neck. Anyway, why are you suddenly down on Clark? What did he do?"

Alice opened the closet, pulled out a mass of tangled Christmas tree lights. "Nothing."

"Did he say something about me?"

"No. What would he say about you?"

"Oh, excuse me, I guess you've forgotten I used to go out with him."

Alice tried pushing the lights aside, trying to get to the brown box that held the paper cups. The Christmas lights kept tangling in her hands. "I know who told him about the party," she said softly.

"Who?"

"You."

Polly let go of the ladder, chuckled. "What?"

Alice glared at her. "Admit it, you wanted him to come tonight. I've broken up with him, and you want to see if you can get him back. Well, he's not coming. I called him not three hours ago and told him he wasn't welcome."

"Why, you little—"

"Listen to me, Polly! Stay away from him. He doesn't just have weird ideas, he does weird stuff. He's dangerous."

Polly found herself trembling. How dare her sister, her *baby* sister, talk to her this way! Such filthy lies! Yet she didn't yell at her. The top of a ladder was no place to fight. There could be an accident, somebody might get hurt. She knew about that sort of thing. She tried to calm herself.

Besides, she was—*curious.* "What sort of weird stuff?" she asked.

Shaking her head, Alice climbed down. "I'm going. Good-bye." She opened the door.

"What about the cups?" Polly cried.

"I'll get them later," Alice called over her shoulder, slamming the door behind her. Polly stood for a moment staring at the bright bulb, even though it hurt her eyes and made her headache worse. She hadn't invited Clark. Why would Alice say that? She was pretty sure she hadn't invited him. And she had a good memory for such things.

Polly resolved not to get the cups no matter who complained. Alice had said she would take care of it, and Alice had to learn to be responsible. But while the ladder was out, she figured she might as well change the overhead bulb. The lamp didn't go on when you threw the switch by the door. She didn't want someone looking for the bathroom stumbling and breaking a leg.

Polly found a package of 100-watt bulbs beside the Christmas lights. Holding the replacements in one hand, she scooted the ladder to the center of the room with the other. Climbing the ladder, she reached around the shade and began to fiddle with the old bulb. She couldn't see it but she could feel it, dusty and delicate beneath her damp fingers.

All of a sudden, she realized exactly how wet her hands were.

Russ must have spilled some beer on me or something.

The light switch beside the door remained in the on position. The bulb couldn't have been completely dead. As she turned it counterclockwise, it flickered on. Water and light bulbs make poor companions. It exploded in her hand, and her fingers slipped directly into the charged socket.

The electric shock shot through the length of Polly's body. Her footing vanished beneath her. She had no chance to brace herself for the fall. She hit the floor on her right hip, hard, the impact sending a jolt through her spine and into her skull. Her headache blossomed from a minor irritation into a red wave of agony.

Then everything turned dark and cool, for how long she wasn't sure. When she opened her eyes next, the ceiling looked miles away. She sat up, shook herself. The fingers of her right hand were bleeding. She slowly got to her feet, using the wall for support. Glass from the shattered bulb lay scattered across the hard wooden floor.

Lord, I could have electrocuted myself.

She needed a bandage for her hand. She could fix the bulb another time. Clark might show up any moment. She did remember now; she had told him to come over late, after most of the people were gone. That didn't excuse Alice's insolence, though, not by any means. She would have to have a word with her about being respectful, for her own good.

Bill Skater didn't talk much. Jessica had always been attracted to the strong, silent type. Like Michael, she had discovered Bill to be an excellent listener. She did wish, however, that he would occasionally volunteer something. Hanging out with him, she often felt as if she were playing bounce with a flat ball.

The Rock, on the other hand, enjoyed talking, and surprisingly, had much of interest to say. He was telling her about the work he did with disadvantaged kids downtown. He had a loud, boisterous voice, and a childish enthusiasm she found appealing. In many ways he was like one of the kids he helped. She and Bill were drinking beer, but The Rock had ten minutes ago recoiled from her offer of one as if she had suggested a deadly shot of heroin. He had quickly reassured her that he had nothing against her drinking, it just wasn't his style.

"We have it so easy in this part of town," The Rock said. "We have the ocean to swim in, the beach to run along. Everything's clean: the stores, the sidewalks. But in the ghettos, those kids have nothing but asphalt, plugged sewers, and drugs. There're dealers everywhere. Crack's the big thing these days, that hard cocaine people smoke." He shook his head in disgust. "Just last week I was approached by a twelve-year-old kid trying to sell me the stuff."

"How did you get involved in the Big Brother Program?" Jessica asked. He had such obvious sympathy for black kids, she wondered how the feud between him and Nick had ever started. She didn't have the nerve to ask.

"I had to pick up a pal at the L.A. bus station. You know where that is, right in the heart of the city? There was this black kid—found out later he was only eight—bumming change at the entrance. He hit me up for a nickel. Imagine, just a nickel! I asked him what he wanted it for. He told me food. I took ahold of his arm. It felt like a chicken bone."

The Rock went on to describe how he took him for a sandwich and learned how the boy slept in a garbage dump. He discovered there were dozens of kids like him all over the city, that they had no parents, no one to help them. His conscience called. He became a Big Brother. To this day, he regularly saw that first boy—Emmanuel.

Then The Rock switched the topic to football, and almost immediately Jessica found her mind wandering, back to the previous Monday morning when Bill had approached her after Mr. Bark's political science class. That morning she'd had to read a paper on why she thought the electoral college system should be abolished. Mr. Bark had given her an A on the piece. She had spent three hours researching the paper in the library the previous day. Bill had wanted to compliment her on a job well done. Those were, in fact, his exact words. She had blushed.

"Thank you. But to tell you the truth, I didn't understand half of what I was saying."

"I thought you were very clear," he said. He had an unusually smooth complexion. The blue of his eyes reminded her of the Mediterranean skies of her vacation. "What was your name?"

"Jessie."

"That's right." They talked for a few minutes about purely inconsequential matters: the weather, the state of the union. Finally the question came. "What are you doing for lunch, Jessie?"

Life was good. Her legs felt weak. She told him she was free.

He took her for Chinese food in the mall. She had fun. Well, she had fun looking at him. They didn't exactly enjoy an instant rapport. Possibly because the team was doing badly, but he wouldn't even discuss football. She still didn't know what his interests were. Since Sara had told her how assertive he could be during student council meetings, she found his shyness confusing. Over lunch, and at other times in the week, he often seemed uncomfortable in her presence. She decided she would have to give it time. She had already made up her mind about one thing. She wanted to have sex with him.

A girl is always supposed to remember her first. Why shouldn't I start with the best?

Jessica was tired of daydreaming about making love. She had been doing that since she was in the seventh grade. It left her feeling unsatisfied, to say the least. It left her frustrated. She wanted the real thing, and she wasn't going to wait till she got married. It wasn't only because she was horny, she was just incredibly curious to see what it was like. When Bill finally asked her out on a real date, if he made a move, she had already decided she wasn't going to stop him. She couldn't wait to see the rest of that hard body. She was already investigating types of contraceptives.

Her decision surprised even her. A year earlier it would have been unimaginable. She had always considered herself fairly moral. For instance, her cheating on the chemistry quiz still bothered her. But her outlook had grown far more liberal in the last year, largely because of her European vacation. When she had first arrived on the beaches of southern France, and seen people nude sunbathing, it had been a shock. But by the end of the week—when her parents weren't around, of course—she had joined the crowd.

But there was still that big question—*when* Bill asked her out. When was that going to be? Clair had to be the reason for the delay. Jessica had never spoken to him when she was around. The one time she had broached the topic of his involvement with her, he had changed the subject.

The Rock wrapped up a story about some opposing lineman whose knee he had cracked in a dozen places and went off to change into his swimming trunks. Left alone with Bill, Jessica racked her brain for something to talk about. Bill continued to sip his beer, watching things go on about him. Suddenly Clair swept back into the room in an unfastened beach coverup and red bikini. In a cheerleader uniform, Clair projected a certain sex appeal. In this reasonable excuse for total nudity, she looked positively nasty. All legs, chest—enough clear brown flesh to exhaust any red-blooded American boy's fantasy reserve. Bill started to stand up. Clair grabbed his hands and pulled him into her arms.

"Let's go big boy," she said. "Time to get wet." She glanced up. "Time to get down."

"All right, I'll be there in a minute."

Clair grinned and asked what on the surface appeared to be a redundant question. "In the pool?"

"Yeah," Bill said.

She patted his rump. "OK, OK, the water first. Hurry." And completely ignoring Jessica, she turned and left.

"Did you want to go swimming?" Bill asked uneasily, setting down his beer.

Why buy contraceptives when I might be able to borrow Clair's?

She had bought a new bathing suit for the party. To compete with Clair, however, she should have purchased breast implants. She smiled, although it hurt to do so. She wouldn't ask what the deal was, not yet. "Another time, maybe," she said.

Alone, she started to search for Michael. She'd seen him come in. She just wanted someone to talk to.

* * *

Summer had come to an end. Feeling the chill of the night-time air as he huddled his shoulders beneath the warm water and fluffy bubbles, Michael felt autumn inside. He always mourned the summer's passing and instantly began waiting for it to return. Somehow, this year, he could tell, it was going to be a long wait. He continued to think of Jessica and Bill together on the couch.

"Marco!" Bubba called, paddling through a bank of foam in the deep end, his eyes tightly clenched, playing the blind-man in the oldest pool game ever invented.

"Polo!" three dozen people replied. Marco Polo in a pool as crowded as this was a joke. You just had to launch yourself in practically any direction and you were bound to tag some-body. Naturally, Bubba had been *it* for the last twenty minutes. Michael suspected he was slyly opening his eyes so he could stay *it* until he could accidentally rip the top off a girl of his own choosing.

"Marco!"

Maria and Nick swam to Michael's side. "You two look like you're having fun," he said.

"The water feels great after working all day," Nick agreed.

"I think we should get out," Maria said, glancing toward the diving board where several of the football players had gath-ered to taunt Bubba into coming their way.

"You might," Michael said.

Nick shook his head. "I feel just fine where I am. Anyway, what can they do to me in front of all these people?"

"They could drown you," Maria said unhappily.

The boys on the team did not try to drown Nick. But they did pull a rather unpleasant stunt. Much to Bubba's obvious displeasure, he bumped into The Rock, and was no longer *it*. As the center of attention, The Rock, with supposedly closed eyes, wasted no time in heading straight for Nick, who made the mistake of moving away from the side of the pool. Several guys on the team suddenly popped to the surface behind Nick. He saw them at the same time Michael did. It did neither of them any good. One grabbed Nick's right arm, the other his left. His head got pushed under and The Rock went diving.

They all reappeared a few seconds later, with Nick thrashing wildly and The Rock laughing heartily. The Rock had torn off Nick's trunks.

"Come get me, boy," he taunted, moving into the shallow end where Nick would have to stay low—*real* low—if he didn't want to be the talk of the school on Monday. Yet Michael felt more afraid for The Rock than he did for his friend. The guys who had pinned Nick's arms seemed to have reassessed Nick's strength in the short time they'd had ahold of him. They backed off, gingerly rubbing their sides, as the other guys on the team watched from a respectful distance. For the moment Nick had The Rock to himself, and Michael could not have imagined such fury in Nick's face. It was out of a similar expression the many ugly rumors concerning his deadly rage must have sprung.

But Nick couldn't move, except on his knees. Bubba clearly recognized the problem, and Bubba loved to watch a good fight.

"Hey, Nick!" he called from the deep end, his hands out of sight beneath the water and bubbles. "Take these!"

He didn't toss him a sword or a knife. Bubba threw Nick a pair of trunks—*his* own shorts. Nick caught them, put them on. The Rock backed into the side of the shallow end, stopped his taunting. Nowhere to go.

"Hey," he said.

Nick launched himself at The Rock, who had decided a fraction of a second too late that the water was not a safe place to be. Nick caught The Rock by the right arm and the back of the neck just as The Rock put one foot on the deck. The Rock started a cry that ended in a strangled gargle. Nick had shoved him under. The festive atmosphere hushed into a tense silence. It was a struggle for Nick—The Rock's feet and hands kept thrashing to the surface—but it was clear he could hold his prey's head under as long as he pleased.

"Stop!" Maria cried.

"No," Nick said.

"You'll kill him!" she pleaded.

"Yeah!" Bubba cheered.

Nick smiled grimly, tightening his grip. "Not yet."

Maria dived toward Nick and pounded him on the back. "Let him go now!"

Nick looked at her strangely for a moment. Then he held his hands up, as if he were displaying his innocence. The Rock broke the surface, his choking gasps material for pity. He lay bent over the steps, sobbing in recovery.

"We can't do this," Maria said wearily. She could have been talking about more than The Rock's dunking.

"He started it," Nick protested.

Maria shook her head sadly. To her, it didn't matter.

Michael watched the next few minutes with a calm fascination. To a casual spectator, the hostilities appeared to be over. The usual chatter resumed across the pool. Yet Michael knew they had merely passed into the eye of the hurricane. Worried about Maria's feelings, Nick paid little heed to the movement of people around him. The Rock was making a swift recovery. He had moved from the steps and now was sitting on the side near the diving board. One by one, his teammates, including Bill Skater, swam to his dangling feet, conferring with him.

"Nick," Michael said. "Nick."

His friend didn't hear, preoccupied as he was with convincing Maria that he hadn't intended to drown the fat slob. Perhaps it didn't matter, Michael thought. Help was on the way. Seconds before The Rock jumped Nick, Alice had been testing the pool's chlorine level. When they had a lot of people in the water, Alice had said, the level could drop rapidly. When

The Rock had attacked Nick, Alice had dashed into the house, the pail of powdered chlorine in her hand. Now she reappeared with her sister holding the chlorine, just as The Rock reentered the water with eleven backups—and began to swim toward Nick.

"Nick!" Michael shouted.

He said violence follows him, no matter where he goes. In the streets, the weight room, the store, the pool . . . Could he be right?

It didn't take long for a person, or a dozen for that matter, to swim the length of the pool. It took Polly about the same interval to stride from her back door to the steps of the pool. When Nick finally did look up, he found himself surrounded by friends and foes alike.

"Get out of the water, all of you," Polly said.

"Sure," The Rock said, a purple welt swelling beneath his left eye. "After we take care of business."

Nick flexed his shoulders, the water reaching to his waist, shooing a terrified Maria aside. "Don't keep me waiting," he said to The Rock.

"My man!" Bubba shouted, off in the corner with Clair. He would be pulling off the bottom of her red bikini next and offering it to Bill. Tabb's quarterback, another upstanding member of the lynch gang, waited expressionless by The Rock's side. Michael edged toward Nick. If he had to fight to save his pal, he decided it wouldn't be bad to get in a stiff kick to Bill's crotch.

After all, the guy stole my girl.

What a laugh. He would probably get his head smashed in, and yet, he was pleasantly surprised to discover he wasn't afraid.

"You better pray you were born with gills, boy," The Rock said, glancing around to assure himself of his support. Nick did not move, but Michael could literally see the dark strength coiling in his muscles.

"No!" Maria cried.

"Get off my property!" Polly shouted at The Rock, jumping onto the first step, the water drenching the bottom of her black pants. She stuck a hand into the pail of chlorine. "Get!"

"Bug off," The Rock said, raising his fist, intent on Nick.

Polly threw a handful of chlorine in his face. Unfortunately for The Rock, he was soaked. The white powder dissolved instantly. The Rock let out a scream, his hands flying to his eyes. Michael grimaced. Chlorine solution could eat out eyes in seconds.

"Put your head under the water!" Michael said. "Get his head under!"

Bill tried to do just that. The Rock jabbed an elbow into Bill's jaw. *Don't you touch me.* Understandably, The Rock was not crazy about having someone submerge him again. He just kept screaming.

"My eyes! My eyes!"

Michael dived forward, grabbed The Rock's wrists. "Go

under water—now—and blink your eyes or go blind!" he yelled in his ear. The Rock nodded once, thrust his head beneath the surface. He came up a few seconds later.

"My eyes!"

"More," Michael ordered, pushing him down. "Stay under a whole minute. Flush them out."

While he was submerged this time, Polly muttered something under her breath, dropped the pail on the ground, and strode back into the house. The others waited quietly. Alice entered the water to stand beside Michael. Finally The Rock reappeared.

"How are they?" Michael asked. "Let me see."

"They sting. They hurt."

And they were a nasty red. "But you can see," Michael said. "Go inside, into the bathroom, and take a shower. Let the cold water run straight into them for a few minutes, but not too hard. Keep your hands away from them. Then get dressed and have someone drive you to the hospital." Michael patted him on the back. "Go ahead, you're going to be all right."

The Rock did not look at Nick as he left. Maybe it hurt too much. The boys on the team dispersed. It seemed to be over, for the time being.

The night deepened. The suds began to vanish. In groups of twos and threes, people got out of the water. Bubba finally gave up his carousing with Clair and consented to wear a towel on the walk to the house. And Nick and Maria were long gone when Michael began to slowly swim laps, on his back, staring at the black sky, wondering if Jessica was inside with Bill hearing about how the tall black dude had tried to kill The Rock for a second time.

Michael was alone with Alice and she was flying through space, like an acrobat, maybe an angel, in her white bathing suit and shining yellow hair, performing dive after dive.

"Watch this one!" she called, jumping onto the board again.

Michael rolled onto his side. Lithe but coordinated, Alice stepped forward, pounced the board's tip, soared upward, gracefully spinning through two and a half somersaults. She disappeared head-first into the water with the faintest splash. Michael waited for her to resurface, ready to applaud her effort. *One . . . two . . . three . . .* Time passed so slowly when someone went under and didn't come up.

"Alice?" he said.

"Eeeh!" She laughed, popping up behind him, throwing her arms around his neck. "Scared you?"

"Yeah, fish brain." He grabbed her and threw her over his head as if she were made of air.

They got out awhile later. From the positions of the stars, Michael knew it must be near midnight. The music continued inside but at a lower volume. No one seemed to be dancing. He could hear few people talking. Handing him a towel, Alice led him around the side of the house to the spot where she had been painting last week. They'd set up a couple of barbecues earlier that needed extinguishing, she explained.

"Do you think Polly damaged that boy's eyes?" she asked, slowly raking the smoldering coals with a black metal stick. She didn't have what most people would call striking features, but at that moment, the burning orange light warm on her young face, she was, to Michael, a child of beauty.

"No. Very little of the chlorine got in his eyes. He's a baby, cries a lot. Don't worry, he'll be fine."

Alice smiled, not like an angel really, more like a mischievous devil. "I told you I wanted to talk to you. Do you know what about?"

"What?"

"Jessie."

"Oh?"

Alice stopped, watching him over the heat radiating from the flaked charcoal. The front of his body was burning, but goose flesh was forming on his back from a breeze that had begun to blow out of the east. He hugged his towel tighter. The tall silhouette of a two-armed cactus stood behind Alice in the garden like a prickly ghost.

"You knew she was the one I told you about," she said.

"Not at first. Not until the football game."

"Why didn't you tell me, after that?"

There was no accusation in her voice, simply curiosity.

"Why didn't you tell her when you found out we were going out?" he said.

Alice nodded, as if to say "well answered." "Neither of us told her. What a coincidence. Or do you think the decision passed unspoken between us?" Before he could respond, she continued, "Yeah, I think so. But I was still disappointed I didn't get to introduce you two, that you found each other without me."

"Why?"

Alice returned to scattering the ashes. "Jessie's always taken care of me. When my parents died, and Polly was in the hospital, she became like another sister to me. No, more like a new mom. I don't think I would have survived without her. And then, when I met you at Christmas, I felt like I had found— Does this sound corny?"

"Not at all, Alice."

She smiled shyly. "I love you, Michael. You know that. You've always been like the other half for me. Jessie and you— I had this dream for a long time. I was saving each of you for the other, for the right time. Then when our schools got put together, I knew that time had come. Do you understand what I mean? Maybe it was selfish, but I thought that you would come together through me, and then—then it would be beautiful." Alice stopped. "You love her, don't you?"

"I hardly know her."

"But you still love her. I can see that. Don't worry, no one else can. I knew you'd love her." She lowered her head, suddenly frowned. "I hope everything will be all right."

He chuckled. "Everything's going to be fine. Why wouldn't it be?" He was glad she had not asked him to verify the truth of her statement. Her certainty, her insight, intrigued him, frightened him. She didn't even care how their date had gone. It was immaterial to her, or rather, it was simply material, and she was talking about something bordering on a spiritual bond. She stood on an edge where she could see in directions others couldn't. He'd known that from their first meeting, and it had drawn him to her. But how fine an edge? He worried for her.

"Because I wasn't there," she said, vaguely confused. "And in my dream, I was always there."

"When Jessie and I met?"

"Yes." She shook herself. "I probably dream too much. That's what my doctor says." She glanced up to the dimly lit second-story window above them. "That used to be my parents' bedroom. Polly cleaned it out a few years ago. Gave away all the furniture."

"You must miss them a lot."

She laughed suddenly. "That's what I'm trying to tell you. I don't! When I'm awake, I have you two wonderful friends, and then, when I sleep, I walk in the forest with my mom and dad. I honestly do." A spark flared between them, distracting her. She wrinkled her nose at the black and burning cinders. "This is something Clark would paint. Looks like hell. But then, he's a weird guy." She set aside her stick and slowly moved her hand inches above the center of the barbecue.

"Careful, you'll burn yourself."

"I'm wet, I can't get hurt."

He had doubts about that. He wished she would stop. Who was this doctor she had mentioned? "Tell me about your dreams?"

She nodded at his question. "I bet you dream, too."

"I do."

"I knew it. I'll have to show mine. We can compare them. I'm going to finish my painting tonight."

"Tonight? You should go to bed."

She took her hand back. If she had burned it, she would never show it. He pushed aside his concern. She was sensitive—true, but also strong. "I'm not tired," she said. She glanced up at the window again. "I'd better go in. This charcoal can burn itself out. I just remembered, I promised Polly I'd get out some paper cups."

"But practically everyone's left."

She stepped around the barbecue, took his hand in her warm one, and led him toward the back door. "With Polly, it doesn't matter." She laughed. "Let's finish our talk later."

All in all, Nick thought, it had been an eventful evening. He'd had an invigorating swim, been in a messy fight, and had received the first kiss of his life from a girl only a few minutes after he believed he had lost her forever. Sitting on the couch in the living room with Maria and Michael, listening to a Beatles album on the stereo, he was glad things had finally slowed down. He didn't wish to disturb his present feeling of contentment—it had cost him too much to achieve.

"It's lucky my parents think I'm asleep in bed at Jessie's house right now," Maria said, nodding toward the polished brass clock on the wall as it struck one o'clock. "At home, I have to be in bed by ten."

"I haven't been in bed before ten since I was ten." Michael yawned, leaning back into the soft deep cushions. He'd dressed, but his hair was still wet from his swim. "I could go to sleep right here. Let's head out in a few minutes, Nick."

"We can leave now if you'd like."

"A few minutes. Where's Bubba?"

"I don't know." For the moment the three of them had the living room to themselves. They had, in fact, only the foggiest idea who was left in the house. Nick had seen Clair and Bill not long ago, heading up the stairs, and Kats wandering around the kitchen searching for a knife. That was it.

Even with the music on, the house *felt* oddly still. Despite Nick's feeling of peace and contentment the sensation was not pleasant. Late at night on the streets, in the worst parts of town, it often felt quiet like this.

"I'm glad I won't have to keep lying to my parents," Maria

said. His reaction to The Rock's attack had terrified her as much as the attack itself. When they had gotten out of the pool, she wouldn't even talk to him. He'd feared that she thought he might one day go off the deep end and throw her around. But then, after she had changed into her clothes, her viewpoint shifted completely. The initial shock must have worn off. She told him how brave he had been. Then she had kissed him, briefly, but on the lips.

"What do you mean?" he asked.

"You're going to meet them," she said.

"Your parents? I thought that was out of the question?"

She wouldn't explain. "You're going to meet them," she repeated, leaning closer toward him.

Sara and Jessica entered the living room from the direction of the game room. Michael sat up suddenly. None of them had seen Sara all night. Maybe she had only recently arrived.

"Why is the music so loud?" Sara demanded.

"Someone must have turned it up," Jessica said. She sat in a chair at Michael's end of the couch. "I was beginning to think you were going to stay in that pool all night," she said.

Michael nodded. "I might have over done it. My eyes are sore from the chlorine."

"They can't be as bad as that jock's in the garage," Sara said, turning down the stereo volume. "That Polly had a lot of nerve."

"The Rock's here?" Michael asked, surprised. "Didn't he go to the hospital?"

"He came back," Jessica said.

Michael frowned. "Why?"

Jessica shrugged, looking tired. "Who knows?"

Wonderful, Nick thought.

Polly came into the room at that instant. Like Jessica, she seemed worn out, only more so. She wandered over to the record player. "I'm turning this off," she muttered. "My head hurts."

"Polly, where's Alice?" Michael asked.

Polly shook her head, trudged toward the back door. "I don't know where no one is." She pulled at the screen. "I've got to check on the chlorine level."

"Leave it until tomorrow," Jessica said.

Polly paid no attention to her, going outside, shutting both the screen and the thick sliding glass door behind her. Nick watched as she walked over to the water and picked up the small, blue chemical test box and pail of white powder she had used to stop The Rock. He had meant to thank her for coming to his rescue. Perhaps he'd do it when she returned—and when he came back from the bathroom. He had been scrupulously avoiding anything alcoholic. He didn't want Maria knowing he had any bad habits. But he had been putting away the soft drinks. His bladder was full. He got up.

"Where's the bathroom?" he asked.

"There's one off the game room," Sara said. "But I think someone's in there right now throwing up."

"Go upstairs," Jessica said. "Polly won't mind. There's one halfway down the hallway before you come to the turn. If that's being used, try one of the bathrooms in the bedrooms."

And so Nick started a walk he would for the remainder of the school year replay again and again in his mind, searching for a clue, for a reason for the horror that came upon them all at the end of Alice's party.

The stairway lay near the front door, close to the kitchen. Putting his foot on the first step, he heard a low moan off to his right. He paused, stretching his head around the tall potted plant that stood between him and the sound. It was Bill Skater, bent over the kitchen sink, his shirt rumpled, his face pale, as if he were about to be sick. Nick wondered if he should go to him, but then he remembered Bill beside The Rock in the pool. He continued on up the stairs.

He probably drank too much.

In the first stretch of the hall there were four doors, three on the left, one in the middle on the right. Jessica had specified the bathroom was in the middle, but had not said on which side. He didn't want to barge in on someone sleeping. He decided to skip the first door on the left, but tried the second door, finding it locked. He thought he heard water running inside. Chances were this was the bathroom Jessica had referred to. Yet he couldn't be sure. The sound could be coming from the last door on the left, or even from the one room on the right. It disturbed him that he couldn't narrow it down more specifically. The harder he listened, the more the faint gurgling seemed to spring from all around him. Of course that often happened with a faint noise in a quiet place. He could not hear the others downstairs.

He tried the lone door on the right. It opened easily, silently; a whiff of night air brushed his bare arms and face. The door led to an elevated porch that overlooked the pool. A dark figure stood alone at the edge of the square space, staring up at the sky, his booted foot resting on the roof's wooden shingles, which went right to the floor of the porch. A blue glow from the lighted waters below danced over his rough leather jacket.

Kats.

Nick closed the door carefully, confident the quirky gas station attendant didn't know he had been there. He moved to the third door on the left.

It was also locked, and had faint stirring going on within. Nick did not intend to be nosy, but he stood long enough and close enough to the door to pick up on the sounds of breathing, of shifting bedsprings. He heard a cough, a sigh, enough, he decided, to keep him from knocking. He walked on, making a right at the turn in the hall.

This part of the hallway presented him with a choice of two doors, both on the left. The first was locked. He almost knocked. There were people inside; he could hear them. What stopped him was a sound of soft groaning. He or she or they—Nick couldn't be sure—seemed to be in pain. Nick thought of Bill downstairs. He wondered if there was a connection. Guilt pricked his conscience. What if someone was hurt, or being hurt?

Yet he walked on. He did not belong in a house this big, with its plush furniture and high-beamed ceilings. He was an outsider still, though for the moment things were going well, with his job and school, with Maria. He didn't want to mess up again. He didn't want to walk in on another fight.

Reasons. Excuses.

His guilt chased him into the final room at the end of the hall. Its door lay wide open, an invitation into a dark place.

Nick reached inside without actually stepping through the doorway, found the light switch turned up. He flicked it down, then up again. The darkness remained. He glanced back the way he had come, uncertain what to do. The last light in the hall was around the corner. At the moment it was of little help.

Come on, after what you've been through, you can't be afraid of the dark.

Yet that was precisely the source of his hesitation. He did not trust the dark. It robbed him of his keenest sense, his first line of defense, and if The Rock really had returned to the party, as Sara suggested, maybe he was waiting inside this room with God knew how many of his buddies, waiting eagerly to pay Nick back for a near drowning and a pair of burned eyes.

At the last moment Nick almost turned and walked away. The reason he didn't was purely physical. Testing every upstairs door had consumed time. Now he either had to get to a place to pee immediately or he was going to have to run outside and find a bush. The Rock was only a possibility—his discomfort, a certainty. He stepped into the room.

It appeared empty, although he couldn't be sure. The illumination through the open windows—they faced east, away from the pool—couldn't have been more meager. Yet the draft pouring in from the outside sent a chill through him. Polly and Alice must love the fresh air.

His eyes adjusted to the gloom. He noted the outline of another set of windows on the right wall, their shades down, and a second doorway off to the left, with a tiny room beyond. He felt his way forward. Inside the small room, his fingers found another light switch. Yet he chose to leave this one off. He had definitely reached a bathroom; he could see the outline of the sink and the toilet. If he put on the light he'd only startle his eyes, and then he'd have to exit into the dark room completely blind.

Nick moved inside, closed the door. He took care of business quickly, flushed the toilet, and reopened the door. He was still in the bedroom, heading for the hall, when he suddenly paused in midstride.

Tommy?

That ominous silence he had noticed downstairs struck

him again, only stronger this time. His head felt strangely full. He wondered for a moment if he hadn't accidentally drunk something alcoholic after all, even though he knew his uneasiness had nothing to do with booze.

My blood brother.

A seed of fear began to form deep in his mind. The feeling of *heaviness*, inside and out, was not entirely new to him. He had experienced it once before, two years earlier. But that had been in the middle of the night in a dark alleyway after a gang fight that had bought his best friend a switchblade through the heart. Later, he had come to understand he must have gone into shock lifting Tommy's head with its blank and staring eyes off the ground, watching the lifeless blood form a dark pool on the dirty asphalt beneath them.

He had not thought of Tommy since he had moved to this new neighborhood. Why now? He did not know. He did not care. He just wanted to get out of the room, back to the others. The breeze coming in through the wide open windows was giving him the shakes.

Nick strode into and down the hallway. He didn't pause at any of the doors along the way.

He had reached the top of the stairs when the shot exploded in his ears.

No. Lord, please, no.

He froze, the bang resounding throughout the house. For several incomprehensible seconds, he did not move an inch.

Then he bolted blindly down the stairs, colliding with Maria on the landing between the two flights, knocking her down. Picking her up, he noticed her eyes were as wide as saucers.

"What?" she gasped, trembling in his arms.

"A gunshot," he said.

She nodded tensely, her eyes going past him, back the way he had come. "Up there," she whispered.

"Stay here," he ordered, turning away from her. She grabbed his arm roughly.

"I'm coming, Nick."

At the sound of the gunshot, Michael did not jump up or let out a shout. Instead, he closed his eyes for a couple of seconds. He did not think of who had died, who it might be, only that someone had died. He knew it to be true with a certainty that went beyond reason. He felt *death* in the house. He felt sick.

When he did look up, Sara and Jessica were already on their feet, holding on to each other. A moment later the back sliding glass door flew open. Polly stood staring at the three of them for a second, her face as white and cold as fresh snow, then flashed by them toward the stairs. Yet Michael was the first to reach the top of the stairs. A gun that had fired once could fire twice. For a moment he tried to hold the girls back. He was wasting his time. They had to see, all of them, no matter how bad it was. They heard Nick's voice around the hall corner. In a tight fearful knot, they stumbled down the first hallway and turned right. Maria and Nick stood outside the last door on the left, peering in at the dark. Michael came up beside Nick, felt for the bedroom light switch.

"It doesn't work," Nick said.

"Is anyone in there?" Sara asked them.

"There's a lamp in the corner of the room," Jessica said. She stepped forward. "I'll turn it on."

Michael grabbed her arm, stopped her. "No, all of you, stay here. I'll get it."

The room was big. He could feel its size although he could not clearly see. He could feel a cold breeze in his face, the blood in his heart. It was cold, too, the blood, and it felt as if it cracked—like ice—when his foot bumped into a soft heap on the floor. A body, a dead body. Michael could smell the blood.

Nick moved up behind him. Nick's eyes were sharper in the dark than Michael's. He noticed the body on the floor before walking into it. He knelt down beside it as Michael was stepping over it.

It. Not her. It. A nothing.

Michael knew who it was before he turned on the light. Why did he turn on the light? Why did he know who it was? The bulb drenched his eyes with harsh whiteness. He closed them again, for a moment, and counted to himself as he had while waiting for Alice to come up from her dive into the pool. He noticed that there was no carpet in the room. They had carpet in the garage, but not here. Nothing soft to land on, like the water. He turned and faced the others.

Statues. Tragic sculptures. Four girls: Maria, Sara, Polly, and Jessica—they all looked the same. Kats came up behind them. He looked different. Somehow uglier than usual. He was moving, that was it. All wired up and jittery. Michael did not want to move. He did not want to look down. But he did.

Alice.

Lying flat on her back. Gun in her mouth. Her lips resting around the barrel. Nick took it out gently. Her lips closed, matching her closed eyes. She looked peaceful. Then a drop of blood appeared at the left corner of her mouth, trailed over the side of her face, plopping in her bright yellow hair. It was still wet, her hair. The drop of blood spread upward along the strand, trying, it seemed to Michael, to get back to her head, back inside.

There was something wrong.

Drop after drop began to trail out of the corner of her mouth. And each one splashed into her hair and spread upward, downward, wherever it found a path. Yet the hair at the back of her head was already soaked red. A thousand drops had already come and gone before they had entered the room. She lay in a pool of red. The reason was very simple.

She had a hole in the back of her head.

"She's dead," Nick said, looking up at him. The gun in his hand and the quiet anguish in his voice hurt Michael almost as much as the sight of the blood. He stepped around Alice and stood close to the girls. Out of the corner of his eye, he saw Polly faint, Sara catch her. The others appeared: Bill, Bubba, Clair, and The Rock—in that order. And he felt Jessica holding on to him, her face buried in his shoulder, the warmth of her tears seeping through his shirt.

"I hope everything will be all right."

Michael didn't know these people. He didn't care about these people. Suddenly he saw and felt nothing that had to do with any of them. There were only the stars that had shone above him while he had swum on his back in the pool, the surprise touch of Alice's wet arms that had wrapped around his neck when he had begun to fear for her well-being.

"I love you, Michael. You know that . . ."

The yellow hair, the red blood, the repose of her sweet face—they all blurred into one ghostly form and began to move upward toward the stars, faster and faster. He chased after her, as best he could, but her arms began to slip away. The spirit began to fade, to fail. The stars went out.

She had put on the veil of his dream. She was gone.

Epilogue

The funeral for fifteen-year-old Alice McCoy was held on the Thursday following her Saturday night party, at twelve o'clock in the afternoon. The McCoy family, though rich, was not large. And despite the many friends Alice had made during her short days on earth, few came to the funeral. People mourn easily the victim, the unfortunate, but seldom the suicide. A notice in the local paper had listed the cause of death as a self-inflicted gunshot wound to the head.

Standing beside the coffin above the open grave, a yellow rose in his hand, Michael looked around and counted, including the black-robed minister, only twenty-eight people.

There should be thousands.

He was in a tunnel. There was a dim glow up ahead, twilight behind, black enveloping walls all around. He had not slept since the party, nor had he been properly awake. Unfortunately, he wasn't in shock. He had been crying too much for that. But only when he was alone. That was how he wanted to be from now on, alone, always alone until the day he died.

He listened to the last words. Old written words—it didn't matter whether they were true or not, he thought, the lines about "life everlasting" and "the valley of the shadow of death." They were still just words. It was foolhardy to believe they could bring any real comfort. They brought him none. It was ridiculous they even had funerals. He was glad when everyone began to leave.

He sat down beside the coffin, near the mound of brown dirt that would cover it. Clouds came and went overhead, and with them, the sun. He couldn't decide whether it was hot or cold. One minute he was sweating, the next, shivering. He still had his flower in his hand. He tried planting it in the dirt but it kept falling over. He couldn't imagine he was never going to see her again.

Time passed, a long time. Someone finally came up behind him. He assumed it was a grave digger, come to shoo him away. You have to go, Bud, we have to stick her in the ground now. But whoever it was said nothing, and finally Michael turned around.

"Hi, Nick," he said. "Were you at the funeral?" He honestly didn't know.

When Nick had come into the store that first day, he had had trouble saying two words. Then he had gone out with a girl and stood off whole mobs. Now he seemed to be back where he had started. He bowed his head, mumbled his words.

"I'm sorry I was late. They just let me out of jail."

"Lieutenant Keller let you out?"

"Yeah."

"That jackass," Michael muttered. "He had no right holding you."

"I wasn't alone."

Michael nodded. The lieutenant had detained The Rock, Russ, and Kats. Michael had spoken to Keller last night on the phone. Kats was the only one he was holding, he said, and that was only because they had discovered a number of unregistered firearms back at the hole Kats called his apartment. Keller did not feel Kats was guilty of murder. "It was a suicide, Mike. None of those kids killed that girl. She put the gun in her mouth and pulled the trigger. Simple as that. Let it go."

Ass.

"I want to talk to you about a few things," Michael said. He hardly recognized the sound of his own voice. His vocal cords felt as if they had been scratched with sandpaper. "Could I see you down by the parking lot in a few minutes?"

"Sure." Nick glanced nervously at the coffin, with its shiny azure-colored paint and inlaid gold flowers. As far as boxes went, it was nice. But who wanted to be in a box. "I didn't bring any flowers," he said apologetically.

"It doesn't matter."

Nick swallowed. "I'll wait for you."

When Nick left, Michael knelt by the coffin, touching it. A final good-bye, that's what he wanted to say. He thought about it a minute, but nothing came. And he knew why. She wasn't here, in this dead body. She had left that night. He had seen her leave.

Nevertheless, he suddenly wrapped his arms around the box as if he were hugging a flesh-and-blood person. He couldn't help himself. He cried as though she had just died in his arms.

Nick was sitting on the curb, next to his bike, when Michael, calm and composed, finally descended from the rows of tombstones. Nick had bought the bike with his first—and last—paycheck from the store.

"I have some bad news for you," Michael said. "While you were in jail, you got fired. I told the bosses you had nothing to do with what happened. They didn't care." He shrugged. "If you'd like, I can quit in protest?"

"No, don't do that." Nick did not seem surprised, nor did he seem to care. "It's always been this way in the ghetto. Go in the slammer, lose it all. Everything."

"Maria?"

Nick nodded.

"She doesn't think you did it, for god's sake?"

Nick winced, turning away. His voice came out small and hurt. "I don't know. She won't talk to me."

"Well, to hell with her then." He went and sat beside Nick

233

on the curb. He had a bad taste in his mouth. He hadn't eaten that morning. He could taste only his bitterness.

"Did you want to ask me something?" Nick said hesitantly.

"Yeah, who killed Alice?"

That surprised him. "I don't know."

Michael sighed. "I'm sorry. I know you don't know. And I'm sorry about Maria. And your job. But I'll speak to some people around town I have connections with. I'll find you another place to work."

Nick nodded, hunched over. "I'd appreciate that." He paused. "I'll tell you everything I know."

"OK."

Nick spoke as if he were repeating something he had repeated endlessly at the police station. "I got up to go to the bathroom. I saw Bill in the kitchen. He was by himself. He looked upset. I went upstairs. I passed the first door on the left. I didn't hear anybody inside. I tried the second door on the left, the bathroom. It was locked. I *thought* there was somebody inside. I heard water running. I tried the one door on the right, the door to the porch. Kats was standing out there, by himself."

"Did he see you?"

"No."

"Go on."

"I tried the third door on the left. It was locked. It sounded like someone was sleeping inside. At the police station, Russ said it was him."

"Yeah, he also said he slept right through the gunshot and all the commotion. I don't see how anybody could have done that." He would talk to Russ himself, to all of them. "Go on."

"I went around the turn in the hall. There were two doors on the left. The first one was locked. But there were people inside. One of them sounded like they were crying."

"Are you sure?"

"No. It sounded weird. I don't know what was going on in there."

"But there was definitely more than one person in the room?"

"I'm sorry, Mike, I couldn't swear to it."

"I understand."

"I went to the last door. It lay wide open. The light wouldn't work. I went inside, anyway, went to the bathroom, and then came back out. That was it. I was on my way back down, at the top of the stairs, when I heard the gunshot."

"You didn't see anyone in the room where Alice died, didn't hear anything?"

"No, but—"

"What?"

"There was something in that room." He stopped for a moment, thinking, then he shook his head. "I can't say."

"Please, Nick. What did you see?"

"Nothing."

"You must have seen something, heard something?"

"No, it— I was scared."

"Scared? Of what?"

He shook his head again, perspiration appearing on his forehead. "I don't know. Just something in that room scared me. It scared me bad."

Nick had grown up in a dangerous environment. He could have developed instincts to recognize a threat, even if it was invisible. "When you turned on the light in the bathroom, you didn't happen to notice anything behind you?"

"I didn't turn on the light. I could see enough without it."

"That's odd."

Nick was worried. "The police thought so, too. They kept asking me about that. But you know, Mike, I'm telling you what I told them. I'm telling you the truth."

"I believe you." He thought of how often Bubba used that same line to call people a liar. Bubba had a way with words. The police hadn't arrested him. "Could Alice have been in the room?"

"I didn't see her. The police think she could have been, waiting to, you know, waiting with the gun."

"Or they think she could have entered the room from the bedroom next to it, right after you started back down? From the bedroom where you thought you heard someone crying?"

Nick nodded. "They say that's probably what happened, that it was Alice I heard crying."

A wave of disgust engulfed Michael. "What did they say

when you told them you thought you heard more than one person in that next to the last bedroom? That you had heard wrong?"

Nick was watching him uneasily. "Mike, they're not trying to hush anything up."

"No! But they're not working overtime, either. They're looking for the simplest explanation. And they think they've found it. Alice put a gun in her mouth and pulled the trigger. Neat. Clean. Fill out the paperwork and close the file."

Nick pressed his knees together, fidgeting. "Who do you think killed her?"

"Someone! Another person. That's all. Or maybe a couple of people." He buried his face in his hands, the tears too close. "She was my friend, Nick. She was full of love, full of life. I know she didn't pull that trigger. I know it."

Nick wisely didn't say anything, letting Michael be. Michael finally sat up. He could feel sorry for himself later. "Lieutenant Keller told me last night where everyone said they were at the time of the shooting. Let me go over it again with you and see if it's any different from what you got out of him." He held up his hand, counting off the points on his fingers. "Bill said he was in the kitchen, having a glass of water. The Rock said he was in the upstairs bathroom, taking a shower. Kats said he was standing on the porch, looking at the stars. Bubba said he was out front with Clair, talking about the stars." Michael clenched his fingers into a fist. "The stars. Kats couldn't even tell you what one looked like, and Bubba and Clair—" He shook his head in disgust. "Is that what Keller told you?"

"In the beginning, they separated us, got each person's story. They always do that. But this morning Keller told me exactly what you just said."

"Did he tell you about the gun and the bullet?"

Nick nodded. "The gun belonged to Kats. It was the same one he pulled on us in the store. Kats admitted it was his."

"Right away? Before we identified it?"

"I don't think so."

"What about prints? Keller told me yours, Alice's, and Kats's were on the gun, but only Kats's were on the bullet shell."

"Same thing he told me. Mike, I honestly don't think Keller's holding back on us."

"I wonder. Did Kats have an excuse for how his gun got in Alice's—hand?"

"He said he had no idea. He had it in his car, in the glove compartment. He didn't say why he brought it to the party. He's one of those strange dudes, you know, always has to have his piece handy."

"If he was out on the second-story porch, how come he didn't get to the bedroom until after us?"

"I don't know. But he's in trouble. He didn't have a license for the gun. Keller hasn't released him yet, and won't until someone bails him out."

"That just breaks my heart." Even if he hadn't pulled the

trigger, if it hadn't been for Kats's weird hobby Alice would probably still be alive. Michael stood. "Thanks for the information. Can I give you a ride anywhere? You bike will fit in my trunk, I think."

Nick got up, too. "No. Being cooped up these last few days—I feel like I need the exercise. What are you going to do now?"

"Go to Alice's house."

Nick was concerned for him. "Why?"

"To look around."

Nick glanced in the direction of Alice's coffin, resting alone on the hill. "She seemed like a real neat girl."

Michael coughed painfully. "I always thought so."

The McCoy residence, from the outside at least, had not changed: high roof, long driveway, steep front lawn—all that money and what difference did it make in the end?

The red sedan parked out front, however, was something new. Michael stopped his car beside it, got out warily. The front door opened before he could knock. The honorable Lieutenant Keller himself.

They'd met the night of the party. He was nothing to look at. Although a trim six feet two and less than forty years of age, he struck Michael as soft, someone on the physical road downhill. He didn't know how to dress. He favored plaids, but the squares on his sports coat were much too big. He had a bald spot he tried to hide by parting his hair low and combing the thin brown strands over it; it only made his head look lop-sided. And he had that grayish skin so often seen on the movie sleaze ball. Michael disliked shaking his hand.

On the other hand, Michael realized, his appearance prob-ably had nothing to do with the dislike. When Keller had arrived at the scene of the crime approximately half an hour after the shooting, he had failed to take charge. True, as Nick said, he did separate them and, along with his fellow officers, had taken down their accounts of the events. But Michael had watched him the whole time, and he never saw the sharp eye, the attention to detail he would expect from a good detective. Also, the lieutenant had appeared to decide right from the start what had happened. To Michael, that showed an unforgivable lack of professionalism.

Yet it would be unfair to discard his positive qualities. He had proven himself sensitive to the stress they were under. He had personally taken it upon himself to make sure Polly was immediately given over into the hands of a psychiatrist who specialized in the care of victims of emotional trauma. He was not a bad man.

He's just not Sherlock Holmes. Or his distant cousin.

They said hello and shook hands. He asked how the funeral had gone.

"Fine, I guess." Michael shrugged. "I haven't really been to a lot of funerals." He nodded at the yellow ribbon in Keller's hands. "What's that from?"

"The doorway to the bedroom. We'd placed it off limits until our investigation was complete."

Michael found the remark ironic. Polly's aunt was staying with a cousin, and Polly was sedated in the hospital. Off limits to whom? His bitterness refused to stay down. "So now you can go home early, I suppose?"

The lieutenant looked disappointed. "Everyone keeps telling me what a sharp kid you are, Mike. They say you could be a genius. Think about it for a minute, the whole situation. Then tell me what you'd like me to do. Go ahead, do it."

"I don't need a minute to know you shouldn't have told the papers it was a suicide. Why didn't you at least say she'd died from an accidental gunshot?"

Keller sighed. "Mike, she had the gun stuck right in her mouth. How could that be an accident?"

Michael wished he would stop calling him by his name. He was going out of his way to be personal when Michael felt like screaming obscenities in his face.

"Right, you felt morally obligated to be a hundred percent honest and to ruin Alice's reputation. But never mind that, your question's a good one. How could it be an accident?"

The lieutenant shook his head. "We went over this last night. The facts have not changed since then."

"I'd like to ask you about a few of those facts."

Keller glanced at his watch. "I have to be at the station in a few minutes. I really don't have the time."

Michael chuckled without mirth. "But you said it yourself, I could be a genius. I might spot something you missed. Or is that impossible, that you might have missed something?"

"Are you always this rude?"

"I must be in a bad mood."

The lieutenant took a weary breath, looked past him over the lawn, northwest, in the direction of Jessica's house. Michael had seen Jessica at the funeral. She'd worn a black dress. It wasn't her color. Although he remembered her saying hello, he was unsure if he had answered her. For reasons unclear to himself, he hadn't even wanted to stand near her.

"You're talking about a locked-room murder, you know that," Keller said. "The screens on the windows in that bedroom were screwed down. Our best man went over them with a magnifying glass. No one's removed them in years. There's an opening to the attic in the bedroom closet, but there's a stack of boxes pressed against it. Those boxes, by the way, couldn't have been moved and replaced in five minutes, never mind five seconds. When you get down to it, there was only one entrance into that room. The door."

"And it was lying wide open. How can you call that a locked-room murder?"

Keller caught his eye. "Do you think Nick did it?"

"No."

"His prints were on the gun."

"Because he took the gun out—away from Alice."

"But if I was the murderer, I would have done the same thing. Touch the gun as quickly as possible so I'd have an excuse for having my prints all over it."

"Nick didn't do it."

"I don't think he did, either. But, from a purely technical point of view, he's the only one who could have."

"That's not true. When the gun went off, he had the entire hallway behind him, all those rooms at his back that someone could have ducked into."

"And how long did Nick take to get from the top of the stairway and back to the bedroom? Three seconds? Four seconds? He ran straight there, didn't he?"

Michael paused. He hadn't asked Nick that specific question. "I would assume."

"He did, he told me he did. And looking at him, I'd wager he can run pretty fast. Face it, Mike, there just wasn't time for anyone to enter the room with Alice, force a gun in her mouth, pull the trigger, and then hide in one of the other rooms."

Michael put his hand to his head. He couldn't think as clearly as he usually did. He needed sleep. "You're overlooking something. You believe Alice entered the room immediately after Nick exited, right?"

"Yes. Or she could have already been in there when he used the bathroom."

"But the first possibility, you feel that's the most probable?"

Keller nodded. "Chances are she was the one Nick heard crying in the next-to-the-last bedroom."

"Let's say she did enter the room right after he left. But let's also say she wasn't alone, that someone was with her, or that someone followed her. And let's imagine he, or she, killed her, but *didn't* leave the bedroom."

Keller frowned. "I don't know if I follow you?"

"The murderer didn't have to rush from the bedroom to hide in one of the other rooms. He could simply have stepped into the bathroom."

"Did you see anyone step *out* of the bathroom?"

"No. But Alice was lying on the floor, and the— Well, in the shape I was in, Kats or The Rock or Clair or Bubba could have slipped into our group without my knowing it. To tell you the truth, I don't know where any of them came from."

Keller thought for a minute. "They came in through the door," he said finally.

"Admit it, you never considered the possibility."

The lieutenant started to protest, stopped. "You are clever, Mike, like they said. All right, I didn't think of it. But I had a good reason. You had Maria, Jessica, Sara, Nick, Polly—part of the time—and yourself, and yet, not a single one of you said anything about someone coming out of the bathroom."

"*We* may have had a good reason. Perhaps the murderer didn't come out of the bathroom until we left the room. That's what we did, you know. None of us could stand to stay in there."

"And then, when you were all back downstairs, did this murderer calmly stroll out the front door in front of you all?"

"No. But he could have gone out onto the second-story porch, off the roof, and into the backyard."

"Are you ruling out those you've mentioned as possible suspects?" Keller asked.

"If the murderer joined our group without our seeing him, no. If he snuck off after we left, yes."

"How did he get ahold of Kats's gun?"

"He took it out of his car. Kats hasn't been able to lock that Mustang in years."

Keller thought some more. This time he ended up nodding. "There is merit in what you say. But it doesn't explain how he was able to get the gun into Alice's mouth and her fingers wrapped around the trigger?"

"That is a problem," Michael admitted.

"And what about a motive? If you don't have that, you've got nothing. Who would want to kill Alice? Who was this outsider?"

"Did anybody tell you about Clark?"

"No. Who's Clark?"

"He was Alice's boyfriend."

"Was he at the party?"

"I didn't see him."

"Then why bring him up?"

"I told you, he was Alice's boyfriend. You asked for a possible motive. He was a weird guy."

"What's his last name?"

"I don't know. I checked around and nobody knows. I even went to the hospital where Polly's being treated. I managed to get a note slipped in to her asking for his last name. She doesn't even know, and she used to go out with him."

"I find that hard to believe."

"He never told her."

"Wait a second, Polly used to go out with Alice's boyfriend?"

"Yeah. I met him once."

"And?"

"He had the strangest eyes."

"Who cares about his eyes. Did he seem capable of murder?"

"Yes."

"Do you know anything about him? Where he goes to school? Where he works?"

"No. All I know is that he's an artist, like Alice."

Keller took out a tiny notepad, jotted down a couple of notes. "How come I never heard about his guy earlier?"

"Clark is only a possibility. The others—they could have motives of their own."

"Such as?"

Michael shook his head. "Not right now. I need to think about it longer. But you could do me a favor. I want a look at the autopsy report."

"What for? She was killed by the bullet that came out of the gun. It's cut and dry."

"I'd still like to see it."

"I appreciate your desire to clear your friend's name. But you are only that, a friend. You're not family. I can't turn over that report to you without permission from Alice's aunt."

"If I get permission, will you give it to me?"

"What do you want it for? You're not going to discover something the coroner missed."

"I like to be thorough. What was the name of the coroner?"

"I'd have to look it up." He glanced at his watch again. "I really have to go now. If you want to talk more, Mike, call me at the station in a few days. Try to get me Clark's full name."

"I'll do my best."

Keller went to close the front door. "I don't have to tell you that what you've suggested is a long shot. From what Jessica Hart said, Alice sounded like a very unhappy girl."

Michael found every muscle in his body suddenly tense. When he tried to speak, he distinctly heard his jaw bone crack. "What did she say?" he whispered.

"How Alice still hadn't gotten over her parents' death. In fact, it was Jessica who gave me the name and number of Alice's psychiatrist." Keller consulted his notepad. "Dr. Kirby. I have a call into her, but she hasn't called me back."

"She wasn't seeing a psychiatrist," he said indignantly. "I knew her as well as anybody and she never said a word about—"

"I probably dream too much. That's what my doctor says."

He lowered his head. It changed nothing. Lots of people saw psychiatrists and didn't kill themselves. That goddamn Jessica, spreading such lies . . .

"Anything wrong?" Keller asked, peering at him.

"No."

"What were you saying about her psychiatrist?"

"Nothing. I'd—forgotten." He needed to change the subject, to get rid of this man. "Could you please leave the front door unlocked? I promise to lock it when I leave."

Keller trusted him. Giving Michael a fatherly pat on the shoulder, he got in his car and drove away.

Hope you have time to stop for doughnuts.

The instant he stepped inside the house, Michael felt slightly nauseated. More than anything, he wanted to turn around and leave. He walked up the stairs slowly, listening to his heart thumping against his rib cage. It was the only sound he could hear. He realized he was holding his breath, and had to make a conscious effort to let the air out of his lungs.

The bedroom door where Alice died was closed. Turning the knob, he half wished it was locked. But it wasn't, and the first thing he saw as the door swung open was the yellow chalk outline the police had drawn on the floor around Alice's body. He hadn't stopped to think how short she had been. He walked into the room and closed the door at his back.

There was another outline on the floor, at the top of the yellow chalk, rounder, darker; blood always left an awful stain.

For a morbid moment, he wondered if any had seeped through the floor onto the aunt's bedroom ceiling.

The rest of the house was furnished exquisitely. This room, except for the lamp and nightstand in the corner, the shades above the windows, was empty. No paintings, ornaments, not even a photograph, hung on the featureless white walls. Alice had told him Polly had simply cleaned it out one day. Why? The parents were dead. The parents had slept here. Alice had died here. Curious symmetry . . .

The police had drawn a small circle of chalk beneath the east-facing windows. A black dot pinpointed the center. Michael knelt beside it. This was where the bullet had gone after it had exited the back of Alice's head.

He peered into the shallow hole. It appeared to go straight into the wall, parallel to the floor. He sat beside it and faced in the direction of the door. The hole was about level with his Adam's apple.

Was she sitting when she died?

The possibility filled him with disquiet. If a murderer had been holding her, it would have been easier for him to do so with her standing up. It would give the others another reason to think she had killed herself.

He noticed an aluminum ladder resting against the wall beside the bathroom. He figured the police had brought it in to assist in studying the room until he vaguely recalled having seen it when they had discovered the body. Why had

Alice or Polly brought a ladder into the room? To get down the paper cups?

He went through the room systematically, verifying Keller's points: heavy closet boxes blocked the attic entrance; dusty screen screws that didn't appear to have been touched in ages. Nothing he found proved or disproved either of the hypotheses he had presented Keller. But there were two things he noticed that struck him as unusual.

First there were the tangled Christmas tree lights hanging from the top shelf of the closet. The police had not pulled them out; he definitely recalled seeing them the night of the party. He wasn't quite sure why he considered it significant. The overhead light had been shorted out. Wires were often used to short out other wires. The connection seemed tenuous at best.

The second thing was not even properly in the bedroom. Peering out the east-facing windows at the overhang of the roof, he noticed that a small portion of a nearby wooden roof shingle—at the very edge of the overhang—was broken off. Indeed, it looked as though someone had broken it off with the heel of a foot.

Did someone enter or exit the room over the roof?

It made no sense. With the screwed-down screens, any approach from the outside was impossible. And yet, when he searched both ways along the roof edge, he saw not a single other damaged shingle. Only this one directly outside the east windows.

He examined the bathroom, found the same immovable screens on the window.

He was leaving the bedroom when he noticed the fine glass shards in the center of the wooden floor. A quick examination revealed them to be from a light bulb. He grabbed the ladder, spread it in the middle of the floor. Going up the steps, he reached up and unscrewed the overhead light shade. A minute later he was staring at a busted light bulb.

But what does it mean?

Probably nothing. That was what he was afraid of.

He went through the remainder of the rooms on the upper floor. When he was done, he sat down at the top of the stairs with a paper, ruler, and pencil he had taken from one of the rooms and drew himself a diagram. He sketched the entire second floor, but only that portion of the bottom floor that seemed pertinent.

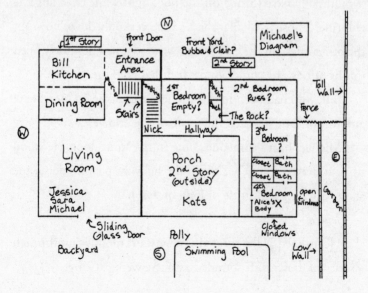

Who had been in the third bedroom appeared, on the surface, the crux of the whole matter. Yet in reality it could be of only minor importance. Alice and the murderer could both have already been in the fourth bedroom when Nick had entered. The guy could have had the gun in her mouth, and been whispering in her ear that if she so much as let out the tiniest sound . . .

Standing on the porch, Kats had had easy access to the roof of the house. Despite the window screens, it was something to think about.

The fourth bedroom had been extremely dark just before they had turned on the lamp. Michael didn't recall any light from the pool entering through the south-facing windows. Had the pool light been off or had the window shades been down? Would Polly have turned off the pool light while checking the chlorine? Those particular shades were certainly down now. Yet the other ones, on the east-facing windows, had definitely been up. Even now, he could almost feel that cold breeze.

Bill, who had been in the kitchen, had taken an inordinate amount of time to reach the scene of the crime.

Michael heard someone come in the front door. He stood up and moved a step back into the hallway, peering down the stairs, catching a glimpse of long brown hair.

Jessica.

He listened as she entered a downstairs room, went through a series of drawers. It sounded as if she were packing.

He had decided he would let her come and go without making himself known when he heard her start to cry. Mingled in with his grief and bitterness, he felt another emotion—guilt. Putting his diagram in his back pocket, he walked down the stairs.

She was standing in Alice's studio, her back to the door, touching a painting on an easel. She did not jump when he said hello. She merely turned, watched him through strands of hanging hair with those big brown eyes that had always worked such strange magic on him. They were red now, and puffy. She still had on her black dress.

"I saw your car out front," she said.

"Why didn't you call for me?"

"I knew you didn't want to talk to me."

He shrugged. "I'm here. We're both here. Why shouldn't we talk?"

She closed her eyes, sucked in a breath, her hands trembling. His tone had not been kind. She turned away. "I came to pick up some clothes for Polly," she said. "I'll be gone in a minute."

"Take your time."

Her back to him, her head fell to her chest. His guilt sharpened, yet so did his anger. "Michael, I don't understand," she pleaded.

The studio was the smallest room in the house. The numerous paintings and sketches were piled one on top of the other. Alice had had a dozen brushes and color trays going at the same time. She hadn't been what anyone would have called neat.

Michael had seen much of the work before. She used to bring her pictures into the store as she finished them: forest animals building a shopping mall in the middle of redwoods; high schools populated with penguin students—bright and silly situations that he had thought made up the best of her private universe.

As his eyes wandered over the room, however, he noticed a row of strikingly different works. A few were of alien worlds: a purple multitentacled creature feeding its hungry babies pieces of an American spacecraft; a hideous shivering skeleton trapped on an ice planet, trying to light a last match on the inside of its naked eye socket.

Before Clark. After Clark. I'll find that bastard.

Michael came farther into the studio, feeling in no hurry to answer Jessica's question. There was no carpet in here, either; and this floor was also stained.

"*I* don't understand," he said finally, leaning against the wall. "Here Alice gets murdered and the first thing her best friend does is tell the cops she killed herself."

Jessica stared at him, shocked, as if he'd slapped her across the face. Then her face collapsed in despair. A tear rolled over her cheek. Then another one. He held her gaze for a long moment, feeling his bitterness beginning to teeter as she began to tremble again. He turned away. This was bad. He had to stop. He wished he could stop. He just hurt so bad—it was as if pain had taken on a demonic character inside him and was demanding he make everyone suffer as he was suffering. But he didn't really hate Jessica.

I should have been there, in that room.

He hated himself.

It should have been me.

For being alive.

"I loved Alice," Jessica said, struggling with each word. "I loved her more than the world. And what I said to the police, I didn't say because I wanted to. It hurt me to say it, as much as it's hurting me now to stand here and have you accuse me of—"

She broke down then, completely, the sobs racking her body like shocks of electric current. He tried as hard as he could to go to her, to comfort her. Yet the insecure ego inside that he had deftly kept hidden all his adolescent years wouldn't let him. He was too afraid if he so much as touched her, he would break down, too. And that he could never do, not in front of her.

He stepped instead to the easel and pulled away the covering cloth.

Go forward, I will follow.

There was no desert, no bridge over a running river. Yet the lush forest and shimmering lake of Alice's final painting strongly reminded him of his dream. The colors were similar, and more important, the painting embodied the *feel* of his place.

He didn't quite know what to think. A lot of people, he supposed, dreamed of a Garden of Eden. That Alice and he shared similar tastes in paradise probably meant nothing.

Nevertheless, the painting somehow evoked the peace he'd experienced in his dream. A faint ray of that peace pierced his heavy pain. He reached out and touched the canvas. Alice had placed the two of them together, walking hand in hand along the grassy path that circled the edge of the clear water. She'd had only to complete the details of his clothing and she would have been done.

Then he noticed something else, a photograph of himself propped up beside the easel. He picked it up, as Jessica began to quiet down.

"I took it the night of the game." Jessica sniffed. "After you helped me with my camera, when you were sitting at the end of the bleachers with Nick. When Alice saw it, she told me she had to have it." Wiping at her eyes with her arm, Jessica gently plucked it from his fingers. She smiled suddenly. "I sort of wanted it for myself, but Alice asked, and she was all excited and—what the heck, I thought."

"Jessie."

"No." She set the picture on the easel at the base of the painting, picked up a small suitcase at her feet. "Let's not talk, not now. I'll leave. I'll talk to you later. I'll see you at school."

He nodded. "Good-bye."

She turned away. "Good-bye."

THE DANCE

Chapter One

I can't wear glasses to school," Jessica Hart said. "I'll look like a clown."

"But you can't see without them," Dr. Baron said.

"I don't care. There's nothing worth seeing at Tabb High, anyway. I won't wear them."

The eye examination was over. Beside her best friend, Sara Cantrell, Jessica was seated on a hard wooden chair in front of Dr. Baron's huge walnut desk. Jessica had been coming to Dr. Baron since she was a child. A slightly built, kindly faced man with beautiful gray eyes and neatly combed gray hair, the ophthalmologist had changed little throughout the years. Unfortunately, neither had his diagnosis. He continued to say her eyesight was failing.

"Jessie," Sara said. "Even with your old glasses on, you almost ran over that kid on the bike on the way here."

"What kid?" Jessica asked.

"I rest my case," Sara muttered.

Dr. Baron, as patient as when Jessica had been six and didn't want to peer through his examination equipment because she feared her lashes would stick to the eyepieces, folded his fine hands on top of his neatly polished desktop. "You may be pleasantly surprised, Jessie, at the number of attractive frames this office has obtained since your last exam. Glasses have recently become something of a fad. Look at the number of models wearing them on magazine covers."

Models on magazines aren't worried about being voted homecoming queen, Jessica thought. "How about if I try the soft contacts again?" she asked. "I know last time my eyes had a bad reaction to them, but maybe they'll be OK now."

"Last time you started bawling whenever you had to put them in," Sara said.

"That's not true," Jessie said. "I didn't give myself a chance to get used to them."

"A few people," Dr. Baron said, "less than one in a hundred, have hypersensitive eyes. The slightest bit of dust or smoke makes their eyes water. You are one of those people, Jessie. You have to wear glasses, and you have to wear them all the time."

"What if I sit in the front row in every class?"

"You do that already," Sara said.

"What if I only put them on when I'm in class, and take them off afterward, at lunch and stuff?" Jessica asked.

Dr. Baron shook his head. "If you start that, you'll be taking them off and on between each class, and your eyes will have to keep readjusting, and that'll cause strain. No, you are nearsighted. You have to face it." He smiled. "Besides, you're an extremely attractive young lady. A nice pair of glasses is hardly going to affect how others see you."

Sara chuckled. "Yeah, four eyes."

"Hardy, ha," Jessica growled. Homecoming was only two weeks away, and she was beginning to have grave doubts about the "attractive," never mind the "extremely." If not for the piercing headaches that had begun to hit her every day after school—and which she knew were the result of eyestrain—she wouldn't even have stopped in for an eye exam. She would simply have waited until after homecoming. But now she was stuck. Sara would hassle her constantly to put on her glasses.

"One thing I don't understand," Jessica said. "Why has my vision gone downhill so rapidly in the last few months? I mean, I don't have some disease that's making me blind, do I?"

"No, definitely not," Dr. Baron said. "But sometimes a stressful period can worsen an individual's sight at an accelerated rate." He raised an inquiring eyebrow. "Have you been under an unusual amount of pressure?"

The memory of Alice's death needed only the slightest nudge to flood down upon her in a smothering wave. Red lips around a black gun. Red blood dripping through beautiful yellow hair. Closed eyes, forever closed. Jessica lowered her head, rubbed her temples, feeling her pulse. It was hard to imagine a time when she would be able to forget. Alice had been with her the last time she had visited Dr. Baron's office. "I suppose," she answered softly.

The good doctor suggested she browse through the frames in the next room while he examined another patient. Jessica did so without enthusiasm, finally settling on an oversize pair of brown frames that Sara thought went well with her brown hair and eyes. Before they left, Dr. Baron reappeared, promising the glasses would be ready the following Monday. Only four days, and it used to take four weeks. Jessica thanked him for his time.

They had left Polly McCoy waiting in the car; Polly had wanted it that way. She was listless these days. Often, she would sit alone beneath a tree at school during lunch and stare at the clouds until the bell rang. She ate like a bird. She had lost twenty pounds in the last two months since she had lost her sister Alice. It was weird, she looked better than she had in years—as long as one didn't look too deeply in her faraway eyes and ponder what might be going on behind them. Jessica worried about her constantly. Yet Polly insisted she was fine.

"Do you need new glasses?" Polly asked, shaking herself to life in the backseat as Jessica climbed in behind the wheel and Sara opened the passenger door.

"She's blind as a bat," Sara said.

"I can see just fine," Jessica said, starting the car with the window up. It was the beginning of December, and after an unusually long, lingering summer, the sun had finally decided to cool it. Heavy gray clouds were gathering in the north above the mountains. The weatherman had said something about a storm in the desert. Flipping the heat on, Jessica put the car in reverse and glanced over her shoulder.

"Watch out for the kid on the bike," Sara said.

"What kid?" Jessica demanded, hitting the brakes and putting the car in park. Then she realized Sara was joking. "I was going to put them on in a second," she said, snatching her old glasses from her bag.

"I seriously doubt a single potential vote is going to see you on the way home," Sara said.

"That's not why I hate wearing them," Jessica said, putting on the specs and wincing at how they seemed to make her nose stick out in the rearview mirror.

"I heard Clair Hilrey's a patient of Dr. Baron, too," Sara said.

"Really?" Jessica asked. The talk around campus had it that it was between Clair and her for homecoming queen. Jessica wondered. The results of the preliminary homecoming court vote wouldn't be announced until the next day, Friday. Wouldn't it be ironic if neither of them was even elected to the court?

It would be a disaster.

Sara nodded seriously. "He's prescribed blue-tinted contacts for her to make her eyes sparkle like the early-morning sky."

Jessica shoved her away. "Shut up!"

Sara laughed, as did Polly, although Jessica doubted Polly felt like laughing.

They hit the road. Sara wanted to go to the bank to get money from the school account. She needed cash, she said, to pay for the band that was to play at the homecoming dance. A month earlier, acting as ASB—Associated Student Body—president, Sara had cleverly talked a local car dealer into donating a car to the school in exchange for free advertising in Tabb's paper and yearbook. The car had been the grand prize in a raffle put on to raise money for Tabb's extracurricular activities. The raffle had been a big success, and Sara now had several grand to put into the homecoming celebrations.

Jessica, however, did not want to go to the bank. She was getting another headache, and besides, she had someone to see. With hardly a word, she dropped both girls off at Sara's house. Sara could always give Polly a ride home. She'd finally gotten her license back. These days Sara was always quick to help Polly out.

Things have changed.

But life goes on—Jessica knew it had to go on for her. She had mourned Alice for two months. She had gone directly home after school each day. She had spent most of her time in her room, neither listening to music nor watching TV. She had spent the time crying, and now she was sick of crying. Alice was gone. It was the most terrible of terrible things. But

Jessica Hart was alive. She had to worry about her looks again, whether Bill Skater found her desirable, whether she was going to pass her next chemistry exam. She had to live. But before she could properly start on all those things, she had to heal the rift between Michael Olson and her. It was time they talked.

She had obtained his address from the phone book. She preferred seeing him at his house rather than speaking to him at school. She hardly saw him on campus, anyway. He came and he went, he said hello and he said good-bye. It was her hope that he would feel more sociable on his own turf.

With the help of a map, she located his place, parking a hundred yards up the street from the small white-stucco house. The late-afternoon sun was ducking in and out of drifting clouds. She looked around: secondhand cars leaking oil on top of broken asphalt driveways; backyards with weeds instead of pools. This wasn't her kind of neighborhood, and she realized the truth of the matter with a mild feeling of self-loathing. Nice things meant too much to her.

His garage was open, but she didn't see his car. She briefly wondered if he was at work, but remembered that he always took Thursdays off. She decided to wait. After pulling on a sweater, she reached for her SAT practice test book. The real test was to be a week from Saturday. With all her studying, she had only begun to score over a thousand. Compared to the average college-bound student, this was a respectable score, but next to the typical Stanford freshman—which she hoped to be this time next year—she was at the bottom of the pile. The math sections were what was killing her. She could figure out most of the problems; she simply couldn't figure them out quickly enough.

They raise us with calculators in our hands and then take them away precisely when we need them most.

Jessica picked up a pencil and set the timer on her dashboard clock. She vowed to run through as many math tests as it took for Michael to show up.

She dozed briefly in the middle of the third round, but a couple of hours later, when Michael Olson's beat-up Toyota pulled into his garage, she was still there. However, she did nothing but watch as he climbed out of his car and stretched in the orange evening light for a moment before disappearing inside. She remembered eight weeks earlier when he had cursed her for assuming Alice had committed suicide. And she remembered her inability to defend herself, to explain how it couldn't have been any other way.

Suddenly she was afraid to see him. Yet she did not leave. She simply sat there, staring at his house.

Chapter Two

How much cash did you get?" Polly asked as Sara returned to the car from a quick stop inside the bank.

"Three grand," Sara said, closing the door, setting down her bag, and reaching for the ignition. She never wore a seat belt. If she was going to be in a major accident, she was already convinced her car would explode in flames. She had that kind of luck. The last thing she wanted was to be tied in place. "I have to pay the band, the caterer, and that circus guy who's renting us the canopy."

Homecoming would be a lot different this year, Sara thought, and a lot better. She again complimented herself on insisting at the start of the year that the dance be postponed until basketball season. The delay had given her time to raise the money necessary to put on a wild celebration that everyone could enjoy for a nominal fee, rather than a stuffy party that only a few could afford.

The plan was to have the dance at the school immediately after the first home game, outside, on the practice basketball courts. When she had initially proposed the idea to the ASB council, they had all told her she was mad. "We come to this goddamn school every goddamn day," the beautiful, bitchy vice-president Clair Hilrey had said. "We can't stage an event as crucial as the crowning of the new queen between the peeling gym and the stinking weight room!"

Naturally, the negative reaction had only strengthened Sara's belief she was on to something. Yet the idea had its potential problems. What if it rained that night? And equally as bad, how could they create a party atmosphere when they would be surrounded by nothing but dark?

It was then Sara had thought of renting a giant tent. What a genius! With a tent the whole school could come; everybody, whether they had a date or not. And they could decorate it any way they wanted, and have a live band with the volume turned way up. Clair had loudly booed the idea, along with every other so-called hip person on the council. But the others in the room, those who figured they wouldn't be going to the dance, had nodded thoughtfully at the suggestion. That was enough for Sara. She hadn't even put it to a vote—she had simply gone about making preparations.

"You were able to get all that money on your own signature?" Polly asked.

"No, it's a joint account," Sara said. "I needed the treasurer's signature, too. Bill Skater signed a check for me this afternoon."

"Before you wrote in the amount?"

"What's your problem?" Sara snapped, before remembering she had promised herself she would be nice to Polly until Polly was fully recovered from Alice's suicide. Polly turned away at the change in tone, nervously tugging on a bit of her hair. Except for a streak of gray that had mysteriously sprung from beside her right ear, she looked—in Sara's truly unbiased opinion— downright voluptuous. That was what happened when fat girls got skinny. Why did anyone pay for breast implants? Probably pigging out for a few months and then going on a fast would work just as well.

"I was only asking," Polly said defensively. "It's not safe carrying around that much cash. It's better to pay people with checks. That way you get a receipt, too."

"I realize that," Sara said patiently. "But take the band. None of them want to declare this money on their income tax. I can dangle the cash in their faces and tell them to make me an offer I can't refuse. And they'll make it."

"Isn't that against the law?"

"I don't know. Who cares? Hey, has that engineer at your parents' company finished designing the float?" Another plus, in Sara's mind, of having the homecoming dance in a tent was that simply by pulling aside a flap, a special platform could be driven in for the crowning. The old custom of having the princesses cruise onto the track surrounding the football field with their papas had struck Sara as—well, old-fashioned. She had envisioned a castle float, with a central tower that the queen would ascend after the opening of the secret envelope. She had stolen the concept from a video on MTV.

"You mean Tony?" Polly said. "Yeah, he called last week. He has it all worked out. He said he can use one of the trucks at the company to build it on."

"Great." That was one thing she wouldn't have to pay for.

"It's going to have to be towed to the tent," Polly said. "And Tony warned me that we'll need a good driver. It'll be hard to see, and the float won't be real stable."

"I'll think of someone."

"I don't want to do it," Polly said quickly.

"OK."

"I don't."

"That's fine."

Polly nodded, relaxing. "All right."

Sara gave her a hard look and sighed to herself. Who was she fooling? Polly was never going to get over Alice. None of them were. Sara hadn't even told Jessica this, but she could no longer stand to be alone. Occasionally she wondered if some sick impulse would suddenly strike her, like a demon whispering in her ear. And, like Alice, she would grab a knife, or maybe a razor blade, and cut open a vein, and bleed all that blood Alice had. . . .

But, no, she was not suicidal and never had been. She was in no hurry to leave this world. Yet she would have given a great deal to see Alice again, even for a few minutes. Two long months, and still her grief was an open wound.

Before pulling away from the bank, Sara noticed the teller had forgotten to stamp the new balance in the ASB council's checkbook. A dash back inside remedied the situation.

On the way to Polly's house, they talked about Polly's guardian aunt. The poor old lady had had a mild heart attack immediately after hearing about Alice, and had only recently returned home. A nurse watched her during the day while Polly was in school, but Polly took care of her the rest of the time: cooking her food, rubbing her back, helping her to the bathroom. Sara admired Polly's charity but didn't understand—with the bucks Polly had—why she didn't hire round-the-clock help. She'd get a lot more sleep that way.

After Sara dropped Polly off, she stopped by the market. Only this market wasn't just any market. It was six miles out of her way, below par in cleanliness, and had an employee named Russ Desmond. She had asked around campus—discreetly, of course—where he worked. This would be her fourth visit to the store. The previous three times he had either been off or working in the back.

Naturally, she saw him practically every day at school, but being ASB president, she thought it beneath her dignity to go chasing after him there.

Starting in produce, her bag in her hand, she went up and down every aisle until she came to the meat section. She didn't see him. More disappointed than she cared to admit, she was heading for the exit when she spotted him wheeling a pallet into the frozen-food section. He had on a heavy purple sweater, orange gloves, and a green wool cap that was fighting a losing battle with his bushy brown hair.

What a babe.

She didn't know why he looked so good to her. Most girls would have thought he had too many rough edges and was too sloppy to be handsome. Actually, she thought that herself; nevertheless, she always got a rush when she saw him. She liked the curve of his powerful shoulders, the insolence in his walk. Yet she didn't for a moment believe she was infatuated with him. She was too cool to be suffering from something so common.

She wanted him to notice her, to call her over. Acting like an ordinary, everyday shopper, she began to browse through the ice cream and Popsicles, drawing closer and closer to where he was working. She had approached within ten feet of him, and still he hadn't seen her. Feeling mildly disgusted, she finally spoke up.

"Hey, Russ, is that you?"

He glanced up. "Sara? What are you doing here?"

She shrugged. "Shopping. You work here?"

"Yeah."

"I didn't know that. I come in here all the time."

"Really? I've never seen you before."

"I usually don't stay long. In and out—you know how it is."

"Huh." He returned to unloading his pallet, bags of frozen carrots. "What are you looking for?"

"What?"

"What are you buying?"

"Oh—Spam."

"Aisle thirteen, lower shelf on the right. You like Spam?"

"It's all right."

"I can't stand it."

Neither could she. "I like the cans." Brilliant. She cleared her throat. "So, what's new?"

"Nothing. What's new with you?"

"Oh, just putting the homecoming dance together. You know I'm ASB president?"

"I remember you said that, yeah."

"It's in a couple of weeks." *Hint, hint, hint.* She didn't exactly have a date yet. Actually, no guy had even spoken to her in the last month. For all he cared. He finished with his carrots and went on to broccoli. She added, "I'm going."

"Huh."

"Yeah, I have to. I open the envelope that announces the new queen." She paused, swallowed. "Are you going?"

"Nah. What for?"

"To have fun. We're going to have a neat band. They're

called the Keys. I heard them a few days ago. They play great dance music. Do you like to dance?"

"Sometimes, yeah. When I'm drunk enough."

She didn't know how to respond to that. Booze wasn't allowed at the dance. She stood there feeling totally helpless for the next minute, reading and rereading the label on a bag of frozen cauliflower—"Ingredients: Cauliflower"—while Russ finished with his vegetables. He began to collect his empty boxes, stacking them on his pallet. "I've got to go in back," he said.

"OK."

He didn't invite her to accompany him, but she followed him anyway. Fortunately, there wasn't anybody else in the back, not beside the frozen-food freezer. Sara could hardly believe the cold rushing out of it or how Russ could work inside it. He began to restock his pallet, his breath white and foggy. He was a superb worker. He never stopped moving. He had excellent endurance. She remembered something she wanted to bring up.

"I hear you're going to be in the CIF finals," she said. It was extremely difficult to even qualify for the CIF—California Interscholastic Federation—finals.

"It's no big deal," he said, going farther into the freezer, disappearing around several tall stacks of boxes. She took a tentative step inside, feeling goose-flesh form instantly. She noted the huge ax strapped to the inside of the frost-coated door.

"Sure it is," she called, hanging the strap of her bag around a dolly handle, cupping her fingers together. She couldn't even see him.

"Lots of people qualify," he called.

"But I bet you win," she called back.

"What?"

For some reason, shouting in the dark—particularly when you were repeating yourself—had always struck Sara as one of the most ridiculous things a human being could do. "I said, you'll probably win!"

"That shows how much you know about cross-country," he said, reappearing with his arms laden with boxes.

That sounded like an insult, and here she was trying to compliment him. "I know something about it," she said. She had been closely following his performances in the papers. He had won his last ten races, improving his time with each meet.

"Sure," he said.

"I do."

"What do you know?"

"That if you break fourteen minutes, you'll win."

He snorted. "Of course I'd win if I broke fourteen minutes. But the finals are down in Newport, on the hilliest course in the city. *Fifteen* minutes will be tough." He dumped his boxes on the pallet, muttering under his breath, "I'm not going to win."

"Don't say that. If you say that, you won't win."

"Who cares?"

"What do you mean, who cares? Don't you care?"

"Nope."

She had begun to shiver. Another minute in there and her hair would turn white. But at the same time she could feel her blood warming—or was it her temper? "What are you saying?"

"That I don't care." He pulled off his gloves, rubbed his hands together. "It's just a goddamn race."

"A goddamn race? It's the city championship! If you win, they'll give you a goddamn scholarship!"

He shook his head. "I ain't going to college. I can't stand going to high school."

"I don't believe it," she said, disgusted. "Here you have this tremendous natural talent that can open all kinds of doors for you and you're just going to throw it away? What the hell's the matter with you?"

He looked at her, frowned. "Why are you always shouting at me?"

"Shouting at you? When have I shouted at you? I haven't even spoken to you in two whole months!"

"Yeah, but the last time you did, you were shouting at me."

"Well, maybe you need someone to shout at you. Get you off your ass. The reason you don't care is because you drink too much. You're seventeen years old and you're already a drunk!"

"I'm eighteen."

"You're still a drunk. I've seen you run. If you didn't down a case of beer every evening, you'd probably be in the Olympics."

He didn't like that. "Who are you to tell me what I should do? You're as screwed up as anybody."

"And what's that supposed to mean?"

He stood. "You're insecure. Every time I talk to you—it doesn't matter for how long—you tell me you're the president of the school. All right, I heard you the first time. And who cares? I don't. I don't care if you're the Virgin Mary."

Sara couldn't believe what she was hearing. Insecure? She was the most together teenager since Ann Landers and Dear Abby had gone to school. She was so far out that she had been nominated for school president when she wasn't even running— Well, that was only one example of how far out she was. There were dozens of others. "Who are you calling a virgin?" she demanded.

He laughed. Why was he laughing? She'd give him something to laugh about. She stepped forward, shoved him in the chest. "Shut up!" she shouted.

He laughed harder. "That's it. That's your problem, Sara. You don't need a date for homecoming, you need a good roll in the hay."

Sara clenched her fists, her fingernails digging into her palms. She clenched them so tightly she knew she'd be able to see the marks the next day. If she hadn't done this, she probably would have ripped his face off. Only one other time in her life had she ever felt so humiliated: the last time she had spoken to Russ, at the end of their ill-fated date. She sucked in a breath, taking a step away from him rather than toward him. "What makes you think I don't have a date?" she asked softly.

He stopped laughing, glanced at the floor, back up at her—still grinning. "That's why you came in here, isn't it? I saw you looking for me."

She smiled slowly, faintly. "I was looking for you?"

"Yeah. I think you were."

"I was looking for a can of Spam," she said flatly.

He lost his grin. "Sara, there's nothing wrong with—"

"Stop," she said, taking another step back, her hand feeling for the edge of the freezer door. "Just stand perfectly still and don't say another word."

His eyes darted to her hand, panic twisting his face. "Wait! The inside lock—"

She slammed the door in his face. On the way out, she picked up a can of Spam in aisle thirteen. She had decided to have it for dinner.

Yet she shook as she drove home. She wasn't worried Russ would freeze to death—if worse came to worst he could always chop his way out—she was worried he had been right about her.

Only much later did she realize she had left her purse in the store.

Chapter Three

The sound startled Michael Olson. Standing in the middle of his garage beside his homemade telescope, he paused to pinpoint its source, then laughed out loud at his foolishness. He had made the noise himself; he had been whistling. He used to whistle all the time, but this was probably the first time since the McCoys' party. He had forgotten what it sounded like to be happy.

Am I? I can't be.

The truth of the matter was that he felt fine, not overflowing with joy, but pretty good. And with that realization came a flicker of guilt. He had promised himself at Alice's funeral that he would never let himself feel again, that he would never give pain such a clear shot at him. But that had been childish, he saw that now. He had actually seen that for a couple of weeks now, although he had not stopped to think about it. He reached out and touched his twelve-inch reflector telescope, the hard aluminum casing, the well-oiled eyepiece knob. To a certain extent, the instrument was to thank for his comeback.

For two weeks after his blowup with Jessica, he had stayed away from school. During that time, he had done nothing: he had not cried; he hadn't thought about who had killed Alice. Indeed, he had hardly thought about Alice at all, or rather, he had thought about nothing else, but without the comfort of allowing her sweet face to enter his mind. He had blocked every happy thought associated with her, picturing only her coffin, the gun, the weight of her dead body when he had accidentally kicked it in the dark bedroom. He had censored his thoughts out of shame—not just because he felt partially responsible for her death.

All his life people had told Michael what a cool guy he was. And in his immense humility—what a laugh—he had always lowered his eyes and shook his head, while at the same time thinking that he must, in fact, be quite extraordinary. He excelled in school. He worked hard. He helped his mother with the bills. He helped lots of people with their homework. He did all kinds of things for all kinds of people who weren't quite so neat as himself.

That was the crux of the matter right there. He performed these good works, but he did so mainly to reinforce his image. This did not mean he was a completely evil person—only a human being. The day of the funeral had made that all too clear, although it had taken him a while to assimilate the full meaning of his behavior. He had handled every sort of emotion since he was a child by bottling it up. But grief—crushing grief—had shattered Mr. Far-out Michael Olson. He hadn't been able to handle it at all. He had lashed out like a baby, attacking Jessica just when she was hurting the most. Yeah, he was human all right, and still in high school.

Exactly two weeks after the party, he'd had a sudden urge to drive out to the desert. The evening had been clear, the orange sand and rocks sharp and warm. When the sun had set and the stars came out, he lay on his back on top of a hill, miles from the nearest person, letting his thoughts wander the course of the Milky Way. Perhaps he had dozed. Maybe he had dreamed. He remembered lying there a long time, enjoying the first real rest he'd experienced since Alice's death. A calm, solid strength seemed to flow into him from the ground, and it was as if *something* else had touched him, something deep and powerful. He would have said it had come from above, from the stars, had it not touched so close to his heart. To this day, he couldn't say what had happened, except that for approximately two hours he had felt loved, completely loved.

By *whom* or *what* he didn't know.

Michael had never thought much about God. At a fairly early age, he had come to the conclusion that there might be one, but that it would be a sheer waste of time trying to prove it. He still held that opinion. But now he did feel there was *something* wonderful out there in the cosmos, or inside him—either place, it didn't matter. His feeling was more intuitive than logical. Then again, it could have been a desperate invention of his overly grieved heart, but he didn't care. It gave him comfort. It allowed him to remember Alice as she had been, without feeling pain.

When he had finally returned home that night, he dreamed of the girl he had dreamed about a couple of weeks before Alice had died. He had been on the same bridge, the same blue water flowing beneath him, the identical desert in front, the forest at his back behind the girl. Again, she had not allowed him to turn to see her, again saying something about a veil. But she had leaned close to his ear, to where he had felt the brush of her hair against his cheek. It had been the touch of her hair that had awakened him. He wished it hadn't. She had been on the verge of revealing something to him, he was sure, something different.

He had started on his telescope the next day, buying the grinding kit for the mirror from a downtown shop, purchasing other accessories as he went along: the aluminum tubing, the rack-and-pinion casing for the oculars, the eyepieces themselves—constructing the stand and clock drive from scratch. This was by no means his first experience at building a telescope. He had put together a six-inch reflector in eighth grade. But doubling the size of the aperture had squared the complexity of the undertaking. Yet working on it did give him much satisfaction.

He returned to school, and the telescope became central to his MGM (Mentally Gifted Minors) project. He designed it with an unusually short focal point, making it poor for high-resolution work—such as would be required for studying the moon and the planets—but giving it a wonderfully wide field of view, ideal for examining huge star groups. He explained to his project adviser that he was looking for comets. That was only a half-truth.

He was actually searching for a *new* comet.

It was a fact that the majority of comets were discovered by amateur astronomers working with fairly modest equipment. The odds against his making such a discovery, however, even after a dozen years of careful observation in the darkest desert nights, should have been a thousand to one. It was a strange universe out there.

Then just two weeks ago, searching from the top of the hill where he had begun his comeback, he charted a faint wisp of light close to the star Sirius that had—as far as he could tell—never been charted before.

He had followed the light for several days, and "followed" was the word for it; the light was moving. It wasn't a nebula or a galaxy or globular cluster. It was definitely a comet. Perhaps it was *his* comet. He needed to complete a more detailed positional record before he could submit a formal application to a recognized observatory requesting verification of his discovery.

Unfortunately, the recent poor weather was frustrating

his efforts. It had been cloudy in the desert the whole past week, and there was no way he could see the sky clearly in the city with all the background light. He was anxious to get on with the next step, but he was learning patience. It had been out there for billions of years—it would wait a few more days for him.

If it was a new comet, he would have the privilege of naming it. Probably that was why he had been whistling while cleaning his telescope. The weird thing was that when he had started building his new instrument, he had known he would find a comet.

He had also gone out for the basketball team. Their old coach had moved onto bigger things in the college ranks and their new coach was a bimbo, but Michael was having fun. Their first league game of the season would be a week from Friday. And the next game, the Friday after that, would be at home, right before the homecoming dance. It would be a good opportunity to show off his new jump shot.

Yet with all this new outlook on life, Michael had not given in to the common consensus that Alice McCoy had committed suicide. He could understand how others believed so, and he no longer blamed them for holding such a belief, but he was, if anything, more certain than ever that she had been murdered. Perhaps it was another intuitive conviction. Or maybe it was the product of dwelling too long on an idea that had come to haunt him:

Whoever had murdered once, could murder again.

Michael left his telescope in the garage and went into the kitchen. There was a call he had been meaning to make. Last night, while falling asleep, he suddenly remembered something very important about the way Alice had painted.

He dialed the police station, identified himself, and asked for Lieutenant Keller. He had not spoken to the detective since the day of the funeral.

"Mike," Keller said with a note of pleasure, but without surprise, when he came on the line. "How have you been?"

"Very well, sir, thank you. How are you?"

"Good. What can I do for you?"

"First I'd like to ask if there have been any new developments on the McCoy case?"

Keller paused. "I'm afraid not, Mike. As far as this department is concerned, Alice McCoy's death has officially been ruled a suicide."

The news was not unexpected, but nevertheless disappointing. "Does that mean you've completely closed the book on the matter? I think I might have another lead."

"Did you obtain the full name of that boyfriend of Alice's you mentioned?"

"No, I haven't. No one seems to know anything about him. But I haven't given up trying. I think long enough has gone by that I can talk directly to Alice's sister, Polly, about the guy."

"Sounds like a good idea." Keller was being polite, that

was all. Michael knew he still thought he was dealing with a distraught teenager. It bothered Michael, but not that much. "What's your lead?"

"Do you have a CRT on your desk?" Michael asked.

"Yes."

"Can you access the autopsy report on Alice McCoy?"

"Yes, but as I've already explained, I cannot divulge that information without written permission from the family."

"I understand. But I'm not asking you to let me look at it right now, I'm just asking you to look at it."

Keller chewed on that a moment. He seemed to sigh beneath his breath. "Hold a minute and I'll punch up the record." Michael listened as the detective tapped on a keyboard. It took Keller three or four minutes to get to the autopsy, an unusually long time. He was probably rereading it first. Finally he said, "I'm looking at it."

"Who performed it?"

"I told you, I can't—"

"How can the doctor's name be confidential?" Michael interrupted. "The list of the city's coroners is public knowledge." Poor logic, but his tone was persuasive. Keller admitted something significant.

"As a matter of fact the autopsy wasn't performed by a city coroner, but by a paid consultant."

"Why?"

"Our own people were probably busy at the time. Look,

if it will make you happy, the gentleman's name was Dr. Gin Kawati."

Michael jotted down the information. "Do you know his phone number?"

"Mike—"

"All right, never mind. But let me ask you something else. You said that Alice's, Nick's, and Kats's fingerprints were all on the gun. Is that correct?"

"Yes."

"Does the report state which hand the fingerprints were from?"

"It does."

"Which hand was Alice holding the gun in?"

"You were there. She had it in her right hand."

"Were any fingerprints from her left hand on the gun?"

"Not that I can tell from this report. What's your point?"

"Alice McCoy was left-handed."

Again Keller paused. "Are you sure?"

"Yeah. I remembered last night how she used to paint. She always held the brush in her left hand. Interesting, don't you think?"

Keller sounded slightly off balance. "Yes, yes, it is. But it doesn't prove anything. She could just as well have held the gun in her right hand and put it in her mouth."

"Are you right-handed, Lieutenant?"

"I am, yes."

"If you were going to kill yourself, which hand would you hold your gun in?"

"What kind of question is that?"

"I know it sounds morbid," Michael said quickly. "But think about it for a moment. Even if a girl is about to commit suicide, she would still handle the gun carefully. She would be worried about getting off a clean shot, of doing it right the first time. She would be nervous. She wouldn't hold the thing in her weak hand."

"Now you're getting into the psychology of someone suffering from depression. For all either of us knows, she could have intentionally done everything backward."

"She wasn't depressed!" Michael snapped, before catching himself. "When you go home tonight, think about it for a while. That's all I ask."

"All right, Mike, I'll do that. Anything else?"

"Yeah. Could I swing by and pick up that permission form you keep saying I need?"

"I have to go in a few minutes, but I can leave it at the front desk for you."

"I'd appreciate that. One last thing. Was Alice's right hand dusted for prints?"

"I can't tell from this report. But during the party, she could have shook hands with any number of people. Such prints would have been meaningless."

"I wonder," Michael said.

They said their good-byes, both sides promising to be in touch. It was four o'clock; the sun set early this time of year. Michael dialed a number that gave up-to-the-minute weather reports. The word was that it would be raining again in the desert. He decided to finish cleaning his telescope and put it away.

The garage was somewhat stuffy. He pushed open the door, deeply breathing the crisp evening air. It was then he noticed the car parked up the street.

Michael had never seen Jessica leave school in her car, but he remembered the silver-blue Celica in her driveway the evening of their date. This car appeared to be the identical make, and someone was sitting in the front seat. Because of the lighting, however, he couldn't tell who it was, whether it was a male or a female even. Well, he had just the thing to solve the mystery.

He positioned his telescope in the driveway behind a bush. With a little maneuvering, he was able to see the person between the branches without being seen. A moment of focusing presented him with a clear view of every detail on Jessica Hart's face.

She was working on something and had a pencil in her mouth. He watched for a minute while she scratched her head, wrinkled her forehead, glanced at her watch, and grimaced. No matter what the expression, to him she was beautiful.

Since he had returned to school, he had gone to great pains

to avoid her, more than he had during the week following their one date. He'd asked and received another locker. He'd avoided the courtyard during both break and lunch. He'd obtained a list of her classes from the computer at school and mapped out in his head where she should be at any particular moment, planning his own routes accordingly.

"I loved Alice. I loved her more than the world. And what I said to the police, I didn't say because I wanted to. It hurt me to say it, as much as it's hurting me to stand here and have you accuse me. . . ."

Naturally, despite his precautions, he had occasionally bumped into her, anyway. But they'd exchanged few words. Hello. How are you? Take care. Good-bye. But he'd seen enough of her to know his longing for her had not died with Alice, as he had thought it would. It had only grown stronger.

She was parked in front of Julie Pickering's house. He hadn't realized they were friends. She was probably waiting for Julie to come home. From what he could see, he guessed she might be finishing up some homework before knocking on Julie's door. She could disappear any second.

He didn't give himself a chance to think about it, to chicken out. He started up the street. He had decided that first night in the desert that he owed her an apology.

Halfway to her car, he saw her notice him. He waved.

"Hi. Jessie?"

She rolled down her window, peeked her head outside, her long brown hair covering her shoulder.

"Yeah, it's me," she said, her smile strained. "Hi, Michael. I guess you're wondering what I'm doing here?"

He nodded toward the Pickerings' residence. "You know Julie, don't you?"

Jessica glanced at Julie's house. "Ah, yeah, Julie. Yeah, I know her."

"Are you two going to study together?" He remembered Julie, like Jessica, was taking chemistry.

"Yeah, that's it. I mean, I didn't know you and Julie lived on the same block?"

He gestured vaguely back the way he had come. "I live over there."

"Oh."

He put his hands in his pockets, looked at the ground. That was the neat thing about the ground. It was always there to look at when you were talking to a pretty girl. He didn't know how to begin.

"I haven't seen you around school much," she said finally.

"I've been around."

"Do you have a new locker?"

"Yeah, they gave me one. Somebody transferred to another school." He shrugged. "It was available."

"I bet you have a lot more room now?"

"You never crowded me."

"Sure I did. With my bag and my makeup and stuff. I don't know how you put up with me."

"I was the one who ruined your sweater."

"You didn't ruin it."

"Yeah, I did."

"No." She reached out, brushed his arm. "Look at me, Michael." He did so, seeing her large brown eyes first, as he usually did when he looked at her. She chuckled. "Don't you see? I have it on."

He smiled. "That's right. How did you get the stain out?"

She touched her chest. "I don't remember. It doesn't matter. It's gone."

"It looks great on you."

"Thank you." She paused, her face suddenly serious. "Did you ask for a new locker?"

He couldn't lie to her. "Yeah."

The word seemed to startle her. She recovered quickly, however, nodding. "That's OK."

"Jessie—"

"No, I understand. It's fine, really, no offense taken. It's just that I sort of, you know—I used to like talking to you between classes." She smiled briefly. "That was fun."

"I'm sorry," he said.

"It's all right."

"No, I'm sorry about what I said to you." He lowered his voice, his eyes. "When we were in Alice's studio. I shouldn't have said—what I did."

She sank back into her seat, taking a breath, putting her

hands on the steering wheel, pulling them off again. Obviously, it was a topic she would have preferred to avoid. "You were upset," she said quietly.

"I was an asshole."

She started to shake her head, stopped. She could have been talking about the stain again. "I don't remember what you said. It doesn't matter, anyway. It's past."

"Do you forgive me?"

"I don't have to forgive you for loving her." She caught his eye. "That's all I heard in that room, Michael—that you loved her. All right?"

She did forgive him, and she was asking him to drop it. "All right," he said, feeling much better. He should have come to her weeks ago. She picked up her papers and books from the passenger seat, glad to change the subject.

"You can see I'm still studying for the SAT," she said. "I have to take it, not this Saturday, but next."

"That's when I'm taking it. At Sanders High?"

She brightened. "Yeah. Maybe we'll be in the same room."

"Maybe."

She nodded to her test book. "I'm not doing so hot on these trial tests. How do you score on them?"

He had not given a thought to the SAT. "I haven't taken any."

"Really? You're just going to walk in there and do it? That's amazing." She glanced at her scratch papers, frowned. "I wish I could do that."

"You'll do fine. Don't worry about it."

"I'm not worried." She laughed. "I'm terrified."

He smiled. "If worse comes to worst, I can always slip you my answers—if you'd want them."

She looked up at him. "Don't tempt me, guy."

"Of course you'd have to pay me in advance."

"Oh! I do have to pay you. I mean, I still owe you a movie." She paused. "Would you like to go to the movies with me?"

He felt much much better. "When?"

"How about tomorrow?"

Tomorrow was Friday, and he *had* to work because he was already taking Saturday off to play in the final practice game of the season. He couldn't do that to his bosses—disappear two days in a row during the busiest part of the week. They'd already given him a break by not firing him when he had stayed at home for days on end after the funeral.

On the other hand, this last preseason game was against a marshmallow of a school. And Coach Sellers was still trying to make up his mind about a couple of guards. If he did call in sick, the team would still win, and the two guys would get more playing time, and have more of an opportunity to prove themselves. By working Saturday, he could rationalize taking Friday off.

"Tomorrow would be great," he said.

They worked out the details. He would pick her up at six at her house and they would take it from there. She squeezed his hand just before she drove away. He decided she had changed her mind about studying with Julie.

He didn't know what was the matter with him. He could never sit around and enjoy a happy moment. His brief conversation with Lieutenant Keller suddenly came back to plague him. He hadn't had enough information to challenge the detective. He needed more. He needed to study that autopsy report.

He got into his car, drove to the police station. There he picked up the permission form. The sooner he got it back to them, the sooner he might clear Alice's name. He headed for the McCoy residence.

Polly answered the door. There were shadows beneath her eyes, and the rest of her features looked drawn and tired. She had lost a great deal of weight, particularly in her face. He had never realized how pretty she was, or how much she resembled her sister.

"Hi, Mike," she said. She had on dark wine-colored pants, a white blouse, a red scarf around her neck. "How are you?"

"I'm all right. How about you?"

"Fine. Would you like to come in?"

"Yeah, thanks." He stepped inside, bracing himself involuntarily. Even twenty years from now he doubted that he would feel comfortable in this mansion. The plush carpet, the high white ceilings—he remembered it all too well. There was, however, a slight stale odor in the air he did not recall. Polly led him toward the couch in the living room where he'd been sitting with Nick and Maria when the gun had gone off.

"I was in the neighborhood, and I thought I'd stop by and see how things are," he said as they sat down.

"That was nice of you."

He glanced about. "It's amazing how neat you're able to keep this place."

"Polly." A thin voice sounded from the direction of the hallway. Polly immediately leaped to her feet, but stopped at the start of the hall.

"It's a friend from school, Aunty. Do you need anything?"

"No, dear, talk to your friend first."

"First? *Do* you need anything?"

"Go ahead and talk to your friend," the old woman said.

Polly shook her head, mildly irritated, and returned to her place beside Michael on the couch. "She'll probably call out again in a minute," she said.

"How is she? Someone told me she'd had a heart attack?"

She nodded. "Yeah. The doctors say it was mild, but she's so old. She hasn't really got her strength back. She has to stay in the downstairs bedroom. The climb upstairs is too much for her."

"Do you have a nurse?"

"I can take care of her. If she'd tell me what she wants. She doesn't know half the time." Polly shook her head again and then looked at him, smiling, pain beneath the smile. He almost decided right then and there not to bring up the reason for his visit. "I'm glad you stopped by," she said. "It gets kind of boring sitting home every night."

"You should try to get out."

Polly glanced toward the front hall, or was it up, toward the bedroom where they had found Alice. That was one room he'd like to look at again. "Not yet," she said.

He cleared his throat. "Polly, I have a confession to make. I did have another reason for stopping by. I have a few questions I want to ask you."

"Would you like something to eat?"

"No thanks. What I wanted—"

"How about something to drink?"

He smiled. "Sure. Juice would be nice."

She jumped up. "What flavor? We have pineapple-coconut?"

"That would be fine."

She was back in a minute with a huge ice-filled glass, a slice of orange stuck on the rim. She hadn't bothered about one for herself. She sat on the couch a little closer this time, her expression now more alert than hurt. "Is it good?" she asked.

He took a sip. "Great." He set it in his lap, stirred the ice with the straw she had provided. "I wanted to ask about Alice," he said carefully.

"We can talk about her," she said quickly. "Jessie and Sara— they think I'll break down if I hear her name. But I won't. She was my sister, after all, why shouldn't I talk about her?"

"That's a good attitude." Man, this was hard. Despite

what she said, he felt as if he were treading on thin ice on a hot day. "What I wanted to say— Do you think Alice killed herself?"

"Didn't she?"

"Do *you* think she did?"

Polly turned her head away, stared off into space for a moment. "What?"

Michael set down his drink on the coffee table. "Do you think she was the suicidal type?"

She frowned. "Do you mean before she killed herself? She only killed herself the one time. At least that was the only time she tried, that I know of."

"Do you think there might have been other times?"

"She never told me about any other time. She didn't tell me about this time, before she did it I mean. But she didn't always tell me everything. We were close, but she had her secrets, which I think is all right."

"Polly."

"What? Did I put too much ice in your juice?"

"No. What I'm trying to say is I don't think she killed herself."

"No?"

"No. I think she was murdered."

Polly was impressed, to a certain extent. "Really?"

"Yes."

"Who murdered her?"

"I don't know. That's why I'm here. I'm trying to find out."

Polly was suddenly confused. "You don't think I did it, do you?"

"No."

She relaxed. "I didn't. I thought she did it. That's what that doctor at the hospital told me. The man with the electricity."

"The man with the what?"

Polly shook her head. "Never mind. I see what you're saying. You think someone killed her on purpose, and not accidentally."

"Yeah."

"And you don't know who it is?"

"Right." He sat up, folded his hands. "Polly, just before Alice died, you went outside to check the chlorine in the pool. Do you remember if you turned the pool light off?"

She nodded. "Sure I remember. I have a good memory. I turned it off."

"After you put the chlorine in the water?"

"Yes."

"How long before you heard the shot did you turn off the light?"

"Not long."

"A minute?"

"Yeah."

That would explain why the room had been so dark. "When you were outside at the pool, did you see anybody?"

"No."

"Did you hear anything? Like up on the roof?"

"No."

"Are you sure?"

"No. Yes."

"What did you do when you heard the shot?"

"Wh— I came inside. You saw me. Don't you remember?"

"I remember." She had been about to say something else. "Tell me about Clark?"

Polly spoke defensively. "I don't know his last name."

"I understand. But can you tell me anything about him? How did you meet him?"

"On a hike in the mountains. I sprained my ankle and he came and drew my picture."

"Where in the mountains?"

"I don't know what the place is called. We took that road that leads up and away from the racetrack."

"The Santa Anita Racetrack?"

"Yeah, we went up there."

"You and Alice?"

"Yeah."

"What school did Clark go to?"

"I don't know if he went to school."

"But wasn't he our age?"

"I don't know. He never talked about school. Alice told me you met him?"

"I did, yeah, at the first football game. Tell me, what did he talk about?"

"Weird stuff. He was a weird guy. But he—he was interesting, too."

"Why did Alice go out with him?"

"He was an artist. He was showing her all kinds of far-out techniques, opening her up."

"Were they romantically involved?"

Polly's face darkened. "What do you mean?"

He had to keep in mind Polly had gone out with Clark before Alice. "Were they boyfriend and girlfriend?"

"You mean, did they sleep together? Of course they didn't. Do you think I would let my little sister have sex with someone like that? I was the one who told Alice not to invite him to the party. If she was here, she would tell you that."

Michael stopped, feeling a chill at the base of his spine. "Did Clark come to the party?"

"What?"

"Was Clark at the party?"

"I told you, I told Alice not to invite him."

"But did he come? Without being invited?"

"He wouldn't have come without an invitation. He was weird, but he wasn't weird like that."

"But—"

"Polly," the aunt called.

Groaning, Polly got up. "Coming," she said, disappearing

down the hall off the central foyer. She reappeared a moment later. "I'm sorry, Mike. I can't talk anymore. I have to—take care of her. I'm really sorry."

He stood up, pulling the permission form from his back pocket. "That's OK, I shouldn't have barged in on you like this, anyway. Maybe we can talk about this some other time?"

"Sure."

"Hey, could I ask a big favor? You see this paper? It's a legal document that gives me permission to review the report that was done on your sister."

"What report?"

He hated to use the word. "The autopsy report."

She accepted the sheet, glanced at it. "You want me to sign it?"

"No, I want your aunt to sign it. She was Alice's legal guardian."

"But why?"

"I feel there may be something in the report that the police overlooked."

Polly folded the form. "I'll ask her to look at it."

"I'd really appreciate it. Another thing. Could you please keep this visit between us private? Don't talk to Jessie or Sara about it? They think—I don't know, that I should just drop the whole thing."

Polly nodded sympathetically. "They're like that a lot of the time."

She showed him to the door. As he was stepping outside, she put her hand on his arm, looked up at him. Again, the pain behind her eyes was all too clear, and he wondered if he'd added to it with his questions. She seemed to read his mind, as Alice used to do.

"I don't mind talking to you about how she died," she said. "She always told me what a great person you were. She told me I could trust you."

Michael smiled uncomfortably. "That was nice of her."

She continued to hold on to him. "Don't go after Clark, Mike. Alice told me about him, too. The night she died— She said he was no good."

"Are you saying he might hurt me?"

"I don't know. I don't want you to get hurt."

"Was he at the party, Polly?"

Now she let go of him, raising her hand to her head, trembling ever so slightly. "I don't remember," she said softly. "There were so many people there. Too many uninvited people."

He patted her on the shoulder, thanked her again for her help. Climbing into his car, he felt vaguely disoriented. If she hadn't loved Alice so much, and if he hadn't seen her go out to the pool immediately before the shooting, he would have added Polly to his list of suspects.

"That's what the doctor at the hospital told me. The man with the electricity."

Chapter Four

It was later. Michael was gone, her aunt was sleeping, and the sun had gone down. Polly sat alone in the dark, the TV on, the sound off. She preferred it that way, watching people she didn't have to listen to. Sometimes at school she felt as if she would go mad, all those people talking all the time. Even her best friends, Jessica and Sara, they never shut up. And whenever she had something to say, they were too busy to listen.

Polly reached for another carrot. She had read that eating a lot of carrots improved your ability to see in the dark. Since she spent most nights awake answering her aunt's calls, it was important to her. Besides, carrots helped you lose weight. That's what Alice used to say. And look how skinny Alice had been. Thin as a stick.

She wasn't sure what she was watching, some stupid sitcom. Practically everything on TV these days was stupid. She didn't know if many people realized it, but the networks were even beginning to rerun the news.

Polly sat up suddenly. What was that sound? She had heard a banging noise. It seemed to be coming from out back. She hoped it was a cat. She was terrified of burglars. She didn't have a gun in the house, only her dad's old shotgun, which she couldn't even find. Getting up, she peeked through the drapes covering the sliding-glass door.

There was nobody there, at least nobody she could see. But with the approaching storm, it was unusually dark outside. She stood still for a moment, listening to the wind, the rustling of the trees. The noise was probably nothing but a branch knocking against the outside wall. There was probably no need to call the police.

Oh!

A bolt of white light split the sky, causing her to jump. Instinctively, she started to count, as she had been taught as a child. The crack of thunder hit between two and three. The rain followed almost immediately, pelting the pool water like sand particles blasting a windshield. Like sometimes happened in the desert when a car went off the road.

Polly bowed her head, leaning it on the glass door. All of a sudden she missed her parents, missed them real bad. *Their* car had gone off the road, right into a ditch, where it had exploded. She had been small at the time, but she remembered exactly how it had happened. There had been an argument about something, and then the car was burning and the doctor was telling her everything was all right. She didn't understand why doctors always lied.

"The wires won't hurt. You won't even feel them."

But she felt everything. Liars.

Polly walked upstairs, headed down the hall, and turned right, entering the last room on the left, her parents' bedroom and the room where Alice had died. The chalk outline the police had drawn had been washed away long before she had returned to the house after her sister's death, but she could still distinguish a trace of it on the hard wooden floor—even in the dark. Sometimes, when she felt sad as she did now, she found it soothing to come into this room and rest on the spot where they had found Alice. Stretching out on the floor, she lay with her eyes open, staring at the ceiling.

Lightning flashed, thunder rolled. The gaps between the two seemed to lengthen. But the rain kept falling, and the storm was not going away. She noticed that the time between her breaths was also growing. She counted ten seconds between inhaling and exhaling, then fifteen. She wondered if her heart was slowing down. Lying there, she often felt as if she understood what it had been like for Alice when they had found her on the floor. It hadn't been so bad. The dead might bleed, but they never cried.

Polly realized she was crying. It was all because she was alive.

They had all gone and left her alone. A wave of despair pressed down on her, but she fought it, fighting to sit up. They hadn't cared about her. They hadn't asked what she wanted with her life. Her dad had decided to drive off the road. Her mom had gone ahead and burned. And Alice had taken that stupid gun and—

No!

Polly leaped to her feet. That banging sound again. Only now it was coming from outside the window. She crept to the shades, lifted it, and peered down, seeing nothing at first but the garden, the rainy night. Then there was another flash of lightning. And there he was! Someone in her backyard!

"Hey, you! What are you doing there?"

The sound of her voice didn't cause him to run away, nor did it startle him. He cupped a hand over his eyes, looking up, his long scraggly hair hanging over his shoulders. She took a step away from the window, her heart hammering. She should have kept her mouth shut, she thought, and called the police. But then he spoke.

"Is that you, Polly?"

Relief flushed through her, followed by a fear of a different sort. "Clark? What are you doing down there?"

"Trying to get in. It's wet out here. I rang the front door-bell a dozen times. Why didn't you answer?"

"The front doorbell doesn't work." It had broken the night of the party.

"I knocked, too."

"I'm sorry, I thought— I don't know. Just a sec. Go around to the back patio. I'll let you in."

He had on the black leather jacket and pants he wore on his motorcycle. For the most part, the rain had left him untouched. Except for his tangled red hair. Soaked, it seemed much darker.

"I was beginning to believe you'd left this big box to the ghosts," he said as she slid open the sliding-glass door that led out onto the roof-covered patio. "How are you, babe? Been a long time."

"Yeah, months. I can't believe you're here. Why didn't you call before coming?"

He wiped at his pale face with his long bony fingers. He had always been skinny. Now he was close to emaciated. "I wanted to see you, I didn't want to talk to you." He grinned. "You look exotic, Polly, real tender."

She beamed, relaxing a notch. She didn't know why she had felt she had to warn Michael away from Clark. Why, here he was right in front of her and everything was cool. "Thanks, you look nice, too. Do you want to come in?"

"Nah," he said, nodding to his mud-caked boots. "Better not. Don't want to spoil the scene. Like to keep pretty things pretty." He turned toward the side of the house where she had first seen him, and the grin seemed to melt from his face as if he were a clay sculpture in the rain. His entire manner changed. "Why didn't you tell me?" he said.

She bit her lip. "I thought you knew."

He looked at her, his green eyes darkening. "I didn't know until I read about the funeral in the papers."

"Did you go?"

"You know I didn't."

"I didn't know. They had me in the hospital."

He was angry. "But I called. I left messages."

"The machine was acting up. I didn't get them."

He shook his head, stepping away from the door, turning his back to her, reaching his palm out from beneath the shelter of the patio. The rain continued to pour down. "Who killed her?" he asked.

"The police say it was a suicide."

He thought about that a moment, then his mood changed again, and he chuckled. "The police. What else do they say?"

"Nothing."

"Did they ask about me?"

She hesitated. "They didn't."

He whirled. "Did someone else?"

She had never been able to lie to him. He had some kind of power over her she didn't understand. "A boy at school."

"What's his name?"

"Michael."

"What's his last name?"

"I'm—not sure." She added weakly, "He wanted to know your last name."

He moved to her, briefly touched her chin with his wet fingers, and it was almost as if an electrical current ran through his nails; she couldn't help quivering. "Remember when we met?" he asked. "On that sacred ground? The Indians buried there believed if you knew a person's secret name, you could make him do anything you wished. Anything at all."

"Is that why you never told me your full name?"

He grinned again. "Do you believe that nonsense?"

"No."

He held her eyes a moment. "I remember this Michael. I met him at the football game. Do you know if he saw me at the party?"

Lightning cracked again, thunder roared, the smell of ozone filling the air. Polly put a hand to her head, rubbed her temple. She didn't feel pain, only a slight pressure and immense surprise. "You were at the party?" she said.

"Yeah, I came at the end like you told me to. Don't you remember?"

"Yeah," she said quickly. "I had just forgotten for a moment, that's all." She really did remember, not everything maybe, but a lot. The three of them had been in the room together. They had gotten into an argument about the paper cups, or why Clark hadn't come earlier, something like that. Then she and Clark had left Alice alone in the room and gone downstairs. He had left on his motorcycle and she had gone out the back to check on the chlorine in the pool. Then Alice had gone for the gun. . . .

The loneliness Polly had experienced in the bedroom suddenly crashed down upon her, and she burst out crying. Clark's wet arms went around her, and she leaned into them.

"All I did was fight with Alice and make her think I hated her when I loved her more than I loved anything," she said. "And now she's gone, and Aunty's here, but she can hardly breathe. Help me, Clark, you've got to help me. I can't live like this. I feel I have to die."

He didn't say anything for the longest time, just held her as he used to hold her before he had started to see Alice. When he finally did release her, she felt a little better, though slightly nauseated. He brushed the hair from her eyes, accidentally scratching her forehead with one of his nails.

"You'll be all right, kid," he said. "You don't have to die. You didn't do nothing wrong. Nothing at all."

"But I—"

"Shh. Enough tears. Mourn too much and you disturb the sleep of the dead. Tell me, does Michael say Alice was murdered?"

She dabbed her eyes. "He's suspicious."

"Hmm. What else?"

"He gave me a paper he wants Aunty to sign."

"Show it to me."

He barely glanced at the form when she handed it over,

folding it and sticking it in his coat pocket. "I'll look at it later," he said.

"If you want, I can read it to you now. I've been eating lots of carrots. I can see in the dark."

He brushed aside her comment, sticking his head in the doorway, sniffing the air. "It stinks in this place. That old lady's still here?"

"Yeah. She's sick. She had a heart attack. I take care of her."

"Why? Old people—when their number's up, they die. It doesn't matter what you do."

"Don't say that!"

"That's reality, babe. Sometimes they choke to death on their tongues. It's a hassle watching her all the time, isn't it?"

"I don't mind. I take good care of her."

He grinned and started to speak again just as someone knocked at the front door. "Who's that?" he snapped.

"I don't know. I'll go see."

"No, wait, I'll go. My bike's parked at the end of your driveway beneath that ugly tree, but it's probably getting wet." He grabbed her by the arm, pulled her toward him. She thought for a moment he was going to kiss her, but then he let her go, gesturing for her to follow him away from the patio. "Come here."

"Out in the rain? I'll get wet."

"Who cares?"

She walked over and stood beside him in the downpour.

The person at the front door knocked again. She hardly noticed. The water felt delicious atop her head, the drops sliding down inside her blouse and over her breasts. Clark took her into his arms again, leaned close to her ear. "I like you this way," he whispered. "Cold, like me." He kissed her neck lightly, and she could imagine how the rain must have drenched deep into his flesh while he had raced through the night on his motorcycle; his lips sent a chill into her blood, a warmth up her spine. "Do you love me, Polly?"

"I-I'm glad you're here."

"Do you want me to come again?"

"I do."

"Then I will." He kissed her again on the neck, took a step back. "I have a secret to tell. Can you keep a secret?"

"Sure."

"First you must promise not to talk about me to anybody." He scratched her shoulder lightly, pinching the material. "You must cross your heart and hope to die."

She sketched a cross over her chest. "I promise. What is it?"

"Michael knows something. But what he knows, he knows it backward. Alice didn't kill herself."

"How do you know?"

"Your sister was too cute to wash her hair with her own blood."

"Who did kill her?"

He stared at her with his bright green eyes. The person at the front door knocked a third time. "You don't know?"

"No."

"Would you lie to me?"

She began to feel a bit sick again. "I honestly don't know."

His face softened with a sympathy she had never seen in him before. "Maybe I can't remember, either. But I paint what I see. Listen closely and ponder deeply. It wasn't you who killed her, and it wasn't me who pulled the trigger."

She smiled at the absurdity of the idea. "Well, of course we didn't."

He turned to leave, spat on the grass. "Stay alive, babe, and stay cold. It's the only way for the likes of us."

He disappeared around the west side of the house, in the direction of the gate. He was such an interesting guy, she thought. She hurried to answer the door.

It was Russ. All he had on was a green T-shirt and blue jeans. Someone had punched him in the eye. The swelling reached to his nose. It was absolutely cool he had come over to see her messed up the way he was. "I need a place to stay," he said.

She had always known he liked her. Suddenly she was quite happy, and not the least bit lonely. All these nice boys wanting to talk to her and kiss her. It should rain more often.

But Clark might not like Russ kissing her. She could see his motorcycle at the end of the long driveway. Her eyes darted toward the side of the house. He probably hadn't even gotten past the gate yet. She reached out, taking Russ by the arm, pulling him inside. "You poor dear," she said. "Let me make you dinner and you can tell me all about it."

She cooked him a steak and fries. There wasn't any beer in the house, but he seemed to enjoy the expensive bottle of French wine she fetched from her aunt's closet. He finished it off before getting to dessert. When she asked who had belted him, he just shrugged, which was OK with her. She wasn't the nosy type, not like a lot of people she knew.

They watched TV. He liked the old "Star Trek" reruns—with the sound on. They talked a little, but then he started to yawn. She led him upstairs to her own bedroom. He was such a gentleman, he didn't expect her to put out right away. He just said good night and closed the door. She crashed on the couch downstairs.

Her aunt kept her up half the night. She didn't mind. It was nice having a man in the house.

Chapter Five

"How could you be so careless?" Jessica asked.

"I took it into the store because I was trying to be careful," Sara said.

"Leaving a purse stuffed with three grand sitting in a supermarket freezer isn't my idea of being careful," Jessica said.

"I didn't just leave it. I set it down and then he chased me out of the place."

First period would begin in minutes. Jessica and Sara were in the parking lot, sitting in Jessica's car. Sara had let Jessica drive all the way to school before admitting she'd lost the majority of the ASB council's money.

"Russ chased you out of the freezer?" Jessica snorted. "More likely you locked him in the freezer. What did you find when you went back last night?"

"Well . . ."

"Did you find your bag?"

"Yes."

"With all the money gone?"

"Yes."

Jessica studied her old friend, suspicious. "What else?"

"The freezer door was gone, too."

"What happened to it?"

"The store manager says Russ chopped it down."

"*What?* You did lock him in! What the hell got into—
Never mind. I don't want to know. Was Russ there when you
went back?"

"No. His boss fired him for ruining the door."

"Did you explain that it was your fault?"

"No. I was trying to get my money back. I didn't want the
boss mad at me."

"Man, you are dumb. You are the dumbest president I have
ever seen."

"I was hoping you would cheer me up."

"You don't deserve it." They sat in silence for a moment.
"He must have taken it," Jessica said finally. Sara only shook
her head. "But you tried to turn him into a Popsicle. Why
wouldn't he have taken it in revenge?"

"Russ wouldn't do that."

"Have you spoken to him?"

"I called his house."

"And?"

"He isn't living there anymore."

"Great. Fabulous. What are you saying?"

"His old man kicked him out. I don't know where he is." Sara scratched her head. "After Russ got fired, a half-dozen people ran in and out of that freezer for a couple of hours. They were moving all the frozen goods to another store so they wouldn't spoil. One of them must have found the bag, and stolen the money."

"A half-dozen employees shouldn't be that hard to check out."

"Oh, yeah."

Jessica drummed her fingers impatiently on the dashboard. "You've screwed up everything. You won't be able to afford the band. You won't be able to pay for the food. Homecoming will have to be postponed again. It'll probably be called off."

"And your crown might start to rust."

"That's not what I'm talking about."

"The hell it isn't! I'm in trouble, Jessie. And all you care about is winning some horse-faced beauty pageant!"

"That's not true!"

"It's all you think about!"

"So! What do you want me to do?"

"Give me some moral support! Quit telling me how dumb I am!"

"You are dumb! You go in to buy a can of Spam and find a date and you end up spending three grand and almost killing a guy!"

Sara gave her a weird look and sat back in the car seat. "You've made your point," she muttered.

Jessica took a deep breath. "I still think Russ must have taken it. I would have taken it."

Sara sighed. "No. I know him. He's not that kind of person. The money's gone, and it's gone for good."

"How much is left in the account?"

"About two thousand. But half of that will be eaten up by checks I've already written." She shook her head. "There isn't going to be enough."

"How about hitting up Polly?"

"I tried that already. I talked to her this morning. She says she needs her aunt's signature to get hold of that much cash." Sara shrugged. "I believe her."

"Could you find another car to raffle?"

"There isn't time." Sara gave a miserable smile. "I'm open to suggestions?"

Jessica thought a moment. "I don't have any."

The varsity tree was at both the physical and social center of Tabb High. A huge thick-branched oak, it stood halfway between the administration building and the library, near the snack bar. At lunch, without fail, at least half the jocks would gather under it to enjoy the good looks of half the girls on the pep squads. For the most part, except for the week before the party when she had been vigorously pursuing Bill Skater,

Jessica avoided the area. Crowds, even friendly ones, often tired her. But today was different. The results of the balloting to determine who would be on Tabb High's homecoming court would be announced from a platform set up beneath the tree.

"Where's Sara?" Maria Gonzales asked. "Isn't she going to read the names?"

"No, I hear Mr. Bark, my political science teacher, is playing MC," Jessica said. "Sara's got a lot on her mind."

Maria was sympathetic. "It must be hard for her to keep track of everything."

"Tell me about it."

"Are you nervous?" Maria asked.

"I feel like I'm waiting to be shot."

Maria nodded to the crowd. "You're the prettiest one here. Anyone can see that."

"Anyone but me." Dr. Baron had been right about the letters and the numbers on the board making more sense when she had her glasses on, but all morning she couldn't help feeling people were staring at her and thinking she looked like an encyclopedia. At the moment, however, she had her glasses in her hand, and for that reason, she wasn't sure if she was hallucinating when she saw the long-legged blonde sitting all alone on one of the benches that loosely surrounded the varsity tree. Jessica pointed to the girl. "Who is that?" she asked.

Maria frowned. "Clair Hilrey."

"What's she doing?"

"Nothing."

Glancing around, Jessica quickly slipped on her glasses. The cheerleader was indeed by herself, and if that wasn't extraordinary enough, she looked downright depressed. "I wonder what's the matter with her."

"She's probably worried she won't be on the court."

"Clair's got the self-confidence of a tidal wave. No, that's not it. Something's wrong." Jessica took off her glasses and hid them away. "Which reminds me. During chemistry this morning, *you* were looking pretty worried."

"I'm fine."

"Come on, Maria. Haven't we been friends long enough? You're not happy. What is it?"

Her tiny Hispanic friend shyly shook her head. "I'm happy."

"Are you still thinking about Nick?"

"No."

After Alice's party, when the police were running in and out of the McCoy residence and questioning them all, Maria's parents had suddenly appeared. When Jessica had called her mom to explain what had happened, she forgot to tell her not to call the Gonzaleses. That had been a mistake. Mr. and Mrs. Gonzales didn't even know their daughter was at a party—and at two in the morning. And then Maria's parents arrived precisely when Bubba was telling a detective about the fight in the pool between The Rock and Nick. Of course Maria had played a vital role in that fight, which Bubba mentioned right in front of her parents. It took them no time at all to figure out that Maria had been dating Nick. And it didn't help that the police chose Nick—along with Russ and Kats—to detain for further questioning. Jessica didn't hear exactly what they said to Maria, but from a quick glance at their faces as they were leaving, Jessica knew it couldn't have been anything gentle.

Parental law was still in effect in Maria's family: For absolutely no reason was she to go near Nick Grutler.

"Liar," Jessica said. She knew Maria was still thinking about Nick.

Maria started to protest again, but stopped herself. "I wish I could choose what to think about," she said sadly.

"It'll work out. It usually does."

Maria had her doubts. "I can't even talk to him about it."

"Sure you can. Your parents won't know. Explain the situation to him."

"How can I say that because he's black, my mom and dad assume he murdered Alice?" She shook her head. "It's better if he thinks I don't like him anymore. It's simpler this way."

Mr. Bark climbed onto the platform. The crowd quieted. Jessica hoped he wouldn't give a speech. A minute more of this waiting and she would scream.

He gave a speech—fifteen minutes—about how wonderful it was to be a teenager and to be alive in such exciting times. Bless him, he even worked in the need for nuclear disarmament. Jessica ground her teeth. Finally he pulled out the envelope.

"And now, the new homecoming court," he said, excited, opening the list. "Princess number one is . . ."

Jessica—Jessica—Jessica—me—me—me.

Mr. Bark paused, perplexed. "There seems to be some mistake. There are supposed to be five girls on the court. . . ." He stepped away from the microphone, spoke quietly to Bubba for a moment. Bubba kept nodding his head no matter what the teacher seemed to ask. Finally Mr. Bark returned to the mike. "The vote has resulted in an unusual situation," he said. "There was a six-way tie for fifth place. It has, therefore, been decided that there will be only four girls on the court this year. They are: Clair Hilrey, Cindy Fosmeyer, Maria Gonzales, and Jessica Hart."

Maria dropped her books and pressed her fingers to her mouth. Jessica let out a totally involuntary scream. Then they hugged each other and laughed with tears in their eyes. It felt good, Jessica thought. It felt better than just about anything had ever felt in her whole life. She couldn't stop shaking.

"I can't believe it," Maria kept saying. "I can't believe it."

"We don't have to believe it." Jessica laughed. "We're living it!"

People they knew and didn't know gathered around to offer their congratulations. Cindy Fosmeyer was one of them. She had huge breasts and a big nose. Jessica gave her a kiss.

Everything seemed to be happening so fast. Pats on the back, smiles, hugs, kisses. But none of them were from Polly or Sara, and Jessica had started to look for them when Bill Skater came up and shook her hand.

"I knew you'd get on the court," he said.

"If you knew, why didn't you tell me!" She giggled, giving him a quick hug, which took him by surprise.

"Well, Jessie, you didn't ask."

She felt brave. She felt like a tease. "So I didn't. So why don't you ask me something?"

Such boyish blue eyes. He gave her a sexy look—with his face, it was the only kind he could give—but his voice was hesitant. "Do you want to go out tonight?"

The icing on the cake. Maybe she'd get a scoop of ice cream later. "Absolutely!"

She was a princess. She had a prince. She gave him her number, another hug, and went to find her friends.

She accidentally bumped into Clair instead, in Sara's locker hall, far from the hustle and bustle. Clair was alone. She in fact *looked* lonely. But they shook hands and she offered Jessica her congratulations.

"Four little princesses," Clair said. "Sounds like a bad fairy tale, doesn't it?"

"It's amazing about that tie," Jessica said.

"I wasn't surprised. Is Maria a friend of yours?"

"Yeah."

"Give her my regards."

"I will." Jessica smiled. "Aren't you excited?"

Clair turned to dial the combination on her locker. "Ask me in a couple of weeks, when they call out my name during the dance."

So that's how it was. "Maybe you'll be asking me."

Clair paused, giving her the eye. And now she smiled, slow and sure. "You may as well know, dearie, I can't lose."

Chapter Six

Unknown to Jessica, Sara had watched the announcement of the homecoming court. But she had shied away from congratulating her best friend for a couple of reasons. First, as she had told Jessica in the car that morning, she thought Jessica had become overly preoccupied with the whole queen business. Second, with the loss of the money and Russ's getting fired, she was in a rotten mood and was afraid she'd say something nasty just when Jessica was enjoying her high moment. The fact that these two reasons were contradictory didn't make any difference to Sara. In reality, she was happy for both Jessica and Maria, and not the least bit jealous. She wouldn't have wanted to be a princess for anything. Being ASB president was enough of a pain in the ass.

She needed money and she needed to get Russ's job back

for him. She didn't know which troubled her more. She was still smarting from his comments. She liked to think she didn't care about being popular. She had always thought of herself as subtle. But if Russ honestly believed—and it didn't matter whether he was right or wrong (although he was most definitely wrong)—she was using her position of authority to seduce him, then maybe there was something lacking in her approach. It was a possibility.

He was not at school today. All right, she'd worry about him the next day. Big bucks and fat Bubba were what mattered now. She followed Bubba as he left the varsity tree after the announcement, watched him disappear into the computer-science room. It was general knowledge that Bubba dealt in the stock market, and after checking around campus, she found out that he did extremely well. He was, in fact, a genius when it came to turning a few dollars into a few thousand. Knocking on the computer-room door and turning the knob, she hoped he didn't charge for advice.

He was already at a terminal, typing a million words a minute on the keyboard. He dimmed the screen the instant she entered, but appeared happy to see her. He offered her a chair.

"What do you think of our new batch of princesses?" he asked.

"I was surprised Maria Gonzales and Cindy Fosmeyer were selected," she said. "Maria's probably the quietest girl in the school, and Cindy—she's not exactly the princess type."

"You mean she's a dog?"

"Yeah."

Bubba nodded. "But she does have big breasts, and those babies go a long way with half the votes in the school." He glanced at his blank screen. "She's always been one of my favorites." He seemed to think that was funny, smiling to himself. "What can I do for you, Ms. President?"

"I have a small problem. I've been told you might be able to help me with it."

He leaned back in his seat, apparently satisfied that it was his reputation that had brought her to him. "Is it a financial or a sexual problem?" he asked.

"You have a lot of nerve."

"I also have a big bank account, and a huge— Well, let's just say I am willing and able to help in either department."

"It' s a financial problem."

"A pity."

"I need three grand, and I need it by next week."

"Why?"

"There'll be no homecoming unless I get it."

"Why?"

"What do you mean, why? I need it to pay for everything."

"Have you already spent the money from the car raffle?"

"No, not exactly."

"What happened to the money? Did you lose it?"

"I—yeah, I did."

"How did you lose it?"

"What difference does it make? I lost it!"

"If you lost it on a guy, then I would have to say you have both a sexual and a financial problem. I like to know what I'm dealing with before I invest my time." He picked up a pen. "Are you going out with Russ Desmond?"

"What business is it of yours? No, I am not going out with him. Look, can you help me or not? Because if you can't, I haven't eaten lunch yet."

"Where would you like to go for lunch?"

"What?"

"I'll buy you lunch. Where would you like to eat?"

She stood. "Nowhere. Thanks for your time."

She was at the door when Bubba stopped her with the line, "I can get you the money, maybe."

"How?"

"Come back here and sit down." She did as she was told. He put aside his pen, leaned toward her, studying her face. "You're cute, Sara."

"How?" she repeated.

He shrugged. "Does it matter? You should be asking what it's going to cost you."

"What is it going to cost me?"

"Sex."

She chuckled in disbelief. "What?"

"Sex."

"Are you crazy? Are you saying you'll pay me three grand for my body?"

He sat back, shook his head. "No offense meant, but I would have to be crazy to spend that much money to sleep with you, or any girl for that matter. No, I said I can *get* you the money. I didn't say I would *give* it to you."

"Where are you going to get it? From your own account?"

"No, most of my money is tied up." He thought a moment. "How much do you have left?"

"A grand."

He considered again. "Can you get to that money this afternoon?"

"Not without Bill Skater's countersignature on a check."

"Do you have a copy of something Bill has signed?"

"Yeah."

"Then you can fake his signature."

"No, I'm not that desperate. I see what you're driving at. You want me to turn over the thousand to you."

"You *are* that desperate or you wouldn't be here. And, yes, I'll need what you have."

"No way. What are you going to do with it?"

"Invest it."

"Can you invest money and get that big a profit that quickly?"

"In the commodities market, you can lay out a hundred dollars today and have five hundred tomorrow."

"But I've heard investing in commodities is the same as rolling dice."

"Not if you know what you're doing. But I only mentioned commodities as an example. I haven't decided exactly what I will do with the grand. I'll have to think about it."

She shook her head. "This sounds pretty thin to me. I told you, I need this money within a few days. If you're not willing to get it out of your personal investments, then I can't take you seriously."

He was amused. "I notice you haven't said anything about my demand for sexual favors?"

"What am I supposed to say? You were kidding, weren't you?"

"No."

She realized she was blushing, and that he could tell she was blushing. "But you need to triple whatever I give you in less than a week," she persisted. "Nobody in the world can guarantee they can do that."

"Nobody in the world can guarantee anything. But I do believe—in fact, I'm almost certain—I can do great things with your money. Now as far as your deadline is concerned . . ." He picked up his pen again, reached for a piece of paper. "Who do you owe?"

"Mainly the caterer and the band."

"I need their names and phone numbers. I'll arrange it so we can pay them later."

"They won't go for that."

"They will after they talk to me. Give me the information."

"Wait! Let me get this straight. I'm going to give you a thousand dollars, and in return you're going to take responsibility for all the homecoming bills?"

"What is this responsibility crap? I'll do the best I can. That's all a man can do."

She swallowed. "And when you pay everything off, I have to sleep with you?"

"Yes."

"How many times?"

"Once."

"Is that all?"

"When it's over, you'll wish there were a hundred times yet to come."

"But you've been through half the girls on campus. God only knows what diseases you have."

"My vast experience has only made me all the more careful. Trust me, Sara, I'll take exquisite care of you." He paused. "Have we got a deal?"

She grimaced. "Has anyone ever told you what a sleaze ball you are?"

Bubba threw back his head and laughed.

Chapter Seven

I f anyone else had chased after him so long to do something he didn't want to do, Nick Grutler thought, he probably would have punched him in the nose by now. But he respected Michael, and he learned it paid to listen to him. Michael was trying to persuade him to go out for the basketball team.

They were near the end of a one-on-one game, playing on an outside court near the girls' baseball field. The storm the night before had left an occasional puddle for them to dodge, but the water was slowing neither of them down. School had ended about an hour earlier, and the varsity team's official after-school practice had been canceled. The new coach had wanted the gymnasium floor waxed, and Tabb High's most recent crop of janitors had never done it before—and probably shouldn't be allowed to do it again;

at the rate they were going, the floor wouldn't be ready for the homecoming game.

Michael had asked Nick to hang around to help him with his jump shot. Naturally they had ended up trying to show each other up. It was no contest. Nick was ahead forty-four to thirty in a fifty-point game. Michael had trouble stopping Nick because Nick was able to palm the ball with equal ease with either hand, hit three-quarters of his shots anywhere within a twenty-foot radius of the basket, and—according to Michael, although Nick thought he was exaggerating—fly.

"But if this new coach you guys have is such a jerk," Nick said, tossing the ball to Michael to take out of bounds, "why should I put myself out for him?"

"You won't be doing it for him," Michael said, wiping the sweat from his forehead. Nick admired Michael's gutsy determination, especially on defense, even though he knew if he really wanted, he could score on him every time. "You'll be playing for yourself."

"On a team sport? Sure you don't want to take a break?"

"I'm all right," Michael said, dribbling slowly in bounds. "I mean you don't know how talented you are. I bet you could average thirty points and twenty rebounds a game if the rest of us didn't get in your way." He paused, panting, his free hand propped on his hip. "Are you ready?"

"I'm ready."

Michael nodded, continuing to dribble at the top of the

key. "You get that kind of stats over the first half of the season and you'll have every college recruiter in the area coming to watch you play. Have you ever thought about that, going to college?"

"I never thought of graduating from high school till I met you," Nick said, not exaggerating. It had been Michael who had gotten him into academics at Tabb. Michael had done it by forcing him to read one book, from cover to cover, each week. It had been quite a chore for Nick because initially he'd had to go over each page three or four times with a dictionary. But he had learned that Michael's belief that the key to success in school was a strong vocabulary was absolutely true. He had found that even in math he could figure out how to work the problems now that he could follow the examples. He had also learned he enjoyed reading—he especially liked war stories—and that he wasn't dumb. Indeed, Michael had told him not more than an hour earlier that only someone with a high IQ could quadruple his vocabulary in the space of two months.

Nick was going to look up the exact definition of IQ as soon as he got home.

"Would you like to go to college?" Michael asked.

"I don't know what I'd do there."

"You would go to classes as you do here. Only you'd be able to major in any subject you wanted." Michael stopped suddenly, let fly with a fifteen-foot jump shot. Nick sprang up effortlessly, purposely swatting it back in Michael's direction. "Nice block," Michael muttered, catching the ball.

"Do people major in history?" Nick asked.

"Sure. You enjoy reading about the past, don't you?"

"It's interesting to see how people used to do stuff." Michael appeared undecided what to do next. "Why don't we take a break?" Nick suggested.

"Only if you're tired?"

Nick yawned, nodded. A week after Alice McCoy's funeral, Michael had called him with a job lead at a vitamin-packing factory. Nick had immediately ridden to the place on his bike. He had been hired on the spot. Only later had he come to understand they'd taken him on as a favor to Michael. Apparently, Michael had once helped the owner's son—Nick didn't know all the details. He was just thankful to have cash coming in so his dad wouldn't throw him out. But the hours were long and there was a lot of heavy lifting. He usually worked swing— three to twelve. He couldn't imagine taking on the extra burden of daily basketball practice. He told Michael as much as they walked to the sidelines and collected their sweats.

"You shouldn't be working full-time," Michael said. "You're only in high school. Does your dad take all your money?"

"Just about."

"That's not fair."

"If you ever met my dad, and he wanted your paycheck, believe me, you'd give it to him. Anyway, *you* work full-time."

"That's different. My mom needs the dough. And that's beside the point. You've got to take the long-term perspective on this. Imagine—you go out for the team, blow everybody's mind, get offered a college scholarship, earn a degree, land a job where you don't have to kill yourself every day for the rest of your life, and you can see how it would be worth it to sacrifice a few hours of sleep for the next few months."

Nick wiped his brow with his sweatshirt, slipped it over his head. "Forget about psyching me up for a minute and tell me this: am I really that good?"

"You're better than that."

Nick shook his head. "I can't believe this." In response, Michael snapped the ball toward his face. "Hey!" he shouted, catching it an inch shy of the tip of his nose. "Watch it."

Michael nodded. "There isn't another kid in the school who could have caught that ball. The best somebody else might have done was knock it away. You've got reflexes. You've got hands. And you've got a four-foot vertical jump. Trust me, you're *that* good."

Nick lowered his head, dribbled the ball beside his worn-out sneakers; he'd had only one pair of shoes in the past three years. "The Rock and a couple of his football buddies are on the team," he said. "What kind of welcome are they going to give me?"

"Oh, they'll try to make you feel like dirt. Especially when you start bouncing the ball off the top of their heads every time you slam-dunk. But I can't believe you'd let *them* stop you?"

"It's not just them. It's—something else."

"What?"

"Somebody's out to get me, Mike."

"Who?"

Nick grabbed hold of the ball, squeezed it tight, feeling the strength in his hands, and the anger, deeper inside, that seemed to give fuel to his strength. Except for brief moments it was as if he had been angry all his life—or alone and unwanted. It was often hard for him to tell the feelings apart. "There's this guy who goes to school here—his name's Randy. I don't know his last name."

"What's he look like?"

"He's ugly. He's got dark hair, bushy red sideburns, and a beer gut. He looks older. You know who I'm talking about?"

"I've seen him. What's he doing to you?"

"He's trying to sell me drugs. I know that doesn't sound like a big deal, but he keeps on me, even after I've told him a half-dozen times I'm not interested. I think he's trying to set me up."

"That serious?"

"Yeah. This afternoon, when I went to my locker, I found a Baggie sitting on top of my books, and a note that said 'On the House.' The Baggie had a couple of grams of coke in it."

"What did you do with it?" Michael asked.

"I gave it to Bubba."

"What did you do that for?"

"He was with me when I found it. He wanted it."

"But Bubba doesn't do drugs."

"Maybe he wanted to sell it, I don't know."

Michael considered a bit. "The fact that he looks older could be important. It might be possible to use the computer to check on— Hey, what is it?"

She was coming out of the girls' shower room, her long black hair tied in a ponytail as it had been the day they first met. Although small and far away, for a second, she was all he could see. "It's Maria," Nick said.

Michael was not impressed. He thought Maria was a phony for dumping Nick simply because the police had detained him at the station after Alice McCoy's death. Michael didn't know about her overriding fear of calling attention to herself, of being found out for what she was—an illegal alien. But maybe the knowledge wouldn't have made any difference to Michael. Often it seemed a poor excuse to Nick, too. Yet there wasn't an hour that went by when Nick didn't think of her.

"She must be feeling like hot stuff being elected to the homecoming court and all," Michael said.

"Not Maria."

Michael glanced at him, then at Maria. "I shouldn't have said that."

Nick rolled the ball in his hands. He would pop it next; he knew he could make it explode. "It's driving me nuts."

"What do you want to do?"

"Talk to her. But she doesn't want to talk to me."

"Have you asked her why?"

"I've tried."

"Try again. Try now."

"No. No, I can't."

"You have a perfect excuse to approach her. You want to congratulate her on making the court. Here, give me the ball. I'll wait for you."

"Mike . . ."

"Go, before she's gone."

He went; he only needed a shove. She saw him coming and turned to wait. He took that as a positive sign.

It wasn't.

"Hi," he said. "How are you?"

She appeared so calm, he thought she must surely be able to see how he was trembling inside. Yet a closer look showed her calmness to be no deeper than the welcome in her expression. She had waited for him out of politeness, not because she wanted to.

"Good," she said. "And you?"

"Oh, I'm all sweaty." He nodded toward Michael, and the courts. "We're playing some basketball."

She nodded, solemn as the day they'd met, only more distant now, not nearly so comfortable. "I saw you. Say hello to Mike for me."

"I will." That sounded like a good-bye. "I hear you're a school princess. That must be exciting?"

Her mood brightened, a bit. "I still don't believe it. I didn't think anyone knew who I was."

"It didn't surprise me. I voted for you."

"You did, really?"

"Of course."

"Who else did you vote for?" She sounded genuinely curious.

"Jessica and Sara and that girl Bubba sees—Clair."

"That's only four people. You could vote for five."

"They were the only ones I wrote down."

She seemed happy, in that moment, standing there listening to his praise, probably replaying in her mind the afternoon's announcement. But it didn't last. She looked at the ground. "I've got to go."

The word just burst out of him. "Why?"

"Because, Nick, because—" She clasped her books to her chest, her head still down. "I have to."

"I see." Then he said something that had been on his mind since the cops had led him to the jail cell with Kats and Russ the night Alice McCoy had taken a bullet through the head. "Is it because I was running down the stairs after the gunshot?"

She jumped slightly. "No."

"You think I killed her."

She turned away. "No!"

"You're the only one who knew I was coming down those stairs." He stopped, and now a cold note entered his tone. "Or are you, Maria?"

Her back to him, she nodded slowly. "I'm the only one. But that doesn't matter. None of that matters." She glanced over her shoulder, her eyes dark, lonely. "I have to go."

He shrugged. "Go."

When he returned to the court, Michael asked him how it had gone. Nick repeated everything that had been said, except the bit about his running down the stairs. It wasn't that he didn't trust Michael, he simply felt guilty for having lied to him after the funeral when they had originally discussed the matter. Back then, after having spent a few days in the slammer, he'd been afraid to say anything even remotely incriminating.

He needed respect, not just from Michael, but from everyone in school. Then maybe Maria would see him as something other than a threat. As they walked toward the showers, he said, "I think I will go out for the team."

Chapter Eight

Although he had been badly beaten on the court, Michael felt better for the exercise. The thought of his date that evening with Jessica wasn't slowing him down, either. He'd had trouble falling asleep the night before thinking about it.

After saying good-bye to Nick, Michael headed for the computer-science room. He'd been meaning to have a talk with Bubba. He decided now would be a good time.

Michael had not purposely avoided his old friend after Alice's death the way he had avoided Jessica, yet since then, he had spoken to Bubba very few times. He suspected Bubba may have been keeping his distance. Whatever the reason, it was time to clear the air between them.

On the way to Bubba, he passed a pay phone and thought of the form he'd given Polly. She hadn't been at school that day.

He decided to give her a quick call. She didn't answer till the seventh or eighth ring.

"You barely caught me, Mike. I'm on my way out."

"I won't keep you then. I was wondering if I could swing by this afternoon and pick up that form I left last night?"

"What form?"

"The permission form I wanted your aunt to sign. Did she have a chance to read it over?"

Polly hesitated. "I don't know. I don't think so."

"Is there a problem? If you'd like, I could explain what it's for to your aunt."

"No, you don't have to do that."

"Do you have any idea when I could pick it up?"

"I'll see. I'll get back to you, all right?"

"Sure. I'll talk to you later."

Putting down the phone, he knew he'd wait a long time before Polly McCoy contacted him.

He was not surprised to find Bubba seated in front of a CRT. Hardly lifting his eyes from the screen, Bubba waved him into a chair. Michael sat patiently for a few minutes before finally asking, "Should I come back later?"

"No."

"What are you doing?"

Bubba continued to study the screen, flipping through rows and rows of figures. "Did you know Tabb High is paying to receive the latest Wall Street numbers over our modem?"

"No."

"Neither does the administration." Bubba pointed to the screen. "Look at Ford. Yesterday it was ninety-five and three-quarters. Now it's down to ninety-two and a half."

"Did you buy an option on it?"

"No. I've been shying away from options altogether. Too risky with the way Wall Street has been dancing since the bond market choked." He tapped a couple of other numbers, then put his finger to his lips, thoughtful. "But when the market's like this, it's also the best time to make a quick killing."

"Are you in some kind of hurry?"

"Greed always is." He flipped off the screen, relaxed into his personal swivel chair, giving Michael his full attention. "What's up?"

"The usual—nothing. How about you?"

"What can I say? The world revolves around me." He paused, giving Michael a penetrating look. Bubba was no dummy. "You want to talk about something, Mike?"

"Am I that obvious?"

"No, I'm that perceptive. Besides, we've known each other a long time. What's on your mind?"

He reminds me we're old friends. He knows I don't trust him.

Michael did not suspect Bubba of murdering Alice McCoy. He realized, however, that Bubba did not have to be a murderer to be a liar.

Nick had heard groans coming from the locked bedroom

next to the room where they had found Alice. Cries of distress, Nick had thought, perhaps mistaking what had actually been cries of ecstasy.

"All right, I did want to talk to you about something."

"Shoot."

"Were you having sex with Clair in the bedroom next to the one where Alice died?"

Bubba chuckled. "Wow, now that's a fine question."

Michael smiled. "Were you?"

"What did I tell the police?"

"That you were outside in the front with Clair, stargazing."

"Then the answer must be no."

Michael leaned forward. "Come on, Bubba, it had to be you. It couldn't have been anybody else."

"How does this tie in with what happened to Alice?"

"If I knew for a fact you were in there with Clair, it would allow me to cross that room out of the whole equation."

"Are you still talking to the police?"

"The police think it was a suicide," Michael said. "I keep in contact with the detective that was in charge of the case. Why?"

"Just wondering."

"I'm not going to go to them with this information if that's what you're worried about."

"I wasn't in the bedroom. I would tell you if I was. Why don't you believe me?"

Michael knew from experience what a phenomenal liar Bubba was. Yet he didn't understand why Bubba would lie to him now. Surely he couldn't be trying to protect Clair's reputation, not after bragging about how many condoms he had gone through with her. On the other hand, the question remained—who could it have been?

Could Bubba have been in the room with Clair and Alice?

Michael sat back in his seat. "I hope Clair enjoyed the astronomy lesson. Did you show her the Little Dipper?"

Bubba grinned. "Hey, that sounds like a personal insult. But I'll forgive you this time. How's the telescope? Discovered any comets?"

No one could change a subject as smoothly as Bubba. Michael decided he would wait and broach the topic later. "I'm still looking," he said. "It's a big sky." He had made a vow to himself not to discuss his find with anyone until it was definite. He nodded to the computer screen. "I need a favor."

"What?"

"Use those codes you swiped from Miss Fenway and call up the files on that Randy guy who's been hassling Nick to buy drugs."

"On Randy Meisser?"

"Is that his name?"

"Yeah. I already have. He's a narc."

"Are you sure?"

"I can't be absolutely sure, but he came out of nowhere.

He has no transcripts. He has no home address. I think he was planted here by the police. They're doing that these days."

"Why do you think he went after Nick?"

"Because he's black."

"What did you do with the cocaine you got out of Nick's locker?"

"Spiked a Pepsi with it and gave it to Randy."

Michael laughed. "Did he drink it?"

"Yeah. He was bouncing off the walls in creative writing. The teacher had to send him down to the office." Bubba yawned. "I'll spread the word about him. He won't last."

Michael thought of Polly and the permission form. "I'd like you to do me another favor. I want a look at the report on Alice's autopsy. I'm having trouble going through official channels. I was wondering if you could tap into the police files and—"

"Forget it," Bubba interrupted.

"Why?"

"The police department deals with highly sensitive information. It's not like the school district. They have experts protect those files. I won't be able to touch them."

Michael had suspected that would be the case. "The coroner who did the autopsy isn't a full-time employee of the county, but a consultant. His name is Dr. Gin Kawati. I checked around at lunch. He has an office downtown." Michael pulled a slip of paper from his pocket, gave it to Bubba. "That's his business address. You can see he belongs to the ARC Medical Group. They're fairly large. They must be computerized."

Bubba fingered the slip. "Even if I'm able to break into the group's files, who's to say the good doctor will have a copy of a report he did for the city in with his private records?"

"There's no way of telling without looking. Can you do it?"

"It all depends on how their system's set up. It may be that I'd have to go down there at night and use one of their terminals."

"You mean break into the office?"

"Yeah. Or I might be able to do it from here." Bubba set the paper aside. "I'll look into it."

"I really appreciate it." Michael shifted uncomfortably. "I suppose you think I'm nuts for keeping up the investigation?"

Bubba turned away, snapping his screen back on. "I understand how much she meant to you, Mike. You don't have to explain anything to me."

"Thanks."

The door burst open. It was Clair Hilrey. Michael got to his feet, went to congratulate her on her nomination to the homecoming court. The words caught in his throat. Her usually bright blue eyes were bloodshot, and she hadn't been out drinking and celebrating. She had been crying. She smiled politely when she saw him, though, wiping a hand across her cheek. "Hi, Mike. Am I interrupting something?"

Bubba had stood up, too, and knocked over his chair doing

so. Bubba jumped for a girl about as often as he went to Sunday Mass. Michael took the hint. "I was just leaving," he said.

"He was just leaving," Bubba repeated, catching Clair's eye. She lowered her head. Michael hurried toward the door.

"I'll leave you two alone," he said.

Obviously he wasn't the only one with a lot on his mind.

Chapter Nine

Polly hadn't lied to Michael—she really had been on her way out when he called. She had to go to the market for groceries, and to the family clinic for contraceptives. If Russ's sexual appetite matched his appetite at the kitchen table, she figured she had better be prepared. All day he had done nothing but watch TV and eat. Her aunt didn't know he was in the house, and since she never left her bedroom, Polly saw no reason for her ever to know. Polly had told Russ to keep his voice down when they talked.

But after speaking to Michael, Polly couldn't find her keys. They weren't where she always left them, on the counter beside the microwave. She was searching in the drawers when Tony Foulton, the architectural engineer at her construction company, called. He had some concerns about the float he was building for the dance.

"As I told you last week, Polly, this is a little out of my line. I think Sara would have been better off hiring a company that specializes in floats."

"I told her the exact same thing. But she says the school can't afford it. How's it coming along?"

"The platform itself is no problem; it's the fact we're building it on top of a pickup truck that bothers me. How far did you say it has to be driven?"

"Only a hundred yards. We can have it towed to the school."

Tony considered. "Would it be possible to rent a real float carrier?"

"How much would it cost?"

"They're scarce this time of year with all the holiday parades, but I could check around town. Less than a thousand dollars."

"A thousand dollars is a lot of money."

"I don't think it would be that much."

"But haven't you already begun construction?"

"We're about half done with it, yes. But it wouldn't take long to pull it down."

Polly knew what her carpenters charged per hour. This was turning out to be expensive. Sara had a lot of nerve putting her people through all this. "But why? It's not going to cave in if someone stands on it, is it?"

"No, it won't do that. But as I said before, it lacks stability."

He paused. "As an engineer, I would feel better if we didn't use the truck."

"Are you going to be in tomorrow, Tony?"

"Yes. I usually work till noon on Saturday."

"I'll come by about ten and look at it. Oh, how's Philip?"

Philip Bart was a foreman who'd been with the company since her father had founded it fifteen years earlier. Recently McCoy Construction had won a big contract in the mountains near Big Bear Lake for a two-hundred-room hotel. Prior to laying the foundation, a hard vein of granite had to be removed from the soil using dynamite. Somehow, in the middle of one of the blasts, Philip had been struck on the head by a flying rock. He'd gone into a coma and the initial prognosis had been poor. Fortunately, in the last couple of days, he had regained consciousness.

"Much better," Tony said, his voice warming. "He's sitting up in bed and eating solid food. He told me to thank you for the check you sent his family."

"It was the least I could do. I'm glad he's going to be all right. Give him my best. But Tony, next time, have everyone stand back a little further, OK?"

He laughed. "I'll see you tomorrow, Polly."

Russ came in the kitchen as she set down the phone. He had not shaved. He looked very masculine. When he had arrived the night before in the rain, he had a suitcase outside in his truck. Now he had on running shorts, shoes and socks, and nothing else. "Where are you going?" she asked.

"I have to run," he said, sitting down and checking his laces.

"Why? I thought cross-country was over?"

"I run year round."

"Where are you going to go?"

"Wherever my feet take me."

"You won't tell me?"

He glanced up. "I don't know where I'm going, Polly."

"But it might rain on you. It rained yesterday."

He stood, stretching toward the ceiling, then reaching for his toes, his powerful back muscles swelling around his shoulder blades. "The rain and I are old friends." Straightening, he headed for the door. "I'll catch you later."

"Wait! I have to talk to you about something."

He stopped, his hand on the knob. "What?"

"Jessica called a few minutes ago. She told me how Sara locked you in the freezer. I never knew she hated you that much. God, it must have been awful for you. I knew last night something was wrong when I saw how red and sore your hands were."

"Yeah, well, it was probably my fault." He nodded. "See ya."

She watched him go. He sure was cool, maybe too cool. He let people walk all over him. She used to have that problem. She hadn't told Jessica where Russ slept last night. She respected his privacy, and hadn't wanted to brag.

Polly never did find her keys, and had to fetch a spare set from her bedroom. Backing out of the garage into the driveway, she rolled down the window, feeling a chill in the air. It had been her practice last winter to always keep an extra sweater in the trunk. Putting her Mercedes in park, she jumped out to check and see if it was still there.

She found the sweater, but that was all she found. It wasn't until she was back in her car and heading down the road that she realized the ax she had taken from Russ the first week of school—and which she had been meaning to give back to him ever since—was no longer in her trunk. She had no idea what could have happened to it.

She screwed up by going to the market first. She bought all kinds of frozen goods and milk and stuff and then realized it would have to sit in the car while she was in the family clinic. It was really a question of priorities, she thought, after deciding not to go home before visiting the clinic: the welfare of her body over the welfare of a few lousy frozen carrots. Obviously, if she was going to have sex like a mature woman, she was going to have to act like one and take the precautions necessary to keep from becoming pregnant.

Walking up the steps to the clinic, Polly congratulated herself for coming here instead of making an appointment with her personal physician. Dr. Kline had known her since she was a child. He was old and conservative and would have asked her lots of nosy questions. Besides, it was more fun this way. She might run into someone she knew.

Polly did precisely that. But first she had a hard time making the nurse—Polly assumed she was a nurse, she was dressed in white—understand what she wanted. They weren't speaking the same language. Sure, she had read about condoms and diaphragms in women's magazines, but all the articles had been written with the assumption you knew what those things were. Polly wasn't even sure which ones the boys wore. She finally told the nurse she wanted a birth-control method that wasn't too gross. The nurse smiled and told her to have a seat. The doctor would see her in a few minutes.

The waiting room was crowded—thirty people at least, and only three of them were guys. The few minutes had become more than a half hour and Polly was beginning to feel restless when Clair Hilrey suddenly appeared through the inside swinging green door. A nurse was holding on to her elbow; she was having trouble walking. The nurse guided her into a chair directly across from Polly, who had never seen Clair with a hair out of place, much less ready to keel over. Before leaving, the nurse asked if she'd be all right. Clair nodded weakly.

Polly sat and watched Clair for several minutes, all the time wondering what her problem could be. The girl was perspiring heavily, her eyes rolling from side to side. At one point, she even bent over and pressed her head between her knees. Polly was relieved when Clair didn't throw up.

"Are you all right?" Polly asked finally.

Clair took a deep breath, rested her chin in her hand, didn't look up. "Yeah," she mumbled. "I'm waiting for someone."

"But you look sick. Are you sick?"

"No, not now."

"That's good. I didn't go to school today, but Jessica told me the two of you were elected to the homecoming court. That's neat."

Clair sat up. "Huh?"

Polly smiled. "Jessica said—"

"Jessica Hart?"

"Yeah, she's my best friend. Don't you remember me? I'm Polly McCoy."

Clair put a hand to her head, dizzy. "Yeah, Polly, yeah. Of course, I remember you." She glanced toward the exit door. "How are you?"

"Great. Just stopped by to buy some contraceptives. You know Russ Desmond? He's staying at my house. What kind of contraceptives do you use, Clair?"

"I don't."

"You don't?"

"I mean, I don't need any." She got up, staggering slightly. Bubba had appeared in the hallway. "I've got to go, Polly. Take care of yourself."

Bubba took Clair by the arm and helped her across the floor. Clair said something to him about his being late, but they were out the door before Polly could hear his response. Polly didn't know why Jessica didn't like Clair. She seemed a nice enough girl.

Chapter Ten

Michael stopped at the gas station where Kats worked on the way home from school. Because of his one-on-one game with Nick and his talk with Bubba, he was late leaving campus. The sun had already begun to set, and he was anxious to shower and get dressed for his date with Jessica. But he had set the investigative ball in motion and felt he had to stop to have a little chat with Kats—just for a minute. If he'd been asked to pick a murderer of Alice, it would have been Kats.

He parked at the full-service isle—something he never did—and got out. Kats appeared from beneath a jacked-up Camaro inside the garage. He had on an oil-stained army-surplus jacket that could have used a rinsing in a tub of gasoline, and a cigarette dangled between his lips. He must have just been in a fight. Michael noticed he was missing a front tooth—and he had been ugly to begin with.

"Hey, Mikey, how come's I never see you anymore? Where you been hanging out?"

"I've been around. What are you up to these days?"

Kats wiped at his greasy black mustache. "Working and going to night school. You know, I'll probably get my diploma when you guys do."

"I didn't know that."

Kats giggled. He might have been high on something. "Yeah, I might be at your graduation! Imagine that!" He lowered his voice. "You wouldn't let me come last year."

"Not me."

"Huh?"

"Nothing." They were the only ones at the station. Michael nodded to his car. "Could you fill it up with unleaded, please?"

Kats paused, eyeing him. "Since when are you too important to pump your own gas, Mikey?"

"Since I started paying for full serve."

Kats glanced at the pump, grinned. "Hey, you're right. You're parked where all the big shots park. Sorry, I didn't see that." He threw away his cigarette and started to unscrew the gas cap. "You mustn't be counting your nickels and dimes anymore. Things going good? They're going good with me. The day I get ahold of that diploma, I'm out of this joint."

"Are you still planning on joining the army?" Michael asked, leaning against the car. He'd opted for full serve, feeling it would give him a psychological advantage while questioning Kats. For the moment, he was the boss.

"You kidding me? Those pussy-foot children?" Kats unhooked the pump. "I'm going to be a marine, or I ain't going to be nothing."

"Have they accepted you already?"

Kats nodded. "Get your schoolin' done and you're in. That's what they told me."

"Was that before or after you got arrested the night Alice McCoy died?"

He had purposely phrased the question to shock Kats. Yet Kats was either too smart to fall for the bait or else too stupid to recognize it. He stuck the gasoline nozzle into the tank, set the grip on the handle to automatic feed. "I don't remember," he said, whipping a rag from his back pocket. "Want your oil checked?"

Michael could have backed off at that point and asked Kats a couple of civil questions about the night of the party. But he decided to push him further. He would get more out of an upset Kats, he decided. The guy had one of those mouths that split wider the greater the pressure inside.

"Yeah, you remember," he said. "It was before Alice died. But the way things are now, I bet the marines wouldn't let you hold an empty rifle in basic training." He knew this wasn't true. The marines were looking for a few good men, but weren't above taking a few good killers. Kats didn't know that. He started to warm to the discussion.

"I didn't do nothing," he said, throwing open the hood. He sounded both hurt and angry. "I didn't kill that girl. I wouldn't do that, Mikey. You know me. We go way back. When did I ever kill a girl?"

Michael followed him to the front of the car. "It was your gun in her hand. It was your bullets. Your fingerprints were on both. Explain that to me, why don't you?"

"I had it in my car. I don't know how she got ahold of it. I told the police that. They had no right to go to my place and take all my pieces."

"A girl dies, and you're worried about your gun collection?"

"I didn't kill her!"

"Who did?"

"I don't know!"

"What were you doing on the roof porch when the gun went off?"

Kats's pride had been offended. He began to sulk. "I wasn't doing nothing."

"But you were on the second floor. Why did you take so long to get to the bedroom after the gun went off?"

"Why should I talk to you? I thought you were my friend. You're worse than the police." He let the hood slam, turned to walk away. "Get your own gas and get the hell out of here."

Michael grabbed Kats's arm, realizing he might have made a mistake with his hard-nosed tactics. Here he thought he was proceeding logically when deep inside he probably just wanted to find someone to blame. Michael realized he hadn't changed from the day of the funeral, not really. Kats shook loose, jumped back a step. "Lay off!" he snapped.

Michael raised his palms. "All right, you don't know anything. Neither do I. But you can still answer the question."

Kats fumed, debating whether to talk to him. Finally he said, "I didn't go straight to the room. I went into the backyard first."

"What? You jumped off the roof?"

"No, I didn't jump off the roof. I'm not that dumb."

"But why didn't we run into you going up the stairs?"

Kats shook his head impatiently. "I was out on the porch. I thought I saw someone in the backyard."

"Polly was the only one in the backyard."

"I didn't know that. I went to the edge of the roof to see who was there. That's when I saw Polly. She was running into the house."

"Yeah, after the shot," Michael said.

"That's what I'm talking about, after the shot. I saw her run through the back door. I figured someone must be after her. I kept looking for whoever fired the gun, but didn't see them."

"Go on."

"Then I went downstairs, and out into the backyard."

"What did you see?"

"I told you, I didn't see nothing."

"Then what are you talking about?"

"You asked me why it took me so long to get to the room and I've told you. I told the police the same thing and they kept me in jail for a week." Kats was disgusted. "I don't know what's wrong with all you people."

Kats must have still been searching the backyard from his vantage point on the second-story porch when they passed his door in the hall. But the main inconsistency in his explanation was so obvious Michael almost missed it. "Wait a second," he said. "We were downstairs, and we could tell where the shot came from. How come you couldn't?"

"Quit hassling me, would ya?"

"But you're supposed to be an expert when it comes to guns. Christ, you've practically slept with them since you were twelve. How could you make such a mistake?"

Kats paused, and he seemed honestly confused. "I don't know."

Could someone have shot Alice from outside?

It made no sense. The bullet couldn't have passed through the screens on the windows. Certainly, it couldn't have penetrated the walls without tearing out the plaster. And she'd had the gun in her hand. No, Kats was either lying or else he needed his hearing checked. There hadn't been anyone in the backyard except Polly. And even if there had been, even if, say, Clark had been somewhere in the bushes, he couldn't have gotten to Alice. The only way he could have put that bullet in her head was if he had been in that room with her. Now that was a possibility.

He paid Kats for the gas and left.

When Michael got home, his mom told him Jessica had called. She wanted him to call her the moment he came in. His heart sank. Something must have come up. Maybe she'd changed her mind. He hadn't realized how much he had been looking forward to being alone with her.

"Don't be so glum," his mother said when she saw his face. "It might be that she wants you to pick her up a half hour later."

"Did she say anything else?" he asked.

"Nothing about why she wanted you to call. But I talked to her a few minutes. She seems like a nice girl." His mother smiled. "She sounds like she likes you."

He blushed. She knew how to embarrass him when it came to girls—she just had to bring them up. She had been a hippie in the sixties and was still extremely liberal. He had to be the only guy at Tabb High whose own mother thought her son was a prude. "What gave you that idea?" he asked, very interested to know.

"The way she says your name," she said. "I notice she always calls you Michael, not Mike. Also, she went on about how smart you are. Of course, I told her you got all your brains from me."

"Take credit where credit's due." There was no mistaking they were related. They both had the same black hair, the same dark eyebrows and eyes. Neither of them had ever had to worry about their weight, and nature had given them exceptionally clear skin, although Michael occasionally wished—especially during the summer when he burned lobster red on the beach—they weren't so fair.

Their mannerisms, however, were quite different. His mom talked enthusiastically, using her hands a lot, while he normally kept his fingers clasped in most discussions and seldom raised his voice. She was a strong lady, although in the last couple of years or so, Michael had begun to feel her secretarial job—what with the traffic she had to fight commuting and the crap she had to put up with from her boss—had begun to take its toll. She always seemed tired, no matter how much she slept.

Yet today she positively glowed. She had on a light green dress and had curled her hair. Plus there was blood in her cheeks that gave her face a youthful sheen. "What is it?" she asked in response to his stare.

"Have you been exercising? You look—alive."

She laughed. "I'll take that as a compliment. But the only exercise I did today was to carry in the groceries." She nodded at her dress. "Do you like it? Daniel gave it to me. I'll be at his place this weekend. I'm leaving in a few minutes." She added mischievously, "You won't need to spring for a motel on your hot date."

He headed for his room and the phone. "I'd be happy to go to a movie with her."

"Mike?"

He paused, saw the sudden seriousness in her face. "What is it?"

"I'd like to talk to you about something."

"Can it wait a minute?"

She hesitated. "Sure. Call Jessie. I'll be here."

He had memorized Jessica's number when she had given it to him the second week of school. Before dialing, he sat on the edge of his bed and took a couple of deep breaths. Then he dived in. She answered quickly. He knew the date was off the instant he heard her voice.

"Hi, can you hold a sec?" she asked.

"Yeah." He listened to his heart pound while she went to another phone. It didn't sound like it was going to break, yet it ached, and suddenly it hit him again, how much he missed Alice. Those hugs she used to give him when she would sneak up on him— He closed his eyes, sat back in the bed, mad at himself. He was reacting like a child. Jessica came back on the line.

"I tried to get you earlier. I talked to your mom."

"Yeah, she told me."

"She's such a cool lady. I hope I didn't give her the impression I'm stupid. I'm not very good at talking to people on the phone that I've never met. I start rambling."

"She liked you."

"Really? That's good." She took a breath. "I suppose you're wondering why I called? Tonight, Michael, it's not good. Something's come up. I have to cancel on you."

"That's OK." Hey, the sun just blew up. That's OK. I can carry on as a collection of cooked carbon molecules. No problem.

But, Jessie, I need to see you. I need you.

"I'm free tomorrow," she said. "Would that be all right?"

He couldn't call his bosses and expect them to rearrange his schedule again. "No, I can't. I have to work."

"Can't you get off?"

"I wish I could."

"Oh, no." She sounded distressed. He began to feel a tiny bit better. "If I had known— Dammit. I'm sorry."

"Don't worry about it. Things come up. I understand." Since she wasn't volunteering what this *thing* was, he thought it prudent not to ask. "I heard the announcement at the varsity tree this afternoon. I was happy to hear your name called."

"Oh, you were there? I was looking for you."

When he had seen her talking to Bill Skater, he had decided he would save his congratulations for another time. "I want to wish you luck with the next vote. I think you'd make a wonderful queen."

"Thanks. How about next Friday?"

"We have our first league game then. I'll be playing."

"Then how about next Saturday? We could go out after the SAT test. We could compare answers! Come on, Michael, I'll need someone like you about then to help put my brains back together."

He had to work next Saturday evening as well. Yet that was a week away. He might be able to swing something with the boss's son. "That should be fine, but I'll have to double-check at the store."

"I'm *carving* you into my appointment book for next Saturday," she said. "If you don't show, I'm coming to your store to get you." She giggled. "How come you're always so understanding?"

"Don't be fooled, I have my days." The words were no sooner past his lips than he realized she was one of the few people who knew precisely what he meant. He hadn't intended to bring up the scene in Alice's studio, not again. He said quickly, "I'll let you go, Jessie. See you at school."

She paused. "Take care of yourself, Michael."

Her last remarks had soothed his feelings somewhat. But now he had absolutely nothing to do. He glanced out the window, at the clouds. They were heading west, toward the ocean. He dialed the weather service. They assured him there would be patches of visibility throughout the night in the desert. Good news. He hadn't seen the comet in weeks. If he could find it tonight, he would be able to construct a yardstick with which to plot its course.

Preparing to spend the night in the desert, he forgot all about his mom's asking to speak to him, not until she came into his bedroom. "What are you doing?" she asked.

"Cleaning my Barlow lens." He held the unusually long ocular up to the light, lens paper in his hand, searching for dust particles. "Use this with any eyepiece and you double its power."

"Are you going to the desert tonight? Is the date off?"

When he'd started his comet hunt, she used to wait up for him, worrying. So he'd taken her with him once, and hanging out with him beneath the stars on the wide empty dark sands, she'd come to realize he was safer outside the city than in his own bedroom.

"We're going out next Saturday." He shrugged. "It's cool."

"You're not upset?"

"I'm fine. What did you want to talk about?"

Her eyes never left his, not even to blink. "I'm pregnant."

He set down his lens. He heard himself speak. "And?"

"Daniel doesn't know. I'm going to tell him this weekend."

"And?"

"I don't know what he'll say." She glanced above his desk at a painting of a kindly mother polar bear feeding a bottle to a cute baby penguin. Clark hadn't completely spoiled Alice's artistic fun. It had been one of the last things she had done. His mother wasn't the type who cried easily, but as she looked at the painting he saw that her eyes were moist. "And this time, it doesn't matter what he says."

Michael smiled. "I always wanted a sister."

She laughed. "They're still making brothers, too, you know?"

"It will be a girl." He *knew* it would be.

"Who was that?" Bill Skater asked. Jessica whirled around. She had not heard him coming up the stairs.

"No one," she said. "A friend." She felt sick with guilt. When Bill had asked her out at lunch, she, in all the excitement, completely forgot about her date with Michael. And then later she had figured she could simply see Michael on Saturday night, no harm done. Naturally, being Ms. Free Time, she had conveniently overlooked the fact that he had other responsibilities. She shuddered to imagine what he must think of her. If she'd had any integrity at all, she would've called Bill and canceled the instant she remembered her original commitment.

But you didn't because you're as phony as that phony crown you're hoping to wear in two weeks.

"I thought I heard you say somebody's name," Bill said, stepping into her bedroom. He had on a turtleneck sweater the identical shade of blue as his eyes. And he had brought his body with him. What a stroke of good luck. She could practically *feel* it beneath his clothes, waiting for her. She honestly believed she was going to lose her vaunted virginity tonight.

That's why I forgot my date with Michael.

"Huh?" she asked.

"Were you talking to Michael Olson?"

"Do you know him?"

He nodded. "He's a far-out guy. Did you invite him along?"

"What? No." That was a weird question. She picked up her bag, knowing her glasses were not inside. She would have to listen hard during the movie and try to figure out what was going on that way. She smiled, offering him her arm. "I'm ready. Let's go."

Chapter Eleven

Aunty's dying, Polly thought. Sitting on the bed beside her, holding her dry, shriveled hand, watching her sunken chest wheeze wearily up and down, Polly wondered when it would be. Next week? Tonight? Now? She hoped it wasn't now. She didn't want to be there when it happened. She had seen enough family die.

"I'll go now and let you sleep," Polly said, moving to leave. Her aunt squeezed her hand, stopping her.

"Are you unhappy, Polly?" her aunt whispered, barely moving her lips. Since the heart attack, it was as if the nerves beneath her already lined face had gone permanently to sleep. Nowadays her expression never changed; it was always old, always waiting for the end, impatient for it even. Only her eyes, the same blue as Alice's, held any life. Whenever Polly entered the room, she felt those eyes on her. Polly, could you do this? Polly, I need that.

"I'm all right," Polly said. "Don't I look all right?"

"No." Her aunt shifted her head on the pillow so that they were face-to-face. Polly felt a momentary wave of nausea and had to lower her eyes. Aunty had lost so much weight, for an instant Polly imagined she was speaking to a skull. Yet, in a way, no matter whom she talked to lately, she felt that way. All that lay between youthful beauty and clean white bone was a thin layer of flesh, she thought, a thread of life. They were all going to die someday, someday soon.

"What's wrong, Polly?" Aunty asked.

"Nothing."

"Are you lonely?"

"Why would I be lonely? I have you to talk to. I talk to you all the time." She glanced at the clock. Twelve forty-five. Russ had been asleep in her bed upstairs since midnight. He had only stayed up for "Star Trek." She was beginning to hate that show. She had told him she had been to the family clinic and he had just grunted. He hadn't asked her why she had gone.

Her aunt tried to smile, her stiff cheeks practically cracking. "You've been very good to me, Polly. You're good to everyone. I remember how you used to watch over Alice." Aunty's eyes rolled toward the ceiling, going slightly out of focus. "Her first day at kindergarten, she didn't want anyone but you to walk to school with her. I remember driving the car slowly behind you. You were holding hands, wearing

bright-colored dresses. Yours was yellow, and Alice had on—"
She paused, trying to picture it. No matter how the conversation started, Aunty always went off on something that had happened years ago. "It was green. I bought them both in Beverly Hills, at a shop on Wilshire. Of course, you wouldn't remember."

"I remember," Polly said. "Why wouldn't I remember?"

Aunty coughed, raspy and dry. "You were hardly seven years old."

"So? I remember when I was two years old. And, anyway, Alice's dress wasn't green. It was red." She was suddenly angry, restless. If she didn't get out of the room now, she felt, she would never be able to get out. She would be trapped there for ever and ever, feeding Aunty, helping Aunty to the bathroom, wiping the spit from Aunty's pillowcase.

"You must miss her terribly. It must be so hard for you."

Polly leaned over and kissed the old lady, smelling her stale sticky breath. "I have you. I don't need anyone else." She brushed a hair from the woman's forehead, and it stuck to her fingers like a strand of steel wool. "Now get some sleep."

Polly had just sat down on the living-room couch when she heard the sound of the motorcycle roaring up the street. She hurried to the front door.

Clark had parked his bike beneath the tree at the end of the driveway. He waved as he walked up the long front lawn, his leather gloves in his hand, his red hair hanging over the shoulders of his black jacket. Polly glanced back inside the house, up the stairs. Russ sometimes snored. Loud.

She smiled. "Hi, Clark. What a pleasant surprise."

He nodded, stepping past her, putting his gloves in his back pocket. But the instant she closed the door, he whirled around, grabbing her, pressing his mouth hard against hers. She could taste his breath, feel it, clean and cold as the night air. She leaned into him, a warm thrill going through the length of her body. Then his finger dug into her lower back, caressing her roughly. She pushed him away, and his face darkened. For a moment she thought he would explode.

"What's the problem, Polly?"

She let go of him, stepped toward the living room. "You surprised me. I didn't know you were stopping by."

"I told you yesterday I'd come back."

"Oh, yeah." She gestured for him to have a seat on the sofa. "Can I get you something?"

He remained standing in the area between the kitchen and living room, near the stairs. "I want you."

She laughed nervously. "What do you want with me?"

He came toward her. "Let's go up to your bedroom."

"No, I can't."

He took hold of her arms. He was thin as a rail, but strong. "Why not? A few months ago you used to take off your clothes to tease me. You were dying for it." He squeezed tighter, moistening his lips with his tongue. "Tonight, Polly, I think you'll die if you don't get it."

"But that was modeling." She tried to shake loose and couldn't. "You're hurting me!"

He grinned, releasing her. "I'm very sorry." He turned and walked into the living room. There were red marks on her wrists, and she massaged them gently, following him. She hated it when he was like this, but couldn't really say she wanted him to leave. Aunty had been right; since Russ had gone to bed, she had been feeling terribly lonely. Clark went and stood by the sliding-glass door, staring out the back.

"What are you looking at?" she asked, coming up beside him.

"The dark. The past. Can you see it?"

"I don't understand."

"Alice's party. All the beautiful people in the pool."

She wished he wouldn't keep bringing up that night. She had thought about what he had said yesterday, as well as what Michael had said, and had decided they were both wrong. The evidence couldn't lie. Alice must have killed herself. "They weren't all beautiful," she said.

"Jessie, Maria, Clair—those three were here that night, and now they're princesses."

"Maria isn't that good-looking."

"But she's Jessie's friend."

"How did you know that?"

"You told me."

"No, I didn't."

He looked at her, along with his faint reflection—*two Clarks*—in the glass door. "Then how did I know?"

"I don't know."

"You can't remember?" he asked.

"I didn't say that."

He nodded, his eyes going back to the night. "Jessie meets Maria, and now she hardly talks to you anymore. Sara becomes president and she only calls you when she wants money. Isn't that true?"

"No. Jessie's my best friend. She called me tonight."

"Why? To brag to you? She's not your friend. None of them are." He raised his palm, touched the glass, almost touching his reflection. The line between them seemed so thin. "Think about it, Polly. If Jessie and Sara had not talked you into the party, your sister would be alive today."

It was a horrible thought, one she refused to consider for even an instant. But before she could tell him so, Russ bumped the wall with his elbow or leg or something in the upstairs bedroom. Clark turned at the sound. "What was that?" he asked.

"My aunt."

He paused, sniffed the air. "Her. She doesn't smell very pretty." He stepped toward the hall. "Where is she?"

"She's in bed, asleep." Polly went after him. "Please don't disturb her. She's not well."

He ignored her, going to her aunt's bedroom door, peering inside. She tried frantic gestures, tugging on his arm, but he refused to budge. He smiled big and wide. Watching her aunt unconscious and fighting for breath seemed to give him great pleasure. "What would you want if you were that old?" he asked.

"Shh," she whispered. "Nothing. I'd want to die."

"Why?"

"I wouldn't want to be sick like that."

"And ugly?"

"Yeah. Come on, shut the door."

"She's no different from you. Inside, she thinks the same way you would if you were inside her." He nodded toward her aunt. "She wants you to do it."

"Do what?"

"Take a pillow, put it over her ugly face, and hold it there."

"Are you mad? That would be murder."

"It would be a kindness."

"Stop it. She's all I have." Polly began to shake, her eyes watering. She could never do anything to hurt Aunty. She would sooner hurt herself. "I'm closing the door."

He let her. He began to put on his gloves, heading for the front door. She followed on his heels, confused. He always had that effect on her. "I'm going now," he said.

"But you just got here. I thought you wanted— Don't you want to see me?"

He grabbed a handful of her hair, tugged on it gently, then let it go. "I've seen you."

"I meant—"

"See you naked? That would be nice. Maybe next time."

"But what's wrong with tonight?"

"You pushed me away." He opened the door, looked at her a last time, his expression hard. "Push me away again, Polly, and I won't forget it. Not as long as you or your aunt lives."

He strode down the front lawn, jumped on his bike, and drove away. Frustrated, Polly went upstairs, took off all her clothes, and climbed into bed beside Russ. His snoring kept her up most of the night.

Looking at Bill, Jessica would never have thought he went in for foreign films. Yet he had taken her to a French movie, complete with subtitles, and she'd had a terrible time discussing it with him afterward over ice cream and pie. The screen had been a colorful blur, the music loud and deceptive. She'd thought it was a war movie, but the way Bill talked, apparently they'd seen a love story. He probably thought she couldn't read.

All that, however, was behind them. They were at his place, sitting together on the couch, his parents asleep upstairs, the lights down low, the last pause in their conversation stretching to the point where she was thinking, *If he doesn't take me into his arms soon, I'll scream.*

He brushed her shoulder. A start. She felt the warmth of

his touch all the way down in her toes. She honestly did. She was one big nerve. "You have a thread," he said, capturing the offensive little thing between his fingers, flipping it onto the floor, and returning his hand to his lap.

"This sweater draws them like a magnet," she said, smiling. She had been smiling all night. Her cheeks were beginning to get tired.

"Magnets only pick up metal, not material."

She laughed. "Very funny."

He frowned. "No, it's true."

She stopped laughing. "Yeah, you're right. My chemistry teacher talked about that in class." Either she didn't appreciate his sense of humor, or else—*it doesn't matter, he's still a babe,* she told herself—he didn't know he had one.

"I never took chemistry," he said.

"You didn't miss much. I have to study all the time. I got a C-minus on my last test." Actually, she had received a B-minus. For maybe the first time in her life, she wasn't worried about coming off as smart.

"You should get Michael Olson to help you. Did you know he wrote the textbook you use?"

The rumor—which Michael had already told her was false—was that he had written the lab manual. "Really? That's amazing."

"He's an amazing guy," Bill said. "When we were in seventh grade and took all those IQ tests, I remember they had to bring out a psychologist to retest him. He kept getting a perfect score."

"I didn't know you knew him that well?" She'd never seen Michael and Bill talking at school.

"We go way back." He looked at her, instead of at the wall he had been admiring for a while now. "How do you know him?"

"We—ah—share a locker."

"But Michael's in my locker hall."

"Yeah. He moved." Her guilt over standing Michael up had hardly begun to abate and talking about him was not helping. She wished Bill would start kissing her and get on with the evening.

He's probably shy. I'll have to make the first move.

She touched the arm of his blue sweater, letting her fingers slide over his biceps. "Do you work out now that football season is over?" she asked.

"No."

"You feel like you do. I mean, you feel strong."

He shifted his legs, recrossing them the other way. Then he scratched the arm she was supposedly stimulating. She took her hand away. It had worked in a movie she had seen. "The season only ended a couple of weeks ago," he said.

"Oh." Somehow, despite a shaky start, Bill had managed to remain the starting quarterback throughout the season. Tabb High had finished next to last in the league. "Are you going out for any other sport this year?" she asked.

"Track."

"That's neat. What are you going to do?"

"I haven't decided yet."

She twisted her body around so that she didn't have to turn her head to look at him, tucking her right leg beneath her left, her right knee pressing against the side of his hamstring. "I had a wonderful time tonight," she said.

"It's late. You must be tired. Would you like a cup of coffee, some tea?"

"No, thanks." She let her right arm rest on the top of the sofa, near the back of his neck. If she put her fingers through his hair, she thought, and he didn't respond, she would feel like a complete fool. "You have beautiful hair," she said.

"How about a Coke?"

"I'm not thirsty, Bill." She contemplated asking him to massage a tight spot in her shoulders, but decided that would be as subtle as asking him to undo his zipper. "That's a beautiful zipper you're wearing," she said.

He glanced down. "My zipper?"

I didn't say that! I cannot believe I said that!

"I mean, your belt, it's nice."

"It's too long for me."

"I thought the longer the better." Talk about Freudian slips. This was getting ridiculous. She leaned toward him, letting her hair hang over his left arm, smiled again. "I'm really glad you asked me out tonight. I've been hoping you would."

"I've been meaning to for a while. I've always thought you were a nice girl."

She giggled. "Oh, I'm not that nice."

"You're not?"

"I'm not exactly the person people think I am," she said, serious now, touching his arm near his wrist, drawing tiny circles with her finger. "Just as I don't think you're the person people think you are."

He sat up straight. "What do you mean?"

"That you're not just some super-great athlete. That you are a real person." As opposed to an *unreal* person? she had to ask herself. "I think the two of us have had to grow up faster than most people our age. I'm not saying that's a bad thing." She tapped his left hand. "It can be a good thing."

Her little speech was not leading him in the direction she planned. He began to grow distinctly uncomfortable. "What are you saying, we've had to grow up faster? Are you talking about what happened at the party?"

The question startled her. "No."

"I don't know what you heard about that night, but none of it's true."

"Wait. None of what's true?"

He stood suddenly, reaching a hand into his pocket. "I don't want to talk about it. I've had a nice time tonight, Jessie, and I don't want to spoil it." He pulled out his keys. "It's time both of us got to bed. Let me give you a ride home."

She didn't even have to fix her bra as she got up. She decided there must be something wrong with his parents' couch.

Bill dropped her off in front of her house. He didn't walk her to the door, nor did he give her a good-night kiss. When he was gone, she stared at the sky, feeling lonely and confused, and saw a bright red star. For no reason, she wondered what its name was. Had he been beside her, Michael would have been able to tell her.

To the inexperienced eye, the wisp of light in the center of the field of view of Michael's telescope would not have looked significant. Because it was so far from the sun, the comet's frozen nucleus had no tail to set it apart from the star field. It was its position—its changing position relative to the unchanging stars—that had initially caught Michael's attention. In time, it was possible it would develop a halo of gas to further distinguish it in the heavens, but he had no illusions about it sweeping past the sun and lighting up the earth's skies. Very few comets came in that close.

He now had an accurate reading on its position and course. The comet was definitely not listed in any astronomical tables he had access to. If no one else had discovered it in the last few months, it would be *his* comet.

Orion—Olson?

He was really going to have to think of a name for it.

And for my sister.

Michael recapped the telescope and took a stroll around the desert hilltop to warm his hands and feet. Although he could see little of his surroundings in the deep of the night, he sensed the serenity here, the silence. Yet perhaps he had brought a measure of contentment with him. He couldn't stop thinking about the baby. He had been surprised when his mother told him she was already three months along. Her due date was the end of June, a couple of weeks after graduation.

Michael had walked down to the base of the hill and was hiking back up to get ready to go home when a brilliant shooting star crossed the eastern sky. He was not superstitious, but he automatically made a wish. It was not for the health and happiness of his unborn sister, which would have been the case had he thought about it for a moment. Instead, he found, even in this peaceful place and time, a portion of his mind was still on that night two months ago.

He had wished for the name of Alice's murderer.

A few minutes later he was unscrewing the balancing weight on the telescope's equatorial mount when he noticed how bright Mars was. He had been so preoccupied with comet hunting, he had forgotten it was coming into opposition. Changing his ocular for one of higher power, he focused on the planet. No matter how many times he studied Mars, the richness of its red color always amazed him. No wonder the ancients had thought of it as the god of war.

Of blood.

The one time he had met Clark came back to Michael then, hard and clear. The guy's hair had been a dirty red, his eyes a bright green. He had spoken few words and what he said had not made much sense. Nevertheless, as Michael remembered, his heart began to pound.

"Where are you from?"

"Why?"

"I was just wondering, that's all. Do you go to school around here?"

"No."

"Where do you go?"

"The other side of town . . . Our team's as lousy as yours. But in our stadium, you can always lean your head back and look at the trees in the sky."

Trees in the sky. What could it mean? Michael didn't know, not yet.

Chapter Twelve

Holden High's gymnasium was older than Tabb's—pre-World War II. It desperately needed an overhaul. The lights flickered, the bleachers had begun to splinter, and the court had so many dead spots it actually seemed allergic to bouncing balls. Crouched in the corner beside the water fountain—exactly one week after her Friday-night date with Bill—her Nikon camera in hand, trying to get a picture of Nick as he leaped to rebound a missed shot, Jessica wondered if a major earthquake might not be the ideal solution for the building's many problems.

"The lighting in here makes everybody look a pasty yellow," she complained to Sara. "Even Nick."

"What difference does it make?" Sara asked. "They're all going to be completely out of focus. Where're your glasses?"

Nick passed the ball to The Rock, who walked with it.

Holden High took the ball out of bounds, going the other way. Jessica set down her camera, glanced at the scoreboard. Tabb 30, Holden 36. One minute and twenty seconds until halftime.

"I can't wear them now," Jessica hissed. "Half the school's here."

"They're watching the game, not you."

Jessica eyed the cheerleaders, bouncing and twirling in front of the stands. All except Clair, who was standing by the microphone leading the cheers. "A lot of them are watching Clair," she grumbled.

"And here I thought you were sacrificing your night out to take pictures for the school annual," Sara said. "You're only worried about getting equal time."

"Well, it's not fair. She gets to wear that miniskirt and flash her goods in front of everyone all night. The election's less than a week away— Wow!" Nick made another spectacular defensive rebound, tossing the ball off to one of Tabb's guards. Jessica positioned her camera to catch the breakaway lay-up. She got her shot. Unfortunately, the guard missed his. Holden rebounded and went back on the offensive.

"That guy's missed everything he's put up tonight," Jessica said. "I don't understand why the coach doesn't put Michael back in." During the first quarter, when Michael had played, she'd used up a whole roll of film on him. It was her intention to plaster him throughout the yearbook.

"That's Coach Sellers," Sara said. "He was the coach at Mesa, remember? I hear he used to coach boxing in a prison until the inmates beat the hell out of him one day."

Jessica needed a fresh roll of film, but decided to let the half play itself out. In the final minute, Holden scored twice more, leaving Tabb ten down. Jessica waved to Michael as the team headed for the locker room. His head down, obviously disgusted, he didn't wave back.

"He's going to hear about it if he hasn't already," Sara said as they walked toward the steps that led to the stands. The air was hot and humid. People poured off the bleachers, heading for the entrance and the refreshment stand.

"He didn't wave 'cause he didn't see me," Jessica said.

"But Bubba will tell him."

"And how will Bubba know I was out with Bill?"

Sara shook her head. "Bubba knows everything."

"Has he taken care of your bills?"

Anger entered Sara's voice. "He's put them off. We'll have food and music, but when homecoming's all over, we're still going to have to pay for it. I swear to God, I think he's already lost the money I gave him."

"You've got to give him a chance."

"Believe me, sister, I'm giving him more of a chance than you can imagine."

"What?"

"Never mind. When's the SAT tomorrow?"

Jessica groaned, feeling the butterflies growing. "It starts at nine."

"That's how it was for us."

Sara had taken the test two months before. She had not told Jessica her score. She was waiting, she said, to hear Jessica's score first. But Jessica had the impression Sara had done fairly well.

"Is Bill here?" Sara asked.

"I haven't seen him." Bill had avoided her all week at school. She wouldn't have felt so bad if it had been because he was feeling guilty for having taken advantage of her. She worried that she had come on too strong. "Is Russ?" she asked.

"No. And don't ask me where he is, I don't know."

Jessica snickered. "Doesn't Bubba know?"

Sara stopped in midstep. "I'll go ask him."

While Sara went searching for Tabb's sole omniscient resident, Jessica rejoined Polly and Maria in the stands. The three of them had come together. But one of the reasons Jessica had gone picture hunting—and Sara, damn her, *had* hit upon another of the reasons—was because Polly had insisted they sit in the middle of the second row, which was precisely three feet away from where Clair Hilrey and her amazing band of cheerleaders sat between cheers. Jessica liked to keep an eye on the competition, but she wasn't crazy about smelling the brand of shampoo Clair used.

At the moment, however, Clair wasn't around. Jessica

plopped down between Maria and Polly. "Enjoying the game?" she asked.

Polly nodded serenely. "I love it. It's not like football. You can always see where the ball is."

Jessica turned to Maria, who was fanning herself with her notebook. Maria had brought her homework to the game. Jessica thought that was why Maria was getting an A in chemistry while she was only getting a B. On the other hand, Maria had not known Nick was playing, and it looked now as though she hadn't been reviewing the methyl ethyl ethers section tonight.

"What do you think of Nick?" Jessica asked.

Maria appeared awed and sad—a strange combination. "He's very good. They should let him shoot the ball more."

"Michael passed it to him practically every trip down the floor." Jessica glanced in the direction the team had exited. An idea struck her. "Maria, you once told me what a Laker fan your father is?"

"He is, yes."

"Next week's game is at home. Bring him."

"My father would never come to a high-school game."

"But you may be crowned queen that night! Both your parents have to come."

Maria was worried. "It wouldn't make any difference."

"Sure it would. When they see what a tremendous athlete he is, they'll forget his color. Look, just think about it, OK?"

Maria nodded, already thoughtful. "I will."

Maria excused herself a few minutes later. She needed some fresh air, she said. The place was awfully stuffy. Jessica amused herself by listening in on the cheerleaders' gossip. Too bad they knew she was listening; they didn't say anything juicy. Clair hadn't returned yet.

Then Polly started to talk.

"I'm glad Clair's feeling better," she said casually.

Jessica paused. She had been unpacking her telephoto lens to use in the second half. "What was wrong with Clair?"

"I don't know, but last Friday she looked pretty sick."

Polly had not been at school last Friday, Jessica thought. "Where did you see her?" she asked carefully.

Polly sipped her Coke, yawned. These days, she lived on sugar and raw carrots. "At the family clinic."

Jessica set down the lens. The cheerleaders, the girls on either side of them—in fact, everyone around them—stopped talking. They were all listening. Jessica knew they were listening and she also knew that if she continued to question Polly she would probably hear things that could hurt Clair, things that could damage Clair's chance of being elected homecoming queen.

Jessica started to speak, but stopped. If Clair had a personal problem, she told herself, it was nobody's business but Clair's. At the same time, Jessica couldn't help remembering how gloomy Clair had appeared last Friday. She'd had something *big* on her mind. And then—what a coincidence—she'd been at the clinic, looking sick.

She had an abortion.

The thought hit Jessica with sharp certainty. She had not a shred of doubt she was right; she had no reason—not even for the sake of curiosity—to question Polly further. She had no excuse for what she did next—except for another idea that struck her with every bit of force as the first.

I am cute. Clair is beautiful. I don't stand a chance against her. I never did.

Jessica closed her eyes. "What were the two of you doing at the family clinic?" she asked in a normal tone of voice.

"I was getting birth control."

She opened her eyes. "*You?* For what?"

Polly appeared insulted. "I need it." She added, "Russ is staying at my house, you know."

Sara had gone to ask Bubba where Russ was, Jessica remembered. She silently prayed Bubba didn't know everything. "I see." She had to push herself to continue, although she could practically hear a tiny red devil dancing gleefully on top of her left shoulder. "But what was Clair doing there? You said she looked sick?"

"Yeah," Polly said. "I was waiting to get my contraceptives—so I won't get pregnant when I have sex with Russ Desmond—when Clair came out of the doctor's office. A nurse was holding her up. She looked totally stoned."

No one leaned visibly closer, but if they had stopped talking a moment ago, now they stopped breathing. "Like she had just had an operation?" Jessica asked.

"Yeah!" Polly exclaimed, the light finally dawning. "Hey, do you think Clair got—"

"Wait," Jessica interrupted. "Let's not talk about this now. We'll talk about it later."

What a hypocrite.

That was fine with Polly. Jessica listened as the shell of silence around them began to dissolve, being replaced by a circle of whispers that began to expand outward, growing in strength, in volume, and—so it seemed in Jessica's imagination—in detail. Then she saw Clair coming back, smiling, happy, pretty, ignorant.

The whispers would soon be a wave, a smothering wave.

The poor girl.

Jessica got up in a hurry, shaking, close to being sick. Grabbing her camera equipment, she dashed down the stairs, past Clair, pushing through the crowd until she was out in the cold night, away from the gym and the noise. Along a dark wing of the school, she ran into Sara, alone, leaning against a wall. Sara glanced up wearily, saw who it was, then let her head drop back against the brick.

"The world sucks," Sara said.

"It's true," Jessica said, leaning beside her.

"Bubba says Russ is staying at Polly's house."

"Good old Bubba."

Sara sniffed. "What's your problem?"

Jessica wiped away a bitter tear. Her victory now would be meaningless. "I'm going to be homecoming queen."

Then she realized Clair's unborn child must have belonged to Bill, and she felt ten times worse.

Michael had just figured out the fundamental problem he had with Coach Sellers. The man was totally incompetent. Yet he wasn't a bad person. He had just asked for their input, something Iron Fist Adams would never have done. Sitting on the concrete floor of Holden High's uniform cage with his teammates, halftime almost over, Michael raised his hand and requested permission to speak. The coach nodded.

"I think we need to make serious adjustments if we're going to win this game," Michael said. "As you've already mentioned, we have to block out more to stop their offensive rebounds. But that's only a symptom of our main problem."

"Oh?" Sellers said. Although only in his midforties, he was not a healthy man. He had a terrible case of liver spots on top of his balding scalp, and for some reason, which might have been connected to the slight egg shape of his head, his thick black-rimmed glasses were forever falling off his nose. He also had a tendency to shake whenever they had the ball—a quality that did not inspire confidence. "And what is our main problem?"

"We are not playing like a team," Michael said. "On offense, whoever has the ball only passes off when he can't put up a shot of his own."

"Aren't you exaggerating a bit, Olson?" Sellers asked.

"No. Everybody's trying to show off." Michael pointed at

The Rock, who was still red and panting from the first half. The Rock couldn't hit from two feet out, nor could he jump, but with his strength and bulk, he was able to maneuver into excellent rebounding position. "The Rock's a perfect example. In the second quarter, Rock, Nick was open a half-dozen times on the baseline when you had the ball, and you tried to drive through the key."

"I made a few baskets," The Rock protested.

Sellers consulted the stat sheet, nodded. "He's scored seven points so far. That's three more than you, Olson."

"But I didn't play the whole second quarter," Michael said, glancing at Nick, who sat silently in the corner, away from the rest of them, his head down. Nick had already pulled down a dozen rebounds, but had taken only three shots, making all three.

"Are you saying if I let you play more, we'd be a better team?" Sellers asked.

"To tell you the truth," Michael said, "I don't know *why* you took me out so early. But that's beside the point. We're too selfish. We have plenty of plays we can run. Why don't we run them? Why don't we help each other out on defense? We're down by ten points."

"I don't think a ten-point deficit is any reason to despair," Sellers said.

"Yeah," The Rock agreed. "Don't give up the ship, Mike. We'll come back. I'm just getting warmed up."

"That's the spirit," Coach Sellers said, smiling. Apparently that was the end of the discussion. He had them all stand and place their palms on top of one another and shout out some mindless chant. Then they filed out to return to the court. Except for Michael. Coach Sellers asked him to remain behind.

"You're a good kid, Mike," Sellers said when they were alone. The uniform cage stank of sweat. The coach removed his glasses and began to clean them with a handkerchief. "I understand that you're trying to help us."

"I am," Michael said.

The curtness of the reply took the coach somewhat back. "You may be trying, but I don't believe you are succeeding."

"Sir?"

Sellers replaced his glasses on his nose. "Let's be frank with each other. You think I'm a lousy coach, don't you?"

The question caught Michael by surprise. "No, I think you're inexperienced." He added, "That's not quite the same thing."

An uncharacteristic sternness entered Sellers's voice. "But if you don't feel I'm capable of coaching this team, how can you be on it?"

Michael considered a moment. He had mistaken Sellers for a kindly klutz. And here the bastard was threatening to drop him! "I'm the best guard you've got," he said flatly.

Sellers looked down, chuckled. "We like ourselves, don't we?"

Michael's pride flared. "Yes, sir, I do like the way I play. I put the team first. All right, I scored four points in the first quarter. Look how many assists I got. Six. Except for Nick, I'm the only one on this team who knows the meaning of the word *pass*, or even the word *dribble*."

"If you are so team-oriented, where were you last week when we had our final practice game?"

"I came to your office and told you I would not be at the game. You said that was fine."

"But you didn't say why you couldn't come?"

"I had personal business to attend to."

"What?"

"It was a private matter."

Sellers shook his head. "I'm afraid that's not good enough. You're a gutsy kid, Mike, I'll grant you that. But you're not a team person. You don't fit in. You're a loner. Basketball's not the most important thing to you right now."

The words struck home with Michael; there was a measure of truth in them. He'd always played basketball for fun, not out of passion. And now the games, along with practice, had become a drag. There really was no reason for him to stick around.

Nick will survive without me.

Still, Sellers had no right to can him. When he was angry, Michael knew how to be nasty. "I played in every game last year on a team that took the league title and went to the CIF semifinals. How did your team do last year, *coach*?"

Mesa High had finished last. Sellers tried to glare at him,

but lost his glasses instead. Fumbling for them on the floor, he stuttered, "I-if you think you're going to play in the second half, Olson, you have another thing coming."

Michael laughed. "Thanks, but I won't be in uniform in the second half."

The coach stalked off. Michael changed into his street clothes. He was tying his shoes when Bubba appeared.

"Are you injured?" Bubba asked.

"No. I'm no longer on the team."

Bubba didn't care to know the details. "Sellers is a fool." He sat beside him on the bench. "What kind of mood are you in?"

"I'm mad."

"Seriously?"

"No. What's up?"

"I've got some good news, and I've got some bad news."

"Give me the good news first so I can enjoy it."

"I went down to your coroner's office today. I told them my dad was a doctor who was thinking of computerizing his office. The chick there believed me. She demonstrated their system. She even left me alone for a minute to get me a cup of coffee. I took notes."

"You can get into Dr. Kawati's files?"

"Yes. I can do it from school over the modem. But it'll take a while. I'll probably have to dump the entire medical group's files onto one of our hard discs."

Michael was pleased. He'd asked Polly about the permission form again and had gotten nowhere. "Can we do it tomorrow?"

"Next week will be better for me."

Michael knew not to push Bubba. "All right. Thanks for checking it out. What's the bad news?"

"You won't like it. Girls—they're all sluts."

He groaned inside. "Jessie?"

Bubba nodded, disgusted. "She went out with Bill last Friday. That's why she canceled on you."

Michael tried to keep up a strong front. He didn't know if he succeeded. The situation was familiar, as was the pain. Yet neither was exactly as it had been before. When he was alone with the thought of Jessica she seemed endlessly charming, always brand-new and different, and perhaps for that reason, he always unprepared for the heartache she could bring. She could come at him from so many different angles.

Or else stay away.

Bubba excused himself to return to the gym. He'd heard about a rumor that needed tracking down. He didn't say what the rumor was.

Michael had not come on the team bus, but had driven to Holden High in his own car. That was one break, and breaks were in pretty short supply right then.

He was heading for the parking lot when he saw Jessica standing alone in the shadows of a classroom wing. He didn't want to talk to her. He didn't trust what he might say. Yet he did not feel angry with her. If anything, he wanted her more.

Then she saw him. "Michael?"

Trapped. "Hi. Jessie?"

She walked toward him slowly, looking small and frail beneath all her exotic photo equipment. He sure could have used one of those cameras to record his comet on film. But he'd already sent in the finder's application to an observatory.

"How come you're not playing?" she asked.

"Oh, the coach and I—we had a difference of opinion."

"You didn't quit the team, did you?"

"Not exactly."

She sounded upset. "But you won't be playing? That's terrible."

"There are worse things." He glanced around. They were alone. The crowd in the gym sounded miles away. "What are you doing out here all by yourself? You know this isn't the greatest neighborhood in the world."

Her gaze shifted toward the gym. He couldn't be sure in the poor light, but it seemed she had been crying. He hoped to God it hadn't been over Bill Skater. "I'll be all right." Then she looked at him, her eyes big and dark. "I'm really sorry about last Friday."

"It's no problem."

"I had no right to do that to you. It was totally inconsiderate of me." Her voice was shaky. "Can we still go out tomorrow?"

He smiled. Maybe Bill had left a sour taste in her mouth.

"You bet, right after the test." He had to work later that night.

A gust of wind swept by and Jessica pulled her jacket tighter. She gestured north, toward the dark shadow on the horizon. "If it's not too late, and it's a nice day, maybe we could go up to the mountains. What do you think? Michael?"

Holden High was approximately five miles south of the mountains. On a clear day, particularly during the winter when there was snow, the peaks were undoubtedly beautiful. Yet there were other campuses, possibly two or three in Southern California, that must be situated within a mile or two of the mountains. At those schools, the mountains would dominate the scene. And the forest trees . . .

Would seem to stand in the sky.

Chapter Thirteen

Dashing down the hall of Sanders High School to the SAT examination room with Michael, Jessica spotted a drinking fountain and stopped to pull a prescription bottle out of her purse. Removing a tiny yellow pill and tossing it in her mouth, she leaned over and gulped down a mouthful of water, feeling the pill slide home.

"Should I be seeing this?" Michael asked, perplexed. She laughed nervously.

"It's just a No-Doz. They're mostly caffeine. My dad always keeps a few in this old bottle for when he has to fly to Europe on business."

Michael looked at her closely. "Didn't you sleep?"

"I counted sheep, thousands of noisy sheep." She took hold of his arm. She was glad they would be together in the same room. She seemed to draw strength from him. She needed it.

She hadn't slept a minute all night. "Come on, we'll be late."

"Are you sure we're going the right way?" he asked.

"I'm positive."

When they reached the examination room, everybody was seated, and the proctor had already begun to explain the test rules. The woman hurried to meet them at the door. Michael presented the letters they had been sent a couple of weeks earlier. The proctor glanced at them, shook her head.

"You're in L-Sixteen," she said. "Go down this hall and take the first right. About a hundred feet and you'll see the door on your left. Hurry, they'll be starting."

Outside, jogging to the room and feeling properly chastised, Jessica said, "I hope they don't ask for the definition of *positive* on the verbal sections."

Michael smiled encouragingly. "You'll be fine."

This proctor wasn't explaining the rules. She had already finished with those, and was about to start the timer when they stumbled through the door. Jessica had only herself to blame for their tardiness. The night before she had made Michael promise he would wait for her in front of Sanders High. Naturally, on her way to Sanders, she had gotten lost. No matter, Michael was true to his word, and was sitting on the front steps when she finally pulled into the school lot. Everyone else had gone off to their respective examination rooms. She couldn't get over how cool he was about the whole thing.

This lady—a prune face if Jessica had ever seen one—was

all business. After scolding them for being late, she asked for their letters and identification. Satisfied everything was in order, she led them to a table at the rear, handing them each a test booklet and a computer answer sheet.

"Print your name, address, and booklet number on the side of the answer sheet," the woman said. "Use only our pencils and scratch paper." She nodded to Jessica. "You're going to have to find another place for that bag, miss, besides my tabletop."

Jessica put it on the floor. Michael sat to her right. There was no one between them, but with the wide spacing, she would have needed a giraffe's neck to cheat off him.

I haven't seen the first question and I'm already thinking about failing.

The proctor walked back to the front. "I didn't know she brought the goddamn tables from home," Jessica whispered to Michael. The lady whirled around.

"There's to be absolutely no talking. I thought I made that clear."

"Sorry," Jessica said. Michael laughed softly.

The lady pressed the button on top of the timer. Jessica took off her watch and lay it on the table beside her computer sheet. Six half-hour tests. Just like at home. No sweat. She flipped open the booklet.

Christ.

Her practice books had stated that the first third of each section would be easy, the middle third would be challenging, and the final third would be outright hard. She couldn't believe it when she got stuck on question number one.

1. WORDS : WRITER
(A) honor: thieves
(B) mortar : bricklayer
(C) chalk : teacher
(D) batter: baker
(E) laws : policeman

She was supposed to select the lettered pair that expressed a relationship closest to that expressed in the original pair. She quickly eliminated *A*, but then she had to think, which was never easy even when she was wide-awake and relaxed. Words were used by writers. Mortar was used by bricklayers. Teachers used chalk, bakers used batter, policemen used— No, policemen didn't exactly use laws. She eliminated *E*. Now what? Mortar and batter were crucial to bricklayers and bakers, but a teacher could teach without chalk. There went *C*.

Jessica swung back and forth between *B* and *D* before finally deciding on the latter. But she had no sooner blacked out *D* when she erased it in favor of *B*. Then she remembered a point in the practice books. If you were undecided over two choices, the authors had said, take your first hunch. She erased *B* and darkened *D* again.

She glanced at her watch. She had to answer forty-five

questions in thirty minutes. That gave her less than a minute a question, and she had already used up two minutes! She was behind!

I'm not going to make it. Stanford will never accept me.

Paradoxically, her panic brought her a mild sense of relief. She had been worried about freaking, and now that she had done it, she figured she didn't have to worry about it anymore. She plunged forward. The next question was easy, as was the third. Then the fourth had to start off with the word *parsimonious.* She skipped it altogether. Not even Michael could know what that word meant. Their proctor had probably made it up and typed it in out of spite.

In time, Jessica began to settle into a groove. She forgot about the rest of the room, even blocking out the fact that Michael was sitting close. But she could not say this tunnel vision was the result of a high state of concentration. On the contrary, she had settled *too* much. She couldn't stop yawning. Finishing the analogies and starting on the antonyms, she found she was fighting to stay awake. She couldn't wait for the break to take another caffeine pill.

It was good to be out in the fresh air again. The stress had been so thick inside, Michael thought, it had been as bad as a noxious gas. He understood why many kids, like Jessica, took the test seriously. Most name colleges, after all, demanded high SAT scores. But for him, it had been a piece of cake. He wouldn't be surprised if he had a perfect score so far.

The team got snuffed last night after you left," Bubba said.

"Serves the coach right after what he did," Jessica said.

"How did Nick do?" Michael asked.

The three of them were standing near Sanders High's closed snack bar. Bubba was taking the exam in another room. They had only a minute to talk. They still had two thirty-minute sections to complete.

"When our guys gave him the ball, he put it in the basket," Bubba said. "But that didn't happen much until it was too late."

"Nick will make his mark," Michael said confidently. "I'm surprised to see you here, Bubba. You say you're not going to college. Why are you taking the test?"

"For fun."

Jessica groaned, taking out her bottle of yellow pills and popping a couple with the help of a nearby drinking fountain. "I can think of a lot of other things I'd rather be doing this morning," she said.

"What are those, morning-after pills?" Bubba asked.

"Bubba," Michael said. Jessica didn't appear insulted.

"They're No-Doz," she said.

"Since when does No-Doz require a prescription?" Bubba asked.

"This is just a bottle my dad puts them in," Jessica said.

"Let me see it," Bubba said. Jessica handed it over. Bubba

studied the label. "Valium," he muttered. He opened the bottle, held a pill up to the light. "You've got the wrong bottle, sister. These *are* Valium."

Jessica snapped the bottle back. "That's impossible. I asked my mom which bottle to take and she said the one on top of the—" Jessica stopped to stifle a yawn. Then a look of pure panic crossed her face and she spilled the whole bottle of pills into her palm. "Oh, no," she whispered.

Bubba chuckled. "How many of those babies did you take?"

"Three altogether." She swallowed, turning to Michael, her eyes wide with fright. "What am I going to do?"

The hand bell signaling the end of the break rang. "You only took the last two a minute ago," Michael said. "Run to the bathroom. Make yourself throw up.

"Better hurry," Bubba said, enjoying himself. "They dissolve like sugar in water."

Michael took hold of Jessica's elbow. "There's a rest room around the corner. Go on, do it."

"I can't! I can never make myself throw up."

"You just haven't had a good enough reason," Bubba said.

"Shut up," Michael said. "It's easy, Jessie. Stick your finger down your throat. You won't be able to help but gag."

The bell rang again. Jessica began to tremble. "I don't have time," she said anxiously. "We have to get back. I might mess up my blouse."

"And I hear Stanford doesn't stand for messy blouses," Bubba said sympathetically, shaking his head.

"What is the normal dosage for those pills?" Michael asked.

"One," Jessica said miserably, close to tears. "I can't throw up, Michael. Even when I have the stomach flu, I can't."

"You've got to try," Michael said. "You're tired to begin with. If you don't get the drug out of your system, you'll fall asleep before you can finish the test. Go on, there's time. I'll wait for you."

Nodding weakly, she headed for the bathroom. Michael turned on Bubba. "Why are you hassling her at a time like this?" he demanded.

"She stood you up last week to go out with Bill and you're worried about her test score?" Bubba snorted. "Let me tell you something, Mike—and I say this as a friend—forget about Jessica Hart. She's not who you think she is. She doesn't care who she hurts."

"What's that supposed to mean?"

"Never mind. I've got to finish the test. If she passes out, be sure to give her a good-night kiss for me."

Michael didn't understand Bubba's hostility. Jessica's going out with Bill didn't explain it. In Bubba's personal philosophy, all was fair in love. Also, Bubba hurt people left and right, and always rationalized his actions by saying the people in question must have bad karma.

Michael decided to wait outside the test room. He wanted to keep an eye on the proctor should she restart the examination before Jessica returned.

He received a surprise when the lady came into the hallway to speak to him. "Are you the Michael Olson who won the work-study position at Jet Propulsion Laboratory last summer?" she asked.

"Yes, that's me."

She smiled, offered her hand. "I'm Mrs. Sullivan. My son is an engineer at JPL—Gary Sullivan. He spoke very highly of you."

Michael shook her hand. "Gary, yeah, I remember him. He was a neat guy. No matter how busy he was, he always took time to answer my questions. Say hello to him for me."

Mothers always loved him. Too bad he didn't have the same luck with their daughters. The lady promised to give Gary his regards.

Jessica reappeared a few seconds before they started on the next section. She didn't speak, just looked at him, her eyes half closed, and shook her head. He should have checked those blasted pills before she had swallowed them. From the beginning, he had wondered if they were really No-Doz. They went inside and sat down and started.

If 2X – 3 = 2, what is the value of X – .5?

(A) 2   (B) 2.5   (C) 3   (D) 4.5   (E) 5.5

On this section, they were allowed slightly more than a minute per question. Michael found he could solve most of them in ten seconds. *A* was obviously the answer to the first problem. He didn't even need his scratch paper. When he got to the end of the section, however, and glanced over at Jessica, he saw she had blanketed both sides of both her scratch papers with numbers and equations. He also noticed she had filled in only half the bubbles on her answer sheet. Her beautiful brown hair hung across her face as she bent over the test booklet. But every few seconds her head would jerk up.

She's hanging on by a thread.

The proctor called time. Jessica reached down and pulled a handkerchief from her bag, wiping her eyes.

"Jessie," he whispered. "Hang in there."

"I can't think," she moaned.

"No talking," the lady ordered.

They began again. Reading comprehension. Michael had to force himself to concentrate. The miniature essays from which they were supposed to gather the information necessary to answer the subsequent questions were distinctly uninteresting. Also, he was peeking over at Jessica every few seconds, worried she might suddenly lose consciousness and slump to the floor.

She's not going to get into Stanford with these test scores.

It was a pity she had waited until now to take the SAT. She would not have a chance to retake it in time to make the UC application deadlines. He really felt for her.

And what are you going to do about it?

Much to his surprise, Michael realized a portion of his mind was methodically analyzing the best way to slip her his answers. Of course he'd have to make a list of them on a piece of his scratch paper. The real question was how to get the paper into her hands without the proctor seeing. He did have a point in his favor. The lady obviously thought he was a fine, upstanding young man. Nevertheless, a diversion of sorts was called for, and the simpler the better.

It came to him a moment later. He immediately started to put it into effect. He faked a sneeze.

During the next fifteen minutes, while he polished off reading comprehension, Michael faked a dozen more sneezes. Then, after penciling in the final bubble, and without pausing a moment to recheck his work, he began to copy the answers. Yet he jotted down only those that dealt with the final two sections. This was his way, he knew, of rationalizing that he wasn't really helping her cheat.

What if you get caught? What if she doesn't even want your precious help?

He had an answer to that. At least he would have tried.

Carefully folding his list of answers into a tiny square, he closed his test booklet, collected his other papers, and stood. There were nine minutes left. The proctor had her eyes on him. She was smiling at how clever he was to be the first one done. He began to walk toward the front.

He was half a step past Jessica when he sneezed violently, dropping everything except his tiny square. "Excuse me," he apologized to the room as a whole as he turned and bent down. Jessica hardly seemed to notice his presence. Both her hands were situated on top of the table. He took his tiny square of scratch paper and crammed it between her tennis shoe and sock. Then he glanced up, and—it took her a moment—she glanced down. Their eyes made contact. Knocking on dreamland's door, she still had wit enough left to recognize his offer. She nodded slightly, almost imperceptibly.

When he handed in his stuff, the proctor proudly observed how he hadn't needed any of his scratch paper. Thankfully, she didn't observe that he was a page short.

"It was nice to have it handy, though," he said. "Just in case."

He waited for Jessica in the hallway. She came out with the group, ten minutes later, and immediately pulled him off to the side. Her big brown eyes were drowsy—he imagined that's how they would look if he were to wake up beside her after a night's sleep—and she was obviously wobbly on her feet, but she practically glowed.

"I would kiss you if I wasn't afraid my breath would put you to sleep," she said. "Thanks, Michael. You're my guardian angel."

"Did you have time to put down my answers?" His big chance for a kiss and he had to ask a practical question. She nodded.

"I had to erase a lot of mine, but I had time." She yawned. "How do you think you did? Or we did?"

He laughed. "Pretty good."

She laughed with him.

He didn't want her driving. She said they could still go to the mountains as they had planned, as long as she could crash in his car on the way up. Even though he protested that he should take her home, she insisted an hour nap was all she needed to get back on her feet.

On the way to the parking lot, she excused herself to use the bathroom. Michael had to go himself. He ran into Bubba combing his hair in the rest-room mirror.

"Did she conk out or what?" Bubba asked.

"She did just fine—thanks for your concern."

Bubba chuckled. "Hey, what's a few Valium before a little test? I made it once with a six-and-a-half-foot Las Vegas showgirl after chugging down an entire bottle of Dom Perignon. Talk about a handicap in a precarious situation. She could have broken my back and paralyzed me." He straightened his light orange sports coat. "So what did you think of the SAT?"

"A pushover."

"Really? I had to think on a couple of parts. I probably got the hardest test in the batch."

"I believe you," Michael said.

Bubba was pleased to hear his favorite line turned on him.

"I'm serious. I think the difficulty rating varies considerably between the tests."

Michael stopped—stopped dead. "What are you talking about? There's only one test."

"No. Didn't you hear what they said at the start? They use four different tests so you can't cheat off your neighbor."

I'm in a bathroom. This is a good place to be sick.

Michael dashed for the door, leaving Bubba talking to himself in the mirror. He had one hope. They had come in late. Perhaps the proctor had not taken the time to select two different exams.

The lady was sorting the booklets when he entered the room. "Forget something, Mike?" she asked pleasantly, glancing up.

He had to catch his breath. "No, it's not that. I was just wondering— My girlfriend and I, we're going to talk about the test on the drive home, and it would be nice to know if we were talking about the *same* test. If you know what I mean? He smiled his good-boy smile that mothers everywhere found irresistible. "I don't want to change any of my answers."

She laughed gaily at the mere suggestion of a scholar like him doing such a despicable thing. "I can check for you, of course. But I'm sure I wouldn't have given you the same series. What's your girlfriend's name?"

"Jessica Hart."

She flipped through the computer answer sheets, found

his first and set it aside, and then picked up Jessica's, placing the two together. "No, you were code A," she said. "Jessica was a C." She smiled. "Don't worry, you'll know your scores soon enough."

"How long?"

"Oh, with the district's new computer system, you could receive the results in the mail in about a month."

"Is there any way of finding out sooner?"

"You could call the test office. They might know the score as early as this coming Friday."

He thanked her for her time. Outside, he wandered around the campus like someone who had swallowed a whole bottle of Valium, the thought *I should have known* echoing in his brain like a stuck record.

When Jessica finally caught up with him, he was standing in the campus courtyard holding on to a thin leafless tree that felt like a huge number-two marking pencil in his hand. She looked so happy that he debated whether or not to give her the next few days to enjoy it. Unfortunately, he was too devastated to psych himself up for a good lie.

"Where did you go, silly?" she asked. "I've been searching all over for you." She grinned. "What's wrong?"

"We have a problem."

She put her hand to her mouth. "No."

He nodded sadly. "A big problem. Our tests, Jessie, they weren't the same."

"No, that's impossible. What does that mean?"

He spared her nothing. "It means you got a zero on the last two sections." He coughed dryly. "I'm sorry."

She stared at him for the longest imaginable moment. Then her face crumbled and her eyes clouded over. She began to cry.

This was another date they were never going to go on.

Chapter Fourteen

On the Thursday before homecoming, Nick Grutler stayed after practice to work on his free throws. In the game with Holden, he had been fouled every other time he'd gone to the basket. The free-throw line, only fifteen feet from the hoop, was well within his range; the problem was, he was supposed to stand relatively still while taking a foul shot, and he had trouble hitting even the backboard when he couldn't move.

Nick put up a hundred practice shots and made half—not bad, but not great, either. He finally decided that when he was sent to the line during the game, he would just pretend he was taking an ordinary jump shot, and not mind what the people in the crowd thought.

Another reason Nick had stayed after practice was because he didn't want to take his shower with the rest of the team.

When the coach was around, and they were working on plays, the guys treated him fair enough. But if Sellers was not present and The Rock—or the other two leftovers from the football team, Jason and Kirk—were in a bad mood, which they generally were, then he got razzed. If only Michael were around, Nick thought. The week before, when Michael had been coming to practice, no one had said so much as boo to him.

Putting away his basketball, Nick briefly wondered if it was all worth it. Here it was four o'clock, and he had to be at the warehouse by five to work an eight-hour shift, and he was already exhausted. Michael had told him he had to take the long view, but that was hard to do when he could barely see where he was going late at night while riding home on his bike. He couldn't see how all this was going to get him into college on a scholarship.

And he had thought being on the team would impress Maria. Yet as far as he knew, Maria didn't even go to basketball games. Even if she did, and he scored a hundred points every night, she wasn't going to talk to him. Why should she risk it? She was afraid he might kill her.

But that doesn't matter. None of that matters.

Maria's own words. They applied to his situation now. He had discovered something last Friday night during the game, the one thing that was giving him the strength to persevere. It had happened four minutes into the first quarter. Michael had passed the ball to him down in low. It had been the first time he had handled the ball on offense. He had two guys on him, and probably shouldn't have put it up. He just did it on impulse, without looking for anyone to pass to. He missed, but managed to get the rebound. Stuffing it home an instant later, hearing the roar of the crowd—roaring for *him*—he felt an intoxicating power flow through his limbs. It was then the realization hit him: he *loved* to play. And it was strange, in the midst of all the hoopla, in a very quiet way, he had felt at home on the court.

He was not going to quit.

Nor was he going to accept the situation lying down. The Rock was sitting on the bench tying his shoes when Nick entered the shower room.

Nick silently laughed when he saw how quick The Rock tried to finish with his shoes, how he put his head down and tried to disappear. It occurred to Nick that, since their first encounter in the weight room, they had never been alone together.

"Hi, Rocky," he said. "Waiting for me?"

The Rock's finger stuck in the lace. He was not so brave when he had no one at his back. "No," he mumbled.

"What?"

"No."

"That's what I thought you said. But I asked twice because, well, you're always asking me the same question twice. It can be annoying, can't it?"

"Yeah."

"What?"

"I said, yeah." The Rock gave up on his shoes, stood, and closed his locker. He started to step by. Nick blocked his way.

"I want to talk to you."

"About what?" He was scared, a bit, but still cocky.

"Sit down and I'll tell you."

The Rock thought about it a moment. Then he sat down. Nick remained standing, propping his foot on the locker at his back so that his knee stuck out close to The Rock's face.

"I never thought," Nick began, "that we would ever work together on anything, so I never cared why you despised me. But now we're on the same team, and I don't want it to be a losing team. I don't think you do, either. What do you say?"

The Rock grunted, uninterested.

"What does that mean?"

"Go to hell, Grutler." The Rock started to stand up. Nick grabbed him by the collar. The Rock's eyes widened. Gently but firmly, Nick sat him back down.

"Now I've put it politely," Nick said, still holding him by the neck of his shirt. "But you're being rude. And that makes me mad. And the last time I got mad at you, I almost killed you. I'm asking you again, are you going to lay off me or am I going to have to finish what I started two months ago?"

Now The Rock was really afraid, and more arrogant than ever. "You would kill me, wouldn't you?"

"I just might."

The Rock sneered. "And you've got the nerve to ask why I hate your guts? Scum like you doesn't give a damn about anybody."

Because The Rock had jumped him twice for absolutely no reason, Nick found his response hard to fathom. He didn't know how to answer. He let go of him and backed off a step. "Are you serious?" he asked finally.

The Rock rubbed at his tender throat, not taking his eyes off Nick now. "You know what I'm talking about," he said bitterly.

"I don't."

"Get off it, Grutler."

"I swear, I don't. Tell me."

"You're a pusher."

Nick couldn't help but laugh. "You think I sell drugs? Man, you are one misinformed slob. I don't even smoke pot. Who told you I'm a pusher?"

The Rock was not impressed with his denial. "I know the neighborhood you come from. I work there as a Big Brother. Before you showed up here, I used to see you at a crack house on a corner. No one had to tell me nothing about you. And none of your lies is going to keep me from wanting to spit in your face."

Nick stopped laughing and went through a five-second period of total confusion. The Rock a Big Brother to black kids? The corner crack house? But then, in a single flash, he understood *everything*. He pointed a finger at The Rock. "You stay here. I'm going to get dressed and then we're going for a drive in your car."

"To where?"

"My old neighborhood."

"Why?" The Rock asked.

"You'll see when we get there."

Nick dressed quickly. It was half past four. It would be dark soon. He would be late to work. If Stanley was at *his* work, however, it would be worth it to clear up this case of mistaken identity.

The Rock had a blue four-wheel-drive truck. Nick gave him directions. Getting on the freeway, they listened to the radio, and hardly spoke. The Rock drove like a goddamn maniac.

They ended up on dumpy narrow streets Nick knew all too well. The sun had said good night. They could wait a long time for the broken streetlights to come on. Nick could feel the darkness inside as well as out. Yet he did so from a rather detached perspective. He had grown up in this neighborhood, but he did not feel as though he had ever belonged in this slum. He didn't know anyone who did.

"Park here," he said, turning off the music. "Under that tree." The Rock did so. Nick glanced back up the street toward the house on the corner. "Is that the place you saw me?"

The Rock twisted his head around, nodded. "There's no use denying it, Grutler."

Nick pulled out his wallet and removed a twenty-dollar bill. He gave it to The Rock. "Go to the house and knock on the door," he said.

The Rock fingered the bill. "What's this for?"

"To keep you from getting knifed." Nick smiled at the alarm on The Rock's face. "Don't worry, they'll be as afraid of you as you are of them. They'll think you're with the cops. They won't want to sell you anything. But ask for Stanley. Say you're an old buddy. Be sure to say Stanley, not Stan. Have the bill out where they can see it."

"What am I supposed to say to this Stanley?"

"Whatever you want, except don't mention my name. You're not afraid, are you?"

The Rock scowled at him, put the keys in his pocket. "You wait here," he said, reaching for the door. He had a hard time getting out. He was shaking.

Nick readjusted the rearview mirror, following The Rock's slow nervous walk toward the house. A stab of guilt touched him. He tried to rationalize that Stanley would not purposely create a messy situation that, could not possibly profit him. On the other hand, Stanley might be bored and just looking for something to piss him off.

That moron had better have the sense to know when to run.

The plain white house had two qualities that distinguished

it from the others on the block. It had no bushes or trees in the yard, not even grass. And the front door was split in half at the waist. They could open the top and look at you, but you couldn't go barging in. It was so obviously a drug den, Nick didn't know why the police hadn't bombed the place.

Nick suddenly wished The Rock had left him the keys or, better yet, had left the car running. They might want to make a quick getaway. He watched The Rock lumber up the porch. He was fifty yards away at this point, and Nick could see the twenty trembling in his clenched fingers. He was going to say something stupid; it was practically a foregone conclusion. Nick leaned over and pulled the wiring from beneath the dashboard. He had known how to hot-wire a car since he was twelve.

When he had the truck running and looked back up, The Rock was at the door talking to someone. Nick couldn't see who the person inside was, but he appeared to be a young black kid with a shaved head.

Dammit!

The Rock was arguing with the boy, obviously throwing his weight around. The kid disappeared, and The Rock glanced toward the truck and smiled. It was the smile—arrogant, as usual—that pushed the red alarm inside Nick. Cursing himself for trusting the imbecile not to alienate the neighborhood in a minute's time, he jumped into the driver's seat and put the truck in gear.

He had turned the truck around and was approaching the house when he saw a long black arm thrust out and grab The Rock by the throat.

The Rock tried to scream. A strangled whimper was all he got out. Nick remembered how strong Stanley was. The long black arm shook The Rock, pulling him off the ground and closer to the door. Nick floored the gas, then slammed on the brakes, jumping out onto the street in front of the house. He needed something, anything to distract Stanley for a second. Nick couldn't quite see his old enemy, but he didn't have to. The Rock was toppling into the door like prime surfer beef into the maw of a shark.

Nick spotted a Coke bottle in the gutter. The top had been cracked off, and Nick briefly wondered as he scooped it out of the dust if the last person to hold it had used it to keep someone with a knife at bay.

There was a narrow window to the right of the front door. Winding up, Nick let go with a wicked pitch. Glass shattered glass. The long arm snapped back inside. The Rock crashed to the porch floor.

"Get in the truck!" Nick yelled, leaping into the driver's seat again. The Rock had never moved so fast on either the football field or the basketball court. Although starting from flat on his ass, he was diving into the back of the truck even as the tall black dude appeared on the porch. Nick revved first gear, leaving a trail of burnt rubber. One look at Stanley had been enough to remind him why he had gone down on his knees and thanked God the day his dad had moved him to the other side of town.

If I look half as scary as that bastard when I'm mad, no wonder people are afraid of me.

The Rock started banging on the rear windshield so Nick would stop and let him in, but Nick left him in the howling wind all the way home on the freeway. It did his heart good to see The Rock go from shaking with fear to shivering with cold. Besides, he was having a great time driving the truck.

The school parking lot was deserted when Nick finally brought the pickup to a halt, turning off the, engine. He half expected The Rock to leap out of the back and start cursing. Instead, the guy got up and opened the truck door for him.

"You drive like a goddamn maniac," The Rock said. "How did you start the truck without the keys?"

"A pusher's trade secret," Nick said, climbing down.

"Oh, that." The Rock turned away. "You've got to admit, he did look a lot like you."

"The only things Stanley and I have in common are that we are both tall and we are both black."

"Then how did you know I was talking about him?"

"Cops have mistaken me for him in the past. White cops. Now, I guess, you're going to tell me we all look alike to you."

"I wasn't going to say that." Finally The Rock was beginning to show signs of shame, faint signs. Sticking his fat hands in his pockets, he shifted uneasily on his feet. "I suppose I owe you an apology."

"Especially if you lost my twenty dollars."

The Rock glanced up, pulled out the money. "I held on to it. He didn't scare me that bad."

Nick chuckled as he accepted the money. "Then do you have a bladder infection or something?"

The Rock started to speak, then quickly removed his hands from his soggy pockets. He had peed his pants. "He was a crazy dude. He could have cut my throat. Why did you send me to the door?"

"I just wanted you to see him. I didn't expect you to make him reach for his switchblade. What did you say to him?"

"I said I was a friend of yours."

Nick groaned. "I told you not to bring me up. You're lucky to be alive."

"Why? What did you do to him?"

Nick sighed. The truth of the matter was, he *had* been irresponsible taking The Rock to that house. Stanley was bad news. It was upsetting to Nick to remember exactly how bad, to remember how Tommy had died. It was weird; they had been such close friends for such a long time and now he hardly ever thought of Tommy. The last time had been . . .

When Alice had died.

No, it had been *before* Alice died, minutes before, when he had gone into that last bedroom on the left. What had been in that room that reminded him of Tommy? The only thing Alice had in common with Tommy was that they'd both died violent deaths.

"It's a long story," Nick said finally. "Can I ask you something?"

The Rock shrugged. "Sure."

"The night of Alice's party—you told the police you came back to the house to thank Mike for saving your eyes. Is that true?"

"No. I came back to kick the crap out of you."

"Why didn't you?" Nick already knew one reason. The Rock had chickened out when he had discovered all his buddies were gone.

"My eyes started to burn again. I didn't totally trust what the doctor at the hospital had said. I thought I might go blind. I jumped in the shower to wash them out some more."

"You really were in the shower when Alice was killed?"

"Yeah. Anyway, I heard she killed herself."

Nick had never been able to understand Michael's conviction that Alice had been murdered. The facts spoke for themselves, and no one had been closer to the facts than Nick. But now, the more he thought of Tommy . . .

There is something connecting those two deaths.

He would have to talk to Michael about the sense of déjà vu he'd had in that dark bedroom. And he'd better tell him the truth about how he hadn't run straightaway to the bedroom—

as he had told the police—but had dashed down the stairs first. All of a sudden, Nick had the uneasy feeling these things might be important.

"I heard she killed herself, too," Nick said finally. "But I changed the subject. You were starting to apologize?"

The Rock shifted on his feet again. "I'm sorry. What else can I say? I thought you had come here to mess up everyone's mind. You can see why I was always on your case, can't you?"

"But you jumped me without any proof I was selling drugs?"

"I told you, I thought I saw you at that crack house." He added, somewhat embarrassed, "I did try to get proof."

"It was you who set that narc, Randy Meisser, after me?"

"You know about him?"

Nick nodded, checked his watch. "Hey, I've got to get to work. You give me a ride and I'll think about accepting your apology. I'll have to put my bike in the back."

"It's a deal." The Rock offered his hand. "No hard feelings, Nick?"

Nick hesitated. "Are you really a Big Brother?"

"I am."

"What's your real name?"

"Theodore."

Nick laughed, shook his head. "God help those kids."

Chapter Fifteen

Sara started her car as she saw Russ jog down Polly's long driveway and turn onto the deserted sidewalk. She let the engine idle for a minute while he headed away from her.

He is living with Polly. I should run him over.

She was cold. She was tired. She had been sitting in her car in the dark for over an hour waiting for Russ to appear, thinking of the way Bubba was brushing her off every time she demanded an update on the money she had given him, fretting over whether the homecoming tent was going to collapse and smother the whole school, and remembering the good old days when she'd had only herself to worry about. She had been a different person then. She had been happy.

No, I wasn't happy. I was bored out of my mind.

Which had been a lot more fun, she decided, than being

downright miserable. She flipped on her headlights and put the car in drive, rolling after Russ.

CIF is in two days, Saturday morning. He won't run far.

Nor, did it seem, was he going to run very fast. She followed him for two miles, out of the housing tract and on to a path that circled the park across the street from the school. He never broke his leisurely jog. He also gave no sign that he knew she was following him. But when he made a sudden U-turn and began to head back toward Polly's house, she momentarily panicked and put her foot on the gas, racing past him. She probably would have kept going if he hadn't waved. Slamming on the brakes, she pulled over to the side of the road and got out. His breath came out white as he walked toward her.

"Have you been following me?" he asked.

"No." She wished more than anything else in the universe that she didn't feel this way when she was with him, that she didn't need him. "Yes," she said. "Aren't you going to say 'Hi, Sara'?"

He wiped the sweat from his face with the arm of his shirt. "Hi, Sara."

"Hi, Russ. How are you?"

"Fine. How are you?"

"I feel like an idiot. How did you know I was following you?"

"I don't go into a coma when I'm running." He came up beside her, gestured to the unlit park, the silent rolling grass hills. "It's late," he said.

"I remember you told me you liked to run late at night."

"Yeah, it's cooler. And you don't have to run into people."

"Not as cool as a freezer, though," she said. He tried to brush off her remark, but she spoke quickly. "I'm sorry I locked you in there. I didn't mean to. I mean, I meant to, but I didn't know you'd have such a hard time getting out." She reached for her car door. "That's all I wanted to say."

"Where are you going?" he asked, surprised.

"You don't like to run into people." She opened the car door. "That's what you just said."

"I wasn't talking about you. Hey, don't go." He closed the door, touching her hand in the process. "Come on, Sara, let's not fight."

She couldn't look at him, not when he was living with one of her best friends and sending that friend out to buy contraceptives in public clinics. "I just don't want to bother you," she said.

He put his hand on her arm. "You're not bothering me."

"I'm not?"

"No."

She whirled on him, throwing off his hand. "Well, you're bothering me! You got yourself fired. You've stopped coming to school. You've got this big race you've got to win if you're going to do anything with yourself. And you're—"

"I'm just sleeping there, that's all," he interrupted.

"Did I say anything? Did I say a word about you having sex

with Polly and the whole school talking about it when they're not talking about Clair's abortion?"

"Clair had an abortion?"

"Yeah, and it wouldn't surprise me if you're the one who got her pregnant!"

He scratched his head, confused. "There you go yelling at me again when I'm trying to be nice to you."

"I'm not yelling at you!" she yelled. Then she stopped. "Why are you trying to be nice to me?"

"I don't know. I guess I like you."

"You don't like me."

He was beginning to get annoyed. "All right, I don't like you."

"I know you don't. Why did you say that you do?"

Russ sighed, sat down on the curb. "Never mind."

She sat beside him, studying his face for a full minute. He looked about as miserable as she felt, but it gave her no satisfaction. A chilly damp layer of air began to creep toward them from the dark park. "You're going to catch cold," she said.

"I don't care."

"I care."

"What do you care about?"

"That you're going to get cold." She hesitated. "And I care about you, you know?"

"No, you don't."

It was her turn to be annoyed. "Are you calling me a liar?"

"No."

"Then what are you doing?"

He rested his head in his hands. "I think I'm beginning to get a headache."

"Oh, swell, thanks a lot. Sorry I had to be born and mess up your evening." She started to get up. He stopped her.

"Would you please quit doing that?"

She brushed off his hand but kept her place beside him on the curb. Her butt was beginning to freeze. "I'm not doing anything. I tell you I care about you and you don't believe me."

"Well, I told you I like you and you don't believe me."

Sara paused. "You're right." Then she smiled. "Do you really like me?"

"No."

She pushed him. "Yes, you do! You're crazy about me. You're just afraid to admit it."

He laughed. "I wouldn't go that far. Stop pushing me!" He grabbed her hands, pinning them together, hard; impressing upon her again how strong he was. Then their eyes met. She didn't think she had ever looked him straight in the eye before. They were dark, intense. They even scared her, a bit. Still holding on to her, he leaned over and kissed her on the lips. She kissed him back.

Oh, my.

He wasn't cold at all. No one had ever kissed her before.

A minute later—or maybe longer, her sense of time went

straight to hell the instant they had made contact—he pulled back.

"What's the matter?" she asked, opening her eyes with a start. She couldn't remember closing them. Nor could she remember him releasing her hands and wrapping his arm around her shoulders. Like his mouth, it, too, felt warm.

"Nothing. I can't kiss you all night. You're new at this, aren't you?"

"No. Why do you say that?" She had a rush of anxiety. "Am I a lousy kisser?"

"Fair."

She started to shove him again. But when he started to stop her, she let him. Unfortunately, he didn't pin her hands or kiss her again. He just stared at her, and she found herself blushing.

"What are you thinking?" she asked finally.

"About something you said."

"What?"

"That I'm a drunk," he said.

"I didn't mean—"

"No, you're right." He took back his arm, rested his elbows on his thighs, his head hanging down. Even in the dark, she could see the gooseflesh forming on his legs. She should let him go, or give him a ride home, back to Polly's house. "I've got to quit the beer," he said.

She nodded. "I wish you would. You'd run a lot faster. The race is Saturday, isn't it?"

"Yeah."

He had kissed her, she thought, her next question shouldn't be hard to ask. Yet it was. "Do you want me to come?"

He glanced up. "Do you want to?"

She spoke carefully. "Will I be the only one there?"

He shook his head, serious. "I'm only staying with Polly because I have nowhere else to stay."

"That's not what she says."

"Then she's crazy."

Sara couldn't argue with that. "Yeah, but she's also my friend. And she just lost her sister." The mention of Alice made her pause. She had all these problems, and somehow, they all seemed connected to that night.

When Alice was alive, it was easy to be tough.

Suddenly she was close to crying. It was true, what people said about how when someone close to you died, a part of you also died. Two months ago she would simply have told Bubba to take a hike. She would never have lost the money in the first place. She wiped at her eyes, fighting for control.

"What's wrong?" he asked.

"Nothing. Yeah, I want to come. I'll be there." She shoved him in the side. "You'd better win."

Chapter Sixteen

The following afternoon, Friday, Jessica left school at lunch to go home. She had called the SAT test office in the morning looking for her scores. When they told her they would have to search for the information, she had asked them to call back and leave the scores on her answering machine. Naturally, she was anxious to check the machine's tape. The big event of the day was over, anyway. Voting for homecoming queen had taken place during fourth period. She had intended to vote for Maria but, at the last minute, had checked the box beside her own name. Clair hadn't been in all week and the gossip going around about her was vicious; nevertheless, Jessica did not want to lose by one vote.

At home, Jessica found both her test score and Clair. She did not, however, notice her rival until after she had run upstairs and listened to the bad news on her answering machine.

"Jessica Hart," a brisk-voiced lady said. "This is Jill Stewart at the test office. Your scores are as follows: Three hundred and seventy on the verbal section, and three hundred and twenty on the math section. If you have any further questions, please feel free to call me back."

Sixteen hundred total was a perfect score. If you got less than four hundred on either the math or verbal section, your counselor usually recommended a community college with a strong tutorial program. Jessica trudged back downstairs and outside and plopped down on the front-porch steps. She thought of all the Stanford yearbooks she had browsed through while growing up. Her father was going to kill her.

"Bad news?" a voice asked. Jessica looked up and stood quickly. Dressed in old, faded blue jeans, and a plain red blouse, not wearing a speck of makeup, Clair strolled up the walkway.

"Clair, you surprised me. How did you know I'd be here?"

"Bubba told me." Clair stopped at a distance of approximately ten feet, gave the house a cursory inspection, then focused on Jessica, her blue eyes cold. "He told me a few things. All about your filthy mouth."

She swallowed. "What?"

"Don't deny it. You started the rumor about me having an abortion."

"That's not true. All I know is what Polly told me."

"Polly nothing. You made her talk. You did it because you're afraid of me. You're afraid I'll beat you out for homecoming queen, and that I'll take Bill away from you." Clair took a big step closer. "But like I told you before, dearie. I can't lose. And as far as Bill is concerned, you can have him. For all the good he'll do you."

Jessica shook her head weakly, as weak as her lies. "I don't know what you're talking about."

Clair drew closer still, pointing a long nail at her face. "When I first met you with Mike, I thought you had class. I thought we could become friends. Now I'm glad I kept my distance. I hope Mike does the same." She flicked her nail at the end of Jessica's nose, scratching it. "You'll get what you deserve, bitch."

Clair turned then, leaving, and Jessica went inside and collapsed on the couch. It was hard to remember when she had felt worse.

"Alice, where are you?" she moaned to the ceiling. Her little friend had always looked up to her, and perhaps because of that, she had always striven to do what she knew was right. Now that Alice was gone it seemed she didn't care who she stepped on.

Oh, I care. But I do it, anyway.

That morning Bill had asked her to the homecoming dance, and she had said yes. Although talk continued to fly about how he had knocked Clair up, he appeared unaffected by it. Indeed, he hadn't even gone to the trouble of denying it, which confused her; she had recently learned from Polly that it had been Bubba, and not Bill, who had picked Clair up at the clinic.

Once upon a time, Bill's asking her to the dance would have meant everything. And she had agreed to go with him because he still had a body that wouldn't quit. But she was no longer infatuated with him. He virtually had no personality, she finally realized. More important, she was interested in someone else.

She was in love with Michael Olson.

When he had told her about the different tests, and in one stroke shattered her lifelong plans, she wanted to die. What she had done instead was sit in the shade of a tree at the back of the Sanders campus. Afraid to leave her in her fragile condition, Michael had sat with her. With the realization that she wasn't going anywhere special after graduation, the Valium had begun to sock it to her. Lying on the grass, Michael sitting quietly at her side, she had wandered in and out of consciousness for what had seemed ages. But each time she had resurfaced, she opened her eyes to find Michael still waiting for her, sometimes writing in a notebook, other times just staring up into the sky. And each time he had looked different to her, as if she were seeing him through different eyes. Each time he had looked more beautiful, more perfect. Each time she had awakened hoping to find his fingers stroking her hair, or catch his eyes fixed on her face.

But he was just being the way he is, kind. I can't expect anything from him.

She kept taking advantage of him. Surely by now he must know why she had stood him up. Bubba knew everything, and Bubba must have told him. Yet he had treated her nicely all week, repeatedly apologizing for giving her the wrong answers on the test, wishing her well on the homecoming queen vote, apparently oblivious to the self-serving gossip floating around that she had set in motion. He had treated her as Alice always had, as if she were special.

Not for the first time, Jessica wondered what he really thought of her. She would have given almost anything to know.

The mountains owned half the sky. Had the school been any closer to the slopes, it would have had to have been built perpendicular to the ground. Temple High was his best bet and, for that reason, Michael had saved it for the last. Parking in front of the administration building, he climbed out of his car and headed up the steps.

The receptionist-secretary was young and Hawaiian, with braided black hair and a dazzling set of teeth that made Michael think of South Pacific islands and warm green swells. It had been cold the past night and, from the forecast, would be colder still the next night for their outdoor homecoming dance. He hadn't made up his mind whether he'd go or not. All week he had been trying to psych himself up to ask Jessica. With the SAT fiasco, though, he felt the timing would be lousy. On the other hand, she had given no indication she had a date. Bubba hadn't heard anything about Bill having asked her, and that probably meant she needed an escort. Maybe he could give her a call, work the conversation around to the dance, and see what happened.

"Can I help you?" the young lady asked, wheeling her swivel chair back from her typewriter.

"Yes, I'd like to buy a copy of your yearbook." He had learned at the previous two schools he had visited that people would immediately get suspicious if he asked for a list of all the students named Clark. That's confidential information, they would say, and where are you from, and all that jive. All he needed was a picture with a name.

"The due date of ordering yearbooks was last month," she said.

"A copy of last year's yearbook would be fine." He had the lie ready. "You see, I don't actually go here. I'm on the yearbook staff at another school. I'm doing format research for our annual." He spoke sincerely. "I've heard Temple's got one of the best yearbooks in Southern California."

Never underestimate the power of school pride. The lady smiled at the compliment and immediately went looking for a book. When she returned a few minutes later with the annual in hand, and he asked what the charge would be, she said it was a complimentary copy. He thanked her and hurried to his car.

Twenty minutes later, after a thorough search of the senior, junior, and sophomore classes, he slammed the book shut in disgust. There wasn't a single Clark in the whole school, much less one with ugly red hair and green cat eyes. Tossing the yearbook onto the passenger seat, he rolled down the window and stared at the mountains. Far above, on a high-altitude breeze, the matchstick trees swayed in the hard blue sky.

He must have been stoned. He must have been rambling.

Michael had a couple of hours before he had to go to work. He wasn't sure what to do next. His mom had said she would be getting off work early that day, and he debated swinging by the house to see how she was doing. She had told her boyfriend, Daniel, about the baby, and the man was excited. Yet he hadn't proposed, not yet. He needed to digest the news, he said. Michael could understand that. He was still digesting the idea of having a dad. At least there was no chance of the baby telling him what he could and couldn't do. His mom appeared to be taking everything in stride.

Not making any progress proving Alice had been murdered had frustrated him. He decided to go by the school and check with Bubba on the coroner's files.

When he arrived back at Tabb, sixth period was over and the campus was almost deserted. Crossing the courtyard, he caught a glimpse between the buildings of the huge tent being erected for the dance on the practice basketball courts. It looked like Sara had been talking to a circus.

He didn't enter the computer room from the outside, but

through the central utility room that connected all the science classes. Just before opening the door, however, he overheard Bubba talking to Clair. Because it was Bubba, and because Bubba had more power than any teenager had a right to, Michael felt it was his moral responsibility to eavesdrop. He put his ear to the door.

"I can't do it," Bubba was saying. "It'll be too obvious."

"Obvious to who?" Clair demanded.

"Mike for one. He knows what I can do. And he likes Jessie."

"Would he talk?"

"He might. And even though the votes haven't been tabulated, the word around town has you way off the mark. If you suddenly won, it could get ugly."

"For who? You?"

"As a matter of fact, yes."

Clair growled. "You're always bragging about your ability to get anything you want. And here I ask you one tiny favor and you say no. I'm sick of it, Bubba. I tell you, I won't stand on that stage and see her crowned."

"I know."

"You know? Then do something about it!"

"I can't."

There was a long pause. Michael could readily imagine the expression on Clair's face and was glad it was not glaring down on him. "You think of something," she said finally, soft and deadly. "Or *I'll* think of something."

Bubba did not respond, or did not have a chance to. Michael listened as Clair stalked out of the room, slamming the door in the process. He waited a respectable length of time before entering. Bubba glanced up from his terminal.

"Hi, Mike. Did you discover Clark Kent's secret identity?"

Michael shook his head, sat down. "The more I chase this guy, the more I think he must be some kind of superman to disappear the way he has." He nodded toward the screen. Bubba was presently in an administrative file he had no right to be in. It could very well be the file where the votes for the homecoming queen had been stored. "What are you working on?" he asked.

"Nothing important." Bubba turned off the screen, thoughtful. "Going to the dance tomorrow?"

"I'd like to see how Nick does in the game. I don't know, I might hang around afterward. Sara's got the price for the dance down to five bucks."

"I don't know how she does it."

"Still no word on Bill asking Jessie?"

"It just came in. Bill nabbed her this morning after political science. The slut was flattered."

"Don't call her that."

"Sorry. A slip of the tongue."

Michael decided he wasn't going to the dance after all. He couldn't bear the thought of watching them moving hand in hand across the floor. He should have asked her himself! He honestly thought she might have said yes. Even though he had messed her up on the SAT test, she hadn't directed one word of blame at him. She had style.

Even when unconscious.

He remembered sitting beside her while she slept off the effect of the drugs, her shiny brown hair spread over her tucked-in arm, her lips pursed like those of a dreaming child, her long, thick eyelashes flickering slightly as her chest slowly rose and fell. If he hadn't fallen completely in love with her before, he had toppled the final distance that afternoon. He had been tempted to kiss her while she slept.

Then he thought of Alice. He always thought of Alice whenever Jessica appeared to be slipping further from his grasp. It was as if he substituted a fresh pain for one locked in memory, some kind of perverted reflex.

"When are you going to try for the autopsy report?" he asked.

"Tomorrow. But I warn you, it'll take a while to copy all the medical group's files over the school modem, twelve hours minimum. That's going to cost a couple of hundred at least."

"I'll pay it. Can you start it in the morning?"

"For you, Mike, anything."

"Thanks." Michael almost made him promise to leave Jessica as homecoming queen if she had been elected to the position. He couldn't believe she had anything to do with the slanderous gossip going around about Clair. But it wouldn't do to hassle Bubba, he decided, until he had that report in his hand. And he remembered Bubba's words to Clair, that nothing could be done to change the outcome of the vote and he was reassured.

Chapter Seventeen

T hat night, the night before the dance and the ruin of a
princess, Polly returned to her big house to find a message from Tony Foulton on her answering machine and a note
from Russ taped to the mirror in her downstairs bathroom.
She had stopped at the hospital after school to check on Philip
Bart—the foreman who had gotten knocked on the head during
the dynamite blast—and was late getting home. Poor Phil, initially he'd made good progress, but he'd lapsed back into a coma
the previous night, and now the doctors were saying he wasn't
going to make it. Polly had run into his wife in the intensive-care
waiting room and the woman had depressed the hell out of her,
crying and carrying on.

But everyone's got to die, sooner or later.

Polly got to Tony's message first, playing it while she
grabbed a carrot from the refrigerator.

"Polly, this is Tony. Just called to let you know the float will be ready tomorrow morning if you want to swing by the plant for a final inspection before we tow it to the school. I'll be at home this evening if you want to reach me."

Then she discovered the note.

> Polly,
> I've found a new place to stay. Thanks for the hospitality. I won't forget it.
> Russ

A tidal wave of emotion began to rush over Polly, and then, as if the wave had suddenly run into a mountain of granite, there was nothing. She stood holding the note in one hand, the carrot in the other, staring at her reflection in the mirror and thinking about absolutely nothing for an indeterminate length of time. During this time, she wasn't the least bit mad or the least bit depressed. She simply wasn't there. Even when she began to think again, she didn't feel much of anything, except an abrupt, intense hunger.

She blinked at her reflection. She hardly recognized herself. She was much too skinny. No wonder Russ hadn't wanted to have sex with her!

Throwing both the carrot and the note into the toilet and flushing them out of existence, she hurried back to the kitchen. There was a two-pound box of chocolates in the cupboard above the refrigerator that some bleeding soul had given her after Alice's funeral. Love and chocolate, she'd once read, were practically interchangeable from a hormonal point of view.

Polly found the box and began to eat, one candy after another. They were truffles: raspberry, strawberry, mint, all her favorite flavors. She couldn't believe how hungry she was! She finished off the top layer and started on the bottom, checking the time. It was late, but maybe a shop would be open, and she could get another box.

"These are good, these are wonderful," she said out loud to herself. "These are just what the doctor ordered. And a little drink. When you eat candies you have to drink, Polly, or the sugar will make you thirsty. Yes, Mommy, I remember. Where is a glass? Here is a glass. Now let me get you a little drink, Pretty Polly."

Polly did get down a glass and did grab a can of Pepsi from the cupboard beneath the sink. But then she thought of the paper cups she had told Alice to fetch from her parents' closet the night of the party. She looked down at her can of Pepsi, also thinking of how soda should always be drunk out of a paper cup and not a real glass, because then it tasted like you were at a party. Then you could pretend the party wasn't really over.

Setting down the glass and the box of chocolates, Polly ran up the stairs and dashed to her parents' old bedroom, where Alice had died. She flipped the switch, but of course the light didn't go on because it was still broken. She didn't care. She didn't need it. She just wanted the cups! Those stupid paper cups. And she knew where they were. She remembered exactly where her mommy had put them. At the top of the closet. And here was Mr. Ladder, behind Mr. Door.

Polly had set up the ladder in the dark room beside the closet and was on the third step going on the fourth when the black figure came up at her back and shoved her hard in the rear, sending her toppling toward the hard wooden floor. For an instant, caught completely by surprise, she didn't throw out her hands to brace her fall. Actually, it seemed far longer than an instant; it seemed as if she fell forever, and had all the time in the world to decide how she wanted to hit the floor, which angle would cause her the least harm. For some reason, the fact she had the opportunity to decide made her furious.

In the end she did throw out her hands, her wrists absorbing the brunt—but not all—of the impact. Her right ankle took a nasty bang. Pain shot up her leg and she let out a cry.

"What is this supposed to be?" Clark demanded, towering over her, a shadow, except for the yellow hall light filtering through his messy red hair. In his hands was Russ's note, torn and dripping wet. For a moment, Polly had the horrible idea that Clark had been hiding deep inside the toilet when she had come home, waiting for her beneath the house with the worms and slimy things in the black smelly pipes. Then she realized the carrot and the paper must have gotten tangled together, and not flushed properly. He had never been one to knock. He must have entered through the garage and gone straight to the bathroom, and found the evidence.

"He's just a friend who stayed here a few days," she cried.

"You're a liar. You've been unfaithful to me."

"No!"

"You've been sleeping with him." He crouched down beside her, grabbing her shirt at the neck. "Now I know why you pushed me away last time. You'd already had your fill."

"He's just a friend," she said, weeping. She could feel his breath, cold and damp, on the side of her face. The pain in her ankle was making her nauseated. She feared at any second he would step on it with his hard black boot.

He paused, his fury momentarily frozen on his face, then he appeared to relax a notch. He leaned forward, draping the dripping letter over her face. "Tell me the truth, Polly," he said softly, tightening his grip on her shirt. "And I will set you free."

"I told you." The water spilt over her eyes, around her nose. It stank.

"Don't tell me, and I will break your ankle."

Polly stopped fighting him. He was serious. "I slept with him," she said quietly.

"Honestly?"

"I swear." It was the truth, the literal truth. It didn't matter that Russ had never been awake to begin with.

"I believe you. Do you want me to set you free?"

"Yes."

"Very good." Clark let go of her shirt, lifted the veil from her eyes. "I can forgive anything, except dishonesty," he said, the anger gone from his face.

"I'm sorry," she whimpered, wiping the gook off her face and rubbing her ankle; it felt as if it might already be broken. "I won't do it again."

"I know you won't." He stood, not offering her a hand, and stepped to the east-facing windows. She was surprised to see they were open, the shades up. She thought she had pulled them down. Clark took a breath of the cold air coming through the screens. "Do you know what will happen if you do?" he asked.

"You'll leave me?"

He turned, his face serious. "I can never do that. If I leave you, I die."

Despite her pain, she smiled. "You don't care that much about me, do you?" she asked hopefully.

"That's not what I said."

"What do you mean?"

He nodded, as if she had answered a question and not asked one, turning back toward the outside, pointing a long bony finger at a damaged wooden shingle a few feet beyond the window. "That's what I will do to you," he said.

She lost her smile. "I don't know what you're talking about."

"You see it, don't you?"

"See what? You're not making any sense." Suddenly it wasn't her ankle that was hurting, but her head—a thick pressure was building inside. "Never mind, I said I won't do it again."

He lowered his finger and almost instantly her head began to feel better. "How is your foot?" he asked in an offhand fashion.

"It's fine," she lied, before remembering what he had said about honesty. "It hurts." Now it was her turn to be angry. "Why did you push me off the ladder?"

"I didn't push you. You slipped." He grinned. "You won't be able to dance tomorrow. You have the perfect excuse." He took a step toward her. "Jessie and Sara will be at the dance, won't they? They'll be on the stage—up there beneath the lights while you'll still be laying here on the floor in the dark. Do you know why that is, Polly?"

"No," she said, defiant. She wished he would help her up, and she wished he wouldn't talk this way. Yet, at the same time, she felt an obligation to listen. Clark had a certain perspective on things that most people didn't have. She supposed that was one of the reasons she liked him.

"It's because of what's in this room," he said, lowering his voice, standing over her again, the windows at his back. "What's *inside* it." He shut his eyes briefly, and it seemed to Polly he was suddenly uneasy; he trembled slightly, and his breathing was heavy. When he opened his eyes again, he was staring, not at her, but at the spot on the floor near the windows where they had found Alice. He added, "What's inside for now. It could escape."

"Clark?"

He dropped his head back and looked at the ceiling, and then stared again at the spot on the floor. Polly couldn't be sure, but it seemed he was mentally drawing a line from high above to far below. "Your aunt's asleep beneath us," he said finally.

"So?"

He tapped the floor with the heel of his right boot. "What's beneath us feels solid. People always think that way. The fools! The ground can drop out from beneath you at any moment, and leave you falling forever. Nothing's real." He nodded toward the floor, and Polly thought she could see the stains in the wood, even though she knew they had been washed away long ago. "Drops of her blood seeped through the floor," he said. "They escaped."

"No."

"Yes. Alice's dead blood. The drops seeped through the wood and dirt, and now one of them has finally landed on your aunt's face, on her lips." He wiped the back of his hand across his nose and glanced down at her. "Do you know what that means?"

She was afraid she might. "She's not going to die!"

"But she is. She's going to smother to death on Alice's blood." He moved toward the door, past her. Desperate, Polly reached out and grabbed his leg.

"No! *You're* going to smother her!"

He regarded her with calm indifference as she clung to his smooth black boot. "It has to be done. Let me go and I can do it now, and it will be over. I'll use a soft pillow."

Holding on to his leg, Polly tried to get up, to put weight on her foot. She screamed in agony when it gave out beneath her. She fell to her knees, her head banging against his knee. Any moment she expected him to shake her off. Yet he continued to stand above her, at ease, watching her crawl at his feet.

"You can't do this to me," she said, weeping. "I'll be alone in this house. There'll be no one to talk to. They'll all be gone. Leave Polly. Who cares about Polly? Please don't do it. I don't mind taking care of her. I really don't, I swear."

"But she won't let you live until she's dead. Besides, she smells." He shook his leg. "Let go, Polly, and I'll set you free of her like I promised."

"No!" she pleaded, tightening her grip, her tears smearing the leather hide of his pants leg. "No promises! Nothing! You don't have to do anything for me! I can do it myself!"

She hadn't meant to say that.

Clark began to chuckle, soft and steady. Reaching down and undoing her grasp, he helped her to her feet, setting her against a wall where she hobbled on one foot. "All right," he said.

She stopped her crying. "All right, what?"

"All right, it's your show."

She didn't like the sound of that. "No."

He nodded, smiling. "Keep your promise, Polly, or I'll be back to keep it for you."

Then he was gone, down the stairs and out of her sight. It seemed like a long time to her before the front door opened, but then she definitely heard him leaving; his motorcycle starting, its motor fading into the distance.

Bastard. Alice was right about him.

Polly crawled downstairs—moaning the whole way—straight to her aunt's bedroom. With relief bordering on hysteria, she found the lady snoring peacefully, undisturbed by all the commotion, her face clean and old.

Only later did Polly discover the message from Tony Foulton on her answering machine had been replayed.

That night there was a lightning storm, and Polly slept poorly, and had a bad dream that went on until dawn. An ax was chopping somewhere above her bed, cutting holes into the ceiling, narrow splintered holes from which drops of fresh red blood dripped into her open mouth.

Chapter Eighteen

A strong wind was blowing off the nearby gray ocean as Sara helped Russ out of his sweats minutes before the start of the Four-A CIF Championship Cross-Country Race. The storm was over, but a few scattered clouds were hanging around, and the grass beneath their feet was still soggy. It would take a few days to dry out before it would qualify as a halfway decent running surface.

They were standing on the high point of the course, a hill located near the center of Hill Park, a place that more than deserved its name. The spot afforded an excellent view of most of the three-mile course. A gold trail of chalk wound near each corner of the park, under trees and along horse paths crowded with spectators. To Sara, scanning the route, it seemed Russ would be running uphill more than downhill. But since the finish line was right next to the starting line, she decided that must be impossible.

"How do you feel?" she asked, folding his sweats and draping them over her left arm.

"You just asked me that," Russ said, spreading his legs and stretching. He had incredible hamstrings, simply incredible.

"What did you say?"

"I feel all right."

"Your back's OK?" she asked.

"Why would my back hurt?"

"The mattress in the guest room is worse than a leaky waterbed," she said. The mere reminder of the fact he was now living at her house—with her parents' reluctant and soon to be revoked consent—made her embryonic ulcer take another big step toward adulthood. She couldn't understand how he could stay so cool. Then again, he hadn't been awake most of the night setting up for the dance.

Where was Jessie when I really needed her?

There was a ton of preparations left to complete.

"My back's OK," he said.

"How about your feet? Never mind, we can't go through your whole body. As long as you feel strong."

"I feel strong."

"That's all I want to know."

Tabb's cross-country coach, and a number of Russ's teammates, came over to wish Russ well. The team as a whole had not qualified for the finals. Russ would be the only one from the school running.

The announcer called out that there were five minutes to the gun. The colorful collection of athletes began to converge on the starting line. Sara followed Russ as he left his teammates and coach behind and made his way through the crowd. Having won his semifinal last week on a different course, Russ had a low number and was given a position at the privileged front of the pack.

"There're so many people to beat," she said, getting depressed.

"There're only three," Russ said. "I know who they are. They know who I am. You'll see them at the finish." He turned, stopping her from following him farther, smiling at her gloom. "You'll see me in front of them."

She chewed on her lip. "I hope so." Poor words to inspire a man going into battle. She could do better. "I mean, I know you'll beat them." She wanted to give him a send-off hug, but was afraid she would accidentally knee him or something stupid like that. She just stood there feeling dumb and nervous while he completed a few last-second stretches. "Well," she said finally, "good luck."

He glanced up as the announcer gave the one-minute warning. "You know what I would like more than anything right now?"

A kiss from sweet Sara.

"What?" she asked.

"A beer."

"Swell," she muttered, turning away in disgust. He stood straight and grabbed her by the shoulders before she could leave. "Wait, Sara. But I'm not going to have one even if I do win. You know what I'm saying?"

"That you don't like beer anymore?" Behind him, beyond the assembled runners, the starter was giving out final instructions. She suddenly had the horrible thought that they would be off without him. "Hey, you better get going."

"I'm saying that you're more important to me."

"That's good, that's great, but they're really getting ready to go," she said, hardly hearing him, shooing him toward the start. Hadn't she done something like this two centuries ago when he had collided with her the first week of school? Why was he comparing her to beer?

"Sara, you're not listening to me," he complained.

"Everybody get ready!" the starter shouted out.

"Russ!" she cried.

He waved his hand indifferently. "That guy always gets everybody set then spends a couple of minutes loading his gun. I have time."

She would just as soon he didn't count on the guy's past habits. "Time for what?" she asked.

Now he was disgusted. "Never mind."

"Well, this really isn't a time to talk. What did you say?"

"Do you want to go to the dance with me tonight?"

Her heart skipped. "Only if you win."

"What if I don't?"

"Then you're out of luck." She leaned over and kissed him quickly on the lips. "Go. Run. Win." She shoved him in the chest. "Now!"

He went, slowly making his way through the runners. But he knew his starters. It was another couple of minutes before the gun finally sounded and the herd stampeded forward. Sara retreated to the spot at the top of the hill. The clouds flew overhead, chased by the wind. She watched as Russ let a quarter of the runners pass him. She was shaking like a leaf.

He warned me he likes to start slow and build momentum.

Nevertheless, it was disconcerting to see so many people in front of him. His buddies on the team had brought a pair of binoculars and they passed them on to her. The mile marker was in the low south corner of the park, close to the choppy sea. Watching through the binoculars, Sara estimated three dozen guys reached it before Russ did. She wished he would begin to make his move soon.

He did, finally, although at first it was almost imperceptible. The midway point was marked by a yellow flag near the entrance to the park. The runners were about half a mile from Sara as they went by it, and this time—she was monopolizing the binoculars, but no one seemed to mind—she counted only two dozen guys in front of Russ.

Faster.

Between the midpoint and the two-mile mark he really

began to turn it on. Heading into the last mile, turning back toward the starting line—and the finish line—he had drawn even with the leaders, a pack of three kids. Sara could actually see their expressions in the binoculars. Each one looked determined to win. But she hesitated to check Russ's face, afraid she would find him whistling to himself.

Pounding into the far end of the valley that lay beneath the hill upon which she stood, Russ accelerated sharply, drawing away from the others.

"Go!" she yelled.

Ten yards, fifteen yards, twenty yards—his lead grew almost as if by magic. Sara was beside herself with excitement. She forgot about being ASB president, about homecoming, about being cool. She started to cheer like a maniac.

"Russ!"

Coming up the hill, running right past her, he twisted his head around and looked at her. His breathing was labored and his red brow dripped with sweat. He smiled, anyway.

Then he slipped on the wet grass, and went down.

"Get up!" she screamed, leaping forward to help him. He had only fallen to his knees, and because he had been coming up the steep hill, his speed had not been that great. He was all right. He brushed off her hands and was on his way again before his lead disintegrated altogether.

He won by ten yards. Sara had about ten seconds to savor the victory before learning he had been disqualified. The coach told her while Russ was recovering in the chute.

"What?" she cried. "What did he do wrong? This isn't gymnastics! Since when do they take off points for slipping?"

The coach's disappointment was obvious. "He wasn't disqualified for slipping, but for receiving outside help during the course of the race."

She was aghast. "Outside help? You're not talking about *me*?"

"I'm afraid so, Sara," he said sympathetically.

"But I didn't help him. If anything, I just got in his way. Where's the race director? We have to talk to him."

The coach stopped her. "It will do no good."

"But it wasn't his fault that I helped him!"

"It doesn't matter. Because Russ won by such a narrow margin, he might have lost if you hadn't helped him. Disqualification is therefore automatic." The coach glanced toward Russ, who had begun to catch his breath. He was shaking the hand of the fellow behind him in the chute. "It's a real shame," the coach said. "He ran a brilliant race."

Sara's voice cracked. "Does he know?"

"He knows."

This is not fair. This is not right. This is not happening.

Sara was afraid to go near Russ. The coach was being cool, but Russ's teammates were looking at her and shaking their heads. Russ would probably want to rip her head off. Had the positions been reversed, she would have wanted blood. She didn't know what to do. She wished she could simply leave, but they had come in the same car. She decided to go to the car, anyway. Maybe he would think she had left or forget she existed and get another ride.

To where? He's staying at my house!

She was as furious as she was hurt. Once inside her car, his sweats lying across her lap, she began to pound the steering wheel with her fists. She still couldn't believe how strict they were. You'd think she'd given him an injection of speed or steroids or something! If they'd covered the course with plastic before it rained, he wouldn't have slipped in the first place. It was all their fault. She was going to write a nasty letter to somebody. She was the president of the school. She was going to . . .

"Hey, I need my sweats," Russ said, standing outside the car door. She jumped in her seat, smacking her head on the ceiling. "It's cold out here."

Keeping her eyes fixed on the ground, Sara slowly got out of the car and gave him his sweats. She stared at his feet while he put them on. There was mud on the bottom of his shoes, and no doubt it would mess up her car, but she wasn't going to ask him to scrape it off if he still wanted to ride home with her. She was afraid she was going to start crying.

"Hey, aren't you going to congratulate me?" he asked.

She glanced up and was surprised to discover he looked very much as he had before the start of the race; a little more tired perhaps, and certainly more sweaty, but far from devastated. "But you lost," she mumbled. "I got you disqualified."

He waved away the remark as he had waved away her concerns about the starter. "Everybody knows I won, I just don't get the trophy. Big deal. This way we don't have to wait around for the award ceremony. Come on, let's go to that McDonald's we ate at when we went out that night. I'm starving."

"You're crazy," she said, her voice incredulous.

He frowned. "What's wrong with McDonald's? They use the same hamburger a fancy restaurant does. They just don't charge you an arm and a leg. You know what your problem is, Sara? You don't know how to find a bargain. Take that can of Spam you bought— Hey, what are you laughing at?"

"You!" she burst out. "You idiot!"

He scratched his head, his frown deepening. "If I'm such an idiot, how come I know how to save money using coupons?"

Sara had to catch her breath to speak. Although from the outside she appeared in much better spirits than a minute ago, she was still upset. "Russ, that's not what I'm talking about. Because of me, you're not the champion. It's not going to go in the records that you won today. College coaches across the country won't know you won. It won't even go down that you placed."

"So?"

"So you probably won't get offered a scholarship."

"Who cares?"

"I care! I care about your future. That you have one. Russ, we're not going to be in high school for the rest of our lives."

He didn't answer right away, but leaned against the car instead, looking out to the sea. The sea gulls were having a great time in the wind, soaring hundreds of feet into the air on powerful updrafts and then diving down at breathtaking speeds to within inches of the choppy water. Russ reached out his arm and hugged her to his side.

"I don't run to win scholarships," he said seriously. "I run because it makes me feel alive. School doesn't do that for me. School isn't where I belong. Sure, I'll graduate and everything, but that's it."

"But don't you want to get ahead?"

"I can get ahead without a fancy diploma." He glanced toward the hill from where she had watched the race. "When I broke away from the pack, I felt something. I felt powerful, like I could do anything." He squeezed her shoulder. "Remember what you said when we were fighting in the store freezer? That I could be in the Olympics? Well, Sara, I think you were right."

She chuckled, not sure what to think, brushing his hair out of his eyes. "You idiot," she repeated quietly. Then she wrinkled her nose. "McDonald's?"

"I like their food. And then, tonight, I'll take you to that dance."

She shook her head. "I'm afraid not, pal."

"Huh?"

"You didn't win."

Chapter Nineteen

Halftime had just begun and Jessica was doing pretty much what she had done the week before at the start of halftime: changing the film in her camera, wondering if all her pictures were out of focus, watching Clair out the corners of her out-of-focus eyes, and listening to Sara complain.

There were, however, a couple of differences. First of all this game was a lot more exciting. It counted in the league standing, and the score was tied. Nick was tearing up the floor: rebounding, blocking shots, slam-dunking the ball. The most amazing thing, though, was he was doing all this with the earnest cooperation of his teammates. The Rock and Nick had been high-fiving it all night. Amazing.

There were also about four times the number of people present. Tabb's gymnasium was far larger than Holden High's, but it was obvious the main reason for the extra numbers was because the dance followed the game. Judging by the clothes of the majority of the crowd, it appeared that practically everyone had come for both events. Like Maria and Clair—and probably Cindy Fosmeyer, wherever she was—Jessica had yet to change into her princess gown. Jessica had had her hair permed and teased, however, and could not believe the abandon with which Clair had led the cheers throughout the first half. Clair did not appear concerned about looking perfect. Indeed, she had seemed quite happy all night.

"You may as well know, dearie, I can't lose."

That worried Jessica.

"Then this idiot with a camera stepped in front of Russ and tripped him," Sara was saying. "Naturally, I grabbed the guy by the arm and pulled him aside. And they called that interference! They disqualified Russ for that! Can you believe it?"

"No," Jessica said, bending over for a drink from the fountain in the corner of the gym. The two of them were down on the floor. The team had left moments ago for the locker room and most of the crowd was heading for the refreshment stand or a breath of air outside. Her date for the dance, Bill Skater, was sitting with his football buddies a couple of rows above where the cheerleaders had performed. Jessica had been searching for Michael all night but hadn't seen him.

"What do you mean?" Sara asked, indignant.

"I don't believe you," Jessica said, finishing her drink and slipping a lens cap over her camera. "What really happened?"

Sara put a hand on her hip, which she often did when her credibility was being questioned. "I bet you think *I* tripped him?"

"Well, you locked him in a freezer once."

"You didn't have to bring that up. That was an accident. And what does it matter how he got disqualified? The fact remains he won the goddamn race and they didn't give him the goddamn trophy."

"Does he care?"

"No."

"Then what's the problem?" Jessica asked.

"There isn't a problem. I'm just making conversation. What a stupid question. The biggest social event of the school year is about to take place and if it bombs it will be totally my fault."

"What about me? I have a shot at the biggest social title of the year, and if I don't win I'll—I'll go out and get bombed."

"You're going to win."

"How do you know? You don't know anything." Jessica glared in the direction of the cheerleaders. "She shouldn't look so goddamn confident." Clair was little more than a blond blur to her at this distance.

"Quit swearing," Sara said.

"Go to hell."

They stared at each other a moment and then laughed. "Bitch of a night," Sara said.

"It's going to get worse. Hey, I've got to check on Maria and her folks."

Sara nodded. "I'll catch you in the dressing room after the game. Remember, HB-twenty-two."

"Good, yeah. Go light the tent on fire."

"Don't tempt me," Sara said.

Crossing the basketball court, her photo equipment stuffed in a bag hanging over her shoulder, Jessica again searched the stands for Michael. She thought he probably wouldn't attend the dance—he had never struck her as the type that went in for big phony get-togethers—but Nick was his friend, he should have come to the game. Maybe if she put on her glasses she'd find him. She didn't just want to talk to him, she wanted to have *a* talk with him. All day long, from the instant she had woken up this morning, a frightening conviction had been growing inside her. She felt she absolutely had to get him alone and confess how she had stood him up, and then tell him how she really felt about him. What made this conviction so frightening—besides the usual reason that she would be risking outright rejection, which was nothing to sneeze at—was that she *knew* if she didn't do it now, she wouldn't be able to do it later. She didn't know how or why she felt this way. She certainly didn't feel lightning was going to strike him or her down. But there was something—something in the air.

What would Alice have wanted?

Alice had known Michael almost a year before her death and had never mentioned him. It still bothered her.

Did Alice feel Michael was too good for me?

That was nonsense. Alice had loved her. And yet, according to Polly, Alice had *worshiped* Michael. Jessica would have given a lot to be able to ask Alice how she really felt.

Bill waved to her as she came up the steps but did not stand or otherwise show any sign that he wanted her to join him amid the herd of jocks. She didn't mind. Besides wanting to speak to Maria, she needed to check on Polly. Poor Polly was limping around like a deer with its foot caught in a bear trap. She had fallen off a ladder the night before, she said. Jessica wished Polly had a date. She was worried how Polly would feel when Russ and Sara danced together.

Maria's parents made a handsome couple. Jessica had been particularly taken by Mrs. Gonzales. The woman had Maria's soft-spoken manner, only to a much greater degree. Jessica wasn't sure how much English she knew. She also resembled her daughter, but was considerably more beautiful, with finer features and wide red lips.

Jessica took a seat on the bleachers between Maria and Polly; Maria's parents were sitting to her far right, speaking quietly to each other. Jessica hadn't told her own parents what tonight was. She didn't want them present if she should lose.

But if I win, I might have the guts to tell Dad about the SAT.

"What do your parents think of Nick now?" Jessica whispered in Maria's ear.

"My dad says he's unstoppable," she whispered back.

"Does that mean he likes him?"

Maria smiled and nodded. "I think so."

"What does your mom say?"

"That he's tall."

"That sounds positive. Ask him to the dance."

Maria looked terrified. "We'll see."

Jessica turned her attention to Polly, who had brought a sketch pad and a number of pencils. This was sort of odd because Polly drew about as well as your average alligator. The pad had belonged to Alice. As far as Jessica could tell, Polly hadn't done anything with it all night. At the moment she was staring off into the distance, her eyes dark.

"Are you all right?" Jessica asked.

Polly blinked and slowly looked at Jessica. "I'm tired. I had a bad night. The lightning." She gestured feebly. "Everything."

The reference to lightning made Jessica pause and remember the days Polly had spent in the hospital after her parents had died. Those had been dark times, almost as dark as when Alice had died. To this day, Jessica occasionally wondered if the doctors hadn't compounded the situation by using electroshock to alleviate Polly's depression.

A lightning bolt across the brain.

Polly wouldn't remember. They knocked you out—so Jessica had read—before they taped on the wires.

"How's your aunt?" Jessica asked.

"Dying."

"Are you sure you're all right? I could give you a ride home?"

"I'm fine, I have my own car. I don't want to go home, anyway. I don't want to use my ankle as an excuse not to dance."

"What? Surely you're not going to dance on that foot?"

"I don't mind the pain." Polly turned away and added wearily, "It's better than lying on a floor in the dark."

Michael was bent over a CRT with Bubba in the computer room when they heard the cheer in the gym. That day, all day, Bubba had run a pipeline—via a modem—between Dr. Gin Kawati's ARC Medical Group and Tabb High. The end result was a packed hard disc and a ton of files they couldn't directly read.

"The second half must be about to start," Bubba said.

"I don't know if I'll watch it. I'd like to look at that autopsy report tonight."

"Tonight might be asking too much." Bubba pointed to the data on the screen. "These are binary files, not text. Our word processor can't access them."

"We can use the sector editor and read them manually."

"Yeah, but we're talking about forty megabytes of data. There must be sixty or seventy files here. You'll have to load in each file individually, do an 'Alice McCoy' search, delete the file, then load in the next one until you find her. That could take a long time."

"I have time," Michael said.

"If that's how you feel," Bubba said, surrendering his seat

in front of the screen. Michael sat down and called up the sector editor while Bubba took down a fresh-from-the-cleaners suit of clothes hanging in the corner of the room. Naturally, it was not an ordinary suit Bubba had selected for the big night. A bright yellow, it came with a green hat. Bubba liked hats. "Will you be coming to the dance?" he asked casually, pulling off the plastic and inspecting the material.

"I doubt it."

"Not even for the crowning?"

Michael glanced at him. "Why don't you just tell me who's going to win?"

Bubba smiled. "I don't know everything, you know." He held out his green tie. "Is this too Irish or what?"

"No one can ever be too Irish. You're changing the subject."

Bubba set aside his suit, spoke seriously. "I knew you were standing outside the room when Clair was complaining to me about Jessie."

"How?"

Bubba shrugged, indicating it wasn't important. "Clair should be homecoming queen. She's prettier than Jessie."

"In your opinion. Anyway, pretty isn't everything. All I'm asking for is a fair vote."

"Why ask now? The name has already been recorded and placed in a sealed envelope. If I'm not mistaken, Mr. Bark has it in his pocket at this exact moment."

"Whose name is inside?"

"You put me on the spot, Mike. Clair did that to me, too."

"Then you did arrange for Clair to win?"

"I didn't say that. What I said was she deserves to win. Jessie resorted to low-level tactics in this campaign."

Bubba wouldn't look at him, and ordinarily Bubba wouldn't mind looking you in the eye while telling you he was sleeping with your girlfriend. "*Did* Clair have an abortion?" Michael asked, remembering how she had come to Bubba the afternoon she had been elected to the court, her eyes red.

"A vile and vicious rumor started by the vile and vicious Jessica Hart. No, she didn't."

"Was it yours?"

Bubba snapped his head up. "No." Then he relaxed, adding with a chuckle, "You know how careful I am about such matters."

"Yeah, you're careful," Michael muttered, confused at Bubba's behavior. He wasn't simply being evasive—Bubba never actually told the precise truth, except when it benefited him to do so, which was rarely—he was uneasy. And ordinarily he would not have been worried about having knocked Clair up any more than he would have been concerned about having knocked Jessica down.

Someone banged at the door. "Yeah," Bubba called out.

Kats walked in, surprising Michael. Kats had changed from his usual crusty jeans and oily army-fatigue jacket into a pair of black slacks, a white shirt, and a red tie. It was remarkable—he looked greasier than ever.

"What are you doing here?" Michael asked.

Kats grinned. "I'm the man tonight. I'm taking care of the princesses."

"Kats is driving the float into the tent before the crowning," Bubba explained.

"Why did Sara pick you?" Michael asked.

Kats scowled. "Is there something wrong with me, Mikey?"

Obviously Kats was still mad at him from the last time they had talked at the gas station. "Kats is a great driver," Bubba said. "Sara chose him as a favor to me."

"What favor does Sara owe you?" Michael asked.

Bubba brightened at the question and picked up his yellow suit and green hat. "Honestly, Mike, you know I'm a gentleman."

Bubba and Kats left together, leaving Michael's last question unanswered. Michael turned back to the computer screen. Hopefully, somewhere in all this data, was the answer to more important questions.

Michael read in a file, set the computer to search for the McCoy name, sat back, and waited. He wished he knew how the files were organized, which ones he should concentrate on. He heard another loud cheer come from the gym and checked his watch. The second half was definitely under way. He had been pleased to see Nick doing so well, particularly with the cooperation of The Rock. Michael had not had a chance to talk to Nick the last couple of days; he didn't know what had changed between the two. But it had clearly been a change for the better. At least somebody was making progress somewhere.

I can't complain.

His mother's boyfriend had finally come to a decision. He had proposed marriage, and his mom had accepted. Michael had to admit she had never seemed happier.

I'm going to have a father. I have a sister on the way, a comet in the sky that belongs to me. What else can I expect?

Nothing. And yet, he was lonely, desperately lonely. Jessica—crazy as it sounded even to him—he sometimes believed he needed her simply to go on living. And he hadn't felt that way even in the depths of his despair over Alice. He kept remembering sitting beside her while she slept under the tree after the SAT. He should have lain down and slept beside her. Then maybe he could have met her in a dream and told her all the things he couldn't tell her when he was awake.

Go forward, I will follow.

That was a dream he hadn't had in a while.

Alice wasn't in the first file. She wasn't in the second or the third. He began to worry that he would go through all the files and discover Dr. Kawati hadn't bothered to put the autopsy reports he did for the county into his business computer.

The fourth file turned out to be huge. Michael prowled the room while the name search went on and on, listening to the sporadic roar of the gymnasium crowd, thinking of how cute Jessica had looked during the first half crouched at the end of the court, her camera balanced on her knee, her long brown hair hanging loose and wonderful. He glanced again at the computer screen, the endless succession of numbers and text creeping by, and decided a quick stop inside the gym wouldn't make any difference.

He felt the tension the moment he entered the building. A glance at the scoreboard said it all: Tabb 56, Westminister 57. Seven seconds left. Tabb had the ball. Nick had just called time out, and the team was huddling around Coach Sellers. The man would probably advise them to dribble out the clock.

Everybody was standing. Everybody except Jessica. Michael spotted her kneeling alone on the court floor behind Tabb's basket, doing a trial focus with her camera. He wondered if he should accidentally try to bump into her when the game was over. But he could imagine Bill coming up if he tried to talk to her, taking her hand, and leading her away to the dance.

I'll just see who wins, and then go back to the room.

Sitting down, Nick grabbed a towel and wiped the sweat from his brow, trying to block out the noise of the cheerleaders at his back while listening to what the coach was saying. He was running on adrenaline, hyped up. He had played hard all night, but with each passing minute, he felt himself growing stronger. He was ready to take the last shot.

"Go Tabb! Go team! Take the ball and stuff it mean!"

To his disappointment, however, he quickly realized Sellers had other ideas.

"Westminster will collapse on Nick the second we inbound the ball," the coach was saying, sketching shaky *X*s and *O*s with a marking pen on a white board on the floor at the center of their huddle. "For that reason, Nick, I want you to line up on the baseline off the key on the left side. Stewart will take the ball into The Rock, here, who will dribble toward you, but then suddenly whip a pass over to Ted, here, beside the free-throw line. Ted, you'll take the last shot."

Ted didn't know if he liked that idea. He was their best outside shooter—after Nick, of course—but he'd been having an off night, hitting four of fourteen from the field. He stared at the *X*s and *O*s as if they were part of a tic-tac-toe game he had just lost. "What if they don't collapse on Nick?" he asked, standing beside The Rock. "Then I could have both their guards in my face."

"Go Nick! Set the pick! Let your best shot rip!"

"Their guards should fall back," Coach Sellers said, not sounding very sure of himself. "But if they don't, you'll have to take the ball higher up and take a longer shot."

"What if I miss?" Ted asked.

"Then we lose the game and you're the goat," The Rock said.

"That's enough of that," Coach Sellers said.

"Go Ted! Use your head! Make the Trojans drop dead!"

"I wish to God they'd shut up," Ted said. "Don't we have another play?"

"Don't you want to take the last shot?" Coach Sellers asked.

"Sure," Ted said. "I just don't want to miss it."

Coach Sellers glanced at each of them, clenching and unclenching his fingers. "*Do* we have another play?" he asked.

"Let me pass the ball down to Nick," The Rock said.

"It's too obvious a move," Coach Sellers said. "He'll have someone in front of him, someone behind him. You'd never get him the ball."

"Ted will never get the ball in the basket," The Rock said.

"Hey, I could make it," Ted said. "Maybe."

"Go Rock! Be a jock! Catch the ball and give 'em a sock!"

"Who writes those bloody things?" The Rock growled.

Nick felt he should speak up. He could line up a couple of feet closer to the basket than the coach wanted, catch the ball on the leap, and spin around and bank it in. The Rock had improved two hundred percent as a passer in the last week. It would be a sound play. The coach was looking at him. They were all looking at him, waiting. Nick glanced behind him, at the jammed bleachers. He'd seen Maria up there when he'd been warming up before the second half. And her parents. He remembered them from Alice's party.

What if I *miss?*

Suddenly, although he had enjoyed their support all night, he could feel the weight of the crowd. This week, for the first time since his move to this part of town, walking around campus had not been an ordeal. Rather than jumping out of his way, people had been stopping him to wish him luck. But would these same people laugh behind his back next week if he blew the team's last chance? He had already had a great game. Prudence dictated he play it safe.

"Whatever you say, coach," he mumbled finally, taking the easy way out and hating himself for it.

Coach Sellers nodded nervously, glanced at Ted. "You'll make it," he said.

Ted swallowed. "Christ."

The time-out ended. Wiping the last beads of perspiration from his hands with his towel, Nick followed his teammates back onto the court, positioning himself near the baseline, to the left of the basket. A moment later Westminster's center came and stood at his back, while Westminster's power forward placed himself a few feet in front, between him and Stewart. Nick knew Westminster's forward would drop back and lean on him, try to box him in, the moment the referee handed Stewart the ball. Both their center and power forward—in fact their whole team—were strong, very physical.

Oh, no! We forgot to tell Ted to get off his shot early enough for me to stand a chance at a rebound.

Nick went to speak to Ted precisely when the referee tossed the ball to Stewart and blew the whistle. That settled that. Stewart now had five seconds to inbound the ball. Ted would have to follow the cheerleaders' advice and use his head.

Westminster's power forward immediately jumped back and sagged into Nick. Their center put a hand on his shoulder, a hand that might have had a hold on his jersey. Nick did not struggle to get free, deciding to wait a moment to see which way—figuratively and literally—the ball bounced.

Free of defensive pressure, Stewart easily in-bounded the ball to The Rock. Unfortunately, as The Rock dribbled toward Nick, only one of Westminster's guards moved to block his path. The other kept his position near the top of the key, near Ted. The seven on the clock slipped to five.

Putting forth a faked shot that probably didn't fake a person in the building, The Rock whizzed the ball over to Ted, who caught it a solid twenty feet from the basket. Then Ted did the strangest thing. He paused to study the ball, as if he were checking to see if it were the brand name he would willingly have chosen to use while risking his athletic reputation. He did this for a grand total of perhaps one second. Given the situation, that was an extremely long time. Never give the ball to someone who's afraid of it, Nick thought. Michael was right, Sellers should coach checkers. The clock went to three seconds.

Ted finally emerged from his important study, but with no clear idea of what he wanted to do next, whether to dribble closer or shoot. The crowd screamed, clearly wishing he would make up his mind. Ted glanced at Westminster's advancing guard, decided to put the ball up. Nick knew it wasn't going to go down before it left his hands. Ted launched it toward the backboard as if he were throwing a stone at an attacking dinosaur.

Nick pivoted to his left, slapping off the hold on him with his elbow, crashing into the key, into perfect position to grab the rebound. Ted's shot didn't even hit the rim, however, and had so much behind it that it ricocheted high off the backboard. Nick not only had to leap as he had never leaped before to catch it, but he had to twist back so that his midsection stretched directly across the face of Westminster's big center.

Time did not slow down for Nick as he had often heard it did in moments of crisis. Indeed, as he rolled prone off the center's nose, the ball balanced precariously in his right hand, the floor five feet beneath the back of his head and getting closer fast, he caught a glimpse of the big red letters on the clock going from two to one. He acted instinctively. He scooped the ball toward the basket, feeling a painful slap to his right arm in the process. The slap, though, didn't hurt nearly so much as his butt did when he hit the floor.

Go in! Go in!

From flat on his back on the floor, Nick watched the ball roll lazily around the inside of the rim. The crowd gasped. The buzzer sounded. The ball rolled out.

We lost.

The disappointment soaked through him like a bitter drink, draining away his energy. He couldn't even be bothered getting up. But there was The Rock, his fat hand out, insisting he do so.

"You can do it, buddy," The Rock said, clasping Nick's

wrist and yanking him to his feet. "Two free throws and this baby's wrapped."

"What are you talking about? It's over."

"You were fouled, man."

The Rock's comment was slightly premature. The refs—and the coaches—were still arguing about it. Nick had never seen Coach Sellers so alive; all that blood in his cheeks.

Standing with his teammates, waiting anxiously for the decision, Nick spotted someone that almost caused him to faint.

His father was standing at the top of the bleachers.

A moment later the crowd cheered. Coach Sellers returned to his seat and began to twitch. Ted and The Rock patted Nick on the butt. The referee handed him the ball. Nick stared at it a moment.

It's a Spalding, Ted. A fine brand.

Nick had trouble locating the free-throw line. It seemed to him someone had moved it back a few feet. He had shot about sixty-five percent from the field tonight, but had taken six free throws and made only two. Standing at the line, alone on the floor—time had officially expired—he bounced the ball a couple of times and listened as the ear-busting din dropped to a heart-stopping silence. This wasn't pressure. This was murder.

Nick glanced up at his father. His father had only remarked upon his going out for the team once; that had been to tell him it had better not interfere with his bringing home his weekly check.

Why is he here?

Nick tried to focus on his grip on the ball, the position of his feet behind the line, the basket, trying to envision the ball sailing through the air and swishing through the net. He dribbled twice more, took a deep breath, and closed his eyes. But he felt himself beginning to sway and quickly opened them. Yet the dizziness did not leave.

I am going to miss.

As it was, feeling the way he did, he would be putting up a couple of shots reminiscent of Ted's last attempt. The problem was, he couldn't jump, pivot, or fall away. Custom said he had to stand there relatively still and either make it or miss it. His decision after practice on Thursday notwithstanding, this was not his world. He was but a visitor. He had to obey custom.

He glanced again to his father. Although faraway—two hundred feet, at least—it seemed to Nick their eyes met. His dad did a little jump where he stood, pumping with his arms and nodding.

Do it your own way, but do it.

Nick turned and took a fifteen-foot jump shot.

He made it.

The crowd cheered.

He took another jump shot. *Swish.* Game over: Tabb 58, Westminister 57. The crowd freaked.

Like a wave bursting a dam, people flooded the court. Nick

felt his own wave breaking inside. He felt, without a speck of worry or pain to blemish it, a clear white euphoria.

He got touched more in the next few minutes than he had been touched in his entire life; guys and girls pumping his hands, slapping him on the back, telling him how great he was. He drank it up like a man dying of thirst would have drunk down a barrel of Gatorade, which, by the way, was exactly what The Rock had decided to pour over Nick's head.

Then his dad was congratulating him, along with Mr. Gonzales. Nick introduced them, sounding to his own ears as if he were babbling in a foreign language, but making enough sense to get them shaking hands and talking basketball strategy.

And somewhere in all this, Maria appeared. Climbing to her tiptoes, she asked if she could speak to him outside. He let himself be led into the cold and the dark, down a hallway, and behind a tree. Here she didn't compliment him on his defense or his lay-ups. She had never been one to talk a lot.

"I'm sorry," she said. "Can you forgive me?"

"No problem," Nick said. In that instant, he honestly felt all his problems were behind him. He kissed her.

Jessica had taken her pictures and stowed her camera when she spotted Michael slipping away from the jubilant crowd out the corner doorway. She jumped after him, but had a few hundred people in her way, and didn't catch him until he was far down a black empty covered walkway outdoors. He didn't stop to see who was following him until she called his name.

"Hi, Jessie," he said pleasantly, turning. "Great game, wasn't it?"

"It was fantastic. But I wish you could have played."

"I'm busy enough these days. Going to change for the dance now?"

"Yeah, I have this long yellow dress I bought." She forced a laugh. "I'll probably be tripping over it all night."

"Yellow suits you. I'm sure you'll look very beautiful."

She wished she could see his face better, see if he was just being polite, or if she really was beautiful to him. She needed courage. There was so much she wanted to say. "You're coming, aren't you?" she asked.

"No, I don't think so. I'm not much of a dancer. And I have work to do."

That must mean he was leaving the campus. Yet he had not been walking toward the parking lot. Her heart was breaking. More than anything, she had wanted to dance with him. "But you can't work on a night like this. It can't be that important?"

"To me it is." He paused. "Did you call and get your SAT scores?"

"Not yet," she lied. And one lie always led to another, and suddenly she realized she didn't have the strength to confess how weak she was, or how strong she could be if he would come with her.

"Let's hope for the best," he said.

"Yeah."

He touched her arm. "It's cold out here. You'd better get inside." He smiled. "Have lots of fun for me."

She nodded sadly. "I will." Letting go of her arm, he turned and walked away. "Michael?" she called.

He stopped. "Yeah?"

I would love to love you.

"Nothing," she said, knowing as she watched him walk away that the moment had come and gone. Gone for good.

Chapter Twenty

As planned, the four girls—Maria, Jessica, Sara, and Polly—met in room HB-22 to dress for the dance. A number of rooms had been unlocked for girls to change in. The game had ended at eight and Sara had already warned the student body via an announcement in homeroom that morning that no one would be allowed into the tent before nine. Parents of the girls on the court, the announcement had further stated, would be welcome to stop by at ten-thirty for the crowning. Sara's own mother had wanted to come to the dance but Sara had told her not to dare. She hadn't been getting along with her parents since Russ had moved in. They were probably worried he was having sex with her in the middle of the night. But so far, she'd had no such luck.

"How do I look?" Jessica asked, a yellow ribbon in her hair to match her yellow gown.

"Wonderful," Maria said, excited, wearing a relatively plain white dress, no ribbon.

"Great," Polly said, still in the clothes she had worn to the game and showing no signs of getting out of them.

"You look like Jessie dressed up," Sara said, thinking that it was Jessica's night, that no one was going to touch her. She glanced down at her own orange dress, which had squeezed her father's credit card for a tidy two hundred and sixteen dollars plus tax. "How about me?"

"Real pretty," Maria said.

"Pretty as a pumpkin pie before you put it in the oven," Jessica said.

"Shut up," Sara said.

They finished with their makeup, gave up trying to convince Polly to go home and put on something nice, and tumbled out of the room for the tent.

"Maria, Jessie," Sara said as they walked down the outside walkway, freezing to death without their sweaters, Polly struggling to keep up with her bad foot. "Check on the band and the servers for me. I want to take Polly and have a look at the float."

"What exactly are we checking with them about?" Jessica asked.

"It doesn't matter. That they're ready. Just talk to them, Jessie."

They split up when they reached the tent, Jessica and

Maria disappearing inside. By this time Polly was really dragging. Sara felt a twinge of guilt that she'd swiped Russ from the McCoy mansion when Polly wasn't looking. Yet Polly appeared unconcerned about Russ's whereabouts and determined to enjoy the night.

A number of students were milling around outside the tent as Sara and Polly circled to the back. Several called out to Sara complaining about the cold and asking why she didn't let them in.

"Go wait in the gym," she said. "And quit hassling me."

The float surpassed Sara's expectations. That Tony Foulton had some imagination. Although she had given him a general idea of what she wanted—"a castle look to go with our queen and princesses"—it was very much his creation. A blue-carnation moat circled the entire float. Lying across the front was a fake drawbridge—a wide sheet of board, cleverly painted with black and gray strips to resemble whatever it was drawbridges were supposed to be made of. In the center of the drawbridge stood the microphone. The plan was for Sara to announce the new queen after receiving the sealed envelope from Mr. Bark, who would emerge from inside the castle proper. It was a fond dream of Sara's that he would hand her the envelope and not feel compelled to make a speech.

Last year's homecoming queen had flown in special for the occasion from an Ivy League college back east. The latest word, however, had her at home sick from a crash fast she had undertaken to lose the forty pounds she needed to lose to fit into the dress she had worn when she had been elected queen. On top of everything else, Sara would now be doing the actual crowning.

The castle had four battlement towers, all at the front, interconnected by a plank that would be invisible to the audience. They were approximately five feet higher than the moat, decorated primarily with chrysanthemums, each a different color: gold, red, green, yellow. Four towers for four princesses.

At the back, inside the castle walls—another six feet higher than the battlement towers—stood the queen's throne. Whoever had her name in the envelope would ascend a hidden ladder behind the castle after the announcement and take up her rightful seat. (Sara had swiped the chair from her own living room.) With the lights flashing and the band playing, Sara thought they could do the MTV video she had stolen the concept from one better.

"This thing isn't going to fall over?" Sara asked Polly.

"It's possible," Polly said. "Anything is possible."

"Swell," Sara said. Yet she trusted Tony's skill.

Kats appeared from beneath the float. Bubba had explained to Sara that Kats bore Tabb High a measure of resentment for the way everybody had treated him while he had been in high school. Playing an essential role in the homecoming festivities, Bubba had thought, would help dispel the resentment. Sara would have preferred a driver who had a positive outlook, but she had decided to be diplomatic about the issue, hoping Bubba would forget the sex contingency he had tied to his assistance. She still didn't know what was going on with the money she had given him.

"It's dark in there," Kats said.

"Will you be able to see where you're going?" Sara asked.

Kats pointed to Polly. "Hey, Alice was your sister, right?"

Polly lowered her head. "Yes."

"I asked you a question?" Sara said, annoyed at his lack of tact.

Kats grinned. "I'll take care of you ladies, never fear."

They left Kats and slipped inside through the folds in the tent. The band was already on the stage. The food, the glasses, the plates, the silverware—everything was laid out. Ringing the entire canvas dance floor were four dozen electric heaters, glowing orange and warm. The temperature inside the tent was variable, with drafts and cold spots, but Sara believed it would even out when all the people were crammed together.

Polly collapsed into a seat near the punch. Jessica came up to Sara. "They're beginning to jam up outside," she said.

Sara glanced at her watch. "It's fifteen minutes early. Oh, what the hell, let's strike up the band and let them in."

"But you don't have anyone stationed to collect tickets."

Sara realized Jessica was right. She had forgotten all about that. "Let them all in." She laughed. "Who cares? Let's party."

* * *

Michael had gone through nineteen files and was initiating a search on the twentieth when he began to believe he was wasting his time. So far, the name *McCoy* had not rung a bell with any of ARC's records.

He could hear the music from the dance, the laughter and jeers of people having fun. He tried to remember when he'd last had a good time through a whole night, and couldn't. He would've liked to have seen Jessica in her yellow dress.

Michael started the search on the file and got up and walked about the room, stretching. Half the overhead fluorescent lights had died moments after he returned to the computer room at the end of the game. His eyes were aching from staring at the bright green CRT letters and numbers. Earlier in the day, someone must have spilt something in the biology room next door. There was a foul smell in the air. He felt vaguely claustrophobic, as if he were being forced to labor in a morgue.

Now that it had come down to it, he almost hoped he didn't find the autopsy report. He felt as if he were trying to dig up Alice's body.

Are these the days everyone says we'll remember as the happiest days of our lives? Jessica wondered. *God.*

Bill had just brought her a drink. Jessica wished he had brought her a real drink. Something to numb the pain. Yet she really shouldn't have been drinking at all. As it was, shaking from nerves over the upcoming announcement, she was running to the bathroom in the gym every twenty minutes to pee. And her stomach was upset. She had tried to eat something, thinking it would help, but had accidentally bitten her tongue, soaking her mouthful of chicken sandwich with blood and grossing out her stomach further. Luckily, Bill had not tried to kiss her so far. She imagined she wouldn't taste very good.

"How's your drink?" Bill asked.

Jessica sipped it without enthusiasm. "Great."

They were standing with a group of football players and their girlfriends at the edge of the dance floor not far from the band. The music was excellent: present-day pop and sixties rock classics. But the volume was way too high; it was giving her a headache. Bill and she had danced once, to "Surfer Girl," slow and close. In his dark blue suit, his blond hair short and clean, he had to be the cutest guy under the tent. He'd put his arms around her and held her to his chest, where she found herself living a fantasy from the early days of the school year, but which now brought her no pleasure.

"Having a good time?" Bill asked.

Jessica smiled. "Super."

It was a night of firsts for Nick. He had never been a hero before, or a boyfriend. Now he was both, and although he couldn't say which brought him more satisfaction, he hoped he was to enjoy the two roles for a long time.

Like Maria in his arms, the music was soft as they slowly

danced over the dimly lit floor. He had never danced before, either, but he had been delighted to find it a lot easier than attempting to shoot a basketball with three guys hanging on to him. The feeling of warmth where Maria's body touched his was flowing straight to his brain, sending his blood and thoughts swimming. His only concern was that she was getting a crick in her neck trying to look up at him.

"I can't believe my father went off with your parents," Nick said, his big hands resting on top of her black hair.

"He's usually not very sociable?"

"Sort of. He hates almost everybody."

Maria chuckled. "Does he speak much Spanish?"

"Some. Do your parents speak much English?"

"A little." Maria smiled up at him. "They'll be all right. They have things in common."

"Basketball?"

"Us."

"Oh." He liked the sound of that little word. It gave him confidence. Yet, remembering she was an illegal alien, he hesitated before asking his next question. "So, Maria, you no longer feel afraid to be seen by people?"

She chuckled again. "I haven't been wearing a bag over my head at school." Then she was serious. "I have Jessica to thank for tonight. She told me to bring my parents to the game. She's the one who put my name on the homecoming court ballot."

"I feel the same way about Mike. He forced me to go out

for the team." Nick laughed. "He forced me to ask you out on our date."

Maria stepped back and lightly socked him, but he grabbed her hand and pulled her closer and they went right on dancing. He rested his chin atop her head. "Are you worried about winning tonight?" he asked after a while.

She poked his chest with her nose. "I've already won."

Not long after Maria socked Nick, Russ tried to kiss Sara in the middle of a dance. Sara held her head back.

"What's wrong?" he demanded. "You kissed me the other night?"

"There're people here." She glanced to the chair on the other side of the floor where Polly had sat the whole night, Alice's sketch pad balanced on her knees, drawing. Sara had brought her some punch a half hour ago and glanced at her work, a rather poor—though elaborate—drawing of the float and the four princesses. Sara had not known what Polly was trying to say by putting a big clock about to strike twelve on the front of the queen's tower.

Does she think all the princesses are going to turn into pumpkins?

"So?" Russ said, annoyed.

"So, I'm ASB president, I can't be seen kissing a boy in front of everybody like an ordinary girl."

"If you don't kiss me right now, I'll fondle your breasts in front of everybody."

Why doesn't he get urges like this when we're alone?

"You wouldn't dare!"

"No?" He went to grab her chest with both his paws. She jumped back and scurried past him.

"Excuse me, Russ, I've got to go beat the bank."

She had spotted Bubba, alone, taking a break from tearing up the floor on every song with Clair. One thing you had to hand Clair, she didn't give a hoot—unlike Jessica—about being seen with a fashionable guy. Personally, Sara thought Jessica would have done a lot better with Michael Olson instead of Bill Skater. You could talk to Michael. From watching Bill in political science, Sara had decided he was essentially a blank sheet.

"Where's the money?" she asked, tapping Bubba on the shoulder. He turned to face her, smiling serenely, alcohol on his breath. Obviously he had brought his own private punch.

"Where's your body?" he asked.

"Why is it that all of a sudden everyone wants my body?"

"Did you sell it to someone else?"

She glared. "That isn't funny. Do you have the money to pay for this dance or not? And don't give me any BS."

"Why the harsh tone?" Bubba gestured to the rest of the tent. "None of this would have been possible without my assistance. Look about you and be grateful."

Sara had to admit he was right; the dance was a stunning success. Three-quarters of the student body must have come, as opposed to last year's homecoming when less than three hundred tickets had been sold. The music, the food, the colorful ribbons and ornaments hanging across the tent—everything was perfect. Everybody seemed to be having a great time. Already tonight, she'd been stopped a dozen times and congratulated on what a fantastic job she'd done.

But he's still trying to screw me.

"It is I who should be disappointed with you," Bubba continued, leaning closer. "I've done all this and received nothing in return. But, I must say, you do seem in a frisky mood tonight, Sara, dear. Why don't we get together at my place after I drop—"

"Can it. You've done nothing for me. I spoke to the caterer and the band. They say we still owe them half their money."

"Then repay me fifty percent tonight. You know what really turns me on and doesn't take a lot of time? Later, in my bedroom, if you could take off your dress and—"

"Stop it! Where's the money?"

Bubba belched. "I lost it."

"You lost it!" she screamed. People—probably more than would have bothered to look had Russ actually succeeded in fondling her breasts—turned their heads. "How could you lose it?" she hissed.

He shrugged. "Money comes and goes, just like girls and bad weather. It's the way of things."

It was a frightening thing, feeling this close to wanting to murder someone. "If you lost it all, how did you pay for any of this?" she demanded.

"Oh, I had to borrow some more."

"From who?"

"Friends of the family."

She had heard rumors about his family. "Are you talking about loan sharks?"

"Shh. They don't like that word. Never use it around them. They might get angry."

She grabbed him by his bright green tie. "You don't know the meaning of the word *angry*! I am not going to pay loan-shark interest rates on a loan you had no right to take out!"

He laughed. "You sure are a spunky little girl."

She yanked on the tie, choking him. "I mean it!"

He calmly reached up and removed her hand, straightening his tie and the green hat on his fat head. "I'm afraid you have no choice, Sara. I told you at the beginning, I'm not going to bring my own personal funds into this matter. But don't despair. I borrowed enough to make the first couple of payments. And it's six months till June, a long time before you'll need big money for another big event. I'll think of something between now and then." He added slyly, "If you're nice to me, that is."

She sneered, absolutely disgusted. "I hate you."

He beamed. "Not as much as I love you, Sara."

Stalking back to Russ, she was apprehended by Mr. Bark.

He wanted her to gather the princesses outside behind the float. It was time to crown the queen.

If it had been cold outside before, it was freezing now. Jessica didn't know if she could stand to wait any longer in her short sleeves with the other girls on the basketball courts. A wind had begun to blow; it kept picking at the hem of her dress, sending goose-flesh up her legs. Maria was the only smart one among them. She had on Nick's jacket, and on Maria it was as good as a full-length coat.

"Won't the truck under the float start?" Maria asked.

Sara had raved to Jessica about how neat the float was, but looking at it waiting in the dark fifty yards off the rear of the tent, its numerous towers reminding her more of an obstacle course than a castle, Jessica wished the announcement were taking place on stage in front of the band. What a joke; Sara was always calling her a snob, and here Sara had obviously put together this float solely for the purpose of being remembered as the greatest president Tabb High had ever had.

"It starts fine; it just keeps stalling," Jessica said. She could hear Kats and Sara arguing inside. It seemed Sara had rigged a hose to the exhaust tail of the truck so the fumes could be funneled away from the float. Kats wanted the hose removed. The fumes kept backing up inside the tail pipe, he said, and were choking the engine.

"Do what he says and let's get this thing over with," Clair

called out, standing near the front of the float with Cindy Fosmeyer. Clair had selected blue for the color of her gown, but even if she'd chosen bright stripes and polka dots, Jessica thought, she still would have been beautiful. But Jessica was finding it difficult to understand how Cindy Fosmeyer had been selected to the court. The girl had lost several pounds in the past week—perhaps as much as half a pound directly off her massive chest—but her large nose had not shrunk in the interim and the ton of makeup she had chosen to plaster over her face had failed to bury it. It was a sad fact, but a fact nevertheless: Cindy was a dog.

After a few more encouraging remarks from Clair—each one containing a few more cuss words—Sara finally relented and did what Kats wanted. She removed the hose, but muttered that they had better hold their breath for the duration of the ride into the tent.

Mr. Bark appeared. An envelope in his right hand, he crouched down behind the queen's castle, while Sara stationed herself inside the moat up front. Clair and Cindy got onto the battle towers on the left. Jessica was the last one up, taking the tower on the far right—facing the float—off to Maria's left. Beneath them, Kats turned over the truck's engine.

"Go slow," Sara called down to Kats, who was invisible beneath their feet. Sara raised a walkie-talkie to her mouth. "We're coming," she said, telling whoever it was inside to start the music and raise the curtains.

What followed next irritated Jessica's finer sensibilities, yet at the same time gave her a big rush. In reality, she was as much a sap for flash and glitter as the next teenage girl.

The float rocked forward. In front, the tent walls began to part, slowly revealing row upon row of couples waiting within a spell of pulsing synthesized rhythms and whirling strobe lights, looking like a futuristic gang of kids partying aboard a huge spaceship.

They passed beneath the ceiling of the tent. A searchlight caught the tip of the float. The true colors of the castle flooded Jessica's eyes, dazzling her. The searchlight rolled over her face and practically blinded her. She could smell the fumes Sara had spoken of, could hear the eerie sci-fi music. But the next thing she actually saw was the float swaying—as Kats brought it to a halt—and Sara stepping up to the microphone.

Heavy stuff.

Kats shut off the truck. The canvas closed at their back, and the temperature leaped into the comfort zone.

"Having a good time?" Sara asked to the crowd, getting an immediate earsplitting "Yeah!" "That's good, that's great," she went on. "I know it's been a while since I last spoke to all of you at once. And there's something I said that day I'd like to take back. Getting ready for this dance with the help of the whole ASB council, I've learned a high school really does need class officers. I've also discovered that you'd have to be out of your mind to want to be one." The audience laughed and

Sara continued smoothly. "But let's get down to business. Let's crown our new queen. I'll start by introducing the members of the court." Sara gestured to her right. "Over here, at a hundred and ten pounds and undefeated in all her previous fights, we have blond and blue-eyed Clair Hilrey!"

Clair—much to Jessica's displeasure—accepted the silly introduction by raising both her arms high like a prizefighter, showing everyone that—besides being able to take a joke—she had the best body on the float. The audience loved it.

Her reputation sure has bounced back.

"Ooh, baby!" Bubba's voice wailed from somewhere at the rear.

"Next," Sara said. "Beloved of the entire male population of Tabb High for her forward-reaching expression and her twin mounds of feminine excellence—Cindy Fosmeyer!"

I cannot believe she said that.

Cindy didn't seem to mind the compliments, no doubt because she didn't understand them. Politely applauding, Jessica wondered what Sara would say about her. But not half so much as she wondered what name was written in the envelope Mr. Bark carried.

Sara nodded to her left. "And now we come to the smallest girl in the group. Small in size, but big in heart. Ladies and gentlemen, Maria Gonzales!"

The applause for Maria was warm but lacked the enthusiasm the previous two girls had enjoyed; understandable, since

Maria was all but unknown on campus outside a tiny circle of friends. Her election to the court made less sense than Cindy's.

The applause died down. Sara grinned wickedly. Jessica lowered her head and began to squirm, feeling sweat forming beneath the layer of deodorant she had rolled on earlier. Sara had just better remember, she swore to herself, that they were best friends.

Oh, no.

"As most of you know," Sara began, "our final princess and I have been best friends for many years. Now I know somebody out there must be asking him or herself the question: 'can we trust good old Sara to read out anybody's name but that of her best friend?'" Sara paused, then giggled. "We'll see, won't we?" She spread out her left arm. "Wish Jessica Hart lots of luck, folks!"

Her heart pounding so hard it was close to skipping, Jessica rated her applause the loudest of the lot.

I'm in. It's me. It's got to be me!

"The envelope, please," Sara said, turning to welcome Mr. Bark as he emerged from behind the queen's tower. The chatter in the audience halted. Jessica raised her head. Sara took the envelope from Mr. Bark—snatched it from him actually—and quickly began to tear it open. Before she could finish, however, Mr. Bark wedged himself between her and the microphone.

"If I may say a few words before the crowning," Mr. Bark began.

"Damn," Sara mumbled under her breath—soft enough

so that no one in the crowd seemed to hear—trying to get the slip of paper out of the envelope while trying to maintain her position behind the mike. Mr. Bark gave her an uncertain glance before continuing.

"I am happy so many of you were able to make it tonight," he said, stretching his head in front of Sara's face. "Homecoming is an important event, not only as a social occasion, but as a time to reflect upon our bigger home, the world we live in. It is a beautiful world but a fragile one. At any instant, on either side of the ocean, a button could be pushed and—"

"How many here are against nuclear war?" Sara suddenly broke in, raising her hand holding the torn envelope. The whole assembly threw their fists into the air and cheered. "Wow, we're convinced!" she exclaimed. "We'll have the petition at the door, and no one leaves here tonight without signing it. A big hand for Mr. Bark, please! Thank you!"

More clapping. Mr. Bark scowled down at Sara, and she smiled up at him. He must have realized he had nowhere to go with his speech now that she had stolen his thunder. He climbed down from the float.

The silence settled again upon the audience, quicker this time, and deeper. Sara, alone behind the microphone—a beam of light bright on her orange dress—finished opening the envelope and took out the slip of paper. Jessica did not have on her glasses, naturally, and therefore did not have a clear view of Sara's face. Yet Sara was only a few feet away, and it seemed to

Jessica she froze as she unfolded the tiny white paper. But only for an instant.

Jessica Hart! Way to go Jessie! Let's hear it for Jessie!

Then Sara turned toward her, catching her eye. Beyond Sara, on the other side of the float, Clair leaned forward. The crowd waited. Everybody on the float waited.

Everybody—except Jessica. Because as Sara had looked at Jessica, Sara's lower lip trembled slightly. Jessica saw it, and knew it was the one thing Sara did to show disappointment.

I can't believe it. I lost.

Jessica lowered her head again, her hair covering her face. She didn't see Sara turn back to the microphone, although she heard her clearly enough.

"Ladies and gentlemen, please welcome Tabb High's new homecoming queen—Maria Gonzales!"

The rest was a blur for Jessica. Maria reached for her first, and Jessica hugged her. She kissed Maria, laughed and cried with her, telling herself she was happy for her. But she cried more than the occasion deserved.

Then the other princesses were congratulating Maria, and Sara was placing the crown on top of her head and wrapping the royal robe around her frail shoulders. Music played, lights flickered. The applause went on and on. Sara directed Maria toward the back of the float. Ascending the hidden ladder, a bouquet of red roses in her arms, Maria reached the top of the tower. There she stood radiant and tall.

But even the small have far to fall.

The thought flickered past the lowest edge of Jessica's conscious mind, disappearing almost before she knew she'd had it.

Maria waved her flowers, wrapped safe in the audience's adulation.

Clair leaned over and whispered to Jessica. "As long as it wasn't you, dearie."

"I feel the same way," Jessica replied.

Michael had found the file; he had reached the cemetery. The computerized search was now leading him through data that clearly made up Dr. Gin Kawati's autopsy reports. Her tombstone was close. Any second now, he knew, he would have to take up the shovel and dig. He was literally trembling with excitement, with horror. He glanced at his watch: a quarter after one. Alice had died just after one in the morning.

Michael stood and again paced the room, as he had done so many times during the course of the night. He no longer felt simply claustrophobic; he felt as if he were smothering. His eyes burned; he hated to think what he would look like in a mirror. Part of it was from exhaustion, but the stink from the biology room had continued to assault his senses all night. He had finally identified the smell—formaldehyde. But he had not gone to wipe it up. For some reason, he was afraid to leave the computer, afraid the information on the disc might suddenly vanish.

He hadn't heard anything from the direction of the tent in the last hour. No music, no laughter. He was surprised Bubba had not dropped by after the dance to check on how the search was progressing. But Michael couldn't blame him. Clair had probably invited him back to her place. Michael would have liked to have known who the new queen was. He hoped it was Jessica, although he realized that would make her even more unattainable.

He was about to return to his seat at the terminal when he became aware of an unusual sound outside. He paused, standing in the middle of the room, and listened. He thought someone must be knocking hard on a nearby door. Then he dismissed that possibility. Whoever it was would have had to have been knocking with a battering ram. The door—if that was what it was—sounded as if it were disintegrating.

Michael reached for the door to investigate further. A beep at his back stopped him. Turning, he saw the word *Found* flashing at the top of the computer screen. He jumped to his feet.

Subject: Alice McCoy. Age: 14. Coroner: Dr. Gin Kawati.

Forgetting all about the sound, Michael began to read.

The dance was history. The cleanup had begun.

Jessica and Sara had changed from their gowns back into the clothes they had worn to the basketball game. Along with Maria, they were trying to undo in a couple of hours what had taken weeks to put together. It was a hopeless task. If the amount of fun had by all was proportional to the amount of mess they had made, then Sara's place in Tabb's history as the best ASB president was already secure.

Polly had hung around at first and tried to lend a hand, but watching her hop pathetically about with plates and glasses balanced in her arms, Jessica and Sara had sent her home. Maria was almost as useless. She had *not* changed out of her dress. She continued to float about beneath the deserted tent as if the crowds were still cheering her to the top of the float, a stoned smile on her lips.

All right, I'm envious. That doesn't mean I'll hate Maria from now on.

Jessica couldn't figure out how the girl had won.

"I'm tired," she complained, stuffing red ribbon in a green plastic trash bag and wiping the sweat from her eyes.

"You can't quit," Sara said, standing on a ladder above her. "This tent has to be ready to take down by tomorrow at noon or I'll have to pay for another day's rental."

"Let them take it down the way it is," Jessica said.

"Sure, right, and leave this pile of garbage out in the open where everybody can see it."

"Ask me if I care, Sara." Jessica threw down her bag. "I've had enough. I'm going to my locker, getting my books, and I'm not coming back."

"Some friend you are." Then Sara stopped, surveying the tons of junk. "Well, I guess you're right. There is too much to do. Go home and rest." She lowered her voice, nodded to the other side of the tent where Maria was gathering the carnations from the tables, smelling each one as if it were a gift from a boyfriend. "But on your way out, ask our little brown butterfly to give me a hand with the last of these ribbons."

"Will do."

Sara stared at her a moment. "You know, Jessie, you looked awful pretty tonight, it should have been you."

Jessica smiled, touched. "Wasn't in the cards, I guess."

Maria hugged Jessica when she told her she was leaving.

"I owe all this to you," Maria said, holding her tight.

"You did it yourself," Jessica said, embarrassed by the twinge of jealousy that was still there.

Maria let go, shook her head. "I lived in a box until you came along. I never went out. I never talked to boys. If it wasn't for you, I wouldn't even know Nick."

Jessica squeezed her arm. "We all get what we deserve, Maria. I really believe that."

Except for Alice, our sweet Alice.

Jessica grabbed her coat and left.

The wind had died. The cold had deepened. She had to get her homework from her locker before she could go home. Outside the tent, striding across the empty basketball courts toward the silent black buildings, Jessica looked up at the clear sky punctured with stars. Thoughts of Alice had come and now they would not leave. Jessica decided not to fight them. Sometimes when she was sad, she would remember everything in her life that had ever brought her unhappiness, and then whatever was depressing her at the moment would appear less significant, and she would feel better.

She spotted the red star she had been wondering about the night she had gone out with Bill. Again, she wished she had Michael by her side to tell her its name.

Strange how she could not remember Alice without thinking of Michael. He was always there, deep in her mind, standing beside Alice, as he had been in the painting her lost friend had been working on before she died.

I'll have to find that picture and hang it above my bed.

Lowering her gaze, Jessica quickened her pace. Soon she was under the exterior-covered walkway, her sneakers squeaking on the smooth concrete, cursing again the fact that Tabb was too cheap to keep a few lights burning throughout the night. With the roof from the class wing above her head and the branches of some of Tabb's oldest trees off to her side, she was in a dark place, so dark she could barely see her hand in front of her face.

As a child, the dark had both fascinated and frightened her. During the day, when the sun was bright, she had loved nothing better than to go exploring with Polly in a big sewer that was the sole source and inspiration for a creek that ran through a jungle of a lot not far from their houses. The lot was later to become a park, and then the site of another housing tract, but in those days, it had been *the* big outdoors. They must have been five or six at the time. The last time Jessica could remember exploring the tunnel with Polly—their legs spread wide so they wouldn't step in the smelly water that ran down the center, their heads bent low, flashlights swiped from Polly's garage gripped tight in each of their tiny grubby grips— had been the time they had brought Alice with them. *That* had been a mistake.

They were farther into the tunnel than they had ever been before. They had been walking forever. They were excited. Of course it was a big dream of theirs to get to the other end of the thing. They had this idea that if they could get that far, then the dimensions of the world—or at least of their neighborhood— would make more sense. Then they would know where they stood in the scheme of things.

They could see no light up ahead. But a noise had begun to throb around them, a slow thumping sound that reminded Jessica of a giant heart—not the heart of a person, but the heart of a huge machine, a machine that she imagined made all the cars and buildings and sewers. When they got to that noise, she thought, they would really know what was happening.

She never did find out what the noise was.

Alice slipped, smack into the slime in the center of the

sewer. Turning to rescue her, Polly dropped her flashlight and broke it. And naturally, in the heat of the moment, Jessica imagined that her flashlight was beginning to fail too. She told the others it was, and the thought of what it would be like to be trapped in the sewer without any light was enough to send them racing back at warp speed.

Oddly enough, however, once they were out, Alice had begged them to try again to reach the other end. But Alice's stinking clothes alerted their parents to what they had been doing. Their subterranean exploration days were over.

The heart of a machine.

Jessica stopped in midstride in the black walkway.

There was a noise coming from up ahead. Not the noise she had heard in the tunnel a dozen years ago. That had been deep and rhythmic. This one sounded like someone chopping wood. Yet as she listened more closely in the dark, holding her breath, her heart pounding steadily harder and harder, the gap between the chops seemed to shorten, to almost disappear altogether, to blur with her heartbeat, until they were practically a single sound, until she was feeling smaller and smaller, and standing, not in a school outdoor walkway, but far beneath the ground, with a machine over her head that made *everything*— maybe even little girls.

The sound stopped. Silence. Her heart could have stopped.

Then Jessica heard the crash. Glass, metal, and wood exploding.

Help!

She turned and ran back the way she had come. But this was not a tunnel, with only two ways to go. Suddenly it was a maze, and she didn't even have a failing flashlight to show her the way. She went right, she went left. She didn't know which way she was going. It was insane; she spent five hours, five days a week at this school. And now she was lost!

Then she froze, holding on to the corner of an exterior wall, on to the tunnel wall. When she was a child, this had never happened to her. Although as a child, she had, like every other child in the world, dreamed it a million times.

Footsteps. Rapidly approaching footsteps.

Someone was chasing her!

Jessica let out a soft moan, remembering how when the three of them had escaped from the sewer into the wonderful sunlight, they'd discovered Alice had skinned her head. How the blood had trickled from the side of Alice's head through her bright blond hair.

And how the blood had *flowed* out the back of Alice's head as she lay dead on her back on the hard floor in her parents' bedroom.

And Michael said she'd been murdered.

Jessica bolted away from the footsteps, around the corner, back down a walkway she had the terrible feeling she had run up a moment ago.

God help me. God save me.

Apparently God only helped those who helped themselves. Or those who had a better sense of direction.

She ran smack into her pursuer.

He grabbed her. She screamed.

Michael was confused, and all because of a paragraph Dr. Kawati had added to the end of the autopsy report. The other ninety-five percent of the information had been much as he had expected.

The coroner had detailed how a twenty-two-caliber bullet had entered through the roof of Alice's mouth, torn through her cerebral cortex, ricocheted off the top of her skull, and finally exited via the base of the skull. In his notes, the doctor referred several times to a sketch he had drawn tracing the path of the bullet, and to X rays he had apparently taken during the examination—neither of which was available in the data Bubba had swiped. But the absence of the sketch and the X rays was not what had Michael stumped. Nor was the analysis of her blood out of line. Alice had had no unusual chemicals in her system at the time of her death, not even alcohol. There had also been no sign that she had undergone a struggle immediately prior to her death: no flesh under her fingernails, which might have been scraped from an assailant; no scratches on her face or arms; and, at first glance, no bruises anywhere on her body.

In conclusion, the doctor had stated that the cause of

death was a severe cerebral hemorrhage brought about by a self-inflicted gunshot wound.

Then he had added a note at the end.

> Because the bullet traveled a complex path before exiting the head, the girl's brain was left in extremely poor shape. It is, therefore, difficult to know if the hemorrhage found in the region of the hypothalamus and thalamus was brought about by the course of the bullet or by the force of the blow to her nasal cartilage. The cartilage has a significant fracture across its entire width, which could not have been a result of the bullet's trajectory. It is the opinion of this coroner that Alice McCoy must have fractured her nasal cartilage upon hitting the floor with her face after shooting herself. As she was found lying on her back, I must assume that someone rolled her over before the police arrived. It is suggested to the investigating officers they pay special attention to this point when questioning all those involved.

A fractured nasal cartilage? That was a fancy way of saying Alice had a broken nose in addition to a hole in her head. Michael was angry—but not the least surprised—that Lieutenant Keller had withheld this information. But Michael did remember the detective repeatedly asking if anyone moved Alice after they had found her. The lieutenant had obviously been anxious to clear up the discrepancy; and yet he had closed the case without doing so.

There were two possibilities. Either someone had moved Alice's body before they reached the room, or else something other than the fall had broken her nose.

Did someone break it for her?

The bullet had clearly snaked around inside her skull before exiting at the base; nevertheless, the bullet hole in the wall had been at best only three feet off the floor. And straight into the plaster. The chances remained that Alice had been sitting when she was shot.

And if that were true, it would be almost impossible for her to have broken her nose in a fall.

Did someone hit her, hit her hard, in the face?

The coroner had also referred to an area of hemorrhage that was possibly unconnected to that caused by the bullet. That raised another question, one that was in many ways far more confusing than the others.

What?

Something large and loud crashed outside.

Michael leaped to his feet. He was out the door before he could finish asking himself the hard question.

The dark caught him off guard. For a moment he couldn't see far enough to know in which direction to run. He paused, straining to listen. It was then he heard the footsteps, racing along the hallway on the other side of the wing that housed the computer lab. He assumed the footsteps belonged to the person who had caused the crash. He set off after him.

Whoever this individual was, he couldn't make up his mind which way he was headed. He was fast, though. Michael chased him up one hallway, down another, without catching so much as a glimpse of him. But the idiot was going in circles. Michael finally decided on a different approach. He stopped and silently jogged the *other* way, away from the guy. The strategy proved effective. A minute later he ran right into him.

"Hold on there, buddy," he shouted, grabbing him by the wrists. The fellow—he wasn't that tall—struggled furiously.

"Let me go! Help!"

Michael let her go in a hurry. "Jessie?"

"Oh, thank God," she whispered, collapsing against his chest, sobbing. "Someone's chasing me, Michael."

"*I* was chasing you." He held her in his arms. He never would have believed a person could shake so much and still remain earthbound. He could hardly see her face, but he could feel her hot panting breath on his neck. He brushed her sweaty hair from her eyes, hugged her tight. "Shh, you're OK. You're safe. No one's going to hurt you."

"There was this strange sound," she said, weeping. "It was like in the tunnel, and then it just blew up, and I started running, and I—I don't know." She pulled back, wiped at her eyes, dazed. "What was it, Michael?"

"Let's go see. I think the crash came from the courtyard."

Jessica grabbed his hand. "Do you think it's all right?"

He spoke calmly, although inside he was not exactly coasting along himself. "We'll be fine." He didn't want to leave her alone, even back in the computer room.

They found the varsity tree—it was lying across the snack bar. The trunk had caved in one entire wall of the building. Branches poked out dozens of glass windows. It was quite simple; someone had chopped it down. They discovered the ax resting in the grass on top of a pile of wood chips scattered beside the splintered stump. Jessica knelt to touch it. Michael stopped her.

"There could be fingerprints," he warned. He glanced about, but didn't see anybody. "Why are you here by yourself this late?"

"I was helping Sara and Maria clean up the mess from the dance. Then I was going to my locker to get my homework. Michael, why would anyone want to kill this tree?"

"I don't know. Are Sara and Maria still at the tent?"

"Yes. I think so."

The tree had not fallen in a random fashion. The angle had been purposely chosen to cause the most destruction possible. Only a crazy person could have been behind this. In the wake of reading the conflicting details surrounding Alice's death, the thought sent a shiver through Michael. "Let's get the girls and get out of here," he said.

Before they left the scene of the crime, however, Michael changed his mind about the ax. Getting a handkerchief from Jessica, he grabbed it by the blade and took it with them.

Sara yawned. She was as beat as Jessica had complained about being. The day had gone on forever. But she was sort of sad it was all over. Russ had been disqualified in his race, Jessica had not been crowned queen, and yet many good things had happened. Ten years from now, she imagined, if she was still alive and the world was still here, she would have fond memories of homecoming.

"Maria, I'm stacking these trash bags together and then I'm out of here," Sara called.

Maria was wandering about on the float, her royal flowers in her hands. Sara had to chuckle. There was someone who was definitely unhappy to see the evening end. No doubt Maria would find it hard to fall asleep, remembering what it had been like to hear her name called out, how it had felt to ascend to the top of the queen's tower with the whole school cheering her on.

"OK," Maria said, disappearing into the back of the float.

She's doing it all over! But can I blame her?

Thoroughly amused, Sara watched as Maria slowly wound her way up the tower steps. Once at the top, Maria set down her flowers and picked up her crown, holding it high above her head in both her hands.

"We should do this every week!" Maria called.

"Somehow, I don't think it would be the same," Sara said, glancing down, twisting the tie on the trash bag in her hands. As a result—with her attention divided—she had only a vague idea of what happened next.

Out the corner of her eye, Sara received the impression that Maria had placed the crown on her head and did a little skip into the air. That was it. Then Maria appeared to dematerialize. The illusion persisted for a fraction of a second. Until Sara heard the scream and the crash, and knew the top level of the float had caved in and taken Maria with it.

She can't be dead. Please, God.

Sara scarcely remembered crossing the tent and leaping onto the float. The next thing she knew, she was staring down into a deep, mangled hole. There was sufficient light to see the worst. Maria lay sprawled over the truck's shattered windshield, her body bent at a grotesque angle. There was blood on the glass and glass in her face. She was not moving.

"I'm coming, Maria," Sara said. "I'm coming."

It was well that Michael and Jessica showed up at that moment and that Michael had an ax in his hands. Sara had no idea how to help Maria without doing more damage. Shouting for Sara to get down, Michael peeped through a crack in the tower wall, and then began to hack away with the blade. Apparently he did not feel it would be wise to attempt to free Maria by coming in from beneath the float. Sara trusted his judgment. Hanging on to Jessica in the middle of the drawbridge, Sara felt more helpless than she had ever felt in her entire life.

Michael was through the wall in a couple of minutes. Pulling away the cracked boards, he stepped down on top of the hood of the truck. Jessica and Sara crouched beside his chopped opening.

"Is she alive?" Jessica whispered, staring in horror.

There was not a great deal of blood. It was the way Maria was lying—her torso twisted like a Gumby; her chest and face pressed into the roof; her legs jammed into the steering wheel—that filled her with dread.

"She's breathing," Michael said, taking her pale wrist in his hands and feeling for a pulse. "She's alive."

"Let's get her out!" Jessica exclaimed.

"No," Michael said firmly. "We can't move her. She could have a spinal injury." He pointed to Jessica. "There's a phone at the entrance of the gym. Dial nine-one-one. Describe the situation and our location." He nodded. "Hurry."

With Jessica gone, Sara carefully stepped onto the hood beside Michael. "It's just like the party," she said bitterly.

He sighed. "It doesn't surprise me."

Pulling her Mercedes onto her street, Polly spotted Clark swinging a leg over his motorcycle parked at the foot of her driveway. Before she could reach the house, however, he had gunned the engine and roared off in the opposite direction. For a moment she contemplated going after him. But even if she had been in a Ferrari, she knew she would never have caught him. He was like a witch on a broom.

Heading up her driveway, she noticed that the front door was wide open. The house was black, and she never left for the evening without turning on at least a couple of lamps.

"Aunty," she whispered to herself, leaping out of her car.

Inside, she couldn't get a light to go on. Either Clark had fiddled with the circuit breakers or else he had broken every bulb in the house. She stumbled into the kitchen, found a candle in a drawer, and lit it on the pilot light of the stove. Creeping down the hall toward her aunt's bedroom, shadows following her along both walls, she started to cry.

Her aunt was lying on her back and staring at the ceiling. Staring without blinking. Polly set the candle down on the nearby bed stand and sat on the bed. Aunty's pupils had clouded over, like cheap marbles that had been left too long in the bright sun. Polly couldn't even tell what color her eyes had been, and this disturbed her a great deal, that she couldn't remember.

Polly picked up the old lady's mottled hand. It was soft, softer than it had been in life, and it was still warm. She had not been dead long.

She was alive when Clark was here.

Polly glanced at the ceiling and didn't see the blood dripping down that he had spoken of; nevertheless, she felt herself smothering, a black panic rising.

She fainted on top of the dead woman.

Epilogue

Jessica drifted in and out of reality trying to sleep on the hard brown vinyl couch in the deserted hospital waiting room. When she was awake, she watched Michael and Nick sitting in the hallway outside the room. Sometimes they would be talking quietly to each other. Other times Nick's head would be slumped back on the wall and he would be snoring softly. But always Michael would be sitting upright, and always he looked as if he were thinking. Not once, however, did she catch him looking her way. And this simple fact filled her with a sadness that went beyond reason. It made her anguish about Maria almost unbearable. There was only pain in waking.

In being alive.

Then there were her dreams. They were mostly dark thundering things without shape or reason. But there was one that had sent a knife through her heart when she had awakened from it; for it had been beautiful and filled with a joyfulness that made her chest ache to recall it.

She was in the tunnel of her childhood. Only now Michael was with her, and they were both fully grown. Alice was there also, and another blond-haired girl Jessica did not recognize. But the two girls were younger, only three or four years old. Together, with Michael leading the way with the aid of an old-fashioned lantern, they were approaching what they knew to be the end of the tunnel.

A warm yellow light began to stream over them from up ahead, making their eyes shine and their hearts quicken. Then the walls of the tunnel started to dissolve, until they could see through them. Suddenly Michael smiled and extinguished the lantern. And they were standing on a sloping desert plain, with a sparkling clear sky overhead and a breeze, sweet with the fragrance of honey, wafting through their hair. In the distance were a cool green ocean and people, old friends of theirs they could hardly wait to meet again.

Behind them, Jessica caught the faint roar of a churning river and realized that the now-invisible tunnel had been a bridge over the icy water. It was, however, only a passing thought, of something that had once concerned her but which she now understood to be of no importance. Michael took her hand—Alice and her friend were dancing ahead of them—and they walked toward the place by the ocean where the day was only beginning.

She felt as if she had just been born.

A bright spot in a dreary night. Fits of reality and nightmares chased her from then on. Until she felt a hand on her arm, shaking her gently.

"Jessie, wake up. Time to get up."

Jessica opened her eyes and discovered Sara sitting beside her on the couch. Sara had begun the vigil with Jessica outside the operating room at two in the morning, but had rushed home after receiving an emergency call from her mother. It hadn't been clear exactly what the problem was.

"What time is it?" She yawned, pushing herself up with an effort, her neck stiff as a board.

"Eight-thirty," a voice said at her back. It was Michael, standing in the hazy sunlight of the waiting-room window. "The doctors say Maria's operation went well. Her parents are with her now."

"But is she going to be all right?" Jessica asked anxiously. "What did they operate on?"

"Her back," Michael said, coming over and sitting on the chair beside them. "It was broken."

"Is she—paralyzed?" Jessica asked.

Michael shook his head, tired. "I don't know. I don't think the doctors like to use that word. One of us might be allowed in to see her in a few minutes. Nick's gone to talk to the surgeon who performed the operation."

"At least she's alive," Sara said.

"Yeah," Michael said. "She was lucky."

"What did your mom want?" Jessica asked Sara. Her old friend grimaced.

"Bad news. The police identified the ax you guys found as the ax taken from the store where Russ used to work. They found his fingerprints on the handle. They've arrested him!"

"You can't be serious?" Jessica said.

"Can't your parents verify where Russ was at one o'clock in the morning?" Michael asked.

"No," Sara said. "He didn't go straight home after the dance."

"Where did he go?" Jessica asked.

Sara hesitated. "He says he went to a bar. But the idiot—he can't remember which one."

"That's bad," Michael said.

"You don't think he chopped down the tree, do you?" Jessica asked.

"Of course he didn't!" Sara snapped. "But while questioning him, the police learned that he'd stayed at Polly's house for a few days. They called her, and she said that she'd had the ax in the trunk of her car until last week, when it disappeared."

"What was Polly doing with the ax?" Jessica asked.

"She says she took it from Russ one night when he was drunk and trying to chop down the varsity tree."

"They believed her?" Jessica asked, amazed.

"Russ agreed with her! Except he says *I* was the one who stopped him back then and took his ax. He's incriminated himself left and right. They're going to lock him up, I swear it."

"No way," Jessica said.

"They might," Michael said. "When that tree fell, it caused a lot of damage."

"He should have kept his mouth shut," Sara said. "Polly should have kept her mouth shut." She sighed, rubbing her head. "I guess we can't blame her, though. Her night was as lousy as Maria's. Her aunt passed away."

Jessica groaned. "It never stops."

Sara nodded. "And to top it off, an old-time employee of her parents' company died yesterday from a work-related accident. She's got two more funerals to go to. I hope they won't be plugging her into the socket again." Sara stood. "I have to get back to the police station. I'm trying to get Russ out on bail."

"Will your parents lend you the money?" Jessica asked.

"No," Sara said. "They're being total jerks about the whole thing." She patted Jessica on the shoulder. "I'll be back later to check on Maria. I guess we should be glad things can't get any worse. See you, Mike."

When Sara was gone, Michael sat beside her on the couch. "Can I get you anything from the snack bar?" he asked.

"Thanks, I'm not hungry. Have you been up all night?"

"Yeah."

"And you don't think it was an accident?"

Her question surprised him. "It's hard to tell from what's left of the tower. Clearing a path to Maria, I messed up the evidence something awful. We may never know if someone tampered with the float."

"But you think someone did, don't you?"

He shrugged. "I'm not sure of anything these days." He glanced at her. He needed a shave. She needed a hug. "What did Sara mean when she made that remark about plugging Polly into the socket again?"

"When we were twelve, Polly's parents died. Alice must have told you. They drove off a road in the desert and their car burst into flames. Polly was with them, but was thrown free. She didn't get so much as a scratch. But she suffered from severe depression afterward, and was in the hospital for a long time. The doctors treated her with electroshock."

"What!" Michael exclaimed. "They used electro-shock on a twelve-year-old girl?"

"Is that unusual?" she asked uneasily. "She had the best doctors money could buy. It seemed to help."

Michael shook his head angrily. "Electroshock has got to be the greatest evil modern psychiatry ever spawned. It alleviates people's depression by causing irreversible brain damage. The patient is no longer unhappy because he can hardly remember what was making him unhappy."

"Then why do they use it?"

"You said it: 'the best doctors money could buy.' It costs the hospital a few cents in electricity, produces superficial improvement, and makes M.D.s tons of cash." He nodded to himself. "The man with the electricity.' Makes sense."

"What?"

"Just something Polly said to me when I was at her house."

"Why did you go to her house?"

He realized he'd made a slip. "You know why."

"I suppose I do." She touched his arm. "Michael, you've got to let it go."

He looked away. "I can't."

"But it's tearing you apart."

"Not like it tore Maria apart," he muttered.

"What?"

"Nothing." He rested his head in his hands, his eyes on the floor. He was thinking again. "She was outside when the gun went off. We're sure of that, aren't we?"

"Who?"

"Polly. The night of the party."

"Yes, she was outside, *alone* in the backyard. And Alice was upstairs, *alone* in her parents' bedroom. Polly didn't kill her. She loved Alice."

Michael sat up. "But a crazy person could love someone and still kill her. She wouldn't need a reason why."

"You think Polly's crazy?"

"I think she's close enough not to make much difference."

"You're wrong. She may be a bit off, but she gets by. I've known her a lot longer than you."

He softened his tone. "I appreciate that, Jessie—that she's

your friend. And I realize you knew her before they attached electrodes to her brain. But tell me honestly, was it the same Polly who came out of the hospital that went in?"

"Of course she wasn't the same," she said, wondering if she wasn't trying to convince herself. "She was a young girl, and she'd lost both her parents."

"I wonder if that's all there was to it."

"But you saw Polly go out to the backyard, same as me," she said, her voice growing constricted with emotion. "And you saw her come running inside when the gun went off. Believe me, I know that house. There's no way up to the master bedroom except the stairs we took. There're no trapdoors, no hidden stairways. It's physically impossible that she shot Alice. It's impossible anyone did."

Michael looked unconvinced; nevertheless, he nodded. "I can't argue with what you say. I'm sorry I brought it up. I didn't mean to upset you."

He was still feeling guilty, she knew, about the time he had yelled at her in Alice's studio after the funeral. She smiled, squeezed his arm. "You never have to apologize to me, Michael."

He blushed, or frowned, or both. "Yeah?"

"It's true. And I'll tell you why it's true."

Because you're the only one I know who's striving for perfection. Who's completely noble and totally unselfish. The only one who's always there when I need rescuing from myself.

The words did not come out, not right away, and not so

much because she was embarrassed to say them, but because she was ashamed that she had stood him up on their date, that she had purposely started the rumor of Clair's abortion and accepted his help on the SAT. That she was unworthy of him.

"Jessie?" he said, waiting for her.

I can still tell him, and let him decide. About me. Us.

"Because, Michael Olson, old locker buddy—"

"Jessie," Nick called, striding into the waiting room, a different person from the guy who had led Tabb to victory the night before. He had huge bags under his eyes. He stuttered when he spoke. "The d-doctor said you can see M-Maria for a couple of minutes."

"Have you seen her?" Jessica asked, jumping up with Michael.

"She wants to see you first," Nick said, tense.

"But how is she?" Jessica asked. "Will she be able to walk again?"

"I don't know," Nick complained. "Nobody will tell me nothing. And her parents have left already."

Jessica followed Nick's directions and ended up in an aggressively green intensive-care ward. The medicine smell made her empty stomach uneasy. The patients' rooms were tiny glass cubicles arranged around a nurses' station packed with enough electronic equipment to pilot a Trident submarine. The RN on duty pointed out Maria's box and reminded her that her visit was not to exceed three minutes.

A white sheet loosely covered Maria's body; it wasn't much whiter than the color of her skin. Quietly closing the door, Jessica noted through an opening in the sheet that a plastic and metal brace was locked over Maria's bare hips. It reached all the way up her side, embracing her slim shoulders. It could not have looked more uncomfortable. Maria had her eyes open— one eye, rather; the other was swollen shut—and was staring at the ceiling.

Where else can she look?

"It's me," Jessica said.

Maria cleared her throat. "I know."

Jessica moved closer to the bed. Bandage covered the right side of Maria's face; out the bottom of it peeked a stitched cut. She would be scarred as well.

But did she sever her spinal cord?

Jessica walked over to take Maria's hand and bumped into her IV. Wires led from beneath the sheet to monitors overhead. She had to fight to keep her voice calm. "How are you, Maria?"

Her single black eye turned toward Jessica. "How do I look?"

She forced a smile. "A little under the weather. But you'll be better soon. This is a great hospital."

"Is it?"

"Oh, yeah. I had my appendix out here when I was thirteen years old. They have the best doctors. Wonderful nurses."

Maria closed her eye. "Since you love it here so much, it's too bad it wasn't you who broke her back."

"Huh?" Jessica had to force air into her lungs in order to speak. "You don't mean that."

Maria smiled, and with her cuts and swollen face, it was truly gruesome. "I remember when you talked me into putting my name on the ballot for the homecoming court. You told me this was America, that anything could happen, that I might even be nominated queen. But you didn't believe it. Had you thought I stood a chance in a million, you wouldn't have let me get within a mile of that ballot."

"You've been through a terrible ordeal," Jessica said, struggling to keep her composure. "You need to rest, to heal. And you're going to heal, Maria."

Maria looked at her again, her one eye a single accusing finger. "It should have been you standing at the top of that float. You wanted to be homecoming queen more than anything. You schemed to go out with the popular boys so you'd be popular. You told lies about Clair. You told me lies."

"Stop it. You don't know what you're saying."

"It should be you lying here instead of me!"

The tears burst from Jessica then and she had to turn away. She went to the huge window by the door. Hanging from a white thread close to the glass was a silver angel—a Christmas decoration. With everything else going on, she had forgotten that Christmas was only a couple of weeks away. She had gotten so caught up in the fantasy of being the most desired girl on campus that she had almost overlooked what had always been for her the most precious time of the year, and the realization made her feel there must be some justice in what Maria said.

I'm no longer a little girl. I've grown up. I'm a bitch.

Searching for a handkerchief in her pocket to wipe away her tears, her fingers ran into a bobby pin. An idea occurred to her. Pulling out the pin, her back to Maria, she scraped off the rubbery black stuff at the ends. Then she stepped to the foot of the bed.

"They'll only let me stay a minute longer," she said, carefully lifting the sheet from Maria's toes. Maria, her eyes again closed, didn't seem to notice.

"A pity."

"I'm still your friend, no matter what you may think right now. I'll be back tomorrow to visit." Holding the pin between her thumb and index finger, she poked it gently into Maria's heel.

She should have jumped. If she could feel . . .

"Don't put yourself out."

She poked Maria harder, again and again. But the girl just lay there. She was paralyzed. Jessica began to back away from the bed, trembling. She *had* lied to her. Maria was never going to heal. Never.

"It's no trouble," she said, her voice choking. "If I can bring you anything, anything at all?"

"There is one thing I would like."

"What?"

"A promise." Maria opened her eye, but Jessica did not believe she could actually see her this close to the door.

"Yes?"

"Promise me I will never have to see you again."

Jessica swallowed hard, tasting her friend's bitterness, her own worthlessness. "Good-bye, Maria. I hope you feel better soon."

Michael was waiting with Nick by the coffee machine in the hall next to the waiting room when Jessica reappeared. Ordinarily Michael did not drink coffee; it gave him heartburn. But since he had been staying awake all night worrying whether a girl was going to lose her life or not, he had considered it sort of absurd to be concerned about minor gastric upset. This was his eighth cup since three o'clock in the morning. Nick had just downed his tenth.

Jessica was crying. Nick grabbed her as she tried to pass them by without stopping. "What's wrong with Maria?" he demanded. "Did she die?"

Jessica stared at him, her eyes big and red. She shook her head weakly. "She wants to see you now."

Nick let go of her and dashed down the hall. Jessica took a couple of feeble steps forward and then sagged against the wall. Michael put down his coffee and placed his palms on her back, over her soft brown hair, feeling her shiver. "Tell me, Jessie?"

"The fall cut her spinal cord."

"You're sure?"

"Yes."

He had feared as much. "That's very sad. But it's not the end of the world for her. She can live a full life. But she's going to need a lot of support. I know you have a lot to give her."

Jessica stood upright, looked at him, her face a mess with tears. "She hates me."

"What? No."

"She told me she wishes it was me who was crippled instead of her."

"She didn't mean it. She's just upset. Tomorrow—"

"There won't be any tomorrow!" Jessica cried. "I told you, she hates me! She doesn't want to see me again. She blames me for what happened to her."

"She came out of surgery two hours ago. You can't take what she says seriously. You didn't do anything to her. You're her friend."

"Like I'm your friend, Michael?" She shook loose from his hands. "You don't know who I am. I screw you left and right and you think I'm Miss Pretty Perfect. Well, I'm not. I don't give a damn about anybody except myself."

"We all watch out for ourselves. We have to because most of the time it seems no one is watching out for us. I know how you feel. You're not a bad person." He took a breath. "If you were, I wouldn't care about you the way—"

"No!" she interrupted. "It's all true. Everything I touch gets ruined. Alice and Maria and Clair—I do it on purpose I think!"

"Stop it. You're carrying on exactly like I did after the funeral." He lowered his voice, tried to hold her. "Jessie, listen to me, I need to tell you something."

"No," she moaned, pushing him away. "Don't touch me. Don't get near me. I'm no good, Michael. I'm not."

"Jessie?"

She wouldn't listen. She turned and fled down the hall. He didn't go after her. Had people chased after him during the days following Alice's party, he might have killed them. He would leave her alone, maybe forever. He would remain alone.

Nick returned a few minutes later. He was pale as a ghost. "Does she hate you, too?" Michael asked wearily.

Nick fell down in a chair. "She wants the person who tampered with the float," he said. "She's flipped out. She thinks there's a plot against her."

"Anything else?"

Nick nodded heavily. "She told me to find those responsible. She threatened me if I didn't."

"How?"

Nick bowed his head. "She said if I didn't do what she wanted, she would tell the police I was running down the stairs, away from the bedroom, right after the gun was fired at the party."

"That's true?"

"Yeah," he croaked. "I lied to you before. I was afraid the

police would hear that and think I'd killed Alice."

It was Michael's turn to use the wall for support. "Why were you running downstairs?"

"I thought the gunshot came from there." He shook his head miserably. "I don't know, I was scared. I'm sorry, Mike."

Kats also thought the shot came from downstairs.

Michael pulled himself off the wall and slapped Nick on the back. "Stay with her, buddy. Love her. It's the best anybody can do. I'm going home."

Nick nodded pitifully, beginning to weep. "She can't feel anything in her legs. Nothing from the waist down."

"I know. I wish—" He wished a thousand wishes, but it didn't make any difference. There was nothing he could say. He left Nick and headed for the parking lot, where he climbed into his car. About to start the engine, he noticed Temple High's yearbook on the passenger seat. On impulse, he reached over and began to browse through it again. He hadn't really searched the book thoroughly the first time. Perhaps . . .

It could have been coincidence, like Kats and Nick both running the wrong way toward a gunshot they were closer to than anyone else.

Michael found Clark in a group photo on the lower-right-hand corner of the first page he turned to. It was a black-and-white, and the bright green eyes and red hair were not in evidence. But it was the bastard; there was no mistaking that twisted grin.

The picture had several people in it. None of them were identified at the bottom by name. Michael flipped to the end of the junior class and studied the list of names of kids who hadn't posed for pictures. There was only one Clark.

Clark Halley.

We're going to have a talk, guy. A long talk.

THE GRADUATION

Chapter One

T he last day of school began early for Sara Cantrell. As ASB president, she had inherited the job of passing out the yearbooks. No one else had wanted to do it. The task called for a crack-of-dawn rising. The books had only arrived the night before and had to be unpacked and sorted into alphabetical order. The yearbook club had been late sending the book to the printers. There had been some concern—so the rumor went—about the quality of the athletic photographs.

The price of vanity. Did I not say it months ago?

Sara smiled with glee as she squatted on the floor of the recently reconstructed snack bar and tore open one of the boxes and pulled out a copy of the annual. The cover was dark blue, featureless except for a silver name tag on the top and a tiny gold rope emblem in the lower right corner, which Sara had to assume bore some relationship to Tabb High's bronco-bull mascot. Quickly she turned to the sports section. A moment later she was laughing her head off.

"Where are your glasses, Jessie?"

"Bug off, Sara."

In the basketball section in particular, and to a lesser extent throughout the football and wrestling pages, every other picture looked as if it had been shot underwater. There was a blurred photograph of Nick Grutler going to the basket with what could have been a swollen pumpkin in his hand.

"I love it," Sara said aloud, noting something else unusual about the basketball section. Michael Olson, who had been dropped from the team at the start of the season, was in more pictures than anyone else. And a couple of those were remarkably sharp. Jessica must have slipped on her glasses for a second here and there during the game against Holden High, Sara decided. No doubt there was going to be talk when the rest of the basketball players saw how he had been favored.

They'll talk all day, and talk all night. Then nobody will see anybody again.

The graduation ceremony was to be held at three in the afternoon in the football stadium. The time had been moved up to accommodate nearby Sanders High's ceremony. Sanders's stadium was undergoing major renovations. Sara thought it was a bum rap that Sanders's ceremony wasn't first. She would have the sun directly in her eyes when she addressed the stands.

She still hadn't figured out exactly what she was going to say in her speech, although she had stayed up half the night worrying about it. She simply had too much on her mind. There was the all-night party aboard the cruise ship she still had to pay for, and then there was Russ Desmond. Last Christmas he had been sent to a juvenile hall in northern California for chopping down the varsity tree, which fell on the snack bar. He was being released—temporarily—to attend graduation and receive his diploma. She was supposed to pick him up in downtown L.A. at the bus station at one o'clock. She hadn't seen him in over five months.

He's probably forgotten what I look like.

Sara set aside the yearbook and, with a razor blade, began to cut open the boxes. Although the books had not been packed alphabetically, she was pleased to see they had been grouped according to class, simplifying her job somewhat. But there was still a lot to do. Tabb High had a student body of over two thousand, and more than half had ordered annuals. She wished she had Jessica to help her, the new clear-sighted Jessie who now wore her glasses wherever she went. But her best friend, bless her lazy hide, was getting her full measure of beauty sleep this morning.

The first knock at the window came two hours later, an hour earlier than Sara had anticipated—she had less than half the annuals unpacked. Two junior girls wanted their books *now*. Sara had no sooner found them than two more students arrived. It must have been because it was the last day—no one came to school this early usually. From that time on she was running. She quickly gave up checking receipts and IDs. If anyone felt he needed to steal a yearbook to be happy, she wasn't going to stand in the way.

Fortunately, before the big rush started around eight-thirty, three sophomores on the student council came to her rescue. Now she was able to take people's names and call them out to her helpers, who would hand her the right book a moment later.

Michael Olson and Clair Hilrey appeared at eight forty-five.

Sara had seen neither of them since January. Both had chosen to leave school at the semester. Apparently both had had enough units; and that was all that mattered, although Michael's GPA must have been about twice Clair's. The word going around was that Clair was making big bucks modeling and Michael was working for the government on some top-secret space laser. But, Sara knew, you couldn't believe everything you heard, although Clair *had* been on the cover of the May issue of *Seventeen*. Looked pretty damn good, too, and hadn't Jessica scowled when she had seen *that* magazine.

Clair had on baggy white shorts and a thin red blouse, perfect for the weather—the temperature was already close to eighty. She'd always had a tan, even in December, but now she was chestnut brown. It went without saying she was gorgeous.

Michael looked different. It was possible he hadn't cut his hair once since he'd left school. Black as night, and now curly, it hung way past his collar, practically onto his shoulders. He had lost weight, especially in his face. He appeared more handsome than she remembered, less a boy, more serious.

"Hi, Mike," Sara said. "Hi, Clair. Been a long time. How are you both doing?"

"We're just as happy as can be." Clair giggled, squeezing Michael's arm. Michael smiled faintly and nodded.

"It's good to see you, Sara," he said. "Busy?"

She glanced past them at the line. "Yeah, but I can take a minute off." She called behind her: "Michael Olson and Clair Hilrey. They're both seniors. And, Lori, take the window for a second." She had their books a few seconds later and carried them with her as she slipped out the side door of the snack bar. The carpenters were still working on the building's south wall; it was covered with plastic instead of stucco. The varsity tree had been awfully heavy.

Clair immediately opened her yearbook to the homecoming court pictures. Michael peered at the page over her shoulder. Clair made a face.

"That photographer—what an amateur," she complained.

"You look fine to me," Michael said.

"I'm supposed to look sexy, not fine," Clair said. She studied the page a little more, then added reluctantly, "But that is a nice picture of Jessica."

"Very nice," Michael agreed.

"Have you seen Jessie, Mike?" Sara asked. Clair quickly glanced over her shoulder at Michael.

"I've got to go," she said, suddenly closing the book. "I've got to find Bubba, Nice to see you, Sara."

"Catch you at graduation," Sara said.

"I'll be along in a minute," Michael told Clair. When she was gone, he said, "No, I just got here. How's she been?"

"Great," Sara said, which was something of an exaggeration. After Maria Gonzales's crippling accident the night of the homecoming dance, Jessica had gone into as deep a depression as she had when Alice died. She hadn't even returned to school after Christmas vacation to finish the semester. If Sara hadn't brought her work to her, Jessica might have flunked out. Her spirits had improved somewhat when she finally returned at the start of the new semester. Yet Sara continued to worry about her. Jessica wasn't interested in going to the movies, going shopping— hardly anything anymore. Sara had had to use every bit of her considerable persuasive skills to talk her into going to the senior prom in May with Bill Skater. Afterward, Jessica told her she'd had a wonderful time, but Sara didn't quite believe her. Jessica hadn't gone out with Bill since.

Not returning to school until the beginning of February, Jessica had missed Michael Olson's last days at Tabb. Sara remembered how Jessica's face fell when she had heard Michael was gone. To this day, however, Jessica denied they were close or that she cared one way or the other about him.

"She's doing real good," Sara continued. "She should be here any minute. Why don't you wait for her?"

He looked doubtful. "I have a lot to do today."

"But you're coming to the ceremony this afternoon, aren't you? I heard you're valedictorian?"

He smiled faintly at the mention of the word. "Yeah, it looks like I am. I have to give a speech."

"You're not the only one. Well, that's great. I'll get to introduce you. But I wish you could stay now. She should be here any sec. I know she'd love to see you."

He glanced down at the closed yearbook in his hands. "I really can't wait. But say hello to her for me."

"I will." She was trying to get rid of the habit of talking people into stuff. Russ had told her—before they had locked him up—that it was one of her least desirable personality traits. On the other hand, she didn't believe Michael couldn't wait a few minutes, any more than she believed Jessica when she had said it was no big deal that Michael had left school early. "She's as pretty as ever," she added.

Michael smiled politely. "I don't doubt it." He turned to leave. I'll be back this afternoon for the ceremony."

"Hey, hold on. Let me sign your yearbook."

"Sure." He handed it over. "Where's yours?"

"I've been so busy with everybody else's, I haven't had a chance to look for my own. You can sign it later on the boat. You're coming to the all-night party, aren't you?"

He hesitated, spoke under his breath. "If need be."

"Huh?"

"I don't know. I didn't buy a ticket."

She pulled a ticket from her back pocket and gave it to him. "It's on the house. The party won't be complete without our class genius." She clicked out her ballpoint pen and turned to one of the blank pages at the back of his yearbook. "I promise not to write anything disgusting," she said.

"Don't let me stop you," he remarked, stuffing the ticket into his back pocket and scanning the half-filled courtyard. Sara thought for a moment and then wrote.

> Mike,
>
> Of all the people in the school, you're the only one I wish I knew better. All the rest, I wish I could forget. Just kidding! What I really mean is, I'll never forget you. You're so smart! Figure out how to be happy and then tell the rest of us miserable slobs. We're counting on you.
>
> Luv, Sara

She returned his yearbook, saying, "Read it later tonight, preferably when you're drunk."

He nodded. "Thanks for the free ticket."

Sara hugged him briefly. "I'm so glad you're here. I think we're going to have a wild time today."

"I think so, too."

Michael left and Sara returned to distributing the yearbooks at the snack-bar window. Bubba put in a typical annoying appearance ten minutes later. He didn't have to say or do anything. Just the sight of him irritated Sara. It had been Bubba who had talked her into renting the cruise ship for the all-night party, even when he had known it was way beyond their means. She was beginning to believe he was purposely prolonging her personal crisis with the school funds to keep her dependent on him. After the homecoming dance, he had continued to pay her creditors just enough to keep them from suing, but not enough to make them go away. Lately he had been hinting at a scheme that would clear up all her money worries. Of course he hadn't said what it was.

"Come for your book?" she asked wearily. The predicted temperature for the day was a muggy ninety-five and Bubba had on an immaculate pair of light blue slacks, a navy-blue sports jacket and a red-and white-striped tie. His choice of hat that day was a wide-brimmed straw sombrero. He looked positively ridiculous and was loving every minute of it.

"No, I've come for you to sign it," he replied, lifting up his yearbook from beneath the counter. The silver name tag on the top read—in unusually big letters—BUBBA.

"Where did you get that?" she demanded. "I didn't give you that."

"I was sent an advance copy." He produced a feathered quill pen. "While you're signing mine, may I have the pleasure of brightening yours with a few words of love?"

"No. Go away, I'm busy."

Bubba glanced at the line behind him, smiled. "No time for Bubba on this, our last day of school? No time to share a precious moment to express our unspoken feeling for each other? Surely you must realize that an occasion such as this—"

"Stop it! I'll sign your stupid book. Lori, fetch my annual, and then do me a favor and take the window again. Thanks."

She met Bubba outside in the same spot she had spoken to Michael and Clair. Before handing over her annual, she said, "I talked the captain of the ship into taking a postdated check like you told me to. Now I want to know if the check will clear?"

"It should."

"What? Two days ago you told me it definitely would!"

"I do not believe I used the word 'definite.' The only things definite in this world are death, taxes, and my good humor."

"But my name's on that check!"

"Better your name than mine."

"Why are you doing this to me? What have I ever done to you?"

Bubba chuckled. "I've done nothing you haven't asked me to. You wanted a party the class wouldn't forget, and I told you how to give them one. I'm only here to serve, Sara."

She started to yell at him again, but couldn't think of anything to say. To her immense horror, she realized it was because what he said was partially true. He'd had no trouble putting her out on another financial limb. All he'd had to do was dangle before her nose another way to impress the school with what a fantastic president Sara Cantrell was.

"How are you serving me this week?" she asked. "Where's the school money?"

"I'd prefer not to say at this moment."

"Why not?"

"I'd rather not make you more nervous than you already are."

"What kind of answer is that? Where's the money?" Sara asked again.

"Do you like basketball?"

"Yeah, it's all right."

"The seventh game of the NBA finals is tonight. The Lakers versus the Celtics. A classic matchup. I grew up with the Lakers. They're my team. I know them better than their own coach."

"Wait a second. You didn't bet our money on a basketball game?"

"I was given excellent odds. We'll double our investment if we win."

"What if we lose?" she screamed.

He shrugged. "We'll still have our good looks." He held up his yearbook and offered her a regular ballpoint pen. "You don't have to go overboard. A few paragraphs and a poem or two will suffice to let me know you care."

Bubba came very close at that moment to losing whatever

good looks he believed he might have. Sara almost poked his eyes out. Only because she was essentially a nonviolent person did she grab his yearbook and pen instead. Inadvertently she let him get hold of her annual in the process. She plopped down on a nearby bench and began to scribble furiously on a back page.

> Bubba,
>
> Words, even the filthiest, cannot convey what I think of you. You are a liar, a thief, and a pervert. You are also the most unattractive slob to ever abuse my eyesight. I consider it the greatest misfortune of my adolescence that I had a chance to get to know you. You will not go far. You will end up in the mud—where you belong—with the rest of the world's slime.
>
> Get There As Soon As Possible,
> Sara

When she looked up, Bubba had vanished. He reappeared a couple of minutes later, her annual in his hand, a beatific smile on his lips. She snapped her book back and tossed him his. He read her inscription with obvious pleasure.

"You have beautiful handwriting," he said. "Very sensual."

"Go to hell."

"Later." He grinned as he walked away. "Later, Sara."

She was back inside the snack bar when she opened her yearbook. Her scream frightened everyone. Bubba had covered the entire inside cover with fat black marking-pen letters. There was no way to tear out the page. She shook as she read it.

My Dearest Sara,

My heart patters at the thought of us making love tonight above the deep ocean swells, our bodies locked in passion, the salty sweat on the burning flesh of our entangled limbs mingling like oil and wine, ready to burst into flaming ecstasy. My head swoons. Tonight, Sara, I promise you, will be our night. The gods will envy our joy.

But we mustn't be foolish. We mustn't forget, in our carnal hunger for each other, certain responsibilities. You would rather float on love-intoxicated perfumed clouds, I realize, ignoring the practical demands the world places upon us, only fantasizing about the pleasure I will send throbbing through your body. Yet we have to be careful. We can have our cake and eat it, too, but only if we don't let the ice cream melt. We have to get some condoms.

As you have probably guessed, anything that will heighten our delight is fine with me. I prefer the natural to the artificial, the tight to the loose, blue to red. Keep this in mind when you visit the pharmacy, Sara, and you will be thanked a thousand times over when the time comes.

Love You Always,

In So Many Different Positions,

Bubba

PS. Or, if you'd like, I can pick up something on the way to the boat?

"What is it?" Lori asked, standing beside her.

If the Lakers should win, would he keep the money if I don't come across?

Stupid question.

Sara slammed the book shut and answered Lori. "Don't ask."

Chapter Two

Michael had never seen Clair so happy. As they walked the familiar hallways searching for Bubba, she kept glancing over at him and giggling.

"What is it?" he asked finally.

"I have a secret I want to tell you, but I can't."

"What if I promise to tell no one else?"

"I still can't tell you. Bubba would kill me."

"He knows the secret?"

"He knows everything." Clair giggled again and grabbed his arm. "Everything!"

"How come he doesn't know we're looking for him?"

She smiled, her blue eyes clear and bright. "Maybe he's trying to avoid us."

"That's probably the truth. How's the modeling coming? Is Bubba really acting as your agent?"

"Yeah, and he's doing a great job. I'm shooting an ad for Nabisco next Monday, and on Wednesday I'm starring in a video with Killer Kids."

"Is that a heavy-metal group?"

"Punk. Their music stinks but the pay's great. I'm making so much money! Bubba's investing it for me."

"Legally, I hope."

She laughed easily, still holding on to him. He didn't understand why she liked him so much, unless it had to do with stuff Bubba had told her, which was hard to imagine. He regretted his initial low opinion of her. She was really very sweet.

"How about you?" she asked. "I hear you're working at JPL?"

He had not planned to leave school in January. But after Maria's accident and Jessica's subsequent disappearance, he began to feel that Tabb High had lost whatever charm it had once possessed. From his freshman year on he had taken a heavy load. He had more than enough units to call it quits. Plus Mr. Gregory, his MGM (Mentally Gifted Minors) adviser, had helped him land another work-study position at Jet Propulsion Laboratory. The job was only twenty hours a week, so he hadn't quit his job at the 7-Eleven to take it—much to the relief of the store owners. The JPL job came with the impressive title aeronautics intern, but it amounted to little more than errand boy to the engineers. It was not that he wasn't learning. Often he was allowed to sit in on discussions relating to the design of future spacecraft, both manned and unmanned. The problem was, the experience was boring him.

Throughout his school days, he had seen himself as a budding scientist. Now he was finding out that the entire analytic approach to the universe left him feeling cold and unsatisfied. This was a critical discovery; it completely threw off his future plans. He no longer knew what he should study in college, or even *if* he should go to college. Looking around at the other kids in his class hanging out in the hallway, signing one another's yearbooks and gossiping about how loaded they were going to get on the ship, he wondered if he was the only one who felt confused. He often wondered that—why he felt so different from everybody else.

"Yeah. The rocket and space business is OK," he replied. "But I've been thinking of starting my own rock-and-roll band. Would you like to front it for me?"

Clair was amused. "I'm totally tone deaf."

"But you can dance. That's all that matters."

"You should get Jessie. She's got a great voice. She's singing at the ceremony this afternoon." She stopped, obviously afraid she might have offended him somehow. "I'm sorry, Mike."

"No problem. That's neat, she'll be in the ceremony and all."

Clair was watching him. "You never talk to her anymore, do you?"

He shrugged, feeling uncomfortable. Bubba must have told Clair how he felt about Jessica. "I never see her."

"You'll see her today."

"I guess."

"Look, I'm being nosy."

"No."

"Well, then, talk to her today. Hey, I said a lot of nasty things about her before—and I still think she deserved them—but she *is* a classy chick. She really likes you."

Curiosity got the best of him. "What makes you say that? You haven't seen her in six months."

"I can tell." She leaned closer. "Do you want me to tell her?"

"Tell her what?"

Clair reconsidered. "Nothing."

"What?" he insisted.

She grinned mischievously. "Nothing."

"Clair."

She shook her head. "I won't say anything." But she had to add, "As long as you say something."

"You've been hanging around Bubba too long. That sounds like a threat."

She gave him a quick kiss on the cheek and began to bounce away. "I've got to talk to my pals on the cheerleading squad. If you run into him before me, tell him I went to look for them in the gym. Think about what I said!"

"You remember what *I* said," he called after her, embarrassed.

He continued to search for Bubba. The first-period bell would ring in a few minutes, but he doubted that many kids would be heading to class. As usual on the last day of school, there was a party atmosphere all over campus. He observed it without feeling it. The hot weather contributed to his mood. He remembered how it had been hot the day he had met Jessica.

Am I looking for Bubba or trying to hide from Jessie?

He bumped into Nick Grutler next outside. They had kept in touch: regular telephone calls, occasional one-on-one basketball games. Tabb High had finished first in the league for the second straight year. Some people were saying Coach Seller was a genius. None of those people had been on the team. The title belonged to Nick. Come next fall, he would be attending U.C.L.A. on a full athletic scholarship. Michael was proud of him.

"Does the old school still look the same?" Nick asked.

"Hey, I haven't been gone that long." Nick had been heading in the direction of the parking lot. "Where you going?"

Nick averted his eyes. He had gained a great deal of confidence since he had stumbled stuttering into the 7-Eleven at the end of the first week of school, but when he was troubled, he reverted to his old habit and looked away. "Maria's coming to the graduation ceremony," he said. "I'm picking her up at the rehabilitation clinic in San Diego."

"How is she?" He knew Nick hadn't seen Maria since she had been discharged from the hospital in February to the spinal injury clinic to begin rebuilding her body. But Nick had talked to her on the phone, although he wouldn't say what they talked about.

"I don't know," Nick said.

"Does Jessie or Sara know she's coming?"

"No."

"I wonder if someone should tell them?"

"I think Maria wants it to be a surprise."

"Why?"

Nick shook his head. "I guess none of us can know what it feels like to be suddenly crippled."

Michael knew he was trying to make excuses for her ahead of time, and felt bad for him. "Tell her I'm looking forward to seeing her again."

Nick nodded. "I will, Mike." He glanced at his watch. He had one now—and a car. His dad had begun to let him hold on to his money, or else the college recruiters had been very generous. "I better go."

They exchanged good-byes. Michael decided he might find Bubba in the computer room. He spotted Polly McCoy as he was on his way there. A talk with Polly was on his list of things to do.

She was sitting by herself on a bench outside on the far side of the girls' shower room. Her dark hair hung long, straighter than before. The weight she had lost following Alice's death had not returned; if anything, she was thinner. She glanced up as he approached, her eyes dark and uncertain. She had been studying her palm.

"Hi," she said.

"Hi, Polly. How are you?"

"Fine . . ." The word trailed from her lips. Then she blinked. "Mike, it's you. Where have you been?"

He sat beside her on the green wooden bench. Her blue jeans were old, skintight, her white lace blouse, long and loose. She had bitten her nails down a fraction too far. The only makeup she wore was lipstick, thick and red.

"I finished school at the semester," he said. "Didn't you know?"

"Jessie didn't tell me. She never tells me anything."

He forced a smile. "I don't think *I* told Jessie. What are you doing way over here in the middle of nowhere?"

"I have a headache."

"Oh, that's a shame. Is it bad?"

"No. It's long."

"Long?" Mike asked.

"I've had it a couple of months." She paused. "I've missed seeing you. I'm glad you've come back to school."

"She was outside when the gun went off. We're sure of that, aren't we?"

He had asked Jessica that question six months ago. The answer was still yes. That was a fact. But he still didn't trust Polly. "Just for the day. You must be excited about graduating?"

"I'm glad it's almost over." She glanced down at her hands

and wove her fingers together. She answered his initial question again. "I like to be alone."

"Do you want me to go?"

"No. But why do you want to talk to me?"

"I like talking to you."

"Did you find him?"

"Find who?" He knew who she was talking about.

"Clark."

"No," he lied. He had found him, he just hadn't spoken to him. He planned to do so today. "Does he know I'm looking for him?" he asked carefully, his heartbeat accelerating.

"I think so," she said, her expression dreamy.

"So you've seen him?"

"Not in a long time."

"When was the last time, Polly?"

"A long time ago."

"You don't remember?"

She jerked slightly, then frowned, concentrating. "It was the night Aunty died. It was raining."

The sun shone bright in their faces, rebounding off the light brown wall at their backs. Michael realized that he was sweating.

Her aunt had died the night of homecoming, but there had been no storm. And since then, Polly had been alone. The court had not appointed her another guardian; apparently she was over eighteen.

"What did he do?" Michael asked, referring to Clark.

"The doctor said she died of natural causes."

"Your aunt?"

"You don't think he killed her, do you?" She could have been talking to herself. "I know you think he killed Alice. That's why you're looking for him. But he says he didn't."

"He told you that?" Michael asked.

"Yes."

"Do you believe him?"

She looked him straight in the eye. Her dreaminess lessened. Indeed, she seemed suddenly cautious. "I do."

"But was he there, the night of the party?"

"He said something about coming at the end."

Michael could hardly contain his excitement. "Was he up in the bedroom when Alice died?"

She became slightly annoyed. "Why are you asking all these questions? I told you, I have a headache."

"I'm sorry, I was sort of pushy. Let me ask just a couple more and then I'll help you find an aspirin."

"I don't take aspirin. They make your stomach bleed. I have to save my blood to donate to the hospital."

"Was Clark in the room with Alice just before she died?"

"No. He left when I left." She put a hand to her temple—as she had done when he visited her last winter—and paled. "I wish you'd stop. Please stop."

It drove him nuts, to be so close and yet so far. "I have to ask you, Polly, if I'm ever to clear Alice's name."

"She's dead. She doesn't care about her name. The dead don't care about anything. The only one who cares is me."

"That's not true. I care."

She paused, surprised. "You do?"

"I really do, Polly."

She thought for a moment, then looked away. "Don't go to the all-night party, Mike."

"Why not?"

"Clark might come," she answered.

"Did he tell you he was coming?"

"No."

"Then why do you think he will?"

"I—I feel it. It's a bad feeling."

"But I want to talk to him."

Polly shook her head. "He won't talk to you."

"What will he do?"

"I don't know," she said, standing, obviously upset. "Excuse me, but I have to go to the bathroom." She looked right and left, confused. "I hate this school. I come here and Alice shoots herself and then Aunty chokes on a pillow. It's an awful place. It makes me want to throw up."

"Polly," he began.

"Just don't get too close," she cried, running away.

Michael wondered if anything she had told him had been accurate.

Bubba appeared a minute later, dressed to kill, except

for an oversize sombrero that bobbled around on his head. Michael had not seen him in over a month. Bubba had lost a few pounds. Must be Clair's doing. He sat beside Michael on the bench, a brown paper bag in his right hand, his yearbook in the left. Michael knew what was in the bag. He immediately glanced all around.

"We're alone," Bubba said.

Michael nodded at the sack. "You got it?"

"I got it. Are you sure you want it?"

"Where did you get it?"

"Kats," Bubba said.

"Bubba! I told you no one is supposed to know."

"You only gave me a few days. Besides, I fed Kats a good story. Don't worry." Bubba glanced at the bag, appearing a tad worried himself. "You know, Mike, you're a smart guy, but I know a lot of smart guys who have done stupid things with one of these."

"I'll be fine."

"If you'd tell me what you want it for, I might be able to give you some sage advice to keep you out of jail."

Michael held out his hand. "The less you know, the better for you."

Bubba reluctantly gave him the package. "Everything's inside. The keys, too."

Earlier in the week Michael had asked Bubba to slip into Polly's school locker, borrow her purse, and make a copy of her house keys. Michael wanted another look at the bedroom where Alice had died, but wasn't fond of the idea of breaking into the McCoy residence. "I appreciate it."

"What are Bubbas for? I hear Maria's coming to the ceremony."

"Did Nick tell you?"

"No. A confidential source. Do you have your speech ready?"

"I haven't given it a moment's thought. Hey, what am I doing as valedictorian anyway? What happened to Dale Jensen? Did he get a C in a class or what?"

"He got busted."

"When? How?"

"Tuesday night. Remember that narc that was hassling Nick before Christmas? Randy Meisser?"

"Yeah. You said you were going to run him off campus."

"I changed my mind. Thought he might come in useful. He busted Dale snorting coke in a bathroom." Bubba took off his hat and fanned himself. "We can't have an ill-mannered druggie giving any long-winded speeches graduation day. Not when it's hot like this."

Michael sighed. "You set Dale up."

"I may have put the white powder beneath his nose, but I did not force him to inhale."

"Were his parents able to bail him out?"

"Yes, and weren't they embarrassed. Relatives flying in

from the Midwest and all. Would you like me to write your speech for you?"

"No, thank you." Michael stood up, gripping the bag, testing its weight. "Clair's in the gym. She wants to talk to you. You probably know that, right?"

"Of course." Bubba got up, too, brushing off the seat of his trousers.

"She said she had a secret to tell me."

Bubba raised an eyebrow. "Did she tell you?"

"No."

He nodded. "She's a good girl. Did you know Kats will be receiving a diploma today?"

"He mentioned something like that once."

"He's also coming with us on our cruise to Catalina."

"Wonderful."

Bubba smiled. "He might surprise you. He might just be the life of the party."

Michael had what he had come for. He had a great deal to accomplish before he returned to the campus at three. He bid Bubba good-bye and hurried toward the parking lot. Crossing the courtyard, extremely conscious of the sack in his hand, he spotted Jessica talking to Sara outside the snack bar. He practically dropped the sack. He stepped behind a tree, peeking around like a frightened lowlife.

"No. Don't touch me. Don't get near me. I'm no good, Michael. I'm not."

Her brown hair and brown eyes. He always saw them first. Long and silky, big and round. Then would come her smile. Yet she was not smiling now. She was as pretty as ever, but it seemed to him, even at a glance, that she didn't smile as often as she had. She was no longer the young girl who had almost wept over the grape juice he had spilled on her sweater.

Her clothes were seductive now—as was her body. She had on a short green skirt and a thin yellow blouse. Her legs were every bit as tan as Clair's. He had dreamed about them the last few months, along with the rest of her body.

Love would not care. It should not care.

Yet Michael did not feel guilt over his sexual desire for Jessica. It was natural, he realized. He could not separate who she was from her body. He didn't want to.

I just want her.

But she did not want him. Bill came up to talk to her then. He put a hand on her shoulder. Now she smiled.

Michael left quickly for the parking lot. In his car he removed the gun from the brown paper bag and opened the box of shells. Pressing the bullets into the clip of the automatic weapon, he wondered if maybe he should have waited for Jessica as Sara had suggested. If maybe Bubba was right, and he was stupid.

He put the loaded automatic in the glove compartment and drove away.

Chapter Three

Jessica Hart was thinking of winning and losing. She had begun the year at Tabb optimistically. She had figured she would earn outstanding grades, be nominated homecoming queen, get accepted to Stanford, fall in love with a cute boy, and enjoy the respect and goodwill of all she met. She hadn't thought she was asking for more than her fair share.

And none of those things came to me. Not one.

She had received a C in chemistry, the same grade she would receive on her report card. She hadn't been able to find a lab partner after Maria got hurt. Her overall grade-point average for the year was a C-plus. In a class of four hundred and sixty-four, she was graduating somewhere in the mid-two hundreds. The ranking would have been lower if they'd averaged in her SAT score.

Her father had held back her application for Stanford. Maybe after a couple of years at a local junior college, he said.

Junior college—it would be like going to summer camp after expecting to climb Mount Everest. Her father had been so disappointed in her. Sara was heading to Princeton.

She had found a boy she sort of liked—good old Bill. But he wasn't a real boyfriend. They'd only been out three times. She didn't love him and she seriously doubted he loved her. She was beginning to doubt there really was such a thing as love. Sex, yeah—she was as horny as anybody else. But where were the couples who cared more for each other than for themselves? She couldn't find them. All she saw around her were boys and girls struggling to boost their egos at the expense of those they supposedly adored. She despised it, particularly since she wanted to do the same thing.

The year died when Alice died. I should have written it off right then and quit.

"I love this material," Jessica said to Bill, feeling the upper sleeve of his red shirt. "It feels like silk."

"It is," he replied. "My mother bought it for me."

"For a graduation present?" she asked.

He nodded. "Yeah, and I got a car. A Corvette."

"I hope to God it matches your shirt," Sara said. Sara had just given them each a copy of the new yearbook. Jessica had no desire to open it; she knew all too well what most of her photographs looked like. The yearbook club had been very disappointed in her. Had they not been so desperately short of football and basketball pictures, they probably would have trashed all her "preglasses material." She didn't care, she told herself, but it did bother her. So, maybe, she really did care. Letting go of Bill's shirt, she pushed her glasses back on her nose. She was never going to get used to wearing them. She hoped the sun burned out soon and everyone could walk around blind with her in the dark.

"It's black," Bill said seriously. "It goes with everything."

Sara winked at Jessica and patted her hair. "My color coordinator says I absolutely should never be seen in a black car."

"That's too bad," Bill said.

"Our parents are sending us to Hawaii next week for our graduation presents," Jessica said, wanting to stop Sara before she got started. Because Polly was now off-limits, Sara got her kicks out of ridiculing Bill. Jessica hated that he never even knew it was happening. "Isn't that neat?"

"They've got great surfing there," Bill said.

"It's the waves," Sara said confidentially. "Something to do with the waves."

"Yeah, that has a lot to do with it," Bill agreed.

"Bill, could you do me a favor?" Jessica said, clearing her throat and looking pointedly at Sara. "Could you get me a book from my locker?"

"Sure. Did you want one in particular?"

No, any old book will do. Just make sure it has pages, a cover, words in it—the usual.

In reality, she didn't care what book he got. She just wanted to talk to Sara alone.

"My political science book," she said.

"We handed those in to Mr. Bark yesterday," Sara said. "Get her something else. Get her a brush."

"Do you want a brush?" Bill asked, and now even he was beginning to wonder.

But Jessica kept a straight face. "Yeah, I'd appreciate it," she said.

When Bill was gone, Sara said, "He's lucky he's so good-looking or we'd have to have him stuffed."

"Leave him alone, he's all right."

"Oh, I think he's great. I love him. I can see why you love him."

"Right, my feelings go real deep."

Sara laughed. "Hope it goes plenty deep tonight." She leaned close, her excitement barely concealed. "You know how I told you the captain wanted the passenger suites on the ship kept locked and off-limits? Well, last night I had a long talk with him and arranged for the use of a couple of adjacent rooms. I've got the keys. Isn't that great? Everything's set."

Jessica was not sure why she was doing this. She supposed that like anything else, virginity got old after a while and—like a hundred percent of the young ladies in her present situation—she'd been a virgin since she was born. Once she had imagined that when she finally did give herself to a guy, it would be to someone she really cared about. She guessed hormones and biology had finally caught up with her. Now all she wanted was to have a good time.

It's all I can hope for at this point.

That was closer to the truth. She wanted a lot more than a roll in the hay, but she felt—until something better came along—that this would give her life spark. The flatness of each day was becoming almost unbearable.

Yet she hoped boredom was all there was to it. She hoped she wasn't attempting to seduce Bill in an effort to prove to herself beyond a shadow of a doubt that she really didn't care about anything.

That was a frightening thought.

And what was even more frightening was that she recognized her self-destructive streak, and its source, and still wasn't able to free herself from it. She had not killed Alice. She had not crippled Maria. She had not chased Michael from school. But somehow she felt as if she had *allowed* all those terrible things to happen. As if she should have known ahead of time. As if someone had been trying to warn her of the dangers and she had not been listening.

Someone . . .

"Everything's set like hell," Jessica said, forcing her thoughts back to Sara and trying to shake off her melancholy mood. "We don't even know if we've got ingredient A."

"Russ will be down. Bill's coming to the party. What's the problem? You think we can't seduce two eighteen-year-old boys?"

Jessica remembered back to senior-prom night. Bill had kissed her long and hard in his car before dropping her off home, yet she couldn't have sworn they had been passionate kisses. He had made no move to grab her or even touch her. It had left her feeling frustrated and with all sorts of doubts about her own sexuality.

"I don't know if the shower routine is what we want," Jessica said.

"What's wrong with it? We have every reason to be in the shower when they get to our rooms. People are dirty creatures—they're always taking showers. It won't look like a setup. They'll see us naked, we'll squeal, and the rest will be history."

"Don't give me that confident B.S. You're scared to death Russ will take one look at your bare ass and bust up laughing."

Sara was insulted. "What's wrong with my ass?"

"I don't know. I've never looked at it that closely. Christ, this is beginning to sound ridiculous. You would think we were hard up or something."

"Yeah, isn't that a ridiculous thought."

Then they laughed at how far past ridiculous they already were. Jessica began to feel a bit better. If nothing else, she had her best friend to share her misery with. Jessica nodded at Sara's yearbook.

"Let me sign it," she said. "And you can be the first person to sign mine."

But Sara held her book back. "Later. On the boat."

"No, let's do it now." Jessica reached out for it, and when

Sara held it farther away, Jessica naturally snapped it out of her hands. "What's the problem with you. What's—" She stopped. Sara's yearbook had a crudely cut rectangle of brown paper pasted over the inside front cover. "What is this?"

Sara grabbed her book back. "I got a defective copy."

"How can you get a defective yearbook for God sakes?"

"All of them are defective, Miss Fuzzy-Film Face."

"Haven't you insulted me enough times about that already this year? I know what's wrong with your book. Somebody wrote something nasty in it."

"Sure, yeah, who would do that?"

"Bubba. That's who. I know that's it."

"I wouldn't let that slime touch my book if he didn't have any hands."

"What did he write?"

"He didn't write anything!"

"Forget Russ and the shower. Bubba will do it with you no matter how many clothes you have on and no matter how flabby your ass is. What did he say?"

Sara sucked in a breath. "I wish, Jessie, for the sake of our long and warm association that you would please change the goddamn subject."

"OK. But you're right—the grease just sweats off that guy. Can you imagine why any girl would go to bed with him?"

"I try not to think about it." Sara stared at the ground, thinking, chewing on her lower lip.

"What's the matter?"

"Nothing."

"What?" Jessica persisted.

"I was wondering if I should tell you this."

"Don't tell me. Play it safe. Keep it to yourself."

"All right."

"Sara?" she said, getting exasperated.

"Mike was here about half an hour ago."

"Michael?" The strength went out of her. She had not been thinking of winning and losing. Only of losing. "Why didn't you tell me?"

"You just got here."

"But where is he?" She quickly scanned the courtyard, almost afraid to find him. "Where did he go?"

"I don't know," Sara said.

"What do you mean, you don't know? Which direction was he heading when he left you?"

"He went after Clair."

"Clair's here, too?"

"Yeah."

She swallowed. "I don't care."

"Jessie, of course you care."

"I don't. So she's got her stupid face on the cover of some stupid magazine?"

"We're talking about Mike. You might be able to find him if you go look."

"First period's going to start in a minute. I don't have time." She shielded her eyes from the bright sun—it was going to be a cooker of an afternoon—searching harder. "Why was he here?"

"He came to pick up his yearbook. He's going to be at the ceremony. He's valedictorian."

"*What?* When did this happen? What happened to Jensen?"

"All I know is Mike is going to be giving the speech."

"Since when have you known this?" Jessica pressed.

"Since yesterday," Sara said.

"Why didn't you tell me?"

"You didn't ask me."

"Why should I have to ask you?"

"Because you keep telling me you don't care."

"I don't care. I mean, what's there to care about? He left school early. He didn't even say good-bye. I hardly knew him. How did he look?"

"Great."

Jessica smiled. "Did he?"

Sara smiled, too. "Yeah. His hair's longer. He's got a tan."

"I always wanted him to grow his hair." She scratched her own hair. "He wasn't with Clair, like in *with* her, was he?"

"No."

Jessica bounced on her feet. "I've got to find him. Talk to you later."

"Good luck."

Unfortunately, she had no luck at all. She was hurrying

down the first hallway when she ran into Bubba. He had on a straw hat so huge it was causing traffic jams.

"Bubba, have you seen Michael?" she asked casually.

"He left already."

"But he's coming back, right?"

Bubba showed a flicker of uncertainty. "I hope so."

Then he grinned and reached out his hand. "May I sign your yearbook, my dear?"

"Yeah." She clasped it to her chest and looked at his fat ink-stained fingers. "Later."

Chapter Four

Ray Bradbury had written a short story called "Rocket Man." Michael had read it in junior high. It told of a man who piloted a rocket for a living. Most of the time he worked alone in space, but occasionally he returned home to earth. He had a wife and son, and although the story was largely told through the son's eyes, it was the wife's point of view that had stayed with Michael. It came to him as he stood in the cemetery at the foot of Alice McCoy's grave.

The wife always worried that her husband would crash into the moon, or die on Mars, or Venus, or on any other planet in the solar system. Then she would never again be able to look up when the moon was in the sky, or when the particular planet was close to the earth. For that reason, she tried to keep distance between herself and her husband. She knew that one day she would lose him, and that from then on there would always be a light in the heavens to remind her of him, and break her heart.

Of course the husband's rocket fell into the sun. It had been a sad story. Yet the Western custom of pumping dead people's veins with preserving fluids, Michael realized, and sealing the bodies in airtight coffins to bury them in concrete-lined holes, affected him in much the same way. One of the reasons he couldn't get over Alice, no matter how often he told himself her soul was free, was that her decaying body was always, in a sense, beneath his feet. He wished they'd had her cremated and thrown her ashes into the ocean, or tossed them onto the wind.

At the same time, he wondered if it would have made any difference.

He had not intended to visit the cemetery. He had many things to do. He had to question the coroner who had performed Alice's autopsy, examine the bedroom again, speak to Clark, and give that silly speech. The fact that he had so many things to investigate all on one day caused him to wonder about his convictions. He could have made his appointment with the coroner months ago. He could have had Bubba duplicate Polly's keys anytime. And he had found Clark three weeks ago, but still hadn't approached him. There was really no two ways about it—he had postponed the investigation. The question was, had he done it because he was afraid to discover a fact that proved she *had* pulled the trigger?

But why would she kill herself?

Even Jessica had not attempted to address that point. Maybe Clark would. Michael glanced back toward his car and the gun safely stowed there. More questions came to mind. Why had he postponed his investigation until this particular day, the last day of school? And why did he feel he could no longer postpone it?

"I feel it. It's a bad feeling."

It was hard to stand beside her grave, but harder still to leave it. He wished he had brought flowers. This was the first time he had been to the cemetery since the funeral. He glanced at the two graves on either side of Alice: Martha McCoy and Philip Bart, Alice's aunt and an employee of McCoy Construction who had died from an on-job accident. The grass was not quite as green around their tombstones. They had been in the ground less time, but perhaps it would always be greenest near Alice.

It was just a thought. He turned and left the cemetery.

Michael had obtained his appointment with Dr. Gin Kawati under false pretenses. He had called the doctor the previous week and explained he was an assistant editor at a local paper in need of technical information on modern forensic techniques for an article his boss was doing on how modern murders were sometimes solved. Michael had given the doctor the impression the name Dr. Kawati would figure prominently in the article if he would help him out. The doctor had sounded interested.

Michael drove to downtown Los Angeles and parked across the street from the ARC Medical Group. This was his first visit to the office, but Bubba had been there before when he swiped certain codes from the physician's secretary. It was those codes that had allowed Bubba and Michael to dump the medical group's files onto Tabb High's computers homecoming day.

The receptionist showed him directly into the doctor's office. Dr. Kawati was of Japanese descent—which was no big surprise given his last name—short and mustached. He was not old—thirty-five at most—and appeared at first glance to be friendly. He gave Michael a warm handshake and offered him a seat beside his cluttered desk. But Michael couldn't help glancing at the man's hands and thinking to himself that here were hands that spent their days dissecting people. Michael couldn't understand how anyone could willingly go into such a gruesome field.

"I wear gloves," Dr. Kawati said. Michael glanced up.

"Pardon?"

"I wear gloves when I perform an autopsy." The doctor smiled. "I have yet to be at a party or any social occasion and not have someone stare at my hands. Don't be embarrassed, I am proud of what I do."

"You read minds?" Michael asked, shaken at his own transparency.

"I read mysteries. The human body is the most mysterious of all God's creations, and when it ceases to work, for whatever reason, it often leaves behind a puzzle more complex than any-thing you can find in a movie or a book." He nodded toward the tape player Michael had brought. "That would be a fine opening for your piece. You might want to turn on your cas-sette machine."

On the spur of the moment, Michael decided to take a big chance. Perhaps the doctor's obviously keen perception gave him the inspiration. "I lied," he said. "I don't work for a paper."

The doctor raised an eyebrow, not fazed. "I'm intrigued. What is your real name and why are you here?"

"My name *is* Mike, and I wanted to question you about an autopsy you performed last fall on a friend of mine. Her name was Alice McCoy." He added, "I realize I deserve to be kicked out, but I really would like to talk to you."

"This Alice—she was a close friend of yours?"

Michael nodded. "Yes."

Dr. Kawati turned to the computer on his desk. "M—C—C—O—Y?"

"Yes."

Kawati called up a file menu, then typed in the name. A moment later an autopsy report appeared on the screen. Michael recognized it; he had, after all, read it a dozen times. Kawati frowned. "I remembered the name McCoy when you said it. A most interesting case."

"Why?" Michael asked.

"A minute, please," the doctor said, taking several minutes

to read the report from start to finish. When he was done, he looked over at Michael. "I believe you are a friend of hers, but why are you concerned about the results of her autopsy?"

"I have serious doubts about the police's investigation into her death."

"Please be more specific."

"I think Alice McCoy was murdered."

"Why?"

Michael hesitated. "I've read your report."

"Did the police show it to you?"

"Not exactly."

The doctor smiled. "You *are* an intriguing young man. I won't ask you how you managed that. I don't believe I want to know." He glanced at the screen, frowned again. Michael spoke quickly.

"She didn't break her nose falling to the floor after firing the gun. She was sitting when she was shot. None of us rolled her body over when we found it."

"You can't be certain she was sitting," Kawati said.

"It is likely when you take into account where and at what angle the slug hit the wall. Also, she had the gun in her mouth, with her hand around it, when we found her. How could she fall and break her nose with that in the way?"

"How could someone have gotten close enough to put the gun in her mouth, wrap her fingers around the handle, and then pull the trigger?"

"Before I answer that, why did you remember the name? What was so interesting about the case?"

"What you mentioned—the fracture to her nasal cartilage."

"Then you don't think it was caused by a fall?"

"I didn't say that," the doctor replied.

"How else could she have broken her nose?"

"Any number of ways. She could have been struck across the face, or rather, struck directly on the nose. There were no scratches on her cheeks, nor any other signs that she had been in a struggle." Kawati paused, intent upon the details, apparently not minding the exchange. "You still have not answered my question."

"In your report you mentioned a brain hemorrhage that appeared unconnected to the path of the bullet."

"It *may* have been unconnected. The bullet followed a twisted route before exiting the back of the skull. The brain was in extremely poor condition. What are you getting at?"

"I have thought about this a great deal. I was there the night of the party."

"Go on."

Michael remembered back to another night, to homecoming, to the moment before the varsity tree toppled and destroyed the snack bar. The idea had begun to form in his mind even then. "I think she was dead before she was shot," he said.

The doctor thought a moment. "It's possible."

"Is it?" Michael asked, realizing he had been holding his breath waiting to hear those exact words.

"Possible, but unlikely," Kawati quickly added. "Why would someone quietly and effectively kill her with a blow to the nose and then put a gun in her mouth and fire a shot that alerted everyone in the house?"

"To give the impression it had not been a murder, but a suicide."

"Why?"

"To give the police an excuse not to investigate, which is precisely what has happened. They threw the file on the shelf and closed the case before they opened it."

"You sound angry."

Michael felt a tightness in his throat. "She was very dear to me." He started to get up. "You've told me what I wanted to know. Thank you, doctor."

Kawati glanced at the screen a last time. "There is one other thing you might want to consider. If someone did strike her, cracking her nasal cartilage and giving her a cerebral hemorrhage in the process, then he must have done it with a baseball bat. Either that or he was a strong devil." Kawati put a hand to his chin, nodded thoughtfully. "Incredibly strong."

Chapter Five

Nick Grutler drove fast down the coast, reaching San Diego in less than two hours. He had never been to the rehabilitation clinic before, but Maria's directions were precise and he found the huge modern, two-story building without difficulty. Since her discharge from the local hospital three months ago, Nick had spoken to her on the phone every couple of weeks. Each time, *he* had called her. Each time, she had sounded much the same, quiet and withdrawn. Yet the bitterness that had unexpectedly arisen after her accident still remained. It had faded, true; nevertheless, it tore him apart to catch hints of it in her voice. Sometimes he felt as if he were talking to a stranger, that he was in love with someone who no longer existed.

She was sitting outside, waiting for him as he walked toward the front stairs. She had a red wool blanket over her legs and a battered tan suitcase by her side. Only she wasn't simply sitting; she was sitting in a wheelchair.

Oh, Jesus, please heal her.

He had prayed the same prayer a thousand times since last winter. Jesus was either keeping him in suspense or else He had already given him his answer. Nick was a big, strong young man but he almost broke down and cried at that moment.

"Hi, Maria," he said. She had cut her hair, her beautiful hair. There was hardly any of it left. It was probably easier to take care of shorter, he reasoned. She smiled briefly, and rolled toward him. He wondered if it would be OK to hug her, if he would hurt her.

"Hello, Nick," she said, glancing up at him before quickly looking down to make sure of her hold on the wheelchair handles. She still seemed to be learning how to get around. "Thanks for coming."

He stood above her, afraid to move. "It was no problem. It's good to see you again."

"It's good to see you." She nodded to her bag. "I'm already checked out. We can go."

He stepped past her and picked up the suitcase. He knew it was all she had to her name. After the accident, her parents had been exposed as illegal aliens in the United States. They had subsequently been deported to El Salvador. Maria's status was still questionable. As long as she needed medical attention that only the United States could provide, she was allowed to stay. She might be deported now that she was leaving the rehab clinic. Michael had helped Nick write a letter to their local congressman pleading her case. So far, there had been no reply.

Nick helped her into the front seat of his car—he could have picked her up with one hand, she was so light—and folded the wheelchair and put it in the trunk. It was a tight fit but he was able to close the lid. He climbed in beside her and started the engine.

"Nice car," she said.

"Thanks. The Rock sold it to me cheap."

"The Rock—I remember him."

"I bumped into him in the parking lot when I was leaving school this morning. He told me to tell you he'd like to see you. Mike also said he was looking forward to seeing you again."

"Good old Mike. Is he still searching for a murderer?"

There was an edge to her question, but not of sarcasm; she really wanted to know. "He doesn't talk to me about it," he said, feeling uncomfortable. He wanted to touch her, kiss her, and comfort her, but he could have made the trip for nothing. She was still a hundred miles away, wrapped in a cool protective shell.

"I bet he is," she said.

"Are you?" He hadn't shifted the car into gear yet. He hadn't intended to ask that question. Maria looked over at him. He noticed a faint two-inch scar near her right eye. She'd had some plastic surgery; she'd need more.

"Yes."

"And you want me to help you find the murderer?"

"You'll help me," she said, implying with her tone that he didn't understand what she was talking about, which was true.

"How?"

She smiled, slow and calculating. "You'll know when the time comes."

Chapter Six

Sara hated L.A.'s downtown bus station, located in one of the worst parts of town. She always felt relieved to get in and out of it without being molested. The whole world was full of perverts. Society was sick. It still infuriated her how the courts locked Russ away for a crime he had not committed. She wished she'd sent him an airplane ticket. Then she could have driven to Los Angeles airport instead. She had suggested the idea in her last letter, but he hadn't answered her last letter, so that had been the end of that.

He didn't answer my letter before that, either.

It didn't matter. He wasn't into writing letters. She couldn't stand to write them herself. The only reason she had sent him so many was that she'd had nothing else to do— only get good grades, keep her mother and father from killing each other, and run the whole school. Actually, she was going to give him hell for not answering her—immediately after she determined if he still liked her. She was worried he might have found someone else.

In a juvenile hall full of boys?

One could never tell. They probably had a buxom secretary or two working in the warden's office. She'd always had the impression Russ could go for an older woman, or a teenybopper for that matter. God help him if he had been unfaithful to her.

He was supposed to be on the one o'clock from Sacramento. She was on time and waiting at the right gate, but when all the people had passed by, there was no Russ. She couldn't believe it. The bastard had missed his bus and hadn't had the decency to call her house and leave word that he'd be on the next one arriving at—she glanced up at the schedule board—three o'clock. Three o'clock! She couldn't wait till then. She was ASB president and this was her last and most important day on the job. That insensitive son-of-a-bitch had dragged her all the way down here *after* getting himself thrown in jail where she couldn't see him at all, and now he had stood her up.

She reached in her bag for her handkerchief. Life sucked. She hated this trying not to care when all she felt like doing was crying. She dabbed at her eyes. Well, that was the end of that. Jessica would get Bill tonight, and there would be no one there to save poor Sara from being raped by Bubba.

Sara blew her nose and headed for the exit. If she'd known

for sure he'd be on the next bus, she would have waited, her important speech notwithstanding. But he had decided not to come, she realized, because he didn't want to see her. God, she hated him!

She ran into him the second she stepped outside. He was crouched on the curb feeding a pigeon a piece of chocolate doughnut, his duffel bag propped against a nearby fire hydrant. They had cut his hair short. They must have been keeping him inside; he had lost his bronze sheen. It didn't matter. He looked incredible, simply incredible.

"Where have you been?" he asked, glancing up.

"Where have I been? You were supposed to be on that bus that just came in. You had me standing there waiting for you like some lost bag lady. You have a lot of nerve asking me where I've been."

He gave the bird the remainder of the doughnut and checked his watch. "It's five past one and you only got here. I've been waiting around a couple of hours. I told you I was coming in at eleven."

"No, you didn't." She pulled his last letter from her bag—it was little more than a slip of paper—practically ripping the envelope in the process. "See, it says one o'clock. You wrote it yourself."

He stood and studied the paper. "There're two ones there."

"What? No, that's not another one. It's just a scratch."

"No, I made it. It's a one."

Now that he mentioned it, the scratch did bear a faint resemblance to a one. "Why didn't you call, then?" she asked.

"I didn't have your number."

"Why not? What did you do with it?"

"I didn't do anything with it. I never had it memorized."

"Is that why you haven't called me since you left?"

"I couldn't afford it."

"You could have called collect," she began to yell.

He stared at her a moment. "You look great."

"What do you mean? Do you mean my body or my face?"

He shook his head. "Never mind."

She pouted. "How come you're not being nice to me?"

"How come you're yelling at me?"

"I'm not." She wanted to reach over and brush a hair from his eyes as she used to, but she couldn't see any hair long enough to give her an excuse. "I'm sorry if I am."

"It's all right." He paused. "Your body's all right."

"It's not great?"

"No."

She started to sock him, but he grabbed her hands and gave her a quick kiss on the lips. A little too quick. She had been hoping for a lot more. As he stepped back and picked up his duffel bag, he averted his eyes. He didn't want to talk, not about why he had been out drinking homecoming night at a bar he couldn't remember. She had the feeling he didn't really want to talk about what he thought of her, either.

"The car's over here," she said. She wished she understood him better.

Chapter Seven

The keys opened the door. Michael knew they would. Bubba was a master when it came to secretive preparations. Glancing down the McCoys' long driveway to make sure no one was watching, Michael quickly slipped into the house and reclosed the door.

I could get arrested for doing this.

That would be a joke. He could share the same cell with Dale Jensen and the local paper could do an article on the shortage of good valedictorians this year. In reality, he wasn't concerned about getting caught. The chances were against it, and even if someone did call the cops and he was carted down to the station, he didn't care. It would give him an excuse not to go to graduation. He still hadn't thought about what he was going to say. Not having gone to the rehearsal a couple of days earlier—he hadn't been valedictorian back then—he didn't even know when he was supposed to speak: first, last, or what.

He had hit traffic returning from the coroner's office and was running behind schedule. He would have to go to Clark's house after the ceremony.

The house was silent in the manner empty houses are prone to be. Yet it was not a comforting silence. It reminded him of the silence that hung in the air following a major argument or an explosion. It seemed to him that acts of violence somehow transcended time. He remembered when he was a boy going with his mother to a bank where there had previously been a holdup and a fatal shooting. He told his mother it was a "bad place" before she had told him what had happened there. The McCoy house now felt like a "bad place."

He paused for a moment at the foot of the stairs, looking toward the kitchen. Standing in this spot, Nick had seen Bill with his head bent over the sink. Bill never explained why he had been standing there upset, before the gun went off.

Michael decided to retrace Nick's steps to the room where Alice had died. He climbed the double flight of stairs and paused at the first door on the left. It had been locked the night of the party, the room beyond silent, and it was the same now. The next door on the left led to the bathroom. The Rock had been there, showering and flushing out his chlorined eyes.

Michael opened the sole door on the right and peeped out onto the second-story porch, where Kats had been getting a breath of fresh air and admiring the stars. It seemed to clear Michael's mind, going through this ritual. This hallway had one more door on the left. Nick had paused there, too, and listened at the door and heard snoring. Russ said he had been asleep inside. Then again, Russ couldn't remember where he had been when the varsity tree had toppled to the ground, or whether it had been Polly or Sara who had taken his ax away the first week of school.

The hallway turned to the right. There were two doors on the left. The first swung open easily, revealing a spacious bedroom with an adjoining bathroom. But it had been locked when Nick tried it, and there had been moans coming from inside. Bubba said he didn't know anything about it. No one seemed to know anything.

Michael came to the last room. The door was closed over, and as he opened it, the hinges creaked loudly, doing wonders for his nerves. The room was bare except for an aluminum ladder set beside the closet. He remembered the ladder from his last inspection the day of the funeral.

The starkness of the wooden floor struck him, as it had before. Nearly every room in the house had carpeting except this one. He found the fact disturbing, although he wasn't sure why. He stepped inside.

The blinds on the windows—those facing east and south— were down. He raised them, letting in more light. The bullet hole in the wall beneath the east windows had not been plastered over. As he knelt beside it, his conviction that she had not broken her nose falling strengthened. It was less than three feet above the floor and straight as an arrow into plaster.

Yet all this was old news. He searched the room and the adjoining bathroom, and discovered nothing significant. The screens on the windows were all screwed down. There were no trapdoors, as Jessica had once pointed out. There was only one entrance into the room, one exit.

If she was dead before she was shot, was she dead long?

He found himself standing at the east windows, which faced the McCoy garden—as opposed to the south windows, which overlooked the pool—pondering what the coroner had said about the strength of her assailant. Clark had been thin as a rail. In a fight, Michael figured he could have taken him easily.

Then he looked up and noticed the broken shingle at the overhang of the eaves outside the east window. It appeared to Michael as it had before, as if someone had been on the roof and stepped too close to the edge and broke off a couple of inches of the dark brown wood with the heel of his shoe. When he thought about how steep the east slant of the roof appeared from the front, however, he began to doubt that the damage could have been caused by a misplaced foot. Only the original roofers, with the help of safety lines, would have been able to stand that close to the edge. Why wouldn't they have repaired the damage? It was the only shingle on the entire side of the house that was broken.

Michael wanted to have a closer look at it. But he didn't

bother undoing the screws on the screens. The overhang was too far for him to reach, even if he were to hang out the window. He hurried downstairs to the garage instead, where he found a tall ladder. After assorted jostling and banging noises—and, thank God, Polly's nearest neighbors were more than a hundred yards away—he had the ladder situated beneath the bedroom window. Unfortunately, it wasn't tall enough for him to reach the shingle.

He had come down the ladder and was returning it to the garage, walking past the pool where Nick had almost drowned The Rock and beside the covered patio attached to the rear of the house, when he spotted the piece of yellowed paper lying in the grass next to the bushes. He set the ladder down and picked it up.

It was the permission form he had given Polly to have her aunt sign so that he could examine Alice's autopsy report. Polly had never returned it to him. It looked as if it had been sitting outside in the elements since that day. He stuffed it in his pocket.

He wasn't crazy about his next plan. He almost hoped, as he searched the garage after replacing the ladder on its hooks, that Polly didn't have any rope. Then he'd have an excuse not to play Mr. Roofer. But in a cabinet above the workbench, he soon found a fifty-foot coil of one-inch cord.

He didn't return to the bedroom, but took the second-story-hallway door onto the porch that overlooked the back-yard. The shingles came directly down onto the tar floor of the porch, giving him easy access to the roof. Climbing up toward the peak of the house, Michael felt the hot sun on the back of his head, the slickness of the wood beneath his feet. He was glad he had chosen to wear his tennis shoes that morning.

If I slip and break my neck, people will say I committed suicide.

At the ridge, he tied one end of the rope to the sturdiest vent he could find, the other end around his waist. With the life insurance in hand, creeping down toward the broken shingle was not nearly so intimidating as he had imagined it would be. He actually found it quite exhilarating. He wasn't even worried about the neighbors. Not many crooks climbed onto a victim's roof in the middle of the day and performed gymnastics.

A moment later he was kneeling beside the shingle, forty feet above the spot where Alice and he had had their last talk over the hot coals of the barbecue. He felt the damaged edge and was immediately taken by its smoothness. There were splinters, yes, but they—

They were turned *upward*.

Strange, very strange. Did the roofers break the shingle while it was lying upside down on the ground, and then install it? He found that hard to believe.

It was fortunate that he had a safety line. His next discovery almost sent him reeling. Placing his head inches from the finely splintered edge, he noticed a number of tiny round metal pellets embedded in the wood. He dug them out with his nail, studied them in his palm.

They were from a shotgun blast.

Chapter Eight

The stadium stands were packed, and the football field was jammed with gray folding chairs and blue-robed seniors. The ceremony would start in minutes. Sara still hadn't finished rewriting her speech. Jessica hadn't decided which song to sing. It was hot and getting hotter.

"Should I bring up the state of the environment?" Sara asked. "People are always talking about pollution. Maybe I could work it into my overall theme."

"What is your overall theme?" Jessica asked.

Sara glanced at her notes. "Isn't it obvious from what I've told you so far?" she asked anxiously.

"No."

"Jessie!"

"Well, I'm hardly listening to you. I have problems of my own. I can't sing the Beatles song I rehearsed."

"Why not?"

"Mr. Bark says it's too racist."

"'All You Need Is Love' is racist?"

"That's what he says. He wants a song with more of a political message, like 'Back in the U.S.S.R.' or something." She took off her cap and glasses and wiped the sweat from her forehead. Her tassel was blue. Sara had a gold one. Both their parents were in the stands. The six of them were supposed to go for an early dinner to an expensive restaurant afterward. Big thrill.

"What if I bring up the space program?" Sara asked. "Everyone likes astronauts."

"What if I sang Bowie's 'Starman'? I know the chords."

"That's ridiculous. You can't sing about spacemen at my graduation."

"Then you can't talk about astronauts at mine." Jessica replaced her glasses and scanned the crowd for Michael. "When is he going to speak?"

"After Mr. Bark."

"I forget, when do I sing?"

"After Mike speaks," Sara said. "It's all there in your program."

"Michael's not even listed in the program."

"Dale Jensen is. You know he's taking his place."

"Yeah, you told me—as of this morning."

"What are you complaining about? I can't even have notes with me when I go up there."

"Why not?"

"I have no place to put them."

"What's wrong with the podium?" Jessica asked, pointing to the stage in front of the folding chairs.

"It's been fixed," Sara smiled suddenly. "You'll see. Mr. Bark wants to talk before me. He thinks he does. What grade did he give you?"

"A B-minus," Jessica said angrily.

"He gave me an A-minus."

"That's so unfair. You fell asleep the first day I was back."

"Well, then, I was obviously most improved."

"You are beginning to bore me. I think I'll leave."

Jessica had another reason for splitting. She wanted to check out the piano—how it had been miked. She was a fair pianist; she'd had lessons since she was six years old and could play most popular songs if she had the music in front of her. She knew dozens of Beatles tunes by heart. Although many people complimented her on her voice, she didn't think of herself as a vocalist. Her singing voice was too similar to her speaking voice, which had always bothered her for some strange reason.

The school piano had a single microphone rigged above it—that was all. Yet the sound appeared to carry fine when she tapped out a few chords. She wondered if it would offend the older members of the audience if she played Alice Cooper's "School's Out for Summer." It annoyed her, being censored by Mr. Bark, especially when he considered himself so liberal.

"Don't worry," The Rock said, coming up at her side, a green plastic trash bag in his hand. "The chance of there being a record producer in the audience is five hundred to one."

She smiled. "I'm not here to get signed. I just want my diploma. What's with the bag?"

She knew without asking. Being a Big Brother wasn't enough for The Rock. A couple of weeks ago he had joined the Keep America Clean Society. He took his membership seriously. Tabb High was now the cleanest school in Orange County, or it should have been. Bubba had organized a counterorganization: It's Biodegradable. Bubba had a lot of friends. The Rock could regularly be seen at break and lunch picking up half-eaten apples and banana peels. Nothing irritated Bubba like a social conscience.

"The gang's getting started early," The Rock said. "I've already collected a hundred beer cans at school today." He sighed and shook his head. "I hope no one falls overboard tonight." He patted her on the shoulder. "Stay sober."

"I'll try." Either that or she was going to get stinking drunk.

She was heading toward the stands to ask her mother for a throat lozenge—she wanted to keep her vocal chords well lubricated—when she caught sight of Michael standing alone by the equipment shed on the far end of the stadium. He had his head down and appeared deep in thought. She hesitated to disturb him. As Sara had mentioned earlier, his hair was a lot longer, and he looked so damn good to her that she felt her eyes water. She found herself jogging toward him before she knew what she was doing.

He did not see her coming. She trembled inside as she came to a halt a few feet from him and spoke his name. "Michael?"

He glanced up with a start. Then he smiled. "Jessie. I love your glasses."

She laughed. She could have cried. She spread her arms wide and gave him a big hug. It might have been the best moment of her life when he hugged her back. Except he had to let her go. What a mush she had become.

"It's good to see you again," he said casually.

"It's good to see you. Oh, God, these glasses. I hate them."

"Why? You look like a scholar in them."

"I do?" He was being serious. She should have worn them all along. She giggled, shaking on the outside as well as the inside. No one in the world made her feel this way. She hated it, but only because she knew, like his hug, that it would not last. He would go away again. He always did. "So, how have you been? You look great. I hear you're building a spaceship at JPL?"

"Not exactly. I'm doing janitorial work."

"Really? No! You're kidding. I know you. Our chemistry teacher told us one day he'd never had a student like you. He said you invented the carbon bond!"

He chuckled. "Now I'm responsible for all the life on this planet. What a reputation. What have you been up to?"

She shrugged. "Oh, the usual. I sleep all day in a velvet-lined coffin and then prowl the streets at night. Hey, Sara told me you're valedictorian. Congratulations! Your mom must be real proud."

Michael nodded past her shoulder. "Here she comes. You've never met her, have you?"

Oh, no, she's going to hate me. Mothers always hate me.

His mom was massively pregnant; she waddled as she walked. Jessica hadn't even known she was married. Michael indicated that they should meet her halfway. Jessica could not believe how nervous she was. One would think she was Michael's fiancée.

"She's due in a couple of weeks," Michael remarked as they walked toward her. "Did you know I have a stepfather now?"

"That's neat."

"I never see him. They spend most of their time at his place by the beach. I'm still at the old house."

That was not news to Jessica. She had driven by his place a couple of times and parked down the street to wait for him to come home. But each time he had appeared, her nerve had failed and she'd driven away.

His mother had his black hair and dark eyes, but little or none of his seriousness. Jessica spotted that the moment she spoke; her voice was light, gay. Jessica could tell at a glance she was looking forward to the baby.

"Mom, this is Jessie. You remember her, don't you?"

"Sure, I do." She offered her hand. "I spoke to you on the phone once. Nice meeting you, Jessie."

"Thank you. Nice meeting you."

The lady turned to her son, handing him a letter. "This came from the observatory this morning. Is it what I think it is?"

"Probably," Michael said, slipping the envelope into his gown pocket.

"Aren't you going to open it?" his mother asked, slightly exasperated.

"Later. We know what it says."

"What is it?" Jessica asked, curious.

"Nothing," Michael said quickly, catching his mom's eye.

"All right," the lady said. "Be that way. Be rude." She nodded to Jessica and laughed at Michael. "She's pretty."

"I know," he said quietly.

Jessica quickly pulled off her glasses, embarrassed. "I have to wear these stupid things all the time."

"You look wonderful with them on," his mother said.

"Like a philosopher," Michael said.

"A professional woman," the mother said, reaching out and fixing Jessica's cap.

"I don't even have a gold tassel," Jessica muttered, trembling worse. The lady brushed a hair from her cheek, then took the glasses from her hands and checked the lenses for dust.

"These are strong," she remarked. "You *do* have to wear them."

"Come on, Mom," Michael said. "Give her a break."

"I know," Jessica said. The lady wiped them on her green dress and then carefully fixed them back on Jessica's nose, momentarily staring into her eyes.

She's checking me out.

"I hope we get to meet another time, Jessie."

"So do I," Jessica replied, a bit confused. Michael's mother turned back to him.

"Daniel and I are sitting near the bottom on the far right," she said. "In case you wanted to know. Be sure to thank your mother in your speech for being so wonderful."

"I'll mention it several times," he promised. She hugged him briefly, and then—to Jessica's surprise—gave her a hug too. When she left, Michael tugged gently on Jessica's tassel.

"Would you like to trade caps?" he asked. "I know you would have gotten an A in chemistry if I'd done a better job structuring the universe."

"Yeah, it's all your fault." She added softly, "No thanks."

"I didn't mean—"

"No, it's fine." She shrugged. "I really messed up this year. It was my own fault." She smiled quickly. "Your mom's neat."

"I'm glad you like her. I'll have to meet your parents."

"That's right. You didn't see them when we went out."

Hint. Hint. Hint. Ask me out again.

Of course he hadn't asked her out in the first place. He

never had in all the time they had spent together. She must be crazy to think he liked her.

In the hospital, however, the morning after Maria's accident, he had begun to say something that had since given her cause to wonder.

"I know how you feel. You're not a bad person. If you were, I wouldn't care about you the way . . ."

She had been crying because Maria had been so bitter toward her. He had probably been trying to cheer her up. She would never know. She had run away from him. She would run away again. She didn't deserve him. She was going to seduce the football quarterback tonight. It was all she was good for.

She suddenly felt as if she were going to cry. Here it was her last day of school, a beautiful summer day. She had everything: rich and understanding parents, perfect health, a bright future. Yet she had nothing. She had no love. Alice was gone. Michael was going. And Maria hated her.

It was at that precise moment that she saw Maria. Had that not happened, she might have been able to push aside her self-recriminations long enough to invite Michael and his parents to have dinner with her and her family after the ceremony. It was an idea, a good idea. But Nick guiding Maria across the track and onto the football field was bitter reality. She froze in midstride. Michael glanced at her face, then followed her eyes.

"I was going to tell you," he said.

"I haven't spoken to her since that morning." Jessica swallowed thickly. "She's in a wheelchair."

"It was a terrible accident."

He lay emphasis on the last word. She found that strange. He had always given her the impression that he didn't believe in accidents. He was trying to dispel her guilt. He might as well have tried to convince her she would gladly have traded places with Maria. But she wouldn't have, not for the world, and so her guilt remained.

"I'll talk to you later, OK?" she mumbled. "I have to get in line."

She walked off the field and hid in the crowd. Maria had asked Jessica never to make her see her again. It was the least she could do for her crippled friend, Jessica thought.

The ceremony began shortly afterward. The huge audience had been seated when the chatty senior class marched in and took their seats. Mr. Smith, Tabb's elderly principal, was the first speaker. Dressed in the same blue robe as the rest of them, he thanked the many parents, relatives, and friends for coming, and then proceeded to praise the group of graduates as the most dynamic in his long academic career. Jessica found his choice of the word "dynamic" appropriately vague. Hitler had been dynamic. Of course, she realized, it had not been a bad year for everyone.

The diplomas were to be presented alphabetically; for that

reason, the seating followed roughly that order. But Jessica Hart had switched with someone so she could sit next to Polly McCoy rather than Larry Harry. Larry not only had a weird name, he also had such consistently bad breath that Sara once remarked that if at the end of his life he donated his body to medical science, he would probably be found posthumously guilty of involuntary manslaughter when the medical students cut open his cadaver and choked to death.

Jessica also wanted to be with her old friend at this special time. Polly had suffered far more than any of them, and Jessica had courageously helped her the last few months by avoiding her. Not entirely, naturally; they continued to talk at lunch and stuff. But they no longer hung out as real friends do. The reason was simple. They were both down, and Jessica had discovered that the truism that the depressed seek out the company of other depressed people to be entirely false. Being around Polly only made her feel worse.

Yet seeing Maria again made Jessica want to atone for her cowardly approach to the situation. Sitting to the far right of the stage, in the back row—twenty rows behind Maria's front-row wheelchair—Jessica leaned over to Polly as Mr. Smith completed his talk.

"He's such a nice man," she said.

"He must be to have put up with Sara all year," Polly said. "Who's that he's introducing?"

"A car-company executive. He's here to inspire us to

go out into the big wide world and get rich." Polly winced slightly, took off her cap, and put her hand to her temple. "I'm already rich."

"Do you have a headache?"

"Yeah."

Jessica wiped the sweat from her brow. "It's this sun."

"It's sunny every day." Polly searched the stands.

"Looking for somebody?"

"No, nobody."

The guest speaker did turn out to be a strong believer in capitalism. His name was James Vern and ten years ago he had swiped—his actual phrase was "drew from the research of"— an invention that improved the efficiency of transmissions in large trucks, and parlayed it into millions. He laughed when he recounted the lies he had told to get financing for his company. Jessica wondered if he knew what a jerk he was. He talked for forty-five long minutes.

Sara came next. People giggled as she made her way to the microphone. Jessica tossed around in her head the idea of singing "Hey Jude."

"Thank you, Mr. Vern, for your enlightening words," Sara said, the tiniest hint of tension in her voice as she adjusted the mike down to her height. "The world of modern business really sounds like a jungle. But I suppose even a snake needs a place to live."

The audience chuckled uneasily. The senior class cheered

appreciatively. Sara smiled and went on more confidently, not using any notes. Jessica noticed for the first time that the top of the podium had been removed. As Sara had mentioned, there was no place to put papers.

"I have written several speeches this last week," Sara said. "I have one on this country's need to remain competitive in the world marketplace. I put a lot of time into it. Then I thought, haven't we been number one long enough? Shouldn't we give someone else a chance? I decided it was all a question of whether we want to be greedy or cool about it. I also had this speech on *our* future. It is my understanding that ASB presidents across the country talk about this subject graduation day. I really got into the idea myself—for a while. Then I realized that the best minds on Wall Street can't tell if the Dow Jones average is going to go up or down a couple of lousy points tomorrow, never mind where it's going to be ten years from now. The earth could get smashed by a huge meteorite this instant and vaporize us all, and then what would we do? Why worry about it? Why talk about it? I'm certainly not going to. Then, finally, I had this speech on the problems facing the youth of America: over-indulgence in alcohol, lack of ambition, sexual promiscuity. But I had to ask myself, Are these things really that bad? Think about it for a second." Sara turned to the class and raised her voice. "Do we really want to give them up?"

The class let out a resounding *no!* Then it burst out alto-gether. The audience—full of real-life parents—didn't know what to think. In the end, though, the crowd joined those on the field, and applauded Sara. She loved it.

"You know what I finally decided?" she said. "Not even to give a speech. Let's get this thing over with as quick as possible and get to the party." She cleared her throat and glanced to the side as the class clapped and hooted. "With that in mind, please welcome our senior faculty adviser, the wonderful Mr. Bark!"

Their political science teacher, wearing a blue graduation gown and a dyed fringe of hair that was supposed to take ten years off his age, strode confidently to the microphone. Sara remained on the stage. Jessica leaned forward in anticipation.

"Mr. Bark and I have had our disagreements this year," Sara said pleasantly as the teacher stood nearby. "But I like to think our trials have brought us closer together. I think, especially in the last month, I have finally begun to understand his commitment to social causes, particularly his concern over the arms race."

Mr. Bark leaned forward and spoke into the mike. "I am happy to hear that, Sara. It means a great deal to me."

"I wanted to show you how much it means to me," Sara said, nudging herself back behind the mike. "I bought you a present, a very special present." She gestured to someone on the left side of the stage. Jessica was surprised when Russ Desmond—Sara had not said a word about the progress of *the* relationship since she had picked him up at the bus station, and Jessica had been hesitant to ask—stood up and strode onto the stage, a small white package in his hands. He gave it to Sara, then hastily retreated. Sara presented it to Mr. Bark.

"Open it," she said.

Mr. Bark beamed. "This is so thoughtful of you, Sara." He began to peel away the paper. "I wonder what it could be." The crowd murmured expectantly. It took a minute to get through all the wrapping, and when he had, he was left holding what appeared to be—from Jessica's admittedly poor vantage point—a black rectangular stone. "Sara?" he said, uncertain.

"It's a paperweight," Sara explained.

"Oh." He grinned as he weighed it in his palm. "It feels like it should be able to handle the job. Thank you."

"Thank *you*, Mr. Bark." Sara muttered the next line under her breath as she turned away, but the mike caught it. "It's a uranium paperweight."

It was perfect. He obviously had a long speech prepared. Undoubtedly it was to be every bit as long as Mr. Vern's. He would talk about how much he had loved working with the kids this year, how sad he was to see them all leave, but how happy he was to know they were going on to bigger and greater things. Then he would bring up the nukes, the goddamn nukes that could destroy all of them at the push of a button.

Yet he had a uranium paperweight in his hand, and although he probably understood intellectually that the level of radiation it was emitting was extremely small—probably one thousandth or one millionth of what he would absorb if he had a chest X ray—he would not be able to stop thinking about it. Jessica watched as he began to speak and then glanced down at the thing in his hand and fidgeted. There was no place to put it, except on the ground. And he couldn't do that. No, that would be rude. He clearly didn't want to be rude.

"I am very happy to be here this afternoon with all you fine people," he began uneasily. "It is always an honor for me when I am given a chance to speak to—fine people."

He paused and glanced again at the paperweight. For a moment, it appeared that he might actually drop it. Jessica could practically read his mind. He was thinking of gamma rays, beta rays, and those always terrible cosmic rays—all those mean nasty things he read about every night in his literature about the mean nasty military industrialists.

"It's always a sad day, graduation day," he mumbled. "And a happy day."

His voice faltered. He moved the paperweight from his right hand to his left, then moved it back. He was probably imagining the different rays penetrating his flesh, Jessica thought, mutating the DNA in his cells, setting him up for a hideous case of cancer five years down the line. His fear practically screamed out at the crowd.

This rock is killing me!

He couldn't take it anymore. He took a step away, realized what he was doing, and then leaned back and spoke hastily into the mike. "And all I'd like to say is, good luck, good luck to all of you kids. Thank you."

He left the stage in a hurry, pausing at his seat only long enough to get rid of Sara's present, then strode toward the end of the folding chairs and off the football field. The audience watched quietly, reacting little. The class members whispered among themselves, relieved to have been spared another speech. Sara returned to the microphone.

"Our next speaker is the rarest of people," Sara said seriously. "He is the smartest individual I have ever met, and the nicest. He is Michael Olson, our class valedictorian."

"You should have gone out with him instead of Bill," Polly whispered as Michael stood up and walked to the microphone. The welcoming applause was the loudest of the afternoon.

"I know." Jessica sighed. "Do you think it's too late?"

"Yes."

"Thank you, Sara, for the kind introduction," Michael said, standing perfectly straight, his hands clasped in front of his gown below his waist, not as relaxed as he could have been but nevertheless in control of the situation. "And thank you, ladies and gentlemen and fellow classmates, for inviting me to speak on this occasion. Like Sara, I will try to keep my talk brief. I, too, have written and discarded several speeches in the last couple of hours. None of the topics I chose seemed right. I suppose that is the problem with selecting any topic. It can only be about one thing, while our lives are about so many things. I finally decided I would simply talk about what is important to me as I prepare to graduate from high school."

He glanced down at a small white card he held in his hand, and Jessica looked down at her shiny white high heels, and the grass beneath them. She was sitting on the forty-yard line, directly above the hash mark. She remembered the first Tabb High football game she had attended, how the team had tried for a first down on this part of the field and failed. Bill had fumbled the ball. She had a picture of the fumble in her files at home. She smiled at the memory, especially at how Michael had inadvertently helped her take the picture when he was demonstrating to her how to fit the telephoto lens onto her camera.

But that had been a long time ago.

Polly's right. It's too late.

"In a way I'm five months late with my speech," Michael went on. "I left school in January, and today is my first day back. Since I've been gone, I've been rather busy, working and stuff. But I've often looked back and thought about what I learned at Tabb. The obvious thing that comes to mind is all the science and math and history I absorbed. The teachers here are really great, some of the best, and now, I think, would be a good time to thank them for their patience and dedication. They always praised me and gave me confidence. But maybe they did too good a job. One of the problems with people thinking you're smart is that you eventually begin to believe it.

I remember all the times in class—how restless I would be for the teacher to get on with the lesson. I've grasped the concept, I used to think, why haven't the rest of the kids? What I didn't realize then is that learning something doesn't just mean figuring it out. It's also the pleasure you get from the knowledge. I didn't appreciate that the teacher would sometimes dwell on a particular subject because he or she loved it. I got mostly A's but now I wish I'd had more fun doing it. I hope this is one lesson I won't forget."

Michael paused and looked over the audience. When he spoke next, it was in a lower voice, and Jessica found herself leaning forward, afraid she might miss something.

She knew he was going to bring up Alice.

"But there is something else high school taught me," he said. "Something I did not know until I was no longer here on a daily basis. Like everybody, I suppose, I knew certain people at school that I didn't really like. They bugged me for one reason or another, and I used to think I'd be glad when I didn't have to see them anymore. Then again, I had friends I loved to be around, people that made it easy for me to get up in the morning and drive here. But the strange thing I've discovered since I've been gone is that I miss both groups of people. And I like to think I've been missed by both groups. I like to think we're all good friends. Maybe I've learned the importance of friendship. Mr. Bark was right—today is a happy day, but it's also sad. We'll all promise to keep in touch, but realistically, many of us will never see one another again. Today is supposed to be the day we grow up, yet in a way, it's a shame any of us have to. Your high-school friends—I think they're your best friends."

Your final friends.

Jessica didn't know why she thought that. There was life after high school. There would be other boys besides Michael.

There was only one problem. She didn't want any other boy.

Michael coughed once and looked down. "In closing I would like to pay tribute to the memory of a very special friend who had her life taken suddenly from her. If possible, I would like her remembered with a minute of silence. Her name was Alice McCoy. She would have graduated in a couple of years."

Michael lowered his head. Most of those present did the same. Jessica closed her eyes and felt a tear slide over her warm cheek. Just one tear. The minute lasted an eternity. Sara's voice made her sit up with a start.

"And now Jessica Hart will close the ceremony with a song."

Jessica stood and glanced at Polly, who in turn stared up at her.

"Was he right about us not having any more friends?" Polly asked sadly. Jessica squeezed her shoulder.

"We'll always be friends, Polly."

Jessica found the piano and sat down. The silence persisted, but a faint breeze had begun to cross the stadium. She felt it in her hair and on her damp cheek. She had no music before her; she had to choose a Beatles song. That was OK. They had composed the perfect one for the occasion, especially since Michael had forgotten to thank his wonderful mother for having given birth to him. Jessica began to sing.

"'When I find myself in times of trouble, Mother Mary comes to me, speaking words of wisdom, let it be. And in my hour of darkness, she is standing right in front of me, speaking words of wisdom, let it be. Let it be, let it be, let it be, let it be, whisper words of wisdom, let it be. . . .'"

She went through the song alone, and when she came to the final chorus, no one in the stands or on the field joined her. That was OK, too. She may not have sung it as beautifully as Paul McCartney, but she sang it as if it were important to her, which it was. When she finished, the silence returned, deeper than before and just for a moment. Then the applause poured down upon her from all sides and she smiled. It was the first time she had felt good all day.

The diplomas were handed out, one by one, with Mr. Smith shaking everybody's hand and wishing each one well. When that was done, Sara squealed something ridiculous into the mike and the class sprang to its feet and cheered. Then five hundred caps sailed into the air, the largest of which was Bubba's huge straw sombrero, complete with gold tassel.

Jessica hugged Polly. They had made it. School was over, and if they wanted, it could be over for good. Sara burst through the crowd and embraced them both. And then they laughed and insulted one another, and it was just as it always had been between them and, she hoped, always would be. Michael didn't know everything after all. Jessica meant it when she had told Polly they would be friends forever.

Jessica didn't find Michael in the crowd, though she looked long and hard. He seemed to have disappeared.

Michael had indeed left the school, but Carl Barber, better known as Kats, had not. He stood in the middle of the joyous crowd, watching everybody hug and kiss, a wide grin on his face, but a scowl in his heart. Nothing really changed, he thought bitterly. He had his diploma. He had earned it attending hours of tedious night classes. He was as good as the rest of them. But how many of them wanted to shake his hand? As many as had shaken his hand last June when he had failed to graduate because of a few lousy grades. Nobody cared about him. Nobody ever had and nobody ever would.

After tonight, though, they would remember him, if they remembered anything at all. Almost the entire senior class would be on that cruise ship when it left the dock for Catalina. But if he had his way—and he would, he swore it—not a single one of them would be on board when it reached its destination. That ship would be a ghost ship.

Chapter Nine

Michael parked down the street from Clark Halley's house and removed the gun from the glove compartment. Checking again to be sure it was fully loaded, he stuffed it inside his sports-jacket pocket. Clark's huge black Harley-Davidson sat at the end of the crumbling asphalt driveway, fuming in the boiling sun from recent exertion. Clark was home. If the place could be called a home. It looked more like a chicken coop, out at the far east end of San Bernardino Valley, where the desert began and the rents plummeted. The place stunk, yet when Michael had finally located the house a month earlier—after a great deal of effort and an equal amount of luck—he had celebrated.

And then I did nothing but watch and wait.

A last name is not the same as an address. Michael discovered that soon after he had found Clark's ugly picture and full name in the Temple High yearbook. The Monday after Maria's accident, he had revisited Temple High and asked to speak to Clark Halley. Turned out the guy no longer went there. He should have been in the middle of his senior year, but he had unexpectedly dropped out at the beginning of October. He had, in fact, disappeared just after Alice had died.

No sweat to find him, Michael had figured. He would get Clark's family address and catch up with him there. Easier said than done. Clark didn't have a family. He lived alone. He was an orphan or his parents had died or something; the secretary at Temple High wasn't sure what the situation was. Using the best of his charm, and a couple of tricks Bubba had taught him, Michael was able to obtain from the secretary—the same woman who had given him the yearbook during his original visit—the address Clark had had his mail sent to while at the school. It proved to be phony—a closed Laundromat.

Michael went back to Temple High at lunchtime, again and again. He mingled, made friends, asked questions, and listened. He led the other kids to believe he went to Temple. He began to build up a picture of Clark Halley, and it matched the one he already had—the guy was a creep.

Clark had kept mostly to himself, but when he did speak up, it had usually been to insult somebody. One girl recalled how he'd asked to sign her cast after she'd had a skiing accident. He'd drawn a tasteless sketch of her stepping into a bear trap, her foot being sliced off at the ankle and bleeding all over the ground. That was one thing everyone seemed to agree on—the dude could draw. He had talent. He might even be a genius.

What he didn't have, and what Michael desperately needed to find, was a friend. Clark didn't seem to have a single one. No one knew where he lived. No one had his phone number. He had attended the school for three years and no one could provide Michael with a single fact about his personal life. Did he have a job? Did he have any brothers or sisters? Did he have a favorite place to eat? Michael heard the same answer repeatedly—I don't know. At one point he began to feel he was chasing a phantom.

Then in mid-March he got a lead. He was on something like his twentieth visit to Temple High and talking to a guy who had gone motorcycle riding with Clark a couple of times. The guy's name was Fred Galanger, and although he appeared to be a pretty tough son-of-a-bitch—he carried thick biceps and lurid tattoos beneath his biker jacket—he spoke of Clark reluctantly, as if he were afraid Clark's ghost might suddenly appear and rake him over with a steel chain. Fred probably knew Clark better than anyone at Temple, which, of course, was not saying much. Michael had cultivated his acquaintance carefully. Then he had tired of the game and offered Fred twenty bucks for a single slice of useful memory. Fred's brain cells had lit up.

"We were out that afternoon I told you about before," Fred said carefully, sliding the crisp bill into his pants pocket and keeping his hand wrapped around it in case it somehow vanished while he spoke of the mysterious rider. "We were hot-dogging these turns in the foothills down from Big Bear. That's a dangerous place to be riding hard, but Clark, he'd have a smile on his face heading into the hood of an oncoming truck, if it came to that. He was crazy. It took guts to keep up with him. I was one of the few guys who could.

"Anyway, we came around this one turn near the bottom of the mountain and there was an oil spill on the road. Clark's front wheel caught the edge of it and he went flying, right off the embankment and into this ravine. I figured he'd bought it right then. But he didn't even have a scratch. Don't ask me how. He was already pushing his bike back up the hill and onto the road before I could get to him. He thought it was the funniest thing in the world. But his leather coat was torn to shreds and he'd crushed his shift lever. It was weird; I went to help him bend the lever back so we could get home, but he wouldn't let me touch it. He said he didn't let anyone near his bike except this Indian who works at a station in Sunnymead. He wouldn't even work on it himself, like it was sacred to him or something dumb like that."

"What's the name of the station?" Michael interrupted.

"I don't know. It's an independent, right off the freeway, I think at Branch. Yeah, it's on Branch. We crawled there at ten miles an hour, Clark's bike stuck in first gear the whole way. The Indian's a mechanic at the station. I don't remember his name—Birdbeak or Crowfoot or something. He must have been in his nineties. You shouldn't have any trouble finding him. They seemed like old friends. He'll probably know where Clark lives."

"Anything else?" Michael asked.

"No. Except if you do find him, don't mention my name. I mean it."

"Why not?"

Fred Galanger wouldn't tell him why. He didn't have to. He was obviously afraid of Clark.

Fred was right about one thing—Michael did find the gas station without difficulty. He also met the Indian mechanic. His real name was Stormwatcher, and although he didn't have Clark's strange pale eyes, he had a similar otherworldly stare that made Michael uncomfortable. Michael figured it would be a mistake to approach him directly for Clark's address. He suspected that Clark was somehow involved with the occult, that he was in fact an apprentice of the Indian. The old guy might warn Clark he was being hunted.

It was the perfect time to go to the police. Michael didn't have the time or the inclination to stake out the gas station day after day, hoping Clark would show up. The police could demand that the Indian tell them what he knew of Clark. But Michael did not trust the police; in particular, he did not trust Lieutenant Keller's detective skills. Keller would question Clark, Clark would tell him about Alice's instability, and

Keller would go away satisfied, confident he got what he had come for.

A month later Michael was still debating how to make friends with one of the teenagers who worked part-time at the station—someone who could alert him by phone if Clark should arrive—when he got another big break. He was getting gas at the station when Clark drove up.

Clark didn't see him—Michael was pretty sure of that. He was off again quickly after exchanging a few words with the old Indian. Michael followed him carefully, but not too closely. Clark drove very fast. Yet he didn't go far before he pulled into the driveway of a broken-down house in a decrepit neighborhood.

And this was the same house Michael found himself sitting outside an hour after he had graduated valedictorian, a gun in his pocket, doubt in his mind. Yet he had sat here before—without a gun but with the same doubts—and he had done nothing.

Clark could say one word, and smash everything I believe.

Michael did not fear Clark so much as he feared Alice—feared who she might have been. When he got right down to it, he hadn't known her that long.

He got out of his car, the sweat sticking to him like a layer of deceit; surely Clark would be suspicious about his wearing a coat on such a hot day. Yet Michael had no intention of lying to Clark about the purpose of his visit.

A cat ran across Michael's path as he walked toward the door. It was brown, not black, but it had green eyes. Most cats did, he supposed. He wondered if he was going to die in the next few minutes.

Michael knocked on the door. Clark answered quickly. He had on a gray T-shirt and black pants. His red hair was shorter than it had been last fall, neater, and he was not nearly so bony or pale. Indeed, Michael wondered briefly if he had the right house. He remembered Clark as a fish dug from a foul swamp. This guy was not unattractive. The eyes gave him away, however; they could have been plucked from the cat that had just crossed the yard. And the southern twang was still there.

"Can I help you?" he asked, standing behind a torn screen door.

"Maybe. I don't know if you remember me. My name's Mike. I met you at a football game at Tabb High? You were with Alice."

"What do you want?" His voice was cautious, but not hostile.

"I'd like to come in and talk to you about Alice. If that would be all right?"

Clark considered a moment. "All right." He held open the screen door. "The place is a mess. It always is."

It was messy only because it was crammed with paintings and artistic paraphernalia: recently stretched canvases, tubes of oils, stained rags, dozens of brushes in all sizes and shapes standing upright in tin cans. Except for the supplies, the house, though claustrophobic, was not bad. There were no half-finished TV dinners or overfilled ashtrays. Clark was not a slob. His place was, in fact, neater than Alice's studio had been.

Michael had part of an answer to one of his questions even before he sat down on a stool beside the narrow kitchen counter. Art had been at the core of Alice's life. Michael remembered how her bright blue eyes had constantly darted about wherever she was, as if she were eternally starved for visual input, of the beautiful or the unusual kind. Here, in Clark's place, she could have drunk up images to her heart's content. Maybe that, and that alone, had drawn her to Clark. The room was the inside of an LSD-gorged brain cell, despite the fact that the bulk of Clark's work was black-and-white sketches and not psychedelic paintings. Michael didn't know how he filled the colorless with color. It was as if he used magic; the mind saw something the eye did not.

A phantom.

The subject matter of the sketches consisted largely of women and *creatures* relaxing together on barren desert scenes. The women were always beautiful. More than a few looked like Alice. The creatures had insect and reptile qualities. They smiled a lot. They obviously liked their women.

"Want a beer?" Clark asked, picking up a can of Coors from the floor beside his chair. Clark appeared to have been reading when Michael had knocked. The book lay facedown on the thin green carpet, a hardback. Michael couldn't make out the title.

"No, thank you," Michael said.

Clark sat down and crossed his long legs at the ankles. "You were a friend of Alice's, weren't you?"

"Yeah. Do you remember me? We met at that football game I mentioned."

"Sort of. I wasn't feeling so hot that night, if you know what I mean."

"You seemed stoned," Michael said. Clark didn't look stoned now. He appeared very alert. He was definitely watching Michael closely. Michael pulled his coat tighter, conscious of the weight of the automatic pistol in his inside pocket.

"I might have been. What did you want to ask me about Alice?"

"Well, she's dead, you know."

"Yeah, I know," Clark said, betraying no signs of grief. "I read about it in the papers."

"Did you come to the party that night?"

"No. Alice didn't invite me. Were you there?"

"Yeah. Why didn't Alice invite you?"

"I don't know. She was mad at me."

"Why?"

Clark took a gulp of beer and set down the can. "What is this?"

"What's what?"

"Why are you here? Who gave you my address?"

"I discovered your address by accident. As to your other question—I have doubts about how she died. The police say it was suicide. I think they might be wrong."

"You think she was murdered?"

"I think it's a possibility."

Clark thought a moment. His eyes never left Michael. "Go on," he said finally.

"Do you think she killed herself?"

"I wasn't there."

"But you were her boyfriend. Did she show any signs she was about to commit suicide?"

"No. When I read about it, I was surprised."

"How come you didn't come to the funeral?"

"I don't believe in funerals."

"That's not much of an answer."

"I wasn't invited." Clark stood slowly and moved toward the kitchen, stopping beside the wall, standing above Michael. "Sure you don't want a beer?" he asked.

"I'll take one," Michael said. Clark stepped into the kitchen, opened the refrigerator, and handed him a can of Coors. Clark had left his own beer on the floor beside his chair. He returned to his spot beside the wall, only a few feet from Michael's stool. Michael opened the can and took a sip. "It's cold," he said.

I wish he wasn't so close.

"Tell me more about Alice's party," Clark said, staring.

"It was big, with lots of people coming and going." Michael felt uncomfortable under Clark's scrutinizing gaze. The guy's eyes were not only bright, but penetrating; naturally an artist as talented as he would be visually perceptive. Michael wondered what he was giving away to Clark. He was getting nothing back from him. Clark was impossible to read. His expression—if it could be called that—was as flat as a dead man's.

"Yeah?" Clark said. He didn't appear overly interested in the details of the party.

"But there were only a few people there when Alice died."

A painting sitting on the floor next to Clark caught Michael's attention. There was a creature and there was a girl—the usual. But this one was in a house, an ordinary room. It looked like an empty bedroom. The girl looked like Polly. The creature was a manfly. It was kissing the girl on the neck, probably sucking her blood. There was a real fly buzzing around the room. It landed on the wall near Clark's head. He took no notice of it.

I'm on fire.

The temperature inside the house had to be over a hundred. Michael was dying to remove his jacket. He thought of the gun, why he had brought it. He wasn't going to kill Clark. He had meant only to scare him into telling the truth. Now *he* was beginning to feel scared. He took another gulp of beer.

"Have you been to the McCoy house much?" Michael asked.

"No."

"Have you been there lately?"

"No."

"Oh." The fly leaped onto the shoulder of Clark's gray T-shirt. Clark continued to ignore it. Michael felt off balance. He had plotted too long against Clark in his own mind. The physical presence of the guy was intimidating the hell out of him. And that stupid fly. He had always hated flies. "Have you been to see Polly since Alice died?" he asked.

"No."

"But I spoke to Polly this morning. She says you were at her house the night her aunt died."

"She's wrong."

The fly crawled toward Clark's neck, pausing beneath his Adam's apple. He mustn't be able to feel it. Or else he liked flies.

Of course he likes flies. He's always painting them.

"Polly also thought you were there the night of the party?" Michael said.

"She wanted me to come at the end, but I didn't."

"So you were invited?"

"Why are you asking me all these questions?"

Michael desperately wanted to move. He wanted to brush away the fly from Clark's neck, and then put more space between the two of them. He also wanted to pull his coat closed tighter. Clark was staring at Michael's coat pocket now, the way it hung down slightly. Michael could feel the eyes of every creature in every sketch in the room watching him. He felt—knowing full well it was a hysterical thought—as if they were Clark's allies.

"I told you why," Michael said.

"The paper I read said Alice died with a gun in her mouth?"

"That's right."

"That doesn't sound like murder to me."

"The gun in her mouth didn't kill her," Michael said, straining to keep his voice steady. The fly crawled around the back of Clark's head and disappeared. But Michael knew it was still there. He could feel it as if it were crawling along the base of his own skull. "She was killed by a blow to the nose."

Clark showed a flicker of interest. He stood away from the wall, moving closer to Michael. "Go on."

He was committed. He would throw everything at Clark that he knew or suspected and see what happened.

He saw plenty happen, quicker than he thought he would.

"It was some kind of setup," he began. "We were downstairs in the living room when we heard this shot. But the shot—"

The fly suddenly buzzed from behind Clark and went straight for Michael. It had chosen a bad time. Michael was in the middle of trying to readjust his coat. The fly made him jerk slightly, as if he were going for something *inside* his coat. Then again, maybe the fly made no difference. Clark obviously suspected Michael was carrying a weapon. Sooner or later, he would probably have lashed out.

Clark snapped his right foot up. He had on heavy black boots. The tip caught Michael in the lower right side of his rib cage, sending him and the stool he was sitting on toppling backward. Michael hardly had a chance to react. Pain flared across his side. The back of his skull hit the wall hard. He fell to the floor at an awkward angle.

Oh, man, this is bad.

Clark loomed above, the manfly painting in his hands. This time Michael definitely reached for the gun. He had his fingers on the handle and was pulling it out when the canvas came crashing down on him. The frame tore into the top of his scalp, the canvas ripping down over his face. He felt the gun slip from his hand. Then another hand—this one had thick numbing fingers—reached inside his brain. He momentarily blacked out. The next thing he knew, Clark was leaning over him, the barrel of the automatic pressed to his cheek. Clark's hair seemed suddenly much redder. Then Michael realized he was seeing him through the film of his own blood.

"I didn't kill her, dude," he hissed, showing some emotion at last. "She was my girl. Maybe it was you who killed her. Maybe I should kill you and bury you in the backyard. What do you say to that, Mr. Mike?"

"Go to hell," Michael whispered.

Clark chuckled. Then he drew back the hand that held the gun and a freight train hit the side of Michael's head.

He came to an hour later. The fly was crawling around his ears. He waved it away, feeling nauseated. His hair and shirt were a mess with sticky, wet blood. Clark was gone. So was the gun. He sat up and groaned, the room spinning at odd angles. He suspected he had a concussion.

He noticed Clark's book still facedown on the floor. He crawled toward it, throwing off the painting wrapped around his neck. *Shakespeare's Collected Works.* Clark had been reading *Romeo and Juliet.*

Michael stumbled outside onto the cracked driveway. The Harley-Davidson had gone for a ride. He checked his watch. The sun would be setting soon.

"Don't come to the all-night party, Mike."

Michael climbed into his car. He had to get down to the dock.

Chapter Ten

Jessica and Sara stopped at the first drugstore they saw when they got off the freeway in San Pedro not far from Los Angeles Harbor. It was after six. The boat was set to sail at precisely seven. They had little time to purchase the contraceptives.

"So what are we going to get?" Sara asked as Jessica turned off the engine.

"Ask the pharmacist for his recommendation."

"No way. I'd be too embarrassed."

"What's the big deal?" Jessica asked. "They're professionals." She added, "I'll wait for you here."

"Hold on a second, sister. I'm not going in there alone. You go in."

"Why me?" Jessica asked.

"You look more innocent."

"More the reason you should do it." She grinned. "You slut."

Dinner with the parents had been far more enjoyable than Jessica had anticipated. First of all the food had been fantastic. Both Sara and she'd had lobster. Then her mom and dad had been in good spirits. They hadn't brought up her future once. The conversation had revolved mainly around the ceremony. Mr. and Mrs. Cantrell had loved her song. Sara's various improvisations had been tactfully forgotten. Jessica's mom had fallen in love with Michael.

"He seems such a nice boy. How come you only went out with him one time, Jessie?"

One sticky spot during the entire meal wasn't bad.

Russ and Bill were riding down to the boat with their buddies. Make that two different sets of buddies. Nobody on the football team would speak to Russ. He had, after all, supposedly wiped out their varsity tree. The situation didn't seem to bother him. During the brief time Jessica had spent talking to Russ after the ceremony, he'd appeared removed from the whole situation. Perhaps that was what came from being locked up too long. Sara and Russ had looked stiff together. Sara still wasn't talking about it.

Jessica's mood had continued to brighten since the applause for her song. But it could have been hormonal. The idea of a sleazy encounter on the high seas no longer depressed her. Indeed, she was now looking forward to it.

"I wish I had more slut in me," Sara said, jolting Jessica back to the present situation.

"Is someone having second thoughts?"

"No," Sara said quickly. "I was just wondering, you know, if it will hurt. I've heard that it can. Have you heard that?"

Jessica nodded solemnly. "I read about this one girl—the first time she had sex, she bled so much she had to have a transfusion."

Sara snorted. "Get out of here."

"Don't worry. I honestly believe we'll find it a deeply moving and fulfilling experience."

"I hope not. I just want to have some fun. So what are we going to get?"

"What are our choices?" Jessica asked.

"In a drugstore, there're condoms, foam, and sponges."

"Guys aren't supposed to like to wear condoms."

"I heard that, too," Sara said. "But they're safer."

"You think Russ caught something at juvenile hall?"

"The place is full of guys."

"That's worse," Jessica teased.

"Please, we just ate."

"Why don't we get all three? None of it can cost much." Not to mention the fact that she wasn't hurting financially. Less than an hour ago, her father had given her an envelope stashed with ten crisp one-hundred-dollar bills. The cash was supposed to be spending money for next week in Hawaii, but she was going shopping this week. Boy, was she going shopping.

"Great," Sara said. "And have Bill put on a wet suit while you're at it."

"We just have to buy the stuff. We don't have to use it all at once. Come on, I'll go with you."

The drugstore was empty except for the pharmacist and a helper. Unfortunately, the pharmacist appeared preoccupied in the back making up prescriptions. Worse, his sole employee was a total babe of around nineteen years old. He smiled as they entered.

"Can I help you find something?" he asked.

"No," they said in unison, looking at each other. Jessica leaned over and whispered in Sara's ear, "Let's go somewhere else!"

"We don't have time!" Sara whispered back.

"This is totally humiliating. I'd rather have a baby."

"You're coming to the counter with me."

"I'm just here to get a toothbrush."

"Jessie!"

"Shh! Tell him our names why don't you."

They huddled into a back row and inspected the store's G.I. Joes and Gumbies. Sara idly picked up a package of pink balloons. "Those won't fit," Jessica warned.

Sara threw the balloons down in disgust. "I'm supposed to be the first one to the ship. I have to talk to the captain about a check I gave him." She glanced toward the counter. "I think I see them."

"Where?"

"Near the cash register."

"All right, here's what we'll do," Jessica said. "I'll call the guy over and get him to help me pick out a toy. You grab the stuff, get the pharmacist's attention, and we'll be on our way."

"Why can't I get help with the toy?"

"Because I thought of it first. Now get away from me."

Sara sulked over to the laxative section. Jessica smiled and waved her hand. The guy saw her and hurried to her side. He had blond hair like Bill's, but was taller and thinner than Bill. She could tell he liked her, glasses and all.

I hope to God he doesn't ask me for my number.

"Looking for something?" he asked.

"Yeah," she said, picking up a brown plastic horse. "I wanted to ask you about this toy."

"Yes?"

"Ah—how much is it?"

He checked the price, which was clearly marked on the side. "Two twenty-five."

"Oh," she said. Sara had reached the proper area and was quickly examining the boxes on the shelves. "What kind of horse is it?" Jessica asked. He took it from her hands and fiddled with the cheap tiny hatch on the underbelly.

"It looks like the Trojan horse."

"Trojans?" she whispered. *How did he know?* Then she realized he was *not*—thank God—referring to the popular brand of condoms. She giggled loudly. "Yeah, that's what it is."

He smiled uncertainly. "Buying it for a nephew?"

"Yeah."

"What's his name?"

"Michele."

"Your nephew?"

"I mean, Michael."

Oh, no, no, no!

Sara had finished making her selection—it apparently didn't take long when one was willing to take everything the store had to offer—and signaled the pharmacist. Unfortunately, someone else had entered the store. No, not another person. An all-seeing, greasy butterball.

"Do you live around here?" the guy asked Jessica.

"Sara, my darling!" Bubba exclaimed, sauntering up to the counter, still wearing his ridiculous gold-tasseled sombrero and blue graduation gown. He must have stolen it.

Sara turned a distinctly unhealthy shade of green and threw Jessica a look of pure misery. She wanted help, Jessica knew. But Jessica wasn't about to give it to her. Bubba hadn't seen her so far and Jessica had no intention of letting him see her. She pulled the young man with her toward the corner, using him as a shield.

"I'd really like to know more about this horse," she said.

"What are you doing here?" Bubba asked, picking up one of the boxes. Devilish delight filled his face. "Sponges! A girl who thinks more of her man's pleasure than her own. Bravo, Sara! Bravo!"

"How old is your nephew?" the guy asked.

"Who cares?" Jessica asked. "I mean, what?"

"I was just wondering if another gift might be more appropriate," the guy replied, not put off by her rudeness.

"Is this all?" the pharmacist asked Sara. Sara nodded stiffly, not looking at Bubba, even though she was obviously trying to dematerialize him by the sheer power of her thoughts. Bubba raised a hand.

"Wait," he said. "We would like a bottle of baby oil." Bubba spoke to Sara. "Usually, after exerting myself in lovemaking, I enjoy a full-body massage. It restores my vital energies that much quicker."

The pharmacist somehow kept a straight face, but it was clear it was only because he had been a pharmacist for many years. "Would you like the oil?" he asked Sara.

"No," she said curtly.

"Is that guy hassling your friend?" the handsome young man asked Jessica.

"I don't know her," Jessica said.

Bubba put his arm lovingly around Sara and spoke to the pharmacist. "This is all new to her. She's embarrassed. Look, she's blushing. Give us the largest bottle of oil you carry."

"My name's Dave," the guy said to Jessica. "What's yours?"

"Why?" she asked, terribly distracted.

"I don't want the oil," Sara said, pushing forward her money. "But I'll pay for this other stuff—*now*."

"I won't hear of it," Bubba said, reaching for his wallet.

"I was just wondering if maybe we could get together later?" the handsome young man asked Jessica.

"I can't," she said.

"Why not?"

"I'm busy," Jessica said. "I'm married."

Sara kept shoving her own money on the pharmacist. He finally showed mercy on her and took it, ringing up the three different boxes of contraceptives, minus the oil. Bubba moved back a step.

"Modern women," he told the pharmacist, shaking his head, not overly displeased. "They think they know what they want, when they haven't a clue what they *need*."

"Thank you," Sara told the pharmacist, grabbing the bag and hurrying for the door. Bubba watched her leave, then turned toward the rear of the store. Jessica tried to duck behind Dave. Too late.

"Give my regards to Bill, Jessie," Bubba called. "But if I were you, I'd keep Sara's receipt."

Jessica gave the Trojan horse back to Dave and chased after Sara. When they were back in the front seat of the car, trying to breathe and not groan at the same time, Sara glanced over at Jessica and remarked, "That wasn't so bad."

Jessica stuck the keys in the ignition, her hand trembling. "We handled it like mature adults," she agreed.

Chapter Eleven

Wrong and right. Dark and light. Polly was confused. She did not know what to do. The flowers in her hands were dying. She had just bought them. Roses—the day they bloomed they began to wilt. She didn't suppose it mattered. Alice wouldn't care.

Polly knelt beside the grave, the grass thick and wet beneath her bare knees. Her headache had returned. The voice at her back didn't surprise her. She'd heard the motorcycle approaching from far off.

"So she really is dead," Clark said.

Polly turned. Clark was all in black. She couldn't remember when she had last seen him in the sunlight. It could have been the day they had met. It didn't make much difference, the time of day; he brought the night with him. He was the only guy she knew who stood in his own shadow. She had not seen him since the night her aunt had died.

"Hi," she said.

"Hello."

"Did you think I lied to you about her?" she asked.

"You lie to me all the time."

She turned back to the tombstone, annoyed. Alice Ann McCoy. Polly could have sworn Ann was her own middle name. "Go away."

"You're not happy to see me?"

"No," Polly said.

"Then why did you call?"

"I didn't call."

"Then why am I here?" Clark asked.

"I don't know."

Clark stepped onto the neighboring grave, her aunt's. He grinned as he looked down, and she thought that he might spit. A green canvas bag hung by a strap over his shoulder. "She finally choked to death, I see," he said.

"The doctor said she went peacefully in her sleep."

"But doctors lie."

"Did you smother her?" she asked angrily.

Clark shrugged. "She was old and ugly."

"I hate you."

He chuckled. "You hated her. You hated taking care of her."

"That's not true! Get out of here and leave me alone!"

Clark circled Alice's grave. He did so carefully, almost as if he feared the spot. He moved to Philip Bart's grave. A rock from a dynamite blast had put him in the ground. Polly had donated the plot to his family. It was supposed to have been her own plot.

Clark slipped the bag from his shoulder and set the strap over Philip's tombstone. His middle name had been Michael. Her father's name had been Michael. But neither her father nor mother was buried in this cemetery. There hadn't been enough of them left to fill a coffin. Their car had burned forever. Ashes and smoke. If she closed her eyes, Polly could still smell it, and hear her father shouting at her to behave in the backseat—right before he had driven off the road.

Polly liked the name Michael. It brought back warm memories. But she still hoped Michael Olson didn't come to the party. Clark knelt beside his bag and began to unzip it.

"I'm not leaving," he said. "Today's your last day of school. It's our last chance."

"For what?"

"To even the score."

"You're not doing anything. They won't let you on the boat."

"You can get me on board."

"Why should I?" she asked.

He let go of the bag. Anger filled his face. "You're sitting on your why."

"They didn't kill her! She killed herself!"

"That's a lie. You're lying to me again."

"Then you killed her."

His anger left suddenly. He grinned. He had ugly lips, like a fish. It made her sick to remember all the times they had kissed. "Closer to the truth, Polly. But not close enough. Go on."

"What?"

"Tell me how I killed Alice."

She stared down at her roses. They'd scraped away the thorns at the florist; nevertheless, she felt a sharp prick—a band of thorns wrapped around her head like the crown of thorns Jesus wore. Bloody red roses. Funeral flowers. A waste of money. Her vision wavered at Clark's question. "I was outside in the backyard," she said.

"All right." He appeared to sigh. He'd wanted her to say something else. He went back to his bag, pulling out a tiny metal clock, black and red wires, and a lump of what could have been orange Play-Doh. "We'll say the party killed her. If there hadn't been a party, there would still be an Alice."

Polly nodded wearily. "Yeah."

"Most of the kids who were at the party will be on the boat."

"What is that stuff?"

Clark tapped the tombstone at his back. "Mr. Bart could tell you."

"You're not going to blow up the boat!"

"Of course not."

"You better not."

He laughed. "I'm just going to put a hole in it." He crawled toward her, his leather-clad legs slithering over the grass like twin snakes. She thought he was going to grab her, kiss her—she didn't want him to kiss her, not that much—but he halted shy of Alice's grave. "You remember the party? All the kiddies were in the pool. They know how to swim."

"Not all of them," Polly said.

"Who doesn't know?" he asked gleefully.

"Jessie." That was a fact. Jessica had grown up with a pool in her backyard and was going to Hawaii next week, but she had never learned to swim. She had almost drowned as a child. She was terrified of the water.

"Who talked you into the party?" Clark asked.

"Jessie. And Sara."

Clark glanced at his bag. There was something black and muddy inside that he had not unpacked. "Sara never did like you."

Polly put her hand to her head. She could feel the blood pounding beneath the skin. She had given blood all year—to different hospitals, more times than she was supposed to—and there was still so much pressure inside. Sometimes she honestly felt the only real way to let it all out would be to take a gun and put a hole in her skull the way Alice had.

"How did you know Jessie couldn't swim?" she whispered.

Clark reached over with his bony left hand—he was left-handed, as Alice had been—and touched Polly's lips with the nail of his index finger. He touched her teeth. He probably would have stuck his finger inside her if she had let him. He was trying to get inside her. He had been trying from the beginning, although he had never wanted to make love to her. She had never been able to understand that. He was one way, and he was another way. She imagined his finger would have felt the same way the cold hard barrel of a gun would have felt inside her mouth. She knew it would have been just as deadly. But that might not be such a bad thing, not if it stopped the pain. Her head was killing her!

"If I tell you that," he said. "I will tell you everything."

He was asking for her permission. "No," she said.

"Are you sure?"

"No."

"I'll kill them. I'll kill them all."

She set the roses down. *For my sister.* "He'll stop you."

"Who?"

"Michael."

"I very much doubt it." Clark stood and put the explosives back in his bag. He held out his left hand. "Come along, Polly. It's time."

She went with him.

Chapter Twelve

Haven was her name, and she was at the end of a long and fun-filled career. In the sixties and seventies, she had been a popular choice for vacationers looking for an intimate cruise ship to take to Mexico's Mazatlan, La Paz, or Acapulco. But that had been before a new generation of vessels—larger and more sophisticated—had pushed *Haven* into an uneconomical no-man's-land; she was too plush to haul cargo, and she was too plain and small to attract parties of the rich and pretty. When Bubba had come to Sara in the spring with the idea of renting *Haven* for Tabb High's all-night senior party, he had never spoken so truthfully as he did when he said it was the chance of a lifetime. Her captain had just decided to rent her out as a party boat, making the trip between Catalina and the mainland. This class party was to be one of his first short cruises.

Bubba had caught Sara at an anxious moment. She had been thinking hard and without success for a way to blow everybody's extracurricular mind one last time, and thus forever ensure their fond memories of her leadership skills. Because neither side was aware of how desperate the other was, the negotiations between the captain of the *Haven* and Sara proceeded with remarkable smoothness. The captain didn't even mind a postdated check.

Yet the cost for the all-night party was unusually high—forty dollars per student, and that didn't include a hotel room to recover in on Catalina. But you only graduated from high school once, Sara had thought. She figured the class should be able to stay awake until *Haven* returned them to the mainland the next evening. From the beginning, the idea of the class bumming around together on the island all day had struck her as the best part of the plan. When she had announced the extravaganza, practically every senior had bought a ticket.

It was only because Sara had taken extra pains to keep the price as low as it was that she found herself in desperate need of an L. A. Lakers victory over the Boston Celtics.

Jessica, however, was blissfully unaware of the financial complications surrounding the evening as she sat on the edge of the bed in "her" cabin and watched as Sara split their drugstore bounty. It was just as well. Jessica already had plenty on her mind, not the least of which was the fact that, although

Haven was still anchored to the dock, she was no longer on dry ground.

They don't have icebergs this far south, Jessica told herself. *The* Titanic *was one in a million.*

Maria's accident had been one in a million. It had been that kind of year. Jessica wished they had gone to Disneyland as a normal school class would. She was afraid to hold her breath and stick her head underwater in her own bathtub. The floor beneath her feet was swaying now, ever so slightly.

"I think we should put the stuff in the bathroom cabinets," Sara said, dumping everything out of their boxes and onto the bed.

"Are you giving me the condoms and taking the foam or what?" Jessica asked.

"No, you take some of each."

"Then I don't think we should put it in the cabinets. Imagine how Bill or Russ will feel if he sees we have a selection. We should make it look like we just happen to have something with us."

"That's a good idea."

"Another thing, don't throw away the boxes. I want to read the directions."

"The stuff is pretty self-explanatory, don't you think?"

"I don't know. I've never seen it before. Have you?"

"No."

Jessica picked up the roll of condom packets. "Let's look at one."

Sara stopped her. "No, we shouldn't waste any."

"We won't waste it opening the corner and peeking inside."

"Yeah, we will. Then it will be contaminated."

"So what? We can just throw it out. What do we have here? A dozen. That's six each," Jessica said.

"Is that a lot? I mean, how many times do people usually have sex when they have sex?"

Jessica laughed. "What a stupid question." Then she thought a moment. "I'm not sure."

"I don't think we should waste any."

"All right. You know what just occurred to me?"

"What?"

"That we don't know what the hell we're doing."

"Do you think they will?" Sara asked, serious.

"Oh, yeah. Bill and Russ have been around. Hasn't Russ?"

"I never asked him. Have you asked Bill?"

"No," Jessica said.

"But you figure he did it with Clair, right?"

"What an awful thing to say! Now you have me worrying how I'll match up."

"Sorry," Sara said. Something outside the cabin's tiny round porthole caught her attention. "Oh, no. Don't look."

"What?"

"Nick's just appeared, and he's got Maria with him."

Jessica stood up from the bed and reached the window in one step. The dimensions of the cabin were going to take some getting used to. The whole room was not much larger than her walk-in closet at home. She could feel her heart pound as she pressed her face to the circle of glass.

"She'll have trouble getting around the ship in that chair," Jessica said. *Haven* sat between the dock and the western sky, throwing a deep shadow over the boarding ramp and the boardwalk beyond. Despite the fact that they were to set sail within minutes, a surprising number of kids continued to mill about the dock. Nick was having no trouble wheeling Maria's chair up the ramp. Jessica had forgotten how small she was.

Her lovely long hair. She cut it all off.

Hair meant nothing next to an injured spinal cord, and yet its loss deeply troubled Jessica.

"Not as long as she stays on deck," Sara said, also peering out the window.

"I didn't know she was coming to the party."

"Who did?"

"Well, she must have bought a ticket," Jessica said in a slightly accusatory tone. She still hadn't forgiven Sara for not telling her Michael was to be valedictorian when Sara must have known way in advance. Jessica had been anxiously awaiting Michael's arrival. Sara swore she had *given* him a ticket.

"The tickets are tickets. They don't have names written on them." Sara paused. "You won't be able to avoid her all night."

The ramp carried Nick and Maria out of sight around the curve of the ship. Jessica came to a decision. "I'm not going to try." She stood back from the window. "Come on. We'll talk to her now, get it over with."

"Whatever you say," Sara replied without enthusiasm. She picked up the contraceptives on the bed and stuffed most of them under Jessica's pillow. Except for Polly, they were the only students who had rooms. Theirs were located toward the stern, adjacent to each other, but unconnected by a door. Jessica wasn't sure where Polly's was. Polly had asked when she had come on board if Sara could get her a place to crash. Sara had been quick to oblige; the evening had yet to begin and Polly already looked wasted.

The remainder of the passenger rooms were locked tight, and would remain so the whole night. Kids who wanted to sleep before they reached Catalina would have to do so outside on the top deck or on the floor in one of the main rooms.

"We'll take care of the stuff later," Jessica said as Sara continued to stare at the label on one of the boxes.

"Do you think he was right?" Sara asked.

"Who?"

"Bubba. About using a sponge and a man's pleasure and all that?"

"Ask him. What did he write in your yearbook, anyway?"

Sara hid the box under Jessica's top sheet. "Shut up."

The corridor to the stairway, or companionway, was narrow. Jessica detected a faint odor of diesel in the air. No nuclear power aboard this vessel. Mr. Bark would have been pleased.

Too bad he was going to be unable to chaperon the party. Word had it that he had developed a sudden unbearable rash on his hands. Miss Fenway, a secretary in the administration building, was to take his place.

A bell rang as they climbed onto the upper deck. The kids loitering on the dock began to walk up the boarding plank. The temperature was still warm, but Jessica could feel it dropping. Cool air over warm water—the fog would roll in for sure. She hoped the captain didn't accidentally miss Catalina on the way out to sea.

"Aren't you going to check people's tickets?" Jessica asked, making a brief futile scan for Michael.

"Nope," Sara said. "If someone wants to come that bad, I ain't going to turn them away."

Nick had parked Maria's chair near the bow of the ship. He was pointing out something of interest on a nearby tanker. Maria appeared to be listening closely.

"Promise me I will never have to see you again."

"Do you want me to come with you?" Sara asked, watching her.

"Yeah," Jessica said.

Nick noticed their approach and alerted Maria. Jessica saw one thing had not changed. Maria's eyes were still dark, still solemn. Yet a smile seemed to touch her lips as their eyes met. Jessica reached out both her hands. Maria took them after a slight hesitation. Their fingers squeezed together briefly, lightly.

"I'm glad you're here," Jessica said.

"Thank you," she said, her eyes fixed on Jessica's face.

"Hi, Maria," Sara said, leaning over and giving her a quick hug and kiss. Jessica wished she had done the same. Maria gently returned Sara's embrace.

"I liked your speech," Maria said.

"I'm having it copyrighted," Sara said. "How are you?"

"Fine."

"You look good."

"Thank you."

It was all too formal. Maria continued to watch Jessica with her dark eyes, and even though Jessica didn't detect a hint of hostility in them, the tension between them was still there.

Why can't we just talk?

A silly question. She could walk and Maria couldn't.

"You got us a big enough ship here, Sara," Nick said.

"Hey, Nicky," Jessica said.

"Hey, Jessie," he replied, chuckling.

Sara moved to his side and wrapped an arm around his waist, saying, "There is one thing I haven't told anybody about this boat."

"What?" Nick asked.

Sara poked his powerful biceps. "How are you at rowing?"

Sara went on flirting with Nick, and Jessica thought it was cute and everything, but she couldn't help wondering why Sara wasn't spending every available minute with Russ. He would be heading back up north come Sunday morning.

Jessica lightly squeezed Maria's hands again and asked if they could talk later. Maria hesitated before nodding. Jessica left her to go stand by the boarding plank, and repeatedly checked her watch. A second bell rang. The last of the people on the dock boarded.

Please be here, Michael. Please God.

"Should be a fun night," Bill said, appearing suddenly by her side. He had on a yellow turtleneck sweater, tan pants, and shiny black shoes. He looked good. He always looked good. The boxes of condoms and foam popped into her mind. She pushed them away. She tried instead to imagine the thrill of having his naked body lying beside hers. The picture wouldn't come. A third bell rang. One of the few crewmen appeared and began to withdraw the plank.

"Yeah, it's going to be great," she said, her heart sinking.

"Is Michael here?" Bill asked.

"Who?"

"Olson?"

"No." She spoke to the crewman. "We're expecting someone."

The sailor went right on pulling in the plank. The end clanged off the dock and hung out limply from the faded white hull. "That's a shame," he said.

"Could I sign your yearbook?" Bill asked.

"Later," Jessica said sadly. Then she spotted a figure striding briskly around a wall of stacked pallets. She almost lost her glasses jumping to her toes. "He's here! He's here! Sir, our friend's come. Put down the plank, please, sir. Thank you. He's here."

Michael was on board a minute later, his yearbook in his hand. Bill gave him a warm slap on the back and complimented him on his valedictorian speech. Jessica felt more than a little awkward welcoming Michael with Bill at her side. Michael didn't seem to mind. Her joy at his arrival surprised even her. Once she had thought she was in love with him. Now she knew she was.

Before the night is over, I have to tell him.

Michael shook her hand and thanked her for holding the boat for him. He seemed to have just taken a shower. His hair looked damp. He moved off to speak with Nick after talking to her for less than a minute.

Jessica left Bill a moment later to be alone at the stern of the boat. A breeze came up from the north and a fine mist rose up over the flat ocean. The anchor was lifted and the ship slipped away, the lights of the harbor blurring in the mist, growing fainter. The western sky went from orange to purple to black. The party kicked into high gear. Jessica felt little inclination to join it. She shivered, looking at the dark water beneath her feet. She had always had nightmares of drowning.

Chapter Thirteen

Although he had been in a hurry to reach the harbor when he left Clark's house, Michael soon realized he could not board the ship with his hair and clothes full of blood. He made a quick stop at his house to wash and change. Fortunately, his mother and Daniel were not there to see what a mess he was. They had been disappointed when he hadn't let them take him out for a celebration meal after the ceremony. He had given them some feeble excuse about work he had to finish at JPL.

Michael was worried his mother would have the baby early. She hadn't said anything, but he noticed after the ceremony that her breathing was irregular, as if she were having pain. If he hadn't felt so close to solving the mystery of Alice's death, he wouldn't have left her.

Close does not count in life and death. Only in horseshoes.

When had the shotgun been fired that had torn away part of the shingle outside the bedroom window? What did that shot have to do with the one that had been fired into Alice's head? Who had broken Alice's nose? Had Clark really been at the party? Why would Polly lie to him?

The endless stream of questions didn't frighten Michael as it might have another investigator. He, in fact, felt as if he had almost enough pieces of information to solve the puzzle; he simply had to arrange them properly and the picture would make sense. But as with a child's puzzle, he knew that one more piece—preferably a big corner piece—would help speed up the process immensely.

Showering at home, Michael had begun to take Polly's warning more seriously. He began to worry that if he didn't return from the all-night party, his efforts on Alice's behalf would be wasted. Cursing his shortage of time, he took a piece of paper and quickly jotted down everything he had discovered, including a half-dozen different scenarios that might cover the facts. The problem was, all of his scenarios had at least one major hole.

But he *was* able to print Clark's full name and address on the bottom of the paper. If nothing else, Lieutenant Keller could follow up that lead.

Sealing his information in an envelope, he took it to the station. The lieutenant happened to be in his office.

"What can I do for you, Mike?" he asked politely, offering

him a seat. Michael was not fooled by the seriousness with which the officer welcomed him. Keller may have respected his intelligence and persistence, but he also had doubts about his emotional stability. Michael did not take the offered seat.

"I'm sorry, I'm in a hurry," he said, handing the policeman the envelope. "I want you to hold this for me until next Monday. If I don't return for it by then, I want you to open it."

Keller glanced from the envelope to Michael's face a couple of times and Michael could see the lieutenant's doubts about Young Mr. Olson's stability being replaced by something far worse—pity.

"What's inside?" Keller asked.

"Information."

"About Alice McCoy's death?"

"Yes."

Keller stood uneasily. Perhaps he was worried Young Mr. Olson was going to follow in Alice McCoy's footsteps and go out with a bang. "Why wouldn't you be back to pick it up?"

Michael smiled to put him at ease. "Who knows? I just graduated today. I might find a girl tonight and elope." Then he got serious. "Please hold it for me. And if, by chance, you still have it Monday, give what I had to say some thought."

"But where are you going tonight?" he asked.

"To our all-night senior party."

The lieutenant relaxed slightly. "Sounds like fun."

"I think it's going to be a wild party," Michael agreed.

Now he stood at the edge of the party and above the ocean. They were an hour out of dock and he had already searched *Haven* from the bow to the stern. Clark didn't appear to be on board. Yet Michael was far from convinced he wasn't there. He had been unable to persuade the captain to let him look in the thirty locked passenger rooms. Granted, if he couldn't get into the rooms, Clark shouldn't be able to. But with so many places to hide, Michael had to wonder. Even without access to the rooms, a sufficiently determined individual could probably have found some hidden corner to tuck into. It was a big ship. Michael was debating whether or not to give *Haven* another going-over when Nick came out of the main lounge and joined him by the rail.

"The game's going to start in a couple of minutes," Nick said.

"I'll watch the second half," Michael said.

Nick stared out over the calm water. The rise and fall of the ship was almost nonexistent. The fog continued to gather. The coast was already invisible and their path through the night seemed to be taking them into a land of clouds.

"It's peaceful out here," Nick said.

"You like the water?" Michael asked.

"I didn't know how much until tonight. Did you know, Mike, when I was growing up in the barrio, I never saw the ocean once?"

"That's amazing."

Nick leaned on the rail. "I hear they have a sailing class at U.C.L.A. I think I might sign up for it." He laughed softly at the thought. "Imagine me on a yacht?"

"Who knows, with the salaries they pay in the NBA, you might be able to afford one someday."

Nick shook his head. "That's a one-in-a-million shot. I'll never play pro ball."

Michael leaned on the rail beside him. He wondered how deep the water was. The thought nagged at him. He wasn't able to relax. "Yeah, you'd be better off concentrating on your education. You sprain your ankle or twist your knee and you're out. But they can't take your degree away from you."

"The day I get it, I'll have you to thank for it."

"You get what you deserve. Good things are going to come to you."

"I read that last book you gave me," Nick said.

"Which one was that?"

"*The Hound of the Baskervilles*—Sherlock Holmes. It was great."

"I'm glad you enjoyed it. I'll give you another one."

"You remind me of him."

"Me? I don't smoke a pipe."

Nick looked at him closely. "What's wrong?"

"Nothing."

"You look kind of down."

"I'm all right," Michael said.

"Have you talked to Jessie today?"

"Not really. How's Maria?"

Nick frowned. "Very quiet."

"Has she told you why she wanted to come tonight?"

"No."

"Has she threatened you again like she did at the hospital?"

"No, nothing like that. But she's got something on her mind. She seems to be *waiting*."

Michael glanced about, feeling he couldn't wait. He tapped Nick on the shoulder. "I'll catch up with you later, buddy."

Above the main lounge, where the bulk of the class had gathered in front of the large-screen TV to watch the final game of the NBA playoffs, sat *Haven's* bridge. Michael looked up and spotted the helmsman—lit a faint blue and red by rows of luminescent dials—turning the wheel several degrees to port. That was another place the captain hadn't let him inspect.

Am I searching for Clark or Jessie?

He found Polly instead. She stood alone against the entrance to *Haven's* galley. Michael could hear kids laughing and carrying on inside. Few were walking the deck. The temperature had dropped steadily since they had pulled out of the harbor. The salty breeze, however, continued to blow soft and easy.

"Is your headache better?" he asked cheerfully.

She jumped slightly at the sound of his voice. She had on a short-sleeve white blouse, a thin red skirt. Gooseflesh covered her arms. "I'm all right," she said.

He had told Nick the same thing a minute ago. He had lied. His head was throbbing from Clark's blow. Worse, his vision continued to blur off and on. It blurred now as he looked at Polly. She went back to playing with her dark hair, watching the fog.

"I'm sorry I ganged up on you this morning," he said.

"That's OK."

"Having fun?"

"I'm cold."

"Why don't you go inside and have a hot drink? I'll have one with you."

She stared at him. "He likes me cold."

"Come again?"

"He told me: 'Stay alive babe and stay cold. It's the only way for the likes of us.' That's what he said. He's weird."

"I saw him today."

It didn't surprise her. "At the cemetery?" she asked.

"No, I went to his house. Did you see him at the cemetery?"

She nodded. "Before I came to the harbor."

"When was that?"

"Five o'clock, six o'clock?"

Clark must have gone straight to the cemetery after knocking him out. "Did he have a gun with him?" Michael asked.

"I didn't see everything in his bag." She chewed on her lower lip, looking exhausted.

"Is he on board?" he asked.

"Yes."

He moved a step closer. "Are you sure?"

"Yes."

"Where?"

"I don't know."

"You must have some idea?"

"I don't. He comes and goes, like lightning."

The simile made him pause. Polly was the only one who even indirectly supported his belief that Alice hadn't committed suicide, and yet, whenever he spoke to her, he didn't believe her. "Why is he here?" he asked.

"I can't tell you."

"Why not?"

"He'll kill me."

"Does he intend to kill me?"

"If you get in his way."

She was doing it to him again—confusing him. He remembered the weather-beaten paper he had found in her backyard. "Polly, back in November, I gave you a form for your aunt to sign. What did you do with it?"

"I gave it to Clark."

"Why?"

"He wanted it."

"Where and when did you give it to him?"

"In my backyard, during the storm." She shivered. "I have

to take a warm bath now before it gets any later, Mike. I don't care what he says. I have to warm my blood."

"I'll see you around," he muttered, distracted, hardly caring how or where she would take her bath. As Polly turned and walked away, for an instant, everything in his immediate surroundings seemed to jump into the air, and land in reverse. He put his hand to his head and took it away and found blood on his fingers. No, it was not a concussion that was making reality dance. She had given him the answer! For an instant, he'd had the entire solution to the night of the party, to the whole crazy year, in seed form in his mind. Not the details of the truth, but the essence of it. Unfortunately, it had gone as quickly as it had come, leaving him more confused than ever; leaving him cold, too, almost as if he had just fallen overboard.

It will come back.

Chapter Fourteen

Either one person had sneaked fifty gallons of alcohol on board or else a fair percentage of the class had ignored the prohibition against mixing ocean cruises and intoxicating substances and had brought enough good cheer onto *Haven* to give themselves and their closest friends a respectable buzz. The air in the main lounge literally stank of booze. Sara was getting drunk just breathing. Unfortunately, the basketball game on the tube was keeping her more sober than she would have liked. Halftime had just begun and the Lakers were down by eight points.

"The Lakers are a great second-half team, aren't they?" she asked Nick, who, along with Maria, was sitting with her in the rear of the lounge. Maria appeared to be enjoying the game, although she hadn't said more than five words since it had begun.

"They are, yeah," Nick said.

"That's good," Sara said.

"But so are the Celtics," Nick added.

A faint creaking sound went through the lounge as the floor dropped a few inches. It was a rare sign that they were far out at sea. The lounge could have been in a bar on the west side of town. It was loud enough. "But an eight-point lead," Sara said. 'That's nothing in a basketball game, is it?"

Nick nodded. "It can disappear in a couple of minutes."

"If you were to put money on this game right now, who would you bet on?" she asked.

"You'd have to be crazy to put money down on the Lakers versus the Celtics. It's always close."

"But just suppose? Who do you think is going to win?"

"The Celtics."

"What? I thought you were a Lakers fan?"

Nick smiled. "Yeah, but you're talking about money."

He was not very reassuring. Sara stood. "I've got to find somebody," she said.

Bubba was sitting on the bar on the far side of the room. Most of the kids who were drinking were doing so from brown-bagged pints barely hidden in their coat pockets. Bubba had a fifth of Jack Daniel's riding his left knee. Every time the Lakers scored, he toasted the room and the basket and took a chug. It really pissed her off that he was having such a good time.

Clair stood by his side. She was not drinking. In fact, she

didn't seem all that happy about his flagrant consumption. She was trying to take the bottle away from him. She was a little late; the thing was three-quarters empty. Then again, it was always said that Bubba could drink a crew of sailors under the table.

Why are people always saying good things about this jackass?

"You've had enough," Clair said, unwrapping one finger from the neck of the bottle only to see the finger before it wrap back around the neck. "It's still early and you're already loaded."

"I'm not loaded," Bubba said, slurring his speech. "I'm merely giving a few of my brain cells a much-needed vacation."

"You're going to end up falling overboard," Clair said, getting annoyed. She gave up trying to be gentle about it and yanked the bottle from his hand. He laughed uproariously.

"That's why I've got to get my drinking done now!"

Sara poked him in the side. "I need to talk to you."

He turned, his jovial smile rolling around his fat face like a goldfish in a bowl. "Sara, how come you've left your post? Who's steering the ship?"

Clair gave her a sympathetic look. "He's impossible when he's like this."

Bubba reached out and grabbed Clair, putting his arm around her, snuggling the side of his head up to her smooth tan cheek. "But nothing is impossible when we're together, darling," he said.

Sara half expected her to shove him away; he was, for all intents and purposes, slobbering on her. But Clair did nothing of the kind. She put her arm around him instead and hugged him back, blushing red and laughing as he turned and whispered something in her ear.

Sara just couldn't understand how such beauty could be attracted to such disgust.

Clair gave him a quick kiss on the forehead as she broke free a moment later, the bottle still in her hand. She began to walk toward the rear exit. "I'm still dumping this poison, Bubba," she called over her shoulder.

"There's plenty where that came from!" he called after her, giggling. He turned back to Sara. "Isn't she wonderful?"

"The Lakers are losing," she said flatly.

He sat back in mock surprise. "No."

"They're down by eight points. Nick says they're going to lose."

"Does Nick want to play?"

"Huh?"

Bubba clapped his hands together. "Yeah! The coach should put Nick in. He's a homegrown boy. It'll be legal." Bubba went to jump off the bar. "I'll radio for a helicopter."

Sara grabbed his arm, keeping him on the bar. "Stop carrying on like a lunatic. We've got a serious problem here."

He eyed her as best he could with his eyes rolling around in a multitude of directions. "We can't have a problem until the game's over."

"But what if they lose?" she cried.

He leaned closer, his breath was enough to anesthetize a

tubful of clams, and raised a fat finger close to her nose. "You know what your problem is, Sara?"

She paused. "What?"

"You don't know how to dress."

"What's wrong with the way I dress?"

He gestured to her orange dress. "You're always in autumn colors."

"So what?"

He turned his head and sneezed. She felt the spray. He went on in a confidential tone. "Autumn is a rotten time of year. School starts in autumn. Leaves fall off the trees in autumn. People hate autumn. They hate people who remind them of it."

She sneered. "Get off it."

He belched loudly. "It's a fact. You send out depressing vibes. Look at me. A minute ago, I was finishing my bottle and singing. Then you showed up." He wiped at his eyes. "Now I'm beginning to feel sad."

"What are you sad about?"

"I feel so unhappy."

"No, you don't."

"I do. I can't bear it."

"Well, what do you want me to do about it?"

He thought for a moment, looking as miserable as he would have her believe he was. Then a wild gleam entered his eyes, and he suddenly reached for her with his grubby paws. "I want you to take your clothes off!"

She dodged him easily. He fell from the bar stool and landed on his face. She kicked him while he was down. He sat up and rubbed his head. "Bubba, you're drunk," she said, disgusted.

He rolled his eyes upward and grinned. "No, Sara. I'm just happy."

She decided she would give him to the end of the game— then she would kill him. She left him giggling on the floor.

Russ was bothering her as much as the game. He was acting like a stranger. No, stranger was too strong a word. He was being friendly and all—but that was the problem. He wasn't supposed to be her friend. He was supposed to be her boyfriend. At least that was her understanding. But she wondered if he knew. He had kissed her. He had told her he liked her. He had let her bail him out of jail. He had written to her while he was away; not so often as she might have wished, but a letter and a postcard should count for something. Yet they had never made any promises to each other. When she thought about it, they had never even *talked*, not really, not for any length of time. And now they were supposed to make love before the sun came up.

What the hell have I talked myself into?

It was a lonely thing, to suddenly realize that maybe she had been suckered all along, not by Russ, but by her own imagination.

He was watching the game with "the boys." That was fair

enough. He hadn't seen his pals from the cross-country team since December. She didn't require every blessed second of his time. But eyeing him from across the room as he was sitting on the arm of a couch and laughing at some fool joke, a beer can in his hand, obviously having more fun than she was, she thought of all the trouble she had gone through to pick him up at the bus station. He owed her something. She strode up to him.

"Hi," she said.

"Hi," he said, glancing over briefly, before continuing with his wild tale of mystery and intrigue at the state's most exotic juvenile hall. "Then I said to him, I said, 'You hide that knife under my pillow again during a shakedown and I'll use it to shred every piece of clothing you've got.' He called my bluff, the idiot. And a month later he was walking around with his—"

"Excuse me," Sara interrupted. "Russ?"

He looked at her again. "What, Sara?"

She smiled. "How are you doing?"

He glanced at the beer in his hand. The rest of his buddies were waiting for him to continue. "I'm fine," he said. "What's wrong?"

"Nothing's wrong. I just wanted to, you know, say hi."

"How about we talk in a few minutes?"

"The game starts in a few minutes."

"Then we'll talk after the game. Would that be all right?"

"Sure. Yeah."

He went to give the punch line of his story, then noticed she had made no move to leave. He smiled uneasily. "I don't know if you want to hear this, Sara."

"Why not?"

"It's kind of disgusting."

"OK. Thanks. I'll take that as a compliment, being told to bug off because I'm not disgusting enough to listen to you." She spun on her heel and stalked away. He called to her, but she didn't slow down till she was standing outside in the damp darkness beside the rail. The fog kept getting thicker. She kept getting more tense. She hadn't wanted to fight with him. She had promised herself she wouldn't. But whenever she was around him, she just wanted to strangle him!

Or kiss him. Why didn't he even kiss me after the ceremony when everybody was kissing everybody else?

She stood there for several minutes, catching her breath and trying to tell herself she was too cool to get upset about a boy. After a bit she began to notice her surroundings. It was a bizarre night. She could hear the splash of the water against the hull, could even smell it. But she could not see the ocean in any direction. *Haven* could have been plowing through the sky above a storm.

"Hi," a nearby voice said. It was that weird dude who worked at the gas station, the one with the greasy hair and mustache, the guy who had owned the gun that had killed Alice. He had come up so quietly that he had startled her.

"Hi," she said.

He grinned. He had incredibly crooked teeth. "You don't remember my name, do you?"

"No."

"You're Sara, right?"

"Yeah. You go by a nickname—Rats?"

"Kats."

"Yeah. Sorry. How are you doing?"

"Couldn't be better. How are you?"

"Fine." He wasn't someone she would have chosen for a late-night ocean-cruise partner. The way he kept grinning at her—it was as if he was thinking about doing things to her she preferred not to know. His next question did not exactly put her at ease.

"Can you swim, Sara?"

"Yeah. Can you?"

He leaned over the rail and spat into the fog. How disgusting! Sara thought she heard the splash of the spit in the water. He must have grime in his saliva glands. "I don't have to," he said. "I know how to float."

"I think I'll go back inside."

She heard him laughing to himself as she reentered the lounge.

Chapter Fifteen

Haven did not ordinarily require an entire night to reach Catalina. Usually the trip took only a couple of hours, but the captain was cruising slowly for the party; the engines were operating at only quarter power. Standing near the diesel-driven turbines, Michael was surprised at how quiet they were, especially since they must have been close to thirty years old. Michael had always had a special admiration for machinery that performed its function year in and year out, and for the men who built it.

Clark was not in engineering. Michael had serious doubts that he was on board.

Haven's chief engineer had explained the fundamentals of the propulsion system to Michael earlier. He was now in the crew's galley having a cup of coffee. Michael had the engine room to himself. There was no wasted space. The turbines were housed in huge, twin white-steel tunnels, out of which sprang a complex array of pipes that stretched about thirty feet along the ceiling and walls before disappearing into a massive black fuel tank. The tank was set in the middle of the floor; it neatly divided the rear of the ship's lowest deck from the front. It was amazing the amount of fuel a vessel like *Haven* consumed. Michael estimated the tank's capacity at over a thousand gallons. If fire ever got to it, the whole ship would blow.

Following the narrow passageway to the right of the tank, Michael left the rhythmic drone of the engines and headed for the storage area. He had been through the place once already, but decided to have another quick inspection before he headed topside.

The crew for the cruise was at a minimum; besides the captain, there were only eight men on duty. It was probably plenty. Although the ship seemed large to most of the class members, he knew it would be dwarfed by a modern cruise ship. Also, the trip out to Catalina was little more than a warm-up for *Haven*. Michael saw no one as he went through the various sections: the janitorial supply area, the linen department, the food stores, finishing with the machine shop. The latter was small but uncluttered. It occurred to him the place might be ideal for the meeting he was hoping to have later in the night.

Another invitation to Alice's party.

He surfaced into the night air at the ship's stern. He was surprised to find Jessica standing alone and staring back the way they had come, staring into nothing; the fog had cut visibility to practically zero. Thank God for radar. *Haven*'s horn blared once from the bridge, sounding lost as it faded and died over the invisible waters. Michael wondered why Jessica had been spending all her time by herself. He tactfully cleared his throat, and she turned around.

"Hi, Michael," she said, smiling, quickly removing her glasses and slipping them in her back pocket.

He climbed the last treads of the companionway and stepped onto the deck. "You should have a jacket on. It's getting chilly." He moved up beside her, the water softly churning beneath their feet. Despite his remark, he liked the way she was dressed—in tight white pants and a light blue sweater, her long brown hair reaching almost to her waist. He supposed she could have had on a canvas sack and he still would have found her perfectly presentable. She tugged at the arm of her sweater and looked at him expectantly.

"I had to wear this tonight," she said. "It's the last day of school."

"Oh?"

"I had this same sweater with me my first day at Tabb. Don't you remember?"

"I do now, yeah. I still don't see how you got the grape juice out. I think you flew over to Switzerland and bought another one just so I wouldn't feel guilty."

Her eyes lingered on him. "Maybe I did."

He laughed softly, feeling uneasy and happy. He was used

to the contradictions she inspired in him. "Why aren't you watching the game?" he asked.

"Why aren't you?"

"No fair. I asked first."

"It's so loud inside. It was giving me a headache."

He nodded. "I'm not a great party person myself."

"I thought you weren't going to come. You cut it pretty tight."

"Yeah, I had some business to take care of."

"What was it?"

"Ah, nothing. Just stuff."

They had a big wooden lifeboat and dull yellow light at their backs. Jessica was staring at his head strangely. She reached out to touch his hair. He stopped her. He knew his head was still bleeding. He wished he'd had time to get it stitched. He couldn't very well bandage it now. He had already wiped it several times with toilet paper.

"Your hair was wet when you came aboard, too," she said, pulling her hand back, her face falling slightly. "You're the one who's going to catch cold. I should find you a towel."

He could just imagine the color he would turn the towel. Fortunately, in his black hair, the blood was hardly recognizable for what it really was, even under better lighting. No one else on board had even said anything about it.

Clark had struck him a nasty blow. Michael was looking forward to repaying the favor. He was still annoyed with himself for having been caught so easily.

"Don't bother," he said.

"It's no bother." She turned. "Really, you must dry it."

He stopped her again, this time grabbing her arm, perhaps a shade too hard. He released her quickly when he saw her startled expression. "I know where a towel is, Jessie," he said.

"OK." She forced a smile. "So, what's new? I loved your speech. It—touched me."

"I'm just glad I got to give it before you sang. You stole the show. How come you never told me you could sing like that?"

"You really like my voice?"

"I do. Have you ever thought of doing anything with it? Like getting in a band?"

She smiled, pleased. "When I was younger, I used to fantasize about being onstage and having everyone chanting my name. Alice used to . . ." She paused. "Alice used to encourage me to do something with it."

"You should think about it."

"Yeah? I don't know. I'll see." An awkward silence followed, during which a disturbing warmth began to spread over the right side of Michael's scalp. He knew what it was. Jessica finally spoke. "I broke the ice with Maria."

"How was it?"

She sighed. "Not horrible, not good. We only talked for a minute. But I felt like—this is going to sound weird—she'd like to talk more, but not yet."

Nick had made a similar comment. Maria was waiting.

Interesting. "Give her time. The fact that she's here says a lot."

"I hope you're right." Jessica shook her head.

"What is it?"

"I was just thinking of that morning at the hospital. It was awful. I couldn't talk to her." She peeked over at him. "I couldn't talk to you."

"You can always talk to me, Jessie," he said, feeling a drop of blood trickle into his right ear. This was getting serious. He turned his head away from the water. He had better get to a bathroom. Jessica shook her head again.

"How? I never see you. You're never at school anymore."

"Well, from now on, you won't be at school, either." Here came another drop. He was lucky Clark hadn't done a lobotomy while he was at it.

"That's what's bothering me," she said. "We're together long enough to become friends, then we have to go our separate ways."

"You'll meet a lot of people at Stanford."

She chuckled sadly at the remark and brushed away a hair. "I'm not going to Stanford."

The blood was a distraction. He had momentarily forgotten the SAT disaster. She never had told him her scores. "They didn't accept you?"

"There was no sense in even sending in my application."

"I'm sorry," he muttered.

"It's not your fault. I didn't mean to give you that impression. I shouldn't have brought it up."

"I should have known they used different tests."

She was getting upset at him. "That's ridiculous. How could you . . ." She paused, staring. "Are you bleeding?"

He practically leaped away from the rail. "I scratched my ear. I think I'll go clean it up. It's nothing big. I'll talk to you later."

"OK. Let's do that. Are you sure you're all right?"

"I'm fine, really."

"I have to sign your yearbook."

"Great." He cupped his hand to his ear and backed away from her over the slippery deck. He had a regular vein pumping over his scalp from the feel of it.

"Michael?"

He stopped, for a second, caught by her eyes. She had the biggest eyes on the whole boat; he could have sworn it. "What?"

She thought a moment. "Nothing."

The cramped and dimly lit bathroom behind the galley was empty. He was lucky, none of the blood had gotten onto the collar of his coat. Locking the door, he grabbed a whole roll of toilet paper and pressed it to the side of his head. The wound was deep and ragged. If he washed his hair in the sink, the bleeding would only worsen. When he had showered at home, the bathtub had been red as catsup. He needed a hat. Maybe Bubba would lend him his.

Michael had stopped the bleeding and cleaned up as best

he could when another spell of dizziness struck. He grabbed the edge of the sink, fighting to steady himself, his reflection in the mirror splitting into two. Before he could force his eyes back into focus, he thought he saw—in the mottled glass—Clark standing behind him. Not the Clark of this afternoon, but the one from last fall, pale and drugged, arrogant and frightening. Michael jerked around frantically, his heart racing, then shook himself for being so foolish. Of course there was no one there.

The lounge was as noisy as Jessica had said it would be. The fourth quarter had just begun. Celtics 82, Lakers 78. Ordinarily Michael would have enjoyed such a game, but tonight was far from ordinary. He was beginning to think the ship was haunted.

Bubba was standing tall atop the bar, a half-empty bottle of Seagram 7 in his right hand, cheering on a Lakers comeback. Michael had once seen Bubba down a case of beer and a fifth of rum and an hour later ski off the top of Mammoth's most dangerous slope. Michael suspected that that was not Bubba's first bottle. Bubba was waving his sombrero around as if it were a pom-pom. Michael tapped him on the knee.

"You're going to kill yourself up there," he said.

"Worry not for the royal Bubba, my dear Mike," he said. "If he should by chance fall, he will surely bounce." Then he let out a howl and thrust his bottle into the air—spilling a few stinging drops of whiskey over the top of Michael's head in the process—as the Lakers cut their deficit to two. "My men!"

"I have to talk to you."

"What?"

"I have to talk to you!"

"Go talk to Sara! She likes to talk!"

"Bubba."

Michael probably would have gotten nowhere with him if the Celtics had not chosen that moment to call a time-out. Bubba apparently had a full bladder. As the players walked to the sidelines, he leaped off the bar, shouting, "Show me to the captain's toilet!"

Michael led him to the bathroom he had used a moment ago. Bubba was not inside long, and when he came out, Michael grabbed him by the arm and dragged him into the galley, to a quiet table in the corner. The lighting in the dining area was low. There was no TV, and few people were present. Bubba looked around in a daze.

"Where're my men in purple?" he asked.

"Give me two minutes and I'll let you get back to your game."

"Where's my bottle?"

Michael had taken it from him on the way to the bathroom and thrown it into a garbage can. "I'll get you a fresh one in a minute."

Bubba pounded the table with his fist, satisfied. "A kingly deal! Speak, Mike, and may your words be inspired."

"I wanted to ask you about the night of Alice's party."

Bubba's joyful demeanor faded. Michael also knew from experience that, although Bubba could drink like a sink, alcohol often brought out a hidden sensitivity. Bubba shook his head sadly. "That poor girl. She was so beautiful. Had she lived, she may have gotten to know me better." Then he paused and eyed Michael. "You don't think I killed her?"

"Of course not."

Bubba nodded, relaxing. "That is good. The Bubba can be nasty, but he only wants to have fun." He burped. "I consider the killing of a beautiful girl to be a sin against the gods and the boys." He glanced about. "What's the score?"

"It hasn't changed. I have a problem about that night, Bubba. I want you to help me with it. The bedroom next to the one where Alice died—who was in there?"

"Was it not the exalted Bubba himself?"

"Was it?"

Bubba hesitated. "Is this a trick question?"

"Were you in the room just before the shot was fired?"

He spoke reluctantly. "It was me."

"Were you with Clair?"

"The Bubba is well known for his discretion and his silence. This is a delicate subject."

"Please, Bubba, I have to know the truth. I have to cross that room out of the equation before I can go on. Was Clair in there with you or not?"

"Yes."

"How about anyone else?"

"No. Yes."

"What does that mean?"

"Bill was in there before I got there."

"With Clair?"

"Yes."

"What were they doing?"

"Nothing. Absolutely nothing."

"And then you entered the room? Right after Bill left?"

"Yes."

"Why didn't you tell me this six months ago? Why did you lie to me?"

"The Bubba is well known for his—"

"Cut the crap."

Bubba lowered his head and took a breath, a breath that seemed to sober him considerably. "I was trying to protect Clair's reputation."

Michael had to laugh. "But you bragged in the car on the way to the party, in front of both Nick and me, how many condoms you used on her before you even went out with her."

"I didn't."

"Yes, you did."

"No. I didn't have sex with Clair on our first date."

"Why did you say you did?"

"At the time I thought the topic made for stimulating conversation."

"If you didn't have sex with her, how did you keep her from killing you when she found out you didn't have any U2 tickets?"

"I gave her a gold necklace," he admitted sheepishly.

"You bought her off?"

"I wouldn't put it in precisely those terms."

"All right, back to the night of the party. How did you just happen to be upstairs and see Bill leaving the bedroom?"

"I was standing outside the bedroom door."

"How's that?" Michael asked.

"I followed Bill up the stairs."

"What were you doing outside the bedroom?"

"Listening."

"Listening to what?"

"To what was going on inside," Bubba said.

"And what was that?"

"Absolutely nothing."

"That's the second time you've said that. What does it mean?" Michael insisted.

"I don't know. Nothing."

"Did Bill see you when he left the room?"

"He bumped into me."

"Was he mad at you?"

"He was upset."

"At you?" Michael asked.

"No."

"What was he upset about?"

"Clair and he weren't getting along." He shrugged. "I went inside to see how she was. I guess it was good timing on my part."

Michael felt as if he were missing something obvious. "Were you and Clair having sex when the gun was fired?"

"Mike! That is a very personal question. I do not feel legally or morally bound to answer it."

"Did you hear anything coming from the adjacent room before the shot was fired?"

"No."

"Are you sure?"

"Absolutely."

"Dammit, Bubba."

"Clair was moaning in my ear," he admitted.

"You were having sex."

"I didn't say that."

"You two were having sex for the first time," Michael said, finally understanding at least a part of the puzzle. "And after doing it, you started to fall for her and feel protective of her."

"Is there something wrong with that?"

"Not unless you have a huge stud reputation to maintain."

Bubba sighed. "It does demand a great deal of my energy."

"Did you have your condoms with you?"

"That's none of your business," he snapped, showing a rare flash of anger. Then he showed something far more rare, perhaps an emotion he had not displayed since before he had mastered the art of "attitude" at the age of two. His face sagged into lines of deep pain. "I didn't," he said softly. "I was careless."

Michael leaned closer. "She got pregnant?"

"Yes."

"Well, that's all behind you now."

"No, it's not." Bubba took another deep breath; he was obviously struggling with intense feelings. "She had an abortion, Mike. I talked her into it."

Michael's instinctive distaste for the procedure rose up. He had to remind himself his views were not everybody's views. "It must have been a difficult decision for both of you."

"For Clair it was. For me it was just another problem to be handled." The transformation was remarkable—he was close to tears. Michael thought an argument could be made for the beneficial effect of periodic alcoholic binges on Bubba's character. Bubba buried his head in his hands. "But I couldn't forget what I'd done. The more I fell in love with Clair, the more I thought about the baby I'd killed."

Fell in love?

"You made a mistake. Everybody makes mistakes."

Bubba looked at him with red eyes. "I murdered my son."

"How do you know it was a boy?"

"Of course it was a boy," he said, insulted. "I would not have a female for a firstborn."

Despite the serious nature of the discussion, Michael

couldn't help but laugh. Bubba had finally begun to accept girls as people, but he was a long way from accepting them as equals. "Bubba, promise me one thing. Ten years from now, when you're ruling the world, please try to remember that it was a woman who brought you into the world."

Bubba was confused. "What about Baby Bubba?"

"What about Clair?"

He brightened suddenly. "We're getting married."

Michael almost fell out of his chair. That was the big secret Clair had been afraid to tell him. *"What?"*

Bubba nodded solemnly. "It's time I settled down. She's a good woman. She understands me." He touched Michael's hand. "I want you to do me a favor, Mike?"

"Anything."

"I want you to be my maid of honor."

"Your best man?"

"Yes. I want you to stand beside me on Sunday."

"You're getting married this Sunday?"

"In Las Vegas." Bubba sat back. "I've thought about this a long time, Mike. It's nothing Clair has talked me into. I've made up my own mind."

"I believe you." Michael offered his hand. "Congratulations."

Bubba beamed. "You're not going to try to talk me out of it?"

"Why should I? Like you said, she's a good girl. I hope you don't drive her crazy. You better not cheat on her."

Bubba waved his hand. "I've canceled my subscription to *Playboy*, that's how serious I am about this."

"Great. I suppose you want to get back to your game now?"

Bubba nodded enthusiastically, then furrowed his brow in concentration, worried. "I haven't told you anything I wouldn't have ordinarily, have I?"

"You've been fine. Oh, there is one other thing. Now that school's over, how often did you use the computer codes to change stuff?"

Bubba scratched his head. "I can't remember."

"Did you make Sara president?"

"No, not that. Sara got elected by a landslide. But I did make Clair vice-president. Don't tell her, though. She doesn't know."

"What about homecoming?"

Bubba looked unhappy. "I don't know if I should talk about that."

"Did Jessie get elected queen?"

He hesitated. "Yes."

"Why did you choose Maria?"

"I couldn't put in Clair. People were too down on her because of the abortion talk. And Clair wouldn't stand for Jessie being queen. Maria was neutral."

"But Jessica should have been queen," Michael insisted.

"Nah. Clair should have been queen."

"Maybe, maybe not."

"I'm glad neither of them won. They're both bigger than Maria. The float probably would have collapsed on them in the middle of the dance."

Did someone tamper with the float thinking it would be Jessie?

"But what about Maria?" Michael asked.

He shrugged. "What can I say? I'm only Bubba; I'm not God."

"At least we've made some progress tonight."

Michael accompanied Bubba back to the lounge. It was good that he did. Along the way, Bubba tried to tightrope-dance on the top of the rail. Had he fallen the wrong way, he would have disappeared into a hazy soup, probably disappeared for good.

Michael just couldn't get into the game, even though the score was close and the end was near. He went out to search for Polly. But he couldn't find her anywhere.

Chapter Sixteen

Polly lay soaking in the steaming tub, staring at her naked body. Her figure was fabulous. She had large firm breasts, a narrow waist, smooth wrinkle-free thighs, and soft creamy skin. Any normal guy, she thought miserably, would have been happy to climb into the tub with her.

The door to the bathroom lay wide open. Clark prowled the room beyond. In the last half hour, he hadn't so much as peeked in. She didn't understand it.

Polly was, however, grateful for the room. Sara had done her a good turn in that regard—for once. Polly didn't know if she could have stood a whole night partying with people who didn't like her. She knew they didn't. She'd known it all along, actually, although she had never understood that, either. She wasn't a bad person. She had been sort of fat once, but now she had a nice body. You'd think they'd want to talk to her more often. The last few months at school, hardly anyone had talked to her. They'd avoided her as if she'd had the plague. She'd had bad luck, true, but a lot of people had bad luck. She wasn't alone in that respect. In fact, a lot of people on this stupid boat were unlucky.

They couldn't have imagined how unlucky they were.

Polly had left the hot water in the tub running in a trickle. A drain prevented the water from overflowing. It was an old trick; it kept the water always hot. She liked it that way, so hot her skin turned cardinal red whenever she took a bath. She'd first learned the trick in a book she had read on the Mafia. It seemed that whenever a mob member got thrown in jail for life, his buddies on the outside would provide for his family if he'd take a hot bath and slit his wrists. Those mob guys were always afraid that anybody in jail would eventually break down and talk. The hot water was important; supposedly when you bled to death, you got real cold, and then nauseated. A good bath made the whole experience much more comfortable. Leaving the water trickling was the key; if you sat all night in a tub with the hot-water faucet turned on a little and your wrists slit, in the morning most of the blood would be gone. No vomit, no blood, and naked as a babe. When Polly thought about it, she imagined it wasn't such a bad way to go. Much better than, say, being trapped in a room overflowing with icy seawater.

An open razor blade rested on the soap tray next to Polly's head. She picked it up and let the overhead light reflect off the sharp edge into her eyes. White light, star bright. Sitting up, she transferred the blade into her left hand. Like Alice, she was left-handed. Some things ran in the family.

Like bad luck.

"You should have got the paper cups when I told you the first time," Polly whispered, taking the blade and pressing the tip into her right wrist. For a second nothing happened, and she wondered if she had a dull blade. Then a drop of blood drew a line down the pink flesh of her inner arm, dripping off her bent elbow into the clear water. It was interesting to watch how the red dissipated when it hit the water, how quickly her blood was lost. Maybe when she was through bleeding, her body would dissolve, too; it would be as if she had never been. She started to push the blade deeper.

"Polly," Clark said. He stood outside the bathroom, a lamp at his back; she could clearly see his shadow on the bathroom door.

"What?" She set down the blade.

"What are you doing?"

"Nothing. What are you doing?"

"I'm waiting for you."

"I'll be out in a few minutes."

Clark thought a moment. "Why are you taking so long?"

She had been hoping he would come in and join her, make love to her before he killed them all. It had really hurt her feelings that he'd had her pose nude all those times and not once stopped painting to touch her. The drops of her blood continued to drip off the end of her elbow. "I don't know," she said.

"I don't believe you."

"Go, do what you're going to do without me. I want to stay here."

"I can't do that."

"Why not?"

"You know why."

She felt a stab of pain across her temple. "I'm not going."

"If you don't come, Alice will have died for nothing."

"I don't care about Alice."

He entered the bathroom. At first she thought he was bleeding, too—from the head. His red hair was ablaze, as were his eyes. But it was only hate. "And where do you think you're going?"

She crossed her arms over her breasts, trying to hide her wrist. The red spilled over her nipples. "I accidentally cut myself."

He strode to the tub and leaned over, grabbing the razor blade and holding it inches from her face. "I'll show you an accident. I'll cut your eyes out."

"No," she cried, suddenly terrified.

"I'll cut your tongue, make you eat it. Then you can bleed all you want."

"I won't do it again, I swear. Stop it, Clark!"

He stood and threw the blade aside. Then he picked up her

hair dryer and flipped it on. "You're getting out of that water this instant. It's too hot for a bitch as cold as you."

He threw the hair dryer into the tub. The electrical shock hit Polly's brain like a fistful of exploding dynamite, just as it had when she had been in the hospital as a child. She began to scream.

Chapter Seventeen

The Lakers had called a time-out. There were ten seconds left on the clock. They had the ball. They were down by two points. Never in her wildest imagination could Sara have dreamed a stupid basketball game could make her feel so miserable.

"What if they don't make it?" she asked Nick, who stood beside her. With the exception of Maria, the whole room was standing. On the screen, the Lakers' coach drew diagrams on a big white sheet of paper while the players huddled in a semicircle at his back and nodded their exhausted, sweaty heads. On the left side of the lounge, Bubba paced along the top of the bar, shouting out encouragement.

"My men!"

"If they miss and don't rebound the ball, they're dead," Nick said.

"But they don't get any points for a rebound, do they?" Sara asked.

"No. They'd have to put up another shot quick. And it would have to go in."

Sara clasped her hands together. "I'm going to kill him."

"Who?" Nick asked.

"You'll know when you see the body."

The time-out came to an end. Both teams walked onto the court. The noise in the Fabulous Forum and the lounge of *Haven* settled down. Sara bit her lower lip. The referee handed the ball to a Lakers player and blew his whistle. Immediately the players of both teams scattered across half the court. A second went by, two seconds. The guy wasn't going to have time to inbound the ball!

"Shoot!" Sara yelled.

"He can't shoot from out of bounds," Nick said.

The player inbounded the ball to a teammate at the top of the key. The guy faked to the right, dribbled to the left. Then he leaped; it was a magnificent leap. He floated through the air toward the basket. Green uniforms sprang up to block his way. Sara thought they were too late. The time on the corner of the screen went to six seconds.

"Shoot!" Sara yelled.

"He doesn't have the ball," Nick said.

Nick was right. The player had passed the ball to a teammate in the left corner. The guy was all alone, far from the basket. He was going for a three-pointer! If he made it, the game would be over! There would be no need for an overtime!

"Shoot!" Sara yelled. The clock went to three seconds.

He shot it. The ball sailed high through the air. It had beautiful arc, seemingly perfect touch.

"No!" Sara screamed along with the rest of the room.

It missed. A Celtic grabbed the rebound. The Lakers tried frantically to foul him. They were too late. Time expired. Sara collapsed into the chair behind her.

I will not kill him. He is fat and slimy, but he has a working heart, functional kidneys. I will force him to sell his organs to pay off the debt.

"Excuse me," Sara said to Nick and Maria, standing and making her way through the crowd to the bar. The mood of the lounge was gloomy, but compared to Sara's mood, the place was in seventh heaven. Yet Sara wasn't exactly angry. The pure fullness of her anger had transformed it into something quite the opposite, into an almost perverse joy. Bubba no longer had a hold over her. She could say what she wanted to him, *do* what she wanted. There were so many things she would do to him.

Bubba sat atop the bar, his head bowed in misery, an empty bottle loosely clasped in his chubby fingers. Clair was not around.

"Bubba," she said sweetly. He looked up, rubbed his red eyes.

"It's you again?"

She nodded. "Outside."

He did not protest. They exited the lounge and stood on the deck. A lot of kids had just come out for a breath of fresh air, however, and Sara decided their "talk" would go better in private. She steered Bubba down a companionway and into a deserted hall. The locked passenger staterooms stretched the length of the boat away from them on either side. Bubba slumped to the floor and leaned against a wall. Sara stood above him, her hands on her hips.

"They should have gone for the tie," Bubba said sadly. He looked up at her as though he expected her to offer him comfort. "I should be coaching that team."

"I don't care about the Lakers."

He was shocked. He was even more drunk than before. "I've followed them since I was a little Bubba."

She knelt in front of him. "Bubba, do you know how close you are to having terrible things happen to you?"

He was interested. "How close?"

She held her thumb and index finger up a quarter of an inch apart. Then she squeezed them together. "This close."

He was *very* interested. "What are you going to do?"

She leaned closer. "I *need* the money you promised me. I *need* you to get it for me. I don't care *where* you get it. Do you understand me?"

Now he was disappointed. He brushed off her remark with a sloppy wave of his hand. "I bet your money on the Celtics."

"What?" Sara fell back on her butt. "I don't believe you."

"You can have all the money you need tomorrow evening." Bubba wasn't much interested in the discussion. He clenched his fist and pounded his knee. "They should have gone for two points."

"Why would you bet against the Lakers? They're your team. You just said it—you grew up with them."

He nodded. "I knew in my heart it was time for them to take a fall."

Sara laughed. Then she did something that could have ruined her reputation for all time had there been anyone around to see it. She gave Bubba a big hug. "I never will understand you."

"My true nature is unfathomable," he agreed.

Sara suddenly remembered the bargain she'd made. She quickly sat back. "I suppose now you'll expect me to put out for you?"

He hesitated. "Does it mean that much to you, Sara?"

"My body?"

He spoke in a regretful tone. "I suppose I could make love to you, give you a night you could carry happily to your grave, but I'd hate to do that to Clair. Faith and trust and not screwing around mean so much to her. Do you understand, Sara?"

"Are you saying you *don't* want to have sex with me?"

"It's not you personally."

Her usual distaste for him returned. "But you've been dying to sleep with me all year? Or was that just an act?"

"Well . . ."

"You don't find me attractive?"

"Now I didn't say that."

Sara leaped to her feet and paced in front of him. "What about me don't you like? Is it my face? Is it my legs? Come on, don't worry about my feelings. I don't care what you say."

He studied her a moment. "I've never liked the way you walked."

She stopped. "I walk just like any other girl. Just like Clair does."

He shook his head. "No, you walk like you're in a hurry. A lady is never in a hurry. Good things come to a lady. She doesn't have to chase after them."

"What else?"

"Your clothes—"

"You said that earlier. I'm getting new clothes for the summer. What else is wrong with my body?"

"Nothing. Your body's fine."

"Fine? China and silk are fine. Come on, what don't you like? Is it my ass?"

"I'd have to see you naked before I would be willing to express an opinion in that area."

"Hold it right there, slimeball. I'm not taking my clothes off for you. No way you're going to trick me into that."

"All right."

"What do you mean, all right? You don't want to see it?"

"Not at the moment."

She sagged against the wall, feeling totally unwanted. "You really don't think I'm very sexy, do you?"

Bubba gathered himself off the floor and put his arm around her shoulder, the odor of a half dozen of the world's most famous distilleries in his breath. "Sara, if I had met you before I met Clair, I honestly believe things would have been different between us. Of course I think you're sexy. You have a great ass. A few private lessons and I'm sure you could have made me very happy."

She realized he was feeding her a crock of pure BS. It was amazing—not to mention ridiculous—how much it meant to her. She kissed him on the cheek. "I bet you're still a virgin."

He reached around and pinched her butt. "If I am, I was born with incredible natural talents."

Chapter Eighteen

I f Nick had been told his first week at Tabb High that he would end the school year as perhaps the most popular person on campus, he would have laughed. Yet, when the basketball game was over and the class gathered in groups to discuss it, the biggest group gathered around Nick. It was true, of course, they were talking about a subject he was an acknowledged master of; nevertheless, had they just watched a war movie, he still would have drawn the most people to him. He knew this without understanding it.

He was the best athlete in the school—he had no qualms about accepting *that* distinction—and he was no longer the shy mumbling ghetto exile he had been last September. He was, however, still soft-spoken and hesitant to express his opinion on any subject, including basketball. Also, his fearsome appearance had not changed with Tabb's capture of the league basketball title. But perhaps Michael had explained Nick's popularity best when he had said that Nick was the only one in the school who even vaguely fit the definition of a hero.

"And people are always searching for a hero, Nick. Just look at who's big in Hollywood. It's usually the actor who can rescue the most prisoners of war in two hours or less. Enjoy it while it lasts. Someone's sure to come along soon and take your place."

Nick did enjoy the adulation, although he found himself shying away from it at the same time. A few minutes of attention from a big group gave him a pleasant high. More than that made him anxious. As soon as was politely possible—after saying for the tenth time that he didn't like second-guessing the Lakers' coach for going for the win instead of the tie— he excused himself from the lounge and wheeled Maria onto the deck. Here there were fewer people; it was now cold and the fog had gone beyond thick to frightening. Nick had once seen a television show on the Bermuda Triangle—a place in the Atlantic Ocean where many ships had disappeared. Had those ships ended up in another dimension, he imagined, it might have resembled *Haven*'s present environment. Complete darkness would have seemed more natural. The damp grayness was spooky.

"Are you cold?" he asked Maria, parking her chair near the rail. The splash of the ocean against the hull could be heard beneath the fog. Maria pulled her shawl tighter.

"No." She looked up at him. "Are you?"

"The fresh air feels good."

A period of silence went by. There had been a lot of those between them since he had picked her up at the rehabilitation clinic. "They like you," she said finally.

"I guess. They like my jump shot, that's for sure."

"I wish I had gotten to see you play again."

The remark warmed his spirits somewhat. Maybe she did still care about him. She had given him few signs one way or the other. "It was a fun season. Making the CIF playoffs was exciting. Track was fun, too. I ran the quarter mile and did the long jump."

"I was told they gave you a trophy at the awards banquet?"

He nodded. "It was for having done well in more than one sport." Coach Campbell had presented the award, the same man who had almost expelled him the first week of school when he had floored The Rock in the weight room. Coach Campbell had given him a big smile and a slap on the back with the trophy, but still no apology. Nick didn't feel any resentment. It was easy to forgive when you were winning. His father had been at the banquet. He had been the first one to stand and clap. The rest of the school had followed suit. Nick had never received a standing ovation before.

"Trophies, fans, scholarships," she said. "You must be happy?"

He looked down at her white tennis shoes lying still on the wheelchair's metal footrests. "I'm not happy, Maria."

"Why not?"

He turned away. "Isn't it obvious?"

Another spell of silence. *Haven*'s foghorn broke this one. Maria touched his leg. "Don't worry about me, Nick."

He chuckled, staring into nothing. "Sure. I'll just wheel you all over the place and forget that you used to walk. How can you tell me not to worry?"

"I don't want you to. I don't know why you do."

A note of anger entered his voice. "You know why."

She took her hand back. "I don't."

He turned on her. "How would you like it if *I* got crippled that night? What if I had gone up for a rebound and came down wrong and broke my neck? Would you even—" He stopped, realized what he was saying. Awful as it was for him to see her paralyzed, it was nothing compared to *being* paralyzed. She answered his unfinished question.

"I would care."

"I'm sorry," he said quickly. His apology had a strange effect on her. She seemed to take up his shame. She turned her chair as if about to leave, as if she were embarrassed to be with him.

"Nick, you don't have to—" she began, getting upset. "I can take care of myself. Really I can."

He touched the handle of her wheelchair instead of her arm, holding on to her just the same; the chair was a part of her now. "What do you want me to do?" he asked, afraid she would respond by telling him to go away. He didn't understand till right then how much he loved her. Maria composed herself and looked in the direction of the lounge.

"Later, when things slow down," she said. "I want you to talk to everybody who was still at the party when Alice died: Bubba, Clair, Bill, The Rock, Kats, Russ, Sara, Polly, Michael, and Jessica. I want you to gather them below, where we can be alone."

"Why?"

"You'll see."

Chapter Nineteen

The night went on. The air grew colder. The fog grew thicker. Around midnight, *Haven* encountered four-foot swells and began to rock uneasily, her hull softly groaning with each rise and fall, the stomachs of many of her passengers doing likewise. A few kids lost their dinners over the ship's rail. Yet the rough waters did little to slow the momentum of the party. Time took care of that. No matter that for many it was the most exciting night of their lives—passing the three o'clock hour, the bulk of the senior class could be found lying curled up in the lounge or the game room on sheets of foam someone had been thoughtful enough to provide. Those who were resting were smart. They would be fresh for the upcoming day on Catalina.

If they lived that long.

Once again, Jessica and Sara were in Jessica's cabin, trying to decide about the contraceptives. Jessica was not enjoying the pitch and roll of the ship. It made it impossible for her to pretend—as she had done most of the night—that she was still on dry land. The way *Haven's* hull kept creaking was particularly disturbing. Sara's reassurances that the sound was natural didn't ease Jessica's mind in the slightest. Sara knew as much about boats as she did, which was precisely nothing.

"I don't see how you can be worried about drowning at a time like this," Sara said, the bottle of foam in her hand. "You should be worrying about how you look."

"Excuse me, but I've heard that when you drown it can affect your appearance," Jessica said, sitting on the bed beside Sara. Jessica had already changed into her bathrobe. Sara was going to have to pop next door in a minute and get ready. Ten minutes ago they had told Bill and Russ—Jessica had told Bill and Sara had told Russ, to be precise—to meet them in their rooms in exactly twenty minutes. Bill and Russ thought they were being invited to a private party.

Just our luck they'll bring their buddies with them.

But it seemed unlikely. Jessica and Sara had both made it clear that they were to come alone.

"I don't think I like the ingredients in this stuff," Sara said, studying the foam label. "Nonoxynol nine, potassium hydroxide, benzoic acid—does that sound like something you want inside your body?"

"It sounds like it'll work."

Sara handed her the foam. "You take it then. If you explode, don't blame me."

"Thanks," Jessica muttered sarcastically. The room had a lamp hanging from a corner of the ceiling. The motion of the boat made it swing back and forth, sending shadows chasing its light, giving Jessica a headache.

"You don't look very excited."

Jessica shrugged. "I'll get excited when Bill gets here."

Sara nodded, thoughtful, chewing on her lower lip. "Can I ask you something, Jessie?"

"As long as it's not about your ass."

"Well, I've been getting a lot of complaints about it lately. Come on, you've taken showers with me in PE."

Jessica groaned. "I just cannot believe you are asking me this. Who's complained about it?"

"Bubba."

"Bubba! Bubba's screwed half the girls in the school."

"Yeah. So he's a goddamn expert on the subject."

"What did he say?"

"It's not what he said. It's what he didn't want to— Look, I'm asking for a vote of confidence here."

"You have a great ass, Sara."

"You're just saying that."

"Please don't make me say it again. I'm changing the subject. How much light should we leave on?"

"I'm turning off all the lights."

"You'll be in the shower when Russ gets there. How can you have all the lights off?"

Sara looked worried. "I guess it would seem strange."

Jessica realized Sara was more scared than she was. Actually, Jessica was surprised at her own lack of fear. She felt more resigned to the event than anything else. One thing had become clear: she was not giving up her virginity in joy. She just wanted to get it over with.

"How are you getting along with Russ?" she asked gently.

Sara snorted. "Oh, we get along fine, as long as we don't talk. So far tonight, we've been doing *splendidly*. He's been with his buddies since he came on board." Sara glanced at her watch. "Well, I guess I've got him to myself now, for a few minutes, anyway." She stood. "You promise to tell me exactly what happens?"

"I'll videotape it."

Sara smiled. "I guess this is it."

Jessica hugged her. "I hope this is it for one of us at least."

When Sara was gone, Jessica stood by the porthole for several minutes, staring out into the eerie night. Alice had loved the fog. Alice had loved everything. Jessica had been trying to tell Sara she had no hope for herself. Not for love.

"I'm going to the movies Saturday night. You won't believe it, I asked the guy. His name's Michael Olson. . . . That reminds me, where's that fantastic guy you were going to introduce me to?"

"Ask me after your date."

725

And then Alice had lain down to sleep.

"I could go to sleep here and never wake up," Jessica whispered, remembering her exact words.

The bathroom was small but neat. Jessica removed her robe and got in the shower. The water came out hot and hard at first, and she jumped back, almost slipping and falling. She had left her hair down, although she didn't want to wash it; she looked a lot better with it down. Well, it was going to get wet, there was no helping that. She wondered how long Bill would be. The shower curtain was translucent; at least it would have been without all the steam. She had read somewhere that steam was supposed to be very sensual. She hoped she started to feel sexy soon.

Several minutes went by. During that time she scrubbed herself from neck to toe using her own soap—just to be sure. The spray of the shower waved up and down in rhythm to the ocean swells. Finally there came a knock at the door. Naturally, she had left the bathroom door open—it was part of the plan. The distance between the two doors couldn't have been more than eight feet.

"Bill?" she called, pulling the shower curtain to the edge of the tile, on the small chance he did have someone with him.

"Yeah."

"Come in."

He opened the door to the suite, paused. She could see his outline through the curtain, but that was all. He was alone. "Jessie?"

"It's all right. I'll be out in a minute. Come in."

He entered, closing the door, and then sat on the bed. She peeked around the edge of the curtain. He had his hands folded in his lap and was staring at his feet. He was being a gentleman. "Where's the party?" he asked.

"It's in Sara's room." She added, "I've been running around all night. I thought I'd grab a quick shower. I won't be long."

"I could go on ahead of you."

"No." He was still looking down. "Just let me wash off this soap."

"OK."

Now what? Sara and she hadn't given this enough thought. It would have been much easier had he come into the bathroom and tried to peek around the curtain or something. There was really no good excuse to invite him into the bathroom.

Fine, I'll give him a lousy excuse.

She turned off the water. "Bill?"

"Yeah?"

"Could you hand me my towel?"

"Where is it?"

It was right outside the shower, on a hook on the back of the bathroom door. She could see it through her crack in the curtain, along with Bill, searching the bedroom. "I don't know," she said. "Don't you see it?"

"No."

"God, there's so much steam in here. Is it on the sink?"

He paused in the bathroom doorway. "I don't see it, Jessie."

She grabbed hold of the edge of the curtain and stuck her head around at him and smiled. He couldn't have been three feet away. He jumped slightly. She pointed to the towel with her wet and dripping arm. "There it is," she said sweetly.

He handed it to her, saving her a six-inch reach. "You want me to come back?" he asked, his eyes down.

"That's all right." She let go of the shower curtain and began to dry her face. "I'm almost done."

"OK. I'll wait for you." He closed the bathroom door and returned to the bedroom. She couldn't believe how proper he was being. In all the teen movies she'd ever seen, guys were always dying to get peeks at cute girls in showers. And she was cute. She had almost been voted homecoming queen for god's sake.

She quickly dried herself, climbing out of the shower and slipping into her bathrobe. Sara had given it to her last Christmas. It was pink, thin, and it clung to her damp body in a number of important places. She glanced at herself in the foggy mirror. Wet, her hair appeared almost black, and the heat of the shower had flushed her face. In her totally unbiased opinion, she thought she looked pretty fantastic.

I just have to get him to kiss me. Just get him started.

She opened the bathroom door. Bill was standing by the window, admiring the fog. He jumped again when he saw her. She smiled to put him at ease. "I didn't know you'd get here so soon."

"You said twenty minutes."

"Oh, that's right, I did." She gestured to the bed and reached for the towel around her neck. "Have a seat, let me dry my hair."

He sat on the bed. She stepped past his knees and sat beside him, on his left. They had the bathroom and its diffusing steam in front of them, the door to the hallway on their right. Bill still had on his yellow turtleneck and tan pants. She reached up as if to fix his collar. Too bad he didn't have a collar. She brushed a hair from his neck, playing the role of the seductress to the hilt.

"I haven't gotten to talk to you much tonight," she said.

"Yeah, where have you been?"

"Oh, I went for a little swim." She giggled. "I wish you could have joined me."

He frowned. "What are you talking about?"

"Nothing." She turned to face him, tucking her right knee under her left leg while pressing her knee against the side of his leg. She had made a similar move months ago on his parents' couch without much success. But now they knew each other a lot better, and her bathrobe was split open and my, didn't her wet legs look fine. "I'm glad you're here," she said.

His gaze strayed to her legs. She was not sure how far up he could see, not exactly, nor did she care. Suddenly she began to enjoy herself. "You're going to catch a cold," he said.

"I'm not cold." She smiled her naughtiest smile and moved her hand into his hair. "Are you?"

"No."

"That's good." She tugged lightly on the hair at the base of his neck. "If you were, I don't know what I would do."

"Jessie?"

"Yes, Bill?"

"What about Sara's party?"

"It'll wait." She leaned closer, her wet hair hanging over the arm of his yellow sweater. "I'm not making you uncomfortable, am I?" she asked.

"No."

She continued to play with his hair, continued to smile as if she couldn't wait for him to kiss her, which was the truth of the matter. "That's good, because I feel real comfortable with you. I mean, I like you, Bill. Did I ever tell you that?"

"Yeah. I like you, Jessie. You're a nice girl."

She gushed over the remark as if he had just sworn his undying love. "Really? Oh, that's neat. I mean, I wasn't sure if you felt that way." She let her right hand slip from his hair to the top of his right shoulder and caught his eyes. "You know what I liked most about the prom?"

"What?"

"When you kissed me afterward."

He took the hint. He kissed her. He might not have intended for it to be a deep and passionate kiss, but the moment his lips touched hers, she tightened her arm around his neck and pulled him close. She had not kissed many guys in her life.

She was unaware of the finer points that constituted a great kiss. Nevertheless, she didn't feel Bill was giving her his all. She felt that way very strongly when he suddenly pulled back.

"It's late," he said.

She laughed, tugging him toward her. "It's early."

They started again and things began to pick up, possibly because they rolled back onto the bed. This had nothing to do with her; it just happened. He put his right hand on her robe near her left breast. The kissing got harder, deeper. Yet she still felt as if she was doing most of the digging. She wished he would touch her breast. His hand kept moving toward it, then pulling away. It was driving her nuts.

"Jessie?" he mumbled.

"What?" She was having trouble with other parts of their bodies as well. Her legs were up on the bed. His feet were still on the floor. She tried swinging her left leg over his hip, but it kept slipping loose. Surprisingly, her robe continued to hold together; she must have tied the belt too tightly coming out of the shower. She took his right hand and put it on the knot, hoping he would work on it.

"Why are we doing this?" he asked, between heavy breathing and kissing.

"Because we want to."

"I don't think it's right."

"Don't think, Bill."

He didn't loosen the knot. He put his hand on her hip

instead. That would have been fine except his hand just stayed there, while his kisses became less and less passionate, until finally she began to feel as if she were chasing a strawberry around an empty bowl with a baseball bat. She had heard him when he said he didn't think what they were doing was right, but she hadn't *really* heard him. When she took his right hand and pressed it to her left breast, his reaction took her completely by surprise. He leaped off the bed and began to yell.

"What are you trying to do?"

She had never seen him mad before. "Huh?"

"You're trying to seduce me!"

She sat up, very slowly. "No. I was just, you know, being friendly." There was something not quite right here. She still hadn't figured out where she had messed up. He looked positively livid.

"Look at you, Jessie. You're practically naked. And you're trying to undress me!"

"No. I was in the shower, and—"

"The shower! You knew I was coming. What kind of girl are you anyway?"

It hit her then—the humiliation. Her voice came out small and shaky. "I'm a nice girl, like you said."

He began to shout again, then suddenly balled his hands into tight fists and turned to face the wall, breathing heavily. She thought he wouldn't speak again, that he'd just leave. But finally he got hold of himself.

"I shouldn't have yelled at you like that, Jessie," he whispered, reaching out and putting his hand on the doorknob. "I shouldn't have come."

"Why did you come?" It could have been a stupid question. She had, after all, given him a legitimate reason to visit her cabin. But she had been a fool to think he had been fooled. He was nodding as he turned and looked at her, nodding to himself, asking himself the same question.

"I wanted to see, I guess," he said.

"See what? Me?"

"No."

"Oh." His remark did wonders for what was left of her ego. And here all these years she had thought she was pretty cute. Oh, well, half the point in this whole seduction had been to run what was left of her self-esteem into the ground. It was funny how she had gotten exactly what she had wanted.

She began to tremble.

"This has nothing to do with you," he said.

She nodded weakly. Of course her being unattractive to him had nothing to do with her. She may as well not have been in the room. She still couldn't believe this was happening to her. He took a step toward the bed, stretched out his arm to touch the side of her face, then thought better of it and pulled his hand back to his side.

"I better go," he said.

She nodded again. "All right."

But he didn't leave immediately. Ignoring her for a moment, he stepped into the bathroom and picked up her brush beside the sink. He ran it under the faucet and began to comb his hair. She had run her fingers through his hair while they'd been kissing, but since he always wore it short, she hadn't really messed it up. From his perspective, however, she must have messed him up bad. Her eyes began to burn. He set the brush down and stepped to the door.

"I won't say anything to anybody about this," he said gently.

She bit her lip. "Thanks."

"Bye."

"Bye."

He left. She picked up her towel and buried her face in it. She began to cry.

A few minutes later someone knocked at her door.

Chapter Twenty

Sara almost froze to death waiting for Russ to appear. The captain must have been scrimping on fuel. There was no hot water, and never before in her life had Sara taken a cold shower. She understood that only monks took those, and that they did so mainly for reasons of celibacy. Just what she needed—a cold shower to make her as horny as a statue and as desirable as a fish.

Why is he taking so long?

She had said twenty minutes. At least forty minutes must have gone by since she had last seen him. Maybe he'd gone with Bill to Jessica's suite. Yeah, the three of them were probably having a great time about now. Disgusted, Sara grabbed her towel and tried to stand at the far end of the shower out of reach of the spray. But every time *Haven's* bow went under, the water splashed her legs. She had gooseflesh on her thighs ready to sprout feathers.

Someone pounded on the door.

"Who is it?" she called, pulling the old gray shower curtain tight. She'd left the bathroom door open, but she was beginning to wonder if that had been a good idea. He might have brought the whole cross-country team with him.

"It's me," he called.

"Are you alone?"

He opened the door. "What?"

"Are you alone?" She was afraid to peek around the edge of the curtain.

"Yeah." She heard the door close. "What are you doing?"

"I'm taking a shower. What do you think I'm doing?"

"Do you want me to join you?" He sounded as if he could have been standing in the bathroom doorway. She couldn't stop shivering.

"No. Close the door."

"Whatever you want." He closed the bathroom door.

He had to choose this moment to do exactly what I said.

She turned off the water and dried herself furiously, trying to get some warmth back into her flesh. All was not lost. She had a cute orange bathrobe waiting to put on. Jessica said she looked like a doll in it, even if autumn colors depressed Bubba. Sara knew as soon as Russ saw her in it, he would want to kiss her.

When she came out of the bathroom a few minutes later, he was lying flat on his back on the bed and staring at the ceiling. He had on blue jeans, a blue Pendleton shirt, and looked so masculine it made her legs weak. He hardly glanced over.

"Are you ready?" he asked.

"Sure, I'm going to go dressed like this." She sat on the bed by his feet. The soles of his running shoes were dirty and he wasn't going out of his way to keep them off the sheets. She had to remind herself that she couldn't fight with him when she wanted him to make love to her. "How are you doing?" she asked.

He yawned. "Tired. I wish I could just stay here and sleep."

"You can."

"What about your friend's party?"

"We don't have to go."

He sat up suddenly. "No, I'll go. Hurry up and get dressed."

She smiled. "Don't you want to talk for a few minutes? I haven't really had a chance to talk to you all night."

"We can talk at the party." He glanced about restlessly. "How come you and Jessie are the only ones to get your own rooms?"

"I'm ASB president."

"So?"

She stopped smiling. "It's me who rented this stupid boat. Why shouldn't I get my own room?"

He shrugged, doing an excellent job of not looking at her. "I guess you're right. Come on, put on your clothes. Let's go."

"No, I want to talk."

"About what?"

She reached over and began to fiddle with the lace on his left shoe. "Have you been able to train up there?"

"They have a track." He was watching her hands. "I run laps."

"But you told me you never liked to run on the track?"

"They don't let you out, Sara."

His saying her name—she didn't know why it touched her so. She squeezed his toes through his shoe and glanced up. He was looking at her now. "It must be hard on you?" she said.

"I can take it."

She was still cold from the shower. The thinness of her robe and the temperature of the cabin were not helping matters. She could have used a long hug. "How come you never wrote me?" she asked.

"I wrote."

"Not really."

"I didn't have anything to say. Every day there is the same."

"But I wrote. You could have answered my letters." She loosened his lace all the way and started to pull off his shoe.

"Don't," he said, jerking his foot away.

"You're messing up the sheets." She hadn't meant the remark to sound harsh. He got up.

"Let's go to the party."

"No," she said, watching as he leaned against the wall beside the bathroom door. His expression was inscrutable, and it depressed her; she'd always believed she could read his mind simply by looking at his face. He had changed while he was away. "What's wrong?" she asked.

"Nothing."

"Then why are you acting this way?"

"I'm not acting any way. You told me you wanted me to go to a private party with you. I'm here to go to the party. Let's go."

"I can't go. I'm not dressed."

"Get dressed."

"You didn't really want to get in the shower with me."

"What?"

"You just said that. You don't really like me."

"What are you talking about?"

She began to speak, but found a lump in her throat. "Nothing. Forget it. Forget the party, too. I don't want to go."

"What do you mean, you don't want to go?"

"I don't want to go!"

"What?"

"And quit asking me what I mean. Isn't it obvious what I mean?"

"No. What do you mean?"

She put her face in her hands. "Get out of here."

Time went by. It could have been a whole minute. He finally sat beside her on the bed. "I'm sorry," he said.

"What are you sorry about?"

He hesitated. "I'm sorry I don't know."

She burst out laughing, although she knew he hadn't meant the remark to be humorous. She laughed until her sides were ready to burst, until she was ready to cry. Of course, she had felt like crying before she had started laughing. "Oh, Russ," she said, trying to catch her breath. "You are a prince."

He didn't respond to her raving, just sat looking at her. "I know I'm not good enough for you," he said without bitterness.

Sara stopped laughing. "What do you mean?"

He glanced down at the dirty shoes she had criticized. "You're ASB president. I'm just a beer-drinking bum out on a weekend pass from juvenile hall."

She stared at him as if she were seeing him for the first time and discovering that he had two heads instead of the one she remembered. It sure was another side of him. "How come you went to a bar after the homecoming dance and got drunk?" she asked. She had always wanted to know.

"Because you didn't want to kiss me."

She knew instantly what he was referring to. Before the homecoming queen announcement, they had been dancing together and he tried to kiss her. She had stopped him because she felt uncomfortable with any public display of affection. At the time she figured he understood. He hadn't seemed upset. "I was joking," she said.

"After my race that morning, you said you didn't want me taking you to the dance."

"I went to the dance with you!"

"We went in separate cars."

"I had to get there early. I had to— You knew I was joking!"

He glanced at her. She wished again they hadn't cut his hair so short. "Were you?"

"Yeah!"

"Oh. I didn't know." He started to get up. "It doesn't matter."

She pulled him back down. "It does matter, Russ. You didn't have to go out drinking that night."

Now she could read his face. It was filled with regret. "I wish I hadn't."

"You do hate it up there, don't you?"

"It's a cage."

"But you didn't cut down the tree?"

"No." He showed a trace of annoyance. "How could I when you took away my ax."

"I didn't take your ax. Polly took it."

"Polly took it? I thought that was you."

"No." She giggled. "Does this mean you're in love with Polly now?"

He was insulted. "Who says I'm in love with you?"

"Of course you're in love with me. Why else would you get all upset because I rejected you? And why would you go out drinking all night and try to kill yourself?"

"I didn't try to kill myself."

"Anyone who drinks so much he can't remember where he

drank is trying to kill himself. Don't be embarrassed. You can love me. You're an incredible person. I'm an incredible person. And I love you." She stopped. "I can't believe I said that. Never mind, I didn't say that."

He kissed her. She didn't see it coming. She quickly decided those were the best kind of kisses. They fell back on the bed and she felt his hands on her body. It was incredible. She couldn't even count the number of places he touched her. It was absolutely the most exciting thing ever! She didn't mind in the least that his twelve-hour beard was scratching the hell out of her face. She was just about to slip out of her robe and give him a night in heaven to make up for all his days in hell when he suddenly stopped and sat up.

"I shouldn't be doing this, Sara," he said.

I shouldn't? She'd thought she'd been doing a few things of her own. "What's wrong?" It was her ass, she knew it. He didn't like it, and he hadn't even seen it yet.

"I'm taking advantage of you. You're not even dressed." He shook his head, ashamed. "I can't treat you like you were just any old girl."

She got up on her elbow, wishing she was a little older. "You've slept with girls before?"

"Oh, yeah, loads of times. But they didn't mean anything to me."

"Not like I do?"

"Well, yeah."

"Do you love me?" she asked.

"Do you love me?"

She thought a moment. "Maybe we should quit while we're both ahead."

He laughed, hard and loud, as he used to laugh a long time ago. "Come on, get dressed. Let's go to that party."

She sat up. "Oh, I forgot to tell you. It's been canceled."

He seemed disappointed. "What are we going to do? Today and tomorrow are my only days out. I shouldn't waste them sleeping."

She had this great idea. On the other hand, she didn't want to be one of *those* girls who meant nothing. She stood, heading for the bathroom and her clothes. "Let's jog around the deck a few times."

She'd have to do some creative thinking about what it had been like. She couldn't possibly tell Jessica she was still a virgin.

Chapter Twenty-One

The late-night hours were hard on Michael. After questioning Bubba and searching unsuccessfully for Polly, he got trapped in a chess game with Dale Jensen—Tabb's first valedictorian to ever be impeached. Dale had not attended the graduation ceremony, but he had boarded the boat with a vengeance. He had sent out the challenge via Bubba: "Meet me in the galley, twelve midnight. We'll see who's so smart."

Michael didn't want to play. He had a lot on his mind and the pain in his head, rather than diminishing as the night wore on, kept getting worse. But Bubba—sobering at a truly phenomenal pace—insisted that Michael play, and Bubba could be incredibly persuasive. He had always despised Dale. He even lent Michael an extra hat to hide his head wound. Michael had finally told Bubba about his run-in with Clark. He hadn't planned to, but Bubba had started to ask about the gun. Seemed Kats was worried about it. Michael hadn't talked to Kats directly about the gun, of course, but as he searched the boat after the basketball game, he felt Kats was following him. Every time he turned a corner, Kats was there.

The galley was packed when Michael arrived with Bubba and Clair at his side. Dale had brought a chess set and cigarettes. Dale chain-smoked, and like everything else he did, he used the habit to irritate people. Michael knew he would have smoke in his face until one of them was checkmated.

Although he had a despicable personality, Dale was not bad looking. Besides Bill Skater, and possibly Russ Desmond, he might have been the most handsome guy in the school. He was half Italian, with thick black hair, dark olive skin, and a wide insolent mouth Clair had once admitted looked mighty tasty. Dale was extremely slim, however, and he also had a chronic cough. He didn't care in which direction he coughed.

Bubba had warned Michael not to underestimate Dale, but Michael thought he would win easily. He had been playing chess regularly on his home computer since leaving school in January. He could beat the most sophisticated programs at the highest levels of complexity. He thought the contest would be over in less than twenty minutes.

He was still playing at one-thirty in the morning. Dale threw him off balance in the first few moves with a strategy Michael had never seen before. That was one of the weaknesses about honing chess skills against a computer; the programs had an almost endless supply of complicated attacks, yet they were often quite predictable. During the first hour of play, Michael had to use all his skill simply to defend his position. And then, when he finally did take command of the board, and his victory appeared certain, he allowed his mind to wander and made a disastrous mistake. He lost his only remaining rook, while getting nothing in return.

"Mike!" Bubba yelled, pounding the table beside the board and upsetting several of the pieces.

"I wanted to make it interesting," Michael muttered, knowing that unless Dale made an equally careless blunder, the best he could hope for was a draw. Dale blew a cloud of smoke in his face.

"You won't be making a speech after this game," he said.

Michael got his draw, but it took him until two, and left him feeling weak and drained. Dale surprised him afterward by shaking his hand and complimenting him on an excellent game. Bubba did not approve of the result or the sportsmanlike gesture.

"Play him again and kick his ass," Bubba whispered in Michael's ear as Dale got up to leave. Michael shook his head. He had to have another talk with Polly.

Unfortunately, once again, he could not find the girl. He decided to search *Haven*'s engine rooms one more time. He was seriously beginning to worry that Polly had jumped overboard. Before he started down, however, he stopped in the tiny bathroom he had used earlier. He needed a gulp of water.

That was the last he remembered for a while.

He regained consciousness on the floor of the bathroom in a pool of red, his heart thumping in his brain, his thoughts a gray fuzz. He must have knocked his cut open again. His watch said he had lost an hour. He was fortunate he had automatically locked the door upon entering. He sat up and stared in the gray-speckled mirror. The ghost image of Clark did not jump out to scare him as it had before, but his own appearance was frightening enough. A vampire could have gotten hold of him. His coat had blood all over it and he had to stuff it in the wastebasket, leaving him shivering in the damp night air.

The effect of the blackout went deep. After cleaning up, he stumbled outside and found he was trembling inside as well as out. He felt defeated, lonely. He had spent the whole year chasing an unseen enemy who might not exist, and running away from a girl who hardly knew he existed. He suddenly felt so weak he wanted to cry.

He had hit rock bottom.

It was precisely then he decided to tell Jessica he loved her.

He went searching for her. He brought his yearbook with him. She had said she wanted to sign it; it would give him an excuse to talk to her. But he couldn't find her either. He couldn't even locate Sara to ask where Jessica could be. He decided to go to Bubba for help. Bubba was supposed to know everything.

Except who killed Alice.

Michael found Bubba and Clair entwined in blissful slumber on a piece of foam on top of the bar. If they were to roll to the right or the left a couple of inches, they would surely get a rude awakening. Michael shook Bubba gently. Bubba half opened his eyes and smiled.

"Cabin forty-five," he said.

"Jessie?" Michael asked.

Bubba closed his eyes. "Forty-five."

"Thanks." Clair touched him with a warm hand as he was leaving.

"Tell her," she mumbled, not raising her head or opening her eyes.

"I'll try," Michael said.

Walking down the long hall that led to Jessica's cabin, Michael bumped into Bill. They had the space to themselves. Bill smiled broadly.

"I loved that speech you gave," Bill said for the second time that evening.

"Thanks."

Bill laughed. He appeared sort of jittery. "So, where's our scholar off to now? Harvard? Yale? Stanford?"

"No place like that. I can't afford it."

"No shooting, Mike? Did you apply for any scholarships?"

"No."

"Why not?"

"I didn't feel like it." And he sure didn't feel like talking to Bill at this very moment. He had to wonder where Bill had just come from. The neck of his yellow sweater was damp and he had water spots all over the arms.

"Does that mean you'll be around for a while?" Bill asked.

"I guess."

Bill nodded to his yearbook. "Hey, let me sign that. I'll give you my number. Maybe we can get together sometime for a movie or something. Just 'cause we're graduating doesn't mean we can't keep in touch. Right?"

"Sure." Michael handed him the book. Bill whipped out a pen and scribbled something on the inside cover. Michael glanced down the hallway. Jessica's room must be at the end. Bill gave him back the book.

"I can run and get mine if you'd like to sign it," Bill said. "It'll just take me a minute."

"That's OK, I'll sign it later."

"You sure?"

"Yeah."

Bill followed Michael's glance down the hall. "Looking for someone?"

"No."

Bill smiled again. "Catch up with you later, Mike." He disappeared up the companionway.

Michael found cabin 45 three-quarters of the way down the hall. He stared at the number for a long time, remembering how he had felt when he had gone to Jessica's house to pick her up for their date. He had been scared then, but he'd had hope. He realized, suddenly, he didn't have a shred of hope now.

"I love you, Jessie."

"That's sweet, Michael. I think you're a very special person, too."

He knocked on the door, waited. No one answered. Maybe she was asleep. He was turning away when he heard a feeble, "Who is it?"

"It's Mike."

There followed a long pause. "Come in."

He opened the door slowly. She was sitting on the bed, wearing a pink bathrobe, a white towel resting on her lap, her hair wet. The air in the room was moist with steam. She must have taken a shower recently. Her eyes, however, were puffy, as if she had just awakened from sleep. She did not smile in welcome.

"I didn't wake you, did I?" he asked.

"No." She glanced toward the bathroom and touched her head as if it hurt. "What are you doing here?"

"I'm sorry. I thought . . . I'll leave you alone."

"No," she said quickly. "Come in, have a seat." She picked up her towel and began to dry her hair, her attention obviously elsewhere. "Please excuse the mess."

The bed sheets were rumpled; otherwise the room appeared neat. A ceiling lamp in the corner swung back and forth with each rise and fall of the ship. It reminded Michael of a hangman's rope. "I could come back later," he said, closing the door.

"No, it's fine. I was just drying my hair. Have a seat."

There was nowhere to sit except on the bed. He did not believe she had on anything beneath her robe. As it was, he could see more of her legs than he had ever seen before. He did not want to sit on the bed. He leaned against the wall near the bathroom doorway. "You said you wanted to sign my yearbook?" He held it up. "I have it here."

"Oh." She set down her towel and glanced around for her own yearbook. It was sitting on the stand three feet from her nose, but it took her several seconds to spot it. They exchanged books. "Do you need a pen?" she asked, reaching for her purse.

"I have one."

She found something to write with and flipped open his book, sitting cross-legged in the center of the bed with her head down, her long hair hiding much of her face. She appeared to be having a hard time thinking of something to say. Michael took his pen out of his shirt pocket. For a moment, he considered telling her he loved her in her yearbook. Then he quickly discarded the idea. Everybody who signed her annual on Catalina would see it.

It was not going well. There was a gloom in the air that matched the gloom in his heart. He was probably the cause of it. His gaze strayed to the bathroom. A wet black brush sat on the counter beside the sink. There were a few hairs tangled up in its bristles. He leaned closer.

They were short blond hairs.

Bill's sweater had been wet.

Bill had been heading up the hall, away from Jessica's room.

Bill had just been here.

They had taken a shower together!

Michael closed his eyes and rolled into the wall, feeling sick to his stomach. The image of them naked together under the hot water stabbed into his mind like a needle. He had never known such pain. A hard knot formed in the center of his chest and choked off his air. There was poison in his mouth. He couldn't swallow. *His* Jessie in Bill's arms— He simply could not bear the thought.

Not here! Get out! Get away!

He was going to cry, but he couldn't cry—not in front of her. He had sworn that to himself in Alice's studio after Alice's funeral. He swore it to himself again now with the last fiber of his shattered will. Yet he couldn't move. He couldn't get his head off the wall. And the tears were coming no matter how hard he fought to hold them back. He couldn't stop shaking.

She'll see you! She'll know!

"Michael?" She was standing beside him. She touched his shoulder. "Michael, what's wrong?"

He tried to speak. He tried to disappear into the wall. It was not fair. They had been in the shower together in this bathroom having sex when he had been all alone in that other bathroom bleeding to death!

"Michael!" Jessica cried. "You're bleeding!"

She pulled him off the wall and he fell sitting on the edge of the bed, his arm tightly locked across his eyes, his head down. "I'm all right," he managed to get out.

"What happened?" she asked, upset, sitting beside him. Her fingers touched the side of his head, cool and soft. He was able to draw in a breath, clamp down on the tears. He let his arm down, lowered his head further. "Michael?" she said.

"It's nothing. I slipped and bumped my head." He tried to get up, not looking at her. "I'll go find a bandage."

She stopped him and examined his scalp gently. He shouldn't have let her. "You've split open your head! We've got to get you a doctor!"

"No." He turned toward her, and although he didn't intend it to be so, a cold note entered his voice. "Don't get me anything."

She took back her hand, her fingers bloody. She swallowed. "I can't let you go like this."

"I'll be all right." He did not believe it. He did not understand why her eyes were moist. He stood. "Good-bye."

She let him go, at least to the door. He had his hand on the knob when she said, "You forgot your yearbook."

He came back for it. Her hands trembled as she handed it to him. Then she burst into sobs, grabbing her towel and burying her face in it. "You can't go," she moaned.

He sat on the bed and put his hands on her back as she bent over. "It's not that bad, Jessie."

"But you're bleeding!"

"It'll stop." He hadn't seen her this distressed since Maria had been hurt. She let go of the towel, looked at him with tears pouring over her cheeks.

"No, it won't stop."

He was too hurt, too confused. He had no comfort left to give. "I've got to go." He picked up his yearbook. "I've got to get out of here."

He half expected her to grab his hand to stop him, to cry some more. Yet, suddenly, she stopped fussing and stared him in the eye. "You can go," she said. "But you have to read it first."

"What?"

"What I wrote."

He opened the yearbook. He had not been passing it around. Few people had signed it so far: Sara, Clair, Bubba, Nick, Bill. Michael found Bill's note before Jessica's—something about getting together for a one-on-one game of basketball. Then he spotted Jessica's small neat handwriting tucked in the corner of a page at the back. It was not a long note.

I love you, Michael.
Jessie

Michael sat down again. People were always writing things like this at the end of the year in people's yearbooks. It meant nothing. "What does this mean?" he asked.

Her eyes never left his. They were a little red, but they were still pretty eyes. He had always thought so. "I love you," she said.

He looked down at the note, shook his head. "I don't know what you're talking about." He really didn't. Jessica couldn't love him. Only Alice had loved him.

"I've loved you for a long time." A tear formed in the corner of her left eye. It was a quiet tear, not like the ones of a minute ago. "I just wanted you to know."

He closed the yearbook and stood. "I have to go."

"OK. Good-bye."

"Good-bye." He made it to the door, had his hand on the knob again. "Why didn't you tell me this before?" he asked, his back to her.

"I was afraid."

He understood that fear. He asked anyway. "Why?"

"Alice didn't want me to meet you. She didn't think I was good enough for you."

Michael turned to face her. She had lowered her head, hiding her face behind her long curtain of hair. "That's not true."

She nodded sadly. "It is."

He returned to the bed, to her side. She was crying softly. Setting down his yearbook, he put his arms around her. "The first day I met you," he said, "Alice came to visit me in the computer room during fourth period. She had to leave the campus at lunch to see her doctor, but she told me about this wonderful girl she wanted to introduce me to at the football game. She didn't tell me her name, but that night, when I went to the game and spoke to you, I realized you were the girl."

Jessica raised her head, sniffled. "It was you?"

He smiled. "It was me."

A look of amazement filled her face. "I'm glad."

He brushed aside her hair and kissed her forehead. "I have something else to tell you about that day."

He had imagined the speech for almost too long. He couldn't live the moment without the memory of it already before him. On the other hand, nothing he remembered was exactly like this. Nothing was this sweet.

"When I met you at our locker that first day, I thought you were the most beautiful girl I had ever seen. I thought about you all that day, and the next day, and the day after that. Finally, Monday morning, I got up the courage to ask you out. You remember that time we spoke under the tree, when we talked about chemistry? I was going to ask you then."

"How come you didn't?"

"You asked me first."

Jessica sat back and put her hand to her mouth. "No. This can't be. All this time— But you didn't ask me out later! Not once did you ask me out. I was the one who kept trying to set up a date."

"Yeah, but only because you wanted to thank me."

"Thank you for what?" She began to laugh. "OK, I wanted to thank you. But I wanted to go out with you, too! Couldn't you tell?"

"No. Couldn't you tell I wanted to see you?"

"No. Every time we talked, you ran away."

"I didn't want to bother you."

She stopped smiling. "Was there another reason?"

He hesitated. "There was Bill."

"Did you know that time I canceled our date, I went out with him?"

He nodded reluctantly. "Bubba told me."

"I thought you might have known." She sighed. "I'm a bitch."

"No."

"Yes," she insisted. "I'm not who you think I am. Did you know Bill was just here?"

He honestly didn't want her to talk about it now, not right after saying she loved him. "It's none of my business."

She spoke seriously. "But you should know about me. Bubba's going to tell you about it later anyway. I set up this whole scam to lure Bill here. I was in the shower. I was going to seduce him. I even stopped at a drugstore on the way to the harbor and bought contraceptives. Does this sound like the sweet innocent Jessie you think is cute?"

"Well." He was beginning to feel a tiny bit sick again. She saw it, and hugged him quickly.

"I did it because I couldn't have you. I don't love Bill."

"He's a nice guy."

"He's not so nice." Her face darkened and she looked toward the brush sitting by the sink. "He told me I was just like all the other girls, loose. He couldn't get out of here fast enough."

"Really?" That was excellent news, and he was glad to be hearing it firsthand from Jessica rather than secondhand from Bubba.

She chuckled. "It happened just before you got here. He started screaming at me! It was so weird. I'm not that repulsive, am I?"

"Oh, no." A faint idea touched the edge of Michael's mind, an idea so ridiculous and mean-spirited that he would have immediately dismissed it had it not been followed by the memory of a remark Bubba had made in the galley. "'Nothing. Absolutely nothing,'" he whispered.

"What?"

"Something Bubba said about Bill."

"Something Bubba said?" It was Jessica's turn to pause. "'But if I were you, I'd keep Sara's receipt.'"

"Did Bubba say that, too?"

"Yes."

"When?"

She blushed. "In the drugstore."

They began to smile together. Then they started to laugh. They laughed so loud it hurt. It was the best laugh Michael could remember. But perhaps Jessica would not have said the same. She was beet red.

"Oh, God," she cried. "I've been trying to seduce a gay guy!"

"We don't know for sure he's gay," Michael protested, trying unsuccessfully to stop giggling.

"Yes, we do! It all makes sense now, the whole year." Jessica doubled up in embarrassment. "I am sooo dumb!"

"Hey, there's nothing wrong with being gay."

"I know that. It's just that I can't believe it," Jessica said, still howling.

"We shouldn't be laughing."

Jessica stopped suddenly, sat up. "You're right. To each his own."

"We shouldn't judge."

Jessica nodded. "I'm sorry."

"He really is friendly."

"He is, yeah." Jessica kept her straight face approximately three seconds. Then she went into another fit. "He's always liked you!"

Michael couldn't stop her. So he joined her. He could feel guilty about it later. If the truth be known, he was absolutely delighted with Bill's choice of lifestyle. Jessica's shower scheme might have ended a lot differently if Bill hadn't been gay.

But Michael preferred not to think about that.

Somewhere in the midst of their laughter, they began to kiss. Jessica started it; Michael had *never* kissed a girl before and would not have known how to begin. He was pleasantly surprised to discover it was easy to do. He had to assume he was doing it well; he was getting no complaints from Jessica.

They lay back on the bed, their arms wrapped around each other. He couldn't get over the fact that she cared for him! Or how warm and soft her body was. He seriously doubted any other girl would have felt like this. He ran his hand through her wet hair and she leaned into him, tilting her head back. Her mouth was a wonder, so soft and warm, tasting like— well, she tasted like toothpaste, which was fine with him. From now on, he knew, whenever he brushed his teeth, he would remember this moment. It was almost too much for him. He could see a *lot* of her legs. The knot in her robe was about to fall apart. He pulled back slightly.

"What's the matter?" she asked.

"Nothing."

She smiled. "I'm not too aggressive for you, am I?"

"No, it's not that." He twisted his head around. "I think maybe I'm bleeding on your sheets."

She sat up with a start; leave it to him to put a halt to the happiest moment of his life. She touched the side of his head gently and grimaced. "What really happened to you?"

He sat up. "I can't talk about it."

"Michael?" she protested.

He raised his hand. "Not now, Jessie. But later, I promise, I'll explain everything."

She continued to worry. "Does it hurt?"

"No."

"Liar. We should clean it at least."

"I can't run water on the cut. It will only bleed worse."

She touched a part of his head where the blood had already dried. "We could wash here, if we were careful. I think it would help." She slapped him on the back. "Take off your clothes."

He laughed. "What?"

"I can't wash your hair in the sink. You're taking a shower."

She was serious. "I don't know," he said.

She leaned over and kissed him briefly on the lips. "Don't be shy. I'll join you." She added hastily, "We don't have to do anything. I know you're not feeling well."

"I don't know," he repeated, feeling a different sort of dizziness. She shoved him in the chest and giggled mischievously.

"Come on, Michael Olson, make my night."

He had a sudden horrible thought of being eighty years old and looking back on this night with a feeling of profound regret. He took her hand. "I'm not feeling that bad," he said.

It turned out to the best damn shower he'd ever had.

Later, when they were dry and dressed, he asked if she knew Polly's whereabouts.

"She's probably in her own room," Jessica said, sitting on the edge of the bed, brushing her hair, a slight smile on her lips.

"She has a room, too? What number is it?"

"Twenty-eight, I believe. Why?"

"Stay here. I'll be back in a minute."

When he knocked on cabin 28, no one answered. He tried the door without calling out Polly's name. It was unlocked.

The room was larger than Jessica's, far more plush. Polly had left all the lights on. An unopened gray overnight bag sat at the end of the undisturbed bed. No one had been sleeping in this room.

He checked in the bathroom. The tub was full. A double-edged razor blade lay in the corner soap tray beside several drops of bright red blood. Michael took a step forward, the joy of his time with Jessica fading rapidly. Sitting at the bottom of the warm tub—the hot water had been left trickling—was a hair dryer. Its plug rested less than two inches from a nearby socket.

"The man with the electricity."

Had she accidentally dropped the dryer into the water while blow-drying her hair during a bath, she would have received a terrible shock. Yet what did any of that mean next to a bloody razor? That nothing had been an accident?

"I have to warm my blood."

She had given Clark the form.

Michael reached down and touched the red drops beside the blade, rubbing them between the tips of his fingers. A strange sensation swept over him, similar to déjà vu but far more disturbing. It was a feeling of stumbling across the obvious and finding it utterly alien, a nightmare of staring into a mirror and seeing someone else. The realization that had hit him on the deck at the end of his conversation with Polly returned. And this time it remained.

He finally understood what Polly had been trying to tell him.

Russ had followed Sara's advice and was jogging laps around the deck in order to stay awake. Not being much of an athlete, Sara had decided to wait in the hall near Jessica's room. When

Michael exited in a rush, Sara immediately ran to Jessica's door. She didn't knock; she just barged in.

"I knew you'd show up soon," Jessica said, brushing her hair in the mirror on top of the cabin's built-in chest of drawers. Sara couldn't help but note Jessica's *glow*. She immediately felt insanely jealous.

"So how did it go?" Sara asked.

"Wonderful." Jessica beamed. "How about you?"

"It was great."

"Did you and Russ *do it*?"

"Of course. How about you and Bill?"

"Three times," Jessica said.

Sara leaned against the wall. "How come I just saw Mike leaving?"

"He wanted to talk to Polly."

"Yeah, but why was he here? I mean, what happened to Bill?"

"Nothing. Bill left, and then Michael stopped by."

Sara thought a moment. "He just stopped by to talk?"

Jessica grinned slyly. "We didn't talk that much."

Sara was shocked. "You didn't screw both of them?"

"What's wrong with that?"

"That's disgusting!"

"No, it was fun. I had a great time. Especially with Michael. Bill just got me kind of warmed up."

Sara almost choked with envy. Then she noticed the blood on the sheets. "Was it painful?"

Jessica shrugged nonchalantly. "It's sort of like having an itch. It bothers you at first, but then, when you scratch it, it feels great." She set down her brush.

"You know what I mean."

"Oh, yeah. Sure, yeah."

Jessica laughed. "I'm only kidding! I didn't have sex with Bill."

"What happened to him?"

"Nothing. Absolutely nothing."

Sara felt a small measure of relief. She hated to think she was missing out entirely. "How about Mike?"

"Awesome."

"If you're lying to me— How many times?"

"Simply awesome."

"How many times?"

Jessica began to count on her fingers, then threw up her hands. "I ran out of all the stuff we bought."

Sara let her head drop against the wall. "And I thought I was amazing."

Michael reappeared a minute later. He looked a little pale. Sara didn't have a shred of sympathy for him. "Hi, Sara," he said.

"Hello," she snapped. He paid her no heed.

"Could you two do me a favor?" he asked. "Could you help me find Polly?"

Jessica sat up. "Why? Is something wrong?"

"No, I don't think so," he replied, his voice odd. "But I want to find her. She's on board."

"Of course she's on board," Jessica said, concerned, watching him closely.

"Yeah," he muttered, thoughtful.

"What do you want with Polly?" Sara asked.

He shook himself. His eyes cleared. "I want to have a meeting of everyone who was at the party when Alice died."

"Michael," Jessica said, anguish in her voice. "Don't."

"Maria wants to have the same meeting," Sara said, confused. "I just ran into Nick a few minutes ago. She's sent him around to gather everybody together. She wants to have it down in the hull in half an hour."

"Maria." Michael chewed on that a moment. "Interesting."

"Why are you doing this?" Jessica asked, upset, striding toward Michael. A look of sympathy touched his features, and he took her hand.

"It's all right. I understand everything a lot better now. It all makes sense to me, almost." He hugged her. "She didn't kill herself, Jessie."

Jessica stared at him in disbelief. "You don't know that."

He touched the side of his head. "You asked what happened—Clark did this to me."

"Clark?" Sara muttered, more confused.

"Alice's boyfriend?" Jessica frowned. "Is he on board?"

But Michael would not say.

Chapter Twenty-Two

In the dark and relatively deserted hull of *Haven*, Polly McCoy, last surviving member of her unlucky family, stood above Clark Halley and watched as he attached a potent charge of plastic explosive to the side of the ship's huge black fuel tank. He glanced up at her as he turned the setting on the timer, his thin, sweaty red hair plastered over the sides of his white bony face like streaks of caked blood, his dry cracked lips pulled back from his huge teeth in a skull's grin of ecstasy.

"I'll set it for an hour," he said. "It will be almost dawn then."

"If the tank goes, hardly anyone will survive," Polly said.

"It can't be helped."

Polly was cold, even though she had on her biggest and warmest jacket. It was waterproof, but she didn't know how well it would hold up in a fire. "When I was coming down here after you," she said, "I saw Maria. She told me everyone who was at the party will be meeting here soon."

The explosive looked like a lump of dirty orange Play-Doh. Twin red and black wires trailed from it to the tiny square clock. Polly had seen similar explosives and detonators at her parents' construction company. Philip Bart had been in charge of the stuff.

"So?" Clark said.

She knelt beside him and put her right hand over his hands. A drop of blood from the incision in her wrist fell onto his clammy skin. "They are the only ones who matter. Let the rest go."

He chuckled. He was in a great mood. He loved twisting the blue dial on the timer. "The boat's going down, babe. Ain't nothing going to change that."

"It could go down slowly."

He looked at her, holding her eyes. She had never realized before how similar their eyes were—both green, both red. "None of them would shed a tear for you," he said. "Not a one."

"Give them a chance. Please?"

He noticed her blood on the back of his palm, and his mouth twisted into a ravenous grin. "I told you a drop of it seeped through the floor." He held up his stained hand proudly. "See, it escaped the room. It's free now."

"I don't know what you're talking about."

He licked the drop away with his long tongue and bade her lean close, whispering a single black word in her ear. "Madness."

"It's you who's mad," she replied angrily.

He chuckled and let it pass. "All right, babe. For you, I'll let the sleeping innocent try to swim back to shore. As long as you swear to keep our party people down here for the fireworks."

"How can I keep them here if they want to leave?"

He showed her a few minutes later, after he had detached the bomb and dragged her into a small colorless room down the hall from the fuel tank. Here there was a tall metal cabinet pressed against the hull; he opened it, squeezing the plastic explosives into the bottom corner.

"It's always darkest before the dawn," he sang as he decided on a final setting for the timer. The bomb couldn't have been more than three feet from the ocean water.

His answer to her question about how to keep the others from leaving was already in the cabinet, in the green sack he'd brought to the cemetery—a double-barreled shotgun, covered with dirt. It looked familiar. He loaded it with fresh fat shells, and then set the weapon on the topmost shelf, almost beyond her reach.

"It belonged to your father," he said. "Before he burned."

"I know."

He looked at her. "Sure you do. I've been telling you that

all along. But it never mattered what you knew. It only mattered how much you cared. Me, I'm free as a corpse. I don't care about nothing." He added softly, perhaps even with a note of regret, "It's too late to start remembering, Polly."

"Too late," she agreed.

He climbed into the closet, turned, and spread his arms. "Love me, babe, before they get here. It'll feel good, like old times."

"If you stay in there, you'll die," she said. Yet she followed him, into his arms, into the darkness. He was a liar. There were no old times. The door closed at their backs. She could feel his breath in her ear, like the whispering breeze in dreams she had long ago forgotten. But she could not feel his arms, only the cold steel of the closet, surrounding her on all sides, like a metal coffin.

"We'll die together," he promised.

Kats strode *Haven*'s deck alone, wearing the thick fog as if it were a cloak personally given to him by the night. The lounge was crammed with unconscious bodies. The few kids still awake had gathered in the galley to await the dawn. Kats felt as if he had the ship to himself, and the thought of it made him giggle. It was true what they said about the taste of revenge being sweet. He had a natural buzz singing cool music between his ears.

Kats knew about Maria and Michael's desire to have a

meeting below deck for all those who had been at Alice's party. Both of them had told him to be sure to come. They hadn't asked him if he wanted to come; they had simply given him the order. It was just like those jerks. Well, he had no intention of attending—at least, not until his plan was fully hatched. Then he might swing by, if only to see them squirm. He could get into that.

Kats leaned over the rail and spat into the fog. The foam tip of a swell caught his eye as it broke against the side of the ship. The waves were riding high; solid five-footers. It would be rough out there on the water.

Kats whirled and headed for the stern. He needed his bag, his equipment. It was almost time to set the trap. He'd hidden his materials well. He knew they'd be waiting for him, safe and ready.

He poked a lifeboat along his way and howled at the invisible sky. He loved it.

Chapter Twenty-Three

The reason Jessica wore glasses instead of contact lenses was because of the unusual sensitivity of her eyes, and this, in turn, was largely the result of allergies. When she was a little girl, she had suffered terribly with a runny nose and itchy eyes, particularly in the spring when Southern California's many olive trees bloomed. Occasionally she had even been bothered with asthma. As she had grown older, she had left the majority of her symptoms behind, but her eyes had continued to remain easily irritated by dust and pollen. Also, probably as a psychological carryover from her few childhood asthmatic attacks, she had a strong dislike of closed and stuffy places. On several occasions during her high-school days, she had left an exciting movie right in the middle simply to get a breath of fresh air.

Haven's lower deck was as bad as a submarine as far as

Jessica was concerned. It was not only cramped, it had an over-all battleship look. There were huge thick pipes running along the gray walls and ceiling, and the door to the room Michael had chosen to meet in had a *wheel* on it. Michael had closed the door a second ago and turned the wheel. He had locked them in. Jessica could feel the tightness in her lungs and had to consciously remind herself to relax.

Why am I afraid? I am surrounded by my friends.

With the exception of Kats, everyone who had been at the party when Alice had died was present. Maria in her wheel-chair sat near the door. Nick stood behind her—it was Nick who had carried Maria and her chair downstairs. To their left were Sara and Russ, sitting on what appeared to be a huge tool-box. Clair and Bubba stood opposite the door, leaning against the steel hull and looking sleepy. Bill was in the corner with The Rock, and he wasn't giving Jessica a lot of eye contact, which was fine with her. Jessica didn't know how Michael had persuaded Bill to come.

Polly was by herself; she was the only one sitting on the floor, a few feet to the right of a tall metal cabinet. Her bulky navy-blue ski jacket dwarfed her undernourished figure, and she'd tied her dark hair back in a ponytail, making her look all of twelve years old. As Jessica watched her, she noticed Polly's gaze drifting between Michael, a red light above the door, and the cabinet to her left. Just these three places, nowhere else.

"Aren't we going to wait for Kats?" Maria asked Michael.

Outside the door, a few paces down the hall toward the rear of the ship, was *Haven's* colossal fuel tank. Beyond that were the engines. Coming down the ladder, they had passed the engineer on duty, a big bearded gentleman taking an openmouthed nap against a control panel. They pretty much seemed to have the space to themselves.

"He won't come," Bubba said.

"I could go look for him again," Michael said to Maria, apparently not bothered by Kats's absence.

"I'd like everyone to be here," she said.

"He won't come," Bubba repeated.

"How do you know?" Michael asked, the white gauze strip Jessica had obtained from the captain wrapped in a single strip around the top of his head. But Bubba simply waved his hand, as he often did when asked a question that wasn't in his self-interest to answer. Although he was being sensitive to Maria's desires, Michael obviously wanted to get on with things. "It's up to you," he said to Maria.

"Maybe he'll show up," she said, glancing up at Nick.

"I told him twice about the meeting," Nick said.

Michael turned and paced in the center of the room, collecting his thoughts. The room fell silent. Watching him from her position in the corner behind the door, Jessica felt both love and fear. She was still sailing the sky from their time together in cabin 45. Of all the strange and wonderful things in the universe that could be true—he liked her! In the shower she had been amazed at how excited she had been, and at the same time, how comfortable; it was as if they had known each other intimately for ages. Yet there was still much about him that she did not understand.

Why didn't he tell me he loved me?

It didn't matter, he'd told her enough to let her know she was important to him, even if perhaps he meant more to her than she meant to him. You couldn't have everything. Yet that was exactly Michael's problem. He wanted the impossible. He wanted to change the past.

"I had a reason for calling this meeting," Michael said. "But before I begin, I'd like to know your reason, Maria?"

"You go first," she said.

"I would appreciate it if you could give me some idea?"

"So would I," Nick said. But Maria never could be hurried.

"Later," she said.

"All right," Michael replied, pausing and scanning the room. "My purpose in gathering you here is to prove that Alice did not commit suicide. I know most of you have heard me say that before, but this morning I hope—with your help—to put together a number of clues I have gathered to show that suicide had nothing to do with it. I'll start by explaining a couple of alternative theories I gave to the police a few days after the party. I won't spend a lot of time on them, though, because I now realize they are fundamentally flawed."

He returned to pacing, and Jessica noticed he was leaning

slightly to the right. She continued to worry about his head wound, and exactly how he had received it.

"I told the officer in charge of the investigation that Alice's murderer could have hidden in the bathroom after killing her, and stayed there until after we left the bedroom. Looking at it from a slightly different angle, I also suggested that the murderer could have stepped out of the bathroom and secretly slipped into our group moments after we found the body. But both of these scenarios have major problems. The murderer would either have had to enter the bedroom with Alice immediately after Nick had been in there, or else the murderer would have had to have been in the bedroom—with Alice—when Nick got there. With the first possibility, the time would have been incredibly tight. Nick was back outside the bedroom only a few seconds later. And with the second—I just can't imagine Nick not knowing someone was in the room, even if it was dark."

"I didn't hear anyone, that's for sure," Nick said.

Michael nodded. "Because that isn't what happened. Let's get into that now. Let's back up. Let's go downstairs before the gun went off. There were three of us in the living room: Maria, Nick, and myself. Then Jessica and Sara entered. Sara, what was the first thing you did?"

Sara thought a moment. "I don't remember."

"You complained about how loud the music was," Jessica said. "Then you turned it down."

"That's right," Sara said.

"The music was loud," Michael said. "I find that interesting. For all practical purposes, the party was over. But let's not dwell on this point right now. Just remember it. Anyway, Sara lowered the volume on the stereo, Jessica and Sara sat down, and the five of us talked a bit. Then Polly came in."

"I remember," Polly said softly, her eyes big on Michael. He crossed the room and stood above her.

"You turned the stereo off," he said. "You said your head hurt. Then you went outside to check on the chlorine in the pool. Isn't that right?"

"Yes."

"On your way out, you shut the sliding-glass door to the patio. I saw you walk over to the pool."

"It needed chlorine," Polly said.

"So you tested the water?" Michael asked.

"Yes."

Michael resumed his striding back and forth. "Let's pick up Nick's story. He asked where the bathroom was. Sara said there was one in the game room, but that she thought someone was using it. She, in fact, said somebody was in there throwing up. Why did you say that, Sara?"

"When I passed it a couple of minutes before, I noticed that the door was closed and the light was on."

"But you didn't actually hear anyone throwing up inside, did you?" Michael asked.

"I was speaking figuratively."

"Did you hear *anyone* in the bathroom?" Michael asked.

"Not really," Sara admitted.

"Was I in there?" Russ asked Sara.

"Shh," she said, and patted his arm. "Stay out of trouble."

"Jessica told Nick to try one of the bathrooms upstairs," Michael said. "So Nick headed for the stairs. Tell us, Nick, about that little walk you took, step by step."

Nick cleared his throat. "I went to the stairs. I saw Bill in the kitchen. He was bent over the sink. He looked sick or upset. He didn't look good."

Bubba glanced at Clair, who took the occasion to stare at the floor. "What was wrong, Bill?" Sara asked.

"I was— I'd had too much to drink," Bill said.

"You hadn't drunk that much," The Rock said. "What was bothering you, buddy?"

"Nothing," Bill mumbled.

"Come on, Mr. Treasurer," Sara insisted. "Tell us what the problem was?"

"This isn't important," Michael interrupted.

"How do you know it isn't important?" Sara asked.

"It's not," Clair said.

"But I want to know," Sara said.

"Sara," Jessica said, not exactly sure how this related to Bill's homosexuality, but knowing it must. "Shut up."

"Go on, Nick," Michael said.

"I went up the stairs, both flights. In the first part of the hall there were four doors: three on the left, one on the right. I didn't know which one led to the bathroom, but Jessie had said it was halfway down the hall, so I skipped the first door on the left."

"Let me interrupt just a sec," Michael said. "The police later checked that door. It was locked from the inside. I'm sorry, Nick, go on."

"I tried the second door on the left. It was locked. I thought I heard water running inside."

"I was in there," The Rock said. "I was taking a shower."

"You come to a party and you take a shower?" Sara asked, still smarting from the rebuff over Bill.

"I was washing out my eyes," The Rock said defensively, glancing at Polly, who gave no sign that she remembered the chlorine she had thrown in his eyes.

"I tried the door on the right," Nick continued. "It led onto a porch that overlooked the backyard. Kats was out there."

"Did he see you?" Michael asked.

"I don't think so."

"But you could see him clearly?" Michael asked.

"Yeah. There was some light from the pool. It was Kats. I didn't say anything to him. I tried the last door on the left. It was locked, too. But I thought I heard someone inside."

"Was I in there?" Russ asked.

"Were you?" Nick asked.

"He doesn't have to answer that," Sara said. "Not when our quarterback won't tell us why he was crying in the kitchen sink."

"I crashed somewhere upstairs," Russ said.

"You were in that room," Michael said confidently. "Please continue, Nick."

"The hallway turns. There were another two rooms, both on the left. I tried the first door. It was locked. There were people inside. I heard someone groaning."

"That was Clair and me," Bubba said without hesitation. "She was acting out a role in a play for me."

"You told the police the two of you were outside looking at the stars," Sara said.

"That was a misunderstanding," Bubba said with a straight face.

"You're not an actress," Sara told Clair.

"So what?" Clair said.

"This isn't important either," Michael said. "All that matters is that Clair and Bubba were together in that bedroom and that they were so occupied that they couldn't hear what was going on in the next room."

"Why couldn't they hear?" Sara wanted to know. This time everybody simply ignored her. Nick went on.

"I went to the last room. The door was wide open. It was dark inside. I tried the light switch, but the light wouldn't go on."

"What was wrong with the light, Polly?" Michael asked.

"It was broken," Polly said, taking her wrist away from her mouth. She'd been holding it to her lips for the last minute. She looked exhausted.

"Had it been broken long?" Michael asked.

"I broke it when I tried to fix it."

"When? How?" Michael asked.

"That night." Polly shivered. "My hands were wet. I turned it, and it went on. Then it broke." Polly lowered her head. "I fell off the ladder."

Michael stopped dead. "You fell off the ladder?"

Polly nodded, her head still down.

"Did you get a shock, Polly?" he asked, his voice falling to a whisper.

"Yes."

"Did it hurt?"

She looked up, her face sad. "Yes."

Michael stood staring at her for a moment and something in his expression softened. Then he seemed to shake himself inside, throwing off whatever troubled him about Polly's remark. He turned back to Nick. "Go on, and please give us as much detail as you can."

"I stepped into the room," Nick said. "It was cold, dark. The east-facing windows were wide open. The blinds were up. But the other windows—the ones that faced the backyard— they were closed. The blinds were down at least. I could hardly tell there was a window there. Polly must have turned off the pool light. I went into the bathroom and closed the door. I didn't even try to turn on the light. My eyes were beginning to adjust a bit. I could see what I was doing. I wasn't in there but a minute." He shrugged. "Then I came back out into the hall."

"Stop," Michael said. "You skipped something. The day of Alice's funeral, you told me that while you were in the bedroom, you felt something. Tell us about that."

Nick hesitated, and it was obvious to Jessica that he would have preferred not to have been pressed on this point. Jessica did not like the course of Michael's analysis. It was too *real*. It brought it all back, the whole night. The claustrophobic dimensions of the room were not the only thing pressing down on her chest. She was beginning to feel—it frightened her as much as it gave her hope—that perhaps Michael *had* uncovered a truth beneath the obvious. A suicide was horrible to contemplate, but a murder—that wasn't something she could simply forget.

Especially if the murderer was in the room with them.

"I felt scared," Nick said.

"Of what?" Michael asked.

Nick moistened his lips. "I don't know."

"You didn't see anything? You didn't hear anything?"

"No."

"What exactly were you thinking when you were scared?"

"What?"

"People don't just feel scared when they're scared. They have scary thoughts. What were you thinking?"

Nick had to stretch his memory. "I was thinking of Tommy. He was a friend of mine. He died in a gang fight." Nick glanced at The Rock. "Stanley killed him."

The Rock scowled. "That bastard."

"Who's Stanley?" Sara asked, for all the good it did. They ignored her again. Something in Nick's remark had made Michael pause once more.

"Were you with Tommy when he died?" he asked.

Nick fidgeted. It must have been a painful memory. "He died in my arms."

"How did Stanley kill Tommy?"

Nick took a breath. "He got him in the heart with a switch-blade."

"I'm sorry," Michael said. "I had to ask."

"It's OK," Nick said. "Should I go on?"

"Please."

"Should I tell . . ." Nick glanced down at Maria.

"It'll be OK," Michael said. "Honestly, Nick, you can trust me on this."

"I trust you," Nick said, uneasy. "Like I said, I left the room and went into the hall. I got all the way back to the top of the stairs. Then the gun went off. I—I froze, for a second, and then ran down the stairs."

"*Down* the stairs?" Sara asked.

"Yes, he *instinctively* ran *down* the stairs," Michael said. "This is very important. He wasn't the only one who ran down the stairs. Kats did the same."

"How come we didn't run into Kats then?" Sara asked. She was intrigued with the way things were unfolding, Jessica could tell. Bubba, also, seemed very interested in what Michael was up to.

"Before starting down," Michael said, "Kats checked out the backyard from his vantage point on the second-story porch. The only one he saw was Polly, running toward the back door. Go on, Nick."

"I bumped into Maria on the landing. I knocked her down. I had to help her up. Then we went back up the stairs. All of you know the rest."

"Not quite," Michael said. "When the four of us—Jessie, Sara, Polly, and me—came up the stairs, we heard you and Maria talking around the turn in the hall. That's why we went straight to the last bedroom. But you also went straight to that room. Why?"

"I'm not sure I understand your question," Nick said.

"You had five doors between you and the last bedroom, four rooms. How come you didn't stop to check any of those rooms?"

Nick was perplexed. "I don't know."

"How come you ran down the stairs?" Sara asked.

"I don't know," Nick said.

"Do you know, Mike?" Bubba asked.

"You'd better," Clair said, nervously rubbing her hands together. "The suspense is killing me."

"I do know," Michael said, stopping beside Polly. "The shot we heard that night did not come from the bedroom. It did not kill Alice. It came from outside, from a spot in the backyard on the east side of the house directly beneath the bedroom window."

No one spoke for a long time. Yet it was interesting, Jessica noted, that everyone in the room appeared to believe Michael. He sounded so sure of himself. Even Bubba, who spoke first, had no doubt in his voice when he made his one-word request.

"Explain," Bubba said.

"Nick and Kats were upstairs," Michael said. "They were the only ones upstairs who were—fully functional. They were the only two people in the house familiar with guns. And when the gun went off, they *instinctively* thought the shot came from *beneath* them. Think about it for a minute. Then think about how the group of us downstairs would have heard a sound originating from the side of the house. The sliding-glass back door was shut. The game room and the aunt's bedroom windows were all shut. But the east-facing windows in the upstairs bedroom were open. The bulk of the sound from a shot fired beneath that bedroom would have reached our ears via the second-story hallway. It was no wonder Sara and Jessie and me—and even Maria—thought the shot came from upstairs."

"Interesting," Bubba said, thoughtful.

"There's more," Michael said, getting excited, pulling a folded square of white paper from his back pocket. "Alice was supposedly killed by a twenty-two shell. Now I'm not a gun expert, but a twenty-two is a pretty small bullet. The shot we heard was loud."

"Fire any gun in a quiet house and it will sound loud," Nick said.

"Yeah, that's what the police told us," Michael said, unconvinced, stepping toward Nick and carefully unfolding his paper. "Look at this."

Nick studied Michael's secret evidence without fully unwrapping it. "Where did you get these?" he asked Michael.

"What is it?" Sara demanded.

"Shotgun pellets," Nick said.

"Fascinating," Bubba said.

"I removed them from a torn wooden shingle," Michael said. "A shingle located at the edge of the overhang of the roof directly outside the bedroom where Alice died."

"How was the shingle torn?" Bubba immediately asked.

"It was splintered upward," Michael said.

"But she had the gun in her mouth," Jessica said, her voice shaky. Suddenly she wished he would stop. Alice was dead. Nothing was going to bring her back. The feeling belonged to a coward, and that was exactly how she felt—as if she wanted to run away and bury her head in the sand. Yet that was only half of it. As Bubba had said, It was *fascinating*. "We all saw it," she insisted.

The reminder of how they had found Alice appeared to dampen Michael's enthusiasm. He leaned against the tall metal cabinet off to Polly's left, and Jessica could not remember when he had ever looked so frail. She wished to God they had a doctor aboard who could examine his wound. He was white as a sheet.

"That's true," he said. "But the question is, *how* did the gun get in her mouth? Let's look at Nick's account just before we heard the shot. He went into the bedroom. It was dark. It was quiet. He couldn't see or hear anything. Yet he was scared. Now why was he scared? He's no chicken. It wasn't the dark that was bothering him. It was something else. There was something in that room that made him think of a stabbing years ago. What was it?"

"He smelled something," Bubba said suddenly.

"Exactly," Michael said. "Nothing was coming to him from his eyes or his ears. But his nose—the dark doesn't affect your nose. He thought of Tommy dying in his arms from a knife wound to the heart because *he smelled blood*."

"And that's why he ran to the last bedroom instead of checking the others," Bubba said, nodding to himself, enjoying the intellectual puzzle.

"Does everybody understand?" Michael asked.

"No," the others said.

"It is clear," Michael said. *"Alice was lying dead in the room before Nick even got to it."*

More silence followed, longer and deeper than the previous spell. And again it seemed that everyone believed Michael. Jessica sure did, and yet she did not know what it meant, other than that everything they had believed about that night had been built on a faulty foundation.

Michael glanced down at Polly, and she stared back at him, or so Jessica thought at first. But Polly's eyes were focused slightly to the side, behind Michael, on the cabinet. Her red lips trembled. She must have had lipstick on—Jessica had never seen them quite so red. Polly was suddenly the center of attention.

"You fired the shotgun," Michael said.

"Yes," Polly replied softly.

"Then you threw the shotgun into your garden and ran into the house."

"Yes."

"Why?"

"Clark told me to."

Jessica jumped from her position in the corner. "Did he shoot Alice?"

Polly nodded.

"Oh, God," Clair said.

"No," Michael said.

"But, Mike, maybe she saw him do it," Nick said.

"No," Michael repeated, still watching Polly. Now she was looking at him, and she may have been looking to him for help.

"I didn't," she whispered.

"How did Clark get the gun in Alice's mouth?" Michael asked. Polly only shook her head. He came and knelt beside her. He wasn't there to help her. His tone hardened. "Where did he go after he pulled the trigger?"

"I don't know."

"How did he get her fingers on the trigger of the gun?"

"I don't remember," she said, begging to be believed.

"Where did he go after he did all these things?" Michael demanded, grabbing her arm. "How come *none* of us saw him?"

"Michael!" Jessica cried. "She didn't shoot Alice!"

Polly had closed her eyes. She was not crying, but Jessica could hear her breathing, shallow and rapid. It was the damn room. No one could breathe in here. It was almost as if they were back in the bedroom with the body. Michael let go of Polly's arm and sat back. His next words went off like a silent bomb.

"Alice was dead before anyone shot her," he said.

Polly pressed her wrist to her mouth. Jessica could have sworn she was sucking on it; a child in desperate need of a bottle. They were all going nuts. Jessica looked again to the locked door with longing. If only there was a window they could open that wouldn't let the ocean in. Michael had finally lost them all with his last remark.

"Did she have a heart attack or something?" Nick asked.

"No," Michael said.

"A stroke?" Sara asked.

"I read the coroner's report," Michael said, his eyes never leaving Polly's. "I talked to the coroner. That night someone broke Alice's nose. They broke it bad. She had brain damage the bullet didn't cause."

"You'd have to hit someone just right to kill them that way," Nick said doubtfully.

"How about it, Polly?" Michael asked. "Did Clark do it?" When she didn't respond, he reached over and grabbed her hand away from her mouth, yanking up on the sleeve of her jacket. Jessica felt dizzy.

Polly's wrist was all red. She had been sucking on her own blood.

"Did Clark do this?" Michael yelled.

She nodded wearily. "He does whatever he wants."

Michael threw her arm down. "Liar."

"He's not here, is he?" Clair asked anxiously.

"He is," Polly said.

"Really?" Michael asked. "Let me see him."

"I can't," Polly whispered.

"Let me see him," Michael insisted.

"Let me see if I can find him," Polly said, giving up, trying to get up.

The madness was still a few heartbeats in the future, but

even before it arrived, Jessica felt the brush of the razor's edge. It was not the same blade that had cut Polly's wrist. It was a sharp point in time. As Polly stood and walked toward the metal cabinet Michael had been leaning against, Jessica felt the weight of the entire year behind her, focusing down upon this one moment. That was why the air in the room felt so heavy, she realized, so hard to breathe. Polly started to turn the handle on the cabinet.

"What is that?" Clair suddenly cried.

"What?" Michael asked, jumping to his feet.

"People are shouting," Nick said, frowning. "Something's happening."

Michael strode toward the door. He was halfway there when the red light above the door suddenly began to blink off and on and a screaming alarm pierced the air.

"The ship's sinking!" Sara cried.

With the exception of Maria, Polly, and Bubba, they all converged on the door. Nick took hold of the wheel and turned it counterclockwise. It didn't open. He spun it the other way.

"It's stuck," he said, pounding the metal with his fist.

"Oh, God," Sara said.

"Let me try it," Russ said, shoving Nick aside.

"No, I'll do it," Michael said, pressing Russ out of his way. He pulled up on a metal lever beneath the wheel and spun the wheel counterclockwise again. The siren continued to wail. The door cracked open. In a tangled knot, the group pressed forward.

"Stop," someone ordered at their backs.

Jessica turned to see who it was. She didn't recognize the voice. She did not know why; it was only Polly, good old Polly, closing the door on the cabinet with her right hand, holding a double-barreled shotgun in her left. She had her finger on the trigger. They were her target.

"Polly!" Jessica cried. "Put that down."

Bubba, standing quietly off to Polly's right, made a sudden lunge for the shotgun. He didn't make it. Even though she was bleeding from her wrist under her jacket, and floating above space mountain between her ears, Polly was still mighty quick. Bubba caught the tip of the barrels on the bulge of his gut. He froze in midstride and slowly raised his hands, giving Polly his warmest smile.

"Never mind," he said.

Polly's face was dark. She herded everyone into the corner of the room opposite the door with a few silent gestures of her gun. Then she reclosed the door with her shoulder and locked it. Trapped in her wheelchair a few feet away, Maria watched calmly, unmoving. Polly slumped against the door, clasping the shotgun with both hands as if it might suddenly vanish into thin air.

"We have to stay," she said finally, her voice barely audible over the panicked shouts from the decks above. Jessica could hear people running, screaming. She would scream next. She smelled smoke. Michael took a step forward.

"Why?" he asked.

"Clark," Polly said. "He'll kill them all if you don't stay."

"But we have to get out of here!" Clair pleaded. "The ship's on fire!"

"No," Bubba said, reaching a hand out to comfort Clair. Then he hesitated, glancing at Polly. He let his arm drop to his side. He had not finished what he was going to say.

"What is it?" Michael asked Bubba.

"Nothing," he replied.

Michael turned his attention back to Polly, took another step forward. "Where's Clark?" he asked.

"Near," Polly said.

Another step. He was practically daring her to shoot. "Tell him I want to talk to him."

"He won't talk," Polly whispered, perspiration pouring over her face. "Stay."

Michael circled to the left, putting the cabinet at his back and drawing the barrel of the gun away from the others. Jessica could not bear to watch.

He'll sacrifice himself to get us out of here.

Jessica stepped out from the group. The Rock tried to grab her hand, but she shook him off. Michael didn't notice; he was too preoccupied.

"I don't really want to talk to him anyway," he said. "It's you I want to talk to. Do you want to talk, Polly?"

"About what?" she asked. Her wrist appeared to be hurting

her. She stopped supporting the barrel of the gun with her right hand and hugged the cut to her side. The red light continued to flash above her head like an unholy halo. The smell of smoke kept getting stronger. Jessica decided to circle to the right, toward Maria's side of the room.

"Alice," Michael said, taking another step toward her.

"No," Polly pleaded. "Stop there. He pushed . . . He told me—I'll have to shoot you!"

"I don't think so," Michael said, ignoring her order to halt.

"But you don't understand," she cried, pulling back on the trigger with her left index finger. "You must stay here!"

"All right, Polly," Michael said, stopping less than a yard from the tip of the shotgun. "Whatever you want."

What followed next happened quickly and was confused. Jessica had closed to within approximately six feet of Polly's left side. When Michael paused and began to reassure Polly everything was all right, Jessica took that as a signal that he was about to try for the gun. Since he had to cover three feet in the time Polly had to squeeze her finger a fraction of an inch, Jessica did not believe he would survive such an attempt. She decided to make a dive for the gun.

Jessica had barely begun to move when Polly swung the gun toward her face. The twin holes at the end of the double barrels were wide and black—very frightening. Jessica froze. Then Michael made a try for the gun. His heroic attempt was also stopped short. Polly was simply too quick for the two of them. She snapped the gun again on Michael, then onto Jessica, back and forth, holding them both at bay.

Then something incredible happened.

Jessica did not see Maria stand from her wheelchair. Maria was just there, up on her two feet, at Polly's side, forcing the gun down. Unfortunately, whatever magic had suddenly given the small girl the ability to walk had not given her an extra dose of strength. Polly threw her off easily. Maria hit the side of her wheelchair, letting out a cry and falling onto her side.

But by then Michael had reached Polly.

He probably could have gotten the gun from Polly quicker if he hadn't been so overly concerned with where it was pointed while he wrestled with her. It was good he took his time. Whether Polly did so intentionally or accidentally, the trigger was pulled.

The shot hit the side of the tall cabinet, ripping through the metal. Jessica thought she screamed. Maybe the whole room did. Except for Michael. He was in control. He had the gun in one hand, Polly's bloody wrist in the other. Jessica noticed for the first time that the shotgun was caked with dried mud.

"Now you stop," he said.

"I can't," Polly moaned, nevertheless collapsing into him as if he had just come to her rescue. Michael tossed the gun to Bubba and wrapped his arm around Polly.

"Let's get out of here," he called.

"You can walk!" Nick exclaimed, helping Maria up.

"Mike, there's something I've got to tell you," Bubba said.

"Later," Michael called, spinning the wheel on the door.

"I *can* walk," Maria said calmly as Nick hoisted her into his arms on the off chance that her reclaimed legs might disappear.

"Did that goddamn Clark light the goddamn ship on fire or what?" Sara yelled over the din as once again they pressed toward the door.

"No!" Bubba shouted.

Everybody stopped. Bubba never shouted. "What is it?" Michael demanded.

Before Bubba could respond, the heavy metal door swung open. It was Kats, grinning the full length of his greasy mustache. He stepped into the room as if he were captain of the ship.

"Are the kids all right?" he asked, pulling the door closed at his back.

Had he been expecting a royal reception, Kats was in for a big disappointment. Michael leaped to a quick conclusion. "You bastard," he swore, throwing Polly to Jessica and drawing back his fist. "What have you started?"

"Hey, Mike, it was only a prank," Bubba said, jumping in front of Kats, the dirty shotgun still in his hands. "Kats just let off a few smoke bombs to scare everybody into the lifeboats. There's no fire. The ship isn't sinking. There's nothing to get shook about."

"We have to stay," Polly moaned softly in Jessica's arms.

"Why?" she asked, repeating Michael's question. Polly's head sagged back on Jessica's shoulder. She looked up at Jessica with eyes both sad and angry.

"You talked me into it."

"Into what?" There was a hard lump inside Polly's jacket. Jessica wondered what it could be. It didn't feel like a gun. Polly's gaze slipped past Jessica to the cabinet where she had gotten the shotgun.

"Go look, Jessie," she said. "You'll see, it's dark in there, like the tunnel we got lost in when we were small."

The shotgun was in safe hands. The fire apparently didn't exist. Yet the fears of the whole night suddenly coalesced above Jessica and fell over her in a smothering wave. Polly's gaze had been moving to the cabinet since they had come down to this wretched room. Had Polly been pointing to something worse than a hidden weapon?

Jessica pulled a handkerchief from her pocket and handed Polly over to Russ, telling him to bind her wrist. Sara quickly moved to help. Everybody seemed to be talking at once. The alarm continued to blare. Jessica hardly noticed. The tall gray cabinet, its side ripped and twisted from the blast of the shotgun, held her attention. She stepped toward it.

The world exploded in her face.

Chapter Twenty-Four

Orange fire. Black water. And a naked fist of thunder. Time could have come to the Bible's cataclysmic end. Except there came pain—terrible pain.

Since she was closest to the cabinet, the shock wave hit Jessica the hardest. Her eyes had no chance to absorb the blinding flash when she was literally swept off her feet and thrown backward. Her moment in the air existed in her mind all out of proportion to reality. It lasted forever, and yet it remained incomprehensible to her. She couldn't fly. *Haven* didn't carry nuclear warheads. What was going on?

Then she hit the far wall, and the agony almost consumed her. It pulsed throughout her body, shrieked inside her right arm. A long thick pipe had whipped loose from the ceiling and pinned her to the wall.

Flames danced in short-lived fury and tried to claim the

ceiling. But the blaze could not go down. The ocean was pouring in. Jessica tried to draw in a breath and gagged on fumes. Dark numbing water swam around her ankles and up her calves. Cries wailed in her ears. Everyone was trying to open the door again, and this time they were in a hell of a hurry.

Jessica could hardly see. She had lost her glasses. There was a lot of smoke and the blast had knocked out the overhead lights. Yet the red light above the door remained functional, throbbing like a maddened heartbeat in the closing darkness. The fire was going out already. The water was rising. A shadow stumbled against her, grabbing onto the wall for support.

"We have to get out of here," Michael said, taking her left hand and giving it a tug. Jessica screamed.

"I'm stuck," she gasped. Out the corner of her eye, she saw the group manage to force the door open against the pressure of the rising water. For a few seconds, the water around her knees dropped. Then something crashed outside the hull and it quickly rose again, faster than before. The cabinet was gone; a gaping hole into the underworld had taken its place. She realized then how close she was to dying.

Michael pulled himself past her and tugged on the pipe pinning her right arm to the wall. It didn't budge at all, and yet the effort somehow shot the pain in her arm into the region of the unbearable. She teetered on the edge of blacking out. It was only the swelling current, and the horror of drowning beneath it, that kept her conscious. Michael called to the others.

"Jessie's stuck. I need help."

Several had already escaped out the door, if it could be called escape; the flood was sweeping away everything that stood in its path, and who knew where it was taking them. Jessica could not find Bill or Clair or Bubba. But Sara and Russ were in the corner to the right of the door, fighting to hold up what might have been an unconscious Polly, and Nick was still hanging on to Maria, trying not to go under. It was only The Rock who seemed to hear Michael. He splashed toward them. Michael pointed to the pipe.

"We've got to bend this back," he said.

The Rock grabbed hold of the pipe with his thick hands and pulled with everything he had. The pipe creaked. Jessica screamed again. The blood must be squeezing back over her shattered bone. She knew it was broken; it felt like a meaty pancake beneath the hard metal. The Rock leaned his head close to her ear.

"Can you pull it out?" he shouted.

"No!"

"Can you try?"

"It hurts!"

"Mike," Nick called, one arm wrapped around Maria, the other hugging another steel pipe that had fallen from the ceiling. "Can you get her loose?"

Maria must have taken in a lungful of salt water; she was coughing horribly. Michael looked to The Rock, and to Sara and Russ struggling to save Polly. "I don't know!" he called back.

"Theodore?" Nick shouted.

Who in God's name is Theodore?

"I'm working on it!" The Rock replied.

"Tell them to go," Jessica said.

"Not yet," Michael said, fighting to get around The Rock in order to grab the pipe from above. "Not till you're free."

"Go!" Jessica screamed at Nick and the others. "Get out!"

"Jessie!" Sara called, flailing in the river flowing through the door. Russ had finally gotten a handle on Polly; he had her swung over his back. He looked as if he could get her to safety, but he glanced over at Jessica before he left.

"Just go!" Jessica yelled. "I'm almost free." Her brave lies amazed her. She had always thought brave people were not afraid. The water was now up to her waist.

Russ left with Polly and Sara. Nick got out with Maria a few seconds later. It was down to the three of them. *Haven's* alarm cried on. It was a death cry. The floor lurched to the side. Jessica could not bring herself to tell The Rock and Michael to also flee. She almost wished Polly's shotgun blast had caught her in the head. The thought of coming to the end choking beneath the sea was too much for her. She had to fight not to faint.

"We have to pull at the same time!" Michael said. He was to her right, his hands on the pipe above her head, while The Rock was directly in front of her, gripping the pipe inches below her trapped arm. The Rock had decided upon a strategy. He had his feet planted to either side of her waist; he would be able to use the strength in his legs to pull harder.

"Let's do it!" The Rock shouted back. "One! Two! Three!"

They pulled. The pipe creaked again, and she screamed again. It made no sense—freezing on the outside like this while she burned on the inside. The water level passed her breasts, heading for her mouth.

"You must pull, too!" Michael yelled at her, probably not knowing he was asking her to pull her bones apart.

"I can't," she wept. "It hurts."

He let go of the pipe and grabbed her chin. Through the pain, the smoke, and the haunting red light, she hardly recognized him. "Please, Jessie," he said.

He was begging her. She couldn't let him down. "I'll try."

Michael repositioned himself. They counted to three again. The Rock leaned back and howled as if he was on a football field. The pipe squealed. Jessica closed her eyes and prayed for it to end. She pulled.

My God.

The pain was not natural. It soared upward like a light beam fleeing the spectrum. Perhaps it momentarily yanked her soul out of the top of her head. She might have blacked out. She didn't feel her arm snap free. The next thing she knew, she was bobbing loose, with Michael holding on to her. She opened her eyes.

"We'll be all right," he said.

"Honestly?" she asked.

They had outwitted the pipe none too soon. Even as they turned to leave—holding on to the wall to keep from being sucked down—the water level passed the top of the door. That was a problem. Not only did she not know how to swim, she did not know how to hold her breath underwater. She was really a pathetic girl to have to rescue. She stopped.

"What is it?" Michael asked behind her. While freeing her, The Rock had accidentally taken in a mouthful the wrong way; he was caught in the throes of a coughing fit.

"I'm afraid," she said. Her one healthy arm was hardly able to hold on against the power of the current pouring through the submerged door. The ceiling was less than two feet from the tops of their heads and getting closer. The red light would go under next and then it would be pitch black. The Rock continued to choke. Michael spoke with amazing patience.

"There is nothing to be afraid of. This is a big ship. It will take a while to sink. Once out of here, we'll be halfway home. Go on, just hold your breath, let go, and duck down. It might even be fun."

"All right," she said. But she didn't move. Michael turned around to The Rock and patted him on the back as if he were a baby needing burping.

"You OK?" Michael asked.

The Rock nodded, although he was obviously far from OK. He had taken in a lot of water. She was killing them all. The Rock motioned for them to get going. Michael reached for her hand that was holding her in place.

"Michael," she said anxiously.

"I'll go with you," he said.

"No. You go first."

"Close your mouth, Jessie."

"But—"

"Close your mouth." He pulled her protesting fingers loose.

She did close her mouth, but forgot to duck down. It didn't make much difference. The current took hold of her and pulled her under. She was in a washing machine set to black and tumble. Water shot up her nose. *Nothing* could have been worse, not even burning at the stake. Panic consumed her reason. She was smothering! She had to take a breath! Not even the knowledge that she would drown if she did could stop her. She opened her mouth, tasting the salty cold, her bitter death. It was over. She couldn't bear it. She started to suck in.

Then she burst to the surface riding a foaming wave toward the huge fuel tank. "Eeh!" she screamed.

Michael had caught the same wave. He grabbed her uninjured arm, and the wall, preventing her from a nasty collision.

"The ladder's around this room," he said, pulling her to her feet. "We're going to be fine."

There were more red lights on in the hall. Fortunately they were not blinking, nor were they about to go under. The water level was about three feet. It was, however, a torrential three feet; it was hard to stand. Glancing back the way they had come, Jessica noticed an equal amount of water gushing from the room beyond the one that had held them prisoners. The blast must have torn through the wall and the hull. *Haven*'s crew was at a minimum. Those on duty must have raced to the top deck the instant the smoke bombs had gone off to help evacuate everyone; obviously, none of the crew had had a chance to return to the hold and seal off the flooding section. Michael was wrong. This ship was going under soon. The floor lurched again as they began to round the corner.

"I hate ocean cruises!" she complained.

"They're usually not this bad," Michael said philosophically.

Someone had forgotten to turn off the engines. The turbines were freezing up and were not happy about it. The grinding noise vibrated the insides of Jessica's skull. It was as if a whale had swallowed them whole and then been harpooned.

"Up you go!" Michael yelled over the noise when they got to the ladder. Every other deck on the ship had stairs except this one. The pain in her arm had not gone away with the pipe. The ladder looked as insurmountable as Mount Everest.

"I'll follow you!" she gasped, trying to hold up her right arm.

"You can do it with one hand," he insisted. "I'll be right behind you if you fall."

The rungs were smooth and wet. Her foot slipped before she had gotten halfway up and she banged her nose. It was a good thing Michael had his hand on her butt.

The next deck was dry. But their pace didn't improve. *Haven* had gone beyond lurching to shaking. Twice they stepped onto the companionway only to be thrown off. Both times Jessica landed on her broken arm. She could actually feel the bones grinding against each other. All around them, the lights went out, including the emergency lights. Tears poured over her face. She couldn't bear to move another inch. In the black, Michael pulled her off the floor.

"Think of the story we'll have to tell our grandchildren," he said, trying to give her courage. She clung to him. She couldn't talk. He dragged her back onto the stairs.

As Bubba might have said, the gods were finally kind. They escaped the darkness, and the lower decks. Stepping onto the top deck, tasting the fresh air, and watching her close friends preparing to launch a lifeboat, Jessica almost forgot her pain.

They almost forgot something else. They were all aboard and lowering the small boat off the davit and over the side when Michael suddenly leaped to his feet.

"The Rock!" he exclaimed. "He's still aboard!"

They were approximately twenty feet beneath the top deck, bobbing against the hull. The fog had cleared somewhat, and there was a hint of dawn in the misty night, but the bow of the ship was still invisible. Working the ropes together, Russ and Nick looked up and shook their heads.

"We can't pull this thing up with everybody on it," Russ said.

"And we're going to have to get clear soon or we'll get sucked under," Nick said.

Michael caught hold of one of the ropes, the side of his head plastered with blood. "I'll climb back up. I can't leave him."

"When did you last see him?" Bubba asked, sitting beside Clair.

"In that room," Michael said.

"You can't go back down there," Bubba said.

"I can do it," Michael said confidently. Jessica grabbed his leg with her good arm.

"No!" she yelled, feeling instantly selfish. The Rock had, after all, saved her life.

"I'll get him," Nick said. But Maria grabbed him.

"It's going to go under any second," she said.

"I'll get him," Russ said, gripping the rope and preparing to hoist himself up. It was Sara's turn to stop her man.

"The hell you will," she said.

"I'll save him," Bubba said gallantly. Everyone stared at him. He waited for a moment without budging an inch, then turned to Clair. "Aren't you going to stop me?"

"You're not that dumb," she replied between chattering teeth.

"Don't look at me," Kats told everybody.

"I'll go," Bill said, getting to his feet.

"If he got caught in that room, he's dead," Bubba protested.

"He's my friend," Bill said quietly.

"I'll go with you," Michael said, undoing Jessica's hold on his leg. But Bill stopped him.

"I can do this alone," Bill said.

"You might drown," Michael said, looking him straight in the eye.

"Maybe," he said. "Maybe not. Stay here, Mike, you can't do everything."

Michael held his eyes a moment longer, then nodded. Before Bill climbed up the rope, he leaned over and hugged Jessica.

"I'm sorry," he said in her ear. She kissed his cheek.

"I'm sorry, too," she said. "Come back to us quick."

Bill had strong arms. He was up the rope and over the rail in a few seconds. Nick and Russ continued to lower the lifeboat. They hit the water a moment later. The swells of an hour ago had vanished. Yet the ocean beside the ship was in turmoil, bubbling like a steaming pool above a geyser about to burst. Nick and Russ disengaged the ropes and shoved off.

"We have to wait for them!" Jessica protested. Michael sat down across from her and shook his head.

"We can't wait this close," he said.

The lifeboat came equipped with two oars. Nick and Russ took them out fifty yards off the stern. No other lifeboats were visible through the fog. They could hardly see the ship. Without her glasses, Jessica was particularly handicapped. Yet five minutes later even she saw enough to know when *Haven*'s tail suddenly dropped.

"No!" she cried.

It happened unbelievably fast. The nose rose up like a great white whale readying to launch toward the heavens. Only this whale had a grievous wound. As they watched in horror, it began to slide backward, bellowing loud blasts of spray as if it, too, felt the pain of drowning.

Then it was gone, and they were alone on the water.

Chapter Twenty-Five

They drifted aimlessly through the strange night. They could have been trapped in the center of an underground lagoon. The water was *flat*, and the fog seemed a thing risen from below, possessed of an evil purpose. It would unfold far enough to tempt their eye, and then suddenly close over, as if it were playing a game of hide-and-seek that only it could win. Yet the hint of dawn continued to gather strength in the mist. It was now no longer completely dark. Far away, Jessica could hear the faint sounds of people shouting to one another. She hoped most of the class had had a chance to get clear. It was Bubba who spoke first.

"Those were pretty powerful smoke bombs you had there," he said to Kats.

"My stuff didn't blow open that hole. Mine only made smoke," Kats said defensively, casting a worried eye on Michael.

"I suppose," Bubba said, frowning, perplexed at the cause of the explosion.

"Could either of them have escaped?" Michael asked Bubba.

"Don't ask me to quote odds."

Jessica was sick with grief, cold, and pain. The Rock and Bill both gone—she couldn't grasp it. She couldn't stop shivering. The lifeboat didn't come equipped with blankets. Her arm hung limply on top of her trembling knees. It was no longer straight. Looking at it made her nauseated.

"What the hell *did* you do?" Michael asked Kats.

"It was just a prank, like Bubba said," Kats replied uncertainly. "I just wanted to scare everybody off the ship."

"Why?" Michael demanded.

"I thought it would be funny," Kats said with a trace of bitterness.

Michael scowled, before turning to Jessica. "How's your arm, Jessie?" he asked.

"It's all right," she lied.

"It looks like it could be broken," he said.

"I'm all right. Don't worry."

"How many life jackets do we have?" he asked the group.

They had four. They were stored in small compartments spaced around the inside of the lifeboat. Clair, Maria, and Sara each put one on. Michael tried to get Jessica into a jacket but she just shook her head; she wasn't sticking her arm through any strap for anything. Michael then tried Polly; she ignored him altogether. She didn't appear completely recovered from whatever blow she had received when the bomb had gone off. Nick took the last life jacket. Apparently he couldn't swim either. Nick still had his big question.

"Since when can you walk?" he asked Maria.

"Since my back healed," she said.

"But you were paralyzed," Jessica said.

"I was, yes, but it was temporary. The fall didn't cut my spinal cord. It merely bruised it. There was a lot of swelling and pressure near where the vertebrae broke. The feeling did not begin to return to my legs until I got to the rehabilitation clinic." She put her hand on Nick's knee. "I'm sorry I couldn't tell you."

"Why couldn't you?" Nick asked, hurt.

She glanced at Michael. "I wanted what Mike did. That's why I called the meeting."

"How could you be sure the person who killed Alice was the same person who tampered with the float?" Michael asked.

"What were the chances Tabb High had two psychotics?" she asked.

"That's logical," Michael said.

"How did you know—how *do* you know someone killed Alice?" Sara asked.

"I knew her for only a short time," Maria said. "But I knew her well enough to know she wouldn't have taken her life."

"What was your plan?" Michael asked.

"I wouldn't actually call it a plan," Maria said. "I thought I'd have you all together in a room, and then I would stand and walk across the room. I would be watching all your faces, and in one of them, I knew, I would see the disappointment, maybe even the guilt. But only if I took you completely by surprise." She spoke to Nick. "You see why I kept silent. I was afraid the truth of my injury would leak out, and then I could never have my surprise, and catch the person who hurt me."

"I would have kept your secret," Nick said.

"I'm sorry," Maria repeated. "I felt I would only have the one chance. And I must apologize to you also, Jessie, for what I said the morning after the dance. I have no excuse—except I couldn't feel anything below my waist. The doctors hadn't explained to me yet that the paralysis might pass. I was scared. I just needed someone to blame, I guess."

"I understand," Jessica said. "But why didn't you write me later?"

It was hard for Maria—who had always been as proud as she was kind—to answer the question. "I was too ashamed," she said miserably.

"But now you've lost that one chance you wanted," Nick said.

Maria looked at Polly, who sat with her head bowed at the end of the raft, holding on to her wrist, silent and unmoving. "Maybe not," Maria said.

"But what about Clark?" Sara asked, confused. She wasn't alone in her confusion. *Haven* had sunk. It may have taken some of them with it. But they had unfinished business to complete. They looked to Michael, thinking he would take them back to the party to finish the investigation. But he went back further, to many years earlier.

"Polly," he said. "We need to talk some more."

She pulled her jacket tighter and did not look up. "I'm cold."

"I want to talk about your parents," Michael said.

Now he had her attention. Polly slouched deeper. "You have the same name," she said.

"That's right," Sara said. "Michael McCoy."

"Does that matter?" Michael asked.

"No," Polly said.

Jessica understood. Polly had idolized her father. She—and not Alice—had been the light of her father's life. Polly was trying to tell Michael to help her, not hurt her. Jessica doubted that Michael cared. It was clear who he thought was responsible for Alice's death.

"You were in the car with your parents when they crashed," he said. "Tell us what happened?"

Polly fingered her cut wrist nervously. "They died."

"Why did the car go off the road?" he insisted.

"I don't know."

"Did you start an argument in the car and distract your dad?"

How could he know that?

Michael was probably using simple deduction. He knew Polly and her parents had been on a deserted road. If a tire hadn't blown, then the father must somehow have become distracted. Michael had hit the bull's-eye. Polly's face crumpled.

"I just wanted another soda from the cooler. That's all I wanted."

"It wasn't your fault," Jessica said quickly.

"They burned," Polly said, distraught. "And I got away. I didn't even get scratched."

"Then why did the doctors keep you in the hospital?" Michael asked. Polly's head snapped up angrily.

"To hurt me! They taped me up with wires. They gave me shots. They tried to make me go to sleep and forget. But I didn't go to sleep. I remember everything that happened!"

Michael apparently had her where he wanted. He pounced hard. "Was Clark in the room with you and Alice?"

"Yes."

"There was a ladder in the room. There were Christmas lights hanging out the closet. Alice told me you wanted her to find some paper cups. Was she up on the ladder getting the cups from the closet?"

"Yes."

"Were the wires in her way?"

"Yes."

"What happened?" Michael asked.

"Clark pushed her! She fell! She landed on her nose!" Polly stopped, horrified with what she had just said, or maybe at the memory of what had happened. Tears filled her eyes. "It made this terrible cracking sound."

"So that's what happened." Sara gasped. "That bastard."

"Wait a second," Clair said. "Who shot Alice?"

"Clark did!" Polly said.

"What else did Clark do?" Michael asked in a mocking tone.

"He took Sara's money!"

"Huh?" Sara said.

"He took it. He hated you and Jessie. He blamed you for making me have the party. He tried to kill Jessie. He tampered with the float!"

"Did he chop down the tree?" Russ asked, interested.

"Yes! Then he went home and smothered Aunty!"

"That's gross," Sara said. "How did he get my money?"

"He can do anything! He's a sorcerer! He has the spirits of dead Indians do whatever he wants!"

"I've got to meet this guy," Bubba said.

"You've already met him," Michael said. He leaned toward Polly, obviously unimpressed with her outburst of information. "Let's go back to the bedroom, Polly. Before Clark shoved Alice off the ladder, was he arguing with her?"

"Yes."

"About what?"

"She wanted him to come to the party, but he came— No, she *didn't* want him to come, but he came anyway." She nodded to herself. "That's it."

"Did you want him to come?"

Polly regarded him suspiciously. "No."

"Polly?"

"Well, he was mine at first. She took him away from me, you know." She added softly, "I just wanted to see him again."

"Did Clark take the form I wanted your aunt to sign?"

Polly hesitated. "I told you he did."

"Did Clark set the bomb on the ship?"

"Yes."

Michael reached into his back pocket and removed a soggy piece of paper. He handed it to Polly. She would not look at it. A strange light had entered Michael's eyes. Jessica didn't like it. He was a hunter closing in on his prey.

"That's the form, Polly," he said. "I found it in your back-yard yesterday."

Polly winced, putting her hand to her head as if it hurt. "He must have dropped it."

Michael got on his knees, rocking the lifeboat, moving close to Polly. "No, Polly. You didn't give it to him."

"Yes, I did." She swallowed painfully. "I did."

"He didn't push Alice off the ladder."

"He must have!"

"Where is he, Polly? Where's Clark?"

"He's there!" she cried, pointing desperately into the fog. "He's there on the ship!"

Michael grabbed her by the shoulders and shook her. "The ship's gone. Clark's gone. He's been gone all along. He never came to the party. He never came to see you after the party. He didn't push Alice off the ladder. It was you, Polly, it was you who pushed her!"

He's been gone all along?

Jessica's brain did a double take. What Michael was saying was preposterous; it made no sense. It was insane . . . yet he was talking about insanity. Something inside Jessica suddenly clicked. Polly had been going on about all the evil things Clark had done, and yet not one person had seen him at the party. No one had seen him at the homecoming dance. And yet Clark *had* to exist. He had to be real. Michael had said Clark was the one who had hit him on the head.

He is saying there are two Clarks: the real one, and the one Polly talks to—an imaginary Clark.

He was saying Polly was insane.

"No," Polly moaned, collapsing in his arms. He would have nothing to do with her. He threw her back into the side of the lifeboat, almost throwing her overboard. A year of pain and bitterness twisted his face and voice.

"She was up on the ladder," Michael said. "You were arguing about Clark. She was trying to get the paper cups down for you. There were the Christmas lights, a bunch of wires. Her hands must have been tangled up in them. She wouldn't call Clark and ask him to come. You were mad. You shoved her. She wasn't able to get her hands out in front of her to brace her fall. She hit the floor with her nose, the hard wooden floor. She died, Polly, and you snapped. You couldn't take it. You had to make it look like she had killed herself. Or maybe you thought you would make it look like Clark had killed her since he was the one that had made you lose your temper. You went to the garage and got your father's shotgun and hid it around the side of the house. But you needed another gun. You knew where to get it. You knew Kats. You used to get gas at his station. You knew he always carried a gun. You went out to his car and stole the gun from his glove compartment. You turned up the music in the living room. You went back to the bedroom. You put on gloves and you stuck the gun in Alice's mouth. You wrapped Alice's fingers around the trigger. But you made a mistake there. You put the gun in her right hand. You should have put it in her left. It didn't stop you, though, that mistake. You got a couple of pillows or something and held them around the gun to smother the noise. Then you pulled the trigger, Polly. You blew a hole in your sister's head. But you weren't half done. You hid the pillows or whatever in the first upstairs bedroom. They probably had gunpowder stains on them. You locked the first bedroom door. Then you came downstairs and turned off the stereo. You wanted to be sure *we* heard the shotgun. Then you went around to the side of the house after checking the pool and fired it off. I noticed on the boat the shotgun had dried mud on it. You must have thrown it into the garden where no one could find it, and left it there. You're pretty clever. When you ran inside, you had the whole house fooled. Is this what happened? *Do you remember, Polly?*"

Polly had listened to Michael's speech with her face buried in the side of the lifeboat. But now she sat up and brushed her dark hair from her green eyes. The gesture seemed symbolic; it was as if her inner vision had just cleared. She looked at Michael.

"I remember," she said calmly. "You're right."

The admission took the wind out of Michael's sails. He was right—it was over. There was no mystery left to drive him on, Jessica saw, and also, perhaps, no reason to be bitter over what had befallen his Alice. He sat back on his ankles and touched his head much the way Polly had a minute earlier. It was still bleeding. He was in worse shape than any of them.

Jessica also knew that he was wrong.

"Why?" he asked.

"I have no excuse," Polly said, unzipping the front of her bulky navy-blue jacket. She had something hidden inside in a clear plastic bag. "I'm a bad girl."

You can't have a soda, you're a bad girl.

He had been so quick to condemn her a moment ago, but now Michael appeared no longer interested in confessions or revenge. He glanced at Jessica, and she believed he was remembering back to the day of the funeral when he had yelled at her in Alice's studio. He had been looking for someone to blame then. He had been through a lot since then. He was wiser. "It was the light bulb," he said to Polly. "The electrical shock. It was—a mistake."

He was referring to the doctors who had treated Polly years ago. Polly heard him, but wasn't listening. Too late Jessica realized what was in the plastic bag: red and black wires, a timer, a lump of orange dough, a detonator. Another bomb. Polly pulled it out and flipped a switch. "I was a mistake," she said.

"Oh, no," Bubba said, sitting up.

"I don't deserve to live," Polly said, her attention on Michael. "I *can't* live with what I remember." She turned the dial on the timer. "You have five minutes. Leave while you can."

"Polly," Jessica said. "Don't do this. You have your whole life in front of you."

Polly was not spaced. She was resolved. "I died in that room when Alice hit the floor. I've been killing time since." She coughed. "I am going to do this. Nothing will stop me. Leave."

"How about if *you* leave," Bubba suggested hopefully. Clair elbowed him in the side.

"Shut up and let Mike handle this."

"Polly," Michael said. "We don't have anywhere to go." He held out his hand. "Give me that thing."

Polly nodded to the fog, to the faraway voices. "There're

other kids out there. You can find them." She glanced down at the timer. "You have four and a half minutes."

There was something in her voice that made Michael take back his hand. He looked at Bubba, who in turn leaned forward and took a closer look at the mechanism Polly held. Michael's unspoken question was clear: *If I pull it out of her hand, will it go off?* Bubba considered a moment and then shook his head.

"Don't try it," he said.

"I don't want to spoil the party," Russ said. "But we should get the girls off the lifeboat now. That thing could blow any second."

"I'm not leaving without you!" Sara cried.

Russ frowned. "Who said I was staying?"

"Oh." Sara turned to Jessica. "You don't have a jacket?"

Jessica gestured vaguely toward her butt. "There's one under my seat."

"Russ is right, Mike," Nick said. "It could blow any second."

It was seldom Michael appeared lost. He quickly scanned the ocean. Then he slapped the side of his leg with his fist. "Dawn's coming and the fog's lifting, but we could be in the water an hour."

"I'd rather tread water that long than be spread all over it," Kats said.

"Bubba?" Michael asked.

"I can float till the Coast Guard gets here." Bubba stood and grabbed Clair. "Let's go for a swim."

"Mike?" Clair asked, tightening her life jacket. They were all waiting for him to tell them what to do. He threw his hands up.

"Go then, get away. Swim toward the voices. There have got to be other lifeboats out there."

The gang jumped overboard almost as one, sending the lifeboat rocking. Nick didn't even stay. Jessica understood. He had to take care of Maria. They disappeared within seconds in the fog. Michael sat back down across from Jessica. "Get out that jacket."

"There's no jacket," Jessica said.

He did a double take. "You're kidding?"

"No."

He glanced anxiously at Polly. She had the bomb hugged to her chest, her eyes half closed. "It doesn't matter," he said. "You'll be OK. Just swim after the others. You can catch up."

"You're not staying," she said.

"I'll be along in a few minutes."

He was a lousy liar. The minute she was gone, he was going to try to talk Polly into giving up the bomb. And if that failed, he would attempt to take it from her by force. He would risk his life in order to save Polly's. "You go after the others, and I'll be along in a few minutes," she said.

His anxiety increased. "This is no time for games. Get out of here, Jessie!"

Holding on to her right arm, she came and sat beside him. He was so beautiful; it made her heart ache to think she'd only been given one night to love him. "My arm's broken," she said.

"*What?* Why didn't you say something?" He whirled in the direction the others had disappeared. "All right, it doesn't matter. I'll go with you. We can still catch them. You can swim with a broken arm."

"No."

"Yes, you can! I'll help you." He stood and tried to take her hand. "Come on."

"I can't swim."

He dropped back down. The life went out of his eyes. "No?"

"No. I have to stay. *You* have to go."

He turned away from her and stared at Polly. A minute went by and he didn't say anything. Then he burst out crying. "I *can't* leave you," he whispered.

She pressed her left hand to the side of his cheek. He was shaking with fear, and she was suddenly calm. The fear was still there, but it was as if deep inside she understood that it was supposed to end this way. Her destiny had come to her. It was a relief in a way.

"She's my friend," she said. "We've been together since we were children. I can't leave her." She wiped at his tears. "It's all right. I love you, and I got to tell you that. I remember the night we went out. You told me you sometimes swim around the pier in the morning for exercise. You're hurt, but you're still a swimmer. You'll catch the others. Now go ahead, get out of here."

He bowed his head and covered his eyes. "You're going to die."

"Nothing's decided yet." She hugged him as best she could. "Please, Michael, before it's too late."

"I can't."

"Yes, you can. You can do it for me. For *us*. Please, go."

He shook his head. He wouldn't look at her. And she suddenly realized he wouldn't leave. Not Michael. Not for anything.

Except possibly to give her some kind of chance.

Polly was watching them. She caught Michael's eye, subtly shifting her hold on the bomb's wires. Polly didn't have to speak the threat aloud. It was there in the air.

If he didn't leave, she would blow the three of them up right then.

"Damn," Michael whispered. Beaten at last, he did turn to Jessica, looking at her for the longest time. And she remembered the first time she had seen his face, how she had admired the warmth and intelligence in his eyes. From that point on, the whole year, she had wondered what he thought of her.

"I love you," he said.

She smiled. "That is good."

He kissed her good-bye once. Then he was in the water and swimming away. The fog swallowed him up as it had the others. She turned her attention to Polly.

"Do you want to talk?" she asked.

Polly had seen everything. "You could have taken Sara's life jacket. Sara can swim like a fish."

"I could have."

"Why didn't you?"

"I wanted to talk to you alone."

Polly looked away. "Oh, Jessie."

"What happened to your wrist?"

"I cut it with a razor blade. I'm crazy."

"You seem sane enough now."

"I suppose I have Mike to thank for that."

"He doesn't know everything. How come you didn't defend yourself?"

"I used Clark for that. But Mike is right. Clark never came back to see me after Alice died. No one came." Polly shrugged. "Mike knows enough."

"You didn't smother your aunt. You'll never convince me of that."

"When I came home, after I chopped down the varsity tree, I thought I saw Clark leaving my house. And then I went inside. . . ." Polly drew in a weary breath. "She was hard to take care of. There were so many times I wished she was dead."

"That doesn't mean you smothered her. She was old. She just died."

Polly paused. "I suppose that's true."

"And you didn't take Sara's money."

"Yes, I did do that. I remember—she had just gotten it out of the bank. She had to run back inside for a receipt or something. She had it less than five minutes when I took it."

"Did you have a reason?"

"I was afraid she'd lose it. She had all cash." It was coming back to Polly in bursts of clarity. "Yeah, I took it out of her bag and put it in mine. And then, when I got home, I put it in our safe." Polly chuckled without mirth. "And then I forgot about it. I forget my name sometimes. I'm crazy."

"Stop saying that."

"It's true."

"You didn't kill Alice."

Polly looked away again, hugging the bomb closer. Jessica wondered how much time was left. She supposed she wouldn't feel anything when it went off. But that remark Kats had made about being spread all over the water . . . She couldn't go out this way—torn to tiny red pieces. She couldn't help thinking of her mother receiving the news. Not everything that was left of them would sink. The calm and silence of the surrounding sea remained, but her internal calm began to waver.

"Get out of here," Polly said.

"I have nowhere to go."

"Well, it's your own fault."

"I don't care how mad you were at Alice. I don't care if everything else Michael said about that night is true. You didn't push her off that ladder. You loved her."

In response Polly yanked open a compartment on the side of the lifeboat. There was a life jacket inside the compartment. She threw it to Jessica. "Get out of here."

"No."

Polly checked the timer, tension spreading across her face. "There's less than a minute left."

"I don't care." Jessica set the life jacket aside.

"What are you doing? Go!"

"Did you push Alice off the ladder?"

"I'm not bluffing!"

"Did you push Alice off the ladder?"

Polly blinked. "No. We were arguing about Clark. Her hands got all tied up in the Christmas lights like Mike said. And then, she slipped. She fell forward. She landed on her nose." Polly closed her eyes and grimaced. "I was always arguing with her about something." Then her eyes popped open. "Oh, Christ."

"That's it. It was an accident. It was an accident your father drove off the road. You didn't do anything wrong."

The immensity of the revelation had Polly stunned. Yet she would not easily abandon her madness. It had a hold on her stronger than the most potent drug on the most hopeless addict. "I sunk the ship," she said.

"The Rock probably got out some way. And Bill's an athlete. I bet he was able to swim clear. What's one old boat? You've got millions. Buy the captain a new one." Jessica paused. "You didn't do anything wrong."

Polly began to cry. "*You're* wrong. I did tamper with the float. I thought you would be elected homecoming queen. I blamed you for making me have the party."

"I forgive you."

"I tried to hurt you! I was jealous of you!"

"Why?"

"Because everybody loves you! I heard what Mike just told you! No one's ever told me that!"

Jessica picked up the life jacket and threw it overboard. Immediately it began to drift away from the lifeboat. "Does this tell you something? You're my friend, Polly."

Polly stared at her in utter amazement. "You'll die."

"Maybe we'll both die. But we don't have to."

"You would do this to Mike?"

"No." Jessica got to her knees and slowly crawled toward Polly, wincing with the pain in her arm, the fear in her heart. "If I die, *that* will be your fault. You're not crazy now. You know what you're doing." Jessica stopped and stuck out her left hand. "Give it to me, Polly."

Polly held her eye. "Alice told me you would end up with Mike."

"Let's not disappoint her. Give it to me."

"I don't even know how to turn this thing off!"

"That is not a problem," Jessica said, losing patience. "Give it to me!"

Polly's anxiety evaporated, being replaced by an indignant expression and tone that was almost comical given the circumstances. "Really, Jessie, you've got a broken arm. I can get rid of it myself." And with that Polly stood and—holding on to the detonator and the plastic explosives as one unit—threw the bomb as far as she could into the fog. Polly's choice of direction seemed commendable; she had thrown it opposite the direction toward which the gang had disappeared. Of course, it was always easy to end up going in circles in the fog.

The bomb exploded. A couple of seconds later they felt the spray. A couple of seconds after that they heard an irate shout. It was Bubba.

"Hey, girls! Lighten up!"

"Come back!" Polly yelled happily. "Come back! Everything's OK! I'm OK!" She plopped down beside Jessica and the two girls laughed and cried together as they used to in the good old days before time had made them into terrible teenagers. But there was one thing Jessica still didn't understand.

"Why did you chop down the varsity tree?" she asked.

"I used to hate seeing all those jocks and cheerleaders gather under the tree every afternoon at lunch. They're such a bunch of snobs." Polly smiled. "That's one thing I don't regret."

There was a reason the ocean had been so flat. *Haven* had sunk less than a quarter mile off Catalina. The swells that had rocked the ship earlier had been effectively blocked by the proximity of the island.

This was fortunate. Not a single passenger or crew member drowned as a result of the bomb. When the sun rose a half hour later and the fog cleared, all of Tabb's senior class—

including The Rock and Bill—could be found either drying out on the beach or floating about on a lifeboat offshore. Some called it a miracle. *Haven*'s captain, though, was quick to credit one passenger with keeping his head in the middle of the crisis and hurrying everyone into the lifeboats. He was Mr. Carl Barber, better known as Kats.

Very few people realized that Kats had started evacuating the ship *before* the bomb went off. From then on, he was considered something of a hero.

Epilogue

It was a different morning from the previous one. There was no fog. There were no bombs. There was nobody on the beach. Michael was glad the school year was finally over.

It was Sunday. He could hardly remember Saturday. He had spent the whole day—and night—in Catalina's small but efficient hospital. The diagnosis had not been too bad. Twenty-four stitches in the scalp and "a moderate concussion." Michael would have hated to have had a serious one. He still had a slight headache. They hadn't wanted to release him so soon. Then he had told them how poor he was.

The sun was an hour into the clear sky, dazzling on the gentle blue Catalina water; he was still on the island. Michael sincerely believed the morning shore was the best place in the world to sit while waiting for someone. He had recently adopted that belief. He stretched his bare feet through the cool grainy sand. Jessica was supposed to meet him soon.

He had a girlfriend. He had a sister. He had vindication.

A good day to be alive. I need a lot more of these.

Lieutenant Keller had called him and asked if he could interest him in pursuing a career as a detective. Keller had sounded properly chastised, but to his credit, he had also seemed happy to be proven wrong.

Michael had a visitor before Jessica arrived. The fellow seemingly came out of nowhere. He wore black leather as if he had been born with it on. His red hair shone in the morning light. He carried a brown paper sack in his left hand.

"Hi, Clark," Michael said, not getting up to greet him.

"Hello." Clark glanced at the white bandage wrapped around Michael's head. He apparently decided to remain standing. Michael felt no fear, not even when Clark removed a gun from his coat pocket. "This is yours," Clark said.

Michael accepted it. Clark had removed the bullets. "Thanks. Just what I need."

Clark gestured to Michael's bandage. "Did I do that?"

"Yeah."

Clark chuckled. "You should have known better than to come to my door in a hundred-degree heat with a sports coat on."

"You knew I had the gun?" Michael wondered what Clark had in the bag.

"Sure. But I didn't know what you were going to do with it."

In his own way, Clark was apologizing. Michael decided he had no reason to hold a grudge since he had been the one who had brought the gun. "I wasn't going to shoot you," he said.

"Should have told me before I clobbered you."

Michael studied Clark's face. He wanted to make sure he had the real one. "I chased you the whole year."

"I knew you followed me from the gas station that one day."

"You were on a fast bike. Why didn't you ditch me?"

"I wanted to know why you were following me," Clark said.

"Were you really stoned that night I met you at the game?"

"Probably. Why?"

"Honestly? You're a weird guy, Clark. I followed you because I thought you might have killed Alice."

"Why would I kill Alice?"

The proverbial question. It was good to finally understand there was no answer to it, that it had been an accident. "It doesn't matter. How come you're here?"

Clark's green cat eyes brightened. "I heard about what happened on the radio. I called the hospital to see how Polly was doing. They referred me to her doctor. He wants me to come meet with him and Polly. He told me she was starting therapy. He thought I could help her." Clark shifted his paper sack into his right hand. "What's the dude talking about?"

Polly must have been placed into the hands of an innovative psychiatrist. Michael approved. Confronting a flesh-

and-blood illusion couldn't be any worse than being struck by lightning.

Clark hadn't actually answered his question.

"I don't want to spoil the surprise," Michael said. "But you definitely should go. You'd find it fascinating."

Clark showed interest. "How's she looking these days?"

"Thin and sexy." Michael had to shake his head. "What did Alice ever see in you?"

Clark was not offended. When he spoke next, though, there was a strange authority in his voice. "She used to talk about you. She thought you were all right. I guess you thought the same about her. But your Alice was not mine. She was an artist. She could have been great. She had my passion." He wiped his nose with the back of his arm. "She couldn't stand me most of the time, but she saw something in me most people don't."

"What was she to you?"

Clark handed him the bag. Inside was an achingly beautiful painting of Alice walking alone on an ocean shore beside a wide desert, wearing a long white dress, a string of jewels around her neck. It was on the small side, twelve inches by twelve inches, and had yet to be framed, but the colors pulsed with life; they literally took Michael's breath away. He understood. Alice had meant a great deal to him.

"You cleared her name," Clark said.

"So you came all the way over here to give me this?"

Clark nodded. "You're right, I'm a weird guy."

He walked away before Michael could even thank him. Michael stood and threw the gun into the ocean. A few minutes later he heard Jessica call his name.

The doctors had put a pin in Jessica's arm. It was a nasty break, they said, but they were optimistic she would have a hundred percent recovery. With her cast in its sling and the wide black-rimmed glasses her mom had brought her from home on her nose, she was a fine sight. She even had her hair pinned up; she hadn't been able to wash it since—well, since she had taken a shower with Michael. But she didn't care how she looked because she knew Michael wouldn't care.

He was sitting on the beach near the water and looking at a paper or book or something. She was amazed at the pleasure it gave her simply to watch him and know that she was going to see him tomorrow, and the day after that. Although they had been in the same hospital, with rooms down the hall from each other, they had hardly spoken since the lifeboat. She raised her left arm and waved.

"Michael!"

Putting away his object of interest in a brown sack, he stood and walked toward her. She was relieved to see he had gotten over his slight limp. She met him halfway. It was cute—the awkwardness in his greeting. He gave her a light pat on the shoulder. She gave him a sloppy kiss on the lips.

"Hi," she said. "Love your hat."

He touched his bandage. "Bubba wanted to sign it."

"How do you feel?"

"Great. How about you?"

"Fantastic."

"You look good."

"Liar. But it's OK— I'm a liar too. My arm is actually killing me. And I just swallowed two of those yellow pills the doctor gave me."

"I hope they weren't Valium."

"Me too! My mom dropped me off, but how did you get out here?"

"Hitchhiked. It's easy to get a ride when you look like a war vet."

They began to walk down the beach, holding hands, Michael carrying his brown bag. *Haven* was underwater but not forgotten. They passed three plates, a chair, one soggy pillow, and a dozen beer cans before they had gone a hundred yards. A gentleman from the Coast Guard had said debris from the sunken ship would wash ashore for a long time.

"I suppose your trip to Hawaii is off?" Michael asked.

"Postponed," she corrected. "Sara and I are going later in the summer. In a way, I'm glad we have to wait."

"Why?"

"It will give you a chance to arrange your schedule so you can come with me." She added quickly, "Sara's bringing Russ."

"Oh, yeah, he's a free man now. How are those two getting along?"

"They're at each other's throats. They're in love. He's helping her with her PPB—Post Presidential Blues. She doesn't know what to do with herself now." She smiled. "You haven't said yes yet."

"What would your parents say?"

"Nothing. I won't tell them you're coming. What would your mom say?"

"That you only live once. To tell you the truth, Jessie, I don't know if I could afford it."

"Do you *really* want to come with me?"

"Absolutely."

"Then it'll be my treat. And don't say no. My parents gave me a bunch of cash for graduation that I've got to get rid of immediately, before I get materialistic."

"I don't know. That's a lot of money."

"Michael!"

"I'll come."

She laughed. "Had to twist your arm, didn't I? That's great. I'll have my cast off. You can teach me how to swim. But you're sure getting the time off won't be a problem?"

"I'm quitting my jobs at JPL and the 7-Eleven. I'm going to bum around all summer and write a book."

"Can you write?" she asked.

"I hope so."

"What's it going to be about?"

"This year."

"Hah! No one will believe it."

"I'll turn it into a novel," he said. "Where did you say you were going to go to school next fall?"

"I'm not. I've been thinking about what you said about my awesome voice. I'm starting a rock-and-roll band. What are you laughing at?"

"I'm sorry. It's such a coincidence. I told Clair Friday morning I was going to start a band. She told me to get you for a singer."

"*Clair* said that?"

"Yeah. Can I be in your band?"

"Can you play an instrument?" she asked.

"No."

"It doesn't matter. I'll teach you piano if you promise to put me in your book and make me real sweet."

"I wouldn't know how else to make you."

"Hang around with me for a while. You'd be amazed."

They had company—a half-dozen sea gulls hunting for lunch in the leftovers from *Haven*'s galley. And far off, perhaps half a mile up the beach, somebody was scouring the sand with a garbage bag in hand.

"Is that The Rock?" Jessica asked, squinting through her glasses.

"Yeah. I spoke to him earlier. He had a story to tell. Right after we swam out of that room, the door closed on him. He had to go out the hole in the hull. I don't know how he did it."

"He deserves his nickname. What about Bill?"

"He says he was still on the top deck when the ship suddenly went belly-up. He was thrown clear."

Jessica pointed down the beach. "What's The Rock doing?"

"He doesn't want a cameraman from a news station coming over to Catalina and seeing what drunks we have for a senior class. He's picking up all the beer cans. Did you know that yesterday when the tide was out people were able to spot the *Haven*'s antennas sticking from the water?"

"Really?"

Michael looked wistfully out to sea. "I'd like to rent scuba equipment and check her out."

"For something in particular?"

"Well, I'd like to find my yearbook for one thing."

She poked him. "Why?"

He blushed. "No particular reason."

"Liar!" she called him again, bouncing away to the water's edge. "I'll write it in the sand with my toes." She kicked off her shoe. "Michael Olson is the greatest *lover* Jessica Hart has ever—"

He stopped her. He was easy to embarrass. They continued their stroll, the sun warm on their faces. They found a yearbook a few minutes later. Talk about coincidences—it was Sara's, and it was sitting next to Bubba's sombrero. Jessica picked it out of the foam and shook it off. The paper Sara had glued over the inside cover had come loose. The handwriting beneath was smeared but still legible.

"Listen to this," Jessica said. "'My dearest Sara. My heart patters at the thought of us making love tonight above the deep ocean swells, our bodies locked in passion, the salty sweat on the burning flesh of our entangled limbs mingling like oil and wine, ready to burst into flaming ecstasy. My head swoons . . .'" She read all the way through, giggling like a schoolgirl by the time she came to the last line. "'Love you always, in so many different positions. Bubba!'"

"Now there's someone who knows how to write."

"Do you think he slept with her?"

"She's your friend."

"I doubt it. She says she did it with Russ when it's obvious she didn't even untie his shoes. Then again, Bubba is *your* friend. What do you think?"

Michael started to scratch his head, but ran into his bandage. "Ordinarily I would say yeah. But Bubba and Clair are getting married tonight in Las Vegas."

"What?"

"Bubba has a ticket waiting for me at Los Angeles airport. I'm flying out there this afternoon. I'm going to be his best man. You should come. Maria and Nick are getting married also."

"This is a joke."

"No. If Nick marries Maria, she is automatically allowed

to remain in the country. They're all eighteen. I think it's great. Nick said Maria wants you to be her bridesmaid."

"You're serious? Who's going to be Clair's bridesmaid?"

"It might be you. As you can imagine, this is all sort of short notice."

"But Clair and I hate each other."

"Pretty girls always hate other pretty girls. It's biological. That's what Bubba says. Maria's counting on you."

"Then I'll come. Clair must be pregnant again."

"Bubba says no."

"I don't believe it."

A smile lit up Michael's face. "I can tell you someone who's not pregnant anymore."

"Your mom! What did she have?"

"A seven-pound six-ounce girl."

Jessica dropped Sara's yearbook and hugged him.

"*Brother* Michael! Are they both OK?"

"Yeah, they're fine. Mom had the baby about the same time we were in the lifeboat."

"What did she name it? No—let me guess. Alice?"

"Mom wanted to, but I said no."

"Why?"

It might have been a delicate question. Michael let go of her hand and looked down at the paper sack he carried. "Life has to go on." He shrugged. "I'm still learning to let her go."

"I understand. I shouldn't have— What's in the bag?"

He showed her, and it brought tears to her eyes, and not just because it was so beautiful. "I had this dream," she said, staring at the painting in her hands. "It was the morning we were together at the hospital waiting to hear about Maria. There were four of us in a black tunnel. You, me, and these two little girls. One of the girls was Alice. When we got to the end of the tunnel, we were in a place like this. Who did this painting?"

"Clark."

Jessica made a face. "The *real* one. Not Polly's imaginary one."

"Yeah," Michael muttered, a faraway look in his eyes.

"What is it?"

He didn't seem to hear her question at first. "I had this dream," he said finally. "I had it many times this year. It started a couple of days after I met you. In it I'm standing on a bridge over a roaring river. There's a desert in front of me and a forest behind me. And there's this girl—I never see her face. But she tells me to go forward, that she will follow." He glanced at the sky. "I always used to wonder if it was Alice."

"Who do you think it is now?"

"My sister."

"How did you feel in your dream?" she asked.

"Happy. But also sad. I felt I was leaving paradise."

"I felt very happy in mine. I didn't want to wake up. I felt like I was being reborn."

Michael was impressed. "Maybe that's how it really was." Then he shook his head. "We'll never know."

She took his hand. "*I* know. I was supposed to meet you. Alice knew it. That's why she wanted you to meet me. She was wise." Jessica smiled. "She knew how far out I am."

Michael smiled, too, briefly. The sadness of leaving paradise, however, was still there. "If there is a design to our lives, and Alice was sensitive to it, then maybe I messed things up. The night of the party, she was upset she didn't get to introduce me to you. I could have let her, you know. She felt as if somehow a wrinkle had been put in the canvas." He took the painting back and put it in the bag. "I don't know why it bothered her then, or why it bothered me later."

"She didn't die because you avoided me. You don't think that, do you?"

He shrugged again. "I shouldn't have brought it up."

"Michael, you have a guilt complex. You've done more good for more people than anyone I know. I grew up with Alice, but I deserted her the night she died like everyone else. I went by the obvious facts. You went by your gut feeling, and you used your head. You saved her memory."

"I was late doing it."

"Not at all. The truth is coming out. It hurts Polly's image, but that's OK. Polly's got something out of all this. Her memory was saved. You gave it back to her."

Michael was doubtful. "I was hard on her."

"You had to be hard." Jessica paused. "She told me to thank you."

"You spoke to her?"

"Late last night, on the phone. She's in another hospital. This one's supposed to be the best." Her voice faltered. "We had a long talk."

"Was it painful?"

Jessica nodded. "But I'm glad we had the chance. Her doctor arranged the call. I understand her a lot better now. We're going to talk again soon." A sea gull ran across their path with a Ritz cracker in its mouth, fleeing from another almost identical bird. Jessica smiled at the sight, although it touched her with strange sadness. Birds of a feather, and best friends—they were sometimes each other's worst enemies. "I asked her why."

"Why?"

"Why Clark. Of all people to dream into her life, why him? Her response really hit me. She said she just needed someone to love her, but that anytime she ever did love someone—in real life—it always brought her pain. She couldn't help who she invented. Her lover had to be her tormentor. Clark was just someone who fit the bill."

"She said that?"

"Yes."

"It sounds to me like she's on the road to recovery. She has you to thank as well. You saved her life. It was you who got the final truth out of her."

Jessica took his hand and pulled him close. "OK, we're

both heroes. Now let's talk about happy things or I'll leave you and go out with Bill again."

"That isn't much of a threat."

She shoved him away. "Hey, he's as big a hero as they're making Kats into."

Michael groaned. "Don't remind me."

"Oh, you never answered my question. What—"

"Ann," he interrupted. "We chose it together."

"Why Ann?"

"Why not? It's a nice name. It's easy to spell."

"Ann was Alice's middle name."

He was amazed. "I didn't know that."

"Are you sure?"

"Positive."

She smiled. "What's in a name? Maybe everything, huh?"

"Let's wait and see who she grows into before we try to answer that one. But speaking of names . . ." He set the painting down and pulled a heavily wrinkled envelope out of his back pocket. "Last fall I built a telescope. I used to take it out to the desert a lot. Anyway, to make a long story short, I discovered a comet."

"You what?"

"A comet. They're these big balls of ice and dust that—"

"I know what a comet is. That's incredible. Are you going to win the Nobel Prize?"

"If Bubba uses his influence." He handed her the envelope.

It looked as if it had been underwater. Jessica realized it was the same envelope his mother had given him before the graduation ceremony. It *had* been underwater. "This is the confirmation of the sighting," he said.

"How come you haven't opened it?"

"I spoke to the observatory on Thursday. I already know what it says. Besides, I wanted you to open it. That's why I brought it to the all-night party."

She let go of his hand and got to work; it was a lot harder getting to a sealed letter with only five fingers. "When will it be visible?"

"It won't, not without a telescope. In fact, it's already passed its closest approach to the earth. It's heading back out into space. But if you want, I can take you out to the desert and show it to you in my telescope." He watched her fumbling. "Need help?"

"I can manage, thank you. Is it like Halley's comet? Will it come back?"

"Sure."

"When?"

"In a couple of thousand years."

"Then you had better take me to the desert soon." She finally got the paper out. There was an official seal on top, and words of congratulation and numerous astronomical notations below that made about as much sense to her as did the name given to the comet. She frowned. "I don't understand?"

"They always let the person who discovers a comet choose

its name." He stopped. "What's the matter? I thought you would be flattered."

"I am. It's just the way you put our names together—"

Michael snapped the letter from her hand. He quickly scanned it and his forehead wrinkled. "I told them to name it Jessica-Michael not Jessica-Olson."

She nodded. "Uh-huh. Are you sure you're not trying to tell me something?"

"No, honestly. It's a mistake."

"Right. Who's getting hitched tonight in Las Vegas? And why is it *I* have to be there?"

He turned red. "I didn't mean that."

"I believe you."

"Jessie!"

"The nerve of the guy. He washes my back in the shower once and he thinks I've got to marry him."

Michael started to protest again. Then he stopped and grinned. "I washed a lot more than your back, sister."

"I haven't forgotten." She kissed him shyly. "Maybe I should marry you."

REMEMBER ME

MOST PEOPLE WOULD probably call me a ghost. I am, after all, dead. But I don't think of myself that way. It wasn't so long ago that I was alive, you see. I was only eighteen. I had my whole life in front of me. Now I suppose you could say I have all of eternity before me. I'm not sure exactly what that means yet. I'm told everything's going to be fine. But I have to wonder what I would have done with my life, who I might have been. That's what saddens me most about dying—that I'll never know.

My name is Shari. They don't go in much for last names over here. I used to be Shari Cooper. I'd tell you what I look like, but since the living can see right through me now, it would be a waste of time. I'm the color of wind. I can dance on moonbeams and sometimes cause a star to twinkle. But when I was alive, I looked all right. Maybe better than all right.

I suppose there's no harm in telling what I *used* to look like.

I had dark blond hair, which I wore to my shoulders in layered waves. I also had bangs, which my mom said I wore too long because they were always getting in my eyes. My clear green eyes. My brother always said they were only brown, but they were green, definitely green. I can see them now. I can brush my bangs from my eyes and feel my immaterial hair slide between my invisible fingers. I can even laugh at myself and remember the smile that won "Best Smile" my junior year in high school. Teenage girls are always complaining about the way they look, but now that no one is looking at me, I see something else—I should never have complained.

It is a wonderful thing to be alive.

I hadn't planned on dying.

But that is the story I have to tell: how it happened, why it happened, why it shouldn't have happened, and why it was meant to be. I won't start at the beginning, however. That would take too long, even for someone like me who isn't getting any older. I'll start near the end, the night of the party. The night I died. I'll start with a dream.

It wasn't my dream. My brother Jimmy had it. I was the only one who called him Jimmy. I wonder if I would have called him Jim like everyone else if he would have said I had green eyes like everyone else. It doesn't matter. I loved Jimmy more than the sun. He was my big brother, nineteen going on twenty, almost two years older than me and ten times nicer. I used to fight with him all the time, but the funny thing is, he never fought with me. He was an angel, and I know what I'm talking about.

It was a warm, humid evening. I remember what day I was born, naturally, but I don't recall the date I died, not exactly. It was a Friday near the end of May. Summer was coming. Graduation and lying in the sand at the beach with my boyfriend were all I had on my mind. Let me make one point clear at the start—I was pretty superficial. Not that other people thought so. My friends and teachers all thought I was a sophisticated young lady. But I say it now, and I've discovered that once you're dead, the only opinion that matters is your own.

Anyway, Jimmy had this dream, and whenever Jimmy dreamed, he went for a walk. He was always sleepwalking, usually to the bathroom. He had diabetes. He had to take insulin shots, and he peed all the time. But he wasn't sickly looking or anything like that. In fact, I was the one who used to catch all the colds. Jimmy never got sick—ever. But, boy, did he have to watch what he ate. Once when I baked a batch of Christmas cookies, he gave in to temptation, and we spent Christmas Day at the hospital waiting for him to wake up. Sugar just killed him.

The evening I died, I was in my bedroom in front of my mirror, and Jimmy was in his room next door snoring peacefully on top of his bed. Suddenly the handle of my brush snapped off. I was forever breaking brushes. You'd think I had steel wool for hair rather than fine California surfer-girl silk. I used to take a lot of my frustrations out on my hair.

I was mildly stressed that evening as I was getting ready for Beth Palmone's birthday party. Beth was sort of a friend of mine, sort of an accidental associate, and the latest in a seemingly endless string of bitches who were trying to steal my boyfriend away. But she was the kind of girl I hated to hate because she was so nice. She was always smiling and complimenting me. I never really trusted people like that, but they could still make me feel guilty. Her nickname was Big Beth. My best friend, Joanne Foulton, had given it to her. Beth had big breasts.

The instant my brush broke, I cursed. My parents were extremely well-off, but it was the only brush I had, and my layered waves of dark blond hair were lumpy knots of dirty wool from the shower I'd just taken. I didn't want to disturb Jimmy, but I figured I could get in and borrow his brush without waking him. It was still early—about eight o'clock—but I knew he was zonked out from working all day. To my parent's dismay, Jimmy had decided to get a real job rather than go to college after graduating from high school. Although he enjoyed fiddling with computers, he'd never been academically inclined. He loved to work outdoors. He had gotten a job with the telephone company taking telephone poles *out* of the ground. He once told me that taking down a nice old telephone pole was almost as distressing as chopping down an old tree. He was kind of sensitive that way, but he liked the work.

After I left my room, I heard someone come in the front

door. I knew who it was without looking: Mrs. Mary Parish and her daughter Amanda. My parents had gone out for the night, but earlier that evening they had thrown a cocktail party for a big-wig real estate developer from back east who was thinking of joining forces with my dad to exploit Southern California's few remaining square feet of beachfront property. Mrs. Parish worked as a part-time housekeeper for my mom. She had called before I'd gone in for my shower to ask if everyone had left so she could get started cleaning up. She had also asked if Amanda could ride with me to Beth's party. I had answered yes to both these questions and told her I'd be upstairs getting dressed when they arrived and to just come in. Mrs. Parish had a key to the house.

I called to them from the upstairs hall—which overlooks a large portion of the downstairs—before stealing into Jimmy's room.

"I'll be down in a minute! Just make yourself at home—and get to work!"

I heard Mrs. Parish chuckle and caught a faint glimpse of her gray head as she entered the living room carrying a yellow bucket filled with cleaning supplies. I loved Mrs. Parish. She always seemed so happy, in spite of the hard life she'd had. Her husband had suddenly left her years earlier broke and unskilled.

I didn't see Amanda at first, nor did I hear her. I guess I thought she'd changed her mind and decided not to go to the party. I'm not sure I would have entered Jimmy's room and then let him slip past me in a semiconscious state if I'd known that his girlfriend was in the house.

Girlfriend and *boyfriend*—I use the words loosely.

Jimmy had been going with Amanda Parish for three months when I died. I was the one who introduced them to each other, at my eighteenth birthday party. They hadn't met before, largely because Jimmy had gone to a different high school. Amanda was another one of those friends who wasn't a real friend—just someone I sort of knew because of her mother. But I liked Amanda a lot better than I liked Beth. She was some kind of beauty. My best friend, Jo, once remarked—in a poetic mood—that Amanda had eyes as gray as a frosty overcast day and a smile as warm as early spring. That fit Amanda. She had a mystery about her, but it was always right there in front of you—in her grave but wonderful face. She also had this incredibly long dark hair. I think it was a fantasy of my brother's to bury his face in that hair and let everyone else in the world disappear except him and Amanda.

I have to admit that I was a bit jealous of her.

Amanda's presence at my birthday party had had me slightly off balance. Her birthday had been only the day before mine, and the whole evening I remember feeling as if I had to give her one of my presents or something. What I ended up giving her was my brother. I brought Jimmy over to meet her, and that was the last I saw of him that night. It was love at first sight. And that evening, and for the next few weeks, I thought Amanda loved him, too. They were inseparable. But then, for no obvious reason, Amanda started to put up a wall, and Jimmy started to get an ulcer. I've never been a big believer in moderation, but I honestly believe that the intensity of his feelings for her was unhealthy. He was obsessed.

But I'm digressing. After calling out to Mrs. Parish, I crept into Jimmy's room. Except for the green glow from his computer screen, which he was in the habit of leaving on, it was dark. Jimmy's got a weird physiology. When I started for his desk and his brush, he was lying dead to the world with a sheet twisted around his muscular torso. But only seconds later, as I picked up the brush, he was up and heading for the door. I knew he wasn't awake, or even half-awake. Sleepwalkers walk differently—kind of like zombies in horror films, only maybe a little faster. All he had on were his boxers, and they were kind of hanging. I smiled to myself seeing him go. We were upstairs, and there was a balcony he could theoretically flip over, but I wasn't worried about him hurting himself. I had discovered from years of observation that God watches over sleepwalkers better than he does drunks. Or upset teenage girls . . .

I shouldn't have said that. I didn't mean it.

Then I thought of Amanda, possibly downstairs with her mom, and how awful Jimmy would feel if he suddenly woke up scratching himself in the hall in plain sight of her. Taking the brush, I ran after him.

It was good that I did. He was fumbling with the knob on the bathroom door when I caught him. At first I wasn't absolutely sure there was anyone in the bathroom, but the light was on and it hadn't been a few minutes earlier. Jimmy turned and stared at me with a pleasant but vaguely confused expression. He looked like a puppy who had just scarfed down a bowl of marijuana-laced dog food.

"Jimmy," I whispered, afraid to raise my voice. I could hear Mrs. Parish whistling downstairs and was becoming more convinced with each passing second that Amanda was indeed inside the bathroom. Jimmy smiled at me serenely.

"Blow," he said.

"Shh," I said, taking hold of his hand and leading him away from the door. He followed obediently, and after hitching up his boxer shorts an inch or two, I steered him in the direction of my parents' bedroom and said, "Use that bathroom. This one's no good."

I didn't wake him for a couple of reasons. First, he's real hard to wake up when he's sleepwalking, which is strange because otherwise he's a very light sleeper. But you practically have to slap him when he's out for a stroll. Second, I was afraid he might have a heart attack if he suddenly came to and realized how close he'd come to making a fool of himself in front of his princess.

After he disappeared inside my parents' room, I returned to the bathroom in the hall and knocked lightly on the door. "Amanda, is that you?" I called softly.

There was a pause. "Yeah. I'll be right out—I'm getting some kitchen cleanser."

Since she wasn't going to the bathroom, I thought it would be OK to try the knob. Amanda looked up in surprise when I peeked in. She was by the sink, in front of the medicine cabinet and a small wall refrigerator, and she had one of Jimmy's syringes and a vial of insulin in her hand. Jimmy's insulin had to be kept cool, and he'd installed the tiny icebox himself so he wouldn't have to keep his medication in the kitchen fridge downstairs where everybody could see it. He wasn't proud of his illness. Amanda knew Jimmy was a diabetic, but she didn't know he needed daily shots of medication. Jimmy didn't want Amanda to know. Well, the cat was out of the bag now. The best I could do, I thought, was to make a joke of the matter.

"Amanda," I said in a shocked tone. "How could you do this to your mother and me?"

She glanced down at the stuff, blood in her cheeks. "Mom told me to look for some Ajax, and I—"

"Ajax," I said in disbelief. "I wasn't born yesterday. Those are drugs you're holding. Drugs!" I put my hand to my mouth. *"Oh, God."*

I was a hell of an actress. Amanda just didn't know where I was coming from. She quickly put down the needle. "I didn't mean to—" she began.

I laughed and stepped into the bathroom. "I know you weren't snooping, Amanda. Don't worry. So you found the family stash. What the hell, we'll cut you in for a piece of the action if you keep your mouth shut. What do you say? Deal?"

Amanda peered at me with her wide gray eyes, and for a moment I thought of Jimmy's expression a moment earlier—the innocence in both. "Shari?"

I took the syringe and vial of insulin from her hand and spoke seriously. "You know how Jimmy's always watching his diet? Well, this is just another part of his condition he doesn't like to talk about, that's all." I opened the medicine cabinet and fridge and put the stuff away. "It's no big deal, is what I'm saying."

Amanda stared at me a moment; I wasn't looking directly at her, but I could see her reflection in the medicine cabinet mirror. What is it about a mirror that makes the beautiful more beautiful and the pretty but not exceptional less exceptional? I don't understand it—a camera can do the same thing. Amanda looked so beautiful at that moment that I could imagine all the pain she would cause my poor brother if her wall got any higher. And I think I resented her for it a tiny bit. She brushed her dark hair back from her pink cheek.

"I won't say anything to him," she said.

"It's no big deal," I said.

"You're right." She nodded to the cupboard under the sink, "I suppose I should have been looking down there."

We both bent over at the same instant and almost bumped heads. Then I remembered that Jimmy was still wandering around. Excusing myself, I left Amanda to find the Ajax and went searching for him. When I ran into him, coming out of my parents' bedroom, he was wide awake.

"Have I been sleepwalking?" he asked.

"No. Don't you remember? You went to sleep standing here." I pushed him back into my parents' bedroom and closed the door. "Amanda's here."

He immediately tensed. "Downstairs?"

"No, down the hall, in the bathroom. You almost peed on her."

Sometimes my sense of humor could be cruel. Jimmy sucked in a breath, and his blue eyes got real big. My brother's pretty cute, if I do say so myself. It runs in the family. He's the solid type, with a hint of refinement. One could imagine him herding cattle all day from the saddle, playing a little ball in the evening with the boys, taking his lady to an elegant French restaurant at night where he would select the proper wine to go with dinner. Except he would mispronounce the name of the wine. That was Jimmy. He was totally cool, but he wasn't perfect.

"Did she see me?" he asked.

"No. I saved you. You were about to walk in on her when I steered you this way."

"You're sure she didn't see me?"

"I'm sure."

He relaxed. Jimmy always believed everything I told him,

even though he knew what an excellent liar I was. I guess he figured if I ever did lie to him, it would be for his own good. He thought I was a lot smarter than he was, which I thought was stupid of him.

"What's she doing here?" he asked with a note of hope in his voice. I couldn't very well lie and tell him Amanda had come over to see him. When I had been in the bathroom with her, she hadn't even asked if he was home.

"Her mom brought her over. She's downstairs cleaning up the mess from the cocktail party. Amanda wants to ride to Beth's party with me."

"Why's she going? Is she a friend of Beth's?"

"Not really. I don't know why she wants to go." I had to wonder if Amanda had had time to buy a present, if she even had the money to buy one. She and her mom didn't exactly enjoy material prosperity.

"Is she still in the bathroom?" he asked.

"I don't know. You're not going to talk to her, are you?"

"Why not?"

"You're not dressed."

He smiled. "I'll put my pants on first." He started to open the door. "I think she's gone back downstairs."

"Wait. Jimmy?" I grabbed his arm. He stopped and looked at me. "When was the last time you called her?"

"Monday." He added, "Four days ago."

"That was the last time you talked to her. You called her

yesterday. You called her the day before that, too. Maybe you should give it a rest."

"Why? I just want to say hi, that's all. I'm not being fanatical or anything."

"Of course you're not," I lied. "But sometimes it's better, you know, to play a little hard to get. It makes you more desirable."

He waved his hand. "I'm not into all those games." He tried to step by. I stopped him again.

"I told her you were asleep," I said.

"She asked about me?"

"Yeah, sure." I wasn't even sure why I was so uptight about his not talking to her. I guess I couldn't stand to see Jimmy placed in a potentially humiliating situation. But perhaps I was just jealous. "We have to leave for the party in a couple of minutes," I added.

He began to reconsider. "Well, I guess I shouldn't bother her." He shook his head. "I wish her mom would tell her when I've called."

"Jimmy—"

"No," he said quickly. "Amanda really doesn't get the messages. She told me so herself."

I couldn't imagine that being true, but I kept my mouth shut. "I'll drop sly hints to Amanda tonight that she should call you tomorrow."

He nodded at the brush in my hand. "Isn't that mine?"

"Yeah, mine broke."

"You have a dozen brushes."

"They're all broken." I gestured to our mom's makeup table behind us. She never went out of the house without fixing herself up for an hour. Some might have called her a snob. I had called her that myself a few times, but never when my father was around. We didn't have a lot in common. "And mom wouldn't let me use one of hers."

"What did Amanda ask about me?"

"If you were getting enough rest." I patted him on the shoulder. "Go to bed."

I tucked Jimmy back in bed so that he could be fresh when his alarm went off at three in the morning and finished getting ready. When I went back downstairs, I found Amanda and her mom in the kitchen discussing whether a half-eaten chocolate cake should be divided into pieces before squeezing it into the jammed refrigerator.

"Why don't we just throw it in the garbage?" I suggested.

Mrs. Parish looked unhappy about the idea, which was interesting only because she usually looked so happy. Maybe I should clarify that. She wasn't one of those annoying people who go around with perpetual smiles on their faces. Her joy was quiet, an internal matter. But if I may be so bold, it often seemed that it shone a bit brighter whenever the two of us were alone together. I could talk to her for hours, about everything—even boys. And she'd just listen, without giving me advice, and she always made me feel better.

Jo, "Little Jo," had given her a nickname, too—"Mother Mary." I called Mrs. Parish that all the time. She was a devout Catholic. She went to mass several times a week and never retired for the night without saying her rosary. That was the one area where we didn't connect. I was never religious. Oh, I always liked Jesus, and I even went to church now and then. But I used to have more important things to think about than God. Like whether I should try to have sex with my boyfriend before I graduated from high school or whether I should wait until the Fourth of July and the fireworks. I wanted it to be a special moment. I wanted my whole life to be special. But I just hardly ever thought about God.

I'm repeating myself. I must be getting emotional. I'll try to watch that. Not everything I have to tell is very pleasant.

Back to that blasted cake. Mrs. Parish felt it would be a waste to throw it out. "Shari, don't you think that your mom might want some tomorrow?" she asked.

"If it's here, she'll eat it," I said. "And then she'll just complain about ruining her diet." I ran my finger around the edge and tasted the icing. I had already tasted about half a pound of it earlier in the day. "Oh, wow. Try this, Amanda. It's disgusting."

Amanda looked doubtful. "I'm not a big cake person."

Mrs. Parish suddenly changed her mind about saving it. "Maybe we should throw it out."

"You don't like cake?" I asked Amanda. "That's impossible—

everybody likes cake. You can't come to Beth's party with me unless you eat cake. Here, just try it. This little piece."

I could be so pushy. Amanda had a little piece, along with her mother, and I had a slightly larger little piece. Then I decided that maybe there was room for it in the refrigerator after all. I didn't care if my mother got fat or not.

Mrs. Parish sent Amanda to check to see if our vacuum cleaner needed a new bag. For a moment the two of us were alone, which was nice. I sat at the table and told her about the party we were going to, while she stacked dishes in the dishwasher.

"It's for Big Beth," I began. "I've already told you how she's been flirting with Dan at school. It really pisses me off. I'll see the two of them together on the other side of the courtyard, and then when I walk over to them, she greets me like she's really glad to see me, like nothing's been going on between them."

"How do you know something *is* going on?" Mrs. Parish asked.

"Because Dan looks so uncomfortable. Yeah, I know, why get mad at her and not at him?" I chuckled. "It's simple—he might leave me and run off with her!"

I was forever making jokes about things that really mattered to me. I doubted that even Mrs. Parish understood that about me. I may not have been obsessed with Daniel the way Jimmy was with Amanda, but I couldn't stand the thought of losing him. Actually, I honestly believed he cared for me. But I continued to worry. I was never really cool, not inside, not about love.

"Is Dan taking you and Amanda to the party?" Mrs. Parish asked, carefully bending over and filling the dishwasher with detergent. She had an arthritic spine. Often, if we were alone in the house, she would let me help her sweep the floor or scrub the bathrooms. But never if anyone else was present. I'd noticed she particularly disliked Amanda knowing she needed help.

"Yeah. We're picking Jo up, too. He should be here in a sec." I paused. "Mary, what do you think of Dan?"

She brightened. "He's very dashing."

I had to smile. *Dashing.* Great word. "He is cute, yeah." I took another forkful of cake, although I needed it about as much as I needed another two pounds on my hips. "What I mean, though, is do you like him? As a person?"

She wiped her hands on her apron and scratched her gray head. Unlike her daughter's, her hair was not one of her finer features. It was terribly thin. Her scalp showed a little, particularly on the top, whenever she bent over, and she was only fifty. To be quite frank, she wasn't what anyone would have called a handsome lady. She did, however, have a gentle, lovely smile.

"He seems nice enough," she said hesitantly.

"Go on?"

"How does he treat you?"

"Fine. But—"

"Yes?"

"You were going to say something first?"

"It was nothing."

"Tell me."

She hesitated again. "He's always talking about things."

"Things?" I asked, even though I knew what she meant. Daniel liked *things*: hot cars, social events, pretty people—the usual. Since the universe was composed primarily of things, I had never seen it as a fault. Yet Daniel could be hard to talk to because he seldom showed any deep feelings or concern for anything but "things."

Mrs. Parish shrugged, squeezing a couple more glasses into the dishwasher. "Does he ever discuss the two of you?"

"Yeah, sure," I lied.

"You communicate well when you're alone together then. That's good. That was the only thing I was concerned about." She closed the door on the washer and turned it on. The water churned. So did my stomach. I pushed away the cake. I'd heard a car pulling up outside. It must be Daniel, I thought. I excused myself and hurried to the front door.

I found him outside opening our garage. Graduation was a couple of weeks off, but my parents had already bought me my present. I can't say what it was without giving the impression I was spoiled rotten.

It cost a fortune. It was fast. It was foreign.

It was a Ferrari.

Oh, my car. I loved it. I loved how red it was. I loved everything about it. Daniel loved it, too, apparently. He hardly noticed my shining presence when I came out to greet him. He fell in love with my car at first sight.

He had taken longer to fall in love with me.

I had officially met Daniel after a high school play in which he played the lead. I have an incredible memory for facts, but I cannot remember what the play was about. That says a lot. He blew me away, and he wasn't even that great. He had forgotten several lines, and he'd been totally miscast. None of that mattered, though. He just had to strut around up there under the lights, and I felt I just *had* to go backstage afterward and commend him on his artistry. Of course, Jo had to drag me kicking and screaming to his dressing room. I was sort of shy, sometimes.

Since we went to the same school and were in the same grade, I naturally knew *of* him before we met after the play. I would like to record for posterity that the reverse was also true, that he had noted with approval my existence the four years we had spent together at Hazzard High. But the first thing he asked when Jo introduced us was if I was new to the area. What a liar. He didn't want me to think I was too cute.

But he asked me out, and that was the bottom line. He asked me out right there in front of his dressing room with Jo standing two feet away with her mouth uncharacteristically closed. Later, it seemed so amazing to me that I wondered if Jo hadn't set it all up beforehand. But she swore to the day I died that it wasn't so. . . .

I must talk about his dashing body. It was smooth and hard. It had great lines, like a great race car. Except Daniel wasn't red. He was tan. He hugged the road when he moved. He had legs, he had hips. He had independent rear suspension. We used to make out all the time in his bedroom with the music on real loud. And then, one warm and lustful evening, two weeks before Beth's birthday party, we took off our clothes and *almost* had sex.

I loved to think about sex. I could fantasize six hours a day and not get tired, even if I was repeating the same fantasy with only slight variations. I was a master of slight variations. But one can think too much. When we got naked together in bed, things did not go well. Daniel couldn't . . . Oh, this will sound crude if I say it, so I'll say instead that I shouldn't have overdone it comparing him to my Ferrari. Yet, in a sense, he was as *fast* as the car. I left the room a virgin.

He was *so* embarrassed. I didn't understand why. I was going to give him another fifty chances. I wasn't going to tell anyone. I didn't tell anyone, not really. Maybe Jo, sort of. But she couldn't have told anyone else and had enough details to sound like she knew what she was talking about. Unless she had added details of her own.

Daniel and I had other things in common, other *things* we liked to do together. We both enjoyed going to movies, to the beach, out to eat. That may not sound like a lot, but when you're in high school, it often seems like that's all there is.

Anyway, when I went outside to welcome Daniel, he was in ecstasy. He had turned on the light in the garage and was pacing around the car and kicking the tires like guys are fond of doing when they see a hot set of wheels. I didn't mind. He had on white pants and a rust-colored leather coat that went perfectly with his head of thick brown hair.

"Did you have it on the freeway today, Shar?" he asked.

"Yeah, but I didn't push it. They told me to break it in slowly over the first thousand miles."

"This baby could go up to one forty before it would begin to sweat." He popped open the driver's door and studied the speedometer. "Do you know how many grand this set your dad back?"

"He wouldn't tell me. Do you know how many?"

Daniel shook his head. "Let's just say he could have bought you a house in the neighborhood for the same money." He went to climb inside. "Are you ready to go? Can I drive?"

"We can't take it. Amanda Parish is here, and she's riding with us. And we have to pick up Jo."

Although Joanne had introduced the two of us, Daniel didn't like her. It would be hard to pinpoint specifically what she did that bothered him, other than that he was a boy and she had a tendency to make the male species as a whole feel inferior.

I had no idea what he thought of Amanda.

He showed a trace of annoyance. "You didn't tell me."

"I didn't know until a little while ago." The Ferrari had no backseat. "We can go for a drive in it tomorrow."

He shut the door, sort of hard, and I jumped slightly. To be entirely truthful, I never felt entirely comfortable around Daniel. He strode toward me and gave me a hug. His embraces were always unexpected.

"Hi," he said.

"Hi."

He kissed me. He wasn't an expert at lovemaking, but he had a warm mouth. He also had strong arms. As they went around me, I could feel myself relaxing and tensing at the same time. I didn't know if other girls felt the same way when their boyfriends embraced them. But when his kisses grew hard and deep, I didn't mind.

"Oh, sorry," we heard behind us a minute or so later. Daniel let go, and I whirled. There was Amanda, as pretty and as unprepared as when I walked in on her in the upstairs bathroom. Her big eyes looking down, she turned to leave.

"No, it's OK," I said, taking a step toward her, only mildly embarrassed. "We should be leaving. Stay here. I'll go say goodbye to Jimmy and Mother Mary. Be back in a moment."

Amanda stopped. "What did you say?"

I suddenly realized I'd brought up Jimmy. "If Jimmy's awake," I said quickly, the remark sounding thin in my own ears. "He was asleep a few minutes ago."

Amanda stared at me a moment. Then she muttered, "Say hello for me."

"Sure."

Jimmy was awake when I peeked in his door. He motioned me to come and sit on his bed. His computer screen was still on, and, as always, I found the faint green light hard on my eyes.

"Why don't you just turn it off?" I asked, gesturing to the CRT.

He smiled faintly, his muscular arms folded across his smooth chest, his eyes staring off into space. He was in a different mood now—more contemplative. "I might wake in the night inspired."

"The way you get around in your sleep, you wouldn't have to wake up."

"I was dreaming about you before I bumped into you in the hall."

"Oh? Tell me about it?"

He had just opened the window above his bed, and a cool breeze touched us both. Later, I thought it might have been the breath of the Grim Reaper. It was a warm night. Jimmy closed his eyes and spoke softly.

"We were in a strange place. It was like a world inside a flower. I know that sounds weird, but I don't know how else to describe it. Everything was glowing. We were in a wide-open space, like a field. And you were dressed exactly as you are now, in those jeans and that shirt. You had a balloon in your hand that you were trying to blow up. No, you *had* blown it up partway, and you wanted me to blow it up the rest of the way. You tried to give it to me. You had tied a string to it. But I didn't catch the string right or something, and it got away. We watched it float way up in the sky. Then you began to cry."

Far away, toward the front of the house, I heard Daniel start his car. He wasn't a good one to keep waiting. But suddenly, I didn't feel like going to Beth's party. I just wanted to sit and talk with my brother until he fell asleep. I pulled his sheet up over his chest. The breeze through the open window was getting chilly now.

"Why was I crying?" I asked.

"Because the balloon got away."

"What color was it?"

"I don't know. Brown, I think."

"Everything's brown to you! What was so special about the balloon?"

He opened his eyes and smiled at me. For a moment I thought he was going to ask me about Amanda again. I felt grateful when he didn't. "I don't know." He paused. "Will you be out late?"

"Not too late."

"Good."

"What's the matter?"

He thought a moment. "Nothing. I'm just tired." He squeezed my hand. "Have fun."

I leaned over and kissed him on the forehead. "Sweet dreams, brother."

He closed his eyes, and it seemed to me he was trying to picture my balloon a little more clearly so maybe he could answer my question about it a little better. But all he said was, "Take care, sister."

People. When you say goodbye to them for the last time, you'd expect it to be special, never mind that there's never any way to know for sure you're never going to see them again. In that respect, I would have to say I am thankful, at least, that my brother and I got to talk one last time before I left for the party. But when I got downstairs, Daniel was blowing his horn, and Mrs. Parish was vacuuming the dining room. I barely had a chance to poke my head in on her as I flew out the door.

"We're going," I called.

Mrs. Parish leaned over as if she was in pain and turned off the vacuum. "Did you bring a sweater?" she asked, taking a breath.

"Nah! I've got my boyfriend to keep me warm!"

She laughed at my nerve. "Take care, Shari."

"I will," I promised.

But I lied. And those little white lies, they catch up with you eventually. Or maybe they just get away from you, like a balloon in the wind.

HERE'S A PEEK AT THE FIRST BOOK
IN THE BESTSELLING SERIES BY

Christopher Pike

THIRST
NO. 1

I am a vampire, and that is the truth. But the modern meaning of the word *vampire,* the stories that have been told about creatures such as I, are not precisely true. I do not turn to ash in the sun, nor do I cringe when I see a crucifix. I wear a tiny gold cross now around my neck, but only because I like it. I cannot command a pack of wolves to attack or fly through the air. Nor can I make another of my kind simply by having him drink my blood. Wolves do like me, though, as do most predators, and I can jump so high that one might imagine I can fly. As to blood—ah, blood, the whole subject fascinates me. I do like that as well, warm and dripping, when I am thirsty. And I am often thirsty.

My name, at present, is Alisa Perne—just two words, something to last for a couple of decades. I am no more attached to them than to the sound of the wind. My hair is blond and silklike, my eyes like sapphires that have stared long at a volcanic fissure. My stature is slight by modern standards, five two in sandals, but my arms and legs are muscled, although not unattractively so. Before I speak I appear to be only eighteen years of age, but something in my voice—the coolness of my expressions, the echo of endless experience—makes people think I am much older. But even I seldom think about when I was born, long before the pyramids were erected beneath the pale moon. I was there, in that desert in those days, even though I am not originally from that part of the world.

Do I need blood to survive? Am I immortal? After all this time, I still don't know. I drink blood because I crave it. But I can eat normal food as well, and digest it. I need food as much as any other man or woman. I am a living, breathing creature. My heart beats—I can hear it now, like thunder in my ears. My hearing is very sensitive, as is my sight. I can hear a dry leaf break off a branch a mile away, and I can clearly see the craters on the moon without a telescope. Both senses have grown more acute as I get older.

My immune system is impregnable, my regenerative system miraculous, if you believe in miracles—which I don't. I can be stabbed in the arm with a knife and heal within minutes without scarring. But if I were to be stabbed in the heart, say with the currently fashionable wooden stake, then maybe I would die. It is difficult for even a vampire's flesh to heal around an implanted blade. But it is not something I have experimented with.

But who would stab me? Who would get the chance? I have the strength of five men, the reflexes of the mother of all cats. There is not a system of physical attack and defense of which I am not a master. A dozen black belts could corner me in a dark alley, and I could make a dress fit for a vampire out of the sashes that hold their fighting jackets closed. And I do love to fight, it is true, almost as much as I love to kill. Yet I kill less and less as the years go by because the need is not there, and the ramifications of murder in modern society are complex and a waste of my precious but endless time. Some loves have to be given up, others have to be forgotten. Strange as it may sound, if you think of me as a monster, but I can love most passionately. I do not think of myself as evil.

Why am I talking about all this? Who am I talking to? I send out these words, these thoughts, simply because it is time. Time for what, I do not know, and it does not matter because it is what I want and that is always reason enough for me. My wants—how few they are, and yet how deep they burn. I will not tell you, at present, who I am talking to.

The moment is pregnant with mystery, even for me. I stand outside the door of Detective Michael Riley's office. The hour is late; he is in his private office in the back, the light down low—I know this without seeing. The good Mr. Riley called me three hours ago to tell me I had to come to his office to have a little talk about some things I might find of interest. There was a note of threat in his voice, and more. I can sense emotions, although I cannot read minds. I am curious as I stand in this cramped and stale hallway. I am also annoyed, and that doesn't bode well for Mr. Riley. I knock lightly on the door to his outer office and open it before he can respond.

"Hello," I say. I do not sound dangerous—I am, after all, supposed to be a teenager. I stand beside the secretary's unhappy desk, imagining that her last few paychecks have been promised to her as "practically in the mail." Mr. Riley is at his desk, inside his office, and stands as he notices me. He has on a rumpled brown sport coat, and in a glance I see the weighty bulge of a revolver beneath his left breast. Mr. Riley thinks I am dangerous, I note, and my curiosity goes up a notch. But I'm not afraid he knows what I really am, or he would not have chosen to meet with me at all, even in broad daylight.

"Alisa Perne?" he says. His tone is uneasy.

"Yes."

He gestures from twenty feet away. "Please come in and have a seat."

I enter his office but do not take the offered chair in front of his desk, but rather, one against the right wall. I want a straight line to him if he tries to pull a gun on me. If he does try, he will die, and maybe painfully.

He looks at me, trying to size me up, and it is difficult for him because I just sit here. He, however, is a montage of many impressions. His coat is not only wrinkled but stained—greasy burgers eaten hastily. I note it all. His eyes are red rimmed, from a drug as much as fatigue. I hypothesize his poison to be speed—medicine to nourish long hours beating the pavement. After me? Surely. There is also a glint of satisfaction in his eyes, a prey finally caught. I smile privately at the thought, yet a thread of uneasiness enters me as well. The office is stuffy, slightly chilly. I have never liked the cold, although I could survive an Arctic winter night naked to the bone.

"I guess you wonder why I wanted to talk to you so urgently," he says.

I nod. My legs are uncrossed, my white slacks hanging loose. One hand rests in my lap, the other plays with my hair. Left-handed, right-handed—I am neither, and both.

"May I call you Alisa?" he asks.

"You may call me what you wish, Mr. Riley."

My voice startles him, just a little, and it is the effect I want. I could have pitched it like any modern teenager, but I have allowed my past to enter, the power of it. I want to keep Mr. Riley nervous, for nervous people say much that they later regret.

"Call me Mike," he says. "Did you have trouble finding the place?"

"No."

"Can I get you anything? Coffee? A soda?"

"No."

He glances at a folder on his desk, flips it open. He clears his throat, and again I hear his tiredness, as well as his fear. But is he afraid of me? I am not sure. Besides the gun under his coat, he has another beneath some papers at the other side of his desk. I smell the gunpowder in the bullets, the cold steel. A lot of firepower to meet a teenage girl. I hear a faint scratch of moving metal and plastic. He is taping the conversation.

"First off I should tell you who I am," he says. "As I said on the phone, I am a private detective. My business is my own—I work entirely freelance. People come to me to find loved ones, to research risky investments, to provide protection, when necessary, and to get hard-to-find background information on certain individuals."

I smile. "And to spy."

He blinks. "I do not spy, Miss Perne."

"Really." My smile broadens. I lean forward, the tops of my breasts visible at the open neck of my black silk blouse. "It is late, Mr. Riley. Tell me what you want."

He shakes his head. "You have a lot of confidence for a kid."

"And you have a lot of nerve for a down-on-his-luck private dick."

He doesn't like that. He taps the open folder on his desk. "I have been researching you for the last few months, Miss Perne, ever since you moved to Mayfair. You have an intriguing past, as well as many investments. But I'm sure you know that."

"Really."

"Before I begin, may I ask how old you are?"

"You may ask."

"How old are you?"

"It's none of your business."

He smiles. He thinks he has scored a point. He does not realize that I am already considering how he should die, although I still hope to avoid such an extreme measure. Never ask a vampire her age. We don't like that question. It's very impolite. Mr. Riley clears his throat again, and I think that maybe I will strangle him.

"Prior to moving to Mayfair," he says, "you lived in Los Angeles—in Beverly Hills in fact—at Two-Five-Six Grove Street. Your home was a four-thousand-square-foot mansion, with two swimming pools, a tennis court, a sauna, and a small observatory. The property is valued at six-point-five million. To this day you are listed as the sole owner, Miss Perne."

"It's not a crime to be rich."

"You are not just rich. You are very rich. My research indicates that you own five separate estates scattered across this country. Further research tells me that you probably own as much if not more property in Europe and the Far East. Your stock and bond assets are vast—in the hundreds of millions. But what none of my research has uncovered is how you came across this incredible wealth. There is no record of a family anywhere, and believe me, Miss Perne, I have looked far and wide."

"I believe you. Tell me, whom did you contact to gather this information?"

He enjoys that he has my interest. "My sources are of course confidential."

"Of course." I stare at him; my stare is very powerful. Sometimes, if I am not careful, and I stare too long at a flower, it shrivels and dies. Mr. Riley loses his smile and shifts uneasily. "Why are you researching me?"

"You admit that my facts are accurate?" he asks.

"Do you need my assurances?" I pause, my eyes still on him. Sweat glistens on his forehead. "Why the research?"

He blinks and turns away with effort. He dabs at the perspiration on his head. "Because you fascinate me," he says. "I think to myself, here is one of the wealthiest women in the world, and no one knows who she is. Plus she can't be more than twenty-five years old, and she has no family. It makes me wonder."

"What do you wonder, Mr. Riley?"

He ventures a swift glance at me; he really does not like to look at me, even though I am very beautiful. "Why you go to such extremes to remain invisible," he says.

"It also makes you wonder if I would pay to stay invisible," I say.

He acts surprised. "I didn't say that."

"How much do you want?"

My question stuns him, yet pleases him. He does not have to be the first to dirty his hands. What he does not realize is that blood stains deeper than dirt, and that the stains last much longer. Yes, I think again, he may not have that long to live.

"How much are you offering?" he ventures.

I shrug. "It depends."

"On what?"

"On whether you tell me who pointed you in my direction."

He is indignant. "I assure you that I needed no one to point me in your direction. I discovered your interesting qualities all by myself."

He is lying, of that I am positive. I can always tell when a person lies, almost always. Only remarkable people can fool me, and then they have to be lucky. But I do not like to be fooled—so one has to wonder at even their luck.

"Then my offer is nothing," I say.

He straightens. He believes he is ready to pounce. "Then my counteroffer, Miss Perne, is to make what I have discovered public knowledge." He pauses. "What do you think of that?"

"It will never happen."

He smiles. "You don't think so?"

I smile. "You would die before that happened."

He laughs. "You would take a contract out on my life?"

"Something to that effect."

He stops laughing, now deadly serious, now that we are talking about death. Yet I keep my smile since death amuses me. He points a finger at me.

"You can be sure that if anything happened to me the police would be at your door the same day," he says.

"You have arranged to send my records to someone else," I say. "Just in case something should happen to you?"

"Something to that effect." He is trying to be witty. He is also lying. I slide back farther into my chair. He thinks I am relaxing, but I position myself so that my legs are straight out. If I am to strike, I have decided, it will be with my right foot.

"Mr. Riley," I say. "We should not argue. You want something from me, and I want something from you. I am prepared to pay you a million dollars, to be deposited in whatever account you wish, in whatever part of the world you desire, if you will tell me who made you aware of me."

He looks me straight in the eye, tries to, and surely he feels the heat building up inside me because he flinches before he speaks. His voice comes out uneven and confused. He does not understand why I am suddenly so intimidating.

"No one is interested in you except me," he says.

I sigh. "You are armed, Mr. Riley."

"I am?"

I harden my voice. "You have a gun under your coat. You have a gun on your desk under those papers. You are taping this conversation. Now, one might think these are all standard blackmail precautions, but I don't think so. I am a young woman. I don't look dangerous. But someone has told you that I am more dangerous than I look and that I am to be treated with extreme caution. And you know that that someone is right." I pause. "Who is that someone, Mr. Riley?"

He shakes his head. He is looking at me in a new light, and he doesn't like what he sees. My eyes continue to bore into him. A splinter of fear has entered his mind.

"H-how do you know all these things?" he asks.

"You admit my facts are accurate?" I mimic him.

He shakes his head again.

Now I allow my voice to change, to deepen, to resonate with the fullness of my incredibly long life. The effect on him is pronounced; he shakes visibly, as if he is suddenly aware that he is sitting next to a monster. But I am not just any monster. I am a vampire, and in many ways, for his sake, that may be the worst monster of all.

"Someone has hired you to research me," I say. "I know that for a fact. Please don't deny it again, or you will make me angry. I really am uncontrollable when I am angry. I do things I later regret, and I would regret killing you, Mr. Riley—but not for long." I pause. "Now, for the last time, tell me who sent you after me, and I will give you a million dollars and let you walk out of here alive."

He stares at me incredulously. His eyes see one thing and his ears hear another, I know. He sees a pretty blond girl with startlingly blue eyes, and he hears the velvety voice of a succubus from hell. It is too much for him. He begins to stammer.

"Miss Perne," he begins. "You misunderstand me. I mean you no harm. I just want to complete a simple business deal with you. No one has to . . . get hurt."

I take in a long, slow breath. I need air, but I can hold my breath for over an hour if I must. Yet now I let out the breath before speaking again, and the room cools even more. And Mr. Riley shivers.

"Answer my question," I say simply.

He coughs. "There is no one else."

"You'd better reach for your gun."

"Pardon?"

"You are going to die now. I assume you prefer to die fighting."

"Miss Perne—"

"I am five thousand years old."

He blinks. "What?"

I give him my full, uncloaked gaze, which I have used in the past—alone—to kill. "I am a vampire," I say softly. "And you have pissed me off."

He believes me. Suddenly he believes every horror story he has been told since he was a little boy. That they were all true: the dead things hungering for the warm living flesh; the bony hand coming out of the closet in the black of night; the monsters from another page of reality, the unturned page—who could look so human, so cute.

He reaches for his gun. Too slowly, much too.

I shove myself out of my chair with such force that I am momentarily airborne. My senses switch into a hyper-accelerated mode. Over the last few thousand years, whenever I am threatened, I have developed the ability to view events in extreme slow motion. But this does not mean that I slow down; quite the opposite. Mr. Riley sees nothing but a blur flying toward him. He does not see that as I'm moving, I have cocked my leg to deliver a devastating blow.

My right foot lashes out. My heel catches him in the center of the breastbone. I hear the bones crack as he topples backward onto the floor, his weapon still holstered inside his coat. Although I moved toward him in a horizontal position, I land smoothly on my feet. He sprawls on the floor at my feet beside his overturned chair. Gasping for breath, blood pouring out of his mouth. I have crushed the walls of his heart as well as the bones of his chest, and he is going to die. But not just yet. I kneel beside him and gently put my hand on his head. Love often flows through me for my victims.

"Mike," I say gently. "You would not listen to me."

He is having trouble breathing. He drowns in his own blood—I hear it gurgling deep in his lungs—and I am tempted to put my lips to his and suck it away for him. Such a temptation, to sate my thirst. Yet I leave him alone.

"Who?" he gasps at me.

I continue to stroke his head. "I told you the truth. I am a vampire. You never stood a chance against me. It's not fair, but it is the way it is." I lean close to his mouth, whisper in his ear. "Now tell me the truth and I will stop your pain. Who sent you after me?"

He stares at me with wide eyes. "Slim," he whispers.

"Who is Slim? A man?"

"Yes."

"Very good, Mike. How do you contact him?"

"No."

"Yes." I caress his cheek. "Where is this Slim?"

He begins to cry. The tears, the blood—they make a pitiful combination. His whole body trembles. "I don't want to die," he moans. "My boy."

"Tell me about Slim and I will take care of your boy," I say. My nature is kind, deep inside. I could have said if you don't tell me about Slim, I will find your dear boy and slowly peel off his skin. But Riley is in too much pain to hear me, and I immediately regret striking so swiftly, not slowly torturing the truth out of him. I did tell him that I was impulsive when I'm angry, and it is true.

"Help me," he pleads, choking.

"I'm sorry. I can only kill, I cannot heal, and you are too badly hurt." I sit back on my heels and glance around the office. I see on the desktop a picture of Mr. Riley posed beside a handsome boy of approximately eighteen. Removing my right hand from Mr. Riley, I reach for the picture and show it to him. "Is this your son?" I ask innocently.

Terror consumes his features. "No!" he cries.

I lean close once more. "I am not going to hurt him. I only want this Slim. Where is he?"

A spasm of pain grips Riley, a convulsion—his legs shake off the floor like two wooden sticks moved by a poltergeist. I grab him, trying to settle him down, but I am too late. His grimacing teeth tear into his lower lip, and more blood messes his face. He draws in a breath that is more a shovel of mud on his coffin. He makes a series of sick wet sounds. Then his eyes roll back in his head, and he goes limp in my arms. Studying the picture of the boy, I reach over and close Mr. Michael Riley's eyes.

The boy has a nice smile, I note.

Must have taken after his mother.

Now my situation is more complicated than when I arrived at the detective's office. I know someone is after me, and I have destroyed my main lead to him or her. Quickly I go through Riley's desk and fail to find anything that promises to be a lead, other than Riley's home address. The reason is sitting behind the desk as I search. Riley has a computer and there is little doubt in my mind that he stored his most important records on the machine. My suspicion is further confirmed when I switch on the computer and it immediately asks for an access code. Even though I know a great deal about computers, more than most experts in the field, I doubt

I can get into his data banks without outside help. I pick up the picture of father and son again. They are posed beside a computer. Riley Junior, I suspect, must know the access code. I decide to have a talk with him.

After I dispose of his father's body. My exercise in cleanup is simplified by the fact that Riley has no carpet on his office floor. A brief search of the office building leads me to a closet filled with janitorial supplies. Mop and pail and bucket in hand, I return to Mr. Riley's office and do the job his secretary probably resented doing. I have with me—from the closet—two big green plastic bags, and I slip Riley into them. Before I leave with my sagging burden, I wipe away every fingerprint I have created. There isn't a spot I have touched that I don't remember.

The late hour is such a friend; it has been for so many years. There is not a soul around as I carry Riley downstairs and dump him in my trunk. It is good, for I am not in the mood to kill again, and murder, for me, is very much tied to my mood, like making love. Even when it is necessary.

Mayfair is a town on the Oregon coast, chilly this late in autumn, enclosed by pine trees on one side and salt water on the other. Driving away from Riley's office, I feel no desire to go to the beach, to wade out beyond the surf to sink the detective in deep water. I head for the hills instead. The burial is a first for me in this area. I have killed no one since moving to Mayfair a few months earlier. I park at the end of a narrow dirt road and carry Riley over my shoulder deep into the woods. My ears are alert, but if there are mortals in the vicinity, they are all asleep. I carry no shovel with me. I don't need one. My fingers can impale even the hardest soil more surely than the sharpest knife can poke through a man's flesh. Two miles into the woods I drop Riley onto the ground and go down on my hands and knees and begin to dig. Naturally, my clothes get a bit dirty but I have a washing machine and detergent at home. I do not worry. Not about the body ever being found.

But about other things, I am concerned.

Who is Slim?

How did he find me?

How did he know to warn Riley to treat me with caution?

I lay Riley to rest six feet under and cover him over in a matter of minutes without even a whisper of a prayer. Who would I pray to anyway? Krishna? I could not very well tell *him* that I was sorry, although I did tell him that once, after holding the jewel of his life in my bloodthirsty hands while he casually brought to ruin our wild party. No, I think, Krishna would not listen to my prayer, even if it was for the soul of one of my victims. Krishna would just laugh and return to his flute. To the song of life as he called it. But where was the music for those his followers said were already worse than dead? Where was the joy? No, I would not pray to God for Riley.

Not even for Riley's son.

In my home, in my new mansion by the sea, late at night, I stare at the boy's photo and wonder why he is so familiar to me. His brown eyes are enchanting, so wide and innocent, yet as alert as those of a baby owl seen in the light of the full moon. I wonder if in the days to come I will be burying him beside his father. The thought saddens me. I don't know why.

ABOUT THE AUTHOR

CHRISTOPHER PIKE is a bestselling author of young adult novels. The Thirst series, *The Secret of Ka*, and the Remember Me and Alosha trilogies are some of his favorite titles. He is also the author of several adult novels, including *Sati* and *The Season of Passage*. Thirst and Alosha are slated to be released as feature films. Pike currently lives in Santa Barbara, where it is rumored he never leaves his house. But he can be found online at christopherpikebooks.com.

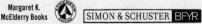